D0057194

 *WOLF HUNTING*

WOLF HUNTING

JANE LINDSKOLD

DISCARD

Uinta County Libraries
Evanston Branch
701 Main St.
Evanston, WY 82930

A TOM DOHERTY ASSOCIATES BOOK
NEW YORK

FEB 1 7 2011

This is a work of fiction. All the characters and events portrayed in this novel are either fictitious or are used fictitiously.

WOLF HUNTING

Copyright © 2006 by Jane Lindskold

All rights reserved, including the right to reproduce this book, or portions thereof, in any form.

This book is printed on acid-free paper.

Edited by Teresa Nielsen Hayden

Map by Mark Stein Studios based on an original drawing by James Moore

A Tor Book
Published by Tom Doherty Associates, LLC
175 Fifth Avenue
New York, NY 10010

www.tor.com

Tor® is a registered trademark of Tom Doherty Associates, LLC.

ISBN 0-765-31288-3
EAN 978-0-765-31288-4

First Edition: April 2006

Printed in the United States of America

0 9 8 7 6 5 4 3 2 1

To Jim, as always, as ever . . .

ACKNOWLEDGMENTS

As always, I want to thank all the folks at Tor, especially my editors, Teresa and Patrick Nielsen Hayden, for their continued enthusiasm for Firekeeper and her story.

My agent, Kay McCauley, kept me on track and honest about my goals throughout this project.

My husband, Jim Moore, read the early draft of the manuscript and indulged me in long conversations about how societies evolve and change in response to external stress.

Finally, I want to thank those readers who took the time to get in touch and share their interest in the series. Those of you who had questions may find a few of them answered in this novel. You can find out a bit more about Firekeeper and her world, as well as learn about other projects of mine, at my Web site: www.janelindskold.com.

DETAIL MAP OF THE LAND OF LIGLIM

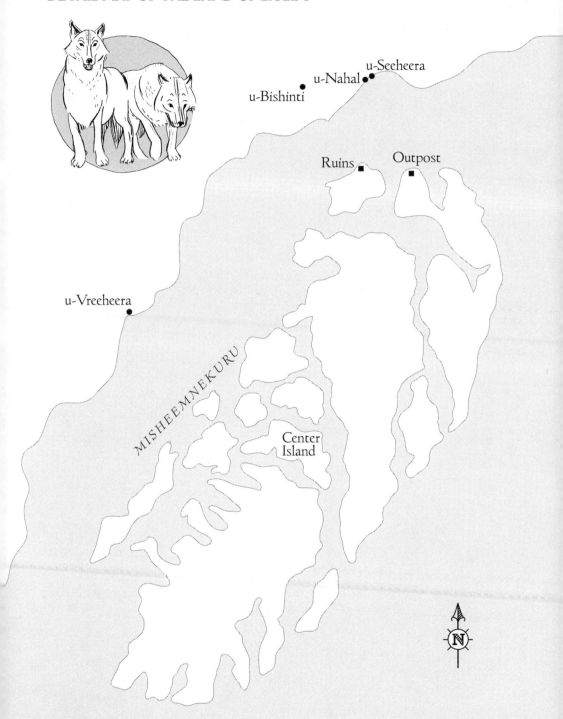

u-Seeheera

u-Nahal

u-Bishinti

Ruins

Outpost

u-Vreeheera

MISHEEMNEKURU

Center
Island

N

BOOK I

I

"HERE, KITTY, KITTY . . . HERE, KITTY, KITTY . . ."

The voice was mocking, but Truth turned toward the sound. Those words offered something she had been without for what seemed like an entire lifetime: direction.

Truth did not hear the voice. Rather the call appeared to her as a physical thing, a strand of certainty amid the chaos of nearly infinite probability. She followed that strand's odor, though she smelled it with her nose no more than she saw it with her eyes, no more than she heard that mocking voice with her round, furred ears.

The jaguar dipped her head close to the ground and took the scent, then followed its trace—for how long? Truth had no idea. The notion of time was one of the first things that had fragmented beyond repair. Even so, she followed, desiring certainty as once she had desired the hot blood of her prey, the attentions of lovers in season, lavish praise or admiration.

Truth followed, hearing a voice that wasn't there, scenting a trail that did not exist, seeing a path that left no mark on its surroundings. She followed, because all these things led her toward certainty.

⚜

FOREVER AFTER, that full year's turning of seasons on Misheemnekuru, the Sanctuary Islands, would remain green in memory for Firekeeper. Events of the summer before had freed her from responsibility for her human companions. Now she ran with the wolves, as free and unencumbered as ever she had been in her childhood.

The wolf-woman even had acquired a pack of her own, she and Blind Seer, for though Moon Frost had won Dark Death back from the doom he had ordained for himself, the season was too early for mating. Instead of dispersing to seek their own territory, the pair ran with Firekeeper. The greatest wonder of all to Firekeeper was that she, she and Blind Seer, were the Ones of this small pack.

Later, another joined them. Young Rascal of Moon Frost's own birth pack followed these first four when they moved on from hunting with his family. The pups Rascal had nursemaided were hunting small game on their own, so neither his mother nor his father held Rascal back from his desire to explore his strengths, though his new teachers would be odd indeed.

Summer was a fat time, as was the autumn that followed. Firekeeper's reputation was such that no wolf pack minded if the wolf-woman's small band shared the hunting in their lands—as long as the five first cried for permission, and granted those who held the territory their due.

When they were not hunting, the wolves usually slept, but Firekeeper—who was wolf and not—often searched out the human ruins that dotted Misheemnekuru. Blind Seer—who *was* wolf, but had run where no wolf had run for a hundred years and more—went with his Firekeeper. Between her questing eyes and his keen nose they discovered many curious things.

Winter was harder, though to Firekeeper and Blind Seer, born farther to the north, the temperatures were comparatively mild. Firekeeper's five joined with another little pack, a mated pair and their first year's pups. When a pup or two who might not have otherwise survived the winter's lean hunting lived because Firekeeper was clever with bow and snare, then to the songs that were already sung of her battles were added those of her generosity, and of her mercy.

When spring came around, Firekeeper and her pack went their way, seeking fresh hunting grounds. Spring had brought with it a small litter, born to Moon Frost, sired by Dark Death. Only two pups survived the birth. There were others, but deformed so that they came forth dead or only breathed a few shallow breaths. This was the curse of Misheemnekuru, and the reminder of it darkened Firekeeper's idyll.

Yet nothing could diminish the wolf-woman's contentment for long. The surviving pups grew strong and fat with only one other to share Moon Frost's milk, and with five adults eager to spoil them, for wolves love their pups and indulge them greatly. Firekeeper had Blind Seer at her side, and a pack with which to sing songs to the Moon.

That summer a few young hunters trying their skill—and some not so young, nor without skill—came to challenge Firekeeper, for as she was wolf and yet not wolf, there were those who doubted Firekeeper's right to walk freely on Misheemnekuru. These battles she won—and the fact that her pack showed willing to fight alongside her counted for much in all eyes.

With the coming of the raven, this time of contentment was shattered forever.

THE RAVEN CAME TO Firekeeper and Blind Seer early one morning at that time of year when the days were hot and heavy, and so—unless the wind came off the water—were the nights. The wolves had been sorting among bits of broken glass and cut stone at what had probably once been a fine estate, but was now little more than an assortment of vine-covered mounds.

When the raven landed on one of these mounds, Firekeeper greeted her with a friendly smile.

"Hey, Lovable," she said. "Come to see if we have found anything that shines?"

The raven lifted her head, angling it to one side to better look at what Firekeeper might be holding, then sank her head between her shoulders and sleeked her feathers flat, so that she looked smaller than she was. This was not very small, for Lovable was a Wise Raven, and like all of her kind, larger than her Cousin counterparts.

"Something that sparkled would be nice," Lovable began, then stopped herself with visible effort, "but that isn't why I have come. The beast-souled, the maimalodalum, asked me to find you and request that you attend upon them at Center Island."

Firekeeper let the bits of stone and glass she had been sifting through her fingers fall to the ground. Blind Seer, who had been lying recumbent, watching Firekeeper as he drowsed, rose in one easy motion. He did not quite challenge the raven, but his posture was defensive.

"What do they want her for?"

"They want both of you, actually," Lovable replied. "Powerful Tenderness, speaking for the rest, said to me, 'Find Firekeeper and Blind Seer. We have learned something that may interest them.' That is what he said."

Blind Seer relaxed somewhat, but Firekeeper, who knew the blue-eyed wolf well, felt he was still suspicious.

"Us alone?"

"You," Lovable agreed. "Though your pack would be welcome, I am sure. But it is to you the beast-souled wish to speak."

Firekeeper rose and placed a hand on Blind Seer's shoulder.

"I would go," she said. "Otherwise, I will wonder what the beast-souled wished to tell us."

"Curiosity," Blind Seer growled. "It is the most human thing about you, Little Two-legs."

Firekeeper did not bristle as once she might have. She knew what Blind Seer said was true. Instead she turned her attention to Lovable.

"What do they want?" she asked.

"I don't know exactly," Lovable replied, and from the set of her feathers, Firekeeper could tell this lack of information annoyed the raven. "All I know is that it has something to do with the jaguar Truth."

AFTER ARRANGING TO have the other three adults follow more slowly with the pups, Firekeeper and Blind Seer set off for Center Island. During the year they had spent on the Sanctuary Islands, they had not often visited this one particular island. They were not unwelcome there, but the island held not only bad memories, but two human residents whom Firekeeper had no desire to know better.

Unlike humans, Firekeeper and Blind Seer did not speculate as to what might await them at their destination—at least not out loud. Privately, Firekeeper did wonder, and she suspected Blind Seer did, too, but they saved their breath for running.

So it was that some days later, as evening was falling, the two wolves climbed the hill to the towers where the beast-souled made their headquarters. Once there had been five towers, each dedicated to one of the five elements worshipped by the Liglimom, the humans who had settled these islands before moving to the mainland. The central tower, the one dedicated to Magic, was nothing but a heap of broken stone. The four that surrounded it stood tall—and in far better repair than their battered exteriors might suggest.

Magic's tower alone had been permitted to deteriorate, but then the beast-souled had little reason to love magic, even though magic had made them what they were.

And what they were was as unlovely a lot as Firekeeper had ever seen: furred, fanged, horned, antlered, these characteristics blended without sense or harmony. Each of the maimalodalum possessed traits taken from at least one human and one animal, but most blended those from three or four. A typical representative of the beast-souled might have the scales of a snake on the torso of a broad-chested man—or perhaps of a bear—in addition to the head of a wolf or great cat. However, there were no typical beast-souled. What was most typical about them was that each was a unique monstrosity.

The maimalodalum were descended from the results of sorcery gone awry. In the generations since a plague had either killed or driven away from the New World those who were most skilled in the magical arts, these mutations had interbred. Their children and their children's children now resided here at the heart of Misheemnekuru, a secret from most who lived on the mainland.

Yet for all their ugliness, Firekeeper respected and even liked the beast-souled. She knew better than most how intelligent and strong-willed were the spirits imprisoned within those mismatched exteriors. As Firekeeper entered the round Tower of Earth toward which a waiting raven guided her, she bowed her head in respectful greeting to those who waited within. Beside her, Blind Seer stretched out his forelegs and gave a sort of bow, a mannerism he had picked up from humans that had nothing to do with the hierarchical groveling of wolves.

"Join us, Firekeeper and Blind Seer," said Hope. Her form blended, not disagreeably, the features of a bird and a human woman. She indicated a space left empty in the seated circle of the beast-souled. "We heard from Lovable that you were coming, and gathered here that we might speak with you. But perhaps you and Blind Seer would prefer to eat or drink before we convene? You have run far. Perhaps you need to rest."

"We hunted," Firekeeper said, "while we waited for the tide to shift so we could cross the inlet to this place. There were springs and creeks enough on the path we followed here. We slept through the worst of the day's heat. There is no need for you to wait your business."

"Is this wolfish efficiency I hear?" asked Hope, her laugh holding a touch of a bird's trill. "Or human curiosity?"

"A bit of both, Hope," Firekeeper said. "You invited us. We came. There seems no reason to delay. Why did you summon us here?"

Hope gave a quick, dipping bob of her feather-capped head. Her gaze, eagle-sharp, scanned her companions and found only listening interest. "Very well. I will begin. You remember Truth?"

"A Wise Jaguar," Firekeeper said. "The diviner. She was driven mad."

Driven mad, Firekeeper thought, *helping me. Had Truth not immersed herself in omens that final time so I might climb Magic's tower before it fell . . .*

But might-have-beens were the stuff of nightmare. Firekeeper knew this far better than most of her acquaintances even suspected. Of those present, only Blind Seer knew that she cried in her sleep and sometimes awoke screaming. In her nightmares, too, she almost remembered her human life, but most of the time Firekeeper was a wolf—a wolf in everything but shape.

Hope continued, "You know that Truth did not return to the mainland after the events here last summer. She was certainly not fit for the honored position she had held. Equally, she could not simply be let roam free. She would have died of starvation. Moreover, she would have been a hazard to any who encountered her."

Firekeeper nodded understanding. Any jaguar was dangerous. A Wise Jaguar, larger and more intelligent than its Cousin-kin, would be more so, even one who was insane—perhaps especially one who was insane.

"Yet we could not simply kill her," Hope said. "Truth had done nothing to earn execution. Her injuries were as much battle wounds as those so many others took to their bodies."

Firekeeper felt a twisting in her gut as she thought about those who had died or been permanently mutilated. She herself bore scars from the battle in which Truth had lost her mind. The least of these marked her body. The deepest were in her heart.

"So you didn't kill Truth," Blind Seer said, perhaps to give Firekeeper a chance to compose herself, "nor let her run free. That must mean you have taken care of her."

"We have," Hope said. "Powerful Tenderness made Truth's care his charge, and to him belongs the next part of this tale."

Attention shifted to where Powerful Tenderness sat—or rather hunkered—on the ground. He was one of the most physically terrifying of the beast-souled. It was impossible for Firekeeper to decide whether his torso was that of a brown bear or merely of a very large, very hairy man. His head bore traces of both ancestries. His toes and fingers ended in claws, not nails. His eyes, when Firekeeper forced herself to meet them, were those of neither man nor bear, but the cold, somehow dead-looking eyes of a snake.

When Powerful Tenderness spoke, a snake's tongue slipped from between too-human lips, and gave his words an incongruous hiss. Yet for all his fearsome appearance, Firekeeper knew, Powerful Tenderness deserved his name as much as she deserved her own. She waited with interest to hear what he would say.

"Bide while I begin with those first days," Powerful Tenderness began, "for only in knowing how Truth was then can you understand what she has become."

Firekeeper inclined her head respectfully, and slung one arm around Blind Seer's shoulders. This was a posture that said "I am not going anywhere. Speak as much as you like," and Powerful Tenderness responded to it as he would have to words.

"At first, I despaired of keeping Truth alive once the fat in her body, the strength in her muscles, was depleted. It was almost impossible to get her to eat, and the few times I restrained her and tried to force her . . ."

He held up one forearm. A scar made a white river through the brown fur. He need say no more.

"Weakness saved Truth," Powerful Tenderness went on, "for when she was weak, she seemed to see this reality more clearly and would eat what I set out for her. But this was not her salvation. Every time Truth ate herself to some modicum of strength, she would again see each possibility in her action and balk at dangers we could not imagine, though sometimes phrases she spat to invisible enemies gave us a clue. She might fear choking, or illness from a faint trace of rot, or even mourn the creature that had died to provide her sustenance. She would again refuse to eat, grow weak, and become somewhat sane, only to fall into madness as she regained her strength. It was not a good time.

"But at last—sometime this spring—Truth broke this cycle. She did not return to full sanity, but she had flashes wherein I know she knew me, knew where she was, and knew, too, that this reality held the foundation from which she derived her omens. Then, just as I was hoping Truth would be with us more often than not, something new happened. Truth seemed to find another . . ."

Powerful Tenderness trailed off, and for a long pause Firekeeper thought he had forgotten what he had been about to say. The other beast-souled waited with such tense watchfulness that Firekeeper felt certain that they, too, had not heard this tale. Hope alone held herself differently. Hope waited, her lips pursed as if ready to prompt her friend, but she held herself silent: a bird on the edge of song.

She knows, Firekeeper thought, *but she does not wish to take this hunt from her friend.*

"It was as if," Powerful Tenderness said at last, "Truth had located another reality, one as solid and as real as this one. I swear I saw her lap as if drinking. There was no water near her, but I saw the muscles beneath her throat fur rippling as she swallowed. Once I thought I glimpsed a drop of water on her whiskers, but that might only have been saliva. Yet, yet . . . It glittered clear and shot rainbows when the sunlight touched it."

Firekeeper fought the urge to lean forward, not wanting to seem like a bird dog straining at the leash. Others of those gathered there, as new to this tale as she was herself, were not so restrained. One, a lean bipedal creature whose tusked boar's head seemed far too heavy for the frame it concealed beneath human-style clothing, made a snuffling, grunting, rooting-in-the-ground noise. Beside him, a voluptuous creature who might have passed for human, except that she had three paired sets of breasts and was downed in thick red fur, twitched her bushy tail uneasily. She wore a fox's muzzle like a mask over human features—though Firekeeper well knew this was no mask.

Another, a man with a stag's head—or perhaps a stag with a man's chest and arms where only a stag's muscular neck should be—dipped his rack as if seeking some enemy he might impale. The stag-man had retractable claws like those of a cat; he was sliding them in and out in his nervousness.

Some few of the nervously listening maimalodalum made even these look normal, for in them the traits of many beasts and perhaps even several different humans were so blended that deciphering their actual heritage was difficult, even impossible. Yet in this company, their oddness went unremarked, for all were remarkable.

The maimalodalum who broke the listening silence resembled either a very short, very fat man with a fat, fluffy tail, or a very large raccoon who had become bipedal. His facial features reinforced the confusion. Although his nose was more like that of a raccoon, his mouth was a bit broader, like that of a human.

When he spoke, it was in the tones of one who is being reasonable, although he knows full well he has excuse to be otherwise.

"Why," the raccoon-man began, "didn't you speak of this before, Powerful Tenderness? You of all people knew all too well the concerns we have harbored this year and more."

Powerful Tenderness's reply held the faintest rumble of a bear's growl mingled with his usual serpent's hiss. "Plik, I said nothing—except to Hope, for she shared some of my vigil with Truth—because there was nothing definite to say. Spend enough time with madness, and you will begin to doubt your own sanity."

There was another round of uncomfortable shuffling at this point, and Firekeeper felt Blind Seer's flanks heave as he swallowed panting laughter. Clearly, while all the beast-souled had agreed that Truth should not die of her mental injuries, only a few had been willing to assume the tedium—and danger—of nursing an insane Wise Jaguar.

Blind Seer said so only Firekeeper would understand him, "Unlike wolves, jaguars are solitary souls. Even Truth's Wise kin would have been unable to care for her properly. Such dependence from another adult would have strained even her own mother."

Firekeeper scratched between the wolf's ears in agreement. She had tremendous admiration for the great cats—both the pumas of her childhood ranges and the jaguars she had met here in the south. One on one, a jaguar could defeat any wolf, but ultimately, she felt that their solitary habits were a weakness.

Plik replied cryptically, "I have not spent time with madness, no, but I have come close. I think you should have trusted us."

Powerful Tenderness flicked his ears forward (they were placed like those of a human, but rounded and furred like those of a bear) in acknowledgment, and resumed his report.

"To this point I have spoken only of supposition. Truth had run from invisible terrors in the past, had hunted insubstantial game. It did not seem unreasonable that she was drinking water where there was none. In fact, Hope and I concluded that Truth might have found some congenial hallucination. Our plans were centered on how to use this to our advantage in her care."

The lean creature with the boar's head grunted, "And then?"

"And then Truth spoke," Powerful Tenderness said simply. "She spoke not muttered phrases nor screams, but clear sentences, meant for our hearing." Powerful Tenderness glanced over at Firekeeper. "You must understand, I only quote."

Firekeeper nodded. "I do."

"Truth said, 'Bring me the bitch. The wolf-bitch. The human-wolf-bitch. She's impossibly stupid at times, thinks the world runs on simple lines, but bring her.'" Powerful Tenderness shrugged. "Truth said this repeatedly. Hope heard her. We both tried to question Truth as to why she wanted you, but we got little more from her. What we did get was not precisely comforting."

"And this was?" Firekeeper asked, keeping her manner casual.

" 'There is a door here,' " Powerful Tenderness quoted. " 'My paws cannot open it. She has hands. She can open the door. She can let me out.' "

Firekeeper frowned. "Do you have Truth caged then?"

"After a fashion," Powerful Tenderness said. "To let her roam free would have been a danger to herself and others. However, where she is there is no door—not so to speak. She is within a walled area that was once part of a house. The 'door'—if you can call it such—is a hole in the wall. I have blocked it with a huge boulder. Forgive me, for I remember you are strong beyond what one would imagine for one so small, but I do not think you could move this stone. Even I need a lever to do so."

Blind Seer tilted his head back as if taking a scent. "So you think that this door of which Truth speaks is no door at all. You think she refers to something else."

The vixen-human yapped excitedly. "Or that this door is in another place, some other place that Truth has found, the place where she found fresh water to drink!"

"So you wish me to speak with Truth," Firekeeper said, "perhaps learn what this door is of which she speaks."

"Yes," Powerful Tenderness agreed. "Not only may it be the means of helping Truth from her delusions, but it may be related to something else that has been troubling us. Would you hear of that now, or go to Truth?"

"Is Truth in any immediate danger?" Firekeeper asked.

"No. She is in one of the quieter portions of her cycle."

"Then let us hear the rest of your tale," Firekeeper said. "If I am not mistaken, this one"—she indicated the raccoon-man with a toss of her head—"has hinted at it already."

Hope stretched, rolling her head as if to loosen tension in her neck. Her arms were adorned with feathers, as if they had tried to turn into wings, but had failed. For the first time, Firekeeper realized that the bird-woman looked weary, and not her alone. Every one of the dozen or more beast-souled gathered here showed signs of weariness. True, they were mostly diurnal, unlike Firekeeper and Blind Seer who were as often active at night as in the day, but this seemed more.

This wasn't just the sleepiness of those accustomed to being awake in the day, forced by circumstances to stay alert through the night. There was tension here, nor was it the drawn tension of a bowstring the archer has pulled back, preparatory to loosing the arrow. This was the tension of a tree bough, overburdened with snow or ice, ready to snap unless something shook that burden free.

Again it was Hope, though among the most physically slight of the beast-souled, who took up the burden of the tale.

"We have told you how, as a result of the peculiar circumstances of our ancestors' creation, many of us are able to sense the use of magic?"

Firekeeper nodded. "The sense varies from individual to individual, but it is like seeing or hearing, something you do without conscious thought."

Hope smiled. "Yes. Though as with any other sense, this ability can be trained so that the possessor has a greater understanding of the various sensory impressions."

Firekeeper nodded again. She did not think her actual night vision was much better than that of a normal human, but because she had lived her life among nocturnal creatures, she had learned to use what she had in order to function when there was relatively little light. Such was also the case with her sense of smell. Compared with a wolf, she was as nose-dead as any human, but compared with a human, she paid far more attention to the impressions she received from her sense of smell.

Hope continued, "When the Tower of Magic fell just over a year ago, all of us sensed a surge of magic. Part of this may have been due to the actions of Shivadtmon. Part may have been due to the release of some passive magics worked into the tower. In any case, we knew that this surge would be perceptible to any creature that shared our ability. Needless to say, we were curious to learn if any would come in response to this surge."

Blind Seer tilted his head to one side in inquiry. "Are you saying that you think there may be others who are attuned to magic? My people—the wolves of my pack—always taught that magic other than the small talents died in the New World with the coming of what the Liglimom call Divine Retribution, the great illness that targeted those who used the magical arts."

"And led to the withdrawal of the sorcerers who founded these New World colonies," Hope added. "Your teaching was, as you know, less complete than you thought before you came here."

"True," Blind Seer admitted, panting white-fanged in laughter. "It certainly did not take you beast-souled into account."

"I think," Hope said gently, "that the Wise Beasts of the northwest—let us call them the 'Royal Beasts,' after Firekeeper's idiom—taught more what they hoped than what they knew. In any case, with a few exceptions like ourselves, that teaching was probably more right than wrong.

"However," Hope continued, "we here perceived the surge of magic as a loud cry or a bright flash of light. We wondered if any others would sense it. We also knew that since Misheemnekuru is an island group, it might be difficult for any to reach us. We have always been alert, but now we were doubly so lest there be a sign and we miss it."

Firekeeper ran her fingers through Blind Seer's fur. "And you have smelled magic, haven't you? That's what he . . ." She tossed her head to indicate Plik, the raccoon-man, who sat hunched over looking more like a raccoon than a man in the firelight. "That's what he was referring to earlier."

Hope trilled approval. "That's right, Firekeeper. Plik is among the best at sensing magic, and he was the first to hear this. We have all done so since, even those whose ability is so slight that they are nearly deaf. It is definitely there, but it is not at all what we expected."

Plik straightened, his semblance to a small, fat man—if one oddly costumed—returning.

"It was . . . Think of it as a sound, if you would. Have you ever filled a bladder with air?"

Firekeeper nodded. Bladders, properly cleaned, were useful for carrying water.

Plik smiled approval. "Then you know the sound they make when the air starts leaking out. A whine that changes as the pressure changes. This . . . this was a little like that. It was not a sound of something building up or being projected. It was the sound of magic draining away. At least that is what we think."

"Could it be something that was in the Tower of Magic," Blind Seer asked, "something broken but not entirely broken?"

"We thought of that," Plik said, "and have checked, but have not found. The 'sound'—which is not really a sound—is not easy to pinpoint. It shifts, ebbs almost beneath detection, then comes clearly again. This is why when Powerful Tenderness began to speak of Truth finding a place . . . a place that was not a place as we know it . . ."

Plik shrugged, the gesture saying better than words, "That was why I think he should have told us rather than sending ravens for you."

In the face of this rebuke, Powerful Tenderness looked as mild as something of his ferocious mien could.

"So you wonder if this 'sound' and whatever place Truth seems to have found might be related. It's an interesting idea."

Hope interjected, looking at Firekeeper and Blind Seer, obviously concerned they might misunderstand. "Now you do realize that Plik is offering a theory only. We have no real proof that these two occurrences—or three if we include the surge that followed the collapse of the tower—are related. It might be coincidence, or two could be related, but not the third."

Firekeeper asked, "Could Truth also have 'heard' this sound and followed it to wherever she is—to this place where there is apparently some sort of door?"

"Possibly," Plik said. "Interesting. The sound did not begin immediately following the tower's collapse. It might not be related as Hope said. All three. Two of the three. No connection at all. We just don't know, but we must try to know."

"Because if we don't try to know," Blind Seer said, "and this magical emanation is something more than a broken artifact leaking away its power, we may miss something important. In my experience, and sadly it is greater than I would like, things related to magic tend to be very dangerous indeed."

"Dangerous," Firekeeper said, "and unpredictable. Come. Someone take us to Truth. She may have the beginnings of answers."

II

PLIK OF THE BEAST-SOULED listened in mingled indignation and apprehension as Hope and Powerful Tenderness told the two outsiders what they had not yet told their own people. He rubbed the furry edge of one ear and tried to consider the matter in all reasonableness.

Was he being fair to view this withholding of information as a betrayal of their community? After all, in the process of telling Firekeeper and Blind Seer, Powerful Tenderness was also telling those of the maimalodalum who were in attendance. Still, Plik couldn't help but feel that Powerful Tenderness should have told his own people first.

Young people, he thought with a sigh. *Always changing things, even when those things have worked well in the past.*

He laughed at his own crotchety mood. Failure to adapt was worse than fearing change. Traditions were fine as far as they went, but if there hadn't been some willing to adapt, to change the way things had always been, he wouldn't have been around to enjoy these seventy and more years.

Plik studied the newcomers. He'd seen Firekeeper and Blind Seer before, of course, but they had not frequented Center Island after the fall of the Tower of Magic. He didn't blame them. They had little but bad memories of the place.

Blind Seer, the so-called "Royal" Wolf, looked much as he had before, a large wolf, mostly grey, though touched with brown and white. His most unusual feature were his blue eyes, so alert and watchful that Plik wondered that any had ever thought him blind.

Firekeeper was something else entirely. When Plik had first seen her the summer before, she had been clad after the style of the local humans. Now the only elements of her attire consistent with that first meeting were the large hunting knife with the garnet-topped hilt she wore belted to her waist and the leather bag she wore about her neck. Otherwise wolf-woman wore mostly dirt, scrapes, and bruises. A skirt of tanned doeskin hung loosely around her waist, a canteen from a strap over her shoulder and between her small breasts. Her dark brown hair was a tangled mess, but about her, despite her general raggedness, Firekeeper emitted an aura of strength.

This last was not magical. Plik was among the maimalodalum's experts regarding things magical. Though he would bet his left ear that Firekeeper had at least one fairly potent talent, magical talents were not the source of her strength. What made Firekeeper someone to be reckoned with was not her ability to speak with animals as easily as—more easily than, if what he had heard was correct—with most humans. Her strength came from having survived ten years in the wild, ten years with no one other than the Royal Wolves to care for her.

"What are you looking at, Plik?"

Hope's chirping voice held just a touch of laughter. Plik realized that he was staring fixedly at the night-darkened greenery. Firekeeper, Blind Seer, and Powerful Tenderness were long gone.

"Nothing. I was just thinking."

Hope touched his arm, her almost human hand stroking his thick fur. Like Powerful Tenderness, she was younger than Plik, part of the rising generation who would dictate the policy of the maimalodalum when Plik had gone back to Earth's embrace. He knew many found her attractive, but she was not his type. This made them easy with each other.

"I know you were offended that Powerful Tenderness didn't speak with the beast-souled first," Hope said, raising the subject that she clearly thought had been occupying his mind. "The fact is, Truth didn't ask for any of us. She asked for Firekeeper."

"Not very nicely," Plik commented, "almost as if she despised the wolfling."

"Jaguars," Hope said, "great cats in general, do not like needing to ask for help."

Plik scratched at a flea. It was almost impossible to be completely rid of them this time of year. He should rub down with fleabane again before he went to sleep.

"Why would Truth ask Firekeeper for help when there are so many others who would help her?" Plik asked. "If the jaguars wouldn't help her, others of the Wise Beasts would. We beast-souled have already provided ample proof of our goodwill."

Hope shrugged. "I don't know. However, I cannot forget that before the events of the past Jaguar Year, Truth was considered among the finest diviners of any of the yarimaimalom, and she from a family known for the gift. I think that even in her madness she must have traced the streams of probability and amid them seen that the chances for success were greatest if Firekeeper assisted."

"Why?" Plik repeated. "Why Firekeeper? She is an outlier, not of our peoples or our faith."

Hope looked up at him. "As you are an outcross? Plik, don't let your own mixed feelings about your heritage color those things to which there is no relation. Firekeeper is from another land, true, but not only has she proved herself our friend, she has proven herself capable of great deeds—even when they mean loss to herself. It is not for moonlight's sake that the wolves sing songs of her deeds."

Plik twitched his ears restlessly. "Firekeeper makes me uneasy. She is so young, so inclined to act without thinking."

"Firekeeper would make anyone of good sense nervous," Hope said with a laugh. "Whatever else Firekeeper is, easy to be around she is not. Now, get some rest. It's late, and I would not be surprised if things grew quite interesting over the next few days."

"Sleep?" Plik said. "Aren't you going to wait to hear what Powerful Tenderness reports?"

"He won't report until morning. Firekeeper won't make up her mind all at once. Blind Seer will be against her involvement in this."

"Why?"

"Blind Seer fears what her curiosity will get her into—her curiosity and her sense of duty to those she views as having done her a kindness. Truth helped Firekeeper when Magic's tower was falling. Firekeeper will feel a debt. Blind Seer will dread what paying that debt will cost her."

"I can't figure out why he follows her so faithfully."

Hope whistled a little screech of contempt. Plik laughed. He knew perfectly well why Blind Seer followed Firekeeper, even as he knew that Firekeeper would follow Blind Seer should the blue-eyed wolf lead.

"If you are so interested in Firekeeper, then cultivate her," Hope suggested, turning into the darkness toward her own quarters in the Tower of Air. "Firekeeper might teach even you, old one, something about how to cope with being different. Now, get some sleep."

"You, too, Hope. No staying up and waiting for dawn's omens."

"I promise," she laughed.

Plik walked stiffly toward the forest. His back ached. There were more and more times as he aged that he wished he were quadrupedal. It seemed the quadruped had fewer back problems. Hips though . . .

He climbed a rough-barked old oak until he came to a hollow that a lightning strike had begun and he had expanded. It wasn't really living quarters, just a nice nest, snug and lined with other people's fur and feathers.

Eventually, the rocking of the tree in the sea breeze sent Plik off to sleep. He dreamed, and, even in his dreams, he listened, though he knew not what it was he sought to hear.

REALITY FRAGMENTED AS FINE AS broken glass began to coalesce into omens: lumps of molten crystal, each holding the reflections of a thousand thousand might-have-beens, might-well-bes, should-have-beens.

"Here, kitty, kitty . . ."

Was the voice louder now?

Determined to find the source of that elusive voice with its mocking call, Truth isolated from all the possibilities that surrounded her those wherein the trace of the caller grew stronger. Her task was nearly impossible, for each effort to search created new probabilities. Even so, the very talent that had doomed Truth to wander—body and soul split, mind encased in the vagaries of insanity—made omens predicting her success surface. She seized upon those traces, and focused her inner vision tightly upon her goal.

First Truth scented a droplet of blood floating free. She followed it, watching carefully until it merged with others streaming through a capillary. She padded alongside this conduit until it joined a vein. She refused to lose the trail when this vein joined into a network of veins and arteries.

She sensed that this circulatory system functioned within a greater body. The voice both was and was not of that body—but it was contained within it, and that was enough.

Truth gathered herself, compacting her strong and stocky body, leaping from the chaos of lostness in which she had been trapped into . . .

She had thought she might leap into herself, had thought she might rejoin the body and mind that had been sundered when she—she could admit it—had gone insane. She had heard insanity defined as losing one's mind. In her case, she knew precisely where her mind was, but that mind was so cut off from her body she wasn't even certain it was still alive. To her the possibility that her body had died and that she was a wandering spirit, a ghost, seemed very likely.

Truth had always enjoyed ghost stories, but now that she might well be a ghost, she wasn't at all sure she liked it.

Where was she? She had thought to leap into her body, but this she had not done, but she had leapt, and she had arrived. She was somewhere. The randomness of probable futures no longer clashed around her. She was somewhere else.

Her surroundings were more silvery than otherwise, full of shadows and repetitions. What interested her more than this was that the voice was again calling.

"Here, kitty, kitty . . ."

The voice came from the waters of a deep pool that Truth had not noticed until this moment. She padded over to it, looked down into the waters. She cast no reflection and this troubled her. It was said that ghosts cast no reflection. Did this mean she was indeed a ghost?

Even so, she was thirsty, and she dipped her head and drank.

"Hey there, kitty," came the voice.

There was motion in the pool. With a flickering of hope—an emotion Truth thought she had discarded long ago as futile—Truth thought she was seeing herself. Then she realized that though the figure within the pool was indeed a jaguar, it was not herself.

"Who are you, there in the water, calling me?" she demanded.

"Who are you to say I am the one in the water?" the other countered. He smelled arrogant and male, and for Truth, for whom this was not the season, very distasteful. "To me, you are the one beneath the water—and I think I am right."

"Why?"

"I know how you can get out from where you are."

"How?"

"You won't believe me, but I've told you this before. There is a door. You must find someone who can open it."

Truth nodded, and felt a shiver when the jaguar in the pool nodded a moment behind.

"Who can open the door?" she said. "You say 'someone,' but I hear you say 'Someone.'"

"I have told you before," the voice said. "There is someone with hands who owes you a favor. Firekeeper. Let her repay you and open that door."

"Firekeeper," Truth said. "Why not?"

"Remember," the voice said, and for the first time the mocking note had vanished, replaced with intense urgency. "You must tell them about the door. Tell them soon. Ask for Firekeeper."

TRUTH WAS BEING KEPT on a portion of Center Island somewhat distant from the towers. Her holding pen was constructed from the partially rebuilt walls of what had once been a large house. The door was an enormous boulder wedged into place.

A ladder had been leaned against the outside of the wall. Firekeeper scampered squirrel-like to the top, where she could peer over and in. Her first thought was that Truth could probably get out of this enclosure if she had a mind to do so. Her second, as she watched the Wise Jaguar's restless pacing, was that Truth seemed to have hardly enough mind to stay on her feet, much less leap a high wall.

Powerful Tenderness had accompanied Firekeeper and Blind Seer to this place. The other beast-souled seemed more eager to return to their usual routines. Then, too, Firekeeper thought she made them a little nervous. Even when she had come to Center Island during her wandering year on Misheemnekuru, most of the beast-souled had kept their distance from her. Only Hope and Powerful Tenderness had regularly sought her out.

Firekeeper didn't know why this was so, but she knew how she hated being pressed when she didn't want someone's company—she thought of her foster brother, Edlin, with a smile—and was not about to force her company on those who did not want her.

Firekeeper described to Blind Seer what she saw.

"Truth paces down there. Her manner is like but not like what we saw that time when Truth was so far gone she would not eat. There is something of the same lack of connection to her surroundings—she just stumbled against a stone anyone with open eyes could have seen was there—but there is not the same rambling. Once you watch a while, you see deliberation."

"Does she hear your voice?" Blind Seer asked.

"Not that I can tell," Firekeeper said. She made her way down the ladder once more and turned to Powerful Tenderness. "Can we go in to Truth? Can you roll back your door?"

Powerful Tenderness nodded, but clearly he was concerned. "I can, but remember this . . ."

He held up his scarred arm in mute reminder. Firekeeper, recalling that among the Center Island wolves there was at least one who had the healing talent, took the warning as seriously as it was given. Truth might be caged, but she was not in the least safe.

"Still," Firekeeper said, "I would go in."

"And I with her," Blind Seer said. "Two of us might deal better with Truth should the need arise."

"Go in as soon as there is room enough for you to pass," Powerful Tenderness said, "and I will close the gap immediately after you again."

The wolves said nothing, but their moving was answer enough. With a grunt and a heave, Powerful Tenderness shifted the boulder. Firekeeper was through in a breath, Blind Seer a breath after. He gave a short, sharp howl, and a moment later the boulder rolled back into place.

That howl seemed to have reached Truth as no sound made from the other side of the wall had done. The jaguar stopped pacing and her rounded ears twitched. Her tail lashed irritably side to side. She took a step, but paused before her paw could touch the leaf mat that carpeted the ground.

"A voice I know," Truth said. "A wolf I know. Where there is the one, then the other."

Her head lifted and her nostrils widened, her mouth opening slightly as was the way with cats when attempting to catch the purest scent.

Firekeeper moved to where the wind would carry her scent to the jaguar. One hand hovered in the vicinity of her Fang, in case upon catching her scent the jaguar attacked. After all, the mutterings Powerful Tenderness had reported had not been precisely kind.

Truth sniffed intently, as if trying to catch a scent weeks old rather than fresh and within the length of her own tail. Thinking how the sound of Blind Seer's howl had helped Truth to focus, Firekeeper spoke.

"I am here, Truth, me, the wolf-bitch you called for. Firekeeper. Blind Seer is here with me. True, the sun yet sleeps, but surely you can catch our scents."

Truth shook her head, hard, as if there was a flea biting her ear, and when next she looked at Firekeeper, the wolf-woman could swear the burnt-orange eyes actually focused on who stood before her. There was something odd about that gaze as well. There was moonlight, but as the moon was on the wane, her light served little. Even so, Truth's pupils were slit, as if she stood in brilliant daylight.

"Truth," Firekeeper said, "you asked for me and I came. Where is this door that I might open it for you?"

Now she was certain the jaguar was aware of her.

"Here," Truth said, "not there. You cannot open the door from there, even though it stands before you."

"How might I find it?"

Truth did not reply, but Firekeeper had the distinct and unsettling feeling that the jaguar was listening to something—perhaps to someone.

After a long pause, Truth said, "Do you remember the house that was no longer a house? The place that had been made to go away?"

Firekeeper was puzzled, but Blind Seer's ears perked and he said, "I do. It was on the island where we spent most of the winter, out at the southern tip. We went there with Rascal when Moon Frost and Dark Death were unpleasant to be around. Rascal fell in a hole or we'd never have known there had been a building there."

"I remember," Firekeeper said. "We wondered at the time if it could even be termed a ruin, as it had been broken down by other than time." She returned her attention to the jaguar. "We know the place, Truth, but what is it to you?"

Truth lashed her tail. "That is where I am."

"Truth, you are here before me on Center Island. I see you clearly."

Truth's tale lashed faster, whipping side to side, but the jaguar kept her gaze tightly fixed on the pair before her. "I am there, I tell you. There is the door that can be opened to let me free. I cannot open it. He cannot open it, but if you come from the outside, you can open it and I can go free."

He? Firekeeper thought. Then she realized what the jaguar's fragmented words had meant. Truth must have been referring to Blind Seer, for if the jaguar couldn't open the door, it was unlikely that a wolf could.

Truth had begun pacing now, and her words were more fragmented. "Bring me with you, else I am lost. Bring me. I know the door."

After that there was nothing sensible to be gotten out of the jaguar—if, Firekeeper thought, they had gotten any sense so far. Powerful Tenderness rolled back the rock, and once the wolves were outside they told him everything they had learned.

"You are sure you know this place of which Truth spoke?" he said at last. "Misheemnekuru is covered with ruined houses."

"I think so," Blind Seer said. "We have looked at many ruins, but this place was different. The others had crumbled from neglect—and maybe because the humans left behind wished to spoil their masters' nests. This one had been wiped away as cleanly as if it had never been built. Even the cellars had been filled with dirt, but the dirt had settled some through time and storm, creating the pit into which Rascal fell."

Firekeeper nodded. "Truth did not disagree when Blind Seer described the location. I think this is the place she meant. What I don't understand is how she could say she is there. She is here—right on the other side of that wall. We have seen her and smelled her."

Powerful Tenderness grubbed in the dirt with his bear-clawed hands. "Perhaps Truth is both here and there. We have spoken of her wandering mind. Remember those water droplets?"

"I do," Firekeeper said, "but I don't understand."

"Nor do I," Powerful Tenderness admitted. "Perhaps there is a cave there, under the earth. Maybe Truth has found some old way there. Legends tell how there were sorcerous routes between places, routes closed since the Divine Retribution. Maybe Truth has paced along one of these and come out at these not-ruins. Maybe she cannot drag her entire self out, but thinks that if mind and body were brought to the same place she would be well."

"What I don't understand," Blind Seer said, looking at the curving patterns Powerful Tenderness had drawn in the dirt, "is why Truth wanted Firekeeper. There are many among the beast-souled who have been gifted with hands. Why not ask one of you?"

"That is a puzzle," Powerful Tenderness said, his cold snake's eyes warming with curiosity, "and not one I had considered. Would you be more willing to undertake this if I went with you? I would not wish you to think that we would ask you to go where we were afraid to travel."

"You would be welcome," Firekeeper said politely, "but we have never doubted you meant us well."

Blind Seer snorted very softly, and Powerful Tenderness pretended not to hear. Firekeeper knew that Blind Seer was weary of people who wanted Firekeeper to do things that they could not. He would have been reassured by Powerful Tenderness's offer.

"Night is ending," Firekeeper said to the towering beast-souled, "and you have gone long without rest. Blind Seer and I will go and hunt, then rest ourselves. Perhaps next evening we can meet and talk this over more."

"And what of Truth?" Powerful Tenderness asked.

"Truth has waited this long," Firekeeper said firmly. "She can wait a little longer."

"YOU WANT TO DO THIS THING," Blind Seer said once they were away and sure of being alone. "Why? What is Truth to us that we should go to such trouble for her? Surely you don't expect thanks from a jaguar."

"Curiosity again, I suppose," Firekeeper admitted with a sigh. "And gratitude preys on me. Without Truth risking herself, I would not have been able to stop Shivadtmon. As it was, I was nearly too late. As Hope said, Truth was wounded in that battle, the same as others. I could not help Sky or Questioner, but I may be able to help Truth."

Blind Seer bumped against her, the wolf's equivalent of a hug. "A year and more gone, and those deaths still hurt."

"They do," Firekeeper admitted. "Questioner's most of all. I had so much to learn from him. I feel like a small fire was kindled then blown out. There's ash in my mouth, dry and bitter."

"Then we go," Blind Seer said. He gave a long, shuddering sigh. "I may not have a diviner's talent, but I think that when we leave Center Island, we will be setting our feet on a longer road than we know."

"FIREKEEPER WILL DECIDE to go where Truth has asked," Powerful Tenderness reported confidently to the gathered maimalodalum the next morning. "I will go with them. Firekeeper and Blind Seer lack the physical power to restrain Truth if the jaguar gets the desire to do something foolish—or violent. Will someone else come to share shifts with me?"

There was nervous shuffling among the group, for most of the maimalodalum rarely left Center Island. What had begun as a long-ago precaution had become habit with the force of tradition behind it. Self-preservation had originated the precaution, and fear maintained it.

The maimalodalum were not cowards, but they knew too well that the unfamiliar bred fear. As each of them was a unique monstrosity, they knew they would always be unfamiliar. Until recently, the humans on the mainland had not known they even existed. Even now, only a few shared the secret. Overall the Wise Beasts were more tolerant, but the yarimaimalom's own precautions against inbreeding made some of them less than kind when confronted with monsters.

Plik remembered his conversation with Hope the night before. He spoke without giving himself time for a second thought.

"I will go with you, Powerful Tenderness. I am not as strong as you are, but weight counts for something. I am also very stubborn and that counts for more. Truth would find it hard to pull away from me."

The human/bear face with those cold snake's eyes broke into a smile as warm as any Plik had ever seen. "Good. I will be glad to have you—and not only for your weight and stubbornness. I will be glad for those sharp ears that hear so much more than sounds. Truth is not telling us everything she knows. Of that I am certain. You may 'hear' something the rest of us will miss."

Plik felt very pleased at this praise.

"I will go with you," he repeated, and wondered what he had gotten himself into.

◑╳◐

THEY DEPARTED CENTER ISLAND late the following day. Had Firekeeper had her way, they would have left with the morning's freshness, for the moon was new and there would not be much light after dark, but there were complications she had not anticipated.

For one, the maimalodalum had decided that Truth must wear a harness and leash, and Powerful Tenderness came to hold the leash's end.

"Otherwise she will climb a tree and be gone before any of us can catch her," Powerful Tenderness said. "I have sent word out and none of her kin will protest."

"None will help either, I suppose," Blind Seer grumbled.

"Jaguar-kind are not social," Powerful Tenderness reminded him. "Let them be what they were made to be. At least they come about their quirks naturally."

Another of the maimalodalum joined them, ostensibly to assist Powerful Tenderness. When Firekeeper saw that the one so chosen was the raccoon-man, Plik, the same who had asked so many questions during the council the night before, she wondered at his intentions, but out of good manners she kept these wonderings to herself.

The two maimalodalum insisted on bringing baggage, not only to assure their own comfort, but in anticipation that the "door" they sought might not be in plain sight. Firekeeper had to admit the maimalodalum had a good idea there. In her years in the wilds, she had jury-rigged tools often enough to fully approve of having them along ready-made.

She felt particularly ready to agree when it became clear she was not expected to carry anything extra. Powerful Tenderness hoisted a large pack onto his back and seemed not to feel the weight.

Rascal, of Firekeeper and Blind Seer's own pack, also joined them. He had arrived two days after Firekeeper and Blind Seer along with Dark Death, Moon Frost, and the pups. The pups were footsore after the longest, fastest trek they had ever made, but Rascal had been held beneath his own growing strength. Even hunting along the trail had not exhausted him. So, although Dark Death and Moon Frost decided to stay with the pups, Rascal insisted on running along.

The ravens Bitter and Lovable completed their number, ostensibly to ease the trail and be there to follow Truth if she did indeed break loose. Firekeeper thought the real reason the ravens were accompanying them was that Lovable had learned they were going to a ruin. Wise or not, the raven had an insatiable appetite for the pretty things—or fragments thereof—that were so often found in these places.

With such a company, the trip should have offered no difficulties beyond those involved in covering the intervening ground in the swiftest time practical. The ebb and flow of the tides dictated when they could swim between the various islands. Once or twice, when the low-tide waters were not shallow enough to allow for safe fording, Bitter, who had status within the Wise Beast community, despite his flutter-brained mate, requested aide from some seals who lived in the vicinity.

Firekeeper found the strength with which the seals moved through the water exciting, but Blind Seer protested the creatures smelled abysmally of fish. Truth loved swimming, so much so that she grew agitated when they took her from the water.

After their first fording, when they were planning their second, Truth slipped her harness. They were contemplating a river, wondering whether to look for a ford or take their chances swimming, when Firekeeper noticed that the leash so firmly grasped in Powerful Tenderness's paw was strangely limp.

Her gaze traced the length and found no arrogant jaguar at the end, just an empty nest of straps. She cast around and saw Plik emerging from the river, wherein he had gone to test the depth. Neither the ravens nor Truth were to be seen.

"Hey! What!" Firekeeper howled. "Where is Truth?"

At almost the same moment there were agitated croaks and quorking raven calls from the deeper tree line.

"Here! Here!" the ravens called. "Truth is here! Hurry!"

They all followed that cry, Plik not even pausing to shake off the water that had soaked into his thick fur. They arrived in an unorganized mob to find Truth lying on a tree limb a good twelve feet off the ground. Her gaze was—for her—clear and direct, though the burnt-orange orbs flickered back and forth, as if seeing things invisible to the rest.

"I want to go fishing," Truth announced sulkily. "My paws are sore, and I am weary of walking."

"I thought," said Powerful Tenderness, his voice charged with the barely contained fury that comes when one has had a fright, "you wished to go to the house that is no longer a house. We will never get there if we keep stopping. Now, how did you get out of your harness?"

Truth looked distinctly puzzled. "How did I get here?"

Powerful Tenderness held up the tangled mess of straps at the end of the harness, suspending it from his broad hands so that all could see not a single buckle had been undone nor strap broken.

"That is what I would like to know," he replied. "We were looking at the river, working out the best way to get across, and the next thing I realized there was shouting that you were gone."

Firekeeper crinkled her brow in thought, remembering tales of Truth drinking water that wasn't there, water that was real enough to dew upon her coat. Had the jaguar somehow gone where that water was for long enough to shed her harness? If so, why did she need Firekeeper to come and open a door for her?

Glancing at Blind Seer, Firekeeper could see that the blue-eyed wolf shared her thoughts. She ran her hand through his fur, a mute request that they not speak of this. It was not that she did not think it would occur to Powerful Tenderness or Plik, but she knew their concern was for Truth, and that they would not welcome suspicions that Truth was being less than completely honest.

Besides, Firekeeper thought, *now more than ever I want to go to this place. What is there that Truth wishes us to see? Perhaps there is indeed a door that she needs opened. Perhaps there is something else.*

Rascal was leaping and snapping at the treed jaguar. Firekeeper kicked him solidly in the shoulder, sending him rolling.

"Fool, pup!" Firekeeper snapped. "You merit an ear cut into ribbons for such behavior. Never taunt one of the great cats. Singly they are a match for any wolf."

Truth liked this praise, and licked a paw complacently. Firekeeper grinned up at her.

"But, Truth," she continued, "no jaguar is a match for three wolves—especially when one of them is quite good at climbing trees. Will you come down, or do I come up after you?"

Truth wrinkled her nose and spat, but she also jumped down and haughtily permitted her harness to be put back on her.

Even so, twice more she slipped her harness. Once was when a young doe bolted out of a thicket, surprising them all. One moment Truth was meandering along in her harness, partly steered by her two guides, the next she was a blur of golden light and compact speed, chasing down the terrified doe.

The second time, they had taken shelter from a violent thunderstorm. Lightning struck a tree nearby and even before the air filled with the smell of burning wood, Truth was away. She came back, embarrassed by her own fear.

"I was elsewhere" was all she would say, "and the sound caught me unawares."

So it was that with a heart filled to brimming with a heady mixture of doubt and curiosity Firekeeper breasted the inlet that would take them to the island that held the house that was no house, a ruin that had, apparently, been ruined by some agency other than the passage of time.

AS ISLANDS WENT, their destination was not among the largest in Misheemnekuru, nor the best positioned. Long and narrow, but sheltered on the whole by one of the more massive islands from the force of the open ocean, it was large enough to harbor wolves, deer, and ample smaller game. Elk, being graz-ers rather than browsers, did not thrive there.

This lack of large game was why the island only boasted a single small pack, and why Firekeeper's versatility as a hunter had been welcome. Bitter and Lovable had flown ahead, and the resident pack had sent their welcome. Bitter must have given the wolves reason to stay away, however, for the travelers landed without the reception Firekeeper had expected.

She drew the raven aside, and he confirmed her suspicion.

"Something is not right with what Truth tells us. I would not involve those who have young to help survive through the coming winter. There are a few resident great cats as well. I have sent word to them of what we are about, for I would not have rumor reach them that we are abusing their kin."

Firekeeper nodded. "I have felt that Truth is hiding something, but I do not know what. Do you have any wisdom you might share with me?"

The raven fluffed his feathers as if feeling cold, though the day was quite warm. "I do not, but cats of any size are sneaky. They rely on stealth rather than force of number for their hunting. This contaminates all their thinking."

Firekeeper, who held similar views, did not protest. Wolves and ravens, whether Cousin or Royal or Wise, were frequent allies, comfortable with the ways of their different peoples.

Indeed, we are not too unalike. They have their flocks, and their mated pairs. So do we. They may be scavengers, rather than hunters, but they are clever, as one who snatches meat from a wolf's jaws must be.

The group had made their crossing as daylight was waning. The beast-souled preferred not to travel by night, though the wolves and jaguar would have been as comfortable after dark. The ravens, though not bound to daylight hours as their Cousin kin were, also preferred daylight. Considering the possi-ble pitfalls concealed beneath the land over which they must travel, Firekeeper decided in favor of those who preferred daylight.

"We will travel on come morning," she said. "The ground here is unpre-dictable, littered with holes as Rascal learned. Blind Seer, do you scent fresh water?"

The blue-eyed wolf tossed back his head and took the scent.

"To the south," he said. "I think I remember the place. Rascal and I will scout ahead. Two alone may have some luck hunting."

They did, and that night the small group dined on rabbit—roasted over a fire for Firekeeper, Plik, and Powerful Tenderness. Plik had proven to be en-thusiastically omnivorous. He located an apple tree laden with fruit not completely ruined by the birds and insects, and brought back a sack from which all but Rascal and Blind Seer shared.

"Tomorrow," Plik said, rubbing his hands together, "I will forage for eggs. We brought oil, and an omelet would be wonderful after all this trail food."

After dinner had been eaten, the three wolves went running, ostensibly to scout tomorrow's route, but mostly because Firekeeper wanted to warn Rascal to be on guard against Truth. Blind Seer needed no warning. If anything, he was more suspicious than Firekeeper.

When they returned, both the beast-souled and the jaguar were asleep. Firekeeper laid her head on Blind Seer's flank as she had done hundreds of times before, but even when she drifted off to sleep, she chased suspicions in her nightmares.

III

THE HOUSE THAT WAS NO LONGER A HOUSE had been built on a rocky promontory near the southern edge of the island. The earth here was mixed with quantities of sand from which grew sharp-edged grasses, prickly shrubs with leathery leaves, and a few scrawny, twisted trees. There were none of the towering forest giants that were elsewhere common throughout Misheemnekuru. Their roots could not grab hold in the porous soil, and the corpses of those who had attempted to reach beyond what the winds would permit lay scattered and slowly rotting.

Someday, if the waters permitted, these dead trees might be the beginning of better soil in which plants that would strengthen the island's hold against erosion and decay could grow. For now, the fallen timber, overgrown with vines and brambles, only added to the general aura of desolation.

The area must have been more inviting when the house that was no longer a house had been built here, Firekeeper thought, for who would have gone to such trouble when there were many other more pleasant places both on Misheemnekuru and on the mainland.

The building or buildings that had stood here had not been the result of a passing fancy—no summer cottage or fishing cabin, as Firekeeper had seen in human lands. The cellar into which Rascal had fallen had been excavated from the surrounding rock. The building stones that remained scattered beneath the vines were large and cleanly cut. She and Blind Seer had found traces of richly tinted colored glass, such as was used for ornamental windows in fine houses. Doubtless the other trims had been equally ornate.

Rascal loped ahead when they reached the promontory, his nose to the ground, his tail alert and straight behind him.

"I found it!" he howled back after a moment. "I found the hole where I fell in."

Blind Seer growled, "Then stay back from the edge, witless. We don't want to have to pull you out again, and the soil will crumble at a breath. I learned the hard way that matted vines only look solid."

Rascal danced back obediently, but Firekeeper could tell the young wolf felt no real fear now that he knew for certain where the hole was. Had she ever been so sure of herself?

No, she thought, *for I was always aware how weak I was in contrast to the wolves. Only among humans did I come to see my strengths.*

Even while watching Rascal frolic, Firekeeper had not neglected to keep an eye on Truth. The jaguar had been more vague than usual during that day's short march, and Firekeeper thought Truth might have gone wherever it was she went when she shed her harness. If so, it was a journey of the mind, not the body. The straps and ties remained snug around the rounded barrel of her body, the collar firmly around her neck.

"So, Truth," Firekeeper said after she and her allies had investigated the area and found nothing that even vaguely resembled a door. "Where is this door you wish me to open for you? This is the place, is it not?"

Truth did not respond. Only the rise and fall of her breath beneath her ribs gave lie to the impression that they were looking at a figure of a jaguar, stuffed and mounted. Her ears did not twitch, even when Firekeeper snapped her fingers directly outside their rounded cups. Her eyes, normally rich orange with the curious golden sheen that gave back light after dark, seemed almost opaque and dull. The pupils did not change in size when Firekeeper held up her hand to block the brilliance of the sunlight.

"She sees somewhere else," Powerful Tenderness said. "This is not good."

"Once before when Truth was like this, I put strong perfume beneath her nose," Firekeeper said, "and that seemed to awaken her. But there is no scent here stronger-smelling than piss—and we wish to awaken her, not offend."

"Toss her in the ocean!" Rascal said, bouncing slightly. "Dunking her would wake her up. Go on! There's water all around us. Truth likes swimming. She won't mind! She might even think it's funny."

Firekeeper had to admit she was tempted to take the younger wolf's suggestion. To come so far just to have the jaguar stand there ignoring them was annoying—offensive, even. Yet Firekeeper didn't want to act merely out of temper. As a compromise, Firekeeper ran down to the nearest beach, a narrow strip, almost as much pebble as sand, and filled her cupped palms with seawater. Some, inevitably, dripped away, but on her return enough remained to solidly splash the jaguar's face.

Droplets beaded on the dense fur, but some rolled into those opaque eyes, into the rounded ears, and down the length of Truth's nose. Truth blinked, spat, and pawed at her eyes. Salt water stings, and the jaguar's inner eyelids had not been closed. Then she sneezed, and as if her spirit came back to her with the next intake of breath, Truth shook her head and glowered at Firekeeper.

"So you are back with us," Firekeeper said. She was already out of reach of those sharp-tipped claws—at least if Truth stayed leashed—but she let her hand drop to her Fang, just in case.

Truth did not vanish, nor did she miraculously shed her harness. Instead she looked side to side, apparently seeing where they were for the first time.

"So we are here," she muttered.

"So we have been telling you," Blind Seer growled. "Now, before you forget us once more, tell us, where is this door my Firekeeper is to open for you?"

Truth wrinkled her lip in a feline sneer. " 'Your Firekeeper'—well, we shall see. As for the door, I will show you."

The jaguar picked her way through the rubble without regard for the pair holding her leash. They scrabbled to follow. Plik, with his round shape and rather short legs, did not have the flexibility to pick his way.

"Here," he said to Powerful Tenderness, and tossed over his leash so that the massive hand-paws held both lines. Powerful Tenderness acknowledged with a grunt, and pulled back. His strength was such that even the Wise Jaguar must acknowledge it.

"Slow," Powerful Tenderness said. "This restraint is for your safety, more than for that of anyone else. Should your mind flee your body once more, someone must have hold."

Truth spat. "Slow is not what I have. This close . . . I am drawn in too many directions. Here now, here . . ."

The jaguar sniffed the ground in an area that Firekeeper had noticed was slightly higher than its surroundings. She dug with one paw, then the other, and was apparently satisfied with what she found.

"Hear me well," Truth said, "for I may not be able to repeat myself. Dig in this place, but carefully. . . . It is a made hole. . . ."

The jaguar was already struggling for coherence. Rascal supplied what she did not.

"A cellar, like the one I fell into."

"Must take out the dirt and stone . . ." was Truth's reply. "Northern wall . . . door . . . locked, sealed. Must open."

"I must open," Firekeeper prompted.

"You will see. . . . You will . . . understand . . ." But the last phrase was little more than a rumble and hiss. When Firekeeper looked more closely, the jaguar's gaze was again opaque.

"Do we splash her again?" Rascal asked, bouncing again. The young wolf looked willing to carry seawater in his mouth if he'd be permitted to spit it in the jaguar's face.

Firekeeper shook her head. "No. Let the cat rest. I wish Truth could be more clear, but there is enough here to go on."

Rascal transformed his bounce into a bound and went to sniff around where Truth had said there was a cellar.

"I don't see any hole, nor smell one." He gave a short howl. "There's no echo either."

Blind Seer bit him on one ear. "Idiot," he growled, letting go. "The jaguar said the hole was filled. Remember the proverb: 'A wise wolf scouts the prey, knows when to hunt, when to stay away.' "

"But we're not going to run away, are we?" Rascal pleaded.

"No, but this is a hunt like any other," Blind Seer replied. "As such, it must be planned. Let Firekeeper take a closer look at what we have found. Otherwise we'll only waste time digging you out again."

Rascal groveled apology, and Blind Seer relented a little.

"Later, you can put some of your mad energy into digging. Meanwhile, maybe you and I should go secure some dinner, and give proper greetings to our winter friends."

The blue-eyed wolf glanced over at Firekeeper and she nodded her approval. She would have preferred to go hunting, but Blind Seer was right. She and the maimalodalum had the best chance of finding what must be found. Still, she had to swallow a sigh as Rascal, not she, followed Blind Seer into the green tangle.

Powerful Tenderness bent and picked up the now inert Truth.

"I will take her to the shade and secure her," he said, "for whatever good that will do. Then I will come and help."

Plik nodded agreement. "As will I. There is no use guarding Truth when we cannot figure out how she vanishes, and I do not think any predator will come stalking her—not with our mingled scents to give warning that she is not alone. My time would be better spent trying to guess what type of place this was. I have gathered some knowledge of the old builders' ways in a long lifetime spent among their ruins."

Firekeeper listened to this with half her attention. She was on her hands and knees, cutting away the tangling vines with her hatchet, then pushing back the accumulated leaf matter and the upper layer of dirt. Here and there she probed with a straight stick until she met resistance. The first few times she dug, all she encountered were stray bits of building stone, but finally her persistence was rewarded.

"I've found an edge," she said. "Building stone, mortared together. It may well be the edge of the cellar."

Powerful Tenderness had begun systematically stripping away vines and moving stray stones. Now he lumbered over and squatted next to her to inspect her find. Plik picked his way across to join them.

"It looks like the edge of a wall," Plik agreed, "but which edge? Truth spoke of a northern wall. That implies three others."

Firekeeper hunkered back, inspecting their surroundings. Unfortunately, the area was flat enough that the mass of the cellar could lie in either direction.

"I think," she said, "that our best bet would be to trace this wall until it comes to a corner, then see which way the corner turns. If it turns south, then we have found our northern wall. If it turns north, however, we have more searching to do."

"Can't we just clear the next wall," Powerful Tenderness asked, "maybe not fully, but enough to find our way?"

"That's probably what we must do," Firekeeper said, "for without any sense of the dimensions of this cellar, we cannot simply pace off a distance and find the next wall. Still, I am hoping that this is the correct wall. Truth led us to this point. I am hoping her sense of direction was precise rather than general."

"That's a big hope," Powerful Tenderness said, glancing over to where the jaguar crouched unseeing and unmoving in the shade of the largest tree he had been able to find.

"It's all we have," Firekeeper said, and methodically got to work.

Her persistence over the next several days would have surprised her human friends, all of whom viewed her as impulsive and impatient, but Firekeeper had not survived for the better part of a decade in the northwestern mountains only because of the loving care offered by the wolves.

The wolves could keep her fed and relatively warm, but they could not do for Firekeeper the dozens of mind-numbing tasks that had been part of her daily routine. Just caring for the knife that had been her most important tool had taken discipline lest the blade rust or become dull.

The wolves could tear into their food without regard, but Firekeeper must skin or scale hers. If she wished to save the hides—as she did whenever possible—then she must take care to preserve and treat them. Her knowledge of tanning had been rudimentary, so the hides had stiffened or rotted more quickly than they would have had she had the skills she now possessed. Therefore, she had been forced to make and remake her clothing.

Fishing augmented the meals the wolves brought her, for unlike a wolf, Firekeeper could not eat once every few days and fast the rest. Nor could she thrive on meat close to rotting, as the wolves did. Then, too, she needed vegetable food. In summer this was fairly simple to find. In winter it meant digging through snow and/or breaking ice as did the deer and elk her people hunted.

Yes. Firekeeper possessed ample patience when it suited her—just not for the things humans thought important and she thought rather foolish.

As she methodically cleared accumulated matter from the top of the wall, she thought of these human friends. She had not seen much of them since soon after the falling of the Tower of Magic. Before the winter shut the ports, Derian had gone north again, and there Firekeeper understood he had taken part in the waltzing for precedence that humans called diplomacy.

Derian had returned south to Liglim in the late spring, and Firekeeper had seen him a few times, but the lure of Misheemnekuru and the life she was making there—and the joy that for the first time in over three years apparently no one needed her to do anything except what she wanted to do—had kept her away from the mainland.

Firekeeper felt a little guilty about this, but only a little. There were many humans with whom Derian could occupy himself, and apparently he was becoming quite important among them. He had his pack and she hers. Moreover, she had the promise of several ravens that should Derian come to harm, she would be told.

As she dug, Firekeeper also wondered about this house that was not a house that they were now excavating. Why had someone gone to the trouble of building what Plik assured her must have been a massive and solid structure only to tear it down again and eliminate even the cellars? The longer she and her allies worked, the more it became apparent that the cellar into which Rascal had stumbled had been little more than a root cellar, and had probably been overlooked in the general effort to eliminate all traces of this building.

Plik was not built well for digging. His hands were as clever as those of a human—or a raccoon. With them, he crafted a sort of sledge, and convinced Rascal to haul away the larger pieces of detritus. Then Plik joined Firekeeper and Powerful Tenderness in clearing away vines and probing for wall edges.

When he grew weary, for with his years Plik could not labor as steadily as the younger ones did, he inspected the scattered stonework. On the first night, he told them that some of the stones had fragments of writing on them.

"It's an old dialect, not one I read easily. I have sent a copy of some of the fragments back to Center Island for translation. If none of the other beast-souled will come, I have asked for a loan of some of the dictionaries. Bitter assures me that between them a couple of the fish eagles can transport even a large book."

"Can you read any of the writing at all?" Powerful Tenderness asked. "I would like to know what manner of place this was. I do not think it was a mere estate."

"I can read a little," Plik said, "and I think you are right about this not being some estate. For one, I do not think that people, even then, so copiously inscribed the stones of their homes. I would guess this was a temple of some sort—but I cannot guess which of the deities were celebrated here."

Firekeeper did her best to hide a shudder. There was ample evidence that the worship practiced by the forerunners of the modern theocracy of Liglim had involved blood sacrifice—and magic.

THE BOOKS PLIK REQUESTED arrived on the third morning of their digging, but Plik did not have much time to spend piecing together stone fragments and translating their texts, for on that same day Firekeeper found a corner. To her delight, the angle turned south, seeming to confirm that Truth had led them to the northern wall.

"We need to be sure, though," she said, "so while the rest of you start digging, Plik and I will make certain that we have the outline of this cellar."

No one protested this division of labor. Blind Seer and Rascal were quite pleased to dig a ditch alongside the inner edge of the wall. Powerful Tenderness, who had brought a shovel blade in his pack and fashioned a handle as soon as digging was clearly in the offing, did deeper clearance. All took turns hauling away the accumulated detritus.

Everyone kept watch over Truth, but it hardly seemed necessary. The Wise Jaguar lay in whatever shade in which she was put, ate when food was put directly under her nose, drank if her muzzle was pressed into fresh water. Otherwise, she did little but dream weird dreams, her paws twitching as she ran who knew where.

By the fourth day, Firekeeper felt certain they had the correct wall and joined Powerful Tenderness in clearing away dirt. The huge maimalodalu did most of the actual digging, but Firekeeper shoveled dirt and stone onto the sledge that Rascal, and now Blind Seer hauled. It had been hard to convince the blue-eyed wolf to take his turn in the traces, but Firekeeper shamed him into the work, showing him her own bruised and blistered hands.

"We are a pack, are we not?" she said, and although Blind Seer did not stop complaining about the indignity, he let Plik harness him up and hauled.

On the fifth day, the soft dirt on the edge of their trench crumpled inward. Had Powerful Tenderness not been so tall, he would have been completely covered. As it was, he was buried right to his chin. Firekeeper uncovered him with all the haste care would permit. After that accident, some of the Wise Wingéd Folk brought heavy sailcloth that could be used along with cut saplings to hold back the dirt. By the sixth day they were ready to continue.

On the seventh day, they found the door, and by that evening, with renewed enthusiasm, they had cleared its surface to the threshold. The door was sheathed in dark metal, unadorned but for some writing stamped into its surface. There was no knob, latch, or keyhole—nothing at all to indicate how it should be opened.

After the door was cleared, Plik very carefully made his way out onto the packed dirt and stone that still filled the bulk of the cellar. Pebbles and dry soil trickled into the trench.

"Careful," Firekeeper warned.

"I am being careful," Plik answered, proving this by very cautiously lowering his bulk so that his weight would be dispersed more evenly. "I want to see what's written on the door. It's the same old script I've been finding on the blocks. Now that I have the dictionaries, I think I can translate it."

"Good," Firekeeper said, mollified. "Can you see the writing clearly enough? The sun is setting."

"I inherited excellent night vision from both my parents," Plik said. "I can manage well enough to make a copy."

Firekeeper found herself wondering who among the assorted beast-souled were Plik's parents—or if they were even alive, for Plik was clearly a mature creature. As no one of the maimalodalum looked unduly like any of the others, she couldn't even guess.

Plik had brought a well-scraped piece of hide with him, and now he copied the inscription with a bit of charcoal. The scratching sound made Firekeeper's back prickle—at least that's what she told herself, refusing to admit her growing apprehension.

" 'Silver,' " Plik murmured. "That word is unchanged from what we use today. So is 'magic.' 'Light' is an older form, but I'm sure that's what it means. There's something here about a cascade, but I can't figure out how that fits."

" 'Cascade,' as in a waterfall, you mean?" asked Powerful Tenderness. He stood beside Firekeeper in the trench, inspecting the door but apparently having no better luck in discovering how to open it.

"Something like that," Plik agreed, "but there seems to be something about 'detritus,' too. It doesn't help that the text is written in one of those archaic verse forms where it seems the author thought it was in bad taste to use verbs. I was never very good at those."

Firekeeper listened, letting the words flow through the edges of her awareness. It occurred to her that, in nature, patterns in the dappling on the fawn's coat or the spots on a moth's wings often served to distract the eye from what was really there. She set her fingers to inspecting the surface of the door, looking for any irregularities that might not be visible to the naked eye. She traced every letter, seeing if it hid more than mere meaning, but found nothing.

When she drew her hands back, she noticed that the pads of her fingers were blackened. When she licked one, the blackening didn't rinse clean, only smudged a bit. Powerful Tenderness noticed what she was doing and frowned.

"Why are you licking yourself, Firekeeper?"

"My fingers," she said, holding them to show him. The black marks were clear even in the fading light. "The door made them filthy, but the marks do not come away easily." She spat. "Licking wasn't a good idea. My mouth tastes like metal."

"Go drink some water," Powerful Tenderness said, but his attention was elsewhere. As Firekeeper climbed from the trench, she saw he had taken a bit of cloth from a pouch that hung at his waist and was using it to rub the metal.

Water made most of the taste go away, and Firekeeper chased away the remainder with a few withered, late-season blackberries before returning. Powerful Tenderness was still rubbing the door, and even in the failing light Firekeeper could see that a section was lighter than the surrounding area.

"The door is made from silver," Powerful Tenderness said in response to her query. "Something Plik said made me think it might be. What came off on your fingers was tarnish, not dirt."

Firekeeper nodded. "Does this matter?"

"It might," Powerful Tenderness replied. He seemed to notice the gathering darkness for the first time. "But this is not the time to worry about it. Plik, let me come up before you move again. If you spill a little dirt in after, it won't hit me."

The raccoon-man didn't look up from his copying, but nodded. Firekeeper turned away, knowing work was done for the day, and looking forward to whatever Blind Seer and Rascal might have hunted up for her dinner. She was tired of rabbit. Maybe they would have taken a deer.

"MAGIC." "LIGHT." Those words hadn't changed too much over time. One verb gave Plik a great deal of trouble. It turned out to be an archaic form of "reflect," little in use these days.

The minimalist verse style had been popular over a hundred years before Divine Retribution had sent the Old World rulers to whatever judgment the deities had ordained. Rather than making Plik's task easier, it made it less so, for even when Plik felt fairly certain he had all the words correctly translated, meaning still escaped him.

Plik finished his translation that night when meals had been eaten and even the three wolves were settled near the fire—though all three sat with their backs to the flame lest their night vision be spoiled. Truth had no such qualms. The jaguar cuddled so close that the occasional spark guttered out in her fur.

"So," Firekeeper said after a long silence, "what do you have?"

"Have?" Plik replied blankly.

"You haven't been writing for some time, but your eyes go up and down over the page. What do you have there that is so fascinating?"

Plik chuckled. He felt a ridiculous urge to toss the paper in the fire rather than subject his efforts to that coolly assessing mind, but he knew he was being foolish.

"I think I know what it says," he replied, "or rather, I have meanings for all the words, but I'm not sure in the least what it means."

"Read it," Firekeeper said, her tone midway between a suggestion and an order.

Plik couldn't think of any reason why he shouldn't, so he complied.

Magic Light
Silver Shine
Reflect
Back, then back, then back, then back
Cascading concourse
Bright shower
Foaming tumult
Carrying detritus
Open way

"Magic light?" Firekeeper said. "Reflecting? If reflecting magic light is what we need, then we must find some other way through. I wonder if we can cut silver?"

"It depends on how thick it is," Powerful Tenderness said automatically, "and how pure. Pure silver is fairly soft as metals go. But it doesn't follow that we don't have magic light. Some of the light panels in the tower on Center Island still work. I suppose that is magic light."

"But would those panels work if taken from the tower?" Plik objected. "Our experiments have shown otherwise. I don't think that could be the answer."

"Why didn't whoever wrote that just say what needed to be done?" whined Rascal.

"Why bury a door underground?" Blind Seer retorted. "There are times I think you might as well be Cousin-kind for all you use your mind. Whoever wrote those words didn't want them to be easy to understand, just as they didn't want that door to be easy to find. I know little of human buildings, but I recall certain things Firekeeper and I saw in New Kelvin. I am sure that even when the building here was standing—before it was flattened to the ground—this door was hidden."

Plik nodded vigorously. "That idea goes well with what little I have been able to understand from the fragments of writing on the building stone. Many of the words seem to be warnings or cautions. This was not a place where the common resident would have been welcome."

"So," Powerful Tenderness said, and Plik worried that the huge creature was angry that his idea had been so quickly dismissed. "If 'magic light' is not to be found in the panels at the towers, where do we find it?"

"Or how do we cut the silver?" Firekeeper muttered, her words probably inaudible to any but Blind Seer, next to whom she sat, and to Plik, whose hearing was unexpectedly good given that his ears were rather small and furry.

Plik ignored the wolf-woman—after all, she hadn't been addressing him. "I've been thinking about the original word used for 'magic.' I translated it as an adjective modifying 'light.' There seemed to be justification in a parallel to the next line."

He heard a faint growl that he was fairly certain came from Firekeeper and hastened on.

"The language is archaic. Forms have changed. What if instead of it being 'magic light,' it is 'Magic's light'?"

The two foreigners looked as baffled as ever, but Rascal yelped happily, "Moonlight! The Moon is Magic's body, and so moonlight would be magic's light."

Firekeeper nodded. "I remember your people's old tales. That makes sense. So this begins to work. Moonlight, reflected, will open the way."

"Not so fast," Blind Seer said. "How then do you explain all of this about reflecting back and back?"

Firekeeper shrugged, but Powerful Tenderness answered.

"If the door is silver, then it would reflect back light cast upon it. However, somehow the light must be handled so that it reflects repeatedly. I can see doing that with sunlight, but with something as weak as moonlight?"

They sat in silence, contemplating.

"There will be a full moon in a few days," Firekeeper said at last. "The moonlight will be strongest then. We should at least try."

Plik stared up at the waxing moon. "I wonder how the ones who built this door managed to get moonlight into a cellar?"

"Maybe that's why the inscription hints at using mirrors," Powerful Tenderness said. "There could have been a window into the cellar."

"It's all very strange," Plik said. "I know we came here to let Truth out, but what is this door? Why was it built here? How did Truth—or some part of Truth—come to be on the other side?"

Rascal cut in, repeating his earlier question. "And why make it so hard to understand the inscription? I know what Blind Seer said—that it was meant to be hard to understand, just like the door was meant to be hard to find—but why?"

Firekeeper shifted uneasily. "Rabbits and foxes alike hide the entrances to their dens so that they will always be able to escape, but this does not seem to be of the same order. This seems like a door that is not meant to be opened except with great difficulty."

Plik knew that Firekeeper had been raised by Royal Wolves, and that the Royal Beasts had as great an aversion to magic as did their northern human counterparts—an amusing parallel, since in all other things the Royal Beasts viewed themselves as in opposition to the humans. Still, Firekeeper surely had heard stories from the old days when magic was still common—and was used by those who ruled humans and annihilated Beasts with equal cruelty.

The maimalodalum had a different relationship with Magic, but more than did the yarimaimalom or the humans who lived on the mainland, their tales included cautionary ones. After all, the beast-souled themselves had been created from an abuse of magic. Plik wondered if Firekeeper's thoughts paralleled his own, but she said nothing aloud, so he spoke.

"I wonder if something is locked away there," Plik said, "something powerful, perhaps, or merely dangerous, but something so valuable that the ones who built this place did not want to destroy it."

"Do we leave it locked away then?" Firekeeper asked, and Plik was fairly certain she would be happy to do so. "If we do, it means abandoning Truth to her madness—or hoping she finds her way back by some other road."

Powerful Tenderness looked at the jaguar who had been his charge for over a year now. "Truth has grown worse, not better since we have come to this place. She is like one in whom fever has split the body and soul. I fear that even if we took her from here she would not recover."

"I agree," Plik said. "Whatever is happening to her is not active magic applied against her. I would 'hear' that, I am sure. I think her talent for divination is splitting her mind from her body, as once it revealed omens for her contemplation."

"So," Firekeeper said, "you do not think Truth will find her way back from this madness."

"No," Plik replied for both himself and Powerful Tenderness.

Firekeeper stretched, rising with the motion. Blind Seer rose beside her.

"Very well," the wolf-woman said. "Then we have two choices. We can do our best to open this door to which Truth has led us and hope she is the only thing that comes out, or we can give up."

"Wolves," Blind Seer added, "find it difficult to give up on a pack member. Truth may not be a wolf, but she has been if not a friend, at least an ally."

"So you wish to proceed?" Plik said.

"We do," Firekeeper said. "I could not sleep well knowing I left Truth trapped."

"Besides," Blind Seer said pragmatically, "we do not know if we can open this door. If we do open the door, we do not have to remove anything from the space behind but Truth."

Plik wished he was as certain they would have the choice. He only had to look at his own reflection to be reminded that even well-laid plans did not end as those who made them might wish.

Sometimes, they created monsters.

IV

FIREKEEPER DECIDED SHE DID NOT LIKE POLISHING silver one bit. Even after Bitter returned from Center Island bearing with him a compound that made the task easier, the job remained filthy, repetitive, and boring.

However, neither Blind Seer nor Rascal could help, for they lacked hands. Plik and Powerful Tenderness took turns, but there was room for only two at a time in the trench. Worse, Firekeeper was the only one supple enough to polish the lower portions of the silver door. As everyone—even she—had agreed that a wholly polished surface was probably necessary, she could not slip away and leave the work to others.

So she polished. That night, while she was trying to wash away the scent of tarnished metal in the cool waters of the bay, she wondered if the moon so high above was laughing at her.

When they were not taking a turn polishing, Plik and Powerful Tenderness experimented with a variety of mirrors, seeing which caught light best, learning how to cup the glow and send it elsewhere. Later, when Lovable returned from Center Island bearing a small sack of polished lenses, they worked on using these rounded pieces of glass to intensify the light.

By the night of the full moon, the two maimalodalum had worked out some possible ways to reflect moonlight "Back, then back, then back, then back," as the verse demanded. Firekeeper had her own ideas about what might be needed, but she kept these to herself, not sharing them even with Blind Seer. Magic made her uncomfortable, and her growing understanding of how the art might have worked made her even more so.

On the night of the full moon, they gathered in the vicinity of the door. The fill dirt that remained in the cellar had settled now, the edges tamped down and shored up so they were less likely to cave in. Powerful Tenderness and Plik were down in the trench. Firekeeper waited above, standing on the packed dirt. Truth, still leashed and harnessed, sat beside her. The jaguar had needed to be carried to her position, her body as limp as that of a doll and nearly as lifeless.

Blind Seer and Rascal flanked the edges of the excavation, ready if needed to spring on Truth, or chase down anything that might get away from the pair of beast-souled and into the night. No one really expected any trouble of the sort, though. The oral history they had gathered from the Wise Beasts agreed that the building that had once been here had been razed before Divine Retribution had driven away the Old Country rulers. If anything alive had been imprisoned behind the silver door, it was unlikely that it had survived well over a hundred years.

PLIK CRANED HIS NECK BACK so he could watch as the moon rose. Last night and the night before they had calculated the arc it would travel through the sky, and he knew exactly when its light—faint and diffuse as it was—would touch the mirror. They would have plenty of time to try their various experiments, and then, if none of them worked, well, the moon would be nearly as full on the next night. They could try again.

Plik held the lenses that he and Powerful Tenderness hoped would help with the repeated channeling of the light. The mirror Powerful Tenderness held was an artifact taken from the Tower of Magic before it had fallen. As far as any had been able to tell, there was nothing magical about it, but they had all thought it was best to use something once dedicated to Magic for this task.

"All" was perhaps not the best way to think of it. He and Powerful Tenderness had agreed that this was the best course of action. Through messages relayed by the now weary-winged Bitter and Lovable, they had the concurrence of the majority of the beast-souled as well. None of them were happy about the need to work with magic, but it seemed necessary.

Firekeeper and Blind Seer had refused to offer any contribution to the process, stating that they knew little about magic. Plik thought the two Royal Beasts were being stubborn and deliberately obstructionist. The lore and traditions that governed magic might have been all but destroyed in their homeland, but he had gathered they had learned something of magical lore in New Kelvin.

However, although Plik had worked day after day beside Firekeeper, he could not say he understood her. He would find himself chatting comfortably with her and Powerful Tenderness, then his tongue would dry as he found himself groping for some idea or concept to bridge the gap between her youth and his age, her wolfish outlook and his own shaped by a life spent as both part of a community and yet ever a little apart.

Blind Seer paced nervously through a narrow route that kept him within his assigned duty station. His hackles were slightly raised, his head up, every line of his grey-furred body alert with tension. Firekeeper was more still, but she too showed tense alertness. Even Rascal, normally mischievous as most young things are when they start feeling their strength, was unduly quiet. The awareness that he was the only thing between the darkness and some unnamed horror had clearly weighed the young wolf down as nothing else had managed to do.

"Here comes Lady Moon," Powerful Tenderness said softly.

He looked at Plik, who replied with a faint nod. They had both agreed that reciting aloud any of the litanies to the Moon, or to Magic, the Child of Water, granddaughter of the Creator Deities, would only make their foreign allies edgy, but they had privately agreed to recite them in their hearts. Prayer could only help appease Magic's darker mood.

Earlier, Powerful Tenderness had drawn aside young Rascal and asked the wolf if he would do the same. The Wise Beasts, unlike their Royal counterparts, shared the religion that was practiced by Beasts and humans alike in this region. Rascal had agreed, and doubtless some of his nervousness was due to this dual role demanded of him. Wolves were interesting, and made good allies and worse enemies, but they were not terribly complex.

Now Powerful Tenderness stretched to catch the moonlight in the mirror. Plik felt a flicker of hope. Against all reason, the moonlight did seem to reflect back, but hope died almost as soon as it had arisen. That pale reflection was not sufficient to touch the silver door, much less be repeatedly relayed.

"We have failed," he said, lowering his own useless tools.

Reassurance came from an unlikely quarter. Firekeeper's husky voice broke the silence.

"Try again. The moon is higher now. Listen. The island's pack is singing to her. Perhaps she will hear us if we join them."

In example, Firekeeper raised her head and howled, a clear sound whose rise and fall made the hairs on Plik's body rise. Blind Seer and Rascal made a chorus of that single howl, and after a slight hesitation, Powerful Tenderness added his own guttural note.

Plik tried a howl or two, but the sounds he made were less than commanding, so he fell silent, listening. The distant howls of the resident pack mingled their notes into the concert, and Plik's sensitive ears caught more distant notes from the next island.

He also "heard" a faint and tenuous vibration that made him wonder if the moon had indeed heard the wolves' call. Perhaps Powerful Tenderness also heard this sound that was not a sound, for he raised the polished mirror toward the moonlight with renewed confidence.

Did the reflected moonlight seem brighter? Plik wasn't certain. He glanced up at the moon to try and gauge differences in intensity. So it was that he witnessed Firekeeper doing something very odd.

She had raised herself onto her left knee, her right leg crooked as if she was about to push herself upward into a standing position. Swiftly, she drew her hunting knife from its sheath. The cabochon-cut garnet in the hilt glinted as it caught the moonlight; then Firekeeper made a horizontal slashing motion against her right leg and blood beaded, then flowed, from the cut.

Firekeeper cupped her free hand to gather the blood, then tossed the liquid forward so it splattered against both the mirror in Powerful Tenderness's hand and the silver door. A few droplets touched Plik's fur as well, and he felt sickened.

Firekeeper caught a bit more blood, and again tossed it to land upon mirror and door. Then she pulled a bit of cloth from her waistband and bound her cut thigh with swift efficiency. Lastly, she cleaned both sides of her knife blade against the cloth and dropped the weapon into its sheath.

The entire process took no more than three or four easy breaths, and Plik was too shocked to make a sound. Blind Seer must have caught the scent of his partner's blood in the air, for his howling faltered, and would have ceased but that Firekeeper shouted:

"No! Keep singing. Look!"

She gestured toward the mirror that Powerful Tenderness held. Not the faintest doubt remained that the reflected moonlight had become brighter, co-alescing and contracting, seeming to focus on the beads of blood—or did the blood focus on the moonlight?

Plik "heard" the faint vibration of magic intensify, becoming a single note that echoed the wolves' song. The silvery light shot forth, and would have been swallowed by the sky, but Powerful Tenderness had recovered his com-posure and directed the beam toward the silver door. The light hit the mirror-bright surface and suddenly the entirety was illuminated, making the surrounding area brighten as if an oil-soaked pyre had burst into cold flame.

The blaze of light made Plik's eyes shut, but he forced them open despite the searing pain. In the new illumination he saw the beam from the mirror an-gling toward the sky as Powerful Tenderness shied away from the radiance. Plik leapt, scrabbling half up Powerful Tenderness as he might the trunk of a tree. He seized hold of Powerful Tenderness's arm and pulled the mirror back into alignment with the silver door.

Plik saw now what must be done. When the mirror slipped from Powerful Tenderness's grasp, he seized it. He caught the light that bounced from the sil-ver door, channeled it back again, running the brilliance along the door's edge, catching it again, and sending it back until the door's edges had all been un-bound.

The light failed with the opening of the last seam, and the door swung open into absolute darkness.

A shrill scream came from where Truth waited on top of the fill-dirt mound. For the first time in days, the jaguar moved with purpose and volition. She leapt into the pit, once again leaving leash and harness behind her.

Firekeeper leapt after, landing clumsily on her newly cut leg. There was a blur of grey as Blind Seer followed her.

Plik was suddenly aware that the howling had ceased, not just that of the three proximate wolves, but elsewhere as well. It left the surrounding area eerily silent. Even the insects and frogs made no noise. Even the waves lapping the beach seemed to do so tentatively, so as not to draw attention to themselves with their grumble and hiss.

Plik realized that the hum of magic that had vibrated his bones a moment before had died with the brilliant light.

"Aren't we going after them?" Rascal said pleadingly, and for the first time Plik realized that the young wolf had been trying to push past, but that he and Powerful Tenderness had unconsciously moved to block the now open door.

"I think we wait," Powerful Tenderness said. "Someone must remain to guard and to keep the door open so they may return."

"Or," added Plik, feeling a tremble of apprehension at the thought, "in case such comes forth that we must close and hold this door forever sealed."

ALTHOUH STILL REELING WITH SHOCK that she had been right—that blood and not mere tools would be needed to unseal the silver door—Firekeeper did not fail to feel Truth surging to her paws and gathering to leap through the now open door.

Firekeeper had expected something of the sort if they did indeed manage to open the door, and without conscious thought she leapt after. When she landed, she felt fresh blood dampen the bandage she had tied around her leg, but no great amount of pain. Abstract pleasure that she had calculated so exactly raised her spirits as she bolted into the darkness that had been concealed behind the silver door.

Firekeeper's night vision was very good, but the brilliant glow that had accompanied the unsealing of the door had left her temporarily night-blind. Truth, gifted as all cats were with an inner eyelid, did not suffer the same penalty and charged ahead.

Behind her, Firekeeper heard a dull thump as Blind Seer landed in the trench, but she did not pause in her pursuit of Truth. Blind Seer could track her by scent. Truth could see in the dark. She alone was handicapped here, and could not give up any advantage. A moment later, she felt the heat of Blind Seer's breath on the back of her legs, a sniff as he checked her wound, the warmth moving beside her as he came around and took point.

She let him do so without protest. That's what pack mates were for—providing strength and skill you yourself lacked. Firekeeper no more lost status for letting Blind Seer go ahead of her than she would have if she let him pull down an elk she had driven into his range.

"Truth's scent is still hot," Blind Seer said. "Can you track me if I go faster?"

"In a moment," Firekeeper assured him. "Go ahead. I will follow as swiftly as I can."

The blue-eyed wolf did not ask if she was "all right," as a human certainly would have done. He trusted the evidence of his nose, but that didn't mean Firekeeper would escape his scolding for her impulsiveness—that would come later. For now there was the hunt, and the hunt was all.

Firekeeper followed, finding that the surrounding area was not completely dark. They had passed from one space into another—she could tell, for the echoing of sound changed—and in this area where sound was more muted, and her feet fell upon what felt like thick carpeting, light glowed dully from above.

Glancing up, she saw pale blocks of stone such as she had seen in other buildings crafted by the Old Country rulers. These were artifacts, used to give light without the need for fire. She had seen such dead and useless, and she had seen such restored to life. These seemed to be nearly dead, but Firekeeper was glad for their faint glow. Had she been reared like the Wise Wolves to pray, she would have offered a brief prayer of thanks. Having been raised without such, she passed under and on, merely grateful.

The light was brighter still up ahead, bright enough that Firekeeper could see Blind Seer as a shaggy outline, though the greys and browns of his coat hardly differed from shadow. Ahead of the Royal Wolf, Truth, either more in the light or the brighter hues of her coat giving the illuminated blocks more to show, was visible. The jaguar was sniffing at something set in the wall, pawing at it as a kitten might a mouse hole, her muscles tight with mindless frustration.

Firekeeper joined the pair, standing in back of Blind Seer, aware that the wolf would do better at stopping Truth if the jaguar's frustration should turn against them. From this vantage she did her best to understand what was before her.

Truth—or Truth's body, for Firekeeper felt certain that body and mind were still not united—stood before another chunk of tarnished silver. This one was set flush into the polished stone of the wall, as if it had been built in when the surrounding room was made.

Although the silver block was tarnished black, Firekeeper thought she could see motion within, as if dull black was giving back a reflected image of the jaguar who stood before it. Instantly, Firekeeper understood. This was another door and Truth's spirit was on the other side, almost close enough to be joined with her physical self.

"Does this mean more moonlight and song and days of polishing?" Blind Seer growled. His hackles were up, making him seem much larger and much more dangerous. "Does this mean more bloodshed?"

"Perhaps," Firekeeper temporized, "but shove Truth away for me and let me try something."

"I will not let you harm yourself," Blind Seer rumbled. "Promise me. No more cutting."

"No more than has already been done," Firekeeper promised.

So Blind Seer stepped forward and shouldered the jaguar a few steps back from the blackened block of silver. Truth did not resist. Perhaps she sensed that the wolf was trying to help her. Firekeeper was glad. A fight between the pair would have been ugly indeed. As soon as she could, Firekeeper slid herself into the narrow space between Blind Seer and the wall.

Deftly, she unbound the blood-sodden rag from about her thigh. It was damp enough to dapple droplets onto the floor, and make the knot hard to untie.

Once Firekeeper had the cloth free, she rubbed the bloody thing against the tarnished silver block. Almost instantly there was a transformation. The blackened metal soaked up the wet blood, seeming to drink it. Where the rag touched the block it left behind a surface that was not only shining, but rapidly becoming transparent. Then it was not there at all.

A breeze moved the air in the enclosed chamber, carrying with it a form as tenuous as moonlight. It leapt over Blind Seer, and sank into Truth. The jaguar trembled from head to tail, stiffened, then crumpled onto the floor as if her paws could not bear the added weight of her soul.

Firekeeper felt the air around her eddy, then still. Glancing back over her shoulder, she saw that the opening had closed once more. Only a shining square of silver remained, twisting the reflection of her worried frown into a mocking leer.

AS BODY AND SOUL REJOINED, Truth fell into darkness, and in that darkness the mocking-voiced one waited. Yet there was no mockery in his voice now, only a dreadful sincerity that commanded her full attention.

"They are going to ask you about this place," the voice said. "Tell them what you know."

"I know nothing," Truth said, sulkily. "Who are you?"

"A friend," the other replied. "Haven't I proved it? All I ask is for you to re-member what I did for you—consider that later."

"Later?"

"Trust me. You'll know exactly what I mean."

"You ask for a great deal of trust."

"I led you out, didn't I?"

Truth felt her body around her, aware of heartbeat and breath as never be-fore, and was forced to agree.

"Remember," the voice said. "And now, I will let you awaken. Until we meet again, Truth."

"Again?"

"Surely you know all things are possible, O gifted one." The mockery had returned to the voice. "And the omens favor some things more than others."

Truth sensed that the source of the voice was gone. In another breath, she smelled—really *smelled*—others around her. There were sounds—real sounds—and she knew them for voices. She opened her outer lids, and the light was not too bright.

Opening her inner lids, she pushed up to rest on her paws and breastbone, aware how limp and sore her muscles were, but then—images from her body's memory flooded her mind—she had hardly moved for days now.

"I'm thirsty," she rasped.

◊❦◊

PLIK HARDLY KNEW whether he was relieved or not when Firekeeper emerged from the dark rooms behind the silver door, the limp body of Truth hanging heavily in her arms. For a moment, he thought the jaguar was dead, even though his nose caught none of the staleness of death.

When Truth awoke, and even spoke and drank, Plik felt joy and relief, but no abatement in his confusion. Blind Seer's account as to how Truth's spirit had apparently come forth from a silver block did not help much. Plik pressed back confusion by concentrating on immediate problems.

"Can someone," Plik said, "tell me what is behind that silver door other than a room with a silver block set in the wall?"

Firekeeper still stood in the doorway, obviously determined that the silver door would not slam shut without warning.

"We did not see much," the wolf-woman said, "for our attention was on Truth, but the door seems to open into a suite or apartment. I think we might risk another, closer look. Blind Seer and I neither saw nor smelled any stranger."

She looked at Truth for confirmation.

"I think exploring should be safe," the jaguar said, "but let us make certain someone stays to hold the doorway. It does not like being open—and I think opening it again will be difficult, at least until the moon is right."

That reminded Plik of another question. "Firekeeper, what made you think of using blood to finish the opening ritual?"

Firekeeper's dark eyes were troubled. "Remember last year? What Shivadt-mon did? What Dantarahma is said to have done? These involved blood, so I thought . . ."

She shrugged, and obviously did not wish to say more. Knowing her aversion to magic—indeed, sharing it after what he had seen—Plik did not press her further, though every part of him wanted to argue with her rather than be in sympathy. Instead, he looked at the jaguar.

"Truth, how did you come here? I cannot believe it was mere chance."

The jaguar lifted her head. "I was guided here, and before you ask, I have no idea who that guide was, nor for what purpose he took pity on me."

"He?" Firekeeper asked, her husky tones focused and fierce. "Then you saw him?"

"Never," Truth replied. "I heard him—a voice, sweet but mocking. He had the arrogance of an eagle screeching contempt at the land-bound."

Plik heard Rascal—safely above the trench—add, "Or a jaguar in her Year."

Truth did not hear, or if she did she did not choose to comment. "That voice was the one solid thing in . . . Do not make me remember where I was when I first heard it. I admit, I am afraid of being drawn back. There was a voice. It called me to it. I followed and found myself in this place, but locked behind the silver block. The voice's owner did not bring me through, but told me that there was a door, and if that door was opened I would be united with myself again."

"And did he name me as the door opener?" Firekeeper asked.

"He might have," Truth said. "Yes. He did. I do not recall asking for you, but I suppose I must have done so, for you are here, and I am free."

Blind Seer growled. Plik thought he did not envy the owner of the voice that had spoken to Truth—no matter who he was or what power he might wield. This voice had earned Blind Seer's enmity, and the blue-eyed wolf would be a deadly opponent.

Something you should remember, Plik reminded himself.

"Could this place be a tomb?" Truth said, so hesitantly that Plik could hardly believe it was the jaguar who spoke. "I remember a little of when it spoke to me. I thought I might be dead and a ghost, and that the Voice was another ghost."

"Tomb?" Firekeeper said. "I know graves, but tombs?"

"Those who came here from the Old Country sometimes built houses for their dead," Powerful Tenderness explained. "The tradition is not common anymore, for it takes much labor, and the modern Liglimom celebrate the living, and remember the dead in their traditional lore, not by sacrifices. I am surprised that those of the Gildcrest lands do not build tombs, for I believe Derian Carter said they worship their ancestors."

"I know little enough about that," Firekeeper said. "They do give them grave offerings, but I don't believe they build them houses. I think the shrines within the homes of the living serve that role."

Blind Seer sniffed at the darkness behind the silver door. "Tomb or something else, we will not know unless we go and look. Who goes with us?"

"I would like to inspect that suite," Plik said. "It and the root cellar into which Rascal fell seem to be the only traces left of what once stood here—and of whoever lured Truth to this place. I see a faint glow. Is there light within?"

"Some, farther in, in rooms to the back," Firekeeper said. "It is the old kind—the glowing blocks, but so dim that it carries not very far. A lantern might be useful—even though your night vision is good. I think you might find things to read."

So there was a delay while lanterns were brought from the camp. Then Firekeeper offered to carry Truth up to a more comfortable place than the trench before the door, but the Wise Jaguar refused.

"I am too weak to walk with you," she said, "but my hearing is very good, and I can follow what happens from here."

"And I," Powerful Tenderness said, suiting action to words, "will be the doorstop. Even if some force beyond what is natural tries to close this door, I think I am strong enough to stop it—at least long enough for you to get out."

Firekeeper looked at Plik. "Blind Seer and I will go with you. Between us three, we should find all there is to find."

Young Rascal did not even ask to cross over the threshold now that he knew his pack mates were safe. Indeed, he seemed quite relieved when Blind Seer set him as sentry above the trench.

The wolves entered first, then Plik, holding the lantern. He had the wick turned low, so as to not spoil his own night vision, and was resolved not to turn it up unless needed. Fire and enclosed spaces were not a good combination.

The dull yellow-red glow provided enough light for Plik to see that he stood in a small entry foyer. Only one at a time might pass through this space, and he wondered at that.

His bare feet touched the rough tiles set in the entryway. When he looked above, he saw an odd "candelabrum," set with quartz crystals where wax candles should have been.

A sorcerer's light, then, but one from which the power was long gone. Plik wondered at this, too, but passed on, hoping for clarification in the larger rooms.

"There are four chambers," Firekeeper said as Plik came out of the entryway. "One seems to be for sleeping. The other three . . ."

She shrugged, and Plik was reminded that in the ways of humans Firekeeper might know less than he did for all she looked so much like a human. Certainly, he knew more of the customs of the Liglimom.

"No cooking place?" he asked. "No place to wash? Is there any place that smells as if a body is enshrined there?"

Blind Seer padded in. "One chamber does have fresh water flowing through it. Another chamber holds a faint scent as of food and fire, but there are none of the pots and kettles humans seem to need to make their food. No body, but then bones have little smell once they are dry. It is a very odd place."

Plik had to agree, and the oddity of the place increased when he had made his own quick tour. He did not think the place had been a tomb. There was no urn nor coffin, no sarcophagus nor niche. No statues, paintings, or other aids to remembering the deeds of the deceased as one would expect. He supposed the place must have been an apartment, but if so, it was the strangest he had ever imagined.

The water chamber could have served for bathing and elimination, but other than a large bowl carved from blue-grey slate it lacked the usual fixtures. There was an iron brazier in another chamber, but rather than coals it held chunks of dark reddish stone—another quartz, he thought.

Fire had been made here, but as with the light in the entryway, it had not been a natural fire. Whoever had dwelled in—or had been imprisoned in—this place had been a sorcerer then, and a sorcerer of no mean power if he, or she, had used magic to supply light and heat and possibly, for not even the wolves' keen noses found any larders, food and wine.

Was this a sorcerer's retreat then? Or perhaps a sorcerer's prison?

Plik shared some of his conjectures with his companions, ending by saying: "But I only felt the slightest vibration of active magic here, and that more of the sort stored in amulets. This place is rife with the tools of magic—more so than I have ever seen in one place."

Firekeeper frowned. "But you have seen magical tools in the past."

"A few, like the light stones," Plik said, "but in this land, as in the north, magical artifacts were destroyed following the coming of Divine Retribution. Those we have at Center Island would not still function today except that Sky-Dreaming-Earth-Bound had some gift for handling energies. Now that he is dead, I suppose they will darken again."

At his words, Plik was pleased to see Blind Seer's hackles smooth—at least a little—and Firekeeper's hand move deliberately from the hilt of her knife. Whether he had soothed the two northerners or merely shamed them, still he felt he had defused a potentially destructive situation.

"There is a secret hidden here," Plik went on. "I am sure of it. There are a few books in this room"—they stood in the first room—"and in the room with the silver block. I could read those . . ."

He heard a faint sigh from Firekeeper, and knew he was pressing her patience. He must remember she was not human and that being underground would not be natural for her.

"But the books can be carried away," he went on. "While I pack them, I would like you to inspect whatever else is here for some indication of who this place was made to hold."

"That is my desire also," Blind Seer growled, "for whoever he is, he seems far too interested in my Firekeeper."

FIREKEEPER DID NOT BEGRUDGE PLIK his desire to take the books away. After all, Truth would have remained locked behind the silver door if the maimalodalum had not preserved some of the old knowledge. She did rather begrudge the way the raccoon-man took each one and shook it, seeking for things hidden between the leaves, before packing it in a sack that had once contained provisions.

Concerned lest she be asked to join him in his wearisome task, the wolf-woman methodically searched the other rooms. She began with the sleeping room. This was perhaps the most normal room of the four, but even so, there were not the things she had come to expect where humans made their lairs.

Blind Seer came in as she was patting down the mattress, looking for anything that might have been hidden within.

"Phew!" he said, sneezing. "It reeks of human male."

He paused and sniffed again. "And yet, not. There is something strange here."

"Strange?"

"I cannot say. How can one compare something to something when one has met nothing like?"

Firekeeper nodded. "Whoever slept here was clean, at least. No fleas, no lice, no bedbugs. Tell me, Blind Seer, have you noticed what is odd about this place?"

"What is not odd?" the wolf countered.

Firekeeper swatted at him, but went on. "I mean there are none of those little things humans accumulate where they live. Derian had them, so did Elise, even when we traveled. Small things of little use except that they reminded the owner of someone else, somewhere else."

Blind Seer studied the room, his blue eyes intent.

"You are right. There are no mementos here—unless the books may be such. Perhaps this place was like an inn, not the den of one man, but used by many."

Firekeeper frowned. "My nose is not yours, but wherever I have searched there has only been one stranger's scent."

"True."

They passed from the bedchamber to the room through which the water flowed. Unlike the rest of the place, which was still and cold and somehow dead, this place was alive with the chuckling of the running water. The waters were clean and fresh, but in the dim light they appeared shadowed and opaque rather than clear.

Firekeeper felt a sudden knowledge.

"I think whoever lived here—whoever it was who called to Truth—must have loved this room and this stream. I wonder that he did not let the waters carry him away with them."

She plunged one bare arm into the water. "Cold, but not too cold."

Still holding her arm beneath the surface, Firekeeper moved to where the water flowed away near the wall and probed. "Ah, the outlet is small, and a grille has been set over it, as if even the stupid fish were to be kept out. How firmly is it set, I wonder."

She leaned forward. There was a current, but not so powerful that she need fear it would drag her under. She located the bottom edge of the grille, found it set as firmly in the stone as the silver block had been in the wall. Her fingers found something else, too: pieces of something hard and solid with many oddly shaped edges. They were no larger than her hand and rolled slightly in the current, confirming that they were not anchored.

"Did he leave his cooking things here to be drawn out when they were needed?" she asked.

"Pull out what you have found," Blind Seer replied practically. "Why guess when you can know? Do you think you can reach what is there without going for a swim?"

"I think so. Yes. One . . ." Firekeeper closed her fingers around something and set it dripping on the stone. "Two. Three. A fourth . . . I think that is all. What do we have?"

Blind Seer had been sniffing at her find. "Stone. Wet stone. That is all my nose tells me. Let us take them where the light is better."

Firekeeper agreed. She could tell the stone had been worked, but in the dim light little more. Shaking off the worst of the water, she gathered up the four pieces and carried them into the room with the silver block, where the light was best.

Plik's feet slapping against the tiled floor announced him. "What have you found?"

Firekeeper was rubbing one piece against her tattered loincloth to dry it. "Carved stones. They were hidden under the water."

She inspected her find. "Plik, my eyes do not always see what humans call art, but I think this is a little statue of a woman."

Plik took it from her. "Your eyes see perfectly well. This is a woman. That broken one is a man in the attire of the Liglimom. See the trouser legs gathered at the bottom and the full blouse?"

Firekeeper had no eye for details of dress. She had been inspecting another piece. It was also a woman, but this time it was a woman she thought she recognized.

"Queen Valora!" she said, and heard her voice break in astonishment.

V

"QUEEN VALORA?" Plik looked at Firekeeper. The wolf-woman's fingers were curled tightly around the stone figurine. "Is this figure a portrait of someone you know?"

Firekeeper nodded slowly. "I have seen Queen Valora. She is not a friend, not precisely an enemy—though I think she would be pleased to do us harm if she could."

Blind Seer had nosed Firekeeper's fingers into uncurling, and was now inspecting the figurine.

"I think I see the resemblance," he said. "Take a look at the base, Firekeeper. Something interesting there."

Firekeeper did so and frowned. "Symbols carved deeply into the stone. Two sets—one is the emblem for the kingdom of Bright Bay. The other, that one also seems familiar, but I am not sure where I have seen it."

Blind Seer snorted. "I remember. It is the emblem of the new Kingdom of the Isles."

"How?" Firekeeper looked at Plik, accusation in her dark eyes. "How did this come here? I thought the Liglimom knew as little of the northern lands as the north did of this place. How did this come here?"

Plik swallowed an involuntary surge of fear. "I don't know. You say you know this woman. She is a contemporary then, not a historical figure?"

"She is alive," Firekeeper said. "Or was, last I heard. Not only does she live, these emblems speak of recent knowledge of her. First Valora was queen of

Bright Bay. About three years ago she lost her right to rule. Since then she has been queen only of the Isles."

"Queen," Plik said, making sure he understood the foreign term. "First Female."

"First Human," Firekeeper corrected. "The One of her pack. After the way of the northern humans, Valora's ruling came to her from having been born to the right parents, not from any deed of her own."

Plik wanted to ask any number of questions about this peculiar concept of government, but a feverish brightness in Firekeeper's eyes stayed him. The wolf-woman was now turning over the other figures.

"This one I do not know—the costume is again foreign. This one here. See, again the dress is northern. A woman again, to judge from the skirts. Her head is missing."

"I think," Blind Seer said, "we should find that head if we can. Would you be willing to check beneath the waters again?"

Firekeeper nodded. Her lips were set so tightly that Plik wondered if she had suspicions as to who that broken figure might represent. Without another word, she exited the room of the silver block. A moment later, they heard faint splashing as she felt around in the water.

Blind Seer had laid down alongside the figurines, his ears cocked to listen. "Plik, do you recognize any depicted in these figurines?"

"No," Plik replied. "Until Firekeeper came to Misheemnekuru, I had only glimpsed humans at a distance, out on the waters in their boats. My kind does not mingle with humanity—and mingles very little with the Beasts."

"Ah . . ." Blind Seer said. "Well, the ravens may be of help there."

The Royal Wolf might have elucidated more of his thoughts, but at that moment Firekeeper re-entered the room. She had shed her loincloth. Water streamed from her naked body and wet hair. She was strapping her leather knife belt back around her waist, the blade in her hand, held away from any chance contact with damp.

Apparently, merely groping around with her hands in the water had not been sufficient. She had gone diving, and, judging from what she held wrapped in the discarded loincloth, her efforts had not been without reward.

"Look at these," the wolf-woman said, dropping the bundled loincloth beside the figurines. It fell open to reveal a few more carved pieces of stone. "I need to dry off."

Plik reached for the first thing that came to hand. A male figure, clad in dress like, but not like that of the Liglimom. He began to dry the stone against his coat, but stopped when his grey and brown hairs stuck to the stone. Instead he reached for a piece of fabric.

Firekeeper returned almost as quickly as she had left, now wrapped in some of the unknown occupant's bedding. Her hair, hastily toweled off to stop the worst of the dripping, stood out at odd, spiky angles. Plik thought for the first time how odd it was that humans, alone among almost all the beasts, had hair that grew without limit. It certainly did not seem to be a useful trait, and he was glad for his own shaggy coat.

Squatting, Firekeeper picked a small bit of broken stone from the wet heap she had just brought in. "I think this is the head that goes with the other northern body. It is chipped but . . ."

She fitted head to body, and held the reassembled whole before Blind Seer. The blue-eyed wolf studied it with thoughtful calm. Then, almost as an afterthought, Firekeeper handed the two pieces to Plik.

"A woman in northern attire," Plik said. "Do either of you know this woman as you did the other?"

Blind Seer replied, "I cannot say I see any resemblance to any we know in that face. The nose is gone for one. But once again there are symbols etched into the base. One is that of House Gyrfalcon, the other that of the land of New Kelvin. There is only one woman I know to whom that pairing would apply."

"Melina." Firekeeper's voice held a flat anger that sealed Plik's questions behind his teeth. "So I thought. Blind Seer, I do not like this."

"Nor I," Blind Seer nosed the heap of stones. "Take these outside and ask Bitter and Lovable if they see anyone they know among those sculpted here."

Firekeeper glanced at him. "You suspect?"

"I do, but I prefer not to say."

Firekeeper dropped the sheet where she stood. Apparently, she was dry enough for her comfort.

"I will go," she said. "Will you stay?"

"Someone should guard Plik."

Firekeeper nodded. "Well enough. Do not remain in here too long. More and more, I fear this is a place wherein we should not linger."

Left alone with Blind Seer, Plik asked the questions he had held back until Firekeeper had taken her anger and agitation away with her.

"This Melina . . . Another northerner you know?"

"Yes. A woman who loved magic too much. She is dead now."

Plik waited, but no further details were forthcoming. He remembered how the one figure had been broken, the other not.

"But this Queen Valora, she lives?"

"She lives. As far as we know, she lives."

Plik waited for more, and when nothing came set himself to work. He had bagged almost all the books. With their northern aversion to magic, Fire-keeper and Blind Seer had resisted his taking the brazier. The bedding was not interesting. He couldn't see a use for the basin in the water chamber. Neither the silver block, nor the light panels would come free without damage.

Then he remembered the chandelier in the entryway. Surely they would not care if he took a stone or two from it. Over a century had passed since magic had been practiced, but Plik knew that sometimes an item could retain the signature of the one who had made or used it. A light crystal was a long shot, but better than nothing.

Blind Seer dragged one of the bags of books forward. Pausing and running his tongue around his teeth, he watched as Plik moved a chair over to beneath the chandelier.

"What are you doing?"

"I was going to . . ." Plik then stopped, realizing something. He removed one of the crystals and held it where the wolf could inspect it. "See anything here?"

Blind Seer sniffed, his ears laying back against his skull, his lips wrinkling back from some very impressive fangs.

"I think I might. These are the same type of stone from which the figurines were made. These pieces are larger, but then they would be."

Plik was inspecting the fixture. "There are a dozen or so crystals missing, mostly from the upper tier. Firekeeper found, what? Five figurines? Six?"

"About that," the wolf agreed. "Either there are others, or not all the stone-cutter's hunts came to good ends."

"I'd bet the latter," Plik said. "We've seen no cutting tools, so he may have had to use what was left to him."

Given his company, Plik did not say "magic," but from how Blind Seer's ears pressed even flatter, the wolf understood.

"We need to take a sample," Plik said firmly, "and, I think we cannot leave the brazier or the bowl. Those wiser than me in the ways magic was practiced may learn something from them."

They had both forgotten Powerful Tenderness and Truth, for the pair had waited silently in the exterior darkness. Now Truth spoke.

"There are no omens indicating harm will come to you for doing this," she said, "but I will be the first to admit that my sight is not what it once was."

Blind Seer gave a shuddering sigh. "Very well. You will have your way, Plik, but be quick about your collecting."

Plik was, and when they had taken all away, even Firekeeper's abandoned loincloth, even the wet bedding, Powerful Tenderness stood out of the doorway. No one was surprised when it closed of its own accord, nor when pale white light rippled across its surface, leaving the silver seamlessly melded into place once again.

"I felt that," Powerful Tenderness said, stooping to lift Truth. "Old magic, like in an amulet, but this was made to renew itself."

"A great expenditure of power must have gone into that making," Plik agreed. "I wish I understood better what this place is."

Truth, passive as a huge toy in Powerful Tenderness's arms, said softly, "A place for keeping in. A place for keeping out. A place where the worlds meet—worlds that perhaps should not meet."

But when questioned, the jaguar claimed to have no idea what she had said. With this the throughly unsettled band had to be content.

FIREKEEPER RETURNED shortly after the door had been sealed, young Rascal romping at her heels. She bore the figurines in a bundle at her waist, balancing the weight of her knife.

"I found Bitter and Precious," she said without preamble. "Our host pack had been hunting, and the ravens stayed to dine. They took time from their meal to examine our finds, though."

She looked at Blind Seer. "Your suspicions. Were they about the other broken figure?"

Blind Seer huffed breath out through his nose in a whuff of agreement.

"You were right then. Bitter swore the figure was a perfect miniature of Dantarahma. The emblem on his base is that of the junjaldisdu."

Plik bleated in astonishment. "Dantarahma? But he died but a year ago. . . . He was the junjaldisdu who . . ."

"Loved magic too much?" Blind Seer's hackles rose, but there was humor in the cant of his ears. "As did Melina—who also is shown without a head.

Queen Valora, too, had doings with magic, but she trusted unwisely and lost her prizes. Trails cross most often when you near the deer yard. What trail is this?"

Firekeeper shuddered. She removed the bundle from her waist and spread out the figurines, lining them up, matching head to shoulders. Two were broken. Three remained entire. Of these, one was Valora. The other, man and woman, wore a style of clothing like, but, as Plik had said, not the same as that of the Liglimom.

"Bitter and Lovable did not know these two," she said, tapping the two with the unfamiliar dress. "Moreover, though they have emblems scratched on them, the ravens did not recognize the emblems either. Perhaps I should say 'emblem.' It looks much the same on both figures."

"We could copy the emblem," Blind Seer suggested. "Plik has a steady hand. If the maimalodalum do not know the symbol, then perhaps one of the Liglimom on the mainland does. We could send a message to Derian."

Firekeeper emitted a soft inaudible sigh, a mere kiss of breath against her lower lip. Blind Seer was always harrying her to learn to read and write. Indeed, she knew he read better than she did, though neither of them were fluent. However, the wolf had rapidly realized that humans used their written symbols as trail markers, as most of the Beasts used scent and more personal signs.

"You would not ignore where a bear has sharpened his claws on a tree trunk," Blind Seer had chided her. "Why do you ignore these signs?"

And Firekeeper had refused to reply, for the entire issue awoke uncomfortable stirrings within her. Although she now knew more of her human kin than she ever had before, in a contrary fashion, she still fled from that heritage.

"I have one more figure," Firekeeper said. "I found it when I went diving, but I kept it back from the others . . . I needed to think."

She reached beneath her knife belt and drew forth an uncomfortable lump from where it had pressed against her flesh. She laid it where the firelight would illuminate both its form and its markings.

This sixth figurine was of a jaguar, and from the cant of the head, something in how the figure stood, even in the rosettes of spots so carefully placed, it was clearly not just any jaguar.

It was Truth.

LONG AFTER THE OTHERS HAD STOPPED TALKING and gone to sleep, long after the fires had been banked to coals, Truth sat thinking about everything that had happened these last few hours.

They had told her she had talked to them, had told them how to find her, but she had no memory of this. They had told her how she had moved her body out of the harness, but she had no memory of this either.

Indeed, her body felt strange to her. After perceiving infinity, it seemed limiting to rely on one pair of eyes, one nose, one set of ears, one mouth. Limiting, but comfortable, too. She could trust those impressions, as she could never trust the others. It was a feeling akin to fullness after starvation.

There had been much speculation about what the presence of those six figurines might mean. If the evidence of the four known figurines could be applied to the two unknowns, then clearly they must be images of contemporary people. How they could have been found in an apartment that had apparently been sealed since before the coming of Divine Retribution had been something no one could explain.

That hadn't kept Powerful Tenderness and Plik in particular from speculating, and Truth had taken some amusement in watching Firekeeper fidget.

That the figurines had been used to focus on individuals seemed evident. Two of those individuals were dead. Though the immediate causes of death were vastly different, the greater cause was frighteningly similar. Both Melina and Dantarahma had investigated the magical arts with more enthusiasm than had been the wont of either of their widely differing peoples. Each had discarded the varying prohibitions of their peoples. Had they been helped to slip the bonds of convention? Had they been prompted to do so? Was the prompter the same as the Voice that had guided Truth?

It seemed all too likely, and Truth was aware that the others held her in some suspicion because of this. Worse, she held herself in suspicion. It was not a good feeling.

Plik had promised he would copy the symbols from the two unknown figurines the next morning. When Firekeeper had protested at the delay, the beast-souled had pointed out that he could not do his best work by firelight. The wolf-woman had subsided. Soon afterward, she and her wolves had gone to run off some of their contained energy.

Truth had heard them singing to the setting moon, their voices mingling with those of the island's resident pack. She wished she had such easy relief for her worries, but jaguars were solitary creatures. With such solitude she must be content.

❦

PLIK AWOKE TO THE SCENT OF FRYING FISH mingled with that of wet
bear. He rose from where he had curled in the long grasses and picked his
way to the camp. Powerful Tenderness, still showing traces of having been
swimming, was frying fish. A Wise Bear and Wise Sea Otter had joined him.
The bear was waiting for the cooking to finish. The otter was eating his share
raw.

"These," Powerful Tenderness said with a toss of his head toward the two
yarimaimalom, "along with the local wolves will arrange to refill the trench in
front of the silver door."

"Good," Plik said, not envying the Wise Beasts their labor—nor their own,
should they decide they needed to look into that apartment again. "Even with
the silver door resealed, I think that place is not a good thing to leave easy to
find."

"The Wise Beasts agree," the bear said. "Not only would younglings fall
into the trench, but we all fear what might come out."

"Or what might be drawn here," the otter agreed. "Magic's pull is not to be
taken lightly. Deep beneath the waves there are said to be fish who lure others
into their very maws with false lights. So it is with Magic's arts. Unlike the
northerners, we do not think Magic intrinsically evil—but she is certainly to be
avoided by those who cannot understand what they find."

Plik wondered what the northern wolves would think of this philosophy,
but there was no trace of the three wolves. Truth was lolling by the fire. The
jaguar, like the otter, had preferred her fish raw, and was eating with messy enthusiasm.

"Taste," the jaguar said by way of greeting. "That I do enjoy having back
again. I had almost forgotten how good it is to taste."

"I'm glad you have found something to enjoy," Plik said. He rummaged in
the packs until he found his drawing materials. "Where are the figurines?"

"Firekeeper has them," Truth said, "all but the two. Those she left for you
to copy."

She tossed her head, spraying the area with little bits of torn fish and glittering scale, indicating a small bundle neatly tied to a tree limb.

Plik wondered if Firekeeper didn't trust them with the rest of the figurines,
or if she was merely possessive. Probably a little of both. After all, she was human, and there was no race ever—not even squirrels and ravens—who so enjoyed collecting useless things.

And she has only scant reason to trust us, Plik thought, forcing himself to be fair. *She is an outsider wherever she goes. I thought I knew something of that state, but compared to Firekeeper . . .*

He let the thought drift, and ambled over to a sapling whose succulent young growth promised a good meal. Between bites, he sketched the emblems etched onto the bases of the figurines. They were essentially the same: roughly triangular, with another triangle set within. The edges of both triangles were repeatedly broken into curving lines that rose upward to new points. Somehow they suggested flame.

Plik shivered. Among the five elements, the most unpredictable—even more so than Magic—was Fire.

The flame/triangle within a flame/triangle did not seem in the least familiar to Plik. He wondered if this was because it was very old—or perhaps very new.

The wolves arrived soon after Plik had finished his drawings, making the raccoon-man suspect that Firekeeper had convinced Lovable, who was easily bribed with trinkets, to stand watch. Blind Seer and Rascal could be of little help, but Firekeeper applied herself with unwonted eagerness to assisting Plik and Powerful Tenderness assemble their gear. She even helped Powerful Tenderness hoist the heavy pack to his shoulders—not that he needed her assistance.

The drawings were sent ahead, carried by Bitter, then the travelers took their leave of the house that was no longer a house. Behind them was the scent of fresh dirt as the bear set about filling the trench. Plik knew that before the night fell there would be little trace of their hard labor—but of their discovery there was much evidence, some of it carried in his own, small pack. Bearing mystery—and perhaps Magic—Plik hurried on the trail back to Center Island.

HOPE SHOOK HER HEAD. "We have spent the last several days since Bitter brought your message researching those two symbols, and although there are ones like them in our archives, we can find none that are the same."

Firekeeper tilted her head to one side in unconscious mimicry of the way the wolves expressed a question.

"You say there are symbols similar to these in your archives," she said. "How like?"

Hope gestured toward sheets of vellum. "I could show you, if you wish. The problem is this: Even a similarity does not mean a relation. Can you understand?"

Firekeeper thought of the two symbols Plik had drawn, and realized that she did.

"It is like scents, is it not? All wolves smell like wolves, but no two wolves smell alike. Moreover, one could not tell a Wise Wolf from a Royal Wolf without more than scent to go on."

Hope gave a little bird-like chirp. "Very good, though not being as nose-driven as you wolves are, I would not have put it that way."

"Among my people," Firekeeper said, almost in apology, glancing to where Blind Seer reclined at her side studying the symbols as if he were memorizing them, "I am nose-dead, but still . . ."

They were seated within the Tower of Air, which housed the communal archives of the maimalodalum. Plik waited to one side. His contained bearing held some complex of emotions Firekeeper could not quite identify, for though the Royal Beasts included raccoons, her contact with them had been limited. Like jaguars, they were not social except with their own kits. That Plik's body combined human and raccoon traits only confused the matter. Of one thing she felt certain: The normally affable maimalodalu was tense and nervous.

When Plik spoke, Firekeeper listened carefully, seeking to garner every bit of meaning she could—both from what he said and what he did not.

"So, now that our resources are exhausted, do we turn this over to the humans on the mainland?"

Hope gave a crisp nod. "I think so. Not only do they have texts we do not, they have contact with peoples we do not. It may be that they will be able to recognize the manner of clothing worn by those two."

Firekeeper noted with fascination that Plik had lowered his head slightly—protecting his throat. She did not think he meant to attack, more that his action was after the fashion of the growls that would rumble in a wolf's belly when the wolf wished to express displeasure.

"And," Plik said, "from there?"

"It depends," said Hope, "on what we learn."

"Precise action does," Plik said, "but surely it is time and enough to discuss what all of us must see . . ."

"See?"

Firekeeper thought that Hope was being deliberately obtuse, but she recognized this tactic. She had seen it used before by leaders who needed to draw forth their followers. Annoying as it was, it was often the mark of a good leader, for only bad leaders thought they knew all there was to know.

Plik glared at the bird-woman. "Shall I spell it out then?"

"Do."

"Six figurines. Two were known to have attempted to use magic. These are dead. One might have used magic—this Valora—but for lost opportunity. Truth . . . Truth is harder to place, but I see her as a link to the others. They were used as she was used."

"By the Voice of which she spoke?" Hope asked helpfully.

"Precisely."

"Go on."

Blind Seer spoke for Plik. "Two others may remain out there—alive. Two others who this Voice has touched. Two others who may be toying with things wise creatures know are dangerous."

Firekeeper nodded. "You beast-souled have better reason than we to know what magic misused can do—and we all know too well what the price is for that use."

"Blood," Hope said. "Yes. Our people know that. The Liglimom long ago banned such among their own peoples. We share your fear of Magic, but we respect her. Our great difference is that your people thought that by ignoring Magic you could make her go away. We did not."

Firekeeper and Blind Seer looked at each other, but they did not deny the truth of this assertion.

Plik returned to the main point. "Out there, somewhere, are two we know nothing about. What has the Voice prompted them to do? Both Melina and Dantarahma believed they did a good and wise thing in trying to bring back the old ways. What do these two believe?"

"You speak with great certainty," Hope said.

"I speak with fear," Plik retorted. "The pattern is there—and though we have Truth back with us, worn but sane, we also must face that something was sealed in that apartment beneath the earth, something that was there recently enough to carve the features of people still living. We have skirted around this matter, but what did we let loose? And what is this 'Voice' going to do now that we have set him free?"

Hope said nothing, but her clear, bright eyes turned and studied Fire-keeper.

Firekeeper nodded slowly. "Twice before, almost unwitting, Blind Seer and I have been part of ending sorcerers. What we have seen them do with their magic has given me no great love for them or their arts. Plik, you said you speak with fear, but there is no shame in fearing a fire. Fire burns, as I know all too well. Magic seems too much like fire to me not to fear its misuse."

Blind Seer rose and shook himself. "Plik, are you looking for reassurance that whatever these symbols show us, this 'Voice'—or at least these remaining tools of his—will not be dismissed as mere curiosities?"

"I am."

"Be reassured. I don't know if we can find the two depicted through these figurines or the source of the Voice that spoke to Truth, but if there is the least hint of a trail, Firekeeper and I will go scenting along it."

"Boldly sworn." The words rasped from the open doorway where Truth had entered, unheeded. "Would you still speak so boldly if you knew you could find what you seek?"

Firekeeper rested her hand on Blind Seer's shoulder. "We would."

Truth's tail lashed. "Then count me in on your hunting. I have very mixed feelings about this Voice. If we find a trail, I will come with you. My talent is mine once more, and I think . . . yes . . . I am almost sure . . . that the binding between myself and this Voice goes more than one way."

Plik's head dipped again. "Do you view this Voice as a friend or an enemy?"

"Neither. Rather say a curiosity," Truth replied. "I am a jaguar, and we do not take kindly to bindings, not even from our kittens once they are grown. I want to meet this one who dared lay hold of me—even if his gain was mine as well. It seems to me that the best way to find him would be to find these two of whom he has also carved figurines. What do you say?"

Blind Seer coughed. "I say we are ahead of ourselves, hunting the herds before they gather. Firekeeper and I have given Plik our promise. Now we have yours, but first we must take these figurines and the symbols to the mainland. I fancy we should go with them ourselves. What do you think, Firekeeper?"

Although she knew her time on Misheemnekuru was ending, Firekeeper felt the words she spoke cut her as sharply as her Fang did hide and bone.

"I think you are right. We must go to the mainland."

Leavetaking from Dark Death, Moon Frost, Rascal, and the little puppies was very hard, but u-Seeheera, the First City of Liglim, was not a place for a wolf pack, especially one with pups too young to demonstrate common sense.

Firekeeper held each of the puppies tightly, making sure each one drank deeply of her scent. Her parting from Dark Death, Moon Frost, and Rascal was no more formal.

"Don't let them forget us," Firekeeper said, hugging each of the wolves.

"We'll tell stories about you," Dark Death promised.

"And some of them will even be flattering," Rascal laughed, "and I'll recite each and every one of Blind Seer's proverbs—those I can remember anyhow."

Blind Seer looked at Firekeeper, and she knew he was aware of her sense of loss. Hadn't her freedom been his as well? Then his jaws gaped in a wolfish grin.

"Going to the mainland means you had better find yourself some new clothing, sweet Firekeeper—that is, unless you wish Derian Carter's skin to blush as red as his hair."

BOOK II

VI

DERIAN CARTER STOOD IN THE INNER COURTYARD of the Bright Haven embassy looking at the note that had been delivered to him by a fish eagle.

Perhaps it said something about his current situation that for most of those in his immediate vicinity his appearance seemed stranger than his courier service. Tall, fair, freckled, and red-haired, Derian stood out among the Liglimom. These were uniformly dark of hair and eye, possessed of skin that while not actually deeply tanned gave—to Derian's eye, accustomed as it was to fairer-skinned peoples—the impression of having been warmly toasted by the sun.

The note Derian had unbound from the osprey's leg was written in the language of Liglim—Liglimosh, as his own Pellish-speaking people had taken to calling it, since the Liglimom used the same word for their homeland and their language. The Liglimom claimed there was a definite difference in stress between the two words that made them easy to tell apart, but Derian had never heard anything to differentiate the words from each other.

The note was in an unfamiliar hand, but the signature, a sketched outline of a human hand with that of a wolf's paw side by side, left him no doubt as to who was the sender. Firekeeper, finding some poor disdu to do her writing for her again, no doubt.

"Fox Hair," the note began without the flourishes and titles that either Derian's own people or the Liglimom would use in a note to one who was, after all, a high-ranking assistant to an ambassador, "We come. Today, with evening. Truth is with us. Can you be at harbor?"

That was all, but those few words gave Derian quite a bit of reason for thought. Firekeeper had only rarely touched the mainland in the past year—and one of those times had been to greet Derian on his own return from a voyage home to Hawk Haven.

Part of her reluctance to leave Misheemnekuru was because after two years spent more or less among humans, she was back among wolves. Part, and Derian smiled slightly as he recalled this, was because Firekeeper became violently seasick whenever she got on a boat. There were drugs that helped her deal with the malaise, but as these had to be mixed up fresh, she could not carry a supply with her, and it galled her to ask any human for help.

Derian glanced up at the sun. Midday. Hours yet before he would need to be at the harbor. He supposed that he should go inform the ambassador that one was coming who, while not really a citizen of either Hawk Haven or Bright Bay—the two kingdoms sponsoring this embassy—certainly had ample claim on the hospitality of both.

I wonder if Firekeeper got news of our new arrivals, Derian thought. *Some seagull or otter or whatever might have passed on a bit of gossip. That might be enough to make Firekeeper interrupt her running about like a wild thing, and come to the mainland. But why would she bring Truth with her? Maybe it would be a courtesy to send a message to the ahmyndisdu. . . .*

Derian thought he'd better clear that thought with the ambassador. The ahmyndisdu was one of the members of u-Liall, the ruling counsel of the Liglimom. Derian had met with u-Liall before, but that had been under different circumstances. Now he was no longer just Derian Carter, victim of some very peculiar circumstances, he was Derian Counselor, and what he said might be interpreted as coming from Bright Haven.

The idea—the entire mess of ideas—still was almost more than Derian could accept. Start with this idea of having the embassy come from Bright Haven rather than either Hawk Haven or Bright Bay—or even a joint embassy from them both. This Bright Haven gambit seemed to be anticipating events just a bit, for the two kingdoms were not supposed to officially merge until both their current rulers had died.

King Tedric of Hawk Haven, well, he was an old man and the Ancestors might issue him an invitation any day now—though Derian sincerely hoped the Ancestors would withhold themselves the pleasure of the king's company a while longer. But even if King Tedric could fairly be said to be in his last years, Allister of the Pledge, ruler of Bright Bay, was a man of only middle years, one who could be expected to reign for a long time to come. Yet it had been Allister, not Tedric, who had suggested this course of action.

"It is the best way I can envision to emphasize our commitment to a pledge that is now—after all—nearly four years in the past. Sending a Bright Haven embassy will help not only our own peoples, but our neighbors adjust to the idea that Bright Haven is a reality—Hawk Haven and Bright Bay are merely convenient fictions, old shoes kept until the new pair can be made comfortable."

King Tedric had agreed, as had the joint heirs. Since Derian was one of a very few from either Hawk Haven or Bright Bay who had been to Liglim, Derian found himself back in Liglim, a place he had not been at all certain he had ever wanted to see again. Nor was he there in his accustomed role, that of a minor advisor to an indulgent monarch—or even that of "kennel keeper" to Firekeeper. No, Derian was here as assistant to a man whose people had been enemies of his own until just a few years past.

But for all his tendency for introspection, Derian was honest with himself. He actually—"liked" wasn't quite the right word—respected and admired Ambassador Fairwind Sailor. Although a scion of one of Bright Bay's noble houses, the ambassador had served in his country's navy before taking up whaling. Later, after he lost one eye in some accident, Captain Sailor had delved with enthusiasm into the land side of the processing and sale of whale oil. There he had shown a taste for innovation. This, added to his familial connections, and the fact that he was sincerely interested in foreign peoples, had made him the final choice from the many considered for the post.

And, Derian thought, *all of the ambassador's professions have made him a stickler for hierarchy. I'd better tell him about Firekeeper's message, and somehow manage to make it sound like her note was meant for more than me.*

Derian headed inside, and immediately felt the temperature drop. Even the humid air felt a trace dryer, for the Liglimom knew well how to deal with their hotter, wetter southern climate.

I wonder if their Old Country was like this, he thought. *For surely they did not invent this all at once when their ships landed.*

Not for the first time, Derian found himself wondering just how the Old Country rulers had gone about parceling up the New World. Had they made agreements in advance? Had it been a race of white-sailed ships, each hurrying to see who would arrive first? Had there been trading of parcels once they had arrived, exchanging parcels of land until all had something to their taste?

It struck Derian as odd that he knew more about the coming of the Old Country rulers to the New World from the point of view of the Beasts than he did from that of the humans, for the humans who resided in the New World now were descended from colonists, not from the rulers. The rulers had left when the Plague—what the Liglimom called Divine Retribution—had arisen.

They had abandoned the colonists to illness and chaos. Those who had survived the upheaval had had no reason to love their former rulers. The stories that remained of them told of their cruelty to the humans they ruled. In the north, where Derian's people lived, the Old Country rulers had first made treaties with the Royal Beasts. Later, when they felt more secure, they had attempted to wipe out the Beasts. Although their genocidal aims had not been achieved, they had succeeded in driving the Beasts west of the Iron Mountains.

Here in the south, the truce had held longer, but even the Wise Beasts, the yarimaimalom, told tales of betrayal. Clearly, the Old Country rulers, rich as they were in the magical arts, were poorer in those of ethics.

Derian knew he was thinking of such things in order to distract himself from worrying about what was bringing Firekeeper to the mainland. However, even as his mind had wandered, his feet had carried him to his destination. He raised the polished brass ring that adorned the door into Ambassador Sailor's office, and rapped it sharply.

"Enter."

Derian obeyed, shutting the door behind him. Fairwind Sailor sat in a chair near the window, the book in his hand tilted so that his one eye might take better advantage of the light. He was a man of medium height with stiff, coarse, iron grey hair pulled back in a braid tied with a ribbon, rather than the loose queue Derian wore. Like Derian, the ambassador wore local dress. The fitted britches, waistcoats, tailored jackets, and the other accoutrements that were common at home would have been stifling in Liglim's damp heat.

Ambassador Sailor's left eye was covered with a patch of black silk.

"Derian Counselor," Ambassador Sailor said, "what may I do for you?"

"A message has come, sir, from Firekeeper—Lady Blysse Norwood. She's due to reach the mainland this evening, and has requested I meet her in the harbor."

"Did she say why she is coming?"

"No, sir, only that she was coming—and that means Blind Seer as well. She also mentioned that Truth, a jaguar, is coming with her."

"Truth . . . I remember being briefed about her." The ambassador tapped his chin with one broad, flat finger. "She was rather important, wasn't she? A diviner, they say. I believe she was retired for medical reasons?"

Ambassador Sailor tried to keep disbelief from his voice as he spoke of the jaguar as if she was a person, but then, unlike Derian, he had been given only a short time to grow accustomed to the idea of intelligent animals. It was one thing to hear stories, another to know the reality for yourself.

Derian didn't mince words. He knew the ambassador would prefer having all the details to being humored. There was much Derian could not tell Ambassador Sailor about the events of the previous summer, but he could say this.

"Truth went insane. I am hoping that this message indicates some improvement in her condition—but it could indicate the opposite. I was wondering, sir, should we send a message ahead to Ahmyndisdu Tiridanti? Truth served with her, and Firekeeper . . . well . . . Firekeeper probably hasn't sent any message there."

"And Truth might not have been able to do so. Yes. We should draft something. I'll ring for my translator." The sharp rap of the brass ring against the door interrupted him. "Wait! This should serve even better. Enter!"

The door opened and a beautiful young woman with pale golden hair and sea green eyes stepped over the threshold. Lady Elise Archer was a close friend to Derian, and more importantly, given the business at hand, to Firekeeper and Blind Seer as well.

"Lady Archer," the ambassador said, rising for her as he had not for Derian. "You have arrived for our language lessons at an opportune time. Counselor Derian has brought some interesting news."

Derian turned to greet Elise, a warm smile coming involuntarily to his lips. Unlike himself and the ambassador, Elise wore a modified version of their native costume. Summer gowns were far less confining, and she admitted that while she rather liked tailored riding trousers, the baggy version favored by the locals left her feeling a bit odd. She did like the local cotton fabrics, though, and her current gown was made from a fabric printed with a pattern that mingled exotic flowers and stylized cats.

Elise and Derian knew each other very well, having traveled together on two rather eventful trips into New Kelvin. Her arrival in Liglim eight days before had lessened Derian's feeling that his station here was an exile rather than an honor.

"News?" Elise said, returning Derian's smile. "Of what?"

"Firekeeper. She's on her way to the mainland. I'm wondering if she might have gotten wind of your arrival, and come to say hello."

"I hope so!" Elise was genuinely delighted. She had been very disappointed to learn that it would be almost impossible to get a message to Firekeeper. "There's something in your eyes that tells me you aren't so certain my arrival is the reason that Firekeeper's coming."

Now that the subject had been broached, Derian pulled out Firekeeper's note and read it aloud in its entirety.

"We were wondering," Ambassador Sailor said to Elise when Derian had finished, "about the mention of this jaguar, Truth. Derian suggested we send a missive to Ahmyndisdu Tiridanti, just in case she doesn't know to expect company. Would you like to help me draft one?"

In reply, Elise gestured toward the desk. She was very talented with languages, and already spoke and read Liglimosh as well as Derian did, having studied not only the teaching primer Derian had brought home with him, but with the Liglimom's ambassadorial staff stationed in Hawk Haven.

Between the three of them, they had soon crafted an appropriate note, and when Ambassador Sailor called in his resident translator to check it, the man assured them that they could have done without his services.

"If you wish, I will arrange to have it taken to Heeranenahalm," the translator said.

"I do so wish," Ambassador Sailor replied. "Come back in an hour or so, would you? I'd like you to review my lessons."

The translator bowed stiffly in the fashion followed in the north, and excused himself.

"He's going to be wearing a waistcoat, tricorn, and brass-buckled shoes soon enough," the ambassador said with a chuckle. "I think he envisions himself transferring to one of the northern embassies and wants to show willing."

"And he's likely right," Elise said. "Now that Bright Haven has opened relations with Liglim, the Isles want their own embassy—and so do Waterland, Stonehold, and New Kelvin. Familiarity with Pellish will see him far in any of those lands."

"Except possibly New Kelvin," Derian said, remembering. "Even when they knew Pellish, they usually didn't admit it."

"I suspect our translator knows that," Elise said. "He's already asked me to teach him New Kelvinese when I have time."

They laughed over this, then Derian said, "Firekeeper asked me to meet

her at the harbor this evening. She wasn't precise about time, but I can probably get an idea from the harbormaster's office when a boat would be likely to
arrive from the outpost. Would anyone like to come?"

Elise nodded. "Definitely."

Ambassador Sailor shook his head. "By all means, bring Lady Blysse back
here if she wishes to come, but my presence would make what should be the
reunion of old friends into something far too formal."

Derian admired Fairwind Sailor's tact, and thought it was time to exercise
some of his own. "Then I'll meet you in the courtyard, Elise. Now, I'll leave
you two to your lessons, and make arrangements just in case Firekeeper—and
Blind Seer, and maybe Truth—decide to stay here."

He took his leave, heart light at the thought of seeing his friends—the eu-
phoria almost enough to banish the apprehension that had come to him the
moment he had unrolled Firekeeper's note.

ABOARD THE LIGHT, fast sailing vessel that was carrying her, Blind Seer,
and Truth to the mainland, Firekeeper sat very still and did her best to keep
from moving her head. Her gaze was fastened on the coastline, and perhaps
only Blind Seer, in whose neck ruff she had locked her fingers, knew how
much of a struggle she had to maintain her composure while her head roiled,
her skin prickled with sweat, and her stomach threatened upheaval.

The cool evening breeze did help, as did the skill of the small crew who
manned the craft, but Firekeeper found herself wondering if she should have
tried to talk a pod of dolphins into escorting her to shore.

Then, of course, she would have arrived naked, with her hair and skin stiff
from the bay's brackish waters, rather than neatly dressed in clothing she had
borrowed from one of the disdum at the Misheemnekuru outpost.

But then again, she could have asked the dolphins to land her outside of the
harbor proper. She could have carried her clothing in a waterproof bag. Blind
Seer and Truth might have had difficulties swimming to shore, but they didn't
get seasick. They could have ridden in the boat. The Liglimom wouldn't have
found anything at all strange about being asked to ferry a wolf and a jaguar.

With such thoughts, Firekeeper kept herself from thinking about just how close to vomiting she was. At long, long last, the sailboat slid smoothly up to one of the many piers that jutted out from the edges of the harbor.

Truth and a sailor leapt onto the wooden planks almost as one. Firekeeper and Blind Seer followed more slowly. Then Firekeeper must wait for the boards underfoot to stop their annoying pitching. Only then could she turn and walk to the shore, alert for sight of Derian.

Blind Seer found him before she did.

"There," he said with a pleased whuff of air. *"And with him . . . Look!"*

Wolves neither bark nor wag their tails, but Blind Seer did the adult wolves' equivalent, giving an almost puppyish yelp of pleasure, and standing with his ears pricked high and forward.

Firekeeper followed the line of his body and saw Derian's tall shape, the red of his hair visible even in the fading light. Beside him stood a slender, fair-haired woman wearing the long gowns favored by women in Hawk Haven, and beside her a man of medium height and build, with dark hair and a distinctly hawk-like profile.

"Elise! Doc!" Firekeeper cried, the remnants of her seasickness vanishing in a wash of pleasure. She hurried down the pier, her bare feet glad for the firmness of the boards.

Wolves are exuberant when greeting those they love, and Firekeeper had spent the last year among wolves. She threw her arms around Elise, then Doc, and lastly around Derian. Each received a squeeze that set them gasping for air and a sloppy kiss—almost a lick on the cheek.

Blind Seer joined Firekeeper in her greeting, bumping himself against the humans, his body wriggling with delight.

"Firekeeper, Firekeeper . . ." Elise said, gasping with laughter. "Gently! You'll have us on the dock."

Firekeeper drew back, folding some of her usual reserve around her, but she didn't bother to hide her pleasure.

"You two, here!" she said, rummaging through her memory for disused human speech. "When?"

"We arrived several days ago," Elise said. "Derian said that you were nearly impossible to reach, but we were going to at least leave a message at the outpost in case you went there."

Firekeeper shook her head. "Not be there. Been at other side of islands. Derian right."

Derian grinned at her. "I see you cleaned up for the trip in. I thought I was going to need to arrange a flea bath. You even had someone trim your hair."

"Disdu, at outpost."

Firekeeper shrugged this away as unimportant, just as she ignored the surrounding Liglimom who were watching the reunion with fascination, though they deliberately went on with their business. She had noticed something interesting in how Elise and Doc were standing, close, if not touching, but without that prickly sense of each being too aware of the other.

Tilting her head to one side, she looked them over. "You two. Here. What Baron Archer think?"

Elise beamed and slipped her hand through Doc's arm. "My father thinks it's just fine, thank you. Doc and I were married at the New Year festivals this spring—married on my family's lands, and later blessed at the castle at Eagle's Nest."

Doc's smile wasn't as open as Elise's but his happiness was just as apparent. "I came back from New Kelvin with some interesting medical information, and then Elise and I decided that the time had come to stop worrying and start doing. Baron Archer was quicker to accept than we had hoped. I think he'd had time to get used to the idea that his heir wasn't going to make a politically advantageous marriage."

"About time," Firekeeper said with a grunt. Elise and Doc had been interested in each other since they had fallen into each other's company in the small circle of those humans who had befriended the wolf-woman. That had been four years ago, and Firekeeper had found their courtship—if such it could be called—both frustrating and confusing.

Derian had begun to lead the way away from the harbor, and the group trailed along together, still talking.

"I think it helped," Elise said, "that my father adopted my cousin Deste, so I am no longer his sole heir. Deste isn't adverse to playing courtship games. In fact, ever since her cousin Ruby made a good marriage to a scion of one of Bright Bay's Great Houses, I think Deste has been panting to have a try at the game. She's turned out to be a better archer than me, too."

Firekeeper considered this news in light of past events. "So is this why you here?"

"If you mean, was I thrown out," Elise said with a laugh, "no, I wasn't. However, I did point out to my father that I would go insane if I did nothing more for the next several decades than apprentice to someday be Baroness Archer. When Derian returned with news of Liglim, I immediately started studying the language and culture. I didn't make the first cut for the ambassadorial staff, but I didn't leave Sapphire much peace, and here we are!"

"Am pleased," Firekeeper said.

Derian had been very quiet, and for the first time Firekeeper realized why. Truth paced alongside him. Derian was more accustomed than most to the Royal, or Wise, Beasts, but even so the proximity of a great cat of such size—and with a reputation for insanity—would quiet the bravest man.

"*Truth,*" Firekeeper said. "*You are with us? I thought you would go to the ahmyndisdu.*"

"*In time,*" the jaguar replied. "*I thought to be with you when you told these about your find. I may not go to the ahmyndisdu in any case. Another has my place in that house. I will probably go to the forests.*"

Firekeeper nodded. "*Fine, but is that any reason to make Derian nervous?*"

Truth's reply was to step slightly farther away and a few steps ahead of Derian.

"Firekeeper, we thought you might have come to the mainland to see Elise," Derian said, "but clearly that's not why. What brought you here?"

Firekeeper shook her head. "Not here. We . . . find something."

Beside her, Blind Seer said, "*Find something or were guided to something . . . Or a little bit of both.*"

"*Find,*" Firekeeper said firmly, remembering how she had had to search for those bits of stone beneath the water, but thinking of Truth's Voice, she wished she were certain.

BEFORE FIREKEEPER COULD SETTLE IN and tell what had brought her to the mainland, she had to meet Ambassador Sailor. She thought the man inoffensive enough. Remembering that he was One of this small northern pack, she did her best to make herself pleasant. She thought Derian approved.

Telling her tale took Firekeeper a long time, long enough that a late meal was brought in and cleared away by the time she had finished.

Part of the reason for this was because Firekeeper had lost a great deal of her facility in Pellish in the time she had been on Misheemnekuru. Part was because of the human predilection for asking questions or requesting clarification or speculating before the information had been laid out in an orderly fashion.

Firekeeper had not forgotten this tendency, but she had forgotten how much it annoyed her. However, she needed these humans' help, and so reined in a desire to growl and snap as she would have at Moon Frost's puppies.

When Firekeeper finished speaking, and the little stone figurines had been passed around and examined by all present, Derian said, "So, you want us to find out if the Liglimom know the meaning of these strange symbols. You're sure that no one on Misheemnekuru knew where they came from?"

He put a slight emphasis on the words "no one," and Firekeeper knew precisely what he was asking, and why he didn't ask more directly. Derian was one of a hand's worth of fingers of living humans who knew about the beast-souled—the maimalodalum, as they were called in the language of Liglim.

"No one," Firekeeper said firmly, "and I ask."

"Of course," Doc commented thoughtfully, "animals' eyes seem to see differently than do ours. They might know the symbols, but not see them as we do."

"True," Firekeeper said, "but they not know. Someone mainland, maybe?"

"The best one to ask," Derian said, rather uncomfortably, "would be the aridisdu Harjeedian. As I recall, he has studied the older languages of the Liglim. He is well placed in his own temple, and his sister is one of u-Liall. Therefore, he will have access to resources unavailable to the average researcher."

These words all came out very quickly. Derian had been intimately involved with Harjeedian's sister, Rahniseeta. Firekeeper knew that Derian had almost refused to return to the land of the Liglim because to do so would mean encountering Rahniseeta again. Only Derian's personal loyalty to King Tedric, and the fact that he was the sole Hawk Havenese expert on the Liglimom, had made him return.

"Harjeedian," Elise said. "I believe we met him at the reception that was held upon our arrival. He's the one who . . ."

Firekeeper interrupted, tired of long stories. She also didn't much like Harjeedian, but agreed with Derian's assessment.

"He bring us here," Firekeeper said. "Yes. Let Harjeedian work for us. Tonight too soon?"

"Tonight is definitely too soon," Derian replied firmly. "Harjeedian is not a personal friend upon whom we can impose at a moment's notice. I can, however, write out a message and send it to him tonight. He knows how impatient you can be, and so won't be surprised."

"Why we care?" Firekeeper asked. "We owe him surprise."

Elise gave Firekeeper a reproving frown. "Is what you have found something you want everyone talking about, Firekeeper? You've stumbled on something potentially volatile. This Voice seems to have been somehow associated with two who dealt in forbidden magic—and we have suspicions that these unknowns may also be involved with magical lore. Do you want Harjeedian's meeting with us and his later research to be noticed so that he must report to his superiors?"

Firekeeper shook her head violently.

"Then a little less haste, a little more care," said Elise, sounding rather like Blind Seer when he was quoting proverbs.

Firekeeper rose, and Blind Seer and Truth rose with her.

"Then if we must wait until tomorrow, we go now."

"We have prepared rooms for you," Derian said with a certain degree of resignation, as does one who makes an offer he knows will be refused.

"No rooms," Firekeeper said. "Night is good."

And with that the three were gone. The building that housed the embassy was near Heeranenahalm, the section of the city where the rulers lived. Forests backed onto this, and Firekeeper and her companions well knew their way into those wooded refuges.

Firekeeper hardly noticed when Truth left them to pursue her own hunting. The wolf-woman's thoughts were a living thicket, one that threatened to snare her. Miserably, she shook her head clear of the thorns. Then she ran with Blind Seer, pretending that they were wild and free for just a little time longer.

TRUTH PADDED OVER THE DUFF, slipping beneath thick curtains of vines, prowling along the trunks of fallen trees, wading in the living waters of running streams. In one of these she caught a large water turtle and cracked open its shell with her powerful jaws.

The fishy flesh tasted very good. The maimalodalum had done their best to care for her, but turtle and tortoise had not been on the menu, although Powerful Tenderness had a bear's fondness for fresh fish. Standing chest-deep in rapidly flowing water, Truth indulged herself by catching and eating the minnows that shot over the polished rock. She missed a great many, and not entirely because she was out of practice—but she didn't think about this. There was too much good to enjoy.

Truth was truly alone for the first time since her sanity had returned to her, and she luxuriated in her solitude as much as she did in the taste of her meal. She concentrated on reality, feeling how the pads of her paws sank into the damp earth, sheathing and unsheathing her claws, licking them clean of mud and traces of blood.

Then she began on her fur, pulling with her teeth at the snags and mats that had accumulated during her separation from her body. Powerful Tenderness had done his best to care for her, but even he had stopped short of grooming a Wise Jaguar.

As her teeth worried at the matted clumps of fur, Truth's mind worried at another, more tangled mess.

The Voice. What was he? Why had he been locked in the strange apartment—assuming it was he who had been imprisoned there, and this seemed likely.

Had he escaped when they opened the door? None of those who had been closest had seen anything. Although all admitted that they had been flash-blinded by the silver light that had attended the opening of the door, all swore with equal firmness that they could not have missed someone slipping past.

Truth was inclined to believe them. She herself had been present—or at least her body had been—and she had no memory of anyone going past her as she dove through the door. That would seem to suggest that whoever had left the apartment—if anyone had done so—whoever had carved those figurines—had been . . .

Truth broke this chain of thought, for it only led to frustration. All the options led simply to more questions. As once she had focused on various streams of probability, now she forced herself from speculation into planning a course of action.

The Voice had led her spirit to that apartment.

The Voice—or at least the tenant of that apartment—had carved a figurine that represented Truth. Had this been used to communicate with her? Likely To control her? Again, reluctantly, Truth had to admit this was likely.

She gnawed at a fragment of claw sheath, working it free, letting it drop into the running water.

What had been done once could be done again. Therefore, she must find the Voice—and upon finding him, she must kill him. Only then would she be freed from the risk of having him dominate her again.

But to find him . . . Firekeeper and the others might learn something from those figurines, but the figurines would lead only to the Voice's pawns. She wanted the Voice, and the only place she had encountered him was a place to which she feared to return.

Once before she had overextended herself to the point of insanity. All too well, Truth realized that the risk of insanity was greater if she reached again into the realm of omens.

VII

AS HE HAD PROMISED FIREKEEPER, Derian wrote Harjeedian before retiring that night. Harjeedian's reply arrived as Derian was finishing his breakfast. So did Firekeeper. Knowing as he did that the wolf-woman often slept in the daylight hours, Derian took this early arrival as an indication of her anxiety regarding the figurines.

"What he say?" Firekeeper asked, reaching to help herself to a wedge of melon from Derian's plate.

"He says," Derian replied, with a firm emphasis on the grammatically correct form, "that he will call here midday, in hopes of finding you returned from your evening jaunt. Word had reached Heeranenahalm of your arrival on the mainland, and he is pleased that you would wish to see him."

"Neither wish nor pleased," Firekeeper said, reaching for another piece of melon, "is not so, but must do."

Derian started to remind Firekeeper that she must be polite to Harjeedian if she expected to have him cooperate not only in this research, but also in keeping what they told him to himself. He stopped himself in mid-breath. Firekeeper's social graces might be nil, but as she had shown last night when meeting Ambassador Sailor, she had a wolf's finely tuned sense of who was important and who was not. Good manners from her were not, as so often with humans, a sign that she liked someone. Instead they were a sign that she respected—or at least needed—them.

So I suppose, Derian thought dryly, *that I should be thrilled that she's eating my breakfast.*

He wasn't, but he didn't slap Firekeeper's fingers away as he might have his sister Dami's. Eating, and priority in eating, were serious matters with wolves. Derian wasn't completely certain that Firekeeper might not snap at him in response to his defending his meal.

He did, however, slide the remaining melon out of her reach.

"I can have the kitchen send you something if you're hungry," he said.

"Not hungry," Firekeeper admitted, giving him a smile that was at least a little sheepish. "But the melon taste very good."

Derian took this as a request, and rang for his runner. It was odd having servants assigned to him, but it did beat having to run down to the kitchens himself.

Firekeeper had never been much for small talk, so once Derian had her settled with her melon, he turned to his correspondence. There was quite a lot of it, both from members of the small Bright Haven community and from local officials. As Ambassador Sailor and Elise were still struggling with their written Liglimosh, the early review fell on Derian. Later, after he had assessed the gist of the meaning, the translator took over, but they had all agreed that it was wisest not to give the Liglimom reason to think that the northerners could be easily deceived.

The Bright Haven contingent mostly consisted of the crew of the *Shine,* the ship that had carried the ambassadorial party south and had then remained. This way, should the ambassador feel it necessary to break negotiations, the northerners would not need to wait for a ship to carry them home. Many of the *Shine*'s crew had been chosen because of their knowledge of trade and other mercantile matters, and they regularly reported their own, interestingly skewed, views of Liglim.

There were less pleasant matters with which Derian had to deal. Two very different cultures could not meet without clashing, and hardly a hand of days passed without a brawl or serious dispute. Then there was the correspondences from locals, all of whom were certain that there was some advantage to them in getting in tight with the northerners before too many rules and regulations were in place.

At one point Derian glanced over at Firekeeper, thinking to suggest that she might enjoy visiting with Elise and Doc, but the wolf-woman was sprawled asleep on the floor, cuddled as close as the hot, sticky weather would permit, to Blind Seer. The blue-eyed wolf was also drowsing, but he opened his eyes at Derian's motion and canted his ears sideways as if to say, "Let her sleep. She's more worried than you might think."

Or he could be saying, Derian thought, *"Bother her and I'll bite you." I wish we could understand each other better.*

Derian finished reviewing the more critical correspondence and made an early report to the ambassador. His report included a vague explanation as to why Harjeedian would be calling. Ambassador Sailor did not press for more details, and Derian found himself wondering just what the ambassador's directives regarding the wolf-woman might be.

Certainly both King Allister and King Tedric had reason to trust Firekeeper. She had acted to their advantage before. Had the ambassador been told to view her as a faithful subject, or perhaps as someone possessing a peculiar diplomatic capacity? Certainly the latter explanation might be more accurate, for if Derian was certain of anything, it was that Firekeeper's loyalties were often torn. She was loyal to those who had reared her, but at least once that Derian knew, she had defied the Royal Beasts' commands to act in what she thought was a wiser fashion.

With this combination of work and speculation to occupy him, the morning hours flew by for Derian. He was mildly startled when one of the servants tapped on his door. The servant bore a tray holding a variety of standard refreshments.

"Aridisdu Harjeedian has just been admitted to the building," the servant said, setting the tray on the table. "I thought you would like a moment to prepare."

"Thank you both for the warning and the refreshments. Feel free to leave the door open," Derian replied. He turned to Firekeeper, who had risen to her feet and was stretching. "Brush off the wolf fur, Firekeeper. Company's here."

Firekeeper didn't brush off the fur, but she did remain standing until Harjeedian entered, Blind Seer at her side, and her hand well away from her knife. Derian decided to be satisfied with this moderate expression of courtesy.

Aridisdu Harjeedian entered a few moments later. Except for his cheekbones, which were high, even among his people, whose features ran to such, Harjeedian was completely average: shining black hair cut blunt to the shoulder, slanting black eyes, skin the warm brown of toasted bread. What wasn't average about him was the aura of contained authority. This, more than the embroidery on his clothing, or the snake coiled around his neck, marked him as a man of importance.

Derian didn't like Harjeedian, but he didn't precisely dislike him either, so he accorded him both a neat bow and the appropriate courteous local gesture indicating welcome. Firekeeper offered neither, just stood, watching and waiting.

"You asked me to come here," Harjeedian said, when the appropriate greetings were concluded.

Firekeeper nodded. "Yes. Thank you."

Derian hid his relief. Harjeedian would fully appreciate those two small words.

"Before we get to business, can I offer you some refreshment?" He indicated the tray with an inclination of his head.

Harjeedian nodded. "Mint water would be very nice. The walk here was rather hot. The air is close. I wouldn't be surprised if we had a thunderstorm later."

"Nothing else?" Derian asked. "There are cookies and fruit. I could also send to the kitchens if you fancy something that isn't here."

"Mint water will be fine," Harjeedian assured him.

Derian nodded to the servant who stood outside the door. "I won't need you for a bit. Feel free to take a break. I'll ring if something comes up."

Derian shut the door. When he crossed back to his desk, he found Firekeeper was pouring for Harjeedian, every bit as polite as Lady Archer when her grand duchess grandmother came to call. Harjeedian wasn't in the least stupid, nor had his increased importance made him unaware of offered courtesy.

"Thank you, Lady Blysse," he said, accepting the tall, pressed glass tumbler.

"I thought we'd sit over here," Derian said, indicating a pair of chairs set by a window that looked over the city.

Harjeedian looked momentarily surprised. After all, there were three of them. Then he saw Firekeeper resume her seat on the floor, and obviously remembered her habits.

"This must be important to bring you from Misheemnekuru, Lady Blysse," Harjeedian said. "I hope no one is ill."

"No one more than is," Firekeeper replied. "I mean, illness no other thing there or to those there is why I come."

Her Liglimosh is worse than her Pellish, Derian thought with accustomed despair. *I bet she hasn't used it for a year, except when she needed to order some disdu to take her to the mainland. Why would she?*

"Perhaps," Derian interjected aloud, "we should speak Pellish. Harjeedian's has only gotten better since last you saw him."

"And my Liglimosh worse," Firekeeper said, switching languages with alacrity.

One good thing about wolves, Derian thought. *They accept justifiable criticism very well.*

Harjeedian forbore from commenting on Firekeeper's language skills, but returned to the main point.

"I am pleased that neither the yarimaimalom nor the maimalodalum need our assistance," he said. "May I ask what brings you here?"

Firekeeper nodded. "Not need to ask. I tell. Pellish maybe better. If any listen outside, they no understand too well."

"Especially if they try to understand your sentences," Derian said. "Do you want to tell Harjeedian, or would you like me to tell him what you told us last night, and correct me along the way?"

"I tell," Firekeeper said, glancing at Blind Seer. Derian wondered if the wolf had told her she needed practice. "You help. Please."

The telling was long and somewhat laborious. Harjeedian had some acquaintance with Firekeeper, but he didn't have Elise, Doc, and Derian's long familiarity with her tendency to view most words as nonessential. Even so, with Derian's help, by the time Firekeeper rocked back against Blind Seer as a sign that she had finished, Harjeedian had a clear understanding of events to this point.

"Astonishing," he said, picking up the broken pieces of the Dantarahma figurine and studying them. "This is quite plainly Dantarahma. I can see why you are certain two of the other carvings are of people you know."

"And Truth," Firekeeper said, indicating the jaguar figurine.

"And Truth," Harjeedian agreed. "So you are hoping I can help you identify these other two. I will tell you directly. They are not anyone I know. As you said, their attire is not precisely that of Liglim. They could be from one of the city-states to the south. Attire there is rather eclectic, a blending of styles and cultures—even as their people are."

"Can you find out," Firekeeper asked. "Can you find out what this eclectic is? I want to find these and . . ."

She shrugged as if to say that she'd figure out what to do with them when she found them. Firekeeper had never been much for advance planning.

"I can try," Harjeedian said. "We do trade regularly with the southern city-states. However, when I said 'eclectic' I did not mean this was a specific style. I meant the opposite. The southern city-states are not really a nation—as Liglim or Bright Haven are nations."

Derian had his doubts about Bright Haven, but he appreciated the diplomacy and courtesy in Harjeedian's statement.

"The southern city-states," Harjeedian continued, seeing from Firekeeper's expression that she was interested in knowing more, "were founded by peoples who either didn't have a nation to which they belonged—or didn't want to belong to their resident nation."

"I have met some like this," Firekeeper said. "They think they do better without Ones."

Harjeedian nodded. "Precisely. The lands to the south are not ideal for human habitation by any means. Some areas are very swampy and breed disease. Others are rocky, without much fertile soil. There are some nice pockets, I understand. Had Divine Retribution not driven the Old Country rulers from these shores, I think the southern lands eventually would have been settled, but why struggle with disease and bad soil when there was so much land elsewhere?"

"I bet there were renegades living in those areas years before the Plague," Derian said. "People who drifted away, shipwrecked sailors, runaway slaves. There wasn't civil war here in Liglim as there was in our homeland, but surely the social order took a while to settle down—and some folks decided to settle elsewhere."

"Precisely," Harjeedian said. "As these city-states are our closest neighbors, we of Liglim have always had some contact with them. Some of our merchants have kept travel journals, and have earned merit by donating copies to the disdum. Others have written short histories of one city-state or another. I may find something in those records, but if I need to do the work alone, it is not going to be quick. How important is secrecy in this matter?"

Derian stared at him. "What do you think? We may have evidence that someone—someone who apparently can communicate through whatever strange time ocean it is where the diviners go—has been manipulating at least two people who turned out to be dangerously interested in magic."

"And," Firekeeper said, "this someone . . . we have no idea where he is. Do we tell this to everyone?"

Harjeedian shook his head. "No. But I should at least report to u-Liall."

"One of u-Liall was this Voice's tool," Derian reminded him. "Dantarahma was Divine Water's representative among the Five who rule Liglim."

"That is not something I am likely to forget," Harjeedian snapped. He pressed his eyes shut, perhaps praying for insight or patience—or both. He opened his eyes and looked directly at Firekeeper. "You trusted me with this."

"We needed to," Firekeeper said bluntly. Then in a more conciliatory tone she went on, "And you are very wise and very full of knowledge."

"Flattery," Harjeedian said, almost smiling, "will not make me able to read faster. I must have help."

Derian turned to Firekeeper. "What about Poshtuvanu of the Temple of the Horse? We know he wasn't in Dantarahma's camp, and if he's been seduced since I'll eat my best saddle."

"Poshtuvanu?" Harjeedian said. "Possible. The Temple of the Horse has an excellent library in u-Bishinti. Many merchants have given them records."

"And Cishanol," Derian went on, "Iaridisdu Meiyal's secretary. He's also of the Temple of the Horse, and we know we can trust him. He's stationed here in u-Seeheera, right up in Heeranenahalm. He could work with Harjeedian."

"Maybe," Firekeeper said. "Maybe. Can't we just give pictures of figures, show clothes, say 'find' and not say why?"

Harjeedian nodded. "We can. We may, but usually secrecy raises more questions, not fewer. For example, I'll need to have some explanation why you wanted to see me. No one will believe you asked for me out of friendship."

Firekeeper puffed a sigh. "Humans make so complicated! But that is not that you is wrong. You is right. Guide me, and I will follow."

They spent the next hour or so coming up with a plausible excuse for the research. Firekeeper's coming to the mainland was explained by her desire to see Elise and Doc. Her desire to see Harjeedian was harder to explain, but finally they decided on a version of the truth. She had wanted an explanation of things she had seen among the ruins, and had thought of him.

"And I will make quite clear that she was an arrogant chit," Harjeedian said, "thinking she could order about one of my high station."

"Thank you for coming," Firekeeper said. "I do think is kind."

Harjeedian blinked, then made a complicated gesture of acknowledgment. "And I appreciate your trust."

"You know of the maimalodalum and never speak," Firekeeper said. "You have showed trust."

On that surprisingly cordial note, Harjeedian departed.

TRUTH WAS FINDING ADAPTING TO LIFE without her second sight very difficult. Ever since she was a kitten she had used her ability to weigh and judge probable courses of action to guide her in making even minor decisions. Now, as she tried not to do so lest she slide again into that stream and be washed away into madness, she discovered a degree of hesitancy she had not known was part of her nature.

To make matters worse, if she did cheat the least little bit, the Voice had a tendency to start talking to her.

"It's not going to work, you know," he said one afternoon.

"What?" Truth replied before she thought about how dangerous this could be.

"They're not going to . . ."

Truth stopped listening. She collapsed, panting and trembling. Fur came off in a cloud when she shook herself. She sat and groomed limb by limb with centered concentration, focusing on every spot, every curve. She'd done a lot of this in the days since their return to the mainland, and her coat looked wonderful. She was even losing some of her former gauntness.

"What isn't going to work?" she asked herself, but she didn't know the answer, and she admitted that she was afraid to ask the one who apparently did.

FIREKEEPER WAS WELL AWARE that pestering Derian and Harjeedian was not going to get her answers any sooner, so she did her best to be helpful. Since the most helpful thing she could do was defuse any sense that her return to the mainland was an omen of some impending crisis, she tried a hand at deception and diplomacy—neither her strongest trait.

Visiting with Elise and Doc was easy to do, even delightful. Elise insisted that Firekeeper speak Liglimosh with her, which Firekeeper found frustrating, but admitted was probably necessary. As Doc didn't share Elise's gift for languages, conversation often lapsed into Pellish, and Firekeeper found herself increasing in her facility in both languages.

They went shopping to replace what Elise insisted on calling "deficiencies" in Firekeeper's wardrobe. Elise's intentions had been to buy a few changes of clothing over what Firekeeper had worn in from the outpost, and maybe a pair of soft shoes—though Elise knew it would be an uphill battle to get Firekeeper to wear them.

Firekeeper, thinking how poorly the local cottons had held up to her use of them, and aware that she was likely to be away from "civilization," had different ideas. She had Elise help her commission some hardier trousers in light but sturdy leather. These were fashioned more along northern styles, cut to below the knee and fastened with buttons. She even let Elise talk her into a pair of lace-up boots. The local tailors were pleased to have the challenge, and vied for the custom work.

The day after Harjeedian's visit, Firekeeper received an "invitation" to call on u-Liall, the governing body of Liglim. She knew perfectly well that she could not refuse, and so accepted with good grace. She did, however, refuse Derian's halfhearted offer to accompany her. She knew he had no desire to see Rahniseeta, Harjeedian's sister, and the new junjaldisdu. Firekeeper smelled no anger from him, but it did not take much for her to imagine how he felt. A year was not long enough to recover from a soundly broken heart.

"I will be very polite," Firekeeper promised, "very formal. I will answer every question, and ask for explanations as if I were the smallest of small puppies before the One."

She did, too, and the interview went, she thought rather smugly, very well.

Even so, there were countless times each day that Firekeeper wanted to rush in to Derian's office and ask "Have you heard anything?" She restrained herself to three times a day: when the morning mail came, after lunch, and before Derian retired to sleep.

On the fourth day following their initial meeting with Harjeedian, Firekeeper went into Derian's office on the heels of the morning mail. She stood waiting as Derian sorted things into piles, and was finally rewarded.

"Harjeedian has sent a note. He says he will call midmorning, unless we send word that we are not available to receive him."

Firekeeper permitted herself a small bounce of pleasure.

"He also says that what he has to report is far from conclusive," Derian said. "That means, don't hope for too much."

Firekeeper nodded acceptance, and tried to remain calm, but her heart was singing at the idea that they might have a scent from which they might find a trail.

Harjeedian arrived promptly. To his own evident surprise—and Firekeeper's—Truth walked in with him.

"Did you invite her?" Derian asked Firekeeper.

"No," Firekeeper said.

"I divined this meeting was to happen," Truth said, *"and that I should be present."*

Firekeeper repeated this. Harjeedian accepted it as a matter of course, Derian a little less easily. Blind Seer, however, was the one to sniff at the jaguar.

"That is not the whole truth, is it?" he said. *"I am no diviner, but my nose is good. You are upset."*

Truth's ears flattened against her skull and she snarled, *"Perhaps I am upset because I already know the outcome of all this labor."*

Blind Seer sniffed again. *"That, I think, has the whiff of truth. Be at peace, great one. I would be the last to doubt your prescience, only the wholeness of what you say."*

Truth's tail lashed back and forth at this, but as she settled onto the rug Derian offered her, Firekeeper thought Blind Seer had probably been right and that Truth had more reason to be there than merely wishing to hear Harjeedian's report.

"May we know what that was about?" Harjeedian asked.

"Truth say," Firekeeper replied, "that she divined this meeting was to happen. This is why she is here. Blind Seer question her and she get upset."

"Not quite a lie, Little Two-legs," Blind Seer said fondly. *"They will think you mean a question about her divining—when rather I questioned the fullness of the reply."*

Firekeeper shrugged. *"Truth has never been less than honest with what she has chosen to tell us. Why malign her before one who honors her even if we believe she holds back a little? You have warned her, and she has all but promised explanation."*

Truth lifted her head from her paws. *"Your courtesy does you credit. I will remember it."*

The two humans, of course, were unaware of the conversation between Firekeeper and the Beasts, and had continued with their own social rituals. Food and drink had been offered, the one refused, the other accepted. Seats were selected, and privacy assured.

"Why not start?" Derian said to Harjeedian. "Firekeeper is being amazingly patient."

Harjeedian did so. "I wish I had more to offer. The summation of our labors is as follows. Neither Cishanol and myself working in the libraries of u-Nahal nor Poshtuvanu working in u-Bishinti were able to make a positive identification of the two people depicted in the figurines. We were not even able to identify precisely in which city-state they might be residents. Moreover, our investigations into the symbols carved into the figurines also went nowhere. They may mean more in the city-states, but they do not belong to any of their major families or ruling houses."

Harjeedian reached into a heavy bag he had carried with him and removed some books, which he set on the low table between his chair and Derian's.

"Lady Blysse, before you ask 'why' and mutter how stupid humans are, please look at these. They should help you understand the difficulty of our task."

"I look," Firekeeper said, moving forward from her spot next to Blind Seer to demonstrate her willingness. Both wolf and jaguar joined her.

"This book," Harjeedian went on, "is a general compendium—collection or gathering—that shows drawings of typical residents of the various city-states. It's quite nicely done, and even fairly current."

Firekeeper looked, concentrating to make the flat drawings real in her mind. She found it easier than in the past, and thought with some satisfaction that her time spent searching among the ruins of Misheemnekuru had not been wasted.

"See how very similar many of the styles of clothing are?" Harjeedian asked.

Firekeeper nodded. "Like Liglim."

"Very like," Harjeedian said. "There's good reason for this. Not only are our climates similar, it turns out that Liglim is a major supplier of textiles to the south. I hadn't realized just how much the city-states rely on Liglim for both fabric and ready-made clothing."

Since Firekeeper had firsthand experience of how difficult it was to make clothing, even from hides, much less from plants, she wasn't surprised at all, but she didn't think it would be good manners to say so.

"So you can't tell by clothing," she said, knowing her disappointment showed in her tone.

"We can tell a little," Harjeedian said. "The closer the city-state is to our border, the more likely the residents are to dress like residents of Liglim. Derian, can you help me with this map?"

The two men unrolled a map, weighting the edges with unused cups and bits of crockery. The map showed odd shapes in different colors. A river separating a long border was painted in a pleasant grass green.

"Since the figurines show people dressed like but not like residents of Liglim, that means they could be from here, or here, or here, or even here," Harjeedian said, pointing to areas on different colored sections of the map. "Each color is a different city-state. The green is the southern border of Liglim. After Divine Retribution, our leaders declared the river there as our boundary, and no one has argued thus far."

He said this with the smugness of the One of a large pack, and Firekeeper didn't blame him.

"Are there any other limiting factors?" Derian asked. "Up north the people of Stonehold look very different from those of my land. So do you people, for that matter."

"As I mentioned earlier," Harjeedian said, shaking his head, "many of the city-states are racially mixed. The figurines are wonderfully detailed, but overall the people seem more like Liglimom than anything else."

"So the trail ends before it begins," Firekeeper said, trying for philosophical resignation, but failing.

"Not quite," Truth said. *"I may be able to take a scent from another wind. Would you hear?"*

DERIAN WATCHED FIREKEEPER'S EXPRESSION CHANGE, resignation giving way to hope as if a cloud had drifted free from the face of the sun.

"What is it?" he asked.

"Truth speaks," came the curt reply. "Wait. I tell."

Derian accepted the promise as it was given, but Harjeedian shifted in his chair impatiently—or so Derian thought until he took a second look at the aridisdu. Before Harjeedian schooled his features back to neutrality, Derian read envy there, stark and bitter.

No wonder, Derian thought. *His life's training has been in reading the signs and omens that would enable him to interpret what the yarimaimalom say. Firekeeper understands more clearly, and does it as easily as breathing.*

"More mint water?" Derian said, reaching for the pitcher containing the sweetened infusion.

"Thank you," Harjeedian said, but although he held his tumbler out so Derian could fill it, his gaze did not leave Firekeeper.

At last Firekeeper stirred and looked up at the two men.

"Is not easy to explain," she said, "because I not all understand, but I try. Truth say she think she can find these two, like with divination. She say that sometime she hear the Voice still in her head. She not like. She think the Voice wish her to do something more for him."

"More?" Derian asked. Then he understood. "That's right, the Voice seems to have been imprisoned in that cellar on Misheemnekuru. In helping Truth, he helped himself—or so it seems. But he's out now—or at least you didn't find him there."

Firekeeper bit her lower lip, then nodded. "We not find. Truth though, she think he not, maybe not a person. Remember the Dragon of Despair?"

"Who could forget that?"

"The dragon there, yet not there. I think, Blind Seer, too, that maybe the Voice is like the dragon."

Harjeedian spoke for the first time. "You think the Voice is a dragon, did you say?"

"No," Firekeeper answered. "I say *like* the dragon in that it lives in another way than we do."

Derian interjected, "I'll tell you more later if you'd like, Harjeedian. Leave it for now that Firekeeper is being precisely accurate. What we encountered in New Kelvin didn't fit any of the rules for a living thing—but that didn't make it any less alive."

"I'll accept that," Harjeedian said. "After all, until Firekeeper and Blind Seer came from the west, your people had no idea the yarimaimalom were other than fireside tales—our people knew about them all along."

"Right," Derian said. "It's interesting. If the Voice had any role in prompting Melina's actions, could he have led her to the tales of the Dragon? It seems possible, especially if they are somehow akin."

Firekeeper held up her hand. "I not say this. Truth not say this. I just remind, so that you not think a person you not see is less a person."

"Right," Derian said, "but there's nothing wrong with speculation."

Firekeeper tilted her head in tentative agreement. "Maybe. But not to think thinking about something is the something."

"I promise," Derian said. "So Truth thinks she may be able to find the subjects of the remaining two figurines. Does she think the Voice will guide her?"

Truth emitted a sound between a cough and a gruff roar. Firekeeper's mouth quirked in a wry smile.

"Truth say she think she track by her divination," Firekeeper replied. "She think that the Voice tell her things, even things she not want to know."

Harjeedian frowned. "Truth, isn't this a terrible risk for you to take?"

Firekeeper translated. "Truth say, 'Yes, is, but I think leaving this thing of the figurines without us knowing who they are and what they do is worth taking risk.'"

The wolf-woman paused and added, "She also say, she not talk so bad."

"I understand," Harjeedian said. "But what if Truth goes insane as she did before? None of us have her gift for divination, nor can we hear the Voice."

Firekeeper paused, then said, "Blind Seer think maybe we should have someone else come with us, someone who scents magic as he does game."

Derian understood immediately. "One of the maimalodalum? I remember they claimed a sensitivity to magic, but Firekeeper, how could one come with us? I thought they wished their existence to remain a secret and . . . well, they are so odd-looking. They'd be hard to hide."

Firekeeper replied, "Some maybe, with clothing over them—like Hope, maybe—could come with us. There are others who are smaller or good in the forests. They might come with us as Blind Seer has in the northern lands, staying hidden most of the time."

"I suppose it might work," Derian said. "It would be useful to have someone along who could assist Truth. Should she need assistance," he added hastily when the jaguar's burnt-orange gaze turned balefully upon him.

"So Blind Seer and I think, too," Firekeeper said, "but you speak as if you would come with us on this hunt."

"I had planned to," Derian said, surprised. "There are times a human or two are useful, and you don't know yet if you would be traveling through human-held lands or not. I think it's likely. Neither Melina nor Dantarahma had the courtesy to work out in the wilds where you are most comfortable."

Firekeeper gave one of the gusty sighs that meant she agreed, but didn't much like doing so.

"And I thought to also offer my services," Harjeedian said. "The lands in which you will initially travel are held by my people. Even when you cross into the city-states, our language and writing are often used for trade."

Firekeeper scowled, "But humans mean things, and things mean beasts to carry things, and all this means roads and . . ."

"You aren't hunting deer, Firekeeper," Derian said. "You're hunting humans. Get it through your head. You're going to need us."

Blind Seer, who had been sitting calmly though the discussion now rose onto all four feet and looked down at Firekeeper. There was absolutely no doubt that he was reprimanding her, and under his blue-eyed stare, Firekeeper wilted.

"I agree," she said. "To hunt humans, need humans. To hunt magic, need maimalodalu. To find these at all, need Truth—maybe Elise, too, and Doc. They like to go places. What a strange, strange pack this will be."

Derian laughed. "Well, as to that point, you won't find me disagreeing, Firekeeper. You won't find me disagreeing one bit."

VIII

HARJEEDIAN STAYED while they drafted a message to the maimalo-dalum. Then he said he should take his leave, explaining he would need to make arrangements with his temple to go off with Firekeeper.

"I would like to tell the full truth as to why I go," he said, "but I would be lying if I said I thought an explanation is necessary. It is enough that Truth is sane again and requests my aid."

"That's how you will explain it?" Derian said.

"That should be enough," Harjeedian said, "especially if Truth herself will come to the Temple of the Cold Bloods."

The jaguar rose, indicating without need of an interpreter that she would be pleased to do so.

Firekeeper also rose. "I give this message to a fish eagle, then I find Doc and Elise. Tell them what we do, ask them to come. Doc's healing talent would be a good thing to have with us, and Elise very much likes strange places."

"Go ahead," Derian said, "but ask them to keep our going close for a bit. I should be the one to tell the ambassador I'm leaving. Honestly, I need to ask his permission."

"If Ambassador Sailor seems unwilling to grant you leave," Harjeedian said, "send me a message. I will have a request come directly from my temple. The ambassador will be reluctant to refuse us your assistance."

"Thanks," Derian said.

"You talk like you not talk to ambassador now," Firekeeper said. "Why?"

"If I leave now," Derian explained, "I can get to u-Bishinti and back again before dark. We're going to need horses and pack animals for this trip—horses and pack animals that won't be troubled by you, Truth, and whatever the maimalodalum choose to send."

"U-Bishinti later," Firekeeper said. "Ambassador first. He not like if you go making plans for horses until he lets you go."

"She's right," Harjeedian said. "Wolves usually are when it comes to matters of precedence."

"You're right," Derian said. "You're right."

AMBASSADOR SAILOR COULDN'T SEE DERIAN IMMEDIATELY, but he asked Derian to join him for lunch. Over fresh sea bass and wild rice, Derian gave an edited version of his reasons for requesting a leave of absence.

"To be honest, sir," he concluded, "I don't really know the full story. It's often like that with Firekeeper. I know that whatever this is has something to do with what brought her from Misheemnekuru. I know that the jaguar, Truth, is involved, and I know it's important enough that the aridisdu Harjeedian has put himself at the jaguar's disposal."

"And you think we should do no less?" Ambassador Sailor asked. "I see. I am reluctant, though. You are my right hand. In all honesty, and I believe in honesty, you are more the real ambassador than I am. Until I manage to acquire a better grasp of local customs and language, I rely on you to keep me from making a bad blunder."

Derian knew this, but he also knew he was more afraid of what would happen if Firekeeper was turned loose on an unsuspecting south than of any political or diplomatic misstep the ambassador might commit.

"I really should go with Firekeeper," he said. "Please don't refuse me right away. At least tell me you will think about it."

Ambassador Sailor nodded, but he clearly wasn't pleased. "I'm also not happy that Lady Blysse is off attempting to suborn Lady Archer and Sir Jared to her cause. What does she think I will do if all of you go?"

"There are others from Bright Haven here in Liglim," Derian reminded him, but he knew the argument was weak. Most of those who would remain would be more merchants than diplomats, and none had his, or even Elise's, command of Liglimosh.

The butler—one of the ambassador's personal household who had accompanied him south—entered the dining room. He cleared his throat, politely indicating he had a message.

"Ambassador Sailor," the butler said, "Lady Archer, Sir Jared, and Lady Blysse have requested permission to join you and Counselor Derian. Shall I tell them you will see them when your repast is concluded?"

"Send them in," Ambassador Sailor said, pushing his plate away. "My appetite is shot. Never happened at sea. Diplomacy is rougher on my gut than any storm. Have dessert brought in and enough plates for my other guests."

"Very good, sir," the butler said. He paused long enough to gather the used plates before going out, his way of expressing disapproval, or so Derian supposed.

The other three—or rather four, for Blind Seer was with Firekeeper, even though the butler had not thought to announce him—came in soon after. Even Firekeeper accepted a chair at the table, a sure sign that she was aware of the tension. She seemed confused, frowning slightly as she looked at Elise and Doc, and from this Derian thought that her interview had—for some reason—gone no better than his own.

"Ambassador Sailor," Elise began after the usual courtesies had been exchanged and dessert served around, "I take it that you are aware that Lady Blysse plans to journey into southern Liglim and possibly beyond."

"That's what Counselor Derian tells me. He also tells me that she plans to strip my embassy when she goes."

Elise smiled. "Not quite, but she did ask Sir Jared and me if we would be able to come with her."

"Strip my embassy," the ambassador repeated.

"Sir," Elise said, "did it occur to you that this mission is, in its own strange way, a diplomatic one?"

"What? I thought you folks would be haring off after some wild goal of Lady Blysse's—excuse me, of Lady Blysse's and the jaguar's."

"I won't deny that the expedition is prompted by their needs," Elise replied smoothly. "However, that does not change the fact that if they go into the southern city-states, as I have been led to believe is almost certain, Lady Blysse is likely to be the first northerner to do so. Tell me, sir, do you really wish Firekeeper to be thought of as a typical representative of Bright Haven?"

Ambassador Sailor gaped, then he grinned, his more usual good humor resurfacing. "I hadn't thought of it that way. You're right. She would be a very, uh, shall we say 'atypical' representative."

"And more importantly," Elise said, "although Firekeeper has been a fine ally of our people, she is not really of our people—for all she comes of our stock."

Ambassador Sailor did not need any explanation. "Again, I admit that you have a point, a good one, Lady Archer. Still, I am reluctant to give up all three of you. You've just proven how valuable you can be—and that you will be more so as you adjust to local customs and language."

"That's all right," Elise said calmly, looking over at Derian with a slight smile. "Sir Jared and I won't be going, but we would like to beg you to consider releasing Counselor Derian to do so."

Suddenly, Derian understood the odd look on Firekeeper's face. Elise must have told the wolf-woman that she and Doc couldn't go, but quite clearly, she hadn't explained why. His supposition was supported a moment later, for Firekeeper, who had been methodically eating melon while she listened, now put a slice down half-eaten.

"Will you tell why not now?" she growled, her voice husky. "I try to say why we need you so much. What is more important?"

Elise answered with two simple words: "Our baby."

The room was quiet for a moment, then Firekeeper broke the silence with what had to be the first girlish squeal Derian had ever heard from her.

"Baby?" the wolf-woman said. "Yours? Yours and Doc's?"

"That's right," Elise said, laughing just a little. "Mine and Doc's. We weren't going to say anything until I started really showing, but then this came up . . . We felt we had to explain."

Doc leaned forward. "We'd appreciate if none of you said anything. The first trimester is the time when a miscarriage is most likely to happen, and with Elise's family history the odds for Elise's carrying to term aren't good."

Ambassador Sailor looked a trace confused. Derian remembered the man wasn't from Hawk Haven, and so couldn't be expected to know the traits of the various Great Houses. Derian started explaining to save Elise and Doc the need to discuss such an unlucky subject.

"Elise's mother was a Wellward," Derian explained. "There's a reason Elise is an only child. The family has long been cursed with difficulty in bearing healthy children."

"Wellward," Ambassador Sailor said. "I remember the name now. Queen Elexa of Hawk Haven was born a Wellward. Didn't she have three healthy children?"

"Three," Derian agreed, "and ruined her health doing so. She's younger than King Tedric, but looks older. Elise's parents decided not to take any risks after Elise was born, saving Lady Aurella's health at the cost of security of their line. Elise's 'sister' Deste is actually her first cousin."

Firekeeper was staring at Doc with gravity at odds with her previous enthusiasm. As soon as Derian stopped speaking, Firekeeper let loose.

"But, Doc, you will keep Elise safe," Firekeeper said, her voice tight with urgency. "Elise and the baby both. You stayed in New Kelvin to learn the lore. You know how."

"I'll try," Doc said. "I'll try my very best to keep them safe. The doctor's first order is that Elise does not go riding off into the unknown. His second order is that he stays right with her so if something does go wrong, he can try and fix it."

Firekeeper nodded. "Yes. Elise not come. Not with a pup . . . a baby coming. How soon will it come?"

Doc hid a trace of embarrassment beneath a manner suddenly very professional. "We, uh, estimate that the baby was conceived on the voyage here, so the moon will turn—we are hoping—seven or eight times before the baby is born. Elise was certainly not pregnant when we left."

"Not much else to do at sea," Ambassador Sailor said with easy understanding. "Well, congratulations to you both, and congratulations to me for getting to keep two such fine advisors."

Firekeeper growled, "Advise, yes. No too much work."

The wolf-woman's mien was threatening, her hand drifting toward the knife she always wore at her waist. Ambassador Sailor was completely taken aback.

"I, of course, I . . ."

His words trailed off and Elise took over.

"Firekeeper, I promise I will be careful. Doc has talked to a lot of midwives since he began his research, and just about all of them agreed that healthy exercise and something of interest are the best things for a pregnant woman. There's a great deal of difference between working around the embassy here and riding cross-country to an unknown destination."

Firekeeper nodded acceptance of this, but the glance she shot the ambassador as much as said that if anything happened to Elise's pregnancy, he'd better have good references or be far away when she returned.

Derian had to admit he was amused, but he did his best to hide it. Being threatened by Firekeeper was not in the least amusing if you were on the receiving end.

"You said 'keep two,'" Derian said to the ambassador. "That is, when you were offering congratulations to Elise and Doc. Does that mean?"

Ambassador Sailor turned to Derian with evident relief. "Yes. I'm going to take Lady Archer's advice and release you from service here to accompany the jaguar Truth and Lady Blysse on this expedition. You would be a good first contact from Bright Haven to any of the city-states. You're already multilingual, know something of the customs, and all that."

And, Derian thought, seeing the ambassador shoot an almost imperceptible glance over at Firekeeper, *I don't tend to threaten people as a first line of diplomacy.*

Aloud he said, "Thank you, sir. If you would detach me as early as tomorrow, I will ride to u-Bishinti and consult with Varjuna and Zira—that is, the ikidisdu and one of the kidisdu of the Horse—regarding appropriate mounts for our expedition."

"By all means," Ambassador Sailor replied. "If you would do me the favor of making yourself available to me or my personal secretary if you have free time before you leave, I would be grateful. You have been handling so many small details. We need to assure a smooth transition."

Derian made his nod a slight bow as well. "I won't leave you stranded, Ambassador. I promise."

Firekeeper looked around the room, her gaze resting with pleased benevolence on Doc and Elise.

"Many promises, today," she said. "Now let us go keep them."

DESPITE FIREKEEPER'S IMPATIENT HOPE that they could be on their way quickly, Truth knew that days would pass before everything was ready. A message was sent over to the maimalodalum, asking them to nominate one of their number to accompany the expedition. The maimalodalum were assured that all efforts would be made to keep the candidate hidden—and promised that if the maimalodalu was discovered, it would be represented as a unique creature, not one of a community.

Truth thought the maimalodalum would agree to send someone, but she did not use her divination to discover who was most likely. Despite her attempts to appear nonchalant regarding the risk she was taking, she did not care to increase the probability that she would find herself flowing into insanity.

Moreover, the Voice did start talking to her as soon as she tentatively dipped her muzzle into the waters where omens took shape.

"I told you it wouldn't work," he said. "Didn't I? Why won't you accept that I mean you no harm?"

"No harm," Truth hissed, "but maybe no good either."

"Can we at least agree that in this matter our paths march side by side?" the Voice said in a conciliatory fashion.

"Jaguars do not march side by side with any."

"Pick another metaphor, then," the Voice said. "I mean you no harm. Yes, as you suspect, I have reasons for wanting you to find those two people—but since you want to find them, what of it?"

Truth couldn't find a reason to disagree.

"So, where are they?"

The Voice sounded apologetic. "I don't see things quite as you do. I can't give a name or address—at least not now. This may change. What I can tell you is that you won't find them in Liglim. They're from one of the bordering city-states."

"Which?"

"I told you. I don't know. Truth, you're probably the first person I've been able to talk with in centuries. Most of the communication I manage I perform through dreams or visions. You meet me, well, call it halfway, though we'd be pushed to say halfway between where and where. I'll be sort of coming with you on this journey, and just as the maimalodalum—a great idea bringing one along—can sense magic, I'll be able to sense other things."

Truth's tail lashed. "And why is it so important to you that we find these? Are they like Dantarahma and this Melina—gone rabid because of your dreams and vision?"

The Voice laughed, "You wouldn't believe me if I told you. Let me keep that to myself for a while. It will keep you interested."

Truth snarled, but she had to admit the Voice was right. Even if he had told her why he wanted them to find these two, she wouldn't have believed him. Moreover, why he wanted them—or who they were—mattered very little to her. What Truth wanted was the Voice, and she was certain that if she walked this trail far enough, she would find him.

And then, she promised herself, she would kill him.

ᐁ

THE DAY FOLLOWING THE MEETING with Ambassador Sailor, Derian insisted that Firekeeper accompany him when he went to u-Bishinti.

"After all," he said, "you're a great part of the problem. Grey Patience isn't here to be bullied into submission, and I'm not sure that Varjuna would approve of such treatment of his animals."

Firekeeper shrugged, but she didn't refuse. There wasn't much to do around the embassy. The maimalodalum would certainly take some time deciding who would be best to send on the expedition—if they agreed at all. She might as well go into the countryside with Derian.

Derian's mount was a splashy bay paint named Prahini, "Rainbow" in Liglimosh. She was a young mare, lacking the steadiness and ready contempt that had permitted Derian's earlier mount, Roanne, to come to some sort of agreement with Firekeeper and Blind Seer. Initially, Firekeeper offered to go overland and meet Derian at u-Bishinti. He refused her offer.

"I don't doubt that you could get there before us, even beat us there if you put your mind to it."

"Feet," Firekeeper teased. "Not mind."

"Whichever," Derian replied, refusing to be distracted. "I want to see how long it takes for Prahini to adjust to your and Blind Seer's company. She was locally born, after all, and the Liglimom do make some effort to accustom their horses to large predators. Thing is, there's only so much that can be done without making the horses vulnerable."

"Remember how you thought the horses were meant to be eaten the first time you saw them?" Blind Seer reminded. *"These Wise Beasts, at least those that live on the mainland, do not have an easy time, do they?"*

Firekeeper grinned at him, but she could see Derian's point. All the way down to u-Bishinti, she ran alongside Prahini, keeping where the mare could see her and grow accustomed to her scent. Blind Seer did the same, staying a bit farther out.

A year spent running with the wolves had put Firekeeper in excellent condition, and as Derian was not one to tire his horse unduly, the wolf-woman was able to settle into the mile-eating jog that enabled the wolves to cover long distances without evident effort.

They arrived in u-Bishinti midmorning, dusty and ready for something to drink, but none of them very tired. Immediately upon arrival, they were met by an older man almost as tall as Derian. He was broad-shouldered, with heavy, bowed legs that spoke of much time in the saddle. The woman with him also showed the signs of being a rider, but life had altered her figure in other ways. She was broad in the hip, heavy in the breasts, marked in a dozen small ways as a mother.

"*Will Elise look so?*" Firekeeper wondered to Blind Seer.

"*I think not,*" the wolf replied. "*This is not a woman to struggle and die while a baby pushes forth. This woman is made for easy bearing. I can see why her mate values her.*"

Firekeeper gave the woman another look. This was Zira, a kidisdu of the Horse. The man was Varjuna, the ikidisdu, or One, of this place. It was clear in a hand of small ways that Varjuna did value Zira, but Firekeeper thought it was for more than breeding purposes.

Zira was not an attractive woman, not even what Firekeeper had heard politely termed "handsome." She was almost ugly, with stained teeth and more breadth to her figure than even childbearing could account for. What transformed her from ugliness into something very like beauty was a contagious vitality.

Firekeeper had met both Varjuna and Zira a time or two before, for they were among Derian's closest friends among the Liglimom, but she did not know them well. Wolfishly polite, she hung back, letting greetings between friends go uninterrupted, knowing she would not be long forgotten—if for no other reason than she and Blind Seer were unsettling some of the nearby horses.

"Don't be shy, Lady Blysse," Zira said, motioning for Firekeeper to come join them. Something about the twinkle in her eyes made Firekeeper think the other woman didn't think her in the least shy. "Derian has been telling us of your upcoming expedition. We're going to need your help on the next part."

Derian had left Prahini in the care of one of the local grooms, and now they walked toward a place that smelled promisingly of food. To Firekeeper's satisfaction, they stopped long enough to wash the dust from their throats and satisfy their appetites with some slow-grilled lamb wrapped in bread.

The matter of outfitting the expedition was resumed as soon as the last bite was swallowed.

"How did you manage with the horses on your other journeys?" Varjuna asked.

"I tell them," Firekeeper said, "I eat them if they trouble me. They believe. Later, when maybe they not believe, there is one or two who not care or not scare so much—Roanne this last."

She managed this explanation half in Pellish, half in Liglimosh, with Derian providing translation. Derian also translated whenever he thought Firekeeper might be missing some element of the mostly Liglimosh conversation.

"So can you talk to horses?" Varjuna asked.

"Not really, not Cousins," Firekeeper said. "To Wise Horses, this would be different."

"I see," Varjuna said. "So you essentially intimidated the others."

"Yes. They are very like prey, and they know this."

"I suppose the same tactic would work . . ." Varjuna began dubiously.

"But I hate the idea of sending any of our horses out under such horrible conditions," Zira protested.

"I do, too, my dear," Varjuna agreed. "However, they will adjust in a few days, when they realize that she doesn't really mean it."

"But what if something happens before then?" Zira protested. "A storm or something else that sets them off? Not only would they be a hazard to themselves, they might well throw their riders. As I understand what Derian was telling us earlier, the horses in Earl Kestrel's expedition had time to get accustomed to Blind Seer's scent."

"That's right," Derian said. "They probably knew he was out there before we did. He and Firekeeper kept their secret until we had crossed the Iron Mountains."

"After that," Zira persisted, "Derian's Roanne was always there to provide a balance—an example that . . . Well, not that there was nothing to be afraid of but . . ."

"She provided an example of courage," Derian suggested. "Horse herds are led by the mares, after all. Roanne acted as herd mare, and the rest followed her lead."

"That's it," Zira said. "However, your group wouldn't have time to get slowly accustomed to the idea of traveling with wolves and jaguars."

"And Pialhini won't make a herd mare," Derian said, "not for a while yet. She has potential, but she's young and flighty at times."

Firekeeper didn't mention that the horses would have more to put up with than just her, Blind Seer, and Truth. Who knew what type of maimalodalu would join them? There was not a one among those hybrid people who would smell like anything else in nature.

All this time, they had been walking, looking at the horses. U-Bishinti, or the Stable, was more than a horse facility, it was a living temple to horses.

The Liglimom had great respect for all animals, wild and domestic, but the only domestic animal used for auguries and divination was the horse. For the Horse, the Liglimom had created a facility that defied Firekeeper's ability to comprehend it for complexity and vastness. She had heard Derian rhapsodize about u-Bishinti repeatedly—most recently, the evening before to Elise and Doc—so she simply took his word that if there was any place to be a horse, u-Bishinti was it.

Derian paused alongside a field that held some mares as wildly painted as Prahini. He stared at them so intently that Firekeeper wondered if he wanted a different mount; then he swung around and spoke in a voice that mixed hesitancy and enthusiasm.

"Varjuna, what about Eshinarvash or one of the Wise Horses? They wouldn't be afraid of Firekeeper or the yarimaimalom. Didn't you tell me that they seemed to have some ability to communicate with what Firekeeper would call their 'Cousin-kind'?"

"They do," Varjuna agreed. "That's an interesting solution, but . . ."

Derian interrupted, surprising Firekeeper immensely, for usually he was polite to a fault with Varjuna and Zira—even when they were disagreeing about some point of horse care or breeding.

"I didn't mean to suggest that the Wise Horses turn out as mounts for us. I mean . . ." Derian colored a brilliant red. "I've had honor enough with the two rides Eshinarvash granted me. I just meant that one of them might come along and, well, supervise."

"It's a very good idea," Zira said, "and if we didn't suggest it, well, that may be because we think differently than you do. We think of them as our neighbors. You remind us that they are part of our community as well. Didn't Eshinarvash all but kidnap you last year?"

Derian's blush was fading, but he looked embarrassed nonetheless. "I was honored to help him and the rest of the yarimaimalom. It's not their fault I can't talk to them."

"Still," Zira said, "it seems to me that if they didn't think it rude to enlist you, we shouldn't think it rude to at least ask them for assistance. After all, didn't this start with one of the yarimaimalom? Shouldn't they be willing to help Truth if we are?"

Zira sounded so much like Blind Seer—who had not yet stopped complaining about Truth being the latest in a series of people willing to enlist Firekeeper to their cause—that Firekeeper glanced at the blue-eyed wolf. He was sitting in a patch of shade, panting his approval.

"When you put it that way, my dear," Varjuna said to his wife, "it does rather make sense. Come. We'll see who the herds have sent as their emissary today. If Lady Blysse will help, I'm sure we'll be able to explain."

"You first," Firekeeper said. "They know you. I have only met one Wise Horse, and that was Eshinarvash just once."

SINCE THE AREA where the Wise Horse emissary typically waited was on the fringes of u-Bishinti, there was a delay while horses were saddled for the three humans. Firekeeper politely refused.

"Horses no like me," she said. "Is this not why we do this running about?"

"You have a point," Varjuna replied, stroking his own mount along the length of its neck to soothe it.

Firekeeper noted that all three horses were remarkably calm given the circumstances. However, this didn't surprise her. She had long suspected that Derian had a talent for working with horses, a talent less under his voluntary control than was Doc's healing talent, but no less real for that. She thought it was likely that Varjuna or Zira—or even both—were similarly gifted.

The horse who trotted up to meet them at the fence that separated the Wise Horse's area from the rest of u-Bishinti was none other than the same Eshinarvash they had been speaking of earlier.

Unlike the Wise Wolves and Jaguars—and many other of the yarimaimalom—Eshinarvash was not markedly larger than a usual horse. He was not a small animal, but he lacked the outsized proportions that made Blind Seer and Truth so automatically intimidating. Moreover, he had a grace and lithe build not common in horses of his size.

Firekeeper knew there was no strict rule as to whether the Wise—or Royal—Beasts would automatically be larger than their Cousin kin. Where size would provide an advantage, the Wise Beasts seemed to possess it, but whereas a gigantic wolf might pull down larger prey, a large horse would simply need more grazing area. Wise River Otters were no larger than their Cousin kin, but Wise Sea Otters, from the few Firekeeper had glimpsed, at least, could get quite large indeed.

Like Prahini, Eshinarvash's coat was wildly patterned. Firekeeper thought he had more black than white, but white stockings, rump, and splotches on his neck and flanks made for a vivid contrast. His mane and tail were bicolored as well, and Firekeeper had to admit that the contrast was quite lovely.

Coming within sniffing distance of the fence rail, Firekeeper and Blind Seer stood back and waited for the Wise Horse to acknowledge them. Etiquette was delicate when predator met with what in other circumstances might be prey. Eshinarvash, however, immediately addressed them.

"*You arrive with friends of mine,*" he said, snorting and shaking his mane. "*Moreover, I know you to be a friend to the yarimaimalom. Welcome, Firekeeper and Blind Seer.*"

"*Thank you,*" Blind Seer replied for them both, stretching out in the hybrid of a human and wolfish bow he used. Firekeeper knew Blind Seer liked the gesture, since it allowed him to show courtesy without demonstrating submission. She inclined her head in something of the same manner.

"*These humans,*" Firekeeper said, "*have something to ask you. They will do better than I would, but if you have questions for me, feel free to ask.*"

Eshinarvash's ears flickered back and forth, indicating puzzlement rather than annoyance, and he turned his attention to the three humans. They exchanged huffs of air, the humans breathing into Eshinarvash's nostrils as if offering their scent, the horse snorting genially at them. These formalities concluded, Varjuna—with ample assistance from Derian and Zira—began explaining their difficulty.

Eshinarvash listened, then raised his head to look over where Firekeeper and Blind Seer waited in a patch of shade.

"*There is more to this than some vague expedition. I scent that Varjuna and Zira truly do not know—one smells of ignorance, the other of curiosity. Derian does know, but he will not say, even before these two who he admires. Would you care to explain?*"

"*We will,*" Firekeeper said. "*Let me tell the humans what I do so they are not impatient.*"

She switched to Liglimosh. "Eshinarvash say he have question for me. I answer now."

Varjuna smiled gently. "By all means."

Firekeeper then returned her attention to Eshinarvash.

"*Truth is a jaguar, so it is likely she has not even told her close kin what it is we are hunting. Still, there are those on Misheemnekuru who know the beginning of the story. Two of these are ravens, and as they are great gossips, the story may fly wide.*"

Blind Seer cut in, "*Even so, although this is not precisely a secret, what we tell you might not be for the common herd—or pack—especially after the unsettled events of last year.*"

They went on then, the two of them together, to retell the whole tale. They left out the long days spent digging and polishing, and concentrated on the finding of the figurines and what they had deduced from them.

"*So you go,*" Eshinarvash said, when they had finished, "*with Harjeedian and one of these maimalodalum to seek the source of these figurines—or at least the subject. It is a bold venture. I wish I could see you all mounted on ones such as myself, but I think it would draw too much attention. One Wise Horse, perhaps, could be explained for the very reasons Varjuna has asked, but more than one . . . It has not been done since the days of Divine Retribution when all was unsettled.*"

Firekeeper would have liked to hear tales about those days, but even nose-dead as she was she swore she could scent the curiosity coming from the humans—especially from Derian and Zira.

"*Then are you saying you think at least one of you could come?*" she asked. "*It would be a great help.*"

"*One, and I think I know which one,*" Eshinarvash replied. "*Unless there is great argument against it from the leaders of my herd, I will join your expedition.*"

IX

THE NEW MOON, Deer Moon to Derian, something incredibly poetic and allusive to the Liglimom, had gone from a sliver to a definite crescent by the time they departed u-Seeheera.

By this time in his life, Derian had planned and equipped several expeditions into unknown territory. He was pleased and even flattered that—other than suggesting a few people Derian might wish to consult—Harjeedian left him to handle the work on his own. Nor was this the aridisdu treating him as a servant. Derian well knew the difference and appreciated it.

Harjeedian for his part had all but moved to u-Bishinti, and was taking some intensive courses in riding and packing. They had decided to do without wagons on this venture, not knowing if where Truth would lead them would even have roads.

Firekeeper made herself as useful as Firekeeper ever did in these circumstances—which was to say, not very useful at all. Derian didn't mind. He knew that her skills would be of immense value once they were away from cities and regular lines of supply.

He learned that in addition to those already agreed upon, their expedition would have two more members: the ravens Bitter and Lovable. He welcomed the two Wise Ravens with enthusiasm. Early in his association with Firekeeper he had learned how useful an aerial scout could be.

"I miss Elation sometimes," he commented to Firekeeper as they departed u-Bishinti. "I wonder how she is?"

"Raising little peregrines, as Elise is to raise little humans," came the reply. "I hear she is well."

There was a long pause, "But I miss her, too."

One of the ravens, Bitter, Derian thought, gave a squawking croak there was no need to translate.

They were well equipped. With Eshinarvash along to act as the oddest wrangler Derian had ever imagined, there had been no need to skimp. There were a riding horse and a spare for Derian and Harjeedian both, and three pack mules to carry their gear. Harjeedian had brought more gear than Derian had anticipated. However, Harjeedian did not bring the one thing Derian had expected.

"No snake?"

"No need," Harjeedian explained. "We have four yarimaimalom accompanying us. They will provide ample omens to guide our actions. In any case, as someone once chided me, travel is not easy for a snake."

"Then this stuff?" Derian asked, indicating what had seemed to him to be religious supplies.

"For divining," Harjeedian said, "and for communicating with the yarimaimalom. Lady Blysse may not always be with us."

"Firekeeper," the wolf-woman replied, with that word granting Harjeedian the privilege of using her personal name. "And what Harjeedian say is true. I not always be with. It is good to have his wisdom."

Derian already knew that Firekeeper was adept at flattering those whom she needed, but her prefacing the compliment with permission to use her name gave a certain sincerity to the statement. He glanced over at her. Never—especially based on the circumstances of their first meeting with Harjeedian—would he have believed Firekeeper would have granted that permission.

"We hunt together," Firekeeper said, seeing Derian's need for explanation. "We are a pack. You would not ask me to leave aside my Fang or bow. I will not ask Harjeedian to leave his tools."

Harjeedian made a hand-pulling gesture and inclined his head, wordless acceptance of the honor done.

"Where do we meet the maimalodalu?" he asked.

"The message say within a day's ride of u-Bishinti," Firekeeper replied, "along the coast road."

Derian glanced over at the last two members of their riding string, two stout, strong ponies. Firekeeper had indicated the size mount they would need, but had admitted that she didn't know if the newcomer—someone called "Plik"—knew how to ride.

"If he's that small," Derian said, "he can ride pillion until he is comfortable in the saddle."

"Not so small," Firekeeper said, gesturing widely with her hand. "Just not so tall."

All of this prepared Derian not at all for what—or rather who—they found waiting for them along the coast road.

The ravens had left them some time before, and now, as the rest of the group came upon a rough building set to one side of the road, the birds set up a racket.

"I think we're supposed to stop," Harjeedian said dryly. "I do not even need my tools to be sure of this particular omen."

"What is that place?" Derian asked. "It doesn't look like a house."

"A shrine," Harjeedian said, "and a cenotaph. There was a horrible shipwreck off the coast here when I was a boy. The shrine is to thank the deities for sparing those they did. The cenotaph is to commemorate those who did not survive."

Derian nodded. After enduring three long sea voyages, it was all too easy to imagine the wreck. Even here in the bay, where the bulk of Misheemnekuru sheltered the shore, he could envision the comparatively calm, sunlight-dappled waters turning rough and ugly.

What waited for them in the shrine was, at first inspection in the filtered light that came through barred window openings, a short, fat man wearing a cloak over clothing in the Liglimese fashion. His head was covered by a slouch hat that hid most of his features. Unaccountably, Derian was aware of the twinkle of two dark eyes beneath the brim.

"Sir," he said in Liglimosh, "I am Derian Carter, called Derian Counselor."

"And I am Plik," came the reply. "Firekeeper knows me. We have journeyed together before, on Misheemnekuru. I think I smell her about."

"She is almost certainly outside," Derian said. "She would find this building a little close."

"Built to my size, not for a wild, roaming wolf," Plik said. He bent and picked a leather pack from the floor beside him. "I wonder if that means that the gods are small, or merely that those who made this shrine didn't wish to spend too much."

"Or," Harjeedian said from where he had been burning something sweet and aromatic on the altar stone without, "that the builders knew the gods cannot be confined or housed in any space made by human hands. Welcome. I am Aridisdu Harjeedian."

"I remember your face from the day Magic's tower fell," Plik replied. "Your sister became junjaldisdu, or so we heard."

"You heard correctly," Harjeedian replied, and though Derian listened for envy in his voice, he heard only pride. "Rahniseeta does well. The disdum teach her, and when she has enough of lessons for the time, she waves her hands and says, 'If the deities thought I needed to know all of that, all at once, I am sure they would not have chosen me. Leave me to meditate for a week.' "

Derian's heart gave a funny twinge, part pain, part something harder to define. That did sound very like Rahniseeta. She had learned to play the role of the submissive maiden, but there was fire in her, fire and storm.

He often wondered what it would have been like to be married to Rahniseeta, even now, over a year after she had rejected him to follow the will of her deities. There were times the wondering turned to wondering if he would always wonder. That was when he usually kicked himself back into sense.

Plik was speaking. "I know the rest of your company, although Eshinarvash only by reputation for his great deeds in the uncovering of Dantarahma's cult."

He made little bobs that might be bows all around.

"What do I do next?"

Derian now fully understood Firekeeper's reasoning that Plik would not ride well two to a horse. Short he might be, but he looked very solid.

"We have two ponies," Derian said, "if you can ride. If you cannot, then we must teach you."

"I cannot ride," Plik said, "not as you do, but if you put me up on the creature that is least inclined to protest, I will do my best to learn."

Derian glanced over at Eshinarvash. "I was thinking the silver-grey."

Eshinarvash snorted and nodded. Derian went and unclipped the pony from its place on the string.

"He is called 'Cuddle Toy,'" Derian said, half-apologetically. "We could call him something else if you would prefer."

Plik chortled. "Cuddle Toy seems just right. He's nearly as round as I am, but vain of that shining mane and tail, isn't he?"

Derian laughed, his hands busy with the tack. "He is rather, but the hair is silky and not at all hard to keep looking nice. Now, if you'd come over here. There is a stone that will serve admirably as a mounting block. . . ."

Plik came over. From the corner of his eye, Derian saw Harjeedian pick up the maimalodalu's pack and add it to the burden of the most lightly loaded mule. The aridisdu made a careful job of fastening the straps.

"Very well," Derian said. He had put hundreds, possibly thousands of people up on their first horse while working in his family's livery stable. "You put a foot here, then I'll just give you a bit of a shove."

He moved his hand toward the plump posterior, and found himself jerking back immediately.

"Ancestors!" he said. "You have a tail!"

A furry length, mostly grey but with darker rings toward the end, came visible, then vanished under the cloak once more.

"And at least as fine a one as does Cuddle Toy," Plik replied with gravity. "I can move it to one side. You will not hurt me."

Derian forced himself to return to his post. Plik's posterior did not feel unduly unlike a human one, but Derian felt fairly certain that not only did their new companion have a tail, he had fur as well.

What did you expect, idiot? he addressed himself. *You knew he was a maimalodalu. He may have fangs and claws as well. You almost certainly worked with him that night on Misheemnekuru. Get ahold of yourself.*

Plik was stroking Cuddle Toy's mane. His hands, at least, looked fairly human, though perhaps the nails were a bit heavier than usual. Derian looked up into the face under the hat brim, and was relieved to find no snarling fangs, no horribly mutated countenance. In fact, if you concentrated on the raccoon traits, rather than the unsettling manner in which they blended with the human, Plik was rather cute.

"Raccoon in your heritage?" Derian asked.

"That's right," Plik said. "It rather shows, doesn't it?"

"Not when you're dressed like you are, and not even until someone gets close enough to look under the hat."

"Which won't be easy given that I'm rather close to the ground," Plik said complacently. "At least that's what I argued when stating why I should come along."

Harjeedian had joined them. "I believe Lady . . . Firekeeper is growing restless. Truth has already wandered off. Shall we follow? We can talk as we ride."

Derian and Plik agreed, and once the pack train was moving Plik asked, "What is our destination tonight?"

"We thought," Derian said, "to camp. The maps show several promising areas. There may be other groups there—trade caravans and such—but the presence of an aridisdu and the yarimaimalom means that they will grant us our privacy."

"Not to mention the presence of a flame-haired northerner," Plik said. "You remind me of one of our number on Center Island. Her heritage is largely fox."

"Firekeeper sometimes calls me Fox Hair," Derian said, "although I have been compared favorably to a chestnut horse as well."

He glanced over at Harjeedian, and the aridisdu unbent enough to smile.

Derian looked ahead to where Firekeeper and Blind Seer were ranging off into the forests. He knew better than to call them back. They would come in time, and doubtless with something for dinner. He smiled at the thought of freshly roasted venison, looked up to where the ravens glided, marking the trail.

It was good to be on the road again.

FIREKEEPER RESIGNED HERSELF to accept steady rather than rapid progress after Plik joined them. If the campground they turned in to as evening drew near was not deserted, it was, from the point of view of maintaining their privacy, the next best thing. It was so busy that no one was particularly interested in a small group heading south.

Firekeeper was wolfishly pleased when Harjeedian's prestige as an aridisdu got them a space, even if they did need to settle for a location a fair distance from the communal well.

"We should remain uninterrupted," Harjeedian reported as he came back from the well. "All the other groups are going north to trade, and they're indulging in a bit of preliminary business now. Further proof that the deities are smiling upon us is that one of the groups is also taking a daughter to be married to an associate in u-Bishinti. They are already celebrating, and have invited everyone else to join them."

"Could you decline?" Derian asked anxiously. He'd been able to conceal his red hair under a hat, and in the twilight his fairer skin was not so noticeable. Those advantages would be lost in close quarters.

"Without difficulty," Harjeedian said. "I told them we were on a pilgrimage and the omens had said we must spend the evening in meditation and prayer."

"Omens," Firekeeper said. "Useful things I think."

She had avoided drawing attention to herself and Blind Seer by entering the campground through the surrounding scrub growth. Truth had joined them. No one noticed ravens in a place like this, and Eshinarvash had agreed to have a blanket thrown over his back. Since everyone knew a Wise Horse would never tolerate such treatment, then by definition he could not be a Wise Horse.

The company was not attempting to travel south in secrecy, but all had agreed that the less attention they drew, the less likely they were to find keeping Plik's rather unusual appearance from drawing comments. Also, they had no idea whether the two people for whom they hunted would be hiding from them. Better to be careful.

On the road that afternoon, they had decided that, if the matter came up, Plik was to be presented as coming from New Kelvin. As far as they knew, no one from Liglim or the city-states had been in contact with New Kelvin for over a hundred years, but stories about the northern lands were spreading rapidly as embassies were exchanged. The outrageous habits of dress and facial adornment practiced by the New Kelvinese should have been exaggerated, rather than otherwise, in the telling.

Now Firekeeper stretched out at the edge of the circle of firelight, luxuriating in the sensations of pleasant tiredness that coursed through her muscles. She drifted off to sleep to the sound of Derian teaching Plik a handful of New Kelvinese phrases.

THE NEXT MORNING the trade caravans departed almost as soon as there was light to see.

"They make me feel lazy," Derian commented, the ripple of laughter underlying the words indicating he felt nothing of the kind, "and we'll be on the road not long after dawn."

"And if we are fortunate," Harjeedian said, "we should reach the border in a few days. I spoke with several of the merchants last night, and they said the roads were in good condition."

The aridisdu was carefully repacking the array of items he had set out when he said his morning prayers—a ritual, Firekeeper noted with uneasy interest, in which not only Plik, but Eshinarvash, Truth, and the ravens as well, had taken part.

The jaguar now padded up to Firekeeper. *"Tell them that when we reach a road that will take us west as well as south, we should leave the coast road."*

"*The Voice has told you to do this?*" Firekeeper asked.

"*I have divined it,*" Truth replied, but something in the very coolness of how she lifted her burnt-orange stare to meet Firekeeper's questioning gaze made Firekeeper think there was more behind her knowledge than that.

Firekeeper passed on the information. Harjeedian and Derian immediately pulled out maps. It seemed that shortly after noon they would pass just such a junction, and this would change where they would cross the border.

The wolf-woman left such planning to them. Instead she padded over to where Plik was busy stretching and squatting.

"You are well?" she asked politely.

"Sore," the maimalodalu said honestly. "My legs do not like poking out around the barrel of a horse, but they would like less walking all those miles. I am not as long in the leg as you, nor am I as young."

Firekeeper agreed without comment. Plik stopped his exercises and looked up at her.

She decided that his face almost equally blended human and raccoon features. His nose and mouth were more like that of a raccoon, even to the damp black leather at the nose's tip. His mouth, however, was shaped so he had no trouble with human speech. His whiskers were more dense, rather like a mustache. What on a raccoon would have been merely white fur over the darker fur surrounding the eyes was instead bushy eyebrows. His fur lengthened at the crest of his head, growing out like hair, although maintaining more the characteristics of fur.

Plik blinked at her, and Firekeeper noticed his eyes had lids and lashes after the human style.

"I was thinking," Firekeeper admitted, "how well your face is made. Sometimes staring is rude. If so, I apologize."

Plik grinned at her. "No insult offered, none taken. May I ask a favor of you?"

"Ask."

"Would you and Blind Seer stay close this morning? I have a tale I wish to tell, and I think it would be better told on the road, where we are not likely to be overheard."

"*What of me?*" asked Truth.

In the way of the maimalodalum, Plik needed no translation. Like Firekeeper, he understood the speech of Beasts, and could speak it as well.

"*I would like you to hear the tale as well,*" Plik said, "*but I planned to ask you myself. You are not Firekeeper's to govern.*"

Blind Seer panted laughter from where he was stretched in cool earth beneath a bush. The season was shifting from summer into autumn, but as they traveled south, the transition was a slow one, and the wolf was suffering under his thick coat. On Misheemnekuru the pack had laid up during the day.

"And Firekeeper governs me?" Blind Seer asked.

Plik laughed in return. *"You know that best of all."*

"I will run with you in the morning," Blind Seer replied, *"but I may well lie up in the worst of the day's heat."*

"I should not need more than the morning to tell my story," Plik promised.

He began the telling almost as soon as they were on the road, and to Firekeeper's surprise, he spoke in good though not flawless Pellish.

"I was one of the keepers," he said, "of the two humans left with us this last year. They spoke little Liglimosh, and the teaching helped fill the colder days of winter."

"Fluency in Pellish," Harjeedian said thoughtfully. "Doubtless another reason the deities gave omens that ordained your selection as one of our companions."

"Well," Plik said modestly, "it is rather nice to have a common language that it is unlikely anyone we pass on the road will speak, especially when discussing sensitive matters."

"Such as this tale you will tell?" Firekeeper prompted. She wondered if Truth understood Pellish, but as the great cat was not complaining, she guessed Truth understood enough.

"And they say wolves have no subtlety," Plik chuckled. "Very well. My tale begins with your own departure from Center Island. Many of the maimalodalum felt we knew too little about the place you have called the house that was not a house. We resolved to learn more. There were two ways we could do this. One, we could send an expedition to the site of the ruins. Two, we could delve into the nature of the books, records, and other items I had taken with me from the underground room.

"We decided to do both. A few of our number who could travel more quickly went to the ruins. Others with a scholarly bent went to work on the records. One or two who have specialized in learning what they can about the few magical artifacts that remain inspected the figurines. I will say right now that we learned the least from these. Perhaps our greatest expert in these things, Sky-Dreaming-Earth-Bound, died last year.

"I'm going to spare you speculation, as well as the various false starts we had and go immediately to what we felt certain about." Plik looked down at

Firekeeper, who trotted at his pony's side. "Some of us might enjoy speculating later, but for now I will stay with facts.

"Those who went over to the ruins agreed with my conclusion that they were ruins not of a residence, but of a temple. What was fascinating is that every trace of to whom this temple had been dedicated had been very, very carefully wiped out. Portions of texts containing prayers remained, but never a hint of the entity to whom those prayers were addressed. Moreover, every piece of visual art had been broken or carried away. All they felt certain of was that the deity in question had not been one of the great five elements, but one of the lesser figures."

"Excuse me," Derian said. "Lesser figures? I didn't know there were such."

Plik looked over at Harjeedian, and the aridisdu took it upon himself to answer.

"There are and there are not," Harjeedian explained. "Officially, we acknowledge only Earth, Air, Fire, Water, and Magic as divinities. Unofficially, there are a slew of lesser figures—some of the disdum refer to them as heroes, others as demi-deities—that the common people acknowledge. For example, Water is a divinity, but many farmers pray specifically to Rain. Rain has been personified as a daughter of Water, younger sister to Magic, and colorful tales are told about her.

"We of the greater disdum simply teach that these figures are aspects of the greater five, not separate deities. However, we feel that divine Water will be understanding of the very human need to focus on one aspect of an element, especially when, as with Rain, the need can be so great.

"Less tolerable are the stories that attempt to connect human heroes to the Great Five, making this warrior, say, a human child of Fire, or that wise teacher an aspect of Air. Least tolerable are those stories that take human failing or . . ." He frowned. "I'm not sure there's a word for this in your language. It is the opposite of failure, but not mere success or achievement. It is rather the pinnacle, the highest example of a trait. An exemplar, though something more."

"I think I follow you," Derian said. "The person you look up to as the best example of what you could be, like when I was a boy and thought 'If only I could ride like my father.' "

"Very like," Harjeedian agreed, "although something more. As I was saying, while the disdum tolerate the personification of portions of the Five Elements, they resist either the deification of humans or the deification of qualities."

"I can see how humans could be deified," Derian said. "I mean, in a sense that's exactly what my people do. We take our ancestors as guides. We believe that after death they move into a state where they are better able to understand matters of greater good and evil. Then we invoke their aid in times of crisis. I don't quite understand about how qualities could be deified."

Firekeeper had been listening to this theoretical discussion with some impatience, but she actually thought she understood this point.

"I think," she offered, reluctant to become involved in a delay. "Is like this, I think 'Give me patience.' These people, they think Patience is some sort of person. They pray to him or her."

Harjeedian looked at her with surprised respect. "That is very good. I did not know you were a student of theology."

Firekeeper frowned and bit her lip, knowing she was in danger of being insulting.

"I not, but where Blind Seer and I are born, wolves have no gods. We sing to the moon because she is pretty, not because we think is listening. Since we come to human lands, we hear of ancestors and of gods."

"Ask the wind. Ask the rain," Blind Seer quoted. *"Empty howling and wet fur are all you earn for your pain."*

Firekeeper repeated this, then said, "So you see, all is new to us. We must student this theology to understand humans . . . and yarimaimalom, and maimalodalum."

Harjeedian nodded. "In whatever fashion you reached it, your explanation is a good one. Let me use your example of patience . . ."

Plik interrupted with a chuckle. "And I'm sure Firekeeper only chose to wish for patience by the merest chance. Not finding an old raccoon too talkative, are you?"

Firekeeper wrinkled her nose in a pretended snarl at the maimalodalu, but she gave Harjeedian her attention.

"If patience," the aridisdu went on, displaying a fair amount of the quality himself, "were a deity, then worshippers could pray to her and if they could not remain patient, then they could dismiss their failures by saying 'The goddess must not wish me to keep my temper.' We of the disdum do not think this would be a good thing. The deities are there, but they are neither examples nor excuses. They are the elements, eternally changeable, and often incomprehensible."

"Except," Plik said, "sometimes through divination."

"That is right," the aridisdu replied, pleased. "That is why the aridisdum study the art, in an effort to comprehend the divine will."

Firekeeper was relieved when Derian turned the conversation back to its original point. "All right. Thank you, Harjeedian. I think I understand. Plik, to what type of lesser figure do your people think the temple was dedicated?"

"Not a hero or exemplar," Plik said. "Not a human at all."

"One of these abstract qualities, then?"

"That's right. In most legends, he is called the Meddler."

Silence met this announcement, silence broken by the sharp hiss of indrawn breath from Harjeedian.

"I know that name," the aridisdu said. "It is from a very ancient story cycle, one brought from the Old Country, one that, happily, has nearly died to nothing here in the New World. Sometimes mentions of the Meddler crop up in unrelated legends, but those legends are not told to the people. Only the most senior of the aridisdum are taught them so that they might recognize them when they are told, and take action to diminish their impact."

Derian turned in his saddle. "Back up, Harjeedian. You speak as if this is a great horror, something as evil as torture or abusing a child. Meddling? There's not a city street, nor even a household that doesn't have someone who loves to meddle. What else are politics and diplomacy, but meddling with others' fates? What else are gossip and matchmaking? Is it a part of human nature."

"Even wolf," Firekeeper said, "do this sometimes. And often raven or raccoon, any of those Beasts that live from cleverness and wit."

Harjeedian nodded, but the intensity in his gaze did not fade. "Now imagine deifying this quality. Imagine having someone else to blame for those times meddling goes awry—a match badly made, a treaty in which dangerous flaws are overlooked, even an idle bit of gossip that turns a marriage sour or ruins a person's reputation. Meddling is dangerous—all the more so when someone other than the one who has done the meddling can be held accountable."

"I see that," Derian admitted. "I can see why your people have suppressed such a belief. It seems that in your own aversion we have found the reason that temple was so carefully destroyed. I suppose that your Old Country rulers must have felt the same way."

Plik nodded, the brim of his hat flapping. "And when they learned this illegal worship had followed them here, they took steps to halt it."

"You may be right about the temple," Harjeedian said, but he did not relax

in the least. "Tell me, good people, who might have been locked in the underground room? Who might have made those figurines and set so much pain
and destruction at play? Who might it be?"

Firekeeper spoke out, feeling confused, "You think this Meddler was there?
But you say there is no Meddler, that this is one of those deities you not believe. Why you say he is there if he is not?"

"What if . . ." Harjeedian said softly, as if to mute the intensity of his own
emotions. "What if we were wrong? What if the Meddler does exist, and we
have been so unfortunate as to set him free?"

X

TRUTH HEARD WHAT PLIK SAID, and when the band of travelers stopped that night, accepting welcome in an outlying temple dedicated to the Wounded Bear, she parted from her companions.

They thought she was going to fish, and so she was, but they might have been surprised in which waters she dipped her paws. First, she did find a massive, sour-tempered old snapping turtle. She broke open his shell with her powerful jaws, scooped out the red flesh with velvet paws. Then, having made the waters safer for generations of short-lived fish and insects, Truth climbed high into the limbs of a tree. There she washed, the rhythmic lapping of tongue against fur soothing her into a state between sleeping and waking.

This was an old trick, taught to every kitten who showed signs of seeing more than one world, one time. Truth had disdained it for many years, her gift being so great that she must only adjust her will to have the means of reading omens open to her. Now she washed, tongue against packed density of fur, almost tasting the dark rosettes against the golden field. She thought of nothing, focused tightly on one thing.

Meddler . . . Meddler . . . Meddler . . .

She asked for nothing, looked for nothing, but felt in the swirling twists a current that tugged at her, offering her a look elsewhere in time. When the current ebbed, she opened her eyes, and saw.

———

THE BUILDINGS WERE TALL and very elegant, crafted of a pale blue stone that glittered as some limestones glitter. Were one to try and carve this stone, however, perhaps to mark it with initials or a personal emblem, they would find that it was harder than steel. The buildings rose into towers of many shapes: round, octagonal, hexagonal, rhomboid, triangular, even merely square. Their rooftops were domed or coned or peaked or flat, made of slate or metal or sometimes of tiles, each tile crafted with a different arcane sign or sigil. No two towers were of the same height, breadth, or width. This was by design, not by lack of skill.

There was an ordered disorder to this city of towers. One needed to study for many years to understand the reason for that fitting of shapes and heights. It was said that many who did come to this treasured comprehension put aside rod, staff, or wand and became instead simple masons, stonecutters, bricklayers, dedicated to the glory that was the city.

And it was also said that those who came to this understanding and did not retire from the practice of magic became the most powerful sorcerers not only of the place of blue stone, but of all the world. So it was that many strove to understand the shaping of the city, desiring to obtain that power for themselves.

See now. A youth comes to this city. He is past the gangly growth of first adulthood, not yet into the strength and maturity of second. His hair is dark and silken. His eyes are long and appraising beneath lashes merely long. Those eyes are the same color as his hair. There is nothing remarkable about this youth in this place of marvels, and the crowd does not part around him. Rather it jostles him, moving him to the shoulder of the road, and there he makes his way, his eyes never leaving the sparkling blue stone and variety of rooftops.

Why is there a crowd? At first glance it appears to be the usual market vendors, driving livestock, hauling produce or handicrafts. At second glance this seems less sure. They pass into a gate, but that gate does not admit them to a market square. No booths are set up, no ropes strung to indicate where goats are being held, where sheep, where cattle. The herds and carts and wagons pass through one wide gate. Those who drove or hauled or pulled come out another.

Enough time does not seem to have passed to permit a sale to have been made, yet those departing do not look dissatisfied. Indeed, all look cheerful, or at least content. All of those but those who weep, and there are not over many of these.

The youth is swept up to the gate. He walks alongside a herd of odoriferous goats, and initially is thought to be among their keepers.

"I am not," he says, and the goatherd is vociferous in seconding this denial. "I am here to enroll with a teacher."

The youth's boots are dirty, the hem of his traveling cloak soiled to the knee, but the pair guarding the gate, one each a man and a woman, do not mock him. Instead they indicate a smaller door, one made all of crystal, cut and faceted with such intricacy that although this portal should be clear it is opaque with rainbows.

"There," the man says.

"Pull the bell-rope," the woman adds.

Then they return to assessing the goods passing through the gate. The youth steps dextrously around a young white and tan kid with short curling horns and evil yellow eyes, and advances on the door of crystal. He never once looks back. As he moves forward, the sounds of the mobile marketplace fade away to a silence broken only by the sound of his own boots on stone.

When he pulls the bell-rope there chimes a cadence so beautiful that some say that those who hear it remember it ever after with the bittersweet joy with which one recalls a beloved one never quite found the courage to address.

The youth stands and listens with pleasure, but perhaps with a certain degree of apprehension as well. A shadow darkens the crystal, dimming the rainbows so they frame the shape of a large man.

A deep voice rumbles, "State your business."

"I am here to enroll with a teacher."

"Know first the terms. If you cross this threshold, you will be bound into service. Even if no teacher will take you, you will still be bound. If your teacher finds you lacking, still you will owe. Only if you find a teacher and pass that teacher's training will you be free to depart, and even then you will be bound by the codes and regulations of this place."

"I still wish to enroll."

"Then push open the door and enter. None does so but under his own power so it cannot be said he has been coerced into this choice."

The youth raises both hands and presses them against the center of the crystal door where there is a smooth place that seems made for the purpose. A sensation of perfect cold embraces him, but he presses forward. Cold sweeps him from hands to wrists to arms, into his torso, down to the earth and up to the top of his head. This happens so quickly that the youth has hardly taken three steps. By the time he has taken five and the door has opened, the youth feels himself to be himself again, and could have imagined that entire winter cold wash a dream—except that he is far too clever to do so.

When he has stepped into the room, he looks about, but no deep-voiced man awaits him, only what he would have taken for a little girl of no more than eight, but that her wide, cornflower blue eyes are overfilled with almost terrifying wisdom.

"You are here," she says, and her voice holds in it something of the music of the bells. "Go. Walk in the city."

"Where should I go to be interviewed by a teacher?"

"Go," she says again, and her flower-bud mouth smiles with neither warmth nor pity. "Teachers do not interview students. Students must interview teachers."

"And where do I find the teachers who are willing to take students?"

The round blue eyes sparkle with tiny lights like stars. "Walk in the city. Find your way—or not."

The youth loses himself in the sparkling glamour of her eyes, and when he draws himself out of their depths, he finds himself standing on a street, glittering blue towers rising around him. The crystal door is gone. So is the girl child with the cornflower blue eyes. He never sees either of them again.

For day upon day upon day, the youth walks the city streets. As far as he can tell, there is no way of marking time. The sun does not pass overhead, nor does the sky darken with nightfall. All is lit in a perpetual golden glow that comes from no direction except that it comes from above.

He sees no one at all, not even an alley cat or foraging sparrow.

When the youth grows tired he covers himself with his dirty cloak and sleeps in a doorway. Sleep comes with exhaustion, but without dreams. He awakens in the morning feeling ravenous and alert, but not rested.

His stomach has guided him to where he can find food. After several meals, he can see some people. After more meals, it is made clear to him that he must labor to eat. He does so, though he understands little of the purpose of the labors he performs.

The youth is in danger of forgetting his purpose when one day, polishing dust from a seemingly endless stack of newly fired roof tiles, he remembers that he had a purpose when he came here. He takes to wandering the streets again, this time forgoing food and even sleep. When he reaches the point that starvation and exhaustion have driven him into what might well be hallucination, he sees a man watching him.

The man is of his own height, but with burnished copper hair and eyes that focus on the youth as nothing has done since he passed the man and the woman at the gates of the city.

"You're persistent, I'll give you that," the man says. "If you want a teacher, you can start with me, but I can't promise you'll finish with me. I'm not one of the great teachers, but a middling fair lesser one."

"What do I call you?" the youth asks.

"Master will do."

"Master," the youth repeats, and with that word he passes from hallucination into the city of towers.

TRUTH AWAKENED FROM HER VISION, pulling herself into the reality of the treetops with such ease that she felt considerable pride. Shifting her weight, she scratched heartily behind one ear, then the other.

Meddler, she thought. *Was that you? Was that some moment in your life?*

There was no answer, though Truth listened very carefully. She lashed her tail back and forth in annoyance. Really! When she wanted the Voice, he wouldn't speak to her. When she didn't, she couldn't get him to keep quiet. Of one thing she was certain now. Allowing for changes in age, one voice and the same had been employed by the youth in her vision and the Voice that had led her out of madness.

She thought she knew what that meant. The maimalodalum had been right in their identification. What the rest of her vision might mean—if anything—she couldn't know.

For now.

Purring with contentment, Truth resettled herself, this time to sleep rather than to dream.

DERIAN WOULD HAVE LIKED TO HEAR more about just what the maimalodalum had found at the ruins of the house that was not a house, but soon after they had finished discussing what the Meddler might be, and why he was not exactly favored by the disdum of the Liglimom, a woman riding a handsome grey with darker mane and tail came cantering up the road toward them.

From the horse's condition, she had been riding long, but not too hard. Quite probably she had left her point of origin when they had their own, but she had traveled with a bit more purpose.

She hailed them when she was a polite distance away, reining in the grey as she did so.

"Greetings," she said. "Others on the road brought word that the aridisdu Harjeedian, honored representatives of the yarimaimalom, and some foreign companions traveled this way. I come from the Temple of the Wounded Bear to ask you to stay your journey there and accept our hospitality."

Harjeedian recited their agreed-upon excuse about their being on pilgrimage, but this woman had been given omens of her own. It soon became clear that while the majority of the group would be permitted their privacy, nothing would stop the disdum of the temple from giving their hospitality to the junjaldisdu's brother.

Harjeedian consulted with the others and they agreed, especially when it became clear that the woman had changed mounts along the way, and that the temple in question was near where they would have halted in any case.

At the temple, Harjeedian was dragged off for a discussion of politics and religion—though Derian doubted the two could be separated where the Liglimom were concerned. The rest were housed comfortably, but Plik refused to continue his tale until all who needed to hear it were present.

Come morning, Harjeedian returned, rested, sleek, and bearing maps and mail.

Derian was pleased to find a thick letter from his family. After skimming it to make certain no one was ill or had died, he tucked it away for more leisurely enjoyment.

Once they were well away from the Temple of the Wounded Bear, Firekeeper loped alongside Plik's pony. He was riding his second-string mount, an adorable brown-and-white-spotted gelding called, incongruously, Formidable.

"Truth say," Firekeeper began, then she glanced over at the jaguar who was running alongside Eshinarvash, "Truth *ask* if you have more stories about this Meddler and if you could tell us more."

"I know a little more," Plik said. "I had opportunity to look through the manuscripts we brought from the house that was not a house before my departure. I had hoped to bring the books with me but . . ." He shrugged. "The paper was old and probably wouldn't have held up long under the abuses of travel."

"But you have something you can tell," Firekeeper asked.

"I do," Plik promised.

They were riding through a stretch of countryside that the ravens had assured them was largely uninhabited, so Plik had put aside his enveloping cloak, though he kept his slouch hat on, just in case.

"Now," he began, speaking in Pellish, "as I said yesterday, the tales of the Meddler come to us originally from the Old Country. Here's a short one that demonstrates a great deal about his personality."

"The Meddler and the Thwarted Lovers"

One day as the Meddler was out walking, going about, just seeing the world as he liked to do, he came to a prosperous farm. The pastures were all fenced in white, the fields were lush with crops. He walked wide stretches where fat cattle contentedly grazed, and saw ponds where duck swam, and fish glided beneath the clear waters.

When the Meddler came to the main wagon road leading into this fine farm, he paused, wondering whether or not he should turn in and perhaps ask for a meal and a bed for the night. While he was paused there, he heard the sound of a choked off sob.

"Who is there?" the Meddler said, casting around, looking beneath the hedges and in the ditches. "Speak up! Are you hurt?"

A young man emerged from a copse of apple trees, wiping his eyes on his sleeve. He was as comely as the sun at noon, his skin smooth and without blemish, his dark hair glossy, his carriage erect. However, his eyes were red from weeping.

The young man made a great effort and hid his grief, then he said to the Meddler, "Hello, traveler. Have you walked far today?"

"Far enough," the Meddler said. "I was in those distant hills when the day began."

"Will you stop and take the evening meal here?" the young man asked. "I am Letu, son of this house, and my parents would speak sharply to me if I did not make you welcome."

The Meddler's feet were aching, and when he thought of the abundant fields and the fat cattle he had seen, his stomach rumbled loudly enough for the young man to hear.

Letu's handsome face shed its sorrow for a moment, and he laughed. "Your belly answers for you. Come and dine with us."

The road up to the house was a long one. Before they had gone many paces, the Meddler pried from Letu what sorrow had brought him to tears. As Letu told him, his eyes brightened once more with unshed tears, but manfully he held back his grief.

"Traveler, I will tell you. I love a young woman with all my heart, but never, never will I have her for my own. My heart breaks as I contemplate an eternity of separation. My despair is so great that my food tastes of sawdust and my drink of brine."

"She must be an extraordinary young woman," the Meddler said.

"She is," Letu replied, his eyes shining with joy as before they had shone with tears. "You can see her in the kitchens. Her name is Vitzi."

(PLIK INTERRUPTED HIMSELF TO SAY, "That's a word meaning 'meadowsweet,' the name of a pretty wildflower.")

"AND DOES VITZI LOVE YOU AS YOU LOVE HER?"

"Vitzi has loved me almost from the first moment we met. My parents will not agree to let us be together. They say it is not right and proper, not suitable."

Now in his journeys from place to place, the Meddler had seen many young people kept apart by parents who had ambitions for them. As he looked around him at this large and prosperous farm, he thought that certainly Letu's parents had ambitions for their son's marriage.

Perhaps there was a neighboring property that was the dower of some plain woman. The Meddler could imagine her, a spinster, doubtless, with a disposition like sour milk and only her wealth to recommend her.

The Meddler vowed then and there that he would not see the handsome and courteous Letu robbed of the woman he so clearly adored.

"May I step around to the kitchen and so gain a glimpse of your beloved?"

"By all means," Letu said. "Do so while I inform my father of your arrival, and arrange to have an extra plate set at the table. Do not speak with her, though. The kitchens will be busy this time of day, and I would not have harsh words spoken to Vitzi for her inattention."

The Meddler agreed to this condition, and when they reached the farmhouse, he slipped around back to the kitchens. There was a great deal of activity there, and he wondered how he might pick Letu's Vitzi from the others. Then he saw there was no need. Not only was there only one girl beautiful enough to have awakened such a forlorn passion in a young man's heart, the head cook was busy shouting orders to her staff.

This one was ordered to pull the bread from the ovens, that one to check the pastries. Finally the cook's command fell on the beautiful young woman.

"Vitzi," the cook said sharply, "put another pie in the ovens. I have just been told another guest will be here for supper."

Vitzi moved to do as ordered, and the Meddler slipped away, thrilled and delighted by the beauty and elegance of the young woman. He resolved to repay Letu's hospitality by making it possible for him to join his beloved.

Letu's father, whose name was Olenu, proved to be a man whose prosperity was evident in how his gut slopped over his belt, but whose calloused hands showed that he still worked hard. He welcomed the Meddler to his table, explaining that Letu's mother was not present.

"My wife has taken most of our children with her into town for market day. She will return tomorrow morning."

"Perhaps I shall pass her on the road," the Meddler said, and he thanked the deities for granting him this relative freedom to act.

When the evening meal was over, Olenu excused himself, repeating Letu's invitation to stay the night. The Meddler accepted, but he refused a room in the house.

"This is too grand a place for me," he said. "I'd be happier outside."

"We have bunkhouses where the harvest crews sleep in season," Letu offered. "They are empty now."

"That would be fine," the Meddler said. "Come and see me when the sun is set and darkness has come. Perhaps we can find a solution for your problem. Bring with you a change of clothing, and whatever money you can lay your hands on without raising suspicion."

Letu looked doubtful, but he agreed. They parted then, and the Meddler went by the kitchens. Vitzi was standing by herself, eating a slice of the pie that had been served for dessert.

The Meddler walked up to her, and greeted her with a smile. "I am the guest who enjoyed that very pie. Tonight I will be sleeping in the harvester's bunkhouse. Come and see me when it is dark. I have spoken with your beloved."

Vitzi's eyes had widened at a stranger speaking so familiarly to her, but at the mention of her beloved, the astonishment vanished.

"I will be there," she promised, and turned away.

The Meddler spent the time before darkness securing a pair of riding horses from one of the fields. He tied them behind the bunkhouse. He found tack and saddlebags, and packed these with good things from the abundant fields. He even made up a cozy bedroll, thrilling a little at the thought of what it would see that night.

After dark, the two lovers came—first Letu, then Vitzi. Both were nervous, but when the Meddler explained his plan, they looked at each other with a mixture of apprehension and anticipation, their hands reaching unconsciously to clasp.

"Can we really do this?" said Letu. "Just ride away?"

"Of course," said the Meddler. "Go to a place where there is a disdu who can link you in marriage. When you are wed by both law and by love, then your parents cannot separate you."

"I know such a place," Vitzi said shyly. "It is a small temple where I stayed when I was coming here to live. The temple is maintained by a kidisdu who prefers the company of birds to that of people, but he is a kind man, and surely he will welcome us."

"It is a good omen," rejoiced the Meddler, "for many birds mate for life. Go there and be happy."

The young pair rode away, and the Meddler slept well, with very pleasant dreams. He intended to be away shortly before dawn, for he did not wish to be questioned about the whereabouts of the young lovers.

But that night there was thunder and there was lightning. The winds howled and the rains fell in torrents. Tornadoes howled and carried cattle and horses into the sky. The Meddler feared to go out in such weather, and so Olenu found him in the bunkhouse when he sought him there in the morning.

"Where is my son?" Olenu bellowed. "Where is Vitzi? You helped them get away. Don't even try to deny it. I have found those among the servants who saw you carrying things here and there, even one who saw you leading a pair of horses. Speak from your own desire or I will have the information beaten from you!"

The Meddler did not doubt this was true, but he held his silence, thinking nobly that every word he withheld gave the young lovers more time to escape.

Olenu raised a hand as if to strike the Meddler, then he lowered it. He ceased shouting, but the levelness of his tone was no less terrible.

"Let me tell you something, Traveler, for I can see in your eyes that you are one of those who would believe himself righteous for taking a beating in silence."

The Meddler straightened proudly, glad he was cutting such a noble figure.

Olenu continued. "Anyhow, I can always beat you later. Would you like to know the history of the girl called Vitzi and why I do not wish my son to marry her? I will tell it to you then. Vitzi is the love child of my wife, the fruit of an indiscretion early in our marriage."

"Early . . ."

The farmer smiled a touch cruelly. "Vitzi was conceived shortly after Letu was weaned. My wife was suffering mind phantoms and dark sorrows, as some women do after a child is born. In this state, she was easily seduced by a man who no longer walks this earth. There was one problem that kept my wife from hiding her infidelity from me. I was serving in the army, far from home, for the better part of a year during the time the little one must have been conceived. My wife and I had reasons to remain married, and so rather than divorce in disgrace and anger, my wife went away for a time. Vitzi was raised by strangers.

"A few years ago, Vitzi's foster parents died. My wife begged me to have the girl brought here for her final training, and in order that a good marriage could be arranged for her. I agreed. My wife had been faithful and good to me in the years that followed her one error, and the deities enjoin us to compassion and mercy. We brought Vitzi here and introduced her as the orphaned daughter of friends.

"Letu became infatuated with Vitzi, but more the fool I, I did not notice. I knew nothing of his feelings until the boy—and I call him one, though you would certainly name him a young man—came to me yesterday, begging my permission to make Vitzi his bride. I refused. He could not wed his own half-sister."

The Meddler straightened and tossed back his head. "And there you were a fool. Since when has refusal ever cooled the heart of love? I found Letu by the gate, sobbing out his heart, doubtless thinking of taking to the road to soothe his aching heart."

"Better if he had," Olenu said with ice in his voice. "I suspect rather that Letu was thinking of running off and putting his suit to his mother, hoping she would see matters differently than did I. Doubtless your finding him crying like a child put shame in him."

"Even so," the Meddler replied, no less proud, "I am glad to have helped the young couple. The deities will not punish them for their innocent love."

"What do you think this is then?" Olenu said, waving his arm wildly at the storms that still raged all around. "Don't you understand even now? I explained the situation to the boy. Vitzi is innocent, but Letu knew. He knew!"

❧

PLIK FINISHED HIS STORY on that dramatic note, and Firekeeper highly approved. There was no need to tell more. The point was made.

"So this Meddler," she said aloud, "is not bad person, but dangerous one, even so."

Harjeedian made a disapproving sound. "Dangerous can be very bad, especially for an organized society."

"True," Firekeeper said. "What I mean is he do what he think is good, but he not learn enough and he cause harm instead. He not think."

"That's how I see it," Plik agreed. "I chose that story from those I have read, because it was fairly representative of the Meddler's actions."

Firekeeper moved to where she could see Truth.

"What about you, great cat? You are the one who may know more than any of us. Have you any wisdom with which to guide us?"

Truth did not reply with so much as a whisker twitch, but Eshinarvash, who had been so quiet for these days of travel that Firekeeper occasionally had to remind herself that he was not one of Cousin-kind, gave a great shuddering sigh and shook out his mane.

"It seems to me that whoever was buried there beneath the earth—although I still have difficulty with the idea that one could be so buried for such a long time and live—it seems to me that the person's plans were very well laid, very carefully thought out. Is this the Meddler's pattern?"

Plik spoke, and Firekeeper jumped slightly. She kept forgetting in this company, where Plik so often spoke in the human languages, that she was not the only one who had the ability. Indeed, Blind Seer had teased her that Plik spoke the human languages far better than Firekeeper did.

"Well laid if we simply look at getting him out of that place," Plik said, *"but perhaps not so if we look at the larger consequences. Remember there were six fig-*

urines. Two of those are broken and represent pawns that have died. One represents a queen driven into exile and a diminishment of power. The last we know of represents a certain jaguar who, if my nose does not deceive me, feels no great love for this Voice who may also be the Meddler."

"True," Eshinarvash said, "and did he—Voice or Meddler—expect the finding of that place to also be the finding of those figurines? As the tale was told, Firekeeper found them beneath running water, hidden away as best anything could be hidden in that place. Could the Voice have known she would grow so curious about the path of running water? I think not."

Blind Seer, who had been suffering some from the heat, and so had fallen silent, spoke with a certain amount of pride. "If the Voice had known my Firekeeper, he would have expected her to look there, but I do not think he knows her—of her, perhaps, but if he knows her it is through the tools she helped to break. Melina, at least, underestimated any who stood against her and that was her undoing. Had she been content to visit New Kelvin quietly, we might never have been sent against her and her hunt for power would have been successful."

Plik raised a paw. "A moment. Our human friends grow restive."

Firekeeper was content to let Plik do the translating. She looked over at Truth. The jaguar's silence was peculiar, more than could be explained by the fact that the jaguar was traveling by day and over a greater distance than would usually be her wont.

Firekeeper wished for a sense of smell acute enough to tell her something of the jaguar's mood. Freshly reminded that there were many who would overhear her should she ask Blind Seer his opinion, she held her questions until they should be alone.

Alone. Firekeeper went to where Blind Seer was keeping up his steady pace. He was panting hard.

"Rest," she suggested. "You can find us again come nightfall."

"Promise you won't do anything foolish?" the wolf asked, already slackening his pace and veering toward the shady growth alongside the road.

"Promise," Firekeeper replied. "At least not without you."

XI

WATCHING THE SHAGGY GREY WOLF VANISH beneath the spreading branches, Plik felt a strong desire to follow. He wasn't habitually nocturnal, but the maimalodalum rarely pushed through the heat of the day as humans seemed to do at need.

But then what need did the maimalodalum have to push and hurry? Their community wasn't huge. Those of the yarimaimalom who hunted regularly shared their surplus. Remnants of orchards planted long ago still gave fruit and nuts. Foraging brought in other foods. Their own garden patches rounded out the rest.

Center Island offered ample habitations, either after the fashion of the yarimaimalom or in the towers or other semi-ruined structures. What maintenance must be done rarely forced the need for working in the heat or rain. Those of the maimalodalum who were scholarly by inclination, as Plik was, found plenty to occupy their remaining time.

In all his long life, Plik could not ever recall a time when he had continued to move on when he was weary, had gone without food or drink because there was no time to stop. Indeed, although his body might manage to masquerade as human, his habits were anything but.

But, he thought as he tried to find at least one part of his backside that wasn't saddle-bruised, *there are compensations for the discomfort of these hours in the saddle. Many compensations indeed. I have heard the eagles and ospreys talk of human farms and fields, but it is another thing to see them for oneself. And the buildings! I know we have bypassed the larger towns and villages, but even the temple complexes where we have stopped are remarkable. No wonder both Harjeedian and Derian referred to the towers on Center Island as "ruins." By their standards, they were.*

As the days of riding passed, Plik was relieved to find that he did adjust to this strange mode of travel. He learned to adjust to the different gaits of his mounts, and he could let go his death grip on the reins and saddle horn to drink from his canteen or snack on some of the goodies he started keeping in his pockets. He might never have Derian's unconscious comfort on horseback, but he no longer felt quite so punished.

Once they crossed the border out of Liglim into the city-states, things changed. The people of the city-states had heard of the yarimaimalom, many had even seen them, but they did not have the Liglimom's familiarity and trust of the intelligent beasts. Blind Seer and Truth inspired a certain amount of apprehension. Eshinarvash awakened envy and covetousness. The ravens simply kept their distance, knowing full well that a raven high overhead was nothing more than black against sky.

However, Harjeedian and Derian proved very competent in dealing with the authorities in each location. Alone but for the watchful ravens, they would enter the governing city. The rest of the expedition was left outside, where the presence of the jaguar and wolf—and Firekeeper poised nonchalantly "in charge"—meant that any local soldiery did not come close enough to penetrate Plik's disguise.

Occasionally, they were taunted by some of the locals who felt a need to prove that their land was not in awe of the looming power across the river. In these cases, Plik was fairly certain that Firekeeper alone could not have guaranteed they remained untouched, but even when they moved farther from the border, stories of the Liglimom's intense reverence for the Wise Beasts had spread. Not even the most arrogant solider would invite certain war to prove that he or she was not afraid of a big, spotted cat.

But despite careful research at each stop, they did not find what they sought in the first city-state they visited, nor in the second, or third. Truth was their guide in choosing each destination, but she was hardly a reliable one.

"How can I guide you to what I myself have not seen?" she snarled one evening when questions at the archives in the second city had garnered them nothing. Firekeeper was restive, and as was often the case at such times, less

than diplomatic. *"I must go by what I feel, and I feel a certainty that we are going in the correct direction. Go back to Misheemnekuru. Run and howl with the wolves if you do not have the patience for a great hunt."*

Needless to say, Firekeeper did not leave, nor did Truth's harsh words soothe her bruised nerves. She took to avoiding the jaguar, hinting less than subtly that she felt the great cat knew far more than she was admitting. Plik agreed with Firekeeper, but he felt it was less than tactful to say so, even obliquely.

Keeping his own doubts to himself, Plik continued his masquerade, wearing a selection of hats and cloaks. He told Meddler tales to distract his companions. When they needed no distraction, he constructed the stories he would tell when he returned to Center Island.

But Plik worried as he watched the tensions build. Everyone knew that when a wolf fought a jaguar, the wolf lost, but what if the combatants were two wolves against one jaguar?

All he knew was that if the matter came to that point, whoever might win the battle, all of them would have lost.

DERIAN WAS ASTONISHED to discover how quickly and efficiently he and Harjeedian worked out a routine for finding out what they needed to know while giving away very little themselves.

At their first stop, the riverside city-state of u-Itura—that is, the Borders—they had very little difficulty getting cooperation. Indeed, the residents were so like the Liglimom that Derian had to remind himself that they were not. Here Harjeedian's prestige as an aridisdu and his relationship to Rahniseeta opened both doors and archives to them. They were able to learn a great deal more about the other nearby city-states, for many of these preferred to trade with the Liglimom through u-Itura rather than do so themselves.

From u-Itura, Truth directed them toward Amseeta—or Rich Earth—a city-state almost directly south. Here the land was nearly flat and very fertile. However, it was poor in metals, and a long policy of clear-cutting for fields meant they were poor of fuel as well. They dried horse and cattle dung for their fires, and lived in a symbiotic state with the next city-state Truth guided them to.

This was Jekuseeta—or Hard Earth—a city-state more to the west. Here much of the soil was rocky, but rich in metals and valuable minerals. Timber, too, was plentiful, for who would cut down forests to create rocky fields? Derian wondered aloud why the two lands did not merge and learned more than he wished about their long-standing religious—or was it political?—differences. As long as each could view itself as getting the better of any deal, the residents lived in a peculiar harmony, but when either drew ahead, then there was ample excuse for war.

Really, it's not all that unlike the situation between Hawk Haven and Bright Bay, Derian thought. *What kept us apart for so long other than the fact that those who founded the lands had reasons to hate each other? No wonder there are times Firekeeper looks at humans as if we all have rabies.*

In each of these city-states, the burden for investigation fell on the two human members of the expedition. Usually, the greater part of the group would wait outside of the city itself—for true to the name the Liglimom had given them, one city ruled the surrounding region, with the majority of the population maintaining a residence of some sort within the city boundaries. Each "country," if they could so be called, was hardly larger than a day's ride in each direction.

I bet the Norwood Grant alone is larger than most of these "states," Derian thought a trace complacently. It was good to know that not every foreign power was immediately a rival.

In the city, Harjeedian would request direction to the nearest temple complex dedicated to the worship of the Divine Elements. There he would usually be welcomed with a mixture of warmth and respect, the one moderating the other depending on those in charge. Harjeedian would begin by explaining that he was traveling as escort to not merely one, but five of the Wise Beasts.

He usually didn't need to say anything more. Quarters would be found for them and the yarimaimalom, and if Harjeedian requested a certain amount of privacy be given his companions, it would be given. In some cases, Derian thought their hosts were just as glad not to be asked to provide lavish hospitality.

In Truflad—the first place they had been where the name did not derive from Liglimosh—they had been offered a lovely river meadow in which to camp. Nor had they been expected to make do with what they had carried with them. The resident disdum had provided several pavilion-style tents, carpets, heaps of pillows, cots, and would have provided servants as well if Harjeedian had not declined.

Somewhere along the line, their hosts would politely inquire about Derian's foreign appearance—Firekeeper and Plik usually kept out of sight as much as possible—and in the process of explaining, Harjeedian would manage to slip in something that would make the resident aridisdum realize Harjeedian's own relationship to the new junjaldisdu. The already ample hospitality would reach near hysterical levels, for no one wanted to offend the brother of one of the rulers of the much larger power to the immediate north—or the ambassador from the still mysterious but evidently warlike powers farther up the coast.

At first, Derian felt a little uncomfortable about letting these people assume he was the ambassador rather than an assistant, then he realized that it didn't matter. Ambassador Sailor had sent him. Moreover, Ambassador Sailor wasn't present. Derian was the one they saw, the one they needed to impress.

Once the expedition was settled in their quarters or camp—the presence of the yarimaimalom, and a desire to cater to their comfort, meant they camped as often as not—Derian and Harjeedian would start making inquiries after both a place where people dressed after the style of the two unidentified figurines, and after the flame within a flame emblem.

Plik had provided good likenesses of both the emblem and the two figurines, and so the actual items did not need to be brought out. Their hosts were eager to be of assistance, but could rarely help them beyond eliminating their own city-state.

So it went until the expedition arrived in Gak. Gak had been named by a doctor who had been particularly influential in the post-Plague years. It was a prosperous city-state, somewhat larger than usual, and rather more to the west than many to which Truth had guided them to this point.

The Iron Mountains—or a kindred range—began farther west throughout southern lands than they did in Derian's homeland, but as in Hawk Haven, the mountain range provided the boundary between "civilization" and wilderness. However, here there was no danger of humanity pressing that unofficial border. Gak was prosperous compared to her city-state neighbors, but there was ample room for growth.

Gak proved more ethnically mixed than any land they had encountered to this point, and for once Derian did not find his red hair and relatively pale skin drawing attention. Although the local language was close to Liglimosh, Derian caught fascinating echoes of what he was sure was Pellish, and what he was almost sure was the language spoken in Waterland.

Their host that night was Amiri, a garrulous aridisdu. Over a lengthy ban-

quet, she and several others among the local disdum sought to offer some explanation for the local mixture of cultures and racial types.

"Gak was a prosperous land even before Divine Retribution," Amiri said.
"Because the Old World rulers sought to flee the disease by returning to their
homelands, they went east. In turn, those who had no wish to be enslaved to
the demands of this sudden exodus fled west."

"Enslaved?" Derian asked.

"Enslaved," a kidisdu replied. "There were not fleets enough to carry the
rulers and their goods back to the Old World. I don't know how it was in your
homeland, but here those who were still strong enough to travel moved to the
coast in a great body. They didn't care about anything but getting away, and
many a private person found himself a slave or worse."

Amiri took up the tale. "Gak attracted a good number of these refugees. We
were far from the coast, and the Old Country rulers had either died or departed
as soon as they felt the hand of Divine Retribution upon them. Refugees were
offered citizenship on the condition that they agree to take up arms to defend
the land against invasion. Our earliest government was a militia of sorts. Today,
we are a republic rather than a monarchy such as Bright Haven or theocracy
like Liglim. Each clan sends a representative to our standing senate. The leaders of the senate are an elected triumvirate, each of which holds office for . . ."

Amiri smiled, pushing back fair hair from a high forehead. "But you do not
care about our local political arrangements, no matter that we are very proud
of them. They have enabled us to stand united, in contrast to some of our
neighbors who are constantly at war over issues of race or religion."

"I am very interested," Harjeedian said. "But," he went on with evident reluctance, "I am also a servant of my duty. We are seeking information about a
pair of people we have reason to believe live in one of the city-states, probably
in one that, like your own, shows some influence from the culture of Liglim."

"The influence is here," Amiri agreed, "but unlike in Liglim, you will not
find our religious tradition the only one—or even the dominant one. This
close to the mountains, the yarimaimalom have never needed to make truces
with humans. Some come—I rather think as missionaries—to serve our needs,
but there are wild ones we never see and . . ."

She lowered her voice and looked uncomfortable. "And who I fear do not
share our faith."

Harjeedian made a gesture indicating she should be at ease. "Once that
would have startled me more than it does now. Contact with the lands to the
north has meant realizing that not all peoples are as fortunate as we in . . ."

He stopped in midphrase. Obviously, what he had been about to say would have been less than completely polite.

Derian waved a hand at him. "Don't worry. I won't take offense. Someday our land's different ways of interpreting what you would call divine will may be a problem, for now I'm willing to accept that you have your way and we have ours."

Amiri looked at him with interest. "Are all your people so tolerant?"

"Probably not," Derian admitted, "but our region contains numerous individual nations, many of which encompass larger populations and land areas than all I've seen of the city-states. It's a rare child who doesn't learn that there are people with other ways—and in any case, each family has its own ancestors and they're no better or worse than the ancestors of their neighbors. Maybe that does lead to a certain degree of tolerance."

"I think we could talk on these matters for days," Amiri said, and those of the local disdum who had joined them for the meal made sounds of agreement. "However, I sincerely doubt that your yarimaimalom companions would tolerate such delay. You said you seek two people. Do you have names for them?"

Harjeedian shook his head. "No names, but we do have what may be a family emblem—or perhaps one associated with a particular church or clan. It is very little to go on, but Truth has given omens that this manner of searching is according to the divine will, and so we follow it."

"And you?" Amiri asked Derian, her gaze shrewd. "Do you also follow the divine will?"

"Not quite," Derian admitted. "It's more like I follow that of Firekeeper."

"The woman you introduced us to earlier," Amiri said, "the one who seems a rather peculiar form of kidisdu."

"That's as good an explanation as any," Derian said. "If we have time before we leave, I'll tell you something of her history. For now, let's leave it at this. She was raised—really—from when she was a very young child until somewhat over four years ago by a pack of Wise Wolves. She is closer to the yarimaimalom than to most humans, and when Truth became obsessed with finding these people, Firekeeper agreed to help."

Amiri's eyes widened, but she dutifully kept to the task at hand. "Can you show us the emblem at least?"

"I brought a copy," Harjeedian said, pulling out one of Plik's drawings preserved in a leather wallet. "This is the emblem. This is the style of dress worn by the people."

Their audience, here as in the other city-states, were members of the disdum. They didn't ask how Harjeedian had learned these things. Doubtless they assumed that he had communicated with Truth through the elaborate divinatory methods their mutual ancestors had relied upon since before coming to the New World.

"The form of attire is certainly one worn in Gak," Amiri said. "The emblem is not one I personally know. . . ."

She looked at her associates.

One, a very young kidisdu, hardly more than a girl, said hesitantly, "I think . . . I've seen it. I don't know where, though, and I could be wrong."

"Please continue," Harjeedian said, seeing the child was embarrassed at the thought she was speaking out of turn. "Even if you are wrong, we would like to hear what you have to say."

"I only just entered the disdum," the girl said. She somewhat resembled the Liglimom, but was more fair of skin and her eyes held flecks of green, "and until a few moonspans past I lived in my parents' house. My mother remains active in the affairs of her birth clan—our family clan."

Derian bit his tongue to keep from asking how it was decided to which clan children of a union belonged. That was almost certainly not germane to the matter at hand.

"Last triumvirate term, my mother was clan representative to the senate," the girl said.

Her expression flitted between pride in her mother's achievement and embarrassment that she might be thought bragging about what must seem a minor achievement to two such great men. Derian didn't know whether he wanted to pat her on the head or throttle her.

"There was a great fuss over some people who wanted to use an emblem that they claimed had historical basis. I think it was that very emblem. I don't know why there was a great fuss."

She gasped a little, flushed, and abruptly stopped.

"Thank you, Petulia," Amiri said. "Now that you mention the matter, I believe I recall it myself. Being of the disdum, I have never been my family's senatorial representative . . ."

Harjeedian made an odd, inquiring sound, and Amiri interrupted herself.

"It was part of the contract established when Gak survived the departure of the Old World rulers," she explained. "We had refugees who practiced many different religions. Rather than attempting to establish one—and doubtless falling into civil war—all religions were permitted to remain, but with the restriction that no one who was of the established hierarchy of a religion could be a representative."

Harjeedian frowned. "Doesn't that mean that you are ruled by those of least faith?"

"Some have argued so," Amiri said, "but the arrangement has worked for a century. We let the arguments continue."

Harjeedian drew his lips into a thin, tight line, but he had the good political sense not to argue. Amiri, pretending as if there wasn't the least tension, returned to the matter of the emblem.

"Petulia, I believe that the issue wasn't merely that these people wished to use the emblem, but that they claimed the right to establish—or reestablish—a clan. They claimed that the clan had existed at the time when the contract was formed, and therefore its rights should be respected."

Derian had not spent the better part of the last four or so years involved in the political intrigues of at least four different nations without learning a thing or two.

"You said that representation in your governing senate was based upon clans," he said. "Effectively, these people were asking for the creation of a new vote. I can see how that wouldn't thrill those who already had the vote."

Amiri nodded. "The matter becomes even more complicated, for if a new/old clan is created based on claims of prior, heretofore unrecognized residence, what is to keep other people from deciding to try the same gambit? The representatives could find themselves doing nothing but reviewing such claims—and the waste of their time would be the least of the problems to come from that."

The kidisdu who had answered Derian's question about slavery now spoke up. "I assume, however, that since we are not amid a cyclone of new clan requests, these people's request was not granted. Even so, it should be easy enough to learn their name. Petulia, is your mother currently in the city?"

The girl bobbed her head in the shyest of nods.

"Then we will send her a message and see if she will entertain our distinguished foreign visitors." He looked over at Derian and Harjeedian. "How soon would you like to speak with her?"

"As soon as is reasonable," Harjeedian replied. "Although Counselor Derian and I would be more than happy to spend several days in your fine city, our yarimaimalom companions are evincing a certain impatience."

As is Firekeeper, Derian thought, swallowing a grin since he was certain that this was what Harjeedian was thinking, but was too diplomatic to state.

"And impatient yarimaimalom, especially those with fangs and claws . . ." Amiri said.

"Don't underestimate hooves," Derian said, laughing, "or the beaks of ravens."

Amiri laughed with him, then sobered. "We would like to ask a favor of the yarimaimalom. This isn't a condition for our aid—that you will have. However, as I mentioned earlier, the yarimaimalom who share our faith are not as common here. Might you ask your companions if the omens favor their spending some time with us, even if only those hours you will be spending speaking with Petulia's mother?"

Harjeedian nodded, and any pique he might have felt at learning that in Gak the disdum were barred from being governmental representatives was clearly appeased.

"I would gladly do this, Aridisdum Amiri. I cannot answer in advance, but I am hopeful that at least one of our companions would agree to spend time with you."

Amiri looked very pleased at this. "Any time of the day or night," she said. "We always have someone standing vigil."

"I will tell them this," Harjeedian said.

The meal drew to a close, and after a final sweet course, Derian and Harjeedian took their leave.

"We have news," Derian explained, "after days upon days of having no news at all. We must share it with our companions."

"We cannot trouble Petulia's mother tonight," Amiri said, "but I will send a messenger tomorrow as early as is polite. Wait in your camp and someone will come to tell you if she will see you. I firmly expect she will."

I bet she will, Derian thought, *out of curiosity if nothing else.*

FIREKEEPER WAS WILD WITH JOY when Derian and Harjeedian returned with the news that they might have found the source of the mysterious emblem.

Even Derian's caution that this might prove to be a dead end could not reduce her pleasure. Blind Seer agreed.

"I feel so certain this will not be another cold, dead trail," he said, *"that maybe I should take over reading omens for Truth. Do you think I should go to the temple tonight and offer my skills?"*

In reply, Firekeeper booted him in the ribs. *"Whatever we think, dear heart, these people take their omens seriously. Do not tease them as Rascal would one of the pups."*

"I know they are serious," Blind Seer replied. *"Ask them if we could attend the meeting with Petulia's mother tomorrow. I would hear for myself what she says about these people who would make a pack from old bones and pictures."*

Firekeeper passed on the request, and Harjeedian seemed pleased rather than otherwise at their interest.

"Certainly," he said.

He looked over at Truth. The jaguar had been asleep on the plushest of the rugs, her upper body gracefully draped over an embroidered pillow. When Firekeeper had relayed Blind Seer's request, her burnt-orange eyes had opened.

"Do you also wish to attend?" Harjeedian asked her.

In reply, Truth rose and stretched.

"Tell him," she said lazily to Firekeeper, *"that I would like to attend, and that I go now to grace the temple with my glorious presence."*

Firekeeper was tempted not to translate, but she knew that if she did not, the unpleasant task would be left to Plik. From time to time she had sensed that for all his cheerful, even jolly, manner, the maimalodalu was finding his extended exile from his place and people hard.

And why should he not? she thought. *When I left my pack, at least I had Blind Seer with me. Plik has no one but us.*

When Truth departed, Bitter rose from where he was perched beside Loveable in a tangled tree. He gave a hoarse squawk that needed no translation. Then he took wing.

"And," Harjeedian commented, "I believe Eshinarvash will grant them a visit come morning. The faithful will find themselves well rewarded for their hospitality."

PETULIA THE KIDISDU CAME TO THE RIVER MEADOW the next morning, and Firekeeper padded out to meet her. Plik had been enjoying a little time free of clothing, and the wolf-woman saw no reason he should not continue as nature had made him.

"You disdu?" Firekeeper said. "Welcome. I am Firekeeper. This is Blind Seer."

Petulia bobbed the local equivalent of a bow, and tried to stammer out a few words. Immediately Firekeeper remembered how very shy Derian had said the girl was.

"Your mother? She will see us? You very kind. I get Harjeedian, Derian, and Truth. We come with you."

While the two humans readied themselves, Firekeeper brought Petulia a tin mug of water and some sweet confection they had purchased in the last city-state.

"For you," Firekeeper said, hoping her sincere desire to put the girl at ease would make up for her own lack of social graces. "It tastes like apple blossoms and honey."

Petulia peered up through her lashes and accepted the gift. Firekeeper could hardly hear her whispered thanks.

The others arrived not long after, saving Firekeeper from having to make any more social overtures. Petulia immediately started leading the way through the twisting streets, moving so quickly that Firekeeper knew Harjeedian at least was pressed to keep his dignity.

"Does she fear you and Truth?" Firekeeper asked Blind Seer.

"I smell no one special fear," Blind Seer replied. *"I think this little one has a field mouse's heart. It beats too fast."*

Firekeeper was no great judge of human habitations, but she thought that Petulia's family was certainly not poor. The house to which they were guided was beautifully maintained, the timber portions freshly painted, the areas between (they looked as if they were made of mud, rather like swallow's nests) tightly chinked and sealed with the same paint.

The door was opened by a woman who exuded confidence as Truth did arrogance. Unlike her daughter, she was purely of the Liglimom type, with shining dark hair and earth brown eyes. Firekeeper wondered what the father looked like to make Petulia.

"Welcome to our home," the woman said. "I am Layozirate, Petulia's mother. Please call me Layo."

She motioned all of them in, Petulia included, but the girl said softly, "I must report back to the temple, Mother."

Layo bent and kissed the girl on her forehead, right at the part of her hair. "Go, little mouse. Be happy."

"I told you she was a mouse," Blind Seer said, *"though I am surprised that her mother would admit what she mated with."*

Firekeeper thumped him gently between the shoulders, but kept her formal manners. This woman Layo seemed to demand them, although she had spoken very few words.

Layo guided them to a spacious courtyard ornamented with a fountain and a small pool. Chairs had been set for the humans, rugs spread for the yarimaimalom. Although a chair had been supplied for Firekeeper, she settled herself on the rug while Blind Seer luxuriated on the cool dampness of the paving stones nearest to the water. Layo was indeed a diplomat, for she did not comment even with the raising of her finely arched brows.

"Aridisdu Amiri," she said, when greetings had been exchanged, and refreshments offered all around, "sent me a long letter explaining the reason for your coming. May I see this emblem? She described it and made a copy from memory, but I wish to be certain."

Harjeedian extended his wallet, and Layo studied it. Rather than reply with words, she turned to a table set near her side and extended a folder of her own. At the top of the papers heaped within was one bearing the very same emblem.

"That's it!" Derian said, and for once Firekeeper could not blame him for stating the obvious. She wanted to romp and howl as wolves did when catching a fresh scent, but kept her dignity.

"Can you tell us more about the people who made this claim," Harjeedian asked, "and how we might find them?"

Layo folded her hands in her lap. "I can tell you about them, but I am not sure I can tell you how to find them. You see, a year or more ago, they left the city. Why they left is part of the larger story."

"It always is," Firekeeper grumbled to Blind Seer, but aloud she said, "Do they live?"

"As far as I know they do," Layo answered. "There were only two who made the claim, a brother and a sister, twins born at the same moment. You may think this is impossible. Certainly one must come forth first, but in their case, the impossible was possible. They were joined side of hand to side of hand, as if they had pressed too close in the womb and their skin had woven together."

She paused as if expecting questions, but the only words that came were Derian's polite "Please go on. This is fascinating."

"The surgeon was summoned, and they were cut apart immediately, for it was reasoned that young flesh would heal more quickly than if there was a delay. There was also a fear that once out in the great, wide world they might do injury to each other. The surgery was successful. By their first year, no mark of it remained but for a thin, silvery white scar.

"However, soon those who cared for the babies could tell that the twins remained somehow joined, although their bodies had been parted. When one stumbled and fell, the other cried, even if they were in separate rooms, or even in separate parts of the city. They were happy together, miserable together, ill together, hungry together—and this persisted even after their weary mother sent the brother for a time into the country with his father, and kept the sister in the city with her.

"Theirs was a small family, not so ambitious that either member was much noticed by their clan. Do you know anything of our system of representatives?"

Harjeedian spoke for them all. "Aridisdu Amiri explained that each clan has a representative, and these form a senate."

"Accurate but not quite fully so," Layo said. "Doubtless she wished to keep her explanation simple, for how could she know it would matter?"

"If you would explain further," Harjeedian said, "at least those points that pertain to the matter at hand, we would all be grateful."

"Certainly," Layo replied. "Each clan is granted a certain number of senatorial representatives based upon the clan's own size. Size is not measured by mere numbers of people, but by families—and a family is defined as a married couple that has produced at least one child. When the couple marries, which clan they will augment is carefully negotiated, and if a divorce occurs, the parent who is born to that clan keeps the children and they remain part of the clan. The other parent is returned to his or her birth clan and resumes a child's status unless he or she remarries."

Firekeeper knew Derian well enough to know that he wished to ask a question, but had decided it was not to the point at hand. Layo, surprisingly, for Derian had hidden his interest very well, also noticed.

"You have a question, Counselor Derian?"

"Oh, it's probably not important. I was thinking that remarriage after one has been married and divorced—especially if you're the one who keeps the children—must be complicated."

"It is," Layo said. "Usually the second marriage partner must agree to join the same clan as the spouse and children, although there are exceptions."

Derian grinned. "I'm sure there are. Whenever someone sets up what seems like a perfectly orderly way of doing things, someone else will find a way to mess it up. But please, go on with the story of these twins."

Layo nodded. "As I said, the twins' family belonged to a clan well enough placed that one family more or less did not make a great difference. This was the mother's clan, by the way. The father came from outside Gak entirely, a first-generation immigrant. As neither parent had any great desire to join into the political game, the years passed in benign neglect from the clan as a whole.

"The twins grew older. With age, their peculiar bond became more and more obvious. The bond of shared physical sensation decreased, but still each knew more about the other than was reasonable. There was gossip as to who would wish to marry either one. Who would wish to feel that the intimacies of their household were known by another?

"So it rested until a few years ago when the twins' mother died during the usual bout of winter ills. The twins' father dealt with his loss by disconnecting himself from his wife's family as much as possible. As I mentioned, he was a first-generation immigrant—or so we thought. Now he told his children the true story of his heritage. His family had old roots in this region, very old roots, right back to the Old World rulers themselves.

"He filled the twins' heads with stories of the power and influence his family had held. He also shared his indignation that his family, as old as any clan and older still, had no place within the representative system. It is my belief that he intended to raise the issue before the senate himself, for now that his wife—who by all reports he truly loved—was dead, there was no real reason for him to wish to remain connected to her birth clan."

Derian gave a humorless laugh. "I guess not, if he thought he could found his own clan. But you say you believe 'he intended' to raise the issue of his family's heritage himself. Didn't he do so?"

"No, he didn't for the simple reason that he died before he could do so—an infection in a cut to his leg spread. The leg was amputated, but not soon enough. The poison was in his blood and killed him."

"And the twins?" Firekeeper asked, concerned that there would be a round of discussion of similar deaths. Humans were fond of such talking, as if comparison made the one incident somehow more explicable. "What they do?"

"They inherited a house in town, a section of farmland outside the walls, and their father's belief that they should be the founders—or rather the reestablishers—of a clan of their own. I will say this for them. They gave a very good presentation. They had inherited some old documents and pieces of jewelry that supported their father's tales. These they bolstered with materials located in private libraries and the city's own archives. However, their request was denied. The official reason was that the government of Gak was established by those who remained to defend and sustain the nation at a time of crisis."

Harjeedian's expression held a cynical cast as he spoke. "But I am certain that another, unstated reason was that the senate was not at all pleased with the idea of needing to incorporate a new voting bloc—no matter how small that might have been initially. It would still have been one more vote, an unaligned vote at that. Depending on how prolific this brother and sister proved to be, and how good they were at negotiating marriages for themselves and their offspring, they might prove a clan to contend with in a relatively short period of time."

"Precisely," Layo said. "I will not trouble you by reciting the increments at which a clan may claim the right to instate a new voting representative, but given the twins' relative youth, by the time their heads were silvering, they might command a very solid voting bloc."

Firekeeper noticed that Derian was fidgeting, and now he blurted out:

"And was no one troubled by the fact that these twins claimed Old World sorcerers as ancestors?"

XII

"SORCERERS?" LAYO REPEATED, evidently puzzled.

"You said they claimed to be descended from the Old World rulers," Derian said, realizing that she had actually not stated that the twins' ancestors were sorcerers. Had he jumped to a conclusion too quickly?

"That's what the twins claimed," Layo agreed. "However, the twins' ancestors had not maintained their holdings, and thus it was judged that they had relinquished claim of citizenship in our rebuilt nation."

"Now," Derian said carefully, "the twins ancestors fled because . . ."

"The twins did not mention," Layo said. "They probably had no idea."

"In our country," Derian said, "the Plague was more severe in its effects among those who had come from the Old Country. Was that true here as well?"

"So the legends say," Layo said. "That is why there was suddenly a dearth of rulers and we had to reorganize."

"Did your Old Country rulers use magic and sorcery to keep their hold?" Derian asked. "That's what they did in the north."

"Here as well," Layo agreed. "How else could a relative few have ruled the growing colonies? It was the very abuse of those powers that brought Divine Retribution upon them. Even those of my fellow citizens who do not share my precise beliefs say something of the kind. The Old Country rulers abused their power, and so were punished for that abuse."

Firekeeper shifted slightly, moving closer to Blind Seer. Like Derian, she had been reared to view magic as very dangerous. Moreover, Derian didn't doubt that she was already ahead of him on this road down which he was slowly leading Layo.

"When the twins said that they were descended from Old Country rulers," Derian said, "you did say they provided proof."

"That's right. Papers. Jewelry. A family genealogy. Their father had been raised in one of the city-states on the eastern seaboard. His learning of his heritage upon the death of his own parents led to him coming west, meeting the twins' mother, and settling down. She may have convinced him not to pursue the matter, because he seems to have left it lie until after her death."

"Rulers," Derian repeated, "not just household staff or trusted retainers or some such that might have left along with their employers."

"Rulers," Layo said. "The emblem you showed me was their crest. It stood for something like 'Land of the Setting Sun.' That is, it indicated that they held a far western portion of the colony."

"Not fire?" Firekeeper asked, and Derian couldn't tell if he read relief or disappointment in her tone. "It look like fire."

"It does," Layo agreed, "but the reason the flames are spaced out like that is because the general shape is meant to represent a cluster of mountains. The ragged flame edge is the color those particular mountains turn when the sun is setting."

"Layo," Derian said very carefully, not wanting to offend this woman who had been, after all, very patient with them. "It seems to me that your representative's concentration on the political ramifications of the twins' request meant that they overlooked something that seems more serious to me—the fact that the twins were also claiming to be descended from sorcerers."

"You said that before," Layo agreed, "and I can see why, but what does it matter? We rose up against the sorcerers, destroyed what they left behind. In any case, the art of sorcery was only taught in the Old World, never here."

"So it was in the north as well," Derian said, "but that doesn't mean that there haven't been things—books, a few artifacts, perhaps other things—that were missed."

Layo was looking very unhappy now, but Derian was optimistic that her emotion was not directed toward him.

"And the twins are very strange," she said. "Some have said their closeness is along the order of a talent—like a gift for healing or a perfect sense of direction—only much more rare. Do you think they may have inherited more than just bits of jewelry and a particularly detailed family tree?"

"Quite possibly," Derian said.

Harjeedian had waited in perfect silence to this point, nodding occasionally to agree with Derian where appropriate, but otherwise not doing anything to press Layo to accept Derian's conclusion. Derian thought he knew why. Harjeedian was very aware of his dual position as informal ambassador and visiting religious authority. He would not wish Layo to feel afterward that she had been forced to a conclusion she would never have reached on her own.

Now, however, Harjeedian evidently felt he could take a more active role.

"So you can see why it is important that we meet these twins," he said. "Can you direct us to them, and perhaps give us an idea how best to approach them?"

Layo spread her hands in what Derian thought might be a universal gesture of dismay.

"I wish I could," she said, "but they left Gak over a year ago. They sold all their holdings, bought horses and other traveling equipment, and departed. No one has seen or heard from them since."

PLIK TOOK A VERY FINE-TOOTHED COMB and worked the dead fleas from his fur. That was one advantage of being a maimalodalu, rather than a true racoon. He could deal with fleas. He wondered why his mother had never realized the advantages, but then she had never minded fleas.

Plik had known when the others returned from meeting with Layo, the former senator, in the early afternoon, that they had not been completely successful. He had sensed that they had not been entirely unsuccessful either. Now he listened and learned the details.

When they finished speaking and the last question was answered, the last speculation made, Plik set aside his flea comb. His fur smelled good, clean, impregnated with the herbal infusion he had used to kill the fleas. He wondered why the wolf and jaguar chose to sit upwind.

"So they are gone," Plik said, "but we now know where they once were. In a sense, for the first time since we have begun this journey we know for certain that they exist. The twins. Tell me, what are their personal names?"

"Isende and Tiniel," Derian replied. "Tiniel is the male."

"The names don't sound Liglimosh," Plik said.

"They are not," Harjeedian said. "Layo did not know their precise source, but she recalled that the father named them. He apparently felt that if they were to be of their mother's clan—he himself not having one—he should at least give them their names."

Derian looked at Plik. "I've been meaning to ask you. Your name, it doesn't sound much like the type of names the maimalodalum have. I mean, the ones I've met."

"You mean like 'Hope' or 'Powerful Tenderness' or some such abstract quality?" Plik asked, wondering if his discomfort showed on his face. He was not yet sure how much of his expressions came through to the humans.

"That's right," Derian said. "But, like I said, it's not like I've met them all. I mean, it's not like my name means anything. It's just one of those Old World names we still keep using. I guess it means something, or did once a long time ago. In my family, though, it's just the name of someone in the family who died young."

Plik was certain his discomfort had come through, and Derian was giving him a way out. All Plik had to do was start talking about ancestor worship or memory or some such thing, and the question of Plik's own name would be dropped. Moreover, Plik knew that Derian would never raise the matter again, no one would.

He opened his mouth to ask the source of Derian's name, but he heard himself saying instead, "You're right. Plik isn't the name I was given at birth. My mother called me 'Misbegotten.' Plik is the sound water makes when a single drop falls onto rock. I liked that better."

Derian reached out a hand, as if he might somehow take back his question. "Plik, I'm sorry . . . I . . ."

Plik patted the big, pink-skinned hand.

"It was a long, long time ago," he said, "before your own mother was born. We have more important matters to discuss."

Firekeeper, who had been silent during all the telling and speculation, spoke for the first time.

"What? The twins are gone. We will track them or not. If you have a story, tell."

Plik blinked at her and switched to the language of the Beasts, *"And if I do not wish to tell?"*

"Then don't," the wolf-woman said, *"but your fur bristles with old memories. I thought telling might ease you."*

Plik switched back. "I will tell the story, perhaps, someday. Now we need to make our plans. There are some hours of daylight left. Do we strike camp and hit the trail?"

"To where?" Firekeeper said. "The twins have gone. Truth say she have no thought where next to go. Do we go back then?"

The wolf-woman looked to where the jaguar lay on her heap of pillows, but though the great cat's burnt-orange eyes narrowed slightly, Truth made no other reply.

Plik shook his head. "We should definitely *not* go back. It seems to me that the tale Layo has told you fits all too well with the pattern you told us has occurred before. Like Melina, like Dantarahma, these twins also were attracted to magic. Whether they were lured into this attraction or whether the Voice—or whoever it was who carved those figurines—was drawn to that attraction and somehow used it, still, we should feel encouraged rather than otherwise."

Plik had everyone's attention now, and continued with increased enthusiasm. "And we have an indication where they might have gone. The emblem indicated that their father's family originally held lands to the far west. Where else would they have gone when their appeal was rejected?"

Derian, who had slumped back against a heap of pillows when he had realized his idle question had brought Plik pain, now straightened.

"You have a good thought there, Plik."

"West is large," Firekeeper said, but her words were not a rejection of Plik's conjecture, only something like an initial sniffing. "Very. But humans know little of it."

"We will go looking," said Bitter the raven, spreading his wings as if he might take flight that very moment.

"Wait," Plik said. "A little research on the part of our human friends may limit your search. Harjeedian must do it mostly, I fear, and even he may need assistance from the locals if the archives are written in some other language than those he reads."

"I will inquire immediately," Harjeedian said, getting up from the camp chair where he had been sitting. "I will see if there is any record where the father's family holdings were—the family that held the grant in the land of the Setting Sun."

Plik nodded. "It may be easier to find than you imagine. Wouldn't such records have been sought at the time of the senate hearing?"

"Very likely," Harjeedian agreed.

"I wish I could help," Plik said, "but as I have promised my people to keep our existence a secret . . ."

"I understand," Harjeedian said.

"If they do not have the records," Plik said, "there is one other thing you can ask to see."

"And this is?"

"Geographical surveys. I am no great expert about mountains. I have never even seen one up close, but I do know something about sunsets and sunrises. We maimalodalum quite enjoy sunsets. Sometimes we would journey to where we could watch the light striking different things, and one thing I do know."

"And this is?" Harjeedian asked very politely.

"Sunset against trees tends to spread and lose its color, but when it hits rock or water, then it paints them in rather fiery hues."

Harjeedian understood, and his usually stern expression brightened. "You are saying that even if our attempts to find the location of the twin's family holdings in the records fail, we might locate them by looking for a geographical survey that indicates the existence of a cliff or barren mountain slope."

"That's exactly what he said," Blind Seer laughed, *"although I am not certain which of you used more words. Plik, however, was certainly more poetic."*

Firekeeper shared the wolf's laughter, and Plik wondered if her human friends had thought her insane for laughing at quips they did not hear. Then again, they probably didn't recognize a wolf's laugh.

"You will do it?" Plik asked.

"I will," Harjeedian said.

"And so will we," Bitter said, *"but we will take your advice and wait until the humans have opportunity to narrow the field. Why should we weary our wings while everyone else sits and grows fat?"*

"So the twins may have gone to ruins," Lovable said, her mind, as usual, flying upon different winds than her mate. *"You can find pretty things in ruins. I wonder what we will find?"*

"Rather," Plik said, not caring that his words would seem strange to those who heard with only one set of ears, "I wonder what the twins have found—and what they have made of it."

"THEY'RE ON THE RIGHT TRACK," the Voice said to Truth. "I thought you might want to know."

Truth rolled over onto her back. She was asleep. The only one awake to notice the unwonted restlessness of that sleep was Firekeeper, who sat awhile, watching the restless lashing of the jaguar's tail in the ruddy light of the coals.

"I suppose," Truth said. "My paws are not like horse's hooves. These long treks are not what I am made for."

"Then why did you come?" the Voice said mockingly. "For all the help you've given them, you could have remained on Misheemnekuru."

"I sent them west," Truth protested.

"A fifty percent choice," the Voice said, "and one they would have likely taken anyhow. The weather is still warm enough that the seaboard lands are fever traps for those who have not grown to adulthood there. Tell me what other help you have been."

"I told them which city-states to visit."

"Many wrongs before you found the right one," the Voice replied, "and even this is hardly the straightest path to your goal. The twins have been gone a good while now."

"So," Truth snarled, "can you tell me more? Are we close enough now that you can give me guidance?"

"Not so long as you screw your eyes tight shut," the Voice said. "I reached you so well before because what you persist in viewing as madness assisted me. Indeed, I worked wonders with you, showed you potential you never knew you had. I could do that again."

"But I must be mad for you to show me this."

"I didn't say that," the Voice replied, "but certainly you must take that risk."

"And if I choose not?"

"Why then, you will never achieve your goal."

"You mean we will not find the twins? I thought you said we were on the right track."

"Ah, but pretty Truth, that is not *your* goal now is it? What I mean is that you must risk madness if ever you will find out if you can kill me . . ."

Truth did not reply. She was hunter enough to know that one dipped a paw into a stream without being absolutely sure that a fish swam there. Did the Voice know her intention or was he merely dipping his paw, trying to learn whether the water had rippled with the passage of a fish, or maybe of a snapping turtle.

She changed the subject.

"You want us to find the twins then? I thought they were your tools. Why would you wish us to find them?"

"My tools?" The Voice sounded as innocent as a skull scraped clean of brain and flesh. "The twins my tools?"

Truth's first inclination was to snap at him, to ask if he had forgotten the sculpted figurines. She drew back. Hadn't one of those figurines been made in her image? Might she be giving too much away?

"You know why we hunt these two," she said instead.

"Because Firekeeper, clever wolfling that she is, went swimming and found some rocks."

"It seemed to us you might know these two, then, for the rocks she found were in your lair."

"Not precisely my *lair*," the Voice said. Truth growled, and he added with a laugh, "All right, not my lair, but certainly a place where I have spent too much time. I'll even admit that I made those pretty figurines. Surely, though, you yourself should be the first to know that a figurine alone is not evidence that the person so depicted is my tool."

Truth felt her upper lip rippling in a snarl, but she lowered her head, licking her forepaw to cover the expression.

"Tool implies something made or used for one's purpose. Firekeeper's pretty Fang is a tool. Her fire-making stones are tools. Surely you, O Truth, are no one's tool. Are you?"

Truth wished she was so certain, but she merely schooled herself to steady grooming. The action was automatically soothing, but if she kept this up, she was going to have a hairball in the morning.

Does one get a hairball from grooming in one's dreams? she thought.

If the Voice could read her thoughts, he made no comment. Instead he went on, talking as if she had responded to his last several questions.

"I might have found a certain, call it sympathy with a few individuals, and I might have crafted figurines to help me focus on that sympathy," the Voice said. "But that does not mean I controlled those so depicted. Would a nice person like me—someone who would help a jaguar rejoin body and soul— would that person condone the actions of Melina?"

"I know no Melina," Truth said, shaking her head to loosen a claw sheath caught on one tooth.

"Dantarahma, then," the Voice said. "How could what he did have anything to do with me?"

"His figurine was broken," Truth said, "so was that of Melina. Perhaps they were your tools. Humans make balls for their games. I have seen these balls roll where the humans never intended. Once, during a festival in Heeranena-halm, I saw a ball thrown over the head of the one who was meant to have caught it. It rolled all the length of the Processional Way, gaining speed until it landed in the harbor. This was not considered a good omen. Could it have been the same with you and Dantarahma? Was he a ball who rolled away?"

The Voice did not reply for a long time, and Truth felt herself drifting into more normal dreams. She was leaping upon the back of a deer when the deer turned its head and spoke to her.

"The twins are not balls. They are two people, out of place, sad orphans, rejected by their kinfolk. Perhaps I wish you to find them because I feel pity for them. Your group is a mixed lot, not likely to judge on appearances alone. Perhaps that is all I wish."

"Hunt for your cubs yourself," Truth snarled, digging in her claws and feeling the hot blood well between her toes. "I am no one's dog."

"Certainly not! Why do you think I asked you to bring the wolves? They're closer to dogs than . . ."

Savagely, Truth bit down and broke the deer's neck at the base of the skull. The annoying Voice ceased speaking in mid-persuasion. Let him read omens in that!

⚛

ON THE SECOND DAY following the meeting with Layo, Harjeedian returned to camp, his expression somber as usual, but shining beneath the studied restraint was what Firekeeper knew was the pride of success.

"Petulia the daughter of Layo was a great help," Harjeedian began. "She has a great deal of organizational skill, and tremendous ability to retain information. It is a pity she feels the omens are directing her to follow the kidisdu's path. She would make a fine aridisdu."

Firekeeper glowered at him with what she hoped would be taken for pained restraint, not merely irritation.

"Give him his moment of glory," Blind Seer advised. *"His kind do not permit themselves a good howl—though I think it would do them good."*

Firekeeper agreed, and kept her peace. She had been busy pulling loose burrs and bits of bracken from Blind Seer's undercoat. He was meticulous about keeping himself clean, but there were things she could do more easily.

"And you have found?" Plik said, putting aside the book he had been reading. "Tell us!"

Firekeeper thought his eagerness genuine, but his manner of expressing it a bit feigned. It reminded her how pups would whine to get the adults of the pack to regurgitate after they returned from a hunt. Smiling inside, she added her own voice to the cry.

"Tell us! These two days I have wished myself able to read and write so I might be as useful to our cause as you are."

Harjeedian settled himself on his preferred campstool and accepted the cup of mint-laced fruit juice Derian poured for him. Truth had awakened, going as far as to roll up onto her breastbone to indicate her willingness to listen. The ravens, scenting news as a wolf might hot meat, glided down from their perch high above the meadow. Eshinarvash trotted in and lipped the grass at the edge of the pavilion.

Harjeedian looked around his assembled audience with satisfaction.

"The estate we seek is in the deep west, in the foothills of the mountains, in a broad plain cut by where the river comes from the heights. It is good land, very good. Significantly, the geographical surveys . . ." Harjeedian paused and inclined his head to Plik, indicating that the maimalodalu's suggestion had proven useful, ". . . note specifically that the land is low in iron ore."

Eshinarvash raised his head and snorted, *"Why does this matter?"*

Harjeedian answered as automatically as if he had actually understood the Wise Horse's words. "Iron seems to have dampened the effectiveness of magic, Eshinarvash. It could not prevent its use, but it did make it more difficult, rather as a muddy road is harder to travel than is a dry one."

Derian nodded. "There's some indications that the presence of lots of iron over a period of time might actually harm a sorcerer. Most of the lore has been lost in my homeland, but in New Kelvin the name given to what we called the Iron Mountains is the Death Touch Mountains."

"Here we simply called them the Barrier Range," Harjeedian said, "and it would be very nice to know if they are precisely the same range as those of which you speak."

"Maybe someday," Firekeeper said, "the yarimaimalom tell us; for now, does the name and nature of these matter?"

"I suppose not," Harjeedian agreed. "What does matter is that I have a fairly good idea where we must head next—assuming that we are correct in our assumption that the twins returned to make some effort to reclaim their family estate."

Firekeeper restrained herself from asking why the aridisdu did not check the omens. She knew he had attempted to do so, and found his deities unequivocally silent on the matter. In any case, her words would be nothing but mockery—and Harjeedian did not deserve such a reward for his labors.

Harjeedian went on to pull out maps and charts.

"These are not the originals, needless to say, but the archives were happy to loan me an apprentice cartographer to make swift copies. Petulia copied salient passages of verbal description while I read ahead."

He offered Plik, the only other member of the expedition who read Liglimosh fluently, his notes.

"Although this seems to have been a rural holding," Harjeedian continued, "even when the original owners were in residence, there also appears to have been a regularly traveled route between this city and the Setting Sun holdings. It was not paved or cobbled, nothing like that, but the route was marked with regularly spaced cairns. We should be able to locate these. A hundred years is a long enough time that we may find the road overgrown, but then again, we may not."

When Harjeedian seemed to be drawing to a conclusion, Firekeeper interrupted before he could start repeating himself.

"No matter how good are these notes and charts," she said, "it seems a long run—longer as we must bring the packs and horses. Eshinarvash will slow no one, but the other horses may do so."

She shrugged. "I think is best if we break into groups. I go ahead with some and find what is there. The rest follow more slowly. Eshinarvash will warn you of the night wanderers even as we would have done."

Bitter squawked, *"Even at your swiftest, wolf, you are slow. Lovable and I should go ahead of the rest. We can fly back and report to you, and even send someone back to inform the slowest goers. Plik can translate."*

"There is good thought in that," Firekeeper said, and she quickly explained what the raven had suggested.

"I think it's a good idea," Derian said. "I mean, it's not like the twins will expect anyone to follow them, and even if they do, they're going to be looking for their mother's kin, not wolves and ravens."

"Unless," Plik said, glancing over at the book he had been reading, "the Meddler somehow lets them know."

Everyone's gaze drifted momentarily to Truth, but the jaguar only stared at them with cool indifference. No one needed a translator to know she had said, "And how would I know?"

"Then we is decided?" Firekeeper asked. "We can leave nearly at once."

"It will be dark before long," Derian reminded her.

"I know," Firekeeper replied, "tonight we only need to run. We not need to look for cairns. The weather cools, but Blind Seer is still hot in the day. Travel by night would be best, and we are very, very well rested. By when we need to look for landmarks, from what Harjeedian say, we will be where is forest and cooler."

Derian nodded. "There's some sense in that."

Harjeedian inclined his head in solemn agreement. "Yes. I have noticed how Blind Seer has suffered—and admired his tenacity. Will the ravens also leave tonight?"

Lovable bounced. Bitter replied with a tipping forward of his body that Firekeeper was certain was meant to imitate Harjeedian's solemn nod.

"We will wait until morning," Bitter said. *"With our swift flight, we will certainly pass the wolves even with their head start."*

Firekeeper translated, then turned her attention to Truth.

"And you, Truth, do you go with us or remain with the humans?"

"I will remain with the humans," Truth said, *"and help Eshinarvash to guard them. Jaguars are not made to travel long distances afoot, chasing after herds as wolves do. We hunt our prey with cleverness, not by roaming all over the landscape."*

Firekeeper let the mild insult go unchallenged, not bothering to include it in the translation she supplied. Plik grinned at her, but didn't question her choice. Let him think she was practicing tact when in fact Firekeeper was quite happy with the idea that she would have the next several days alone with Blind Seer. Although they had been gone from Misheemnekuru for only a bit over a moonspan, it seemed much longer.

"Then we are decided?" she asked, rising to her feet.

"I suppose we are," Derian said. "You will take a canteen with you at least, won't you?"

"And a hatchet, and rope, and a few other useful things," Firekeeper promised. "I do not wish to be slowed where tools can help."

"Let me help you find what you'll need," Derian said.

Over where their packs had been stowed, they had some small amount of privacy. Derian rested his hand on Firekeeper's arm.

"You will be careful," he said. "Promise?"

"I promise," Firekeeper replied.

"No running off and forgetting that we need you?"

Firekeeper grinned at him. "Only running off, no forgetting. These twins is my hunt, too, remember."

She grew grave. "And you be careful, too. Stay near Eshinarvash and look for his signs. Prey creatures—though I not be first to call him so within reach of his teeth—they are even better than hunters at knowing when danger is about."

"I've noticed that," Derian said. "Tell me. Is Eshinarvash, well, enjoying this trip?"

"He is. He goes where his people have not gone for long years, and sees many things—and he also likes being admired."

"Who doesn't?" Derian laughed. "I know I find myself staring at him. Familiarity doesn't make him any less the finest horse I've ever seen."

"Let him know," Firekeeper advised. "Horses is herd animals, as wolves need pack. You stand off and stare, but remember, he is lonely some."

"I hadn't thought of that," Derian admitted. "I've been trying so hard not to be less than respectful . . ."

"You have proved respect," Firekeeper said. "Now show friendship. Plik, too. He not say, but I think he, too, is some small bit lost."

Derian looked at her. "You've changed, Firekeeper. Once you wouldn't have said any of this."

"Have I changed?" Firekeeper replied. "Maybe this world we think we know so well—both you and I—maybe it changed around us and now those things we think truth bend until we are not sure they are truth."

"Maybe both you *and* what we know have both changed," Derian said. "One thing is certain, though."

"What?"

"Your Pellish and your Liglimosh both have gotten better from steady use. Don't forget how to talk while you're away."

Firekeeper grinned at him. "I not."

While they talked, they had assembled the kit she wanted. Now Blind Seer surged to his feet. Bumping Derian with his head, he turned and padded toward the darkness.

Firekeeper ran eagerly after, but she paused long enough to wave good-bye.

XIII

THE PATTERNS OF THE STARS, the pathway of moon's pale sliver, the scents in the wind, and a dozen other small things guided Firekeeper and Blind Seer as they ran that night.

When morning came they located one of the cairns of which Harjeedian had spoken. The stones had been mortared together with an angular one set on the top pointing the direction. From the dead bracken—mostly vines—piled at the base, much more than one year's growth could account for, Firekeeper guessed that the twins, traveling this same route over a year before, had pulled living vines down to make sure of their path.

"Good," she said to Blind Seer, "the others will find their way better marked than I feared."

"The young growth has pushed up where the road once ran," the wolf replied. "Indeed, except where the deer have kept a trail clear, what was once a road is more tangled than the way to either side."

"Never mind that," Firekeeper said, hoping Blind Seer was not going to suggest they stop and clear away brush. "With Eshinarvash's help, Derian can easily get the horses and mules through."

They continued on, treasuring the coolness and planning to lie up when the sun rose high. Here and there they found a cairn, and pulled the vines free so that the bare stone would reassure their nose-dead human friends that they had passed this way.

A stream with some pretensions to being a river slowed them for a time.

What had been marked as a ford would no longer serve, the living water having shifted as water will over time—indeed, as it will from season to season.

They located a place where they could cross without difficulty, and where Firekeeper felt certain that Derian could get the horses across as well. While they were testing this, hoarse cries from overhead announced the passage of Bitter and Lovable heading west.

The ravens did not stop, and from this the wolves knew that the rest of the expedition must be on schedule. Had there been reason to expect delay, the ravens, great gossips that they were, would certainly have dropped down to gossip.

Firekeeper marked the ford as Race Forrester had taught her to do, slicing away a hand-sized swatch of bark from the trunks of a conspicuous tree or two, exposing the whiter wood below. No one had taught her to do what she did next, climbing into the tree boughs and cutting away some small branches to create a gap that would be obvious to those who flew above. She didn't blame Race for not teaching her this trick. He'd never had to blaze a trail for a bird.

At the next ford, the following day, she did the same, and when she joined Blind Seer she found the wolf a short distance away, snuffling the ground at the base of one of the cairns with audible intensity.

"What have you found?" she asked.

"Human scent," he replied. "Very faint. It is hard for me to believe that it might belong to those we seek. Were we not told they left Gak over a year ago?"

"So we were told," Firekeeper agreed, "but who is to say that they have not returned this way again?"

"True," Blind Seer said, "but I would wonder that any scent, even that of blood, would linger so long."

"Blood?" Firekeeper asked.

"So I said," the wolf said, stepping back and shaking, then turning to scrape dirt over the spot with stiff jerks of his paws. It was the action a wolf might take to cover the scent of a rival or invader into his territory, and Firekeeper found it unaccountably unsettling.

"Then there is our answer," Firekeeper said soothingly, leading the way along the trail. "The twins decided to return to the city, perhaps admitted that they had been impulsive or foolish. One was injured. We are a fair distance from the city, especially at the paces humans travel. Instead of continuing their journey to the city, they returned to their camp. When the injured one had healed . . ."

"Or died," Blind Seer muttered.

"They decided to remain, the momentary impulse to cowardice squelched."

"I suppose," Blind Seer admitted, "that is a possible explanation."

"Or," Firekeeper said, falling into the same game of supposition she so frequently found irritating in her human associates, "one twin wished to return and the other did not wish to return. They fought here, and the one who wished to remain won the battle and took the other back."

"That also makes sense," Blind Seer agreed, "but we will not know until we see with our own eyes. Shall we go on?"

Firekeeper nodded, picking up her pace. She was glad she had reassured Blind Seer enough that he was willing to continue forward, but she had to admit she shared his disquiet. There was something not right here, something that she had sensed almost as soon as her feet had touched the soil across the second stream, but for all she cast about, she could not discover what it was that troubled her.

The birds still sang their idiot songs announcing territorial claims or ritual challenge. Insects chirped and chittered their dry, late summer chants. Here, farther south as they had come, autumn was only beginning to make itself felt, and that mostly in cooler nights.

Squirrels could be seen in the tree branches above, darting about, filling their hoards, stopping to chatter impotent rage at the two passing below, secure in squirrelish certainty that nothing so large could reach so high.

Firekeeper thought it beneath her dignity to take out her bow and teach the rodents just how long her reach could be, but the thought amused her.

After fording the first stream, they had begun traveling more by daylight, making certain they did not lose the road. It was not that they needed the road themselves, but Firekeeper was very conscious of her promise to Derian that she would not simply run off, very conscious of her responsibility to scout for the more cumbersome group that followed.

It was as they were lying up during the hottest part of the day that Firekeeper became aware that Blind Seer was only dozing, his head thrown slightly back, his slit blue eyes studying the sky.

"What is it?" she asked.

"Those ravens," he said. "They should have passed this way on their return. I looked for them yesterday. They are swifter than we are, and can take their meals from almost anything. As I remember the map, we are a day or so's good running from this estate we seek. The ravens should have cleared the distance, seen what was to be seen, and returned to brag of their knowledge."

"Could they have missed us?" Firekeeper asked, apprehension twisting her gut most unpleasantly.

"We have kept near the road, dear heart," Blind Seer replied. "Those bright eyes would not miss us."

"Perhaps they went back to the others, wanting to fill them in on what they found."

"And not tell us first?" Blind Seer snorted. "When we will reach this 'Setting Sun' before the rest? Besides, ravens are too fond of telling a tale, especially one wherein they feature as the heroes. Lovable would need to tell you, even if only to hint at some pretty she wanted you to get for her. Bitter has too good an opinion of himself not to take the opportunity to share his discoveries with us. I fear something has happened to them."

"What could have happened?" Firekeeper asked.

"I saw you thinking about putting an arrow or so to the squirrels," Blind Seer said. "Perhaps one of the ravens has been shot. Humans are jealous of any who would share their crops this time of year—and the twins would be more protective of their own than is usual given that they cannot have any great stores set by."

"As was the case with the settlers at Bardenville," Firekeeper said. "Still, I cannot believe either Bitter or Lovable would have been so careless. They were with us when the Tower of Magic fell, and I know they are aware of the danger offered by arrows."

"Still, these yarimaimalom are accustomed to being privileged," Blind Seer said. "I have heard the ravens brag that farmers will let an entire flock forage rather than risk harming one of them. Might they have grown careless?"

"I suppose," Firekeeper said. "Let us tread carefully. Where there may be arrows for birds, there may also be snares and pits."

Blind Seer did not comment that he was always careful, Firekeeper noted. Rascal would have done so. Not too long ago, *she* would have done so.

Maybe Derian is right, she thought. *Maybe I have changed. Well, if I have done so, I think it is for the better—a little less puppy brash, a little more awareness that if a trap is laid then to be of any use it must also be well hidden.*

She thought of times past when others had paid the penalty for her actions.

Never again, and especially never when Blind Seer is the one who sheds blood for my foolishness.

They padded on then, sometimes side by side, sometimes in single file, sometimes splitting up, never outside of howling distance.

They found nothing, but time and time again, Blind Seer would raise his head and sniff the winds.

"Something isn't right here."

"SOMETHING ISN'T RIGHT HERE," Eshinarvash said to Plik and Truth.

Plik noticed that Derian glanced over, as if he was aware the Wise Horse had spoken, though there had been little enough for a human to detect.

"Is it anything about which I need to warn the humans?" Plik asked.

"Nothing specific," Eshinarvash replied. This time he raised his head, nostrils flared, seeking a scent that was apparently too faint for him to isolate. He shook his mane, shrugging his skin as if he felt flies.

There were no flies. The day was pleasant. The breeze was strong enough to keep the insects away without becoming an annoyance in itself. Earlier that day they had forded a stream at a point Firekeeper had marked.

"The stream is on the map," Harjeedian had said, as if this mention on a map drawn a hundred years or more ago made the waterway more real. "Some time tomorrow, if we progress with good speed, we will come upon another stream. Then, if I read the maps correctly, we will be within the outer territory associated with the Setting Sun estates. From what I can tell, it was wild land even then, but had Divine Retribution not swept the Old Country rulers away, we might today find a prosperous little town there."

They had yet to reach that second stream, and Plik sniffed, hoping for the scent of water and finding instead a faint trace of the "scent" that he had come to associate with magic. Could this be what was causing Eshinarvash's uneasiness?

Plik reminded himself that the Wise Horse was comparatively young. Eshinarvash probably had little training communicating his sensory impressions to other than the members of his herd.

"Tell me what has you unsettled," Plik said. Then he had another thought. *"Wait. Truth, have you sensed anything peculiar? Unsettling?"*

Truth replied with a candor Plik suspected she would not have used if the Royal Wolves had been present.

"I have been unsettled since I came to myself outside the silver block. Even the winds in the trees seem unsettling. I am learning to see without what had been more essential to me than my eyes—and I fear that this has blinded those eyes that remain to me."

The jaguar looked as apologetic as a jaguar could—which was not very much. *"I will see what I can sense, but first, Eshinarvash, tell us what you know."*

Eshinarvash nudged one of the spare riding horses that had decided it simply must sample some of the thick grass that had sprung up where the road had once been. His ears flicked back in reprimand, and the horse immediately decided it wasn't hungry after all.

"I have been looking for yarimaimalom," Eshinarvash said at last. *"I did not expect to find horses, not here, but surely there would be some Wise Beasts."*

Plik scratched where the brim of his hat irritated his scalp. He supposed he could do without the hat here. There were not likely to be many humans—if any at all—but he did like how the brim shaded his eyes.

"Are there yarimaimalom everywhere?" Plik asked. *"I had thought the majority dwelt on Misheemnekuru."*

"We have journeyed much farther south," Eshinarvash reminded him. *"Even if many from this area emigrated, more than a century has passed since the time of Divine Retribution. Plenty of time for the area's population to replenish."*

He nipped at one of the mules and went on, *"What troubles me is that initially I did see the occasional yarimaimalom. The presence of the stranger wolves and jaguar sent most prudently afield, but there were those whose curiosity brought them near, even if not to converse. There was a bear . . ."*

"I scented the bear," Truth said. *"And a family of otters skimmed away when I went fishing last night. I am sure that a hawk who paced us a while yesterday when the old road was more open to the sky was not Cousin-kin. You're right, Eshinarvash. These woods have been full of life, but today I have seen no sign of yarimaimalom."*

Plik scratched again and decided that the hat had to go for now. It was shady enough under the trees.

"Harjeedian," he said in Liglimosh, "how far away does your map say that second ford is?"

Harjeedian reached for the casing tubes and unrolled the appropriate map. Like Plik, he had become much easier in the saddle, and the cumbersome task gave him no trouble.

"Based upon the number of cairns we have passed," Harjeedian said, "we are closer to the second stream now than we are to the first ford. We may even reach the stream banks this evening, although I think we would be wise to wait to cross when we have good daylight."

"I agree," Derian said. "This string is just about the best behaved I've ever dealt with, but where the footing is bad even the best behaved horse or mule can twist a leg. I'd rather have good light, and leisure to lead the animals across one by one since the stream bottom is likely to provide chancy footing."

Plik nodded. "That seems wise to me. Thank you."

Derian fidgeted, then said, "Forgive me if I intrude, but I have had the sense you three have been discussing something for a while now. Is it anything we should know about? If it's some private matter, I apologize in advance for being nosy, but I'm getting worried. We haven't seen either of the ravens yet, and I would have thought at least one of them would have come back by now."

Plik frowned. He hadn't considered that the ravens were overdue, but then he hadn't really grasped the distances involved just from looking at the map. Since he had joined the expedition, they had crossed the equivalent of Misheemnekuru from island tip to island tip again and again. True, passage over these distances had been helped by good roads and strong riding animals. Even so, for one accustomed to traveling afoot on rather short legs, the journey had been enough to destroy his perspective regarding distance.

The raccoon-man glanced over at Eshinarvash and Truth. Seeing that neither seemed adverse to their speculations being shared with the two humans, Plik gave a quick summary—leaving out Truth's confession that she might not be being as much use as she might. He sensed the jaguar was grateful, but resolved that if her restraint seemed likely to put them all in danger, he would show no such consideration for her pride.

"No yarimaimalom," Harjeedian said when Plik concluded, "and only since this last day's passage. The open space of road Truth mentioned came earlier today. Ask Eshinarvash if he began to sense this wrongness before or after the sun was at its height?"

"*After,*" Eshinarvash replied. "*My kind are always alert to those who begin to come abroad when the sun westers. I think I was half listening for a local wolf pack or some great cat or even a fox who might tell us what to expect from the local Cousin-kind predators.*"

"Very strange," Derian agreed. "Tell me. Can any of you tell whether this region is the typical range of the yarimaimalom? I'd like to know if they have fled for some reason—perhaps our own approach—or whether they have been absent for some time."

"Some time," Eshinarvash said, and Truth gave tail-lashing agreement.

"As much as a year," Truth said. *"My kind marks its territory with claw marks to trees as well as scent. I have seen no recent marks, but thought nothing of it until Eshinarvash raised the matter."*

Plik thought that if she had been human, the jaguar would have shrugged.

"After all," Truth went on, *"my kind are solitary, and I am here, so I did not think to look for another."*

Plik translated, adding his own question: "So do we continue on, or do we try and find some of the locals and ask a few questions?"

"Continue," Derian said firmly. "Firekeeper and Blind Seer won't know if we stop. Certainly, the ravens will return soon, and we will be able to relay messages. Until then, I don't see why we should delay."

"Certainly," he says, Plik thought. *Why does that sound so much like "hopefully" to my ears?*

BLIND SEER REMAINED SO RESTLESS that the wolves cut short their midday rest and set off again, pacing themselves along the remnants of the road. They were seeing more signs now of the humans who had once inhabited this area: remnants of buildings fallen into ruin, tangled meadows that had once been cultivated fields, places where the road they now followed had been crossed by others. At each of these road junctures, a cairn stood.

"I suppose that years ago these rock heaps were marked in a fashion that meant something to those who lived here," Firekeeper said, as Blind Seer sniffed around the base.

"I suppose," the wolf agreed. "What I find strange is how few of the local beasts have marked these cairns. They would seem natural markers, being located as they are along what is still used as a trail. The Wise Beasts might even find humor in marking their territory where the humans have already done so."

"But you find no such signs," Firekeeper said, "and last night we heard no pack sing, though this would be good territory for a pack—especially if, as Harjeedian's maps told, there is an open plain not far ahead. This is more than a little strange. Shall we go back?"

"We go on," Blind Seer replied, setting action to word. "The others follow, and trust us to scout. We have little enough to report but conjecture and concern. Moreover, if something has happened to the ravens . . ."

"They trust we will follow," Firekeeper said, finding her feet had increased their pace of their own volition. "Suddenly, it is all I can do not to run."

BLIND SEER SCENTED THE OPEN AIR that heralded the promised plain shortly before a faint, hoarse cry led them to the ravens.

The wolves heard the call in the same breath, a harsh, rasping sound that came then faded, came again, faded and came again. It was as if the one making that sound had been calling for a long, long time, and would continue calling until breath and body parted company for all time.

"Over there," Firekeeper said, turning in the direction of the sound. "That thicket."

For a good time now they had noticed an increase in dense briars, both along the path and clustering between the trees. Such tangles were not uncommon in these southern woods, but the increase—and especially of this one type of plant—had been worthy of comment.

"Walk carefully, dear heart," Blind Seer cautioned. "Those plants know too well how to bite."

Firekeeper grunted agreement. The calloused bottoms of her feet were as tough as most shoe leather. She worried less about what she might step upon than what would grab hold of her exposed skin. Then she saw the ravens, and she forgot any worry for herself.

They perched high above the ground on the limb of an oak, the trunk of which was well-swaddled in the green briar. What was disturbing was that the limb in question was also well swaddled, the viney growth stretched out along it like some vegetable serpent. The ravens were caught within this serpent's coils. One about body and chest, the other encased to the head.

"I smell blood," Blind Seer said. "Fresh."

Firekeeper nodded, already assessing how she might climb that tree without leaving too much of her own blood behind. She didn't like how the ravens had been snared. They were too clever to have landed in this mess. How might they have been lured?

Now, however, was not the time for conjecture. The raven's call had been coming faint and fainter, still at those horribly regular intervals. Lovable, Firekeeper thought. She was the one caught only to her midsection. The other then, so horribly enshrouded, must be Bitter.

"Scout," Firekeeper said to Blind Seer. "I will see if I can get them free. You will be no help in that matter, but you can keep anything from coming upon us without us knowing."

"Take care," Blind Seer said, "as will I. We do no good for any if we lose both ourselves and the ravens in trying to set them free."

Firekeeper had located a broad section of tree branch, still thick with limp leaves. It looked to have been torn free from its parent plant during some summer thunderstorm. She lifted this and, balancing it against her shoulder, carried it to where she could use it to bridge the worst of the tangle at the oak tree's base.

This done, she ran across, taking her lessons from squirrel, who know better than to pause and let the bough dip and shake them off. Without waiting to think about how much this next step would hurt, Firekeeper embraced the tree trunk, leaping as high as she could above where the briars twined, and missing the thickest portion. Even so, the meeting of flesh and thorn hurt tremendously.

She had considered throwing her rope over the limb that held the ravens and climbing that way, but had not cared for how the jolting of her progress would affect the imprisoned birds. Nor had any other limb been low enough to provide her with a perch, for this oak was of the type that shed lower limbs in its climb to the light.

Now the wolf-woman went up, rough bark and sharp thorns tearing her, but she thought even then that the thorns were not as sharp as she had expected. They were green, as if newly grown, and bent a little, rather than piercing as deeply as they would when more mature.

Lovable had finally noticed Firekeeper's approach and her croaking cry broke its rhythm.

"Care," she said. "Take care. They cut and tear and move."

Firekeeper didn't spare word or breath to question this odd warning, but she did manage a small sound of reassurance before asking the question she had been dreading.

"Does Bitter live?"

"He lives," Lovable replied, "barely. I bite away the stems when they push too hard."

"Do you think you can fly?"

"If my wings were free, but I will not leave Bitter."

"No. I would not ask that. If I promise I will carry him with me?"

"Then I will fly."

Firekeeper was level with the branch on which the ravens were held, and now she drew her Fang. No need to creep out over thorns when she could cut them away. She could not cut out the entire mass, lest its falling weight drag the ravens with it, but at least she could remove a few sections.

She set to work, cutting not only the briar from its link to the root, but from its link to the part farther along the tree. The vine was fresh and stringy, slicing apart with relative ease. Firekeeper pushed the mass to the ground and slid out along the branch, keeping her weight flat and evenly dispersed. This brought her even with the cut end of the briar remaining along the branch, and in the sap she saw something that made her heart beat faster with horror.

Mostly the sap was a translucent liquid, not unlike what she had seen in other plants, but this held a thin thread as bright red as fresh blood. Indeed, Firekeeper did not need to have Blind Seer's sense of smell to feel certain that it was fresh blood—raven's blood, mingled just maybe with a trace of her own.

"Lovable," she said, "I am going to loose you first. When you fly free, make sure you go clear of the mass of vines at the base of this tree."

"I won't leave Bitter," came the querulous response. "I have sat beside him, biting the vines. I will not leave."

"You are between me and him," Firekeeper said. "Fly or I will throw you."

She heard a faint croak from within the shrouding tangle about Bitter. It sounded like "Fly . . ."

"I will fly," Lovable said.

Firekeeper cut away the briars, moving with surgical care so that she did not nick the raven beneath. Her task was made harder in that the vines had tightened, as if they would strangle what they could not pierce. More than once Firekeeper encountered cut ends, the vine above them still green but wilted, and surmised that Lovable had cut her own bonds as well as Bitter's.

But he must have been more tightly held. Firekeeper thought, *and could not break free—or perhaps he was badly injured. Lovable would not leave him, even though it meant remaining in pain and fear. She is more faithful and brave than ever I could imagine such a bubble head to be.*

When the last briar was loosened from around her, Lovable raised her wings. The action took tremendous effort. Firekeeper saw dots of blood, red-black against the battered plumage, red where they dripped and stained the bark. She could only guess at the raven's pain.

But pain or not, Lovable stayed true to her promise and half flew, half glided to safety, perching on a low shrub, well away from the briar oak. She was greeted by a low howl from Blind Seer, and Firekeeper, reassured that both were safe for now, turned her attention to Bitter.

The male raven was so wrapped in thorny vine that Firekeeper had to cut away several pieces before she could clearly see the bird beneath. What she saw made her retch, a slight, involuntary gag. The vines had cut deeply into Bitter's flesh, breaking the long feathers on wing and tail, pushing through the delicate ones closer to the body. Blood oozed from these cuts, but far worse was the damage done near to the head.

Bitter's eyes were squeezed shut, the baggy lids covering the orbs below, but Firekeeper felt certain that at least one of those eyes was ruined beyond saving. It seemed to indicate a horrid sense of humor on the part of the vines, to rip out the eyes of a raven, a creature renowned for dining on eyes.

"But only of the dead," Firekeeper muttered. "Only of the dead."

She worked carefully, remembering everything Doc had ever taught her about the treatment of wounds.

"Hurry, Firekeeper," Lovable croaked.

"Patience," Firekeeper said absently, her attention on Bitter.

There was a thorn rooting in toward the heart. She pulled it loose with great care, hoping she would not cut through any of the many blood carriers that nested near to this organ.

"Cut through the vines," Blind Seer suggested. "Remove their hooks when you are more safely on the ground."

Firekeeper didn't reply, but she thought his idea a good one. She had the most severely rooted out, and now she cut the others free a hand's width from Bitter's body. He neither moved nor made an sound, but his blood leaked like that of a living creature, and Firekeeper took faint comfort from that.

When she had him free, she tucked him inside her shirt so that she might have both hands for climbing.

When Derian gets here, she thought, *I can get a clean shirt from the packs. The reek of this one would frighten every game animal within a day's run.*

Then Firekeeper slid her way out toward the end of the branch, and when it dipped beneath her weight, she lowered herself very carefully to the ground, hardly jolting her passenger at all.

"There," she said with satisfaction. "Bitter lives, and perhaps will thrive once I get these thorns out of him."

Blind Seer canted his ears in approval. "Believe me, dear heart, I did not hurry you for no reason. Look, and see why Lovable and I were so impatient."

As Firekeeper looked back, she saw what the others had taken care not to tell her lest she be distracted from her task.

From the mass at the base of the oak tree, the briar stems were moving, putting out new vines, climbing up, slowly to be sure when measured by the speeds of the beasts, but with incredible speed for a plant.

XIV

"SHALL I TELL YOU what the others wish to know?" the Voice asked. "Shall I tell you where your companions are and what has become of them?"

Truth, dozing near the fire circle after another footsore day of travel, did not awaken, but she did reply.

"I am too tired for games," she said. "Tell me or do not tell me, as you wish."

"You are a contrary soul, Truth."

"I am who I am."

"You are less than who you were," the Voice replied.

"I am more than what I was. At least now I have body and spirit joined. This is a great improvement over the year and more I spent apart."

"But before then," the Voice prompted. "Can you truly say that you now are more than who you were then?"

Truth could not, so she did not. She wished the Voice would leave her alone. She did not care at all for the fashion in which it made her think.

"I am here," she said, then went on with more honesty than ever she would have when awake. "I am sane. Voice, I dread that bodilessness. I am not like you. I was born a creature of flesh and blood. Whatever other things I later attained, this came first. But can one such as you even understand?"

"One such as me?" The usual mockery was gone. If anything, the Voice sounded sad. "What do you think I am?"

"Plik tells tales of the Meddler," Truth responded. "He calls this Meddler a deity, and though Harjeedian may argue and theologize over precise definitions, I can smell his sweat. Harjeedian fears you so much because he fears that you are indeed a deity."

"I am . . ." The Voice fell silent in midphrase.

Truth, suddenly impatient, snarled, "Tell me this. One answer, straight and clear. No visions. No evasions. Are you indeed the one Plik names 'the Meddler'?"

"I have been called that name," the Voice replied. "Others have borne it, but, yes, fairly it is mine as well."

"So you are a deity."

"The one does not follow the other. You are called 'Truth,' but you are not 'truth,' nor are you the only one to have been so called."

"But you speak to me in dreams. You send visions. You are bodiless, formless. Do you deny this?"

"How can I deny what is evident? You chide me for telling you so little. Fine. Let me tell you more, but know this: I tell you not for your comfort, but as a challenge. Do you wish me to continue?"

Truth licked a dream paw with a dream tongue. Real tongue mimicked the motion, but she felt it not at all.

"Challenge?" she said. "Do you tell me that to make me back away?"

"I tell you," the Voice said, "because otherwise you will claim I tricked you. I will not have you weasel out that way."

"Weasel? I am a jaguar. We do not slide and slip. We stand and fight."

"So you take my challenge."

"I take your explanation. If that comes with a challenge, well, I will decide what to take and what to leave.

"Well enough. Then I tell you with no evasion, no prevarication, nothing but the absolute . . . truth."

Although there was no sound to herald it, Truth had the feeling the Voice was drawing in a deep breath. The jaguar waited, alert, listening, but otherwise not making his task any easier than she must.

"Like you I was born with a body," the Voice said. "You have called me 'Meddler,' and meddling was in my nature. I had power, too, and power combined with an optimistic spirit can be dangerous to the security of others. I made enemies. They imprisoned me."

"Why didn't they just kill you?"

"They did, after a fashion. They slew my body, but made sure my spirit would live on."

"Why not just kill you outright?"

"Because, like you, they had their suspicions that I might be a deity. Imprisoning deities . . . Well, that has a long tradition. Killing them, however, especially when you are mortal, even when you are sorcerers, that is something not to be done lightly."

"Sorcerers?" Truth licked her paw. "Yes. We suspected that. After all, the place where we found your buried lair was covered with their marks."

"I protested once before when you called that my lair," the Voice said reprovingly. "It was not my lair. It was my prison. It was the one place on all the great wide world where I could manifest my physical body, but those who so imprisoned me took care that I would not be able to use my power to do anything but survive. They left me the means of creating heat and light, but I must use power to do that. They left me books to read—many about my own past exploits, to mock me with my lost greatness."

Truth tried hard not to feel pity, for she knew pity was a great manipulator of other's emotions. The Meddler might as easily have been called the Manipulator, if the tales Plik had been telling them as they traveled were any indication. Even so, she could not help but feel a little pity.

"The only place you could manifest a body," she said. "Does that mean your spirit could roam freely?"

"No, it could not. My spirit was as bound as my body, but in many ways its imprisonment was far worse. At least my body could read or prepare food or bathe or even sleep. My spirit was bound in a restricted space about the size of that 'lair' you uncovered. It was lit in a pale silvery greyness, just enough to make it impossible for me to forget my limits, but not so bright as to be in the least cheering."

Truth did feel pity now. Her insanity had at least been interesting. Too interesting sometimes, but better than disembodied captivity.

"Did they mean to drive you mad?" she asked.

"I think they meant to drive me to suicide," the Voice said frankly. "They wanted my death, remember, but could not bring themselves to murder one they feared was divine."

Truth recalled something about which she had wondered.

"You must be a deity, to have lived so long. Divine Retribution chased the Old Country rulers from our land over a century ago. All the signs were that you had been buried far longer."

"Far longer indeed," the Voice agreed. "But I am neither divine nor immortal. In killing my mortal form, my enemies separated my spirit from the ruin that the passage of time makes on physical things. I have aged, but having no body to wear out, and having held on to my sanity thus far, I have not died."

"But you escaped that prison," Truth said. "Didn't you? How else would you have found me? How else would you have known something of what has gone on in what you term 'the great wide world'?"

"Clever, Truth. Yes. I did escape—a little—but that comes later. First there were long, long years during which I walked on the borderlands of madness and into the countries near death. I suspect there are times when I was truly insane, but I do not remember those times clearly, except as one remembers dreams—in fragments, out of order and incomplete."

The timber of the Voice changed, and Truth knew the challenge was at hand.

"But, Truth, I overcame this madness. I had been told how I might manifest a body for myself . . ."

"Who told you?" Truth asked.

"My enemies. After all, they wanted me dead, and how could I kill myself if I lacked a body?"

"Sensible. Cruel but sensible."

"Indeed. Maintaining that body was exhausting, though, and I soon realized that not only would I need to learn to live without a body, I would need to learn to thrive in that state."

Truth did not wait for the Voice to add whatever clever and cutting statement he undoubtedly had planned.

"And that is your challenge for me, is it not? You have risked insanity and overcome it, so I should prove I can do the same."

The Voice had the grace to sound a little ashamed.

"Something like that. Yes. That will do."

Truth huffed her breath out through her nostrils.

"Tell me how you came to escape your prison."

"It was not," the Voice said in tones of refreshing honesty, "completely by my own merit. I believe that what you call the Divine Retribution had a great deal to do with it. When people fear for their lives, suddenly, even an old enemy—especially one who is rather well known for taking things in hand . . ."

"For meddling," Truth growled.

"As you say," the Voice agreed cheerfully. "When people fear for their lives, even a Meddler looks good. Some came and made an effort to contact me. They did not free me—that would have come later—but they, let us call it 'opened a window' so that we might converse. While we were negotiating, some came who thought that treating with me was worse than the plague. These did their best to close that window, but before they could do so fully, they were interrupted."

"Interrupted?"

"Attacked, to be frank. Some died. Some fled. Some may have escaped back to the Old World. I don't know. What I do know is that the window was left open the merest sliver. That pretty much ended any inclination toward suicide on my part. I spent years, decades, sliding that window open enough that I could get a look outside my prison. As you can imagine, I found the world much changed. I also learned that I was still firmly tethered to my prison. As entertainment to fill my lonely hours, I took to looking out that partially open window and . . ."

"And you started meddling again," Truth said. She couldn't manage a growl. Could she blame the Voice for his actions? Could she say that she herself would have acted any differently?

"I did," the Voice agreed. "My first thought was that sorcery had imprisoned me, so I needed sorcerers to free me. Unfortunately, there didn't seem to be any in the immediate vicinity.

"Here and there I found those who were attempting to resurrect the art, but they were like children who have found their father's bow and a quiver of arrows. They have some idea how the device should work, but they lack the strength to string the darn thing, much less knowledge as to how to fit the arrow and make it fly."

"And you set out to teach archery," Truth said, "to Dantarahma, and to this Melina and this Valora of whom the others tell, and to these twins."

"Well, yes."

"And me? How do I fit in this?" Truth felt the prickle of her hackles rising, her tail lashing, and wondered if she did this in body as well as spirit. "As we know, two of your students were willing to commit murder. We'll never know what Valora would have done—and you've been very cautious about your intention for the twins."

"Well, they . . ."

"No!" Truth roared. "No evasions. What did you intend for me?"

"Why the same as for the others, good Truth. I saw the potential in your situation."

"For sorcery?"

"Not quite. For untapped potential. I also saw something else."

"What?"

"Remember that window I mentioned?"

"Yes."

"When your friends opened the door for you, they finished opening the window for me. My range is still limited. I have a lot of learning to do, but I am managing much better. How do you think I can talk with you so easily now, with your body and soul together and you so dreadfully sane?"

Truth lashed out, why and at what, later she was not sure, but the violence of the motion brought her to full wakefulness. Upon awakening, she noticed immediately that her body no longer lay where she had gone to sleep. She hadn't moved far, but was outside of the camp, and could hear Eshinarvash stamping his awareness that something was new in his surroundings.

Truth called to the horse, "It's just me. I had a nightmare, and am going to run it off."

The Wise Horse settled. "Bad things, nightmares. Good hunting, then."

Truth's paws remained sore, so instead of hunting, she found herself a tree and hung over a branch, trying to make sense of what had happened. The Voice had seemed honest, but the more he told her, the more she feared him. The more she feared him, the more she hated him for making her his tool.

So unsettled was Truth that the stars had moved visibly in their nightly dance before she realized that whatever it was the Meddler had intended to tell her regarding their missing companions had been forgotten by them both.

Or had that merely been bait to make her listen to him?

Truth shook her head so hard that her small round ears rattled like leaves on a gale shaken tree.

Bait. That's what it had been. Bait. Bait to make her go and do what she didn't wish to do. Bait to make her take up his challenge. She wouldn't take it.

Truth shook her head again, seeking to dislodge an uncomfortable feeling, as if with mere motion she could assure herself that the secure join of body and spirit would never be threatened again.

THEY HAD RETREATED north and east, Firekeeper cradling Bitter in her arms, Lovable riding on Blind Seer's back. Beneath the dense forest foliage, color was giving way to shadow with the coming of evening.

"We must warn the others about these creeping briars," Blind Seer said.

"Yes," Firekeeper agreed, "but the ravens cannot be moved quickly. Bitter is gravely wounded."

"My nose tells me you are not merely trying to save yourself what will be a hard run," Blind Seer said, but the cant of his ears and tail failed to transmit the humor of his words. "Let us find you someplace secure. Then I will run as fast as these four feet can carry me. If the others have kept the trail, with Plik there to translate my message for me (you really should have learned to write, Firekeeper), I should be back to you before the next sunset."

Firekeeper nodded. She didn't question why Blind Seer wanted to find her some sort of lair. He would not be the only hunter with a nose sharp enough to scent injury and pain. No predator hunted what would fight when that which would not was easily found.

Lovable might not be able to do more than glide, but her alert memory recalled what she and Bitter had noted during their earlier passage. She directed them toward the ruins of a one-roomed stone structure standing alone in a small clearing that showed ample sign of grazers and browsers both. The stone of the house was thick with honeysuckle vine, but there was no trace of the hook-thorned briar. The few trees were slim saplings that might be eaten by the deer this coming winter.

"The walls are thick and high," Blind Seer said with satisfaction as he sniffed about the structure for sign that any other laired within it. "You can guard the hole where the door once was."

Firekeeper nodded. "And what there is of a roof looks stable enough not to fall—at least not tonight—and nothing larger than a squirrel would trust itself to that shaky bridge. I can block the window holes with dead wood. They were never large to begin with."

"And don't forget fire," Blind Seer said. "Fire will do you more good than all the rest together."

"I won't forget," Firekeeper promised. "I could as soon forget my name."

Lovable hopped from Blind Seer's back and walked stiffly to where Firekeeper had set Bitter on the duff-covered floor of the stone house. Blind Seer looked at Firekeeper.

"Would you have me stay until your fire is kindled?"

Firekeeper knelt so she might embrace him around his neck. Holding him tightly, she spoke into the thickness of his fur.

"I kindled fires before you were born, Blue-Eyes. Go. I'll be fine, but hurry back. Harjeedian may be able to send something to help Bitter—and I will miss you."

Blind Seer licked the side of her face, then he shook himself free from her hold. He stood for a moment, staring at her. Then he turned away. Swift and silent as the approaching night, he was gone.

FIREKEEPER PREPARED THE FIRE FIRST, building it within the shelter of the stone house. She considered building another outside, but the light would ruin her night vision, so she decided to do without.

As the fire was catching, Firekeeper alternated between feeding the growing flame and dripping water into Bitter's beak. The raven swallowed, which she took as a good sign. His wounds no longer bled freely, and though she longed to wash them she did not. Doc had taught her a clean wound healed best, but Firekeeper feared that even gentle tending would start fresh bleeding.

Lovable watched these tendings with anxious alertness. In the firelight, Firekeeper could see anew how battered Lovable was. She had thought to ask the raven to sit watch above the lintel, but now she knew the raven needed sleep as desperately as did her mate.

"I'll make Bitter a sort of nest," Firekeeper said, "close enough to the fire for the warmth, but not too close. Will you sit with him? I think even in his sleep your scent would be a comfort to him."

Lovable agreed, hopping to the assigned place and settling in as if she were brooding her eggs. Firekeeper left long enough to fetch fresh water from a spring to the rear of the house. The area surrounding the spring showed some signs of human adaptation. Firekeeper suspected that the spring was why the house was here, and why the forest denizens still frequented the area. Otherwise, the stone house would likely have been covered by vines and growing things, visible only in winter when the leaves died back, and then only as a shapeless mass suggesting something large beneath.

She scrubbed blood and sap from her skin, and set snares in the surrounding tangle. Bitter had swallowed water. He would probably get even more benefit from blood. For that matter, Lovable could probably use a solid meal—and so could Firekeeper herself.

Firekeeper ranged just a little farther in case the scent of fire drove away the small game that certainly lived in this area. She set a few more snares, silently thanking Race Forester for his teaching. Her childhood would have been much easier if she had known more about such things.

Then she hurried back to the stone house. Lovable was alert and watchful. Once again Firekeeper found herself amazed at the tenacious spirit housed within one she had liked, but had always thought rather frivolous. Most who knew the ravens thought that Bitter had been drawn to Lovable as an antidote to his own somber personality. Now Firekeeper was suspecting Bitter had known of his mate's inner strengths as well.

Never going too far from the stone house, Firekeeper built up a supply of wood for the fire, both green to feed it slowly and dry for light without smoke. She blocked the window apertures. In her wood gathering, she uncovered any manner of bugs and grubs. Some of the fatter ones she ate, for hers would be a long night's watch. Most she gave to Lovable. They both agreed that Bitter was not ready to eat anything so solid.

Before Firekeeper had completed her self-assigned tasks, evening had given way to night. She checked her snares and found a rabbit in one. Bitter swallowed the still warm blood. Lovable and Firekeeper split the rest, the raven eating the viscera, the wolf-woman the flesh.

Yet although food, fire, and some promise that her patients were not losing ground should have been a comfort, as the night drew on, Firekeeper felt increasingly tense and apprehensive. She sat outside the doorway where her shadowed form would blend into the stone and listened, her bow against her knees, her quiver close to hand.

From time to time she rose and patrolled the vicinity, telling herself that she must not fall asleep, that she must not let her muscles grow stiff from immobility, knowing that she was searching for something, though she knew not what. Blind Seer would not return this night. She couldn't be listening for his return, so for what was she watching?

During one of her turns inside to feed the fire, Firekeeper arranged the wood so that embers, not flames would result. She went to check on the ravens while her eyes adjusted again to darkness. Bitter seemed to be resting easily— or more easily than before. Lovable was awake, alert, and glad for the water Firekeeper poured for her. Bitter accepted more water, but did not appear to fully waken.

"You're restless," Lovable said as Firekeeper was making Bitter comfortable in his makeshift nest. "The feeling belongs to this land. Restless. We felt it in the warm air that lifted us over the fields, but we saw nothing. We thought that full night would show something. Humans make lights, you know."

Firekeeper thought of her redly glowing fire. "I know."

"We went to rest in a tree. You know what happened."

"So you saw nothing."

"Nothing but grass, scattered trees, insects, birds. All the something that is nothing when you are looking for more."

Firekeeper placed a bent finger against her lips and bit down gently, as if the mild pain would clear her thoughts.

"But there *is* something," she said.

"We thought so. You think so."

Firekeeper reached and gently sleeked down the raven's feathers. "Thank you. I was wondering if I was overtired, imagining enemies as a puppy stalks his own tail."

"I don't think you are," Lovable said, stroking Firekeeper's hand with her heavy beak. "I know we weren't."

"Good."

Firekeeper went back to her post alongside the door. She settled in, leaning back against the solid wall, allowing her gaze to unfocus into watchfulness, comparing almost unconsciously features seen before with what she saw now. She stiffened. Something had changed.

The moon was nearly gone, a thin sliver that gave no light. In contrast, the stars were brilliant against the pure blackness of the sky. It was in the patterns of shadow and shape against this star-filled backdrop that Firekeeper detected change.

The stone house stood in a small clearing. Early in her vigil Firekeeper had memorized the shapes that the surrounding trees made against the sky. None of these had changed, yet there was something, something new: new shapes in the foreground, things approaching with such infinite slowness that had she not looked carefully, had she not had eyes trained to see dark against darkness, they would have been invisible to her.

Moving very slowly, Firekeeper strung her bow, fit arrow to string, and aimed at the nearest of these shapes. She longed for a proper wolf's sense of smell. Try as she could, all she scented were the blended scents of late summer vegetation dominated by the sweet perfume of honeysuckle. There was no rank scent as of the great cats, none of the sweet mustiness of bear, none of the clean, bright smell of wolf.

Yet the shapes that moved in the darkness were of that size. That one seemed almost a bear raised on hind legs, shuffling slowly forward. That one seemed a great cat, a jaguar, perhaps, its head too heavy, body too stocky to be a puma. Surely those three on the far left were wolves, the lean, beloved lines heart-twistingly familiar.

Firekeeper wanted to scream out loud, to howl her fear and frustration to the skies, but she ground her teeth together and swallowed the sound. The only fit reason for howling was when a pack mate might hear. Here she was alone but for two birds, neither of whom would be any help against opponents of such size.

Her own best choice would be to slay one or more of these opponents without warning. Like most wolves, Firekeeper was without false modesty. She knew she was very good with a bow. Even in this light, she could probably take out at least two before the others moved.

Practicality suggested that the wolves would be her best targets. Bear were notoriously hard to kill. She had never hunted great cats. She had never hunted wolves either, but she had grown up among them, wrestled with them, slept beside them, tended them as puppies, and nursed them as injured adults. She knew their vulnerabilities better than those of any other creature—except, possibly, for humans.

Firekeeper stood frozen, bowstring digging into her fingers, the dull ache a reminder that she must either loose or relax the pull. She raised the bow, aimed at the foremost of the three wolf-like shapes, and knew that she could not fire without warning into those so like her kin.

"Hie!" she said, normal speaking tones like a shout against the routine noises of the night. The insects and night birds that to this point had not ceased their chittering fell silent.

"Hie!" Firekeeper said, the sound sharper now, between yap and howl. "Who are you?"

Her only response came from within the stone house.

Lovable squawked, "What is it?" Then she screamed, "Snake!"

Firekeeper's held arrow loosed as of its own choice, thudding into the throat of the foremost wolf. The creature made no sound, no cry of pain, nor did it fall.

Firekeeper stared a moment longer. Then she fell back. There was confused motion from the right side of the house where she had made the ravens their nest. Lovable was flapping her wings and squalling something about snakes. Firekeeper now trusted the raven's good sense far too much to think she was hallucinating, living out in dreams some portion of the previous night's captivity on the tree limb.

Light would be an asset now, light and fire. Firekeeper stumbled back.

Dropping her bow, she grabbed one of the many sticks she had set at the edge of the coals, knots of pine that would serve as torches. Her motion dropped loose wood into the coals and they flared. In the brilliant orange-yellow light, Firekeeper saw the face of their enemy.

Except the enemy had no face, nor eyes, only shape.

With the first flare of light, Firekeeper wheeled to see what Lovable was screaming about. The raven was half-aloft, beating with her wings, tearing with her beak at a shape that did indeed resemble a snake. This snake, however, was made of twisted vines, the blood-drinking briar snaking through ropes of honeysuckle.

Where the head should be was a dense mass of vines, twisted thickly enough to be solid. This swung at Lovable like a club, moving slowly enough that the raven could easily have dodged it, but that she was determined not to leave Bitter's side.

Bitter remained in the nest Firekeeper had built for him. His one eye was open, but clearly he was too weak to do any more than watch the horror attacking his mate. He could not even move away from the tendrils of briar that were sliding from the greater mass, sliding wormlike to fasten in his flesh once more.

Unlike a human, Firekeeper did not think about the impossibility of something happening in front of her eyes. Instead she leapt forward, swinging the torch in her hand, smoke stinging her eyes, tears blurring her vision. She contacted hard with the body of the snake. Sparks flew, singeing her skin, landing in her hair.

She did not pause to beat them out, knowing they should gutter on their own, but swung again and again with her torch. The twisted mass of vines turned its questing head from Lovable to Firekeeper, and then Firekeeper gripped it firmly with her free hand.

The thing was more honeysuckle than briar or she might not have been able to grab hold. Even so, the thorns cut into her flesh, and Firekeeper imagined she could feel the vine gaining strength from her blood.

"Eat while you can!" she howled, hauling the mass toward the fire. She thrust it head first into the bed of coals and had the satisfaction of seeing it begin to smoke, then catch fire. She placed a foot upon its back lest it pull out, forcing more and more of its length into the fire.

The stone house was becoming uncomfortably smokey now, and Firekeeper tensed, some buried memory reminding her that smoke could be as dangerous as fire. Moreover, she had not cleared away many years of accumulated leaf litter within the ruined hut. Quite likely the fire would spread to fill the interior. When it did, the remaining roof would not last long.

"Lovable, can you move?"

"Not without Bitter!"

"I'll carry him," Firekeeper promised. Bending quickly, she retrieved her bow and threw it over the wall. If she lived, she would find it later. For now she needed the torch more—and a free hand to carry Bitter.

The raven's one eye held stoic understanding as she scooped him up. Lovable flapped and landed on Firekeeper's shoulder.

"I cannot fly," she said, "nor walk fast enough."

Firekeeper replied by moving, adjusting her balance to her dual burden. Now she thought she understood the lack of scent from those who had stalked the stone house. Like the snake, they must be made from plants. Would the fire and the fate of their comrade have frightened them away?

Wolves do not count on dreams to catch their dinner, so Firekeeper was not dismayed when she saw the shapes remained. As the fire within the stone house consumed the snake, it spread to the gathered wood. Consequently, Firekeeper hardly needed the torch—at least not to see.

The creatures remained, but as seen in brighter light their resemblance to wolves, jaguar, and bear became cloud-shape fantasies. Thickly packed greenery created their forms. The hook-thorned briar was woven throughout, moving frantic tendrils as if urging these odd steeds to greater motion.

The monstrosities did move a bit faster, but even so Firekeeper was swifter. Had it not been for the two ravens, she could have easily outdistanced them.

But then if it were not for Bitter and Lovable, I would not be here. Or perhaps it would have been myself and Blind Seer who were strangled as we slept.

Firekeeper retreated to the spring and set Bitter on a shelf of rock that some human had doubtless made to hold his things clear of the dampness in the ground. Lovable fluttered down to stand beside Bitter, and Firekeeper ran back at the briar beasts.

These were more sophisticated than the snake had been. The bear had paws with which to swipe. These were tipped with claws that resembled curving briar thorns as long as the longest finger on Firekeeper's hand. The bear's jaws gaped, but instead of teeth its mouth was lined with briar thorn so tightly packed that Firekeeper was reminded of the teeth of a shark.

The jaguar also had claws and fangs. The wolves had to settle for fangs, but their motion was the smoothest and swiftest of the lot. The bear lumbered in an awkward two-legged gait. The jaguar crept, belly-close to the ground, as if it had forgotten that the time for secrecy was past, but the wolves loped forward, their pace nothing like that of real wolves, but equivalent to that of a walking man.

The lead wolf had an arrow sticking out from its throat, and Firekeeper did not need to look at the fletching to know her shot had gone home.

None of these monstrosities were swift, nor did they seem to have much purpose beyond attacking Firekeeper and her charges, but to this purpose they kept with terrible deliberateness. They advanced on the wolf-woman paws swiping, jaws snapping in a parody of lifelike motion.

Firekeeper held her smouldering torch in one hand, all too aware that it was beginning to gutter, that the fire raging in the stone house would not last much longer.

Then the first of the wolves surprised her by leaping, almost as a real wolf would have done. Firekeeper fell back, her feet going out from under her. She landed hard, kicking up, knowing if she failed, Blind Seer would return to find three tortured bodies drained of blood, and maybe, for plants were very thorough, not even that.

XV

"YOU HAVE CALLED ME 'MEDDLER,'" the Voice said. "Tell me, is that bad?"

Truth growled. "Is not once a night enough for you to torment me?"

"I left without telling you what I came to ask. I meant to ask you if you wanted to know what has happened to your friends. Now I am back to ask what would you give to have me meddle on their behalf."

"Give? Their behalf? Riddles!"

"Let me be direct then. Three of your friends are in grave danger. Without assistance, I would wager that one alone may survive to speak with you again."

"One?"

"The raven called Lovable. Her mate Bitter would surely not survive the night. And Firekeeper . . . She could survive, but she will not leave them undefended."

"What of Blind Seer?" Truth realized that she felt fear and sorrow that the blue-eyed wolf might be dead. "He would not leave Firekeeper in danger."

"Nor would they leave you and those with you to come unwarned into danger. Someone had to carry the message. For now Blind Seer runs free and fast. You should see him by dawn. By then it will be too late for any of you to help the other three."

"You said you would meddle on their behalf."

"I did, but I also asked what you would give me to do so."

Truth's ears folded flat to her skull and she snarled, but the memory of what she had felt when she thought Blind Seer already slain was too fresh for her to deny how she would feel if the other three perished and she might have helped.

"What is the price of your meddling?"

"Come with me, half into madness if you must, but take back your heritage—and possibly more."

"Done. If those three live come morning and if there is evidence to my eyes and ears that you have aided them, then I will let you put a collar about my neck and lead me where otherwise I would not go."

"Done," the Meddler replied. "And done. Will you keep your promise, I wonder, or will you try and say I have not proved my aid to your friends sufficiently for your taste?"

"I will keep my promise, never fear, but Firekeeper is very brave and very strong. She might win this battle on her own, and I would not be bound to you if so."

The Meddler laughed. "That Firekeeper is different, isn't she? Heart in one world, body in another—rather like a certain jaguar."

Truth could not deny the truth of this. As she felt the Meddler fading from her dreams she called after him.

"Tell me, now that you have had your meddling with me, would you have acted to save the others without my making a bargain with you?"

"Oh . . . I might have intervened anyhow. That Firekeeper interests me a great deal. It would be a pity to have her die before I could have opportunity to know her better."

FIREKEEPER KICKED OUT WITH HER FEET and caught the leaping wolf directly in the belly when it would have landed on her. The briar thorns could not harm her calloused soles, thus the monstrosity received the full force of her blow. She flung the wolf back over her body and had the satisfaction of seeing it fly through the doorway into the stone house. There was a red glow, followed by a whiter flash as the "wolf" fed the inferno within.

Unlike real wolves, which either would have paused to assess the changed situation or rushed to take advantage of a downed opponent, the two remaining "wolves" merely continued their slow movement forward—as did the bear and the jaguar.

Firekeeper retrieved her fallen torch. One end smouldered red and hot. Darting forward and to one side, she thrust it directly into the midsection of the bear. The vines and wood from which it had been crafted were green, but the leaves began to smoke, the smaller twigs to catch fire.

Unfortunately for Firekeeper, the bear did not seem to realize its own danger. It continued shuffling toward her, arms opening and closing as it sought blindly to grasp her in a classic bear hug. As the jaguar and wolves continued their own slow advances, Firekeeper realized she was in grave danger of becoming trapped between the briar creations and the fire-filled stone house.

With the new infusion of fuel, the fire burned hot enough that some of the stones popped and cracked. Heat welled forth, a physical force pushing against Firekeeper's back. If she were to go much closer, she risked the cotton of her shirt catching fire.

So far she had been lucky. When the roof had caught, it had collapsed inward. The enclosing walls of the stone house were acting like a chimney, sending all but a few licks of flame upward. Were the wind to shift, though, the fire might escape. The four remaining "beasts" would be little enough threat in the midst of a forest fire.

Best then not to feed that fire further, but what could she do? Her Fang could not cut those creatures apart fast enough. Her hatchet still hung at her belt, but it was a little thing, about the length of her forearm—a tool, not a weapon.

"Feeling hedged in?" a sardonic voice asked.

The Voice seemed to come both from somewhere behind her, perhaps a bit to the right, and inside her head. Firekeeper started to turn and the jaguar, passive to this point, reared on its hind legs and struck with a thorn-tipped paw. It caught Firekeeper on the left upper arm, drawing blood.

Unlike a real jaguar, the monstrosity did not follow up the strike, nor leap back. Instead it stood there, claws anchored in the flesh of Firekeeper's arm. The pain was sharp, then Firekeeper hardly felt it at all. She lashed out with her Fang, catching the jaguar along the side of its head and tearing up, trying to cut as many vines as possible. She doubted these monstrosities had brains as such, but even plants died when you cut them from their roots.

She tried hard not to think how long it took some downed trees to wilt.

The Voice spoke again. "Don't waste your time on that! Get the claw out of your arm. The briars anesthesize you so you don't feel the pain."

Firekeeper suddenly understood how Bitter could have sat still while being slowly mutilated. She ripped the jaguar's paw from her arm. The jaguar dropped to all four paws and moved to clamp her jaws around Firekeeper's thigh. Firekeeper brought her knee up, pushing the head back.

"I suggest," the Voice said, "you grab hold and shove it past you into the fire. Otherwise it's just going to keep coming."

"Forest fire," Firekeeper gasped. She had no idea who was talking to her, but right now she wasn't going to waste breath asking. This close to the stone house, smoke was making breathing difficult enough.

"The wind won't change or rise. I've seen to that."

Firekeeper decided to trust that odd assertion. She grabbed the jaguar on the head, her fingers catching with peculiar painlessness on the thorns. When she had a solid hold, Firekeeper dragged the thing forward, pulling, then pushing it through the doorway of the stone house. She was helped by the fact that the jaguar never once seemed to realize its danger. It kept tearing at her, but as Firekeeper did her best to keep its head and paws below her waist level, the leather trousers she wore kept most of the thorns from cutting through.

As she did this the Voice spoke again. "Now, I can help with the others. You've already done for the bear. It just doesn't know it. The wolves . . ."

In the brighter light as the jaguar caught fire, Firekeeper looked at the wolves and saw they looked somehow furrier. Wiping her streaming eyes, she saw why. The briars were writhing, unweaving themselves from the other materials from which the wolves were made.

Pulling her hatchet from her belt, Firekeeper darted forward and started chopping. The image of the snake was vivid in her imagination, and she didn't like the idea that these briars might work themselves free and create other monsters. Even a few steps gave relief from the raging heat of the stone house, and she set about her task with renewed vigor.

Dead wood and vine soon littered the ground around her, yet the briars did not drop to the ground and lie still as they should have done. Pieces clawed at her lower body, but her feet were tough and the fabric of her trousers protected her from most injury. Usually, after a few moments, the briar fragments too would lie still. Only those that drew blood persisted, and Firekeeper took care to pull these loose and toss them into the fire.

Once, when chopping through a particularly thick section of briar, she glanced over at the "bear." It had stopped moving and was now clawing at the smouldering mass that was spreading through its interior. The mass wasn't precisely catching fire, but the bear certainly wasn't going anywhere, nor did it seem to offer a particular danger to its surroundings.

The Voice did not speak while Firekeeper dismembered the wolves and tossed the pieces into the interior of the stone house. The bear didn't seem to notice her when she came near it, so she moved behind it and with weary persistence pushed it directly through the doorway.

Firekeeper wanted to collapse and assess her wounds, but even more she needed water to cool her throat and rinse her eyes. She needed to check on the ravens, too. What if there had been another snake?

But she found Bitter and Lovable well and safe where she had left them—or at least as well and safe as could be expected. Lovable was agitated. Bitter had fallen into a shocky stupor, but he was still breathing and there was no rattling to the sound.

Firekeeper applied a wet compress where the jaguar had clawed her arm. The numbness was fading, and the pain that followed was sufficiently severe that Firekeeper almost wished for a piece of fresh briar so she could numb it again.

Almost. Whenever she remembered the thin thread of blood running through the plant's sap, she shuddered and wished instead that she might never see another such plant again.

The Voice spoke again as the fire within the stone house was burning out and a certain freshness in the air suggested that dawn might be approaching.

"Tell Truth I kept my part of the bargain," it said.

Firekeeper felt a dreadful certainty who her ally might be, and she wondered if she might have done better to lose this fight. She kept her thoughts to herself, but answered as politely as she would the One of some great pack.

"May I know what to call you?" she asked.

"Truth thinks of me as the Voice," he replied, "but you have heard a different name for me. I am the Meddler. Or a Meddler . . ."

"Where are you?" Lovable croaked, reassuring Firekeeper that this was no hallucination brought on from having her blood drunk and replaced with briar poison.

"I am here," the Meddler replied. "Look at the stone house."

Firekeeper did, and drew her breath in so sharply through her smoke ravaged throat that she started coughing. Against the stone backdrop a figure was taking shape. It was tall as a man and shaped roughly so, but her eyes must have been watering for it seemed to her that the head could not decide how it should be shaped. The image shifted between that of a stern-featured man with iron grey hair and that of a handsome, amber-eyed wolf.

DERIAN THOUGHT HE'D BEEN HARDENED to surprise since the day he had ridden west with Earl Kestrel's expedition, but he never imagined that he'd be riding horseback with a wolf in his lap.

Blind Seer had come running up to intercept them shortly after they had crossed the second ford. That he was close to exhaustion was obvious. His flanks were heaving. Foam frothed around his mouth. When the group reined in their panicked mounts, Blind Seer collapsed in a heap on the ground. Even so, from how Plik reacted, the wolf was clearly giving some sort of report.

"Blind Seer says," Plik translated after a moment, "that he and Firekeeper found the ravens late yesterday afternoon. Bitter and Lovable were in very bad shape, and Firekeeper remained behind to protect them while Blind Seer came to warn us, lest we fall into similar harm."

Plik then went on to tell, with admirable concision given the peculiarity of the tale, how the ravens had come to harm. As he concluded, Blind Seer struggled back on to his feet. Derian noticed with nauseated fascination that the wolf's pads left red stains on the leaves. No wonder, if Blind Seer and Firekeeper had pressed west most of the day before, and then the wolf had retraced their day's travel and more.

Limping and showing a tendency to favor his right front paw, Blind Seer moved to the lead and began heading back from where he had come.

"Hey!" Derian called. "Stop. You need something to eat, and someone should look at your feet."

Blind Seer turned his head to look back, and Derian didn't really need Plik's translation.

"I have left my Firekeeper alone in forests stranger than we have ever seen. I will not leave her any longer than I must."

"You'll do her scant good," Derian protested, sliding from Prahini's saddle and striding toward the wolf, "if you collapse from exhaustion. Be reasonable!"

Blind Seer growled, but from the cant of his tail Derian thought the wolf knew he was right.

"Look," Derian went on, "you don't handle heat well, and today's only going to get hotter. You're already dehydrated."

Blind Seer's tail drooped, then, incongruously rose to what Derian thought was an optimistic angle. A moment later, Derian smelled horse and felt a velvet nose nuzzle his neck. He looked up and found Eshinarvash towering over him looking quizzically at the wolf.

The Wise Horse's ears were slightly back, but when he shook his head and shivered his skin, Derian had the feeling he was indicating distaste rather than anger or fear.

"Plik?" Derian said. "Is Eshinarvash suggesting what I think he is?"

Plik nodded. "He is. If Eshinarvash carries Blind Seer that certainly would solve both of Blind Seer's problems. Can you rig something so the wolf doesn't tear up Eshinarvash's back? As Truth has just so kindly reminded us all, wolves lack the ability to retract their claws."

"I can try," Derian said, already mentally sketching out alternatives. "Blind Seer, go lie down in some shade and let Harjeedian look at your feet. This is going to take a minute."

The wolf agreed and Harjeedian, who had been trying very hard to maintain his usual dignified air of superiority, dismounted and rummaged in his saddlebags for salve.

Shortly thereafter they were back on the trail. Blind Seer had not proven able to stay even on Eshinarvash's broad back—at least not without using more effort than he would have done when running. Eshinarvash himself had suggested their current arrangement: Derian astride, somewhat farther back from the withers than he would usually ride, Blind Seer draped horizontally partially across the horse, enough in Derian's lap that Derian could steady him if needed.

So situated, they made good progress. They paused as infrequently as possible, even going to the extent of having the humans and Plik eat their meals in the saddle. Blind Seer went without eating rather than delaying to hunt and Derian, aware that the wolf had probably not eaten since the previous afternoon, amended his earlier thought: he was riding with an enormous, *hungry, worried* wolf in his lap. And he was riding the most beautiful horse he had ever seen.

Despite their haste, evening was drawing on before they reached Firekeeper. Before they found her, they smelled smoke. Truth, who had been unusually cooperative, reassuring Blind Seer (else the wolf would not have agreed to be carried for more than an hour or so) that according to her visions Firekeeper was alive, now informed them that although the fire scent had something to do with Firekeeper's night, that Firekeeper herself was fine.

"Fine" was not what Derian would have called the wolf-woman when they came upon her a short time later. She sat on a fallen tree trunk near the side of the trail, Bitter in her lap, Lovable perched beside her. Firekeeper was all over scratches and scrapes. Her shirt was in tatters and looked somewhat singed. Her leather trousers showed signs of similar abuse, the fine surface gouged in countless places, torn right through in others. Even the tops of her feet were red and bloody, but her dark eyes seemed to light from within when she saw them coming.

Especially, Derian thought, as Blind Seer pushed himself off Eshinarvash's back—incidentally leaving a couple of good scrapes on Derian's thigh—*because she sees Blind Seer is alive. Whatever happened to her last night, she's been wondering if something like that happened to him.*

But Firekeeper's first words were not for the wolf, nor about herself. Standing, holding Bitter very carefully so that her motion did not disturb the raven's sleep, she looked at Harjeedian.

"Please," she said. "Bitter is very bad. I give him blood and he drinks a little, but I think there is fever in him. Don't let him die, not after all of this to save him."

For the second time that day, Harjeedian dismounted and went directly to his medical kit.

"I'm not your Doc," he warned Firekeeper, motioning her to a clear space where a boulder would serve as a table. "I don't have his talent. I brought with me every medicine every kidisdu could recommend, but I cannot work miracles."

Firekeeper nodded understanding, but Lovable, gliding down from her tree limb, and walking stiffly over to Harjeedian, looked up at him with eyes clouded with worry—and possibly illness of her own.

"Please!" she croaked in a fair facsimile of human speech. "Please!"

Derian felt his throat tighten, and no shame that tears stung his eyes. He looked over at Harjeedian.

"Could you use a spare pair of hands?"

"I could," Harjeedian said shortly, "but if Plik would assist me—his hands are smaller."

The maimalodalu looked surprised, pleased, then a little frightened, but he got heavily from his pony and without saying a single word about what had to be tremendous stiffness from a long day's ride, went over to Harjeedian.

Firekeeper spoke, "I remember Doc and I make hot water to wait. Do you wish?"

Harjeedian actually smiled, the expression making his eyes almost vanish between his high cheekbones and brow.

"Wonderful! How much do you have?"

Firekeeper measured out a space in the air with her hands.

"I find an old pot near stone house. Clean very well with sand and cold water first."

"Wonderful," Harjeedian repeated. "Let's have half of it in one of our cook pots. Plik and I can clean our hands. I'll keep the rest back. Can you put more on?"

"I have coals," Firekeeper said.

Derian slid from Eshinarvash's back. Muscles unused to either such a broad back or riding without stirrups screamed at him, but he followed Plik's stoic example.

"I'll unpack our gear," he said.

It turned out that Firekeeper had chosen this spot deliberately, both for the boulder and because there was a source of fresh water nearby. She had laid out a small camp, and gathered wood for the fire. She even had some rabbits cleaned and hanging from a tree limb. These went immediately to Blind Seer with the assurance that she had snares set.

"Better than watching every breath Bitter makes," she confessed to Derian. "The fire not good for him."

"The fire," Derian said. "You look pretty bad yourself. What happened?"

She told him while they set up the camp and tended to the horses. Work over Bitter seemed to be going very slowly. As the daylight faded, Harjeedian requested a lantern. Derian brought one, and carried Harjeedian and Plik drinking water. Otherwise the best thing seemed to be to stay out of their way.

"Let me clean your cuts, Firekeeper," Derian suggested after they had done all they could. "I don't like the sound of those briars."

"You not like their feel even more," Firekeeper said with a lopsided grin. "Actually, they not hurt except at first. This is very bad."

Derian had to agree. Firekeeper had made a good effort to clean those wounds she could reach, but her back looked like she'd been the centerpiece of a cat fight. The deep cuts on her arm that had been inflicted by the "jaguar" were puffy and inflamed.

After her wounds had been cleaned, Firekeeper donned a fresh pair of trousers and a new shirt. Methodically, she tore the old ones to strips and fed them to the flames. While she was doing so, Plik came over and wearily sank down next to the fire.

"We've done what we can to help Bitter—at least for tonight," he said. "One eye is beyond saving. We cleaned out what remained."

He raised a hand to his throat as if to force back a moment of nausea. "There was infection there and in some of the larger weals. We cleaned it out as well as we could. Harjeedian has some poultices that he says may help."

Harjeedian came over at that moment, cradling Bitter.

"We'll make a nest for him from clean fabric—probably from some of the bandaging, since that's less likely to stick. He's going to need to be given water regularly—or blood. Liquids in any case. If he makes the night, I'd say he has a chance, but if the fever rises or the infection shows other signs of raging . . ."

"We'll all take turns watching," Plik said, and Derian had the feeling he was translating.

"I start," Firekeeper said. "You all travel all the day. I just sit here."

"How much sleep have you had?" Derian asked sternly.

"Much," she said, tossing her head to indicate the broad limbs of one of the trees bordering the campground. "I go there, with ravens. But first I check very careful to see no briars."

Since Blind Seer didn't protest, Derian decided she must be telling the truth. The wolf could probably smell a lie—or at least exhaustion.

"Fine," Derian said. "You first, but wake Harjeedian if there is any change for the worse."

"I promise," the wolf-woman said. "All the night and all the day, I wish for someone to help. I not forget now."

Not for the first time, Derian thought that the fact that wolves were pack animals really was useful in its way. He wondered if Truth would be so quick to admit need.

As if she had read his thoughts, the jaguar—who had vanished soon after they had camped—returned. She half carried, half dragged the carcass of a medium-sized pig. From the looks of it, it was probably a feral one, gone wild after this area had been abandoned by the humans.

"Dinner!" Firekeeper said with satisfaction, and set about the butchering with practiced efficiency.

The only difference in her routine was how she carefully drained the blood into the largest container they could spare.

"For Bitter," she said worriedly, as if the rest of them would want to drink warm pig's blood. "So he get strong."

❧

BITTER SURVIVED THE NIGHT, but Plik thought that the optimism with
which both Firekeeper and Lovable chose to view this development was unwise. Then again, he had not seen the raven at his worst. Maybe there really
was some improvement.

In any case, with the group as a whole rejoined and everyone aware of what
had happened to the scouts when they had gone ahead alone, there was some
protest raised when with dawn Firekeeper insisted that she and Blind Seer
should continue the search for the twins.

"Either this," the wolf-woman said, *"or we go back. I am not ready to go back
knowing so little and fearing so much."*

"I agree," Truth said. *"We must find them and learn how they have turned
the plants into their defenders."*

"And," Harjeedian said, when this had been translated for the humans,
"what other defenders—or weapons—they might have. But is it wise for only
two to go forth, especially when the two of you are now, with Truth, our best at
what I suppose we must term forestry?"

"Should we send those who are not good?" Firekeeper retorted. "We are
warned. We will not go to sleep. And . . ."

She turned to Plik. "Will you come with? Maybe briars that drink blood are
natural as bugs that do, but the creatures I fight last night—the wolves, jaguar,
and bear—if they just growed that way, then I have hair as pale as Elise's and
three times as long."

Plik had never seen this Elise, but he understood Firekeeper's point.

"You want me to come and see if I sense some sort of magic at work."

"Yes. Blind Seer scent the wind, but you can scent this other."

Truth said, *"I will remain here and guard the humans and ravens. No harm
will come to them while I have life."*

Firekeeper had told them all of her encounter the night before with the
Meddler, and Plik thought he knew why the jaguar was being so cooperative.
Even so, after moons passing with nothing but surly silence and haughty
stares, the change was unsettling.

"And I," said Eshinarvash, *"will carry Plik as far as is necessary. Perhaps the
stone house would be a good place for you to begin your search."*

"Or the meadows beyond," Firekeeper said, speaking in Pellish so the humans would understand. "The woman in Gak, she talk of the twins' father's
kin building Setting Sun place in a plain."

Derian gave a gusty sigh. "Can Harjeedian and I gather that you have set-tled this without us?"

Firekeeper shrugged. "What is to settle? Can you hold me if I would go? Can you hold Blind Seer? There is no One here."

Harjeedian pressed his fingers to his eyes. "There are times I wish there were. Will you at least share your arrangements with us?"

Plik noticed Firekeeper had the grace to look at least a little ashamed at this reminder that the humans had not understood all the discussion.

"We go, Blind Seer and I. We take Plik with us. This way we scout very, very carefully. Plik can sense magic for us. We not go to sleep, not without guard. Maybe we even come back by tonight. Eshinarvash say he carry Plik ahead then come back to help Truth guard you humans and ravens."

"All very neatly arranged," Harjeedian said. "And if you vanish?"

"Then three vanish," Firekeeper said somberly. "And six escape. Better than nine all vanish."

"She has a point," Derian said. "I'll accept the plan with one addition."

Firekeeper looked as if she was about to ask the redhead how he would stop her, but waited politely.

"You're leaving at dawn today," Derian said. "At least one of you must come back to report by midday tomorrow. As you tell it, this stone house and the field aren't that far away. Fair?"

"Fair," Firekeeper agreed after glancing at Blind Seer and Plik to see if they had any protest to offer. "If not one of three reports by midday tomorrow, you may worry."

She grinned, "But not before. Before rest and make Bitter well."

"And find forage for all these horses," Derian said, his apparent grumpiness an obvious cover for deep concern. "They won't thrive on leaves."

AT THE STONE HOUSE, Eshinarvash left them. The remaining three spent some time inspecting the area, looking for traces of where the briar creatures that had attacked them might have come from, but even Blind Seer's nose could find nothing.

"Smoke," he said. "Who can smell anything through all this smoke?"

Plik might have made something from the remnants of the creatures, but Firekeeper had thrown them all in the fire.

"They not move then," she said, "but later? I did not wish them come for us again. Once was almost too much."

From the stone house, they moved on to the edge of the open meadows. Plik carefully inspected the briars clustering around the foot of the oak tree where Bitter and Lovable had been attacked while Firekeeper watched with such tense anxiety that he thought she would burn the mass as a preventative.

"There's magic there," Plik reported, "but almost nothing. I sense more from Derian, and he hardly controls his talent so his aura's about as nonmagical as a talented human's can be."

Plik noticed Firekeeper was fingering the bag about her throat where she kept her fire making equipment. "Will you burn them?"

"I wish to," she said, "but last night I was lucky the forest not catch. I cannot risk setting such a fire, not now, not ever."

Plik, who knew that Firekeeper's human family had been killed in a fire, understood the tremor that touched her voice as she spoke.

"Then I suppose," he said, seeking to distract her, "we move on. The question is, where?"

"Lovable," Blind Seer said, "told us she and Bitter flew over the immediate area and saw nothing out of the ordinary. But they felt something."

"A restlessness," Firekeeper recalled. "Lovable told me about it the night we were attacked, reassuring me that I wasn't wrong in what I sensed."

"Ravens scout mostly by vision," Blind Seer continued. "In this they are very like humans."

Firekeeper nodded. "So if humans hid something, ravens might not see it because the humans would hide just what the ravens would seek. I remember now that Bitter and Lovable were going to try again after dark because they thought they might see lights."

"That's not a bad idea," Blind Seer said, "although I can't say I really like the idea of being out here after dark. It's very exposed."

"We might be safer than under the trees," Firekeeper said. "Harder to sneak up on us."

Plik interjected himself into what was beginning to sound too much like one mind reflecting its own thoughts back and forth and refining on them.

"I'm interested in this feeling of restlessness," he said. "Do you feel it now?"

Firekeeper considered. "No. I don't think so, at least not much more than I have . . ."

"Since we crossed that second ford!" Blind Seer completed. "I remember. The cairn that smelled of blood. I started feeling uneasy then. I could sense that you did as well."

"A cairn that smelled of blood?" Plik asked.

Blind Seer explained, concluding, "I didn't think to mention it before because it seemed like an isolated incident and there were many reasons it might have smelled that way, but now that this feeling of restlessness may indicate something . . ."

Plik nodded. He had left his hat and the rest of his human disguise at the camp, and he was still enjoying having his vision and movements unrestricted.

"I didn't notice the cairn," he said, "nor any particular restlessness, but by then my companions and I were all getting very worried. Why don't we try this? Let's pick a direction and move that way. We'll scout just as usual, but if anyone feels that 'restlessness' intensify, speak up."

The other two indicated agreement.

"Let's start to the west," Blind Seer said. "The maps Harjeedian copied weren't very specific about the location of the residence proper, but it seems to me it was to the west."

Firekeeper agreed by turning and beginning to walk west. Plik hurried after. He wondered if all wolf packs behaved like this, or if it was just these two.

The meadows were thick with summer grass, too thick, Plik thought after slogging along for a while. They should have shown some signs of being grazed upon, of animal tracks, but signs of anything larger than a rabbit were scarce. What hunted here that had so scared the game so that nothing larger than a rabbit remained?

He asked Blind Seer and the wolf replied, "I smell nothing—no one. This land would be fine territory for any wolf. It is broad enough to support a pack or two, and hangers-on as well, but there are no wolves. Once I thought I scented a puma, but the odor was old and fleeting. Rabbits there are aplenty, small game of all types, but both the larger grazers and the larger hunters have gone away."

"But they were here," Firekeeper said, indicating a heap of deer droppings. The oval pellets were faded and losing shape from exposure to the weather. "A year ago, I would say, they were here."

"A year ago," Blind Seer echoed. "The twins came here a year ago or so. Coincidence?"

"Perhaps," Firekeeper said, but her entire body said she did not believe it.

They continued on through the deep grasses. Plik was sufficiently tall that he could see over the greenery, but even so he felt claustrophobic. When they spotted a copse of trees in the near distance, they angled toward it by unspoken agreement. As they drew closer, Plik found himself feeling tense. He longed to get away from that looming forest, to stay here in the open, or better, to return to lands he knew. He thought of Misheemnekuru with longing, wishing for his familiar hollow tree, for the leisurely evening discussions of past history and philosophy.

"Wait," he said. Firekeeper and Blind Seer immediately did so, the woman moving to string her bow, the wolf's head tilting back as he scented the wind. "No, no, I haven't seen anything," Plik said, "but . . . Have either of you been feeling a strange desire to avoid that copse of trees?"

They looked at him, and from their expressions, Plik could tell that they had shared his odd feeling.

"Don't you think that peculiar?" he asked. "I mean, we're all forest creatures of one sort or another. Your pack lived in wooded lands—you weren't creatures of the plains. I certainly am not, neither by heritage or habit. Why should we feel driven to avoid those trees? The more I think about it, the more I *think* I should be welcoming the approach, but what I *feel* is completely different."

Firekeeper looked at him, her dark eyes thoughtful. "I had thought I dreaded the briars. They are not here, but they will be under the trees. I also had thoughts of fire, and of how bad the fire could have been."

"And what," Blind Seer went on, "might happen if creatures such as you fought last night reappeared and we need resort to fire again? I kept recalling the Burnt Place from which our pack took you when you were a child. Even years later, after I had been born, the signs of damage were terribly visible."

"Not restlessness this time," Plik said. "Apprehension instead. Interesting. Restlessness might make a raven fly farther afield, not stop to take a closer look. Apprehension might make us inspect the copse quickly and then move on."

"So," Firekeeper said, "we will not move on. We go there and we look very closely, checking for every detail."

"But with care," Blind Seer said, his hackles rising. "With tremendous care."

XVI

FIREKEEPER RUBBED HER HANDS across her eyes as if in doing so she could clear her mind of whatever it was that intruded upon her thinking. It didn't work. Images of fire and of clawing briar invaded her thoughts until they became almost more real than the grass that prickled the soles of her bare feet and the sun upon her face and hands.

She straightened. Very well. Fire she knew and respected. The briars she had defeated. She would continue on and find what was in that copse—find and either learn why she should respect it, or defeat it.

Although no words had been exchanged, it seemed to Firekeeper that Plik and Blind Seer were both awaiting her decision. When she stepped out, they did so as well, Blind Seer to point, then Plik—for Firekeeper's greater height would block his own ability to see—then Firekeeper.

In this way they crossed the intervening distance, closing until Firekeeper could identify the various trees by the shapes of their leaves and the pattern of their branches. With each step, the sense of apprehension became more powerful and, oddly, for Firekeeper, easier to put aside. She was far from fearless, but she did not possess the human tendency to dread in abstract.

This is a trap for humans, not for wolves, she thought, looking over to where Plik advanced, his short legs never faltering in their steady pace, *nor for maimalodalu, though I think Plik is having a more difficult time than Blind Seer and me.*

She thought no less of Plik for his fear. Fear was a good thing, except when it crippled you, and Plik was not crippled.

As forests were judged, this one was very small, yet it contained a wide variety of species of trees. There were several towering oaks, maples with their broad-palmed, sharp-tipped leaves fluttering in any passing breeze. The spear-point-tipped leaves of elms, fan-like hickory, needle-tipped holly, and sassafras with its thumb-like lobe were all well represented. The understory was filled with brush, some in fruit. The shady places were carpeted in thick moss.

Two things were missing: any small creatures, wingéd or not, and the briar that had been so omnipresent in the borders of the forest land across the fields.

"There's something wrong here," said Firekeeper at last, "and not just that the little creatures are so silent."

"No," Plik agreed. "I have been wondering—where did such variety of plants come from? I could understand that if this copse was closer to other plants, but out here? Acorns do not fall far from the tree, so you do not find oaks away from oaks. Unless some creature carries them, there should be a grandmother oak. Now, I suppose this could be an oak forest, and the other plants later intruders, but then the oaks—or at least a few oaks—should be well ahead of their fellows. These all appear to be close to the same age."

"And the scents are wrong," Blind Seer said. "When I sniff for the bitterness of oak, or the sweet-sour scent of maple, then it is there, but if I do not try to isolate it, then there is simply the scent of 'forest.'"

Plik sniffed. "I catch the same scents. Very odd."

Firekeeper had been thinking hard about this; now, almost without thinking about what she did, she dropped back several paces, as if the trees might hear her and take some sort of action.

"This is like an idea of a forest," she said at last, "a human idea, and the idea of a human who does not know forests well or think about the fashion in which they grow. Holly Gardener would never think this is a forest. I do not think Race would either. It startled us enough for us to slow and not plunge in. Would it have stopped Derian or Harjeedian? I think not. Like the other—the apprehensions—this is a human trap, meant for any humans who were not dissuaded by the sensation of fear."

Blind Seer raised his head and studied the copse.

"Do we walk in then? Enter this trap? Or is this where we turn around?"

Firekeeper considered; then she unslung and strung her bow.

"If you do not mind, I am thinking of something in the middle of these two things. I could fire an arrow into that greenness and we could all track its course."

"And see what it tells us," Plik said. "Something might come rushing out, but . . ."

"But then we can bite it or talk to it," Blind Seer said. "The more I look at this copse, the more I think of paintings I have seen in human homes. At first the representation seems right, then you start noticing what is not, and before long the very flatness of the thing is its most salient point."

Firekeeper chose an arrow meant for hunting birds. The head was light and small, more easily replaced than some of her others. Moreover, if there was a creature or human watching from concealment, she did not wish her test shot to cause any great injury.

She drew back the string, seeking to let the shaft fly as long a distance as possible. She gave no warning before she loosed. Plik and Blind Seer's watchful readiness was almost a tactile thing.

The arrow flew straight on the course she had set for it, over the small shrub growth, between two maples, then into a thick clump of saplings. She was not looking to hit any one thing, but to hit several small things.

The result was remarkable.

When the arrow hit the first bit of greenery, the leaves tore as they should, but Firekeeper would have sworn that those in the next clump tore slightly more slowly, and those behind more slowly still. The difference would not have been seen except by one looking to find it, but to her it was a certainty. When she turned to Plik and Blind Seer, she saw from their expressions that they too had witnessed the anomaly.

"The sound was wrong, too," Blind Seer said. "I would swear there was none at all until after the arrow had begun its passage through the clump of saplings."

"I don't know what this is called," Firekeeper said cheerfully, keeping her bow strung and selecting a heavier arrow. "But I think it is something we can tell the others."

"Then we are returning?" Plik asked.

"I think that is wisest," Firekeeper replied. "We have something to tell, and I have no good plan for what we should do next."

"I thought," Plik said, gesturing at the arrow in her hand, "you were going to shoot again."

"Only," Firekeeper said, staring into the tangle of apparent foliage, "if someone comes out after us."

TRUTH WAS ALMOST LOOKING FORWARD to the Meddler's next invasion of her privacy. She'd thought of a few questions she wanted to ask.

"I have been wondering something," the jaguar said, knowing that to exterior appearances she was among those asleep in their camp. Derian was on watch, and if she concentrated she was aware of his soft-footed patrol at the camp's edges. "How did you manage to manifest a body for yourself? Those who imprisoned you left you with very little. My understanding is that nothing can be made from nothing."

"I didn't quite have nothing," the Meddler replied without a trace of the evasion she had expected. "I had a great deal of ability and a certain amount of personal power—the same qualities that so frightened those I would have befriended. Using these qualities, I could make myself a short-lasting version of a body. From this I would take blood. I would use that blood to create food to further sustain the body. Drink there was aplenty. Living, running water provides a special sustenance, separate from its purely physical qualities—and those are essential enough. What I did was not easy. It was very painful, but I managed to manifest. Later, I even managed to store some power for future use."

"You used your own blood?" Truth thought of things she had learned about those who used blood to create magic and her tail twitched. "Are you then a sorcerer?"

"Yes. What else did you think I was?"

"Until a short time ago," Truth said, "I thought you a manifestation of my own returning insanity. Then Plik told us you were some sort of god. Then you told me the circumstances of your captivity, and I decided that I had no idea what you were."

"So you asked, a levelheaded thing to do, one that demonstrates just how very sane you are."

"Your flattery is never without reason," Truth said. "What is it you desire?"

"My flattery is never without truth," the Meddler said, "and as for what I desire . . . I desire to teach you a skill you will need quite soon. By sunrise tomorrow—if they are careful—your three scouts will return with an amazing tale. I wish to teach you something that will enable you to go where otherwise you cannot."

"Does this teaching involve permitting myself to be disembodied?"

"Only briefly." Reassurance dripped from the Meddler's voice. "And you will not 'be disembodied.' You will disembody yourself."

"Agreeing to accept your teaching was our agreement," Truth said. In her dream she rose and stretched. "Therefore, I agree."

The Meddler reached out a hand and stroked her between her ears. "Oh, honorable creature, if only you believed in my honor as much as you do your own."

Truth stared at him, keeping her burnt-orange eyes unblinking. Then she said, "Shall we begin our lessons? Perhaps as you teach me, you can tell me why you wish me to go where otherwise I could not. Indeed, you can start with telling me to where I am going."

"You came here in search of the twins," the Meddler said. "What I will teach you will make it possible for you to reach them."

MUCH OF WHAT THE MEDDLER EXPLAINED to Truth that night made sense with the sort of logic available only in dreams. She learned to separate some essential element of herself from her body in a fashion that was similar to what she had used to find omens, but was in key ways quite different.

From this point, she needed to learn to move within glimmering golden green spaces that were frighteningly familiar. From this she knew she had stumbled into them during her time of madness.

In these places Truth encountered Bitter.

The raven looked far better here than he did in the camp where he slept in his makeshift nest, wakening only for his regular feedings, then slipping back under again.

Here he had both eyes, and Truth wondered if he was aware of his loss. Almost as quickly she resolved that she would not be the one to tell him.

"Hey, jaguar," the raven quorked, his voice here familiar and throaty. "Did you bring me to this place? I can't seem to find my way out."

Truth blinked at him, then decided that a partial answer would serve. "I did not bring you here. I think you brought yourself here."

"Why would I do that? I am needed. Lovable would worry."

"You were injured," Truth said. "Do you remember nothing of that?"

Bitter preened the flight feathers on one wing. "I do remember something. Briars, wasn't it? Yes. I remember . . ." He shuddered and puffed out his feathers so he was twice his usual size. "They would have strangled me, but Lovable kept clipping them back. Did she fly?"

Truth was puzzled. "She escaped if that's what you mean."

"Close enough. I remember telling her to fly. I'm glad she listened."

The raven's feathers suddenly went sleek and flat. His wings flew wide as if he was about to fly away from some threat.

"Truth, did I die? Is that why I am here?"

"You are not dead," Truth reassured him, "but sorely wounded. Perhaps you fled here to leave the pain in your body."

"I was wounded that severely," the raven said, not as if asking, but as if confirming something he already suspected. "That severely."

"Lovable will miss you," Truth said awkwardly. She never quite knew how to discuss pair bonds. "She watches over you, waking and sleeping."

The Meddler, whom Truth had not been aware of all the time she was speaking with Bitter, was there. He looked like a human, his hair thick and grey as old stone, but other than this he looked no more than of middle years. He hunkered down on his haunches to come level with Bitter.

"Let me be honest with you, Bitter."

"Who are you?"

"I am the one you helped set free from imprisonment, the Voice that guided Truth from madness into sanity, the ally who helped Firekeeper win her battle against creatures given life through briar thorn and blood magic."

Bitter flicked head feathers up to make little horns on his head. "You are the one Plik calls the Meddler."

"I cannot deny I am a Meddler," the other responded. "I wish you would believe I am your friend. I am going to tell you something now, and if that is meddling, well, so be it. You are here in this place for the reason Truth suggested. Your spirit could not bear the pain of your wounded body, however, you had reasons not to die."

"Lovable," the raven croaked softly.

The Meddler did not acknowledge this private confession, but went on. "Your friends have kept your body alive to this point, but without your spirit it will fade and die. The longer you remain away in any case, the less complete the healing will be. If you wish to live, if you wish to fly again, you cannot remain away."

"And if I do not return?"

"Your body will die, but your spirit may remain trapped here. This is a more pleasant place than that into which I was condemned. Some, like Truth here, may pass through from time to time and give you company. Most of the time you will be alone, though."

"And?"

"I cannot say. You may fade into gradual death. You may persist without any sense of who you are. You may retain a sense of identity. You may go insane. Remain here long enough and you will encounter spirits who have experienced all these things. Not all of them will be pleasant to meet—in fact, most will not be."

Bitter fluffed his feathers, sleeked them flat, and began hopping about.

"Sorely wounded," he said to Truth.

"Very."

"Immense pain," he said to the Meddler.

"Enough to separate body and soul," the human replied.

"Flight?"

"If you return before the muscles stiffen and weaken much further. You lost a great deal of blood."

"I must think," the raven said.

Without further comment, Bitter spread his wings and with a few hard, fast beats launched into the greenish gold sky. He was a black dot against it for a moment, then nothing.

"Did he go back?" Truth asked.

"I don't think so," the Meddler replied. "Distances here are not the same as elsewhere. When a spirit is sufficiently strong-willed, a wish to be away is as good as any other effort."

"Ah . . . Are you going to teach me more now?"

"The next part will be most difficult," the Meddler replied, "and it would be best if you were away from the others when we attempt it. Rest now, the true rest of deep sleep, and I will return to you tomorrow night."

"Will I never get a quiet night's sleep?" Truth grumbled.

"Quiet," the Meddler replied, "is not all it's made out to be. Death is said to be quiet: a very quiet, very long night's sleep."

ALTHOUGH HE HAD BEEN UP part of the night, Derian asked to be awakened early for the simple reason that none of the beasts could boil water. Harjeedian might have done so, but the aridisdu had experienced an even more interrupted night than Derian's own, waking every hour except during Derian's watch to dribble some liquid or other down Bitter's throat.

Derian knew Harjeedian despaired of saving the raven's life, though he said nothing—especially where Lovable would hear. To lose a comrade would be horrible for any of them. They were not soldiers trained to accept such as part of the course of duty. Derian thought it would be particularly terrible for Harjeedian, for he had grown to manhood as part of a religious hierarchy that considered the Wise Beasts as direct links to the divine forces to which the disdum had dedicated their lives.

Derian was scaling some fish Truth had brought back to the camp—the heads had already been chomped off—when soundlessly as ever Firekeeper emerged into the camp, Plik a few steps behind her, Blind Seer coming in last.

"We have finded things," Firekeeper announced happily.

"Found," Derian said, grinning.

"Does Bitter . . ." Plik asked. The raccoon-man looked very tired. He took a seat on the ground near the fire and started rubbing his feet.

"Bitter's alive," Derian replied. "But no better than when you left." He lowered his voice, "And maybe worse."

"I will bring hot blood for him," Firekeeper said, "if Truth has not."

Harjeedian came from where he had just finished feeding the ravens. With a silent nod of thanks he accepted the mug of rose hip tea Derian poured for him.

"Truth has hunted well," the aridisdu said. "But Bitter will only swallow so much, and his body needs not only to sustain itself but to grow stronger. We started this race behind, and are falling further back."

The jaguar uncurled slightly from where she had been sleeping, her coat admirably blending in so that until she moved she had seemed just another bit of shadow-dappled sunlight. She raised her head, blinked at Firekeeper. Firekeeper shrugged and moved to the fireside.

Without asking, she took the fish from Derian and finished cleaning it. He didn't protest. His mother had rarely served fish, not trusting the cleanness of the River Flin where it ran near the city, and not trusting the fish vendors—all of whom claimed their fish came from upstream. Firekeeper was far better at scaling and gutting than he was.

While her hands moved, without preamble, Firekeeper began her report.

"We goed first to the place where the fire was, but there we find nothing. Blind Seer have a memory though, and this proves good."

She went on, hands moving rhythmically as she told of their investigations. When she moved to start frying the fish, Plik took over the narration. Derian had become so accustomed to thinking of the maimalodalu as a sort of hairy human that he was startled when Plik not only accepted but ate with enthusiasm a share of the raw fish guts.

"And that's where we left our explorations," Plik concluded. "Firekeeper showed what Blind Seer assures me was uncommon restraint in coming back here to report rather than probing further on her own."

The wolf raised his head from his paws, laughter obvious in his openmouthed pant. Derian found himself grinning in return.

"Ask Blind Seer to tell you about the time Firekeeper went into a sewer alone at midnight."

Firekeeper said nothing, but concentrated on her portion of fish. Her dark gaze periodically strayed to where Bitter was, and Derian didn't need to know her as well as he did to know she was thinking that she did not wish to risk another companion. She might not have been so cautious if Plik had not been with her and Blind Seer.

Harjeedian set down his own plate, and added honey to his mug before pouring more tea.

"So what should our next move be?" he asked. "It seems evident that the copse is not what it seems to be. I would even hazard that it somehow conceals the location of the twins' refuge, but dare we enter? What if it also conceals a tangle of those blood-drinking briars? I have too much respect for the damage they can do to send anyone in to them lightly."

"I agree," Plik said. "We could scout elsewhere, see what else we find. I remain troubled by the absence of yarimaimalom. Surely if we go farther afield we may find them." He rubbed his feet again. "I do not recommend myself for this, but Eshinarvash would move quickly out on the plains, and so would Blind Seer."

Derian was trying to decide whether he should volunteer to go with Eshinarvash, or whether he would look like one of the stable boys, eager to make any excuse to exercise some noble's horse, when Truth padded over to join the group around the fire. She sat up straight, in a position more like that of a house cat than her normal sprawl.

She's letting Harjeedian and me know she has something to say, Derian thought.

In a moment, Plik started translating.

"I have had—that is Truth has had, not me—some odd experiences of late. You all know that the Meddler has troubled my dreams, and that he is the Voice who guided me, the one who aided Firekeeper. He has some interest in the twins, some interest that goes deeper than anything he has claimed to this point—even to me. Of this I am certain."

There was a pause, and Plik said softly, "Blind Seer wants to know what proof. Truth admits it's more of a hunch than anything else, but states that she's a diviner and knows how to read omens. Wait, she's getting back to her point.

"Truth says that the Meddler is teaching her something that he says will enable us to reach the twins, but that her lessons are not yet complete. She suggests that we wait in patience for her to be ready." Plik's tone changed. "Oh-ho, that was a mistake. Firekeeper wants to know who made Truth the One of this pack."

"Great," Derian groaned. "Firekeeper, don't you dare go rushing off just to prove that Truth can't boss you."

Firekeeper looked at him, brown eyes all innocence. "I not rush off, Derian, but I think we have more to do than wait for Truth to get enough sleep."

Plik raised a paw. "Are you going to insist on rushing that copse then?"

Firekeeper frowned. "No, but maybe as was said, we go and look more, for yarimaimalom, for other things. I think you is right, Plik. More scouting, especially on those plains where Harjeedian's maps say these twins' family once have this Setting Sun."

Eshinarvash snorted, and Plik translated.

"Eshinarvash says he would run with Blind Seer, but perhaps it would be wisest to send two groups. He thinks that he could carry me. Firekeeper and Blind Seer could check in another direction. No one would stay out longer than during the daylight hours."

Plik made a gesture that indicated he was now speaking for himself. "I appreciate the suggestion—and I know Eshinarvash was thinking my sensitivity to magic would be useful—but I do not think I can stay astride his back for a long stretch. I can barely manage a pony. My legs, quite honestly, are not long enough. I had trouble during our walk through the forest yesterday."

Eshinarvash snorted, shook his mane, and stomped. Plik's eyes widened slightly.

"Eshinarvash just suggested that he could carry both Derian and myself. This would strip the camp, but if Truth would remain with Harjeedian to guard the ravens . . ."

Truth licked her paw and Derian was not surprised when Plik said, "Truth says, of course she would stay here and guard. Tearing around the landscape does not suit her either."

Derian tried to keep an excited tremor from his voice. "Do we go today? It's not even midday yet."

"Tomorrow, please," Plik said. "My legs ache from walking all yesterday—walking when I didn't ride. Remember, I am far older than you. Although they would never say so, I bet Firekeeper and Blind Seer would like a rest and a chance to eat something larger than a rabbit."

Firekeeper didn't say anything, but Blind Seer rose and stretched, his languid motions making words unnecessary.

"Tomorrow, then," Firekeeper said. "If Truth is not ready to find the twins yet."

Truth looked at the wolf-woman, yawned, and with insulting deliberateness strolled into the sunlight and became as sunlight and shadows once more.

"YOU SHOWED ME BITTER ON PURPOSE, didn't you?" Truth asked.

They were in the green-gold spaces. The Meddler was no longer just a voice, but was a completely visible human. Truth thought about asking why, then decided it wasn't important.

"You always think the worst of me," the Meddler replied.

"But I notice you don't deny it. Why don't you ever give a straight answer?"

"Why didn't you tell your companions as soon as you began to suspect that your 'Voice' was also the Meddler?"

"That isn't an answer."

"Humor me."

Truth licked between two front toes. "I wasn't precisely certain, and also . . . You speak of them as my 'companions,' but actually I don't know them very well."

"And?"

"And I am unaccustomed to venturing into something as volatile as that revelation would be without being able to check the omens as to what the response would be."

"So it is for me," the Meddler said. "I have been a prisoner for a long time. You people are new to me. Sometimes I ask a question to try and find out what you are really asking."

Truth rose. "And sometimes asking a question of your own permits you to avoid answering my question. I think you showed me Bitter in order to tempt me back here."

"Did you need tempting?"

"I might have done so."

The Meddler sighed. "I wish you could think well of me. Maybe I wanted to encourage Bitter to return to his body, and I knew that he would be suspicious of a stranger but trust a friend."

"So you admit that you manipulated the situation!"

"I arranged that you should meet, yes."

Truth yawned, showing every one of her teeth. "The night is growing no younger. I now know how to get here without your guidance. What is next?"

"Next you must learn to travel through this space. It is not quite the same as traveling in those spaces into which you were born."

Truth bent her ears to listening. She could already tell it was going to be a long night, and she was doubly glad that she had suggested the others do some further scouting.

She might be able to catch up on her sleep during the day.

ACHING MUSCLES MADE PLIK'S SLEEP that night less than restful. He had never thought himself a sedentary creature, but he had been forced to adapt his assessment. The walk back from the copse had been taken at what the wolves clearly felt was a leisurely pace. Blind Seer had even wandered off to do a bit of hunting. Even so, by the end, Plik was wondering just how much scorn he would garner if he asked one of the others to call Eshinarvash.

Now the two wolves slept close to each other, almost unmoving, and Plik found himself resenting the ease of their relaxation. He was aware of other things, too, of the time close to dawn that Truth returned to the camp, evidently weary to the point of exhaustion, yet bearing no signs or scents of exertion.

He was aware how during his turn at night watch Derian spent hours going over his tack, polishing the leather to satin shine and increased suppleness. He was aware how Harjeedian rose time after time, forcing liquid food and water into Bitter, and how each time Lovable awoke as well and hovered anxiously, crooning almost musically over her mate.

The camp started stirring at dawn, and by the time the first clear sunlight had penetrated the forest canopy, they were ready to go. Eshinarvash had insisted he would permit a saddle. Part of Derian's handiwork over the night had been rigging a sort of sidesaddle pad for Plik.

"It's not that I don't like you," the young man grinned, "but you're awfully big and hairy to sit all day on my lap."

Plik found the seat remarkably comfortable and secure. The day ahead—during which he had envisioned that tortured muscles would be further stretched—no longer seemed so impossible.

It was an oversimplification to say that the plains ran east-west. They filled a river valley and probably had their origin in long-ago flooding from the river that emerged from the mountains to the west. Using the copse as a center point, Firekeeper and Blind Seer volunteered to go to the west—thereby passing the copse (although they promised this would be from a distance). The group carried by Eshinarvash settled for the eastern route.

"After all," Eshinarvash said, "who wants to play games of precedence with a pair of wolves? Young wolves at that?"

Plik agreed, but he was willing to credit Firekeeper and Blind Seer with a certain amount of protectiveness as well. The thick grass meant the wolves should be able to pass below the line of sight from the copse. There was no way that Eshinarvash could manage to hide.

To further permit them to pass without being noticed, Eshinarvash kept to the forest for the first part of their journey, emerging from the trees only when the natural rise and fall of the land blocked direct line of sight from the problematic copse.

"Of course," Plik said, "if whatever is there—if anything is there—has the ability to scout from above, then we've gone to a great deal of trouble for nothing."

Derian, his excitement at riding Eshinarvash only apparent because his companions could smell it in his sweat, turned to Plik, an easy grin lighting his features.

"If there's one thing I've learned over these last couple of years it's that it's usually worth taking the trouble to check the area out. I've rarely felt stupid afterwards when nothing happens—only when something happens that I could have prevented if I'd been more careful."

He went on to tell a tale from his first trip into New Kelvin, a tale involving an attack by some very nasty bandits. Plik felt his fur rise as he listened, and he wondered what would have happened to him if he'd been there. Nothing good, of that much he was certain.

Eshinarvash seemed to be having similar thoughts, for his skin kept rippling as if to chase off imaginary flies.

Listening to the tale actually increased their alertness rather than diminishing it. They located the remnants of what Derian said looked like farmsteads. They stopped for lunch in what had obviously been an orchard. However, although they found ample signs of the former human inhabitants, they found none of the other inhabitants who should have been there.

"No large predators," Eshinarvash said, scenting the wind, his nostrils flared. "No great herds, though these plains are an invitation to browsers and grazers alike. Have you noticed that even the larger birds are not evident? There are ample songbirds, a few crows, but no hawks, no eagles, no ravens. Where have they gone? What has driven them away?"

Derian, who had been refilling their canteens from a spring, scanned the horizon as if his hazel eyes might see what the horse's sense of smell had missed.

"I wish I knew," he said.

"I wonder if you do?" asked a voice from up in one of the trees. "I really wonder if you do?"

Derian looked startled, and Plik realized that the human had not heard words, only a drawn-out sound rather like "shiiish."

However, when Eshinarvash raised his head and snorted, the human reached for the sword he wore at his waist. Plik's heart skipped a beat in his excitement. What was there? How had they missed it?

"Who's there?" he asked. "We do wish to know. We have come searching for those who should be here."

The rasping hiss took on a deeper, snoring note.

"But you travel with a human. Surely you are not to be trusted."

"He is a human," Plik said. "That is true. What does that matter?"

"Humans happened here," came the reply. "Two humans, so battered and insignificant that none worried much about their coming. A few warned us that humans are dangerous. They warned us that bad things would happen, especially when the newcomers began poking around the old buildings, but we did not listen—much to our misfortune."

Derian was looking very disturbed now. "Plik, I can tell you and Eshinarvash are talking to someone. Can you tell me what's going on?"

Plik raised both hands to stroke the white line of his eyebrows. "As soon as I know, you'll be the first person I tell."

XVII

THE NOISES THAT WERE COMING from the leafy cover of the pear tree under which they had sat to take their lunch made Derian's skin crawl. They were hoarse and rasping, terse and truncated, and sounded full of barely suppressed anger.

Plik and Eshinarvash seemed more excited than afraid, and Derian soon gathered why. At last they had found one of the missing yarimaimalom.

The creature in question turned out to be what Derian had grown up calling a barn owl, although the creature in question apparently took great offense at the term with its implications that her people depended on humans for nesting areas. She—the creature in question turned out to be female—was a lovely creature. Her facial feathers were pure white, deep-set, and unusually flat, even for an owl. The contrast of this elongated white face to her rusty-brown upper plumage and pale under plumage was striking and oddly unsettling.

She introduced herself with the name Night's Terror, but she seemed more terrified than terrible. Whenever Derian so much as looked directly at her, she rutched up her feathers and made horrible noises. Eventually, when Plik and Eshinarvash had worked her story from her, Derian didn't much blame Night's Terror for her reaction.

Night's Terror had been born in the forests that bordered this plain and had rarely had reason to leave the area since. She had never even seen a human until the arrival of two who must have been the twins a year or so before. Several of the wingéd folk who kept a wider range knew what humans were, and explained that they could be dangerous, but other yarimaimalom noted that these two humans looked like a breed that had been typically found to be favorably disposed to the Wise Beasts.

"A few of our kind," Night's Terror went on, with Plik translating for Derian, "great arrogant beasts of that type that fear little in any case, went to call upon these newcomers. These self-appointed ambassadors were immediately recognized by the humans as Kind rather than Cousin, and given fair welcome. The humans made clear that they had no intention of harming the current residents, and even made some effort to ascertain which beasts they would be permitted to hunt and which they must avoid.

"To be honest, we rather welcomed these two humans. They were amusing and interesting, something new to gossip about during the dull stretches of winter. The humans experienced some difficulties during the winter, for they were singularly ill adapted to survive, but when there was game to spare the predators dropped something by. Even I dropped off the occasional mouse or vole."

Derian hid a grin at the thought of how those two humans must have reacted to finding dead mice on their doorstep, but then he recalled the rare times Firekeeper had talked about her childhood. She had spoken about the thin times of winter when even the wolf pack's assistance had not been enough to keep her from starvation. Perhaps the twins might have appreciated those mice more than Derian had first supposed.

"Something changed soon after the coming of spring," Night's Terror went on. "I cannot say what it was, for I was busy with fledglings and had little time or attention for anything else. However, those who had befriended the humans said that they scented strange things in and about the place the two humans had taken for their lair. A few of the keener-nosed claimed they scented other humans, but we all knew this was impossible. No human could have entered this territory without our knowing."

Plik raised a hand and said something he immediately translated for Derian. "Night's Terror, earlier you said that these strange humans 'poked around old buildings.' What old buildings? We have seen nothing that would qualify, only some roofless foundations."

Night's Terror ruffled her feathers. "You force my tale out of turn. One of the strangest things that happened was when the buildings wherein the two humans had made their nest began to change. The first change was social rather than otherwise. The yarimaimalom who had taken to visiting the pair of humans found themselves no longer invited in past the main entry.

"Next many noticed that the plant growth had become thicker. At first nothing much was thought of this, for those who had visited human lands related how humans had a special art for making plants grow where they desired and often rather more swiftly than one would expect. Later, however, when trees that should have taken several years to grow appeared overnight, then questions were asked, but by then it was too late to ask them."

Night's Terror paused and swiveled her head around so that even Derian knew she was waiting to be prompted. Eshinarvash did so with a snort and a stamp of one hoof.

"The two humans had ceased to go abroad," Night's Terror went on. "Nor did they speak with the yarimaimalom any longer. Where once there had been a large building in rather better condition than any other building in the area there was now a copse of trees."

"A copse of trees," Plik repeated. "You mean that strange one to the southwest, nearer to the river?"

"That very one," Night's Terror agreed. "You know how curious certain Beasts can be. Where I was willing to leave well enough alone, others had to pry. Some went into that wood. None ever returned."

"None?" Derian asked in surprise.

Night's Terror flapped her wings at the sound of his voice, but deigned answer after Plik translated.

"None. I think it was some sort of cat that went in first, though it might have been a bear. The humans had a gift for making sweet things the bears quite liked. In any case, whichever beast it was didn't come out again, nor was a body found, nor was blood scented by those who claimed they would have known. These foolish first ones had friends, and these risked themselves to try and find their friends. These too vanished.

"Soon after, other bad things began to happen. Briars that seemed to have a taste for living meat started growing at the verges of the forest. Beasts wise and not so became their prey. Then—and I tell you this is true, though I don't expect you to believe me—there came creatures with the form of beasts, but made of vine and twig."

Eshinarvash pawed the ground, drawing a trench through the moldering pear leaves with his hoof.

"We have some knowledge of these," Plik translated faithfully. Derian realized that though there was little reason he should have done so, he had understood the Wise Horse.

"You have?" Night's Terror asked, and made herself into a feathery oval.

Plik stroked a hand along the white line of his eyebrows and said to Derian, "Wait while I tell her what Firekeeper saw."

After a time, the maimalodalu resumed translating.

"I thought I saw smoke," Night's Terror said, "but those forests have become so unpleasant now that I did not go and check. As long as the smoke remained among the trees, I would be safe, isolated here as I am."

She smoothed her feathers, preening to calm herself, then resumed. "You do not need to stretch your imagination to realize that soon this had become too dangerous a place for most to reside. The herds left first, Cousins leading the way, for they had no curiosity to keep them, only a strong sense that this was no safe place to raise their fawns and calves. The Wise who often dwell among their Cousin types followed, and soon the predators who relied upon these for their meals also went."

"But you remained," Eshinarvash said. "Why?"

"My mate, Golden Feather, strayed into that copse," Night's Terror replied. "There was a night of storm and in his eagerness to take refuge he mistook that copse for another. Like all the others, he never emerged. I would have given him up for lost and gone on with the others, but for some reason I could not. Fault me for being irrational, but I could not leave without knowing."

Plik said, "Not knowing can be worse than knowing. Believe me, I understand that. I think you are very brave."

"Very foolish," the owl said. "Very, very foolish. I know this, but for some reason I cannot leave until I know."

"Are you the only yarimaimalom who remains?" Plik asked.

"Not the only," Night's Terror replied. "Some others have stayed, but almost all either smaller creatures—littler cats, foxes, I believe a raccoon or so— or those with wings. We keep loose contact with each other, but this is no time in which numbers bring safety."

"I wonder why we've seen no one else?" Eshinarvash asked.

"Because you travel with humans," Night's Terror replied bluntly. "Humans brought this wrongness to our land. Those of us who remain will have nothing to do with humans."

Derian felt very uncomfortable, but he didn't protest. Quite honestly, he wanted very little to do with those twins himself. What had they done? Had they discovered some old magics and awakened them to life?

As much as Derian dreaded this possibility, this seemed the most likely explanation for what had happened. He wished with all his heart that he and his companions could simply turn away as if they knew nothing of any of this, as if they had never heard of the twins, as if the Meddler had never come to haunt Truth's dreams. Derian knew, however, that like the owl, he and his companions would not leave until they knew what dwelled there in that impossible copse.

❧

THAT NIGHT, after Derian had reported on his band's explorations, Firekeeper lay half awake considering what they had learned that day, and feeling a certain dissatisfaction that more of what had been learned had not been the result of her and Blind Seer's efforts.

Of course, now she knew that the reason none of the local yarimaimalom had approached them was because they had reason to fear humans, but that hardly made Firekeeper feel any better.

Night's Terror had spoken to Plik and Eshinarvash, even though Derian had been with them. Why had no one taken the chance on her and Blind Seer? Could it simply be that she and Blind Seer had not chanced so close to an active lair, or might it have been that to any who watched they might have been taken for a woman and her dog?

Firekeeper reached over and rubbed Blind Seer behind one ear and was rewarded by the wolf continuing to sleep. Were any other to come so near he would be on his feet in an instant, fangs bared, a growl in his throat, but he trusted her.

And was his reward for that trust to be taken for a dog?

Firekeeper lay there beside the wolf, listening to the night sounds, thinking about what they had learned, wondering just how they were going to get into that copse. Actually, getting in seemed to be fairly easy. Getting out was apparently the problem. Truth said she might be able to supply a solution, but that she was not yet ready to explore the matter further. Even Firekeeper's dead nose had smelled the acrid tang of the great cat's uneasiness, and she had not pressed the matter.

Gradually, between breath and breath and breath again, Firekeeper became aware that the night was quieter than it should be. The insect noises had faded away to almost nothing. Only a single obnoxiously persistent cricket continued to court the night. There was an odd feel to the air as well, a stirring where there should not be.

Firekeeper placed her hand on Blind Seer's shoulder.

"Wake, dear heart. Something stalks us."

The wolf was alert in a moment. He did not leap to his feet, but slowly rolled to rest on his breastbone, his ears pricked, his nose raised to catch changes in the wind.

Firekeeper knew this because she knew him. She was no longer at his side, but had slipped to waken Plik, then Eshinarvash. Only when these who lived more as Beasts than humans were awake did she move to where Harjeedian and Derian slept, their bedrolls framing Bitter's sick-nest.

"Hush," she said, placing her hand on Derian's arm where it jutted from the wrapped blankets. "Something is out there. Wake."

Derian, trained by now in her manner, did not fill the night with questions as he once might have done. Instead he slowly unwrapped himself, reaching for his sword. Firekeeper moved on to Harjeedian. Harjeedian had not slept a night through since he had taken over Bitter's care, but he woke readily and with little prompting reached for the curved blade that served him as a weapon.

Firekeeper's motions woke Lovable and Bitter. The ravens knew better than to croak. Lovable was clearly curious, but although she could fly a little now, she did not take to the safety of the trees. Instead, she settled herself near Bitter. The male raven had become more alert over the last day or so, but his pain was so intense that there was no way he could fly, much less defend himself. He waited, his one remaining eye moving abruptly in its socket as he sought to identify the source of their danger.

"What is there?" Lovable asked with fluffed head feathers.

Firekeeper shrugged, tossed her head back as if catching a scent, touched her ear, then moved on.

The eerie silence had spread. Even the cricket had fallen still. It was the silence of the forest when every living thing seeks to hide from prowling hunters, but from the fashion in which Blind Seer and Eshinarvash continued scenting the wind, they had not identified who these hunters might be.

Firekeeper bent her bow stave, and while she was stringing it, Plik came over to her.

"Is Truth back?"

Firekeeper shook her head. The jaguar had gone out into the forest to do whatever it was she did at night instead of resting.

Plik made a soft chuffing noise. He was not armed except for a sturdy club. Before this journey, there had been little reason for him to fight. He had hunted much as a raccoon did, fishing in streams, stealing eggs, but he had also had the farms of the maimalodalum, their poultry and goats to sustain him. Still, looking at Plik as he stood there with his fur puffed and his face set stern, Firekeeper remembered that old boar raccoons were formidable opponents indeed.

Eshinarvash caught the stray scent first.

"The air smells of broken branches and crushed leaves mingled with green sap. At first I thought something had been broken by those who stalk us, but the scent grows more intense."

Firekeeper remembered the creatures made from vines and branches. From their sudden watchfulness, from how Derian and Plik moved as one to stir up the coals in the hearth, she could tell the others did as well.

Blind Seer backed from the camp's edge, his hackles raised, a faint growl rumbling in his throat. Wolf-like, he was not challenged that another had caught the scent before him. He accepted the horse's expertise in telling one plant from another. Indeed, if they survived this, he would probably compliment Eshinarvash.

If they survived.

Firekeeper moved to the fire.

"Take care!" she warned. "I could use fire because I could keep it contained. Here, if it is carried into the trees, we may well all burn to death."

Derian shuddered. "But how can we defend ourselves without fire?"

Firekeeper considered. "Cut at the vines, not the branches. I think these are sinew and tendon to them. But there is better way than cut. If these things have animal form, break the carrying limbs. No matter what foul life they have, if they cannot move . . ."

Derian gripped his sword more tightly and nodded stiffly, his head moving back and forth as he scanned the tree line for whatever might emerge. Knowing the vines could be turned into enemies, they had cleared the area surrounding their camp both of shrub and vine, but they could do nothing about the trees.

These and the darkness provided ample cover for whatever was stalking them.

"Perhaps they are only scouting," Harjeedian said, and Firekeeper was surprised to hear hope tight in his voice. She was so accustomed to the aridisdu's acting as if he knew everything that it had never occurred to her that Harjeedian might be afraid. "Perhaps they are returning our visit of the day."

Firekeeper said nothing, knowing the human talked to keep his spirits up.

The Beasts had positioned themselves around the perimeter, close to the fire, but not too close. Plik stood with the humans within this first circle. The ravens simply waited.

Eshinarvash shifted uneasily. Like the wolves, he was accustomed to being with a larger group of his own when predators must be fought. Still, like the wolves, the horse knew that it was the place of those without young to defend the weaker members. He would stand.

But we could use Truth, Firekeeper thought. *I would even settle for that Meddler right now.*

They waited until the end of patience and beyond. They waited until each one doubted that there was anything out there in the darkness, but each doubt was stilled by the continuing silence of the insect world. Imagination might be tempted, patience tried, but nothing fooled those small watchers.

Something was there. Moreover, whatever was there was doing something other than waiting, else the insects would resume their songs. Firekeeper watched her section of the forest, keeping herself alert through faith in a cricket.

When the creatures showed themselves, it was not as they had done before. This time there was no slow, steady creeping forward, no attempt to fool the eye into believing it saw just another tree or shrub. Later, Firekeeper would think that the bracken beasts must have crept until they reached the edge of the grove in which the camp was made. At the time, all she knew was the moment that silence ended and the forest itself seemed to rush forward in a snarling mass of fangs and claws.

She found herself confronted by three: a pair of wolves and a lumbering two-legged bear. The two wolves were racing forward, one centered on her, the other on Plik.

Firekeeper crouched, hands spread, ready to meet her opponent. When it rushed her, she got beneath its body, scooping it up and heaving it toward the other wolf. She had angled herself so that the first wolf's momentum would aid her throw, and she was pleased when a crash of branch and bracken announced her success. Her Fang would do little good here, but she had made note of a piece of firewood that would serve as an ideal club. With this she bashed at the long pieces of wood that served the "wolves" as legs and necks until she had reduced two opponents to a seething mass of timber and vine.

When she looked, she saw that Eshinarvash and Blind Seer were working as a team, the wolf biting and snapping, worrying at their opponents, while the horse reared and trampled. It was a fight in which the wolf's natural strengths meant little, for the throat tear or gut rip by which a wolf downs his prey could do nothing to a creature with neither guts nor throat. However, when the blood briar wriggled free of its frame and sought to cripple the Wise Horse by hooking in his legs, then did the wolf come into his own—and then did the trust between the two show itself at its finest.

The humans were actually doing better in this fight than Firekeeper might have imagined. Both Derian and Harjeedian had taken up clubs. Plik was feeding the fire, letting it flare just enough to give the humans light without risking blinding those who saw well in shadows. Someone had moved the ravens into that protective ring and none of the bracken creatures seemed interested in attacking them. Lovable hopped about, plucking at small things on the ground, probably scattered bits of briar, though Firekeeper was too pressed to investigate.

That was all Firekeeper saw, for her attention was claimed by a creature with a vague resemblance to a lynx, though no lynx could boast of so many claws so long and so horridly hooked. In them, Firekeeper recognized the blood briar, and kept a careful distance when she could. Despite this, she must close and when she did, the thorn claws bit, and where they drew blood her skin went numb.

But despite the company's good and valorous defense, they might have lost the battle had not Truth returned. The bracken beasts kept coming and coming, as if the dark forest itself was birthing them, then urging them forth to fight.

Firekeeper was battering at the midsection of a serpent that was straining toward Blind Seer, all too aware that yet another bear was lumbering toward her and that her strength was failing her. The next moment there was a scream of feline rage and Truth was there by the campfire, rushing forward, leaping on the bear so that it went crashing to the ground beneath the jaguar's weight. There was a sharp crack as jaws powerful enough to break a snapping turtle's shell snapped the heavy branch that gave the "bear" a spine. The entire construct went tumbling down, and Truth's paws ripped apart the tangled mass before it could re-form in some practical fashion.

Truth's arrival gave them all heart. Derian managed a cheer, Blind Seer echoed with a howl. Truth did not acknowledge except by fighting even more furiously. The jaguar seemed to be everywhere, crushing a support limb of this creature, knocking another creature backward, then rearing on her back legs and slashing out with both paws. Never before had Firekeeper been aware of the power in that compact body, and never before had she had so much reason to be grateful for it.

At long last they realized the darkness had no more monsters to send, and they limped back to the brightness of the fire to assess their wounds. It was then that they realized Plik was missing.

Before much energy could be wasted on either speculation or fruitless search, Bitter the raven stirred himself and made the loudest sound he had yet managed.

Harjeedian, his cotton shirt ripped in dozens of places and bits of briar still hanging from the ruin, moved rapidly and crouched near his patient.

"What is it?" he asked, then glanced at Firekeeper. "Well?"

Firekeeper realized with a start that she alone remained to serve as translator. She crossed the camp in a few quick strides, kneeling near the raven so that he would not need to exert himself too greatly.

"He say . . ." She tilted her head to one side, indicating that Bitter should continue.

Lovable was the one who spoke. *"I saw it, too. No need to talk."*

Bitter subsided, though the ruffling of his feathers said more clearly than words, "Then tell them, fluff head!"

Lovable went on as if Bitter had not spoken, *"During the fighting, I stayed here. The briars at first had no thought for us—if they have thought at all—but as the rest of you shredded the first creatures, the briars that remained undamaged began questing for easier prey. I cut many of these with my beak, but there were too many for me to battle alone. Plik saw this quickly. Being so much smaller, he could not fight the monsters as you larger ones did, but he had managed to take out a carrying limb or so. Now he left this, and joined me in trampling and breaking the small briars. It was his thought that we toss them in the fire, and this served double purpose, ending their motion and lighting our fight.*

"Even so, our task became not easier but more difficult as the battle progressed, for every great creature that fell gave forth many, many of the wrigglers. Both Plik and I were snagged many times by the thorns—he more often than I, for I at least could flutter a little above the ground.

"Do you recall that last rush of attacks, right before Truth arrived? There was one other attacker, one those of you concentrating on those who came from outside the firelight never saw. Remember how I told you that me and Plik were trying to destroy the loose briars?"

Firekeeper wanted to growl that she couldn't possibly forget, but she made herself be calm.

"I remember," she said, speaking Pellish, for she had been translating as Lovable spoke.

"Here we saw something horrible happening. The briars stopped acting as individuals, but began twisting onto each other, forming a sort of snake. It wasn't as big as the snake that attacked us at the stone house, but it was big enough. It twisted around Plik and began dragging him into the forest. He ripped at it—tore it nearly in half at one point—but it just re-formed. You all were providing plenty of material for it from your own fights."

"Why didn't you call us?" Blind Seer said. "I certainly could have been some help."

Lovable collapsed on herself. "I thought it wanted Bitter! I put myself between him and the snake, and bit at it as ferociously as I could. It was only after it had a coil or two around Plik that I realized that it was doing other than subduing a formidable opponent."

"And Plik," Harjeedian said when Firekeeper finished translating this, "doubtless didn't cry out because he had taken a large dose of the briar poison. Bitter's experience makes me believe that in small doses it numbs surface area, but that in larger doses it may cause a state similar to a coma."

Firekeeper didn't understand most of Harjeedian's words, but she gathered the sense. An odd prickling of hope raced along her nerves.

"Plik may be alive, then," she said. "Those who come here did not try and carry us off. They tried to hurt, to kill."

She held up her own lacerated arm, though no one present really needed that testimony.

Derian nodded. "Plik they didn't try to kill—at least at the end there. It's possible the briars needed a source of blood to get out of here, maybe to shape other creatures . . ."

Firekeeper shuddered, imagining that somewhere in the darkness new briar beasts were forming, reducing fat, round Plik into a shriveled husk inside his fur.

"We check," she said.

Blind Seer shook himself. "I will go, Firekeeper, and perhaps Truth . . ."

"I will," the jaguar agreed.

"Firekeeper, you will stay," Blind Seer continued. She made a sound of protest, and he bumped his head against her arm. "We no longer hunt with a pack where only you and I need to understand each other, dear heart. There are others here who require you to be their voice."

Firekeeper nodded, reluctantly accepting this as the right allocation of their abilities, knowing she would be less than a wolf if she refused to serve where the pack needed her.

"Be careful, dear heart," she said, stroking the wolf.

Blind Seer replied without words, for there were no words in him to give a promise that could not be kept. He would be as careful as the situation permitted, no more, no less.

Then wolf and jaguar ventured into the darkness. Firekeeper remained, watching and waiting for the coming of dawn.

XVIII

THE FIRST THING PLIK WAS AWARE OF was the screaming thunder of surf so loud that it blocked everything else from his hearing.

It was not a sensation conducive to thought, but when he did think, Plik's first assumption was that he had come home to Misheemnekuru and that the islands were being battered by a truly horrible hurricane. He wondered that he did not feel whatever tree or tower in which he had taken refuge bending and tossing beneath the force of that storm. At the same time he was grateful. The violence of thundering surf was such that already he felt physically battered. He did not think he could bear much more.

Then the illusion was broken by a solid thump followed by a metallic click, the sounds so clear and crisp that Plik realized that the sensation that continued to batter him was not being heard by his ears. For the first time he recalled he had other senses, and forced his eyes open.

He was in a room lit by the green glow of daylight filtered through leaves. He lay on his side on a bed made after the human design, his head resting on a cotton-cased pillow filled with goose down. The thump and click he had heard were the sounds made by the door to this chamber being opened by the young human who now entered. There was a clatter as the human lowered the latch into its place again, a chiming jingle of china on a metal tray as the human set the tray down on a table some paces from the bed. Plik smelled an infusion of rose hips mingled with honey, baked oat cakes, and chilled butter.

Plik's senses seemed to be working well, but the sound, if sound it was, still thundered in his head, rising and falling with erratic yet regular pulses, very like the sound of waves against a shore. The intensity of the "sound" was paralyzing, dominating Plik's will so that he studied the human who had borne in the tray with mild interest. In contrast to the battering sound nothing else seemed very real.

"You're awake," the human said. "That's good."

Plik studied the creature. It was, he thought, forcing the thought through the reverberations, a human not long past childhood, but certainly no longer a child. It was a female, colored rather oddly by his standards, for until he had met Firekeeper and Derian, Plik's idea had been that all humans were colored much like deer or bear, in shades of brown.

This young woman—the word came to Plik with a small flash of triumph—was browner-skinned than Derian, but not as brown as Harjeedian. Her hair was a new and interesting hue: too fair to be brown, to brown to be fair, but somewhere immediately in the middle. Her eyes were a warm brown, like those of a fawn.

Plik found that if he concentrated hard on something else, the thundering in his head faded, so he studied the young woman with new avidity. There were things about her that suggested that she had passed a long time indoors. Despite the natural brown hue of her skin, a pallor underlay it. The gown she wore was of a very simple cut, but excess flesh strained against the fabric, as if it had been sewn when she carried less weight.

Plik supposed that the gown might have been made for another person and appropriated by this young woman, but he did not think this was so. It had not the look of attire someone would appropriate. Her hair—from what he could see, for it was pulled back and braided—was of one uniform shade top to bottom. This also suggested a great deal of time spent indoors. Even beasts' coats faded in the sun. Plik had noted how Derian and Firekeeper's hair was lighter at the end of its growth than where it was new.

The young woman was pouring tea now, and Plik's stomach made grumbling noises. He realized he was very hungry, but when he tried to bring himself upright so he might accept the cup being brought to him, he found his limbs did not obey him.

The young woman noticed and smiled kindly at him. It was a nice smile, warm and not without pity.

"I'll hold you up, if you don't mind," she said. "The blood briars leave one weak."

She spoke as from experience, and Plik wondered how she had acquired that experience.

"My name is Isende," the young woman went on.

Isende! Plik thought. *That is the name of the girl twin. I must have been carried within the copse. We were right that they were hiding there.*

He studied Isende as she carried a cup of tea over to the bed, set it on a nearby stand, then seated herself on the bed. She lifted Plik with a certain amount of effort and then began to carefully feed him tea.

I feel like a doll, Plik thought, trying not to resent Isende's manner. From the way his body was soaking up the tea, from how he could feel the honey invigorating him, he needed the beverage desperately.

Isende fed him two cups of the tea, then broke one of the oat cakes into small pieces.

"See if you can chew these," she said. "Sensation often returns to the trunk first, then to the limbs."

Plik found he could manage, but only if Isende fed him the pieces. He realized he could not feel his fingers or toes at all, and that his arms, legs, and tail felt as if they had been encased in stone. Sensation was there, but muffled. Plik wondered if the surf still thudding somewhat less aggressively in his head had anything to do with the numbness, or if the two were unconnected.

When Plik indicated that he was finished eating, Isende dusted him off, then brushed crumbs off the bedclothes.

"I imagine you'd like to try sitting up," she said, "but I'm going to ask you to be patient. The briar poison will disperse more quickly if you are all at one level."

Plik decided to attempt talking. He tried to ask "Why was I brought here?" but all he managed was a bleat. Even so, Isende decided to take this as an invitation to chat. She brought a chair over by the bed, positioning it so that Plik could see her without moving his head. This was a good thing. Without the meal to concentrate on, the thundering in his head was growing worse again.

"I wonder what manner of creature you are?" Isende mused, not really asking him. "At first we thought you were a raccoon—one of the yarimaimalom, of course. But when we took a closer look, it was quite evident that you were not a raccoon."

Plik made a noise that was intended to be "We?" but came out as another bleat, differently pitched. He supposed he should be grateful for that small difference.

"My brother, Tiniel," Isende replied, encouraging Plik with this indication of understanding.

Isende looked as if she was about to add something else, but then she shut her mouth firmly, pressing the lips together. After a longish pause she resumed speaking again, her tones forced and bright.

"I wonder if you came here looking for us or merely by chance? You're with others. We know that, but we don't recognize any of them. They aren't from Gak. One looks like he's from Liglim, but the other two humans . . . They're odd-looking."

She gave a light, giggly laugh.

"But then Tiniel and I are odd-looking, too. Our father and mother were from two different peoples, one fair, one dark. We came out as sort of a mix of the two. There's no one like us in all the world—other than each other. We're twins, and except for him being a boy, we're really very much alike. Tiniel is a little taller than I am, and broader in the shoulder. And me, well, I'm a girl, so I'm lots different, but when we were children, and even now if we dress in the right kind of clothing, it's hard for people to tell us apart."

Isende's chattering, the words spilling over each other like water over rocks, was almost enough to drown out the pounding of the surf in Plik's head. Plik wondered how long it had been since Isende had someone to talk to other than her brother. The twins had left Gak over a year before, in the late spring, or so Layo had said. That was a long time for even the most devoted brother and sister to have only each other for company.

Plik listened as Isende chattered about a favorite pet, a grey squirrel she had raised from a kit; about a walking trip with her mother when she was six; about building cities from wooden blocks with Tiniel.

Although Isende talked copiously, a veritable flood of words, Plik began to notice what she did not say. She never once mentioned the bond that Layo had told them made it possible for the twins to share experiences. Plik did not think it at all odd that Isende did not mention this directly. The twins must have learned early on that this ability made others uncomfortable. However, he did think it rather odd how carefully Isende edited any allusion to this bond. If she was doing so deliberately, then she was far more intelligent than she appeared to be.

He also wondered that she did not mention anything at all regarding the twins' departure from Gak, their long journey to this place, and the year and more they had managed to survive on their own, just the two of them, with a little help (so he knew from Night's Terror) from the local yarimaimalom.

As sensation returned to his body, Plik discovered he could turn his head side to side. Immediately, Plik noticed something odd about his surroundings. He had thought he was within the ruined house that Night's Terror had mentioned, the one that had stood where the copse now seemed to be. Now he began to wonder. If this room was anything to judge by, either the twins were well trained in carpentry and masonry, or the sealed house had survived the passage of over a century impossibly well.

He noticed other odd things as well. The daylight was not being filtered through leaves as he had initially thought. The glass in the window was slightly tinted, creating a similar effect. An odd choice, surely, but humans often did odd things.

The thundering in his head was rising again, and the rambling narrative of Isende's chatter was not enough to press the sound back. Then Plik noticed something that shocked him so much that for a long moment the pounding vanished completely, leaving him with thoughts uncluttered and focused.

There was a tree branch outside the window. It looked to be from an oak, but it might have been from some other tree inclined toward rough bark and gnarls. Plik couldn't tell for sure, for the tree was mostly bare, shorn of all but a few brown rags of leaf and one tight knot that held a hint of russet and yellow. The green filtering was provided by the leaves of the blood briar that grew in a light tracery over the window opening.

Plik recalled the appearance of the copse perfectly, and not only of the copse, but of the forest in which they had camped as well. Despite the relative lateness of the year, the deciduous trees had still been in leaf, and mostly in green leaf at that.

The company—especially those members who had thick fur and would have welcomed the cooler weather of autumn—had mentioned how odd this continuing greenness seemed to them. In the land of the Liglim at the time of their departure there had been one or two signs of the coming autumn, whereas farther south the trees retained their summer leaves. The only sign of the lateness of the season was a certain raggedness about the foliage, as if the leaves were tired, ready to be shed and renewed.

But here without a doubt was an autumn bough, and a late autumn bough at that. It might be that the tree outside the window was dead, its ragged leaves banners from a summer gone by, but somehow he felt certain that this tree was alive.

And if it was alive, where did that leave him? Plik struggled for explanations, and as he did so the pounding in his head rose, pushing him under, shoving him beneath a wave of sensation so powerful that he drowned.

❧

THE REPORT BLIND SEER and Truth brought back after sunrise the next morning was discouraging. They had found ample evidence—broken branches, bits of vine, a trail blazed directly through the undergrowth—that Plik had been taken to the copse. That was where the trail ended. What was disturbing was how that trail had ended. It had not ended because wolf and jaguar had been unwilling to follow, for Derian suspected that Night's Terror's ominous reports of the many who had vanished in that copse would not have stopped them if they had thought they could bring Plik back with them.

No. The trail had ended as neatly as if it had never been. There it was, the signs of something heavy going through the tall grass evident to the eye, Plik's scent mingled with the sour blood scent of the briars evident to the nose. Then the trail had simply stopped.

"Wiped out," Truth said, through Firckeeper, "like a wave wipes paw prints from the sand. Gone."

"But not like it was covered," Harjeedian asked. "Wiped away as if it had never been."

"Exactly," Firekeeper said, translating for Truth, her tone capturing an arrogant bluntness that Derian was certain was the jaguar's own, for it had been present in Plik's translations as well.

"They looked up into the trees," Firekeeper went on. "I ask. Truth and Blind Seer both thought Plik might be carried there, but there were no signs above. Bark would have been ripped, leaves broken if something so heavy as Plik go up, but there is nothing."

Blind Seer nudged her with his nose and Firekeeper added, "To make sure they find Night's Terror and she looks, too, though she will not go into copse. She see nothing."

Harjeedian, who had been making a noisome paste that mingled strengthening herbs and deer's liver for Bitter, gave his pestle rest.

"So do we go after Plik?" he asked. "If we do, I say we go all together. There is no need to send two, then two more, then two more until those remaining are left wondering whether there would be greater wisdom in going forward or back."

"I agree," Derian said, "but didn't Truth have some plan she was working on? Something that would get us safely into the copse?"

Firekeeper looked over at the jaguar, and as before Derian noted something subtly challenging about the wolf-woman's posture.

Firekeeper said in Pellish, "Well, Truth?"

The jaguar licked between her toes.

Firekeeper bristled, apparently insulted, but she kept speaking in Pellish.

"You say you learn something—from the Voice, from the Meddler. There was a deal you make. What is that deal?"

Derian felt the skin on his back prickle as a voice, deep, compelling, and masculine, spoke from just beyond the curtaining line of trees.

"What the deal is remains our business, until Truth chooses to speak of it, but I now offer you free of any cost a chance to talk with me. I think I owe you that much since you took the time to set me free. May I join you?"

Firekeeper growled, "Come."

The figure that stepped from the forest cover looked somewhat like one of the Liglimom, except for his hair which was thick, iron grey, and somewhat more coarse than was usual. His eyes were golden brown, and his smile somehow familiar. After a few moments, Derian realized the man—the Meddler this must be—was also slightly translucent. The dark shapes of the trees and rocks were visible through him, though smaller things seemed to fade into his general form.

The Meddler moved to a vacant spot in their circle, a spot Derian realized they had unconsciously left for Plik.

"Now," the Meddler said, seating himself cross-legged on the ground with an ease and grace that didn't go at all with his grey hair. "I've met three of you, and know who the rest are. You already know—or at least think you know—who I am. Shall we go from there?"

"Three?" Firekeeper growled.

Bitter croaked something, and Firekeeper listened, her brows lifting in obvious amazement.

"Bitter say that the Meddler speak with him when he was most hurt and tell him things that make him try harder to live."

"Not," the Meddler said in that fluid, easy voice, "that I could have done much good without the care Bitter was receiving on this side of things. That's what really mattered."

Harjeedian, who had been spooning out liver paste for Bitter, did not seem suddenly won over by this graceful compliment.

You're going to have to work harder to undo whatever damage to your reputation those legends Harjeedian has heard did long before he thought you were anything but legend, Derian thought with an inward smile.

Harjeedian wasn't an easy man to like, but even when they had been ene-mies, Derian had seen traits to admire. Moonspans on the road together had done nothing to undermine Derian's sense that the aridisdu was a strong-willed man indeed.

Firekeeper had moved to sit closer to Blind Seer than was her wont when the weather was warm, her knee pressing into the wolf's fur. Blind Seer didn't seem to mind. Derian was fascinated to note that the wolf's hackles were ever so slightly raised. Eshinarvash and Truth watched with a controlled calm that was less hostile, but no less guarded. Lovable and Bitter seemed to have no at-tention for anything but Bitter's meal, and that said something in itself. Nor-mally, the ravens were the most inquisitive members of the company.

I guess, Derian thought, *it's going to be up to me to get this started. The Med-dler doesn't seem to have many friends here—not even Truth, for all Firekeeper seems to think there is something between them.*

"What can you tell us," Derian said, adopting the easygoing tone he used when getting ready for a good barter session, "about what happened to Plik?"

"You mean what happened that you don't know already," the Meddler said. He flashed a grin at Derian, and with that smile Derian knew exactly what had seemed so familiar.

His father had a brother who smiled like that. Uncle was a complete rascal who could charm the skirts off a girl or the horse out from under a rider. De-spite that, he was a likable fellow, probably Derian's favorite relative outside of his own immediate family.

"That's what I mean," Derian said, keeping his own grin alive. He had a strong feeling that showing any annoyance would lose him marks in a game in which he didn't know the rules. "We know Plik was taken from here into the copse. What have you got to add?"

"That he's quite probably alive."

If the Meddler had expected cries of joy and excitement at this, he was dis-appointed. Stony stares met him from all eyes but Derian's, and Derian just waved a hand and laughed.

"We'd figured that out on our own, and the good noses of Blind Seer and Truth confirmed it. What else do you have to put on the table?"

The Meddler's grin didn't fade. If anything, he seemed pleased. "You're wondering what's inside that copse. I can tell you what was there, but I'm go-ing to be up-front with you. I don't know what's there now."

"What do you mean?" Derian asked sharply.

"I'm being literal," the Meddler said. "I have some idea what was there before, when the twins first arrived and set up camp, but after the copse arose, well, that's where my information ends."

"Might be of some use," Derian said. "I don't suppose you could sketch us a map."

"I'm a little insubstantial now," the Meddler said, sweeping his fingers through the coals of their fire. "But I can tell you what I know and you can draw from that."

"We can work with that," Derian said, "but before we get to mapmaking, I've got a question for you."

"Ask."

"What's your part in all of this?"

"All of this?" the Meddler feigned confusion.

"We found figurines in your apartment."

"Prison."

"Whatever."

"Figurines of people we knew and of a couple of people we've since learned were the twins. We have our speculations, but before we let you draw us a map and chase us into that copse, I think you'd better tell us about your involvement with Melina, with Dantarahma, with Valora . . . and why with those three fine examples of your handiwork we should have anything to do with you and your twins."

"To rescue Plik?" the Meddler suggested.

"To make sure we have a chance of rescuing Plik," Derian countered. "I'm not charging in there until we know a whole lot more."

FIREKEEPER LISTENED WITH ADMIRATION as Derian began to attack the Meddler. She didn't like or trust the strange wolf-headed human, but she also was all too aware that what he was willing to tell them might make the difference when they went after Plik.

Her approach would have been to threaten, try to bully, even to trade—all tactics a wolf knew well. Derian's bullying took a different approach. He had managed to twist things so that he made it sound like the Meddler needed to do something for them.

Blind Seer swished his tail through the dry leaves in gentle applause, and they settled down to listen.

"I don't know why I should try and explain myself to you," the Meddler said. "You're not going to believe anything I say."

Derian grinned. "Still, you might as well have a chance to present things as you'd like us to see them. Otherwise, we'll just be conjecturing from incomplete information."

The Meddler began by recounting the circumstances of his long imprisonment, how he had been locked away by those who did not trust either his motives or his power. Harjeedian stirred restlessly during this part of the account, no doubt because the Meddler made quite clear that his opponents were sorcerers, not divine beings. Since the sorcerers were widely viewed as those who abused divine Magic, that put the Meddler squarely on the side of the deities Harjeedian served. No wonder the aridisdu was uncomfortable.

The Meddler presented his centuries of captivity in a manner that Firekeeper couldn't help but find moving, even as she looked at that wolf's head on those human shoulders and felt herself prickling with distrust. She noted that the Meddler had a long wolf's tail as well, and that he sat leaning forward, arms resting on his knees, so as not to inhibit its motion.

Eventually, the Meddler began speaking of how the bonds of his prison began to fail.

"But not enough to set me wholly free," he admitted. "At first I was overcome with joy, for I had some freedom. Later, I felt worse than I had before. I had grown somewhat resigned to my captivity. Now, glimpsing hints of the world, having occasional contact from some drifting mind, I felt the sharp pinching of my bonds once more.

"Magic had bound me, and my initial thought was that magic was what I needed to be free. I probed, fishing on a very insubstantial line for those minds that were interested in the ways of old magic. I will not bore you with the number of times I felt a nibble, only to feel that nibble drop away. Time for me was not what it is now, but I think my first 'fish' was Dantarahma. Not only did he reside closest to my prison, but he was eager for power and that eagerness made him bite.

"Dantarahma was very important to my growing awareness of the outside world. He sensed the maimalodalum's awareness of his probings into magic and sent out spells to dampen their ability. I have no idea why, but his attempts to dampen the maimalodalum also managed to dampen the forces that restricted my roaming. I ventured farther. To the north I found and hooked Melina. Through her mind I learned of the three artifacts, and decided I needed Valora as well. However, through my contact with Melina and Valora, I learned how acutely fearful of magic the northern lands could be. Therefore, I quested elsewhere and, to the south, I found Isende and Tiniel.

"You know what happened with Melina, with Valora, and Dantarahma as well. Your interest—and mine, I'll admit it wholeheartedly—is with the twins."

The Meddler spoke with such earnestness and intensity that Firekeeper found herself almost forgetting his reputation. A trapped animal will gnaw off a limb to escape. How was what the Meddler had done any different? Then the wolf-woman remembered the lives that had been ruined because the Meddler had meddled, and she hardened her heart.

The Meddler glanced at her, his golden brown eyes seeming to say that he knew she still doubted his good motives and that he was wounded. What had he done that she would not had their situations been the same? But he said nothing direct, and went back to his tale.

"Those figurines in which you place such significance are not dreadfully magical in themselves. They are aids to concentration, that is all. I used them to focus on what my chosen subjects were doing. When—as in the case of the artifacts stored in the castle at Silver Whale Cove—I learned of something that I thought might assist my subjects to enhance their magical abilities, well, I did my best to encourage them to do so.

"So when I realized that Isende and Tiniel were not only possessed of a peculiar sensitivity, but were also through their father direct heirs to magical ability, I grew quite excited. For the longest time, I could do nothing to stir the twins from their own purpose, for they were intent upon getting their family recognized as a voting clan within their resident city-state. Only when that plan failed and the twins were discouraged could I prompt them to seek some other way of claiming their rightful heritage.

"It wasn't easy, not in the least, nor will I expect you to sympathize with my fear as the twins made their way alone through wild lands. They took with them no servants, no guards, only what provisions they needed, and the knowledge of where their family holdings had been. Had the distance been greater, had they been less careful, they might never have succeeded, but they came to what had been the Setting Sun land grant. Within a few days they located what had been the residence of their father's ancestors."

Derian interjected. "Wait a moment. We came well guarded, and with several companions who are more than a little skilled with weapons—or at least with claws and fangs."

"And you have barely managed to survive," the Meddler said. "One of your number is crippled, and all of you are scarred."

"Right," Derian said. "Did you protect the twins?"

"I did not," the Meddler said, "for there was nothing much to protect them from. The blood briars did not grow here, nor did the bracken beasts prowl. This was a forest much like any forest. The weather was kind, and the twins' hardest labor was clearing a trail for themselves and their pack animals. Both had some skill with the bow, and they had brought with them a pair of bird dogs. Really, they faced little more of an ordeal than any pair of campers might."

Firekeeper frowned. "What of the Royal Beasts—or the Wise Beasts? Didn't these object to the twins' coming?"

"These are southern lands," the Meddler said. "Gak, the city-state in which the twins were born, has residents who are closer to Liglim in their religious practices than otherwise. The twins behaved respectfully. In turn, the Wise Beasts watched the twins, but they did not see two such pitiful young humans as invaders."

"Even our pack," Blind Seer said, "would not have felt that two alone were such a threat. If they had tried to settle down, then perhaps, but the policy that guided us when we guarded our own border was always to let those hunters and trappers who dared cross the Iron Mountains come and hunt . . . as long as they went. We hid from them, so they would not bear tales, and warned the other Royal Beasts to do the same."

Firekeeper nodded. "So these twins came, and nothing harmed them, and they went to the old lair. What then?"

The Meddler stretched as a man might, and went on. "This 'old lair,' as you call it, had not been built merely as a place to eat and sleep and store away a bit of food. It had been built to be the heart of a farming community—and as a bit more. Remember, those who came here practiced sorcery, and their dwelling must be a place where those arts could be practiced. It held a library and a workshop and other things as well. When the Plague came and the residents fled, they could not take everything with them. It may be that they had learned of the general uprising against the magical arts and all those who practiced them. Communication over distances was not as difficult then as it is now.

"In any case, they took care to seal the main stronghold as well as they could, and to hide away those things they could not take with them. Remember, you know that the Plague would end the rule of magic in the New World, but they did not. They thought this sickness would set them back a season, maybe a year or two, and then they would rebuild. They did not know this was the end.

"As in the north, the Beasts were active in destroying things of magic, and when the humans had gone, they broke into the estate and destroyed what they could. Outbuildings were burned and even portions of the main stronghold were damaged beyond use, but a few places remained sealed, hidden behind fallen timbers or simply unrecognized for what they were.

"When Isende and Tiniel came, they initially despaired. If I did anything at this point, I merely gave them courage to continue. I gave them images of the indignities they had suffered in Gak, reminded them of their resolve. I did nothing but restore to them their own hearts when those hearts might have become broken by despair."

"How noble," Derian said, and Firekeeper could hear the sarcasm in his tone.

The Meddler apparently did not. He inclined his head as in thanks, and continued.

"The twins found shelter in the ruins, made friends with some of the yari-maimalom. Later, they found remnants of old orchards and such that enabled them to extend their stores. Even while they concentrated on building a home for themselves, they did not lose sight of their larger goals. Each day they reserved a time when one or both of them would explore the ruins. Usually, they would find nothing but some tool or bit of goods that would make their stay more comfortable, but on one memorable day Tiniel found the library. It was not a magical library—by a pact among many nations those were not permitted in the New World—but it was a library that had belonged to sorcerers. Here they found knowledge that had been lost, hints of how magic could be performed."

Harjeedian interrupted, frowning. "This is something I do not completely understand. We have fine libraries in u-Nahal, but I do not think we have books such as these."

"You might be surprised, Aridisdu," the Meddler said, "what is known to the iaridisdu of your temple. But that is neither here nor there. Let me explain. Let us say you have never seen dancing and you find a book in which a dance is described. This description would not be enough to tell you how to perform that dance—not unless the book was quite unreasonably detailed—but it would give you some sense that dancing involved movement to music, movement of both hands and feet, perhaps in coordination with a partner."

"I see," Harjeedian said, and from his tone Firekeeper thought the Meddler's taunt had stung more than a little, "and it was this sort of book that the twins found?"

"That type, and more than one of that type," the Meddler agreed. "And this is where my own knowledge of what happened here in the south becomes less clear. This is around the time that you, Harjeedian, brought Derian, Firekeeper, and Blind Seer south with you and all of Dantarahma's well-laid plans began to go awry. I was already somewhat aware of these three, and more than once I have wondered if someone acting against me arranged for you to learn of them."

"Eh?" Firekeeper said, suddenly acutely interested. "What is this?"

"Probably nothing more than paranoia on my account," the Meddler said. "After all, there were very reasonable and logical reasons that the disdum would learn about you, and once they knew of you, nothing was more reasonable than that they would seek to know you."

Firekeeper decided that the Meddler had a point, and if she wanted to rescue Plik they need not follow such a tenuous trail.

"Go on," she said, "your tale is interesting, but Plik needs us."

The Meddler nodded. "He may indeed, but I, for one, take hope in the fact that he was taken alive."

"As do we all," croaked Bitter. "Now, tell on."

"I have told you that the figurines were aids to concentration on my part, and from this you have surely surmised that I could not concentrate easily on all my subjects at once. By this time, Melina was no longer a matter of concern. Valora was useless to me, and the twins seemed to have settled into a life of contented reading and foraging. I put all my attention into watching Dantarahma, endeavoring to contact him and put the idea into his head that the solution to all his problems could be found on Misheemnekuru. I had not counted on the severe resistance I would meet. Rationally, Dantarahma could work his mind around to the idea that there was nothing sacred about those islands, but emotionally the resistance persisted, he would not go there himself. What he did do—and I assure you this was all on his own—was evolve the idea that there was something on those islands that was opposing him."

"And," Truth said tartly, "we know what happened then. Destruction and the death of many good folk, both beast and otherwise. And, of course, the minor side effect of my being driven insane. But you had nothing to do with this . . ."

Again the Meddler seemed immune to the sarcasm.

"I'm so very glad that you understand," he said. "Again, you know the details of those days far better than I do, for I only experienced them at a distance and through Dantarahma's perspective. When it was all over and Dantarahma gone to answer for his deeds, I turned again to the twins. You can imagine my complete astonishment when I discovered that they were gone."

"Gone?"

The exclamation came from every throat.

"Gone. I could not touch their thoughts as once I had done, nor could I find their physical bodies. My freedom—as I have already told some of you—had been somewhat enhanced by the events surrounding the end of Dantarahma and the fall of the Tower of Magic. However, even with this expanded perspective, I could not find any trace of the twins. What I did find was a copse in place of the cluster of buildings in which they had made their new home. That copse resisted my probing so completely that I knew it was not a natural forest at all, but a barrier meant to keep out any who pried. Moreover, the forests in the surrounding area had changed. The yarimaimalom had not yet abandoned the area completely, but the retreat had begun. The blood briars were twining through the forests, and the bracken beasts prowled.

"I will admit that I was close to despair. Despite all I had done to gain my freedom, I remained trapped. Most of the hopes I had nurtured were either dead or vanished. Only Valora remained, and she was queen of an isolated island realm. Valora's experiences with Melina had enhanced her native distrust of magic. Even so, I probed after her again, hoping to detect some indication she had changed. While I was probing after Valora, I came across a faint trace or scent that led me to Truth.

"Valora proved hopeless—at least for my purposes—so now I focused on Truth. I hoped that if I set in motion the means to return this Wise Jaguar to her sanity, I might make myself an ally. I cannot say I have done so, not as I might have wished, but now at least your company shares a goal with me."

"Oh?" Firekeeper said, and heard herself echoed by throats human and not. "How so?"

The Meddler smiled. "I wish to find out what happened to the twins. They were my associates after a fashion, and I am concerned about them."

Firekeeper did not believe concern was the full reason for the Meddler's interest, but oddly she did not doubt that it was at least a partial truth. In all the accounts they had been told of the Meddler, his greatest flaw seemed a tendency to become passionately involved.

Derian said, "And you think that if we go looking for Plik, we'll learn what happened to your twins."

"That's right," the Meddler said. "And I would like to know what happened to them."

"And perhaps," Harjeedian said, "find out what skills they may have acquired."

"Oh," the Meddler said, "that would be nice, for the twins certainly have learned something. Haven't they?"

XIX

THE MEDDLER VANISHED SOON THEREAFTER, again promising them his aid and assistance.

"I wish we knew for certain he was gone," Derian said, looking around uneasily. "He seems a nice enough fellow, reasonable, eager to help, but—maybe it's being able to see through him from time to time— he makes my skin crawl."

Truth sniffed the air, then said to Firekeeper, "I have taken scent of both here and the other here. I think the Meddler is gone. He may not be completely honest with us, but in one thing I am sure he is—even freed from his prison, he is not as strong as he should be. I think his effort to make contact with all of us wearied him."

Firekeeper nodded and made a quick translation that got across the gist, but left out Truth's elaboration. She could tell the jaguar was annoyed, but she didn't care. She had other things to think about.

Harjeedian was frowning at Derian. "Do not let yourself be fooled into thinking of the Meddler as a 'fellow' of any sort. You heard the legends Plik related. He is not a creature to be trusted in the least."

"Those were good stories," Derian said, "but I don't know if they're exactly history."

"They are not unlike those I learned as sacred lore," Harjeedian said in a lofty tone that Firekeeper thought might have worked if Harjeedian was speaking as aridisdu to the faithful, but was sure to annoy Derian. "The Meddler is not to be trusted. This is what we are taught."

Firekeeper interrupted, "What language you hear the Meddler talk?"

Harjeedian and Derian turned from their nascent argument and spoke almost at once: "Pellish" from Derian, "Liglim" from Harjeedian. Then they stared at each other.

Firekeeper looked at the Beasts.

"I did not think of it," Eshinarvash said. "He spoke, I understood."

"The language of Liglim," the ravens said.

"He spoke to me as in my dreams," Truth said. "I'd never considered him speaking any particular language."

"Liglimosh," Blind Seer said.

"And I heard Pellish," Firekeeper said. Then she translated for the humans what the Beasts had said.

"This is very strange . . ." Derian began, but Harjeedian interrupted.

"This odd power is proof of what I said. The Meddler is a deific figure of some sort."

Firekeeper huffed annoyance at him. "Hush. Tell me this. We all saw him. Derian speaks of being able to see through him. Was this so for all?"

Various sounds and gestures of agreement followed. Firekeeper took a deep breath.

"And what did he look like to you?"

"A man of my race," Harjeedian said, "of perhaps middle years, his clothing and the style of his hair after the way such was worn before the coming of Divine Retribution."

Eshinarvash said, *"Also a man of Harjeedian's people, but dressed like those at u-Bishinti."*

"He looked like someone from Liglim," Derian said, "but he smiled just like my father's brother, the one everyone knows isn't quite honest, but who you can't help but love."

"A wolf," Blind Seer said, *"with yellow-golden eyes and fur perhaps a bit darker than my own. He was larger than me, although not by much."*

The ravens and Truth had seen the Meddler much as Eshinarvash had, although in Truth's visions the Meddler's hair had been iron grey.

Firekeeper considered what the others had said and was startled from her reverie when Derian said, "And you, Firekeeper, what did he look like to you?"

"Like a vision from a dream long ago," Firekeeper said deliberately, "although not wholly so. He had the head and tail of a wolf, but walked upright like a human. His eyes were yellow-brown."

She did not add, "He was strangely handsome," but she wondered from how Blind Seer sniffed at her if he, at least, guessed. She stroked along his back in a quiet bid for forgiveness.

"Why all these faces and languages?" she asked.

"The Meddler is not to be trusted," Harjeedian snapped. "Surely this is yet another proof."

"Maybe because, as he told us," Truth offered, *"he lacks a body of his own and so must furnish one from our imaginations."*

"I think Truth's right," Derian said, "but so is Harjeedian. Not one of us saw a vision that was frightening or repellent. In the case of my being reminded of my uncle, that made me even inclined to like him a little."

"But why," Harjeedian said, mollified somewhat, "did Blind Seer see him as a wolf when none of the other yarimaimalom did so?"

Blind Seer replied, and Firekeeper translated, "Perhaps because I am not of your people, nor did I listen too closely to Plik's tales along the road. Indeed, I think I missed several when I was resting from the day's heat or scouting the road."

Harjeedian listened, then said, "Perhaps the reason we all heard and saw as we did is as Truth suggested—because the Meddler lacks a body and relied upon our minds to give him one. However, it is possible that he deliberately manipulated us in some fashion, hoping to make us see him in the most favorable light possible."

Derian grinned at the aridisdu. "It doesn't seem to have worked with you."

"I have training and education precisely against such dangers," Harjeedian replied stiffly.

Firekeeper ignored the exchange, hearing nothing more than puppy growls in their verbal sparring. Instead she looked at Blind Seer.

"Do we trust this Meddler? Or do we go ahead and try to rescue Plik without his aid?"

Blind Seer looked very unhappy. *"I think we must see what aid the Meddler can offer. We know that there are dangerous things in this forest. Plik and the others saw that the copse was strange even before Night's Terror or the Meddler told how it had come to replace the house in which the twins laired."*

Firekeeper turned her attention to Truth. *"You are the one who has had the most contact with the Meddler. Do you think he has any knowledge that will be useful to us?"*

"*I will ask,*" the jaguar replied. "*I will ask.*"

EVENTUALLY, THE WOLVES LEFT TO HUNT for game larger than a rabbit, for someone the size of Blind Seer was not sustained for long on small game.

Truth wished them luck, but hoped they would take their time about the hunt. She wouldn't mind a chunk of freshly killed pork or venison herself, but she was not as fast a traveler as the wolves. In any case, she could turn the time to better use. Concentrating on the lessons the Meddler had been teaching her was not easy at the best of times. However, she found the manipulations harder when she was aware of Firekeeper's critical gaze. Even when Truth went off into the forests alone, she could feel that watchful waiting. It troubled her and broke her concentration.

"You're aware of Firekeeper," the Meddler said, appearing as he always did, unannounced and without warning, "because our Firekeeper has a very strong sense of herself. You have something she wants—the secret to how Plik might be safely pursued. In a sense, then, you've become a part of her personal sphere."

Truth didn't like the idea of that one bit. She was a jaguar, free and independent. Her life was her own, no extension of the wolf-woman's. Judging from the way the Meddler's lips twisted in an ironic smile, he knew—or guessed—what she was thinking.

"You've encountered people like that before," the Meddler said, "back when you still did divinations. People around whom the currents kept eddying, people who made currents rather than being carried by them."

Truth gave a dismissive sneeze. "Perhaps. What I want to know is if you are truly going to offer us any assistance, or whether we must go after Plik on our own."

"I have something to offer," the Meddler said. "Don't you think I've been working on the problem?"

Truth licked the edge of one paw. "I think you must have been. As you tell the tale, that copse appeared moonspans ago. How to get in and out of it must have greatly occupied your imagination."

"And so it has."

The Meddler seated himself beside Truth. They were not precisely in a place, but the longer Truth had contemplated those golden green spaces, the more she had become aware of them having characteristics. This was a comfortable place, more solid than the one where they had encountered Bitter. It was a place that invited lounging.

"So what can you tell me?" Truth said.

"The copse," the Meddler said without the evasiveness she had expected, "is probably an illusion—thus the anomalous trees and such. It is someone's idea of a forest grove, not a real one."

"You speak very matter-of-factly of something that is impossible," Truth said. "At least of something that I have been taught was impossible."

"Since the Divine Retribution," the Meddler agreed, "such things have indeed been impossible. Anyone who attempted magic on such scale would have been burnt from inside. In the old days, before I was imprisoned, such things were not common, but they were not unknown either."

Truth may not have been given an aridisdu's education, but she had lived most of her year amid the temples of Heeranenahalm, and she had heard more stories than most.

"Go on," she said.

"What I suspect is that the twins stumbled upon an artifact that generates the illusion," the Meddler said. "The illusion would have been meant for defense of the estate, hiding it from those who might mean the inhabitants harm."

"And?" Truth said, perking her ears and lashing her tail as she might when readying to pounce.

"And," the Meddler went on, "I wonder if that illusion field was part of a larger defensive system, one that has also created the bracken beasts and spread seeds for the blood briar."

"Convenient," Truth said, "for this theory leaves your pets guiltless of the deaths that have come since."

"Logical," the Meddler countered, "for how could Isende and Tiniel, unschooled in magic as they are, have managed so much in so little time?"

"So what do you think happens to those who walk into that copse?" Truth asked.

"I think that the outer edges of the copse act like a spider's web—they send warning and snag any who would intrude. Once the intruders have been seen, they are inspected. If they are judged to offer any threat, then the bracken beasts or blood briar come forth. The intruders probably are overwhelmed before they can flee, maybe snared by the briars."

"Probably killed," added Truth, who had a cat's lack of romanticism regarding such things. "And the victims' blood would feed the spell or artifact, enabling it to continue guarding those hidden within."

"Precisely my own thoughts," the Meddler agreed.

"And what plan do you suggest," Truth asked, "for getting through this trap?"

"I think," the Meddler said, "that if the spider's web was not touched, then the defenses would take longer to become active, if they activated at all. That delay could be used to advantage."

"What advantage?" Truth asked.

"How can I know without having been inside?" the Meddler said, exasperated. "Nor can I see inside. Such barriers would have been constructed with creatures like myself in mind, for bodiless scouts were not unknown. I would alert the 'spider' if I pushed through, just as you would if you walked through."

"But your tone says you think there is some other way," Truth said. She thought she knew the answer, and her fur rose at the thought, but she had to hear him say it. It might be the Meddler had something else in mind.

He didn't.

"I have told you already that you are extraordinary in your ability to move between places. I have been showing you how to do so without leaving your body behind. Now this was a rare talent, even in the old days, and I do not think the web will be set to snare one who uses it. It will be like a door that has been barred and locked—but only against those who come from without. You will be within, and none will raise claw or blade against you."

"That's why you came for me," Truth snarled. "All this time you've been planning this. That's why you came for me. You thought I could get into the copse."

The Meddler blinked. "And what's wrong with that? Does it change the favors I have done you?"

"You could have asked . . ."

"Would you have believed? Would you have acted? Would you have cared?" The Meddler made a dismissive gesture. "Rip out my lungs when Plik is safe, not before. I tell you, I think this is the best way to go after him. You can carry with you one other—I would suggest Firekeeper—and then either disarm the trap or guard the others as they come through. Then with your full force, you can rescue Plik."

Truth considered saying many things, her tail lashing as it might before a battle with some creature who threatened her cubs, but in the end she said, "Show me how this can be done."

◈

WHEN PLIK NEXT AWOKE, the light had shifted.

I've slept a day and a night and part of a day, he thought. His mouth was dry and his stomach rumbled complaint, but that was better than the vagueness he had felt before.

He struggled to sit up, and a familiar voice said, "Let me help you. You're not as steady as you think."

Isende, who had been reading near a window, rose from her chair and came over to the bed—at least his first impression was that this was Isende. When the person drew closer, Plik realized that this must be Tiniel.

Tiniel had the same not-brown, not-golden hair as his sister, the same warm, brown eyes. He was, like her, soft and somewhat overweight, and this further blurred the distinctions between male and female. However, his movements were those of a young man, full of contained energy, and even beneath the fat there was a sense that he would grow into lines and angles, where Isende would incline to curves.

"Tiniel," Plik said, and was delighted to hear himself speak a word, not a bleat. It was a poor excuse for a word, dry and croaked, but an honest word.

"Tiniel," the young man said, "and you are Plik. Would you like some water?"

"Please."

Tiniel poured a cupful from a heavy pottery jug. Then he came and propped Plik up, half holding the cup while the maimalodalu sipped.

"More?"

"Please."

After a second cupful, Plik heard his bowels rumble audibly.

"There's a pot behind that screen," Tiniel said, and helped Plik over without further comment, nor did he extend his solicitude to checking on him. When Plik emerged from behind the screen, feeling immensely better and completely ravenous, Tiniel gestured to a low table.

"I can bring you a meal. Nothing too heavy, but sincerely sustaining. The blood briars take a lot out of one."

Plik wondered if Tiniel spoke from experience, but he decided not to ask. He was remembering how Isende had wondered what manner of creature he was, and thought he might as well pretend to be just a bit simple. People weren't threatened by stupidity. In fact, they often grew fond of it, as long as it did not become annoying. Plik had noticed that people—and in this he included humans and maimalodalum and yarimaimalom all entire—tended to talk more freely to those they thought just a little stupid, not at all threatening.

Cute, furry, and utterly uncomplicated, Plik thought, seating himself, and noting that the fit of table and chair with his build were fairly comfortable. *That's me.*

Tiniel returned after a short time with a tray on which the centerpiece was a brown broth in which dark green vegetables had been lightly cooked. There was a loaf of wheat bread and a pot of what tasted like a goat cheese, though not seasoned in any fashion Plik had encountered before.

"The soup is good for rebuilding blood," Tiniel said. "Try to finish it. I can bring you more if you can stomach it."

Plik nodded, and obediently began spooning up the soup. It was flavorful, so getting it down was no great trial. When he began eating, Tiniel stood indecisive. For a moment, Plik thought the young man was going to return to his reading. Then he drew his own chair over and sat back a little from the table.

"Good?" he asked.

"Very good," Plik said.

"So you don't mind eating meat, then. We didn't think you would."

Plik made a noise indicating genuine confusion.

"Your teeth. They didn't look like the teeth of an herbivore, more like those of an omnivore."

Actually, Plik thought, *rather like those of a raccoon, with a bit of variation toward the human in a few odd places. At least that has been my assessment. It isn't easy to look at your own teeth, even with a mirror.*

His fur rose, just a little, at the idea of Tiniel and Isende inspecting his teeth while he slept—or more accurately was drugged. It bothered him that he remembered nothing of it, and he wondered what else they had done.

"Where am I?" Plik asked. It was a reasonable question. It would have been odder if he hadn't asked.

"You're in the place Isende and I have made our new home," Tiniel answered. "You were brought here by the bracken beasts—by one of them. Your friends broke most of the others."

"Are my friends here?" Plik asked. He didn't think so. He hadn't scented them, but then they could be being kept elsewhere.

"No, they are not," Tiniel said, and his tone forestalled further questions on the subject.

Plik decided it was best for him to looked cowed and a little frightened. He did so, eating his soup, and then, when it was done, starting on the bread and cheese.

"Would you like more soup?"

Plik nodded, not quite raising his head and looking up through his lashes. He had rather good ones, and knew the expression (Hope had teased him about it) made him look vulnerable and forlorn.

When Tiniel left, Plik strained to gather any stray sound or scent that might tell him something more. Almost immediately, the surf-like pounding resumed, so powerfully that Plik smashed the bread he was still holding between thumb and forefinger. He squeezed his eyes shut, and, dropping the bread, covered his ears, focusing inward on himself. The horrific pounding began to dim, fade, then diminished entirely.

Slowly, cautiously, Plik opened his eyes again, uncovered his ears. The pounding did not return. He picked up the smashed bread and bit off a chunk, began chewing thoughtfully.

What happened there? I tried to get some idea, any idea of what was out there. Yet my eyes are fine now, my hearing is unimpaired. I can eat and drink. The disorientation is gone.

He thought more, then realization hit him. When he had reached out to sense, he had done so with *all* his senses, including the undefined one the maimalodalum used to detect magic. He had done so on reflex, opening his awareness to the full.

And I opened that awareness to the full because rarely has there been anything for it to find. When it has, then the sensation has been fleeting and distant. Last year when the tower fell, that was different, more like a scream. This was like a pulse. A magical pulse, and a steady one at that. What powers do these twins have? How have they awakened them so quickly?

Plik thought about the huge washes of power he had sensed during the battle. As he and his fellows had fought the bracken beasts he had opened his senses to the full, looking for any advantage that might help find a weakness in the seemingly innumerable host that attacked them.

And when I fell unconscious—or rather was doped by the blood briars—I did not cease my attempts to sense. Indeed, I may have tried even harder as I was struggling against the drug. Then when I came conscious, it was as if a bright light shone in my eyes or drums were being pounded alongside my head.

Tiniel returned with another tray and a second bowl of soup. This one, like the first, was excellent, the crispness of the vegetables suggesting that they were added to the broth shortly before serving. It was not a style of cooking with which Plik was familiar, but he was already developing a taste for it.

"Good," he said, sopping up some of the broth with a piece of bread. "Very good. You make?"

"I'm glad you like it," Tiniel said. "It isn't difficult to make. Tell me, what do you usually eat?"

Plik considered. "Fish. Shellfish. Turtles. Water plants. Eggs. Other plants."

"You seem to like the cheese."

"It tastes good."

"Do you make cheese?"

"No."

"Have you eaten cheese before?"

"Of course. My friends and I carried cheese. Hard cheese. It makes a good trail food."

"But it isn't part of your usual diet."

"No, but I like it." Plik proved this by smearing more on another piece of bread. His midsection was feeling tight, but he also felt more energetic and a bit encouraged to play.

"What do you eat?" he asked Tiniel.

The young man blinked, startled to be interrogated in turn, but answered willingly enough. "Pretty much anything. I don't like really spicy food, and I'm not fond of liver. Do you like liver?"

Plik wrinkled his nose. "Sometimes."

"But you can eat it."

"I can."

"Good. It's another food that's good for rebuilding blood."

"You know a lot about this blood building," Plik said, hoping he sounded innocent, not accusing.

"It's necessary," Tiniel said. His tone wavered as if he were trying to sound authoritative, but some doubt lingered beneath.

Plik decided not to press this point. He didn't like where it might take them. What if they were restoring his blood so they could use him to feed the briars? It was not a comfortable thought.

He frowned, a stray thought trying to claim his attention. He ate another mouthful of soup, and realized what it was. This was definitely beef broth. The maimalodalum did not keep cattle. Goats were better suited to their island. Therefore, he had tasted beef for the first time during this trip, and he knew he was not mistaken about the taste. Nor was this soup made from dried beef. There were a few small pieces of meat mixed in with the vegetables, and they were not rehydrated.

Had Night's Terror said anything about the twins driving cattle with them? He didn't think so. They must have had pack animals, and he supposed one of them might have been an ox. Horses, though, would have made more sense— or mules, but one could breed horses, while mules were sterile. Derian had talked about the matter along the trail, for apparently mules were superior to either of their contributing kin in many ways, but as they could not breed with each other, they remained unfavored by many.

Plik spooned up a slice of meat and chewed it thoughtfully. It certainly tasted like beef, but he supposed it might be horse or mule. They had eaten neither this trip out of deference to Eshinarvash—and, Plik gathered, to Derian as well, for the young man was very fond of horses.

Well, then. Plik decided he would not further investigate this stray thought at this time, but he would remember, and if he had a chance, he would scent the air for cows. They were strong-smelling animals, with a scent that had nothing about it to recommend itself. Horses smelled better, and Plik felt an unexpected pang as he thought of his own two fat ponies. He hoped nothing had happened to them during the battle. He hoped nothing had happened to his friends.

Somehow, he thought, at least some of them must have survived. That might explain the guarded way Tiniel had answered. The twins, for all their apparent quietude and gentle courtesy, might be expecting to be attacked. Since they knew their bracken beasts had been destroyed, they should have the sense to fear those who would be coming after Plik.

And they will come, Plik thought. *All of them—but for the jaguar—are creatures of packs or herds or flocks. I am one of their pack, and they will not leave me.*

Comforted, Plik continued his meal and waited for the next question. Tiniel was less direct than Isende, but he was no less curious.

Plik treasured that curiosity, for as long as the twins remained curious, he was likely to be kept alive.

FINDING ANYTHING HOT-BLOODED and larger than a rabbit proved more difficult than either Firekeeper or Blind Seer had imagined it would be. There were a few wild turkeys, but neither wolf felt these counted as proper eating.

"I want a deer, a fat doe, not too old," Blind Seer rhapsodized as they ran, "but I'd settle for a young elk. Perhaps a boar, fat from eating all the best acorns and mushrooms. That would be best."

Firekeeper couldn't help but agree. She didn't need the red meat the way the wolf did, but during her year on Misheemnekuru she had been spoiled with good hunting and a pack that could easily pull down the best prey. Fish filled the belly. Rabbit was savory, but she also longed to gorge until she could eat no more, then to sleep, wake, and gorge again before the meat got high.

She didn't even feel they were abandoning their friends. Truth had smelled sour with tension. Clearly she would do whatever she needed to do better without the wolves' help. Eshinarvash had said quite frankly he'd sleep better once their bellies were full—and that he would guard the others. Moreover, Lovable was flying easily now, and had promised to find them if any trouble arose. They had agreed to leave signs the raven could follow so she would waste no time in locating them.

Yet although the forest, as soon as they were away from the plains that held the copse, seemed as fine and healthy as any in which they had run, the wolves did not find big game until they were nearly a full day away. Then they took down their prey.

Their kill was not the fat boar of Blind Seer's fantasy, but a yearling sow possessed of a very nasty temper. Firekeeper stung it with arrows from the safety of a tree, and Blind Seer finished the kill when the sow began to stagger.

They ate well and drank well, and if they sung the moon a bit more loudly than should two alone, well, perhaps they would have welcomed any who would come to challenge their effrontery.

But none came, not wolf nor fox, or even a snide and slant-eyed lynx. It was as if the forest had not a predator in it—or, worse, that something had these forest rulers so intimidated that they lay low and would not defend their territory against interlopers.

After they had slept, Firekeeper constructed a bundle from the sow's hide. She had cooked some of the meat over the coals of her night's fire so it would keep a little longer. Blind Seer devoured the rest for his waking meal.

"You smell like King Tedric's banquet hall," Blind Seer teased as they began the run back to the main camp the next night.

Firekeeper tried to grin at him, but she knew her attempt lacked heart. Things were all wrong—not just here in these forests so empty of beasts, even in some way between her and Blind Seer. She didn't know how to address that wrongness, and knew that he would not.

It is like when Blind Seer ran with Moon Frost, Firekeeper thought. *Only this time it is my mind that has done a little running. I feel guilty, though I have done nothing—even as Blind Seer did nothing in which I could find fault and so there was no bone to fight over, no way we can talk.*

Not for the first time, Firekeeper found herself wishing that Elise or Wendee were near enough to confide in regarding her confused feelings. She thought that if presented with this strange situation, those two might understand and have some wisdom to set her heart at rest.

Lacking this good counsel, Firekeeper opted for running. At journey's end would be a good fight, and, though she hated to admit it, her heart thrilled a little at the thought of seeing the Meddler. Perhaps she could find the answer to the confusion that filled her soul in his amber eyes.

XX

BY THE TIME FIREKEEPER AND BLIND SEER RETURNED, bearing with them several very solid chunks of pork to round out breakfast, Derian was aware, even without the aid of a translator, that things were in readiness.

In fact, they had not had to do completely without a translator during Firekeeper's absence. Harjeedian's training as an aridisdu included interpreting omens. During Truth's year as the representative jaguar for the ahmyndisdu, she had learned the conventions as well. Between them, they managed basic communication quite nicely. Almost immediately, Eshinarvash and the ravens began to offer their own comments, and Harjeedian was kept quite busy.

Derian was rather glad about this. He had found being thrown into Harjeedian's company very trying. For one thing, there were times he still flat-out didn't like the man.

Harjeedian was arrogant, scheming, certain of his place, and equally certain that his superiority should be acknowledged. For Derian, who came from a completely different social structure, this acknowledgment did not come easily or automatically.

It's like this, Derian said, carrying on an increasingly complex internal dialogue. *When Harjeedian does something admirable—like pushing himself to learn to ride or working so hard to save Bitter's life—then I have no trouble telling him so. He on the other hand thinks I should bow and scrape to him because he's an aridisdu, and I'm just not set that way.*

And, Derian admitted, *I get just a little tired of the fact that Harjeedian isn't exactly ready with the compliments for me. He's like the worst of the nobles at home, the ones who think their birth makes them better than you automatically. In Harjeedian's case he earned his place, and I guess it wasn't easy, but I've earned mine, too, and by the Horse I'd like it acknowledged. I mean, if things had been a little different, we'd be brothers-in-law, and then he'd be working hard enough to find good in me, if for no other reason than that I'd be kin to him.*

When he was honest with himself, as he was inclined to be, Derian knew that his fuming was in part fed by his feeling of complete uselessness. Plik had been missing now for several days. There was good reason to believe the maimalodalu was alive, but that didn't mean he was happy or comfortable or even well. Derian found himself remembering how Edlin and Peace had looked when they had finally escaped captivity beneath Thendula Lypella. In his imagination, Plik was reduced to the same emaciated, haggard, beaten state.

Relax, Derian Carter, he reminded himself sternly. *Plik's too fat to fade away so quickly.*

But Derian was relieved nonetheless when, near dawn, Firekeeper and Blind Seer trotted into camp. Firekeeper was a complete mess—as usual, after such a venture. Her hair was tangled, and her clothing was greasy and bloodstained. It remained a mystery to Derian how Blind Seer kept so immaculate.

Over pork, reheated over the fire and shared with everyone but Eshinarvash, Firekeeper began translating the plans that had been too complex for Truth to relate through Harjeedian.

"Truth knows how," Firekeeper said, "to go into copse without touching copse. It is something like how she go from her harness when we take her to the Meddler's den on Misheemnekuru."

That tale had been related long ago, so Derian only asked, "Does this have something to do with what the Meddler has been teaching her?"

"Yes," Firekeeper replied. "Before she do because talent is there and time and place and all that not mean much to her because she is insane. Now she know how to do without being too much insane."

Truth snarled.

"At all insane," Firekeeper corrected.

Derian looked for some indication in Firekeeper's expression that would indicate that she had teased deliberately—perhaps to learn how closely the jaguar was attending. Certainly, Truth seemed restless.

"When we inside copse," Firekeeper continued, "then we break enough to let you rest in."

" 'We'?" Harjeedian asked.

"Truth think," Firekeeper said, "that she can carry one with her. I am best to go, we think."

This time no one questioned the "we," but Derian thought that—judging from the cant of Blind Seer's tail and ears—the blue-eyed wolf was less than pleased with this decision. No wonder, as it meant putting Firekeeper at risk, and no Blind Seer being there to protect her. Derian wondered if there might be something more. He hadn't forgotten Firekeeper's description of how the Meddler had appeared when seen through her eyes, and he found that perfect melding of wolf and human a little suspicious.

For as long as Derian had known her, Firekeeper had never hesitated to express her wish that she had been born a wolf, not a human. Now here was someone showing her the image of a perfect hybrid, possessed of a wolf's acute senses without the need to relinquish the advantages of human hands or upright posture.

Add that to the list of reasons not to trust the Meddler, no matter how helpful he may be, Derian thought.

Harjeedian had asked, "Why do you think this way of going in will be better than our walking in together through the sides of the copse?"

"Is like spiderweb," Firekeeper said. "This way we go in without waking spider. Is like when door is opened from inside. There are no locks."

It wasn't the best of explanations, but several moonspans of travel where the humans were in the minority had made both Derian and Harjeedian quite talented at filling in the gaps.

"A door," Derian said, "is not locked or barred against those who are already inside, only those who come from without. Is that what you mean?"

Firekeeper nodded. "So we do this? Three of us may be enough to fight, but if Plik is hurt, I would like Harjeedian there, and Derian is good in many things."

Eshinarvash snorted, and Firekeeper nodded, then gave her answer in Pellish. "Yes. We hope you would take charge of horses and gear. We have it all packed so we can run away swiftly with Plik."

Lovable croaked, and Firekeeper frowned.

"What say you all," she said. "Lovable say she come and scout high for us. I think not, since is building within."

"A raven could spy through a high window," Derian reminded. "If she feels up to it, I think she would be very useful."

Loveable strutted a few steps, then fluttered to perch alongside Bitter. The other raven was doing much better, even capable of a sort of halting, swooping flight, but nothing would replace his one eye, and Harjeedian had expressed concern that scarring might keep the bird from flying normally even when he was healed.

No wonder Firekeeper is so eager to have Harjeedian and me along. She knows perfectly well that we may need to carry Plik away.

"It seems like a good plan," Derian said aloud. "When do we begin?"

"How long to pack up camp?" Firekeeper asked.

"Not long, if everyone helps," Derian replied, looking meaningfully at her. Firekeeper had a tendency to disappear when menial tasks were at hand.

In reply, Firekeeper began gathering the items dirtied by their recent meal, clearly intending to wash them.

"Then when we packed," she said, "we go."

PLIK STILL WASN'T CERTAIN how long he'd been captive, because he had no idea how long he'd slept either the first or last time. He was a captive, too, for no matter how politely either Isende or Tiniel waited on him, he was not permitted outside of his room.

It was a large room, especially for a small person like himself. Plik never heard anything either moving above or through the walls, so he began to think he might be in a small cottage or hut. There were windows, but his view was truncated by the lustrous growth surrounding them. This was not a growth that tempted him in the least to lean out and take a better look. Closer inspection had confirmed his initial impression that the plants that surrounded his windows were blood briars.

There were four windows, but the view outside of them was much the same. Beyond the window was what might be termed a lawn, although less well tended than those he had seen in their journeys. Beyond that lawn was a thick, tired-looking hedge interwoven with more blood briar. Of all the plants, only the blood briar looked lustrous.

Blood briars are certainly a most cooperative plant, Plik thought morosely. *They seem to grow everywhere.*

Because he did not wish to invite the blood briar in, Plik made no effort to open his windows. The room had a chimney. It was too narrow for him to even consider using as an exit, but since there was no fire lit upon the hearth and the winds were gusty, sometimes interesting scents were carried down to him.

He sniffed hard, hoping to catch the scent of wolf or jaguar. A few very exciting times he did so—and caught the scents of other animals besides. But none of these scents seemed to belong to those Plik knew, so they unsettled him rather than otherwise. He had not forgotten the tales Night's Terror had told about those who had gone into the copse but had not returned. Did these scents belong to some of that vanished company? If so, why did he not hear their howls and snarls?

Plik caught human scents, too, but other than those of Isende and Tiniel, these did not belong to any he knew. Indeed, they were so elusive that they might well belong to either of the twins and have been diffused or corrupted before they reached him. Perhaps if he had been a wolf, Plik might have read more, but although raccoons had a good sense of smell, it was not the equivalent of a wolf's—nor was Plik entirely a raccoon.

When Isende returned, Plik decided to let himself speak bluntly. He could get away with doing this, because the twins had already dismissed the possibility of plotting or calculation from their assessment of him. He knew this from how they no longer shut the door quickly when coming from outside his room, how they would set the food tray down before locking the door behind them, from other little casual lapses.

"Isende," Plik said, "who are the others here?"

Isende, who had brought some form of yarnwork with her, looked up from what she was doing, her lips still moving in a deliberate count.

"Others?"

"I smell others. Animals and humans, both."

"I expect you smell the animals in the forest," Isende replied, speaking with care, her mind obviously groping with whether or not she should address his question in full. "Are you sure the humans you smell aren't my brother and me?"

Plik just stared at her, trying to make his gaze appealing, that of a child who doesn't want to argue, but doesn't quite believe. The twins had no means of judging his age, and treated him as if he were seven years old instead of as many decades and more.

Isende frowned and began picking at her yarn. His question had distracted her enough that she had lost her count, that much was certain.

"When can I go outside?" Plik asked. "I'm sure the blood briar poison is gone from me. I'm restless. I want to climb a tree or go fishing or something . . ."

"You can't go outside," Isende said, her tone permitting no argument. "It would be unwise."

For all the severity of her tone, Plik also heard something like longing in her voice. He studied her and found confirmation in the manner in which Isende's gaze went to the window and lingered.

Plik looked at his captor afresh. A new, frightening perspective on the situation rose in his mind, making him struggle to keep from crying aloud in frustration and astonishment.

From their very first meeting, Plik had noted that beneath the natural brown of their skins, the twins were pallid, that despite their youth, they were both fleshy, bearing extra weight. Coming from a loose-skinned, loose-furred stock, he had not considered the implications of these traits, but now he compared Tiniel and Isende with the other humans of his acquaintance.

These were not many, true, but even Aridisdu Harjeedian had lost his remaining fat and gained muscle as the hardships of travel exacted their toll. Now none of the three humans carried any extra weight at all. Even Plik, beneath his fur, had toughened, but his heritage did not lend itself to leanness—and autumn's abundance combined with traveling with several excellent hunters had meant that he had never to go long without food.

But Tiniel and Isende were both running to fat, and both showed ample signs that they were out of condition. How could this be? They had brought no servants with them when they left Gak. Nor had they carried any tremendous supplies of food. Hadn't Night's Terror related how over the preceding winter the local yarimaimalom had fed the newcomers out of curiosity and pity?

So why did both twins show no signs that they were working at all to sustain what was obviously a comfortable—if not opulent—lifestyle? Why did Isende look so wistful when Plik lamented his own desire for physical freedom? Was there another reason for the hard note in her voice when she told Plik he could not go outside of his room? Might she, too, desire a chance to go outside?

All this time, Plik had thought of himself as the prisoner, and these two, for all their solicitude, as his jailers. What if the situation was quite different? What if they were prisoners as well? If so, who was it that kept the prison?

֍

ALTHOUGH THE DAYS HAD GROWN markedly shorter since their departure from u-Seeheera, and even since they had crossed the border from the land of the Liglim into the city-states, there was ample daylight for their venture when camp was packed up, and the group had gone to the segment of forest that grew closest to the copse.

"We will leave from here," Firekeeper said, "Truth and I. Do not leave this cover until you see or hear our signal."

She spoke with more confidence than she felt, wishing with heart and soul that Blind Seer could go with them. She had asked Truth, but the jaguar had replied rather tartly that she was not entirely certain she could move Firekeeper, let alone Firekeeper and Blind Seer.

"How will we know?" Derian asked.

"I will howl," Firekeeper said, "or some such thing. Let Lovable hide high in tree branches, well behind leaves so no one see."

Harjeedian nodded. "I agree there is no need for a subtle signal. Your opening the door into the copse may be enough—if not, our crossing in will be."

Firekeeper tried not to glower at the aridisdu. She knew he only spoke in that way to cover his own concerns—for those who went ahead, about what might await. Harjeedian might be the one most out of his depth in these matters. His training had never been intended for this. Neither had Derian's, but Derian had become very adaptable over the last few years.

Without a word, Firekeeper embraced this oldest human friend; then she knelt and hugged Blind Seer so hard the wolf whuffed mild protest in her ear, but from how he licked her when she released him, he didn't really mind.

Offering the others a polite inclination of her head by way of farewell, Firekeeper turned to Truth.

"If you are done acting like you'll never see your pack mates again," the jaguar said, *"we can go. I must say that your behavior does not express tremendous confidence in my abilities."*

Firekeeper walked over to the jaguar and straddled her as they had planned. She did not sit on Truth as she might have on a horse, but let her legs grip against the jaguar's flanks.

"If you're going to do it," she replied, speaking Pellish for the benefit of those who listened, "then do it before the briars bear word of our being here."

The jaguar growled something deep and wordless in her chest, a vibration that carried up Firekeeper's legs and rumbled in her very bones. Then everything changed.

She had no idea what she expected. When Firekeeper had asked so she might be able to prepare herself, Truth had not been able to tell her, saying that there were no words to describe the sensation. Nor, after sharing the experience herself, did Firekeeper disagree.

There *were* no words for the sensation. Firekeeper might say she felt an icy breath of cold all around her, but she would be equally accurate were she to say she felt feverishly hot. She might say she was smothered by clinging darkness so heavy she could roll it between her hands, but she would be equally accurate to say there was a flash of brilliance that seared rainbows on her inner eyelids and gave colors tastes and textures.

What Firekeeper knew was that the experience was not the same for her and for the jaguar. Truth could navigate through this confusion of sensations, navigate and with some skill. When Firekeeper was next certain of what her senses told her, she was still standing over the jaguar but the forest edge was gone. In its place was a stone wall, its iron gate hanging open and slightly lopsided. Beyond the gate was a towering structure built mostly of stone, except for the shutters that covered its windows. These were wooden, and showed what more than a hundred years of passing seasons could do to wood. Even so, they had kept their trust well. The old house stood solid and strong—and decisively empty.

"We have come to the right place," Firekeeper said, not wishing to phrase this as a question lest she anger the great cat she held so dangerously close.

"We have," Truth replied. "See, it is not so without sign that others have been here as I first thought. Look around the side. There is a trail as would have been made by daily foot traffic."

"It doesn't look as if it has been used for a good time," Firekeeper said. "Nor do I smell wood smoke or any of the other signs humans leave. Do you find more?"

"No," Truth said. "But this is the place. I know it as surely as I know I bore us here. Do we investigate, or do we see if we can bring the others in?"

"Bring the others," Firekeeper said. "They will worry, and the humans may see signs that would be invisible to you or me."

"How then might we open a gate without letting those who guard this place know?" Truth asked.

Firekeeper thought the great cat was musing aloud, but she heard the distant touch of the Meddler's voice in her ears, and realized the jaguar spoke to purpose.

"Turn slowly, side to side," the Meddler said. "Show me what you see, and I may be able to interpret it for you."

Truth did so, moving out from beneath Firekeeper, but not before Firekeeper saw how her fur lifted. From this, she knew the jaguar detested the Meddler's contact.

We may have that jaguar figurine the Meddler carved, Firekeeper thought, *but he has kept some link with her. Will it be so with the twins, I wonder?*

She said nothing aloud, but turned her attention to studying the undergrowth that framed the derelict estate. From within the copse was more clearly a false front. If she concentrated, she could even see the tall grasses growing without.

"There!" the Meddler said triumphantly.

"I really think," Firekeeper said dryly, "we might have figured this out on our own."

Truth snorted, and for the first time in quite a while Firekeeper felt a friendly connection with the Wise Jaguar.

What they had both located was a place along the copse's edge where a section of otherwise unremarkable greenery was flanked by a pair of the bracken beasts. They were dormant. By someone who had not battled them, they might be taken for shrubs clipped into ornamental shapes. One was a bear standing on its hind legs. The other was a great cat of some sort, though specifics of species could not really be told.

The bracken beasts were positioned to face the same direction. It did not take much to imagine them coming to life and lumbering out what must be a door.

"But why a door?" Firekeeper wondered. "If all this forest is false, wouldn't anywhere do?"

The Meddler's voice, tinged with mockery, sounded in her head. "So you do not know everything, then, sweet Firekeeper?"

"I never claimed to," she replied, bristling inwardly. "I only said I thought we could have found this place with our eyes."

"Why a door?" the Meddler said, not really acknowledging her clarification, a thing Firekeeper found very annoying. "For much the same reason as there are doors in the walls of other structures. It is better for the continued existence of the structure. The analogy is not precise, because what creates the image of a copse of trees here is closer to a fabric than to a wall of stone or wood."

Truth, who liked both pillows and rugs very much, understood. "And a fabric can only be torn so many times before it begins to fray."

"Correct. This door was created to enable passage through the fabric that would not destroy the fabric itself."

"Good," Firekeeper said. She was eager to get out and bring Blind Seer to her, and afraid, just a little, of what this continued intimate discourse with the Meddler might bring. Once the door was open, she could tell him to stop bothering her. "So we open the door—or better, I think, push aside the fabric."

"And why do you think that?" the Meddler asked.

Firekeeper gestured at the two waiting bracken beasts. "These not have hands for turning knobs or lifting latches, but they—and we—can push."

She hefted a sturdy piece of hardwood. "Truth, you push. I be ready to hit."

The jaguar agreed, padding between the two bracken beasts, shifting her head from one side to the other, letting her sensitive whiskers test what she found.

Firekeeper watched, waiting for the slightest twitch from either "bear" or "cat," but they stood as unmoving as the garden sculptures they seemed to be.

Truth gave a satisfied hiss, and then her front end began to vanish through what now looked very much like a curtain printed with the image of a group of trees—though no printed image had ever shifted with the passing wind. When Firekeeper thought that the curtain was sufficiently raised, she gave her promised howl.

"Come," she called to the others waiting outside, "but carefully. We will need to guide you through."

Blind Seer came at an all-out run, a ripple in the grass, halting beside Truth. The jaguar gave instructions, and the wolf passed safely under the curtain. He stopped almost immediately, sniffing curiously at the air.

"This place is empty," he said. "Empty of all but bugs and little things that live in the dirt."

"I know," Firekeeper said. "Scout, dear heart, but take great care. I will guide the others through, then send Lovable with a message for Eshinarvash."

"I can go," Truth said, "then come in as I did before."

"Good," Firekeeper agreed, moving to take Truth's place holding up the curtain. The sensation was as if thousands of bees walked over her skin, delicate buzzing accompanied by the prickling of tiny feet.

Truth slipped under, gliding away through the tall grass just as Derian arrived.

"What's with her?"

"She goes to speak with Eshinarvash. Walk beneath the curtain."

"What curtain?"

Firekeeper immediately grasped that the curtain could not be seen from without. It made sense of a sort—as much as anything was making sense of late.

"You will understand," she promised. "For now, pretend I have a fine woven curtain held up over my arm. Duck under it, coming close to me so you do not touch cloth."

This wasn't easy, for Derian was quite tall and he bore with him a pack of things the humans had thought might be needed. He tossed the pack through first, then bent and went under. Firekeeper smelled him, familiar and comforting, clean man sweat mingled with that of horse.

When Derian was through, Harjeedian followed. He was shorter than Derian, though not a short man, but his passage was more complicated. While Firekeeper and Derian were comfortable with each other, despite all the days he had traveled with them, Harjeedian still kept himself somewhat apart. Nonetheless, he managed to get under without touching the curtain. Lovable strutted under after him. Firekeeper trusted that Truth could make her return as promised and carefully lowered the curtain into place.

The bracken beasts had not yet stirred, so Firekeeper hoped they had run this course undetected. She realized something else. With Truth's departure, the sense of the Meddler touching her mind had also vanished. Either the Meddler had gone to watch his student, or in his wearied state he needed the jaguar to help him bridge the gap between his spirit existence and this one.

"You're right," Derian said, "the entire copse is like a curtain. This part of the estate is nothing like what I expected. It looks deserted."

Blind Seer came up at that moment. *"Deserted now, but there are signs of past denning, and denning since the days when this place was sealed behind the illusion of trees. Come. I will show you."*

Firekeeper translated, but she laid a hand on Blind Seer's shoulder in sign that he should wait.

"First," Firekeeper said, "we must set rules."

Derian grinned at her, and she knew why. Usually, she was the one who balked at rules, but she had learned some things when leading her pack on Misheemnekuru, and one was that rules kept pups alive—and in this place, not one of them could be counted less than a pup.

"First, as before, speak Pellish and only that. If any listen, they may know Liglimosh, for Harjeedian's people are a great pack even in these lands, but they may not know Pellish.

"Second, stay close to each other. No flying high and clever or running fast. Each here has different senses, and we will need them all.

"Third, no courage, only care. Many, many yarimaimalom disappeared in this place. We are no greater than they, and maybe lesser."

She looked around, but saw no protest, not even in the lines of Truth. The jaguar had flickered into sight as Firekeeper had begun speaking, and had waited with listening patience. Now Truth spoke.

"Eshinarvash knows that we have not found either Plik or the twins as we had hoped. He plans to drive the horses with their packs back to beyond the second of the streams we passed. None of us can recall having seen the briars before that point. Then he will return."

"The packs will give the horses sores!" Derian protested.

"Eshinarvash knew you would be concerned," Truth said, "and told me to tell you that he is rather clever with straps and knots. He thinks he can remove the gear if needed."

Derian looked as if he wished to argue the matter, but knew there were things more important here than a pack horse getting a sore.

Firekeeper resumed. "Blind Seer and Truth will lead. I will take behind. But first one thing . . . Derian, you have rope?"

"I do."

"Good." She gestured back to the watching bracken beasts. "Blind Seer tell me he have looked, and these are only two here. Perhaps we have broken most, and more must grow. I not want to break these. That might alert someone, but I not think we must make easy their coming after us, or after Eshinarvash."

With Derian's help and a considerable quantity of rope, they rigged a sort of snare. Should the bracken beasts move, either to go through the curtain or to come deeper into the stronghold, they would trip a line and that line would bring down upon them a sizable chunk of timber.

"If they not move," Firekeeper said, slapping her hands against her pants legs to remove the worst of the dirt, "they be fine, if they move . . ."

"They'll be flattened," Derian said, looking quite pleased.

"Now," Firekeeper said, gesturing for Derian to take his place in their loose ranks, "let us go see what this strange place holds."

XXI

DERIAN COULD NOT HELP being nervous as they moved through the open iron gate and into the Setting Sun estate's interior. In many ways, the layout was familiar to him. The main house, which could serve as a second fortification as needed; outer buildings, including an outside kitchen, a smokehouse, various workshops, stables, and even a chicken coop.

There was a walled-off area that looked like it had been a garden, containing a well and a small pond. That last might have been ornamental, but Derian would have been willing to bet, based upon its location, that it had been used to keep fish fresh for the table.

They walked around the outside of the main house first, and Blind Seer showed them signs that someone—probably the twins—had camped here. There were burnt areas from old, but not ancient, fires. One of the workshops had clearly been used as a residence, another as a stable. The original stable proved to have a collapsed roof. The wolf's keen nose even found where a privy had been dug.

Wood had been cut, timbers moved, and vines pulled down. One section of the kitchen garden, after close inspection, proved to have been tended.

"Mints and other hardy herbs," Harjeedian said. "Either they brought seeds with them, or they found a few surviving plants and cultivated them."

"There's every evidence," Derian said, "that the twins intended to stay. Where are they now?"

"Someone," Firekeeper reminded him, "took Plik. If not the twins, who?"

"I think," Derian said, "that the twins camped out here—probably using that shop as temporary quarters—while they worked out how to get into the main house."

"Not so hard," Firekeeper said. "Now."

"But I think it would have been harder then," Derian said. "If you look at the windows and doors, the upper ones were shuttered, but the lower both shuttered and nailed shut. My guess is that the people who lived here couldn't take everything with them, and were hoping to keep looters out."

Harjeedian interrupted, "Truth wants our attention. I believe she has found something."

What Truth had found was an entrance into the main house. Closer inspection showed that it had apparently been unsealed, then sealed again.

"And this time," Derian said with mingled satisfaction and frustration, "sealed from the inside rather than out—though they took some care to try and make it look as if the place had not been opened."

Blind Seer was snuffling around the doorsill.

"Someone has been in and out of here, recently, too," Firekeeper translated. "It's a shod foot, which makes judging time a little harder. Male. Extreme fondness for some sort of very smelly herb I don't recognize. Interesting. There have been others as well, but the herb-eater's scent dominates."

Truth was also taking the scent, her mouth hanging slightly open as cats did when trying to gather finer details.

"Blind Seer, go beneath the human spoor," Firekeeper translated. "There is something older, yet heavy enough that even the season's turning hasn't completely eliminated it."

Blind Seer lowered his head closer to the doorsill; then, to Derian's complete astonishment, his hackles rose.

Firekeeper, moving to place a comforting hand on her pack mate's shoulder, nonetheless continued translating.

"Beasts! Frightened. No. Terrified. There's a reek of blood, too. Someone must have scrubbed to remove the stain, but the scent lingers."

"Wise Beasts?" Firekeeper asked, and from her intonation, Derian knew she spoke for herself.

Truth's tail lashed, and Firekeeper translated her response.

"Telling such by scent is not simple, but I think that it takes a mind that can think to generate such absolute terror. What we smell here, Blind Seer and I, is not just fear, but a horrible despair that makes me want to flee—and I am not easily driven away."

"For the first time," Firekeeper said, "in all my life, I think I am truly glad to be nose-dead. Still, we must go ahead. Derian, Harjeedian, do your eyes see how this door opens? Truth, do you see anything like the curtain—some thing we should avoid?"

Plik's being kidnapped, Derian thought as he stepped forward to inspect the door, *may be the best thing that ever happened to Firekeeper's command of spoken language. Being forced to translate has really helped.*

But even as he smiled inwardly at his own joke, Derian found himself marveling over the changes in Firekeeper. More must have happened to her during that year spent on Misheemnekuru than he had ever imagined. She was learning to be a leader, rather than an impatient force of nature content to let others do the planning, then follow or not according to her whim.

Is this the difference between a head wolf and merely a member of a pack? I wonder.

Harjeedian had taken the lead in inspecting the door, and now he turned to Derian.

"See how these boards are placed? They look as if they are nailed tightly down, but they are actually quite loose. Most of the nails have been cut off so only the heads show."

"Probably can be lifted into place from the other side and fastened," Derian agreed. "We should be able to lever it off."

He turned to Truth. "Truth, have you found anything?"

Firekeeper held up her hand in signal that they should wait. Her brow furrowed as she listened, her lips shaping distaste.

"Truth say," she said, "Meddler say, that door is fastened with something like the curtain. It look like the door wood, but is not."

So much for her Pellish, Derian thought ruefully. *That Meddler really must make her uncomfortable.*

Aloud he said, "We weren't here when you figured out how to 'open' the curtain so we could pass under it. Do you have any ideas?"

Firekeeper moved to join them, making the stoop, broad as it was, a bit crowded. Derian stepped back and looked over her head as she bent and studied the door.

"Other was easier," she said. "We could look through and see grass. This is wood on wood. Still . . ."

Harjeedian gave a gasp of pleased astonishment. "That's very clever, Firekeeper. This is wood on wood, but whoever did it wasn't completely careful.

The boards that were used to seal the door were old and splintered. Look down here, a double image where it doesn't match."

He was pointing to a section about waist-level on Firekeeper. Firekeeper looked up, grinning.

"Good. You see good. I step away. You look. Find edge, then peel back. You will feel it on fingers like the song of bees."

She stepped back, and Harjeedian knelt, studying the door closely, then pointing. "Do you see it, Derian?"

Derian did. In one place, a long splinter could be seen through a sort of mist of undamaged wood. In another, a swirl of "wood grain" didn't match that which it overlapped.

"Now," Harjeedian said, "we must find the ultimate edge."

He placed his fingers very lightly along the edge, and his expression changed.

"It does rather feel like bees buzzing. Shall I lift?"

"Truth say, 'Do,'" Firekeeper replied. "Carefully, not to bend but to peel back." She paused, "Like skin from dead prey."

"Charming," Harjeedian said. "Gently but firmly. I think I can manage that."

He did, starting on his knees and slowly rising, his hands firmly closed over something Derian could see, but just barely.

"I'll hold this while someone forces the door," Harjeedian said, glancing over at Truth.

The jaguar's ears flattened momentarily; then Firekeeper spoke in what Derian was coming to think of as her "Truth voice." It was slightly higher than Firekeeper's own, and touched with the faintest hint of a feline whine.

"That would be best. Those who created it would have had a means of 'hanging it up,' but we don't know how, and the Meddler says there is risk we will set off the alarm if we try."

So Harjeedian stood there, holding his hands up rather awkwardly, and Derian bent under the nearly invisible barrier.

"The door isn't that good," he said. "I'll get rid of this outer planking, then . . ."

"Then" proved to be Firekeeper getting impatient and bursting the door open with her shoulder to the wood. The lock wasn't strong, and snapped at the pressure. Then, one by one, they filed inside. Harjeedian came last and lowered the camouflage carefully back into place.

Derian had lit a lantern, but it wasn't all that necessary. Light seeped in where the shutters had warped. Above, the ceilings bulged where water had leaked in and ruined the plaster. Bits of debris were everywhere, with a few promising traffic patterns from other rooms into this one breaking the clutter of sawdust, leaf litter, and less definable trash.

"The floor's solid," Derian said, thumping his boot heel on flagstone. "This looks like a winter kitchen. It's probably built right on the ground with maybe a root cellar beneath. Which way do we go from here?"

Blind Seer and Truth were sniffing the various paths.

Blind Seer raised his head, and Firekeeper said, using a voice a touch deeper than her own and even huskier, "Humans have been here. More than two. There is the Herb Man I scented on the doorstep, but I have a woman who smells of smoking weed, and three or four others."

"Old scents or new?" Firekeeper asked, then shifted her voice to translate the exchange that followed.

"Mostly old, but months old, not years, certainly not since the Plague. One or two, maybe days."

Truth added, "And beneath the humans, the older scent of terrified beasts remains. Bear and wolf, jaguar and puma, deer and boar. Many, many came through here, and not a one was unafraid."

"I have Plik's scent!" Blind Seer announced triumphantly. "He must have been being carried, but here someone set him down."

"He was alive?" Harjeedian asked.

"He did not smell dead," Blind Seer reported. "It is a brief trace, so he must have been lifted again."

Derian hadn't been precisely relaxed when they came into this place, but Truth's continual mention of fear made it somehow important to him that he not seem so.

"So which way?" he asked again. "Even I can see there are several trails. Is there one where Plik's scent shows up?"

"No," Blind Seer replied.

"One trail runs deepest," Firekeeper said, although in truth the floor showed no grooving. "Broader" might have been more accurate, but Derian really didn't feel like correcting the wolf-woman's language skills just now.

"Shall we go that way?" Derian said, and when no one protested, he lifted his lantern and followed Firekeeper and Blind Seer into the depths of the twilit stronghold.

He felt a touch upon his shoulder as he did so, and discovered Lovable perched there. The weight unbalanced him slightly, but Derian found himself strangely comforted.

FIREKEEPER WAS GLAD that the floor below her feet remained solid stone. She had some bad memories of floors in old buildings falling away beneath her feet. This floor, though, was sound. Enough light drifted in from odd areas that she could see her way, and with Blind Seer beside her, that seemed enough. The main corridor was wide, with somewhat narrower ones branching off of it, but she did not let herself be distracted.

"All the beast scent trails go down this wide way," Blind Seer said, *"and many of the humans as well. Smoke Woman and Smelly Herb Man came back and forth many times. I also scent the blood briar."*

Firekeeper didn't bother to translate. She was frankly tired of being the voice for so many. Indeed, she was glad for Lovable's unwonted silence. Perhaps the raven missed her mate, worried at leaving him alone with only Eshinarvash for protection. Certainly, Firekeeper might have been tempted were the choice hers to stay where she could guard and protect a loved one or go on and fight.

But you have done otherwise, a voice said, and she could not honestly tell if it was her own thoughts or the prompting of the Meddler.

"Outer air," Blind Seer said, a moment before Firekeeper caught the fresh scent herself. *"This trail leads outside."*

Firekeeper reported this development, and Harjeedian said, "Many of these strongholds had an inner courtyard. We may find another well there. We walked around the house and saw no gate leading in. What would bring anyone here—and apparently regularly enough that they have worn a visible trail in the dust and debris?"

"We find out," Firekeeper said, halting in front of a heavy door. "This one is not locked. Truth, does it show that spiderweb?"

The Wise Jaguar studied for a moment then said, *"I see nothing, and the Meddler assures me there is nothing there. Whoever cut this trail must have felt that their way was secure."*

Firekeeper translated, and Derian said, "Secure at least from someone entering undetected. Without Truth, we would have tripped two warnings: one at the copse's edge, and one at the door."

"The other doors are probably warded as well," Harjeedian said.

Firekeeper listened while she inspected how the door opened. She was actually coming to like human prattle. It was rather sweet how they kept trying to give reason to a situation that was only reasonable in its very unreasonableness.

"I can open," she said, "easily."

She did so without further delay.

The weight of the door and its iron bindings further testified that it was meant to secure the stronghold's interior from wind and weather—as well as against possible uninvited guests. However, the door did not stick nor did the hinges creak when she pushed against it.

"Someone has kept it oiled," Harjeedian said, "and mended the upper hinge. You can see where the fresh metal doesn't match."

Firekeeper stepped through the open door, Blind Seer pacing her. The portal could have admitted the two of them and Truth as well without crowding, and she wondered why. Exterior doors were often wide so that furniture and other large items could be accommodated, but she had noticed that interior doors were almost invariably narrower. This door was, if anything, wider than the one through which they had entered the house.

But she did not let such musings distract her. Even her dead nose caught the sour scent of the blood briar here, and with it a trace of blood. She found her hand drifting to the hilt of her Fang, and didn't stop herself.

Yet the area they stepped into was a rather pleasant place: an airy, rectangular garden, nearly as wide as the stronghold itself. The well Harjeedian had promised was there, and many feral plants reseeded from their domestic progenitors. Growing from the mold was a young apple tree heavy with russet fruit, doubtless thriving from its elder's death. Grapevines mingling with honeysuckle had claimed one wall.

Oddly, though Firekeeper looked carefully, in all this tangle there was no trace of the blood briar. She found one hank of briar vine holding a cluster of dry leaves, but this was all.

This was in the center of the courtyard. Here weeds pushed through the gaps between the flagstone paving, but interestingly all the weeds but those at the farthest edges had been beaten down by what must have been fairly frequent traffic.

The path through the wild growth that showed the most foot wear was not the one leading to the well, nor the one to the smoothly polished granite bench near the apple tree. The path worn most deeply headed toward what was in all appearances a solid wall overgrown with some sort of innocuous ornamental vine.

The vine's flowers were vaguely familiar to Firekeeper. She thought she might have seen them in the castle garden in Eagle's Nest. These had mostly gone to seed, each seed tipped with a tiny bit of vegetable down meant to carry it away on the wind.

"Clematis," Harjeedian said, surprising them all. "Why would they go to all this trouble to look at a wall covered with clematis?"

Blind Seer and Truth were reading the ground and air, but Firekeeper ignored their muttered comments to motion the others closer.

"Look," she said, "the wall is not all covered. There is a place in the center that is strangely open."

"The shape is rather like an arched doorway," Derian said. "A few vines drape over it, but they never touch the wall."

"And at least one has been broken," Harjeedian said, "as if someone tall walked into it."

He moved closer and inspected the edges of the vines. "Others of these have been cut as well. This is no chance clearing."

"It's a secret door," Derian said, his voice quickening with excitement. "Perhaps to a treasure vault or a hideaway."

"And the twins are in that hideaway," Harjeedian said, "and Plik with them."

Firekeeper was moving forward to see if she could discover how this door opened when Truth's voice froze her in midstep.

"It is a door," Truth said, and her ears were flat against her skull, *"or rather a gate, a magical portal between this place and somewhere else."*

"DID YOU KNOW?" Truth snarled at the Meddler within the safety of her skull. "Did you know and lead us here as the others were led to your temple on Misheemnekuru?"

"You are always so ready to think the worst of me," the Meddler replied.

"But, no, I didn't know. I spoke honestly when I said that I had no idea what was within the copse."

"You had looked into it before," Truth persisted, "when your precious twins first came here."

"At that time I could see little that they didn't see with their own eyes," the Meddler replied. "And they had not passed through this door. They had barely penetrated the interior of the house, for that matter, and were quite occupied in figuring out if they could last the winter, or whether they must return to Gak with their tails held low."

"But you knew what that opening was as soon as my gaze rested upon it," Truth said.

"As you would know a snapping turtle by the lumpiness of its shell," the Meddler replied. "These gates were not everywhere, but they were common enough, at least to one such as I who practiced the magical arts."

Truth replied with a growl that held such unameliorated menace that her companions all turned and looked at her as if they expected her to pounce upon one of them.

And why should they not? Truth thought in the part of her mind quite safe— she hoped—from the Meddler's intrusion. She had agreed to let him use her eyes and talk inside her head, but had drawn a firm line at anything else. *After all, I have been mad in the past.*

Certainly her current habit of consulting a Meddler who was not visible to any of them had to seem a bit unsettling. It helped that they all had evidence that he existed, which was at least one reason, she was sure, that he had exhausted himself to show himself to them. He had others, she was certain. A creature like the Meddler would never have only one reason for anything.

"Can you tell us how to use this gate?" Truth asked.

"In general, yes. In specific, though, I'm afraid not. And before you get all suspicious and start questioning my motives tell me . . . Wait, you're familiar with door locks, right?"

"I am."

"Good. The problem with any form of portal, from the hole into a rabbit's burrow to the most elaborate magical gate, is that while it lets the creature that created it go in and out, others could use it as well. I can't tell much about this particular gate just from looking at it through your eyes, but I can tell you a few things."

"Please do."

"My guess is that this gate will only take those who pass through it to one place. I also suspect it will be nearly impossible for you or your companions to open this gate from this end. These gates were routinely locked, and without the proper key they could not be opened."

"Is this key something we might duplicate?"

"I doubt it. Usually some minor ritual would be involved. The chances that you would stumble upon the correct combination of words or gestures is minimal."

"But we must go after Plik. The scent trail ends here."

"You may need to wait until those who carried him away return."

"If," Truth said somberly, "they return. Let me tell the others what you have said. They will not be pleased."

"Say what you will. I will do some scouting on my own."

Truth explained what the Meddler had said about magical gates, doing her best to answer questions for which she did not really have the answers. A moment came when humans and beasts alike looked at each other, and each one showed some element of despair.

"We've come so far," Harjeedian said, "since Firekeeper first brought word of the Meddler's machinations. I cannot believe we are to be stopped here. There must be something we can do."

Firekeeper tossed the core of the apple she had been eating at the clematis-framed section of wall. It hit hard, leaving wet pulp against the stone.

"We only have the Meddler's word this is a gate. Maybe it not. Maybe it is like Derian say."

Truth wished this were so, but she knew the Meddler had not lied—not in this, at least.

"The Meddler spoke honestly about this," she said. "Think. It matches what we have already sensed. Where are the twins? Where are those many beasts whose scents layer the floors?"

"From where," Blind Seer added, "came those other humans we scented? Truth is right, sweet Firekeeper, we cannot waste energy hunting a trail where we would like it to run. We must follow where it goes."

"But we cannot follow!" Firekeeper said.

She spoke loudly and in Pellish, and the two humans who had been unaware of the argument in progress looked away from their inspection of the stone wall in astonishment. Firekeeper switched to the language used only by the Beasts.

"I do not wish to turn away," she said. "Plik is gone. We owe him more search than this."

"I agree," Truth said. "This is my suggestion. I will wait here and guard. You and Blind Seer go and do a fast scout of this building's interior. When you are assured there is no one else here, then perhaps Harjeedian and Derian can search. They may find some indication of how this gate is opened."

Firekeeper translated this, and the two humans agreed.

"In any case," Derian said, "we need to decide where we will camp. I'd say here, but those clouds look like rain—and I'd rather not sleep out if we can get under a solid bit of roof."

"One suggestion," Harjeedian added. "Can Truth go and tell Eshinarvash what we have learned?"

Truth nodded after the human fashion, then added to Firekeeper, "Tell the humans I will go after you wolves have assured us this stronghold is empty of all but ourselves."

Lovable made a surprisingly soft coo for a raven.

"May I come with you, to see my Bitter? You carried Firekeeper, and I am much smaller."

Truth considered. "I think I can do it easily, especially if you perch on my back."

The wolves' scouting confirmed that the group was alone in the stronghold. They also reported having found where the twins had apparently set up their housekeeping.

"The area has been cleaned out pretty thoroughly," Blind Seer said, "but the scent lingers."

"Proof," Harjeedian added when this was translated for them, "that the twins left of their own choice, not by some accident."

"I'd like to be so positive," Derian said, "but they could have gone through, then this Smelly Herb Man or whatever Blind Seer calls him came back and took their stuff."

"True," Harjeedian conceded. "Very well. Then we at least have proof that the gate works both ways."

"Which," Firekeeper growled, "we already suspected. Come. We found a room of papers. The twins' scents are heavy there."

"Meanwhile," Derian said, "I'll set us up a camp here in the corridor. It's wide enough, and the ceiling above seems solid. We'll be close to fresh water. We can make our fire in the courtyard, and keep watch on the gate by its light."

❧

PLIK DID NOT SLEEP WELL the night following his insight into the possible truth of his situation in relation to Isende and Tiniel. All through the long hours of darkness he tossed and turned, unable to find a position in which his limbs did not ache. The room, previously comfortable, if somewhat confining for one who had known the freedom of Misheemnekuru, now seemed unpleasantly hot and close. The air was so choking that he considered opening his window and letting the blood briars in.

Morning brought Tiniel, bearing with him the tray containing Plik's breakfast, and once again reality as Plik had thought he understood it underwent a transformation.

"I've brought you some fresh fish," Tiniel said, pulling the cloth from over the tray, "and some late season grapes as well. Come along, don't sulk."

Plik wasn't sulking. The fish and grapes both smelled rather nice, but he couldn't seem to convince himself to move. His stomach growled with hunger, but his throat felt tight, and he didn't think he could swallow anything, even a grape peeled of its skin. Conversely, he craved something cool and wet, and tried to push himself upright so he could get at the pitcher and heavy stoneware mug that rested on the table next to his bed.

Tiniel moved to his side with unusual speed.

"What's wrong, Plik?"

"I feel . . ." Talking made Plik's throat hurt abysmally, but he forced himself. "Sore. Hot."

Tiniel reached to check Plik's forehead as he might have a human's. He hesitated, then found some unfurred skin above the shagginess of the eyebrows. He touched it with the back of his hand, and frowned.

"You are hot. Your throat hurts. Do you have muscle aches, too?"

Plik nodded, grateful not to have to speak. Tiniel asked several other diagnostic questions, and with each nod from Plik his expression grew more and more grave.

"Tell me," he said, "and you must answer honestly. Your life could well depend on this. Do you have anything that could be considered a magical talent, no matter how slight?"

Plik, thinking of how the maimalodalum all could sense magic, nodded.

Tiniel rose. "I must go and consult . . . someone. I will send Isende to you."

"Might catch," Plik managed.

Tiniel smiled grimly. "If you have what I think you have, Plik, we've already had it. It isn't the type of thing you catch twice. Either you live through it—or you die."

XXII

NOTHING CAME THROUGH the gate that night, and Firekeeper did not know whether or not to be relieved. She would have enjoyed having someone to hit, someone to ask the many questions that troubled her. The area within the copse felt dreadfully confining, all the more so for the reminder that they could not be certain what was as it appeared, and what might be overlaid with some nearly invisible web, the touching of which could have unpredictable but doubtlessly unpleasant consequences.

The paper-filled room had proven to be the remnants of a library, as Firekeeper had thought, but Harjeedian did not hold forth much hope for it producing an answer to the workings of the gate.

"Even if that information was here once," he said, "the twins must have found it and used it—and then carried it away with them."

"But you will look," Firekeeper said. "You can read this type of writing."

"I can. Much of the text is in what you like to call Liglimosh. Much, unhappily, is not. I've asked Derian to examine those documents I cannot identify, but he has found no Pellish. He thinks a few documents look as if they are written in New Kelvinese script, but those are unintelligible to us both."

"The twins' father's people?" Firekeeper asked.

"Who knows?" Harjeedian said. "What I do know is what slim chance I have of learning anything is diminished by your interfering with my studies."

So Firekeeper left. Truth had already sent her away so she could sleep, promising she was trying to dream a solution to their problem. Derian, who had taken the watch before dawn, was napping. Lovable, contented now that she had assured herself that Bitter was well, sat in the apple tree eating grubs and watching the gate.

Restless, Firekeeper paced outside, Blind Seer with her. The light drizzle was a welcome antidote to the closeness inside, and Firekeeper felt her head clearing as they paced the perimeter, looking for anything they might have missed earlier.

They were making their third or fourth circuit of the stronghold when Blind Seer paused. Firekeeper stopped beside him and found him studying the dormant bracken beasts. These remained much as Firekeeper had first seen them, waiting with vegetable patience for invaders who had already taken up residence within the guarded pale.

"I have a thought," Blind Seer said, "as to how we might manage to open that gate after all."

"What?" Firekeeper said excitedly. "Tell!"

"Those creations . . . They are awakened, or so we guess, by someone penetrating the boundaries of this copse."

"Yes."

"I wonder, are they the only ones who are alerted? What if the copse also has the means to send forth a howl to those whose scent we have traced?"

"An alarm," Firekeeper said. "Would that open the gate?"

"It might not open the gate precisely," Blind Seer said, "but those who were alerted might well come to check what raised the alarm. How else would they get here but through the gate?"

"I like it!" Firekeeper said. "Do we race outside and come back through?"

"You know better," Blind Seer chided. "I can smell your own trepidation balancing your eagerness. We will do nothing so foolish, even though we both would enjoy pulling the tail of those who have taken Plik and put us in this situation. Rather, let us go and speak with the others, and find out what they think."

Firekeeper agreed. Once she might have argued, but she had seen the price of her impulsiveness paid by others, and had no desire to see that happen again.

Inside the stronghold, she woke Derian and Truth, brought Harjeedian from the stacks of moldering papers, and almost before all were present set before their gathered strength Blind Seer's plan.

"So, you see," Firekeeper concluded, "we need not wait. We set ourselves to pounce, then one goes and comes in the copse wrong. I was thinking Lovable, since she fly and not touch down."

"But what about the bracken beasts?" Derian asked. "This would awaken them. What about the blood briars? They're out there, if not in here."

"There are only the two bracken beasts," Firekeeper reminded him, "and they are trapped with deadfalls hanging over them. So the trap will be tripped and they will be broken. The blood briars move slowly. Lovable fly fast."

"But if we try this plan," Harjeedian said, "whoever comes through the gate will expect trouble. If we wait, they will come through unsuspecting."

"Expect trouble outside building," Firekeeper persisted. "Not inside. If this is like spider and web, then spider knows where web is touched. They feel outside web and think we come in there. They not know we have seen outside web and inside both and have pass through without touching."

"Truth?" Derian said. "Do you or . . . uh, your advisor . . . have any thoughts about this?"

Truth stopped licking between her toes and said, *"I have had many thoughts, but never one so simple and direct. It must be how wolves think. I do not know—and neither does the Meddler—whether this alarm exists, but the Meddler admits that it is likely. Or rather, that in his day such would have been likely. He has no idea what to expect now."*

Firekeeper translated this, then said, "So, do we try?"

Derian frowned, and Harjeedian looked very uncertain. Lovable had sleeked her feathers down very flat and sat looking small, no doubt contemplating the dangers of flying through that copse and possibly awakening the very blood briars that had come so close to taking her life once already.

"The stories told in my land of the might of those who used magic are frightening," Harjeedian said. "I have wondered as I read what things other than the bracken beasts the twins—and these others the Wise Beasts have scented—might have rediscovered."

"If we worry about the elk kicking," Firekeeper protested, "then we will never have the hunt!"

"We can wait," Harjeedian said, "and be as spiders inside their web. Surprise will give us an edge over whatever they may bring with them. How can we give up what may be our only strength?"

Derian nodded. "Harjeedian has a point, Firekeeper. Besides, we've already discussed that Plik is probably alive and well. Why not wait and see if they will come to us? We have nothing to lose, and a great deal to gain."

Firekeeper looked over at Truth, but the great cat's burnt-orange eyes were opaque and uncommunicative. Lovable looked distinctly unhappy, and even Blind Seer seemed to have lost enthusiasm for his own plan.

"We wait," Firekeeper agreed reluctantly. "But Plik must wonder."

"Plik is fine," Harjeedian said. "They would not have taken him alive if they did not intend to keep him so."

PLIK'S FEVER GREW WORSE as the day went on, nor did it break when evening brought increasing coolness. One of the windows into his room was opened to admit the outside air. When Plik panicked and gestured wildly at the blood briars that twined without, Isende reassured him.

"They are trained not to touch anything on this side of the windowsill," she said, "and you need fresh air."

Despite Isende's reassurances, in his feverish hallucinations Plik imagined he saw the blood briars writhing over the sill, snaking down into his bed, anchoring their claws in his flesh, and siphoning off his blood until their green stems turned scarlet. Once he distinctly felt a bite on his arm and cried out in shock and alarm.

Plik's eyelids—which he had not realized were closed—flew open and in the light of a fresh day he saw a new person standing alongside his bed. He was flanked on either side by Isende and Tiniel, their postures showing both familiarity and some undefinable element of uneasiness.

The newcomer was a human male as fair as Derian, windburned and ruddy, with a long-jawed, clean-shaven face, and sparse black hair on top of his head. Plik found it completely impossible to guess the man's age. All he could tell was that this was a man grown, but not yet an elder with the detailed network of lines experience would etch in his skin.

The newcomer proved responsible for the biting sensation on Plik's arm. He was pinching the loose flesh and looking at the mark left by the pressure. He also ran his hands over Plik's torso in a fashion Plik found overly familiar, even going so far as to bend in order to press his head against Plik's chest.

The newcomer said something to Tiniel in a language Plik didn't know.

Tiniel took a note on a slate he held, while Isende reached for the water pitcher. As she was doing so, she noticed that Plik's eyes were open, and drew this to the newcomer's attention.

The other leaned over and inspected Plik's features closely, but with a complete lack of recognition for Plik's new alertness.

He said something terse and clipped.

Isende nodded rapidly, then immediately turned to Plik. "This man is a doctor. He says you should know you have an illness that causes a very high fever. If you hope to survive, you must drink a great deal of water, and permit us to do what we can to keep you cool."

Plik managed a stiff nod. He actually felt somewhat better than he had earlier, detached and distanced from his body and its suffering. He was old enough to know this was a very dangerous thing.

"Did . . ." he asked, his voice rasping dry, "blood briars cause this?"

Isende worried her lower lip between her teeth. She said something to the doctor, presumably translating Plik's question. He had been turning to leave, but now he stopped. He stroked his square chin as a bearded man might a beard, and said something. Then, with a distantly courteous nod to Plik, then another to Tiniel and Isende, he left.

Plik stared at the twins, knowing they would not have forgotten his question. Tiniel took it upon himself to answer.

"You have what the doctor would call 'burning down the wick,' if I were to give the words their literal translation. The people of Liglim call this disease by a name you may recognize. They call it Divine Retribution."

Plik gaped, unable to make a sound, and Isende spooned water into his mouth. He swallowed automatically, and though he suspected the water was room temperature, it felt wonderfully cool and soothing.

"How?" he whispered.

Tiniel sat on the foot of the bed, his fingers folding back and forth a section of the coverlet. Isende reached out and patted her brother's hand, then gave Plik a brave smile.

"How? How did you catch it? How do we know? Well, let me start with something you should know first. It doesn't seem like the disease is as deadly as it once was. The doctor is right in warning you this is a dangerous illness. You could die, but if we're careful, you'll live."

Tiniel said in a tight voice, "We had it. Both of us. We're alive. The doctor had it, too."

Isende frowned at her brother as if his words held some information other than the simple meaning Plik heard. Tiniel subsided back to folding and unfolding the edge of the coverlet, and Isende continued speaking.

"If we're to believe the stories from the New World, the disease . . . Let me just call it by its name in the doctor's language. It isn't as creepy as calling it 'Divine Retribution.' In the doctor's language it's called 'querinalo.' "

Plik nodded carefully to show he understood. He also indicated the water. When Isende resumed talking, she fed him delicately measured spoonfuls. Plik wished he could just have a cup, but he wasn't sure he could lift one.

"The stories we were told," Isende said, "and I think you must have been told—and everyone in the New World knows by heart—tell how querinalo came and those who had magic of any sort became very ill and died. Those with moderate magics took longer to get ill. We were told that many of these escaped back to the Old World, so we don't know if they lived or died. In the New World, anyone with a talent sickened and some of these died, but not all. Is that about what you know?"

Plik nodded.

"Good. Now, one thing we of the New World have always wondered is what happened to the Old World rulers, the people who started all these colonies. Some people thought they fled querinalo and feared to come back. Most thought that querinalo must have spread to the Old World, too, because the Old World rulers have never come back and it seemed unlikely that they would have waited more than a hundred years to do so if they could."

Plik felt question after question rising to be asked, but his sore and swollen throat made it necessary that he wait and listen, hoping Isende would anticipate his questions in the course of her tale.

"The Old World rulers haven't come back, in case you're wondering," she said, perhaps in response to a little squeak that had slipped out. "That's an entirely other story . . ."

"Finish telling Plik about querinalo," Tiniel said. "He needs to know."

Isende looked as if she might rebel. Then an expression that strangely mingled anger and pity warmed her brown eyes and she nodded.

"Very well. As I said earlier, it seems as if querinalo isn't as severe as it used to be. People live through it now, but rarely without serious damage either to body or—more usually—to, well, remember the doctor's name for the disease? 'Burning down the wick'?"

Plik nodded, feeling every bone and muscle ache at the effort.

"His people called it that because they realized that magical ability was the thing the disease fed on—like the flame of a candle centers on the wick. They believed that once the disease destroyed that wick, then it began to diminish, unable to tap into the rest of the victim's strength. That's why those with just talents tended to survive—though often with the talent reduced or lost altogether. Talents are minor magics, hardly more than an extra sense. Major magics, those that can be trained or adapted to multiple uses, those are really intertwined with all parts of the person. If querinalo runs its course, it burns out the person's magical ability. Usually, that ability doesn't return or if it does, it's diminished."

Tiniel interrupted, his words rushing out as if they had been dammed behind his breath.

"That's what happened to Isende and me. If you came searching for us, you must have learned something about us first, about how from when we were small we were aware of each other in a way no other people were."

He raised his hand and revealed the small white scar along the outer edge. "We were connected at birth. Even after that physical bond was severed, we remained connected. The connection changed and altered as we grew, but it was always there. Then we caught querinalo, and when we recovered the connection was gone. Isende doesn't like calling the disease Divine Retribution, but I wonder, I wonder! We had something special. I wasn't satisfied. I wanted . . ."

Isende glowered at her twin and Tiniel halted in midphrase, gulping breath. When Tiniel continued, his voice reminded Plik of a horse under tight rein.

"I wanted to add to it. I thought my ambition gave us the right to investigate, to probe our heritage. When Gak refused to name us a clan—although I still think the right was ours—I came up with this idea. Come here. Find our heritage. Find something . . . I wanted to go back and show them . . . show them that they were wrong to dismiss us as minor members of a vast clan. Isende didn't care how the others felt about us. At least she didn't care as much as I did. Now look what we've done!"

Plik stared at Tiniel, half certain this outburst was another of his own feverish hallucinations. Then he felt Isende's hand—still automatically feeding him water—tremble, felt the water splash onto his fur, and knew that this was no hallucination.

I should have known, Plik thought. *They behaved so normally. They summoned each other by voice or gesture. There was no special link between them. They were close, true, but no closer than would be usual for two people who had dwelled together all their lives. The very normalcy of the situation hid its signif-*

icance from me. But for them, poor children, for them there is nothing normal in this lack of connection. It is as if they have lost speech or hearing. They are crippled for life, and Tiniel blames his ambition for this injury, and for . . . I am sure there is something more. I must have the rest of the tale.

Plik waited until fresh water had washed his throat, then croaked, "Where? Who?"

Unlike when he had asked this a few days before, Isende no longer pretended not to completely understand.

"Plik, we're in the Old World. The doctor you saw, the others you said you smelled—they're residents of the Old World."

"Worse," Tiniel said, his self-loathing making him blunt. "Worse than residents. They're Old World sorcerers. Now, for the first time in over a hundred years, they have a route to the New World—and it's my fault that they do."

"Oh, stop it!" Isende snapped at her brother. "That's your problem, always taking too much on yourself, assuming others feel as you do. They were already here, trying to make the gates work. Maybe we sped things along but . . ."

Plik reached out and tapped her arm. Immediately Isende softened.

"I'm sorry," she said. "I've spilled water all over you, and you've a fever, and our shouting must make your head ache. Do you want me to let you rest?"

Plik shook his head. "Tell more," he whispered. He wished he could tell them about the Meddler. Maybe knowing how that being had pressed the impulse that had fired the twins' exploration would soothe some of Tiniel's guilt, but telling them about the Meddler would have to wait until he could speak more clearly.

Isende put her hand to Plik's forehead. "If Tiniel would get some cool compresses, then I will continue talking. By the way, Zebel, that's the doctor, told us water alone—no food—is best for you at this stage of the illness. Food will just feed the fever, give it fuel to burn hotter. He says you're rather fat, so you can do without eating for a day or two."

Plik tried to smile. He didn't feel in the least hungry, but he could tell that Isende was troubled at having to deny him food.

"Tell," he whispered.

Tiniel brought cool compresses and put them at points where Plik's fur was thinner: forehead, wrists, feet. They felt very good. Plik let himself drift away from the discomfort of his body, but kept himself firmly anchored with the thread of the tale Isende began to unfold.

"We came to our ancestors' stronghold," she said, "for pretty much the reasons Tiniel mentioned—except that he forgot to mention how terribly lost we felt when our father died. Our father was the last person who didn't think of us as very strange—or at least that was how we felt at the time. We came out here, and really it was sort of a relief having to work hard to establish ourselves. We didn't have energy left to tear ourselves up with grief. We mourned, but we didn't mope.

"After we became acquainted with some of the local yarimaimalom, we even began to have some hope we could make our venture work. They spared us a lot of searching for things we needed. They showed us where old orchards were, for example, brought us meat. In return we made clear we wouldn't set up pit traps or snares that might hurt any of them. We weren't quite friends with them, but I think we might have become so in time.

"When winter came we couldn't roam as much. We had moved into the stronghold by then, so we had a good roof and solid walls to keep out the weather. We'd stocked up on food. There was ample water. Useless old furniture gave us more firewood than we could burn in five winters. At last we started investigating the heritage our father had told us about. We'd located the library early on. While we'd pulled out bits and pieces of documents, we hadn't really searched systematically. Now we did.

"That's when we realized that this place had been more than the residence of a sorcerous family. It had housed an important magical artifact—a gate for traveling between the New World and the Old. I wasn't joking when I told you before that we're in the Old World. We are, and we came here by means of that gate.

"Remember all the stories about how the Old World sorcerers took to their ships and fled when querinalo spread? Didn't it ever seem strange to you that they managed so organized a retreat, and managed to get so much of their stuff away with them?"

Plik rocked his head side to side, trying to indicate he hadn't really ever thought about it.

"I did," Isende said, "not because I was terribly practical or anything, but because I kept hoping that someday I'd stumble on a hidden treasure—gems and gold and beautiful jewelry, not magical artifacts—that the sorcerers couldn't get away in time. One of our nursemaids when we were little was full of stories like that, and when she moved on I made up new ones for myself and Tiniel."

Tiniel sighed in fond exasperation. "You've gone off again, 'Sende. Plik doesn't want to hear about our childhood games."

Actually, Plik didn't mind, but he did want to know how the twins had managed to get themselves from a dilapidated stronghold in the western foothills into the Old Country.

Isende stuck her tongue out at her brother, but she did resume the main point of her narrative.

"According to what we learned—both then and since—there weren't a great many of these gates between the Old and New Worlds. Apparently, they are very, very difficult to construct. However, back then the sorcerers were growing weary of long sea voyages. Their initial desire to keep all the secrets of greater magic from the New World was ebbing in their desire to travel more easily. A compromise was reached. A few gates were constructed in semi-isolated areas like this one. In order to keep those who didn't like the idea at all at least somewhat appeased, the gates all opened to one place, a central nexus.

"This nexus already existed, and was one of the most highly protected and guarded and otherwise watched-over places in the Old World. It didn't belong to any one nation, but was a neutral space. I can't say I understand all the reasons, but they had something to do with not wanting rivals to be able to use gates to attack each other, or to march armies through and all.

"When all the parties involved—and don't ask me who they were because I don't really know—finally agreed that there would be gates made between the Old and New Worlds, they also agreed that the gates would arrive in the Old World at a new complex attached to the existing nexus. That way they could be protected from abuse along with all the rest. And when querinalo came, well, who would take a long sea voyage when they could use a gate? And the sick came through the gates and brought querinalo with them."

Tiniel interrupted. "Some think querinalo was already here. That it started here, and that the gates spread it the other way—back to the New World."

Isende sighed at him, and Plik wondered if they had disagreed this much when they were still linked. If so, there must have been a huge number of barely audible arguments.

"Tiniel has a point," she said, "but wherever querinalo began, what's important is that the gates helped it to spread more quickly. And the gates made possible the removal from the New World many artifacts and valuable texts—not to mention more mundane valuables—that would otherwise have been left behind."

Although, Plik thought, *if the tales I heard were true, this wouldn't have mattered much. Between the remaining humans and the Beasts, very little that even faintly resembled an artifact was permitted to survive. Magic was too much feared and hated.*

"And when," Isende went on, "someone finally realized what was happening, the gates were closed down and sealed. In the confusion, no systematic effort was made to eliminate all mention of them. That mention is what we found in the library. There was nothing so neat as a formula for how to use the gates. Our first reference was an old journal, and for the longest time we thought that this place just had rather a lot of visitors for someplace in the countryside. Tiniel was the first to wonder."

The young man looked as if he were about to say something along the lines of "Woe is me, cursed with such curiosity" but a glare from his twin stopped him.

"I," Isende said firmly, "located the gate itself. I'd wondered about that central courtyard. It didn't seem quite right—those big corridors leading to what was basically a dead end. The cold weather helped by killing back the vines. We were still going out there for water, and on one of those trips I noticed the markings on the walls. You probably can't see them now that the plants have grown thick again, but the stones in the gate area are incised with some really intricate patterns. Tiniel and I were fairly bored with each other by then, so we set about figuring out what the patterns stood for, and, well, one thing led to another.

"We realized we had found a route to the Old Country. It was like one of those nursery tales. We imagined an entire land, empty of human inhabitants but for some decorously laid-out skeletons in tattered robes. There would be heaps of jewels lying about. Old tomes explaining how to achieve wonderful powers. Empty castles.

"We grew positively fanatical about finding out how to open that gate, and yet it was mostly luck that we found the . . . well, call it a key, but it's really more like a dance or a recipe. Anyhow, something full of elaborate steps and stages. We never would have found it, but it seems that one of our ancestors was just learning magic when querinalo came. I think he may have died fairly quickly, because no one knew that he'd left crib notes for his studies in his room. If they had known they would have found and destroyed them, for among other things, they contained the key for opening the gate. He'd copied it down without his teachers knowing. He thought he'd impress them by getting it letter-perfect."

Tiniel got up and began changing Plik's compresses. "I guess that's something that runs in the family—the desire to impress."

Plik coughed a very quiet laugh, and Isende grinned in shared understanding behind Tiniel's back.

"So," she continued with mock brightness, "we opened the gate, but what we found on the other side was nothing at all like our imaginings. What we found were the Once Dead and the Twice Dead, querinalo, and, really, pretty much the end to our freedom."

"Who?"

Isende forced a smile. "Plik, that's a long tale in itself, and you need to rest."

Plik knew he did, but he had to try and reassure her.

"My friends," he whispered. "Free us."

Isende nodded. "I know you're hoping to be rescued, but really you shouldn't. Tiniel and I were curiosities, and so are you. As such, we have been kept alive and treated not too badly, but the Once Dead are as arrogant as their ancestors when it comes to those that they view as lesser beings—and by lesser they mean anyone who is not part of their tradition."

She went on gently, seeing his distress, "The best thing you can hope for your friends is that they do not find the gate, and that if they do, they cannot find their way through. You see, if they do not die fighting against those who are already here, then certainly any of them with a scrap of talent will catch querinalo."

"And," Tiniel added somberly, "even if they survive, they will be so badly 'burnt' by the disease's fire that they will surely wish themselves dead."

XXIII

DERIAN TURNED THE APPLES he was roasting at the edge of the coals, making a mental bet with himself how long would pass before Firekeeper and Blind Seer went outside to pace again. Unless they were asleep, the wolves rarely remained indoors long enough for the mud on Firekeeper's feet to fully dry.

The scraps of documentation from the stronghold's library that kept Derian amused—for a few had turned out to be written in Pellish—and Harjeedian deeply absorbed meant, of course, nothing to the barely literate wolf-woman.

When Harjeedian had dryly suggested that this might be an opportunity for Firekeeper to start learning to read more than the ten or twelve Liglimosh symbols she had memorized a year or so before, Blind Seer had so obviously agreed that Firekeeper had begun an effort to at least memorize the Pellish alphabet.

However, her gaze rose so frequently from the characters Derian had written with charcoal on a piece of broken lumber that Derian doubted she would remember much. He thought Blind Seer might be learning more. At least the wolf's blue-eyed gaze remained more fixed on the characters, but then he might have simply been daydreaming. It was hard to tell.

Derian was about to ask if Blind Seer wanted reading lessons when a man flickered into sight across the fire.

Firekeeper leapt to her feet, blade in hand. Blind Seer went from drowsing contemplative to snarling monster before the apple Derian had dropped hit the ashes. Lovable squawked alarm from her watch post in one of the trees in the courtyard.

Only Harjeedian and Truth did not react: Harjeedian because he was too absorbed in his reading to notice the disturbance, Truth because she all too obviously recognized their visitor—and perhaps was the only one to have had warning of his coming.

"Good to see you all so alert," the Meddler said. As before, his form was mostly solid, but if Derian concentrated he could see the wall through the image. "I'm sorry to disturb you, but I saw most of your company was here and . . ."

Firekeeper slid her Fang back into its sheath and resumed her seat on a blanket folded on the flagstone floor. Blind Seer's snarl was slower to fade. He remained standing, his hackles raised. Harjeedian looked up now, and Derian found himself reluctantly admiring the aridisdu's poise, for surely Harjeedian had been as startled as the rest of them.

"You have returned," Harjeedian said. "Truth has told us such manifestations are draining for you. Therefore, there must be some important reason for this honor. I would offer you a seat, but . . ."

The Meddler leaned back against the nearest wall—or at least gave the impression of doing so. Derian saw that his shoulder actually sunk a half-finger's depth into the stone. The Meddler must have noticed, too, for that error was corrected almost as soon as noted.

"I have come to share with you," the Meddler said, "some information that may color your decisions regarding an attempt to rescue Plik. Truth has done me the great courtesy of keeping me briefed, so I know what you have found here, and even of Blind Seer's clever plan for bringing someone to you from whom you could then learn the key to opening the gate."

Blind Seer did not relax at this praise. If anything, he became more guarded. No one else commented, and the Meddler continued.

"As I said earlier, I did not know this stronghold contained a gate, but I do know something of gates. When I realized that you were unlikely to find the key to the gate here in this stronghold, I resolved to see if I could learn anything at the other end."

"Other end?" Derian said. "You mean you know where this gate leads?"

"I had a suspicion," the Meddler said, "and my researches make me think my suspicion is correct. May I say a few words about the nature of gates?"

"If you have the strength," Firekeeper replied, with something almost like courtesy.

"For this, I do," the Meddler said, favoring her with a warm smile.

Derian remembered that Firekeeper said she had seen the Meddler with a wolf's head, and wondered how that expression translated.

The Meddler's smile faded, and his tone became a mimicry of Harjeedian's pedantry. "First, you must understand that these gates, while rather wonderful, are as limited as any other tool. I kept those limitations in mind as I began my research."

Truth gave a long, elaborate yawn for which there was no need of translation.

The Meddler grinned and shrugged. "Very well. I will spare you the details of my research. Simply put, gates enable a vast amount of distance to be crossed, but the destination point must be fixed. In other words, gates are much like any other door, only the threshold between rooms is wider. Even in the great days of magic, when sorcerers ruled all the nations of the world, the gates were almost impossibly expensive to construct, both in terms of the magical power that must be expended and the physical components that must be used. Therefore, it was unlikely that any person or group would contemplate construction of more than one. This meant the gates were of limited utility until someone came up with the bright idea of having all gates share one destination."

"One?" Harjeedian said. "Wouldn't people risk crashing into each other?"

"One general destination," the Meddler clarified. "A nexus. The creation of a nexus meant that if someone, say, from here wanted to go to Hawk Haven— assuming there was a gate in Hawk Haven—they would not go directly to the Hawk Haven gate, but first to the nexus. Then they would walk to the gate that had an endpoint in Hawk Haven and leave from there."

"Interesting," Derian said, "and practical. Since each gate could have only two endpoints, the use of the nexus would save a lot of redundant construction."

"The arrangement was practical from more than one standpoint," the Meddler agreed, "and before the lovely spotted lady yawns again, I would like to stress that I *am* getting to the point. The other reason this nexus system was very practical was that—as those of you with suspicious minds will have already thought—gates could be very dangerous indeed in, say, time of war. Why bother to load armies onto ships or mount them upon horses if the soldiers could march one by one through a door and end up hundreds or even thousands of days' journey distant?"

"Would this nexus stop them?" Harjeedian asked. "Couldn't a private gate between destinations be constructed?"

"You are forgetting the expense involved in building such gates," the Meddler said. "However, assuming that some power was rich enough not only to prepare an invading force, but also to build a gate into the area to be invaded, the nexus system provided another safeguard as well.

"Use of the gates created a ripple or surge that could be detected by those who were skilled in this form of magic. The governing body of the central nexus employed those who could do this. Initially, they did this in order to anticipate use of their facility. However, soon they realized the fringe benefit that these watching sorcerers would be fairly certain to detect the use of a gate, even if it was not tied into their network."

"And as the building of a secret gate would be rather suspicious," Harjeedian said, "in and of itself—no matter what excuses the builder made—international security would be assured."

"That," the Meddler agreed, "was the idea. Well, needless to say, this nexus could not belong to any one nation. It was built on neutral territory, on an archipelago of large islands surrounded by nothing but sea. Despite the isolation, supplying the inhabitants was not difficult. There were the gates, after all. Nor did those who worked there suffer from the loneliness of their post. If they chose, they could go to their homelands at almost any time.

"Despite this relative oneness of purpose, security on many levels was fierce. The oceans were reported to have been stocked with monsters. I don't know if this was true, but enough people believed this that no captain lightly took his ship into the forbidden areas. The magical security was also excellent. As you know from Truth's demonstration a few days ago, there are ways other than the use of gates by which one can travel over intervening distances without physically passing through the space. Precautions were taken so that even those possessing that specialized ability could not reach the nexus. Should they try, it would seem to them as if they had smashed against a wall of stone. There were other precautions as well, marvelous and complex, but I will spare you the details, for I cannot believe that most of these still exist.

"What matters is this. When I learned there was a gate here in this stronghold, I made the logical assumption that this gate, like all the rest, went, if not to the nexus I had known, then to one very much like it. However, given the security arrangements that were already in place at the nexus, I believed that when gates to the New World were created, they would terminate at the same point."

"Makes sense," Derian said. "After all, my bet is that most of those who used that gate out in the courtyard didn't want to go to another point in the New World. They would have wanted a fast way to get to some place in the Old World. That nexus would have been perfect."

"So," Firekeeper's husky voice interjected, tight and impatient, "you go there, Meddler? You go this nexus? You go how Truth goes?"

"I tried to reach the nexus," the Meddler said, "and I failed, but even that failure told me a great deal. You see, the reason I failed was that the barriers against entering the nexus remain intact. They might not have been quite as elegant as in the days I remember, but they were quite enough to stop a bodiless fellow like myself. Moreover, I could sense that the power maintaining them was not latent—not left from the days before the Plague. It was new power, unpolished by the standards I had known, but no less a barrier."

Derian nodded. "A finely finished granite wall without a visible seam, and a heap of roughly mortared rocks both will serve to keep an invader out."

"Correct," the Meddler said, giving Derian one of those smiles that so reminded him of his uncle. "And that rough stone wall might even do a better job since all the effort is going into making it strong, none into making it pretty."

Harjeedian set beside him the papers he had been holding. "So after all this time, the nexus remains active. How, I wonder? Did the Divine Retribution not slay those who dwelled there? I would have thought they would have been particularly susceptible, for all of them must have had some skill in magic."

"Not all," the Meddler said. "There were lots of sweepers, garbage collectors, cooks, and such. Transit between the gates took time to prepare. Sometimes travelers would stay a day or more to sightsee. Negotiations—financial or diplomatic—were held there, too, for the nexus was neutral ground. There was a marvelous marketplace on one of the islands in the archipelago. Expensive, yes, but often one could find things there that could not be had elsewhere."

"Even so," Harjeedian said, "there must have been a huge number of sorcerers at this nexus. Worse, there must be sorcerers present today or that barrier which you encountered would not be in place."

"As to that last," the Meddler said, "you are certainly correct. As to whether they have been there all along, or whether this occupation is a new development, I do not know. I have rather been out of circulation for quite a while."

For a long time, Derian thought, *long enough that the world of which you speak is an alien one to all of us. You talk about it and your voice is full of wonder and longing. But sorcery is a thing of nightmare to me and my people, and to Harjeedian and his, and maybe even more so to Firekeeper and Blind Seer. The Royal Beasts have no love of magic.*

Aloud Derian said, "My guess is that the twins would have known nothing of this elaborate system of gates and all the rest. At least we have found no mention of it in our research—nor did any mention remain in the tales I was told as a child."

"Nor in those of my land," Harjeedian said. "I am not surprised this is so. The Old World rulers did their best to keep ignorant all but those few they chose to teach."

Derian nodded. "If the twins did open the gate—and it was not opened without their doing—they probably expected to find a deserted building on the other side, a vacant stronghold to match this one. They may not have even realized their end point would be in the Old World."

"I don't know," the Meddler said with disarming honesty. "I can't even speculate. Have you learned anything in your research?"

"Little enough," Harjeedian admitted. "My guess is that this library has been picked over time and time again. The original inhabitants would have borne away what they could. Then there may have been looters, perhaps a succession of them over time. Then the twins came and hunted about. Lastly, I suspect, those whose scents Truth and Blind Seer reported—the strangers whose scent is not that of the twins—probably carried away anything left. What I have been reading is interesting in its own way, but useless regarding the gate."

"Then," the Meddler said, "Blind Seer's plan may be the best choice—that is unless you wish to wait here until one of those on the other side decides to come through."

"No," Firekeeper growled. "That could be forever. Why would they come here now?"

"How old are the scents?" the Meddler asked, glancing at Truth and Blind Seer. He clearly understood the answer given, for he said, "So some humans have been here fairly recently, recently enough that they are probably responsible for the blood briars and the bracken beasts being set on you. They may well have had someone staying here as a guard all along."

"Not when we come in," Firekeeper said. "Not that we see. No one here."

"The guard may have retreated," the Meddler said. "You alone, Firekeeper, then you and your fellows destroyed a small army of those bracken beasts. They're not the most complex of constructs, but nothing magical is easy to make. You probably set their creators back several moonspans of work—if not more. The blood briars would be easier to set. Probably the ones that hurt the ravens were passive guards, but there is no way the bracken beasts were."

"You suggested," Harjeedian said, "that we should follow Blind Seer's plan. By that do you mean we should trip whatever alarm may be interwoven into the borders of the copse and hope someone comes to investigate?"

"That is precisely what I mean," the Meddler said.

"I have been wondering," Harjeedian continued, "is it likely that they have been spying on us all along?"

The Meddler grinned, his candor disarming any sting implied in Harjeedian's words. "You mean like I spied on my candidates? I don't think so. For one, scrying like that is another specialized skill. Even I needed physical tools to help me maintain long concentration. For another, the nature of that barrier around the nexus is such that any magic has trouble getting through it. That's why in the old days they employed sorcerers to watch the gate ripples. It was more reliable than any other way of knowing what was coming their way."

"I admit to being relieved," Harjeedian said. "I have been worried we were putting on a show for unseen observers. Still, my concern is that if we deliberately alert whoever is on the other side, those who come will arrive expecting trouble."

"There's no way I can see to avoid that," the Meddler said. "If they have learned anything about the gates, even your using one may well provide an alert. However, I doubt they will come through more than two at a time. Unless gates have changed tremendously from my day, there will be a pause between sendings."

"That's something," Derian said. "The gate's big enough that I had imagined gangs running through waving clubs or firing bows—or worse."

Firekeeper had been listening with that dark-eyed concentration Derian knew meant she had accepted the necessity of a fight.

"Tell us," Firekeeper said, "everything. One time you say you make us map of here. Can you make one of there—of this nexus place?"

"A very outdated one," the Meddler said, "but surely the bigger landmarks will not have changed."

"Good. Do this. Tell us all. Then we will go hunting."

✤

LATE THAT NIGHT, Plik's illness reached a crisis. He hurt everywhere, even to the roots of his teeth. As his fever rose, he began shedding voluminously, but at the same time he shivered with cold, as if the very marrow in his bones had turned to ice.

His muscles ached so that he could hardly open his mouth or swallow, but he craved every droplet of the water the anxiously attentive Isende forced into his mouth. Tiniel brushed the bare portions of his skin with alcohol. During one lucid moment, Plik heard the twins discussing the possibility of putting him in a bath, but as he alternately sweated and shivered, they didn't dare take the risk.

Later the hallucinations began. He held long conversations with the distant maimalodalum, telling them what he had seen, of the kindness he had met from his traveling companions, from Isende and Tiniel.

"Maybe," he said to Hope, "we were wrong to think that humans would view us as monsters."

"Maybe," Hope said, "but the reality is, we *are* monsters."

Later, Plik rested on a cloudy plain, leaning back against a heap of clouds. He felt exquisitely comfortable, but distantly he was aware that he was also racked with pain so great that his body twitched and convulsed. He would have fallen to the floor if Tiniel had not held him down. His mouth tasted of pine, and he realized there was a stick in his mouth, pressing down his tongue so he would not bite it.

"Nice place, isn't it?" a voice said.

Plik blinked, realizing for the first time that he was not alone. Another sat with him, a chubby raccoon-man like himself, so much like that Plik thought it his own reflection come to visit. Given some of the conversations Plik had had that night, he was not in the least surprised.

"It is nice," he replied, but he felt rather guilty as he said so.

"You've heard of me before," the other said, "but I don't believe we have met. Your friends call me 'the Meddler.' "

Plik was interested now, remembering the many stories he had read. "And what would you call yourself?"

"The Meddler will do, though I think of myself as a Meddler. Certainly, I am not the only one who has ever meddled."

"Are you meddling now?"

"In a sense. I haven't been able to reach you before this, although I have been trying."

"Practice makes perfect."

"Actually," the Meddler said, "the reason I can speak with you now is less than perfect. I think you should know—you're in rather immediate danger of dying."

Plik thought about this. The idea did not terrify him as much as he thought it would. Living, especially when he allowed himself awareness of what was happening to his body, was rather more frightening.

"You're not afraid of dying," the Meddler said.

"Is there a reason I should be?" Plik asked. "You seem a spirit yourself. What can you tell me of the afterlife?"

"Very little. I've never been there. This is a between place, where the dying often come. I left means of being notified if you showed up."

"You'd think it would be more crowded," Plik commented.

"It is quite crowded," the Meddler said, "but as everyone is alone in dying, so you are alone here. I'm rather intruding."

"That would be in keeping with the stories told about you," Plik said agreeably. "You always get into places where you shouldn't be—and you always have an excuse."

The Meddler nodded. "My reason for seeking you is this. Your friends are preparing to come rescue you. Originally, all I hoped was to learn something of your situation, anything that would help them find you."

"I am in a cottage," Plik said, "being tended by two who have no idea just how great a role you have played in their recent, unhappy lives. That's all I know. I haven't been outside. Oh! And the cottage is somewhere in the Old World. We reached it by some sort of gate, but as I was unconscious at the time, I have no memory of this."

The Meddler rubbed his raccoon hands over his chest ruff.

"Well, it would be nice if you knew more, but if you don't . . . Tiniel and Isende are well?"

"Alive, but I think they are as much captives as I am. I have been extremely ill since my arrival, first with blood briar poison, now with querinalo. Needless to say, I have learned less than I would like."

"Captives?"

"Of some people they referred to as the Once Dead and, again, as the Twice Dead. I don't know anything more. I think I saw one of them, though. A doctor. Polite enough. Professional. Seemed completely alive to me."

The Meddler straightened. "Alive! That's right. You need to make a decision, and, although time runs somewhat differently here than it does where your body is, you need to make that decision soon."

"Decision?"

"To try and live or to stay here and let your body die. You're half dead already. In a way, you're already dead, your body just doesn't know it yet. If you don't return your spirit to its residence, the dying will be complete."

Plik fell back into his body just a little and was met with a wash of pain. The surf sound had returned, and the pounding in his head was more than he could take. He slipped back to his cloud-pillowed refuge again.

"Dying doesn't seem so bad," he said.

"I doubt I can stop the others," the Meddler said, "even if I tell them the truth. They don't trust me, you see. Even if they do believe me . . ."

"Believe you?"

"If I tell them you have died," the Meddler said, and Plik knew he was being deliberately harsh. "Even if I tell them you have died, then they will still insist on knowing for themselves. Will you leave them nothing but sorrow as a reward for their efforts?"

Plik fell back into his body again. A second time the pain, the pounding in his head, the burning heat that lit his skin, the freezing cold that drilled through his bones, a second time these drove him back to where there was no pain.

"Will you?" the Meddler asked.

Plik thought he would. What sorrow would they feel for him, maimalodalu, monster, rejected child of the only parent he had known? They were chance companions who had known him for a handful of moonspans. Surely their mourning would not be deep.

Then Plik remembered, remembered how each and every one of them had sorrowed while Bitter struggled for his life. The sour raven was hardly the best of companions, but not a one of them had not glanced with almost every breath over to where the raven lay. Plik remembered the joy they had felt when Bitter had begun to move again, when he had first flapped wings still stiff from wounds, but slowly healing.

Plik could no longer deny that his companions would mourn him. They would grieve all the more deeply for feeling they had somehow failed him. Time and again they would ask: "If we had come sooner?" "If we had fought harder?" "Would anything we could have done made a difference?" No matter how many times they were told that the choice had been his, they would not believe.

And on Misheemnekuru a community that not so long before had lost several of its small number would also mourn, wondering once again if all contact with the world outside their islands must end in grief.

Plik glanced at the Meddler. "I believe I must at least try to live."

Then, taking a last sweet breath of painless air, he descended back into the tortured hell of his dying body.

For a long, long while after, Plik was aware of nothing but that pain. Then, perhaps because he had been given some rest in the place of dying, he found he could sort through the pain, place it in categories. He remembered what Tiniel and Isende had told him about querinalo's nature. Burrowing through, he looked for the wick along which the fever burned. It was there, pulsing with the sound of the surf, a sound he now knew to be his own ability to sense the presence of magic.

Plik saw that in order to preserve itself from being turned into ashes, the wick was sucking up his bodily strengths, feeding on them as a candle wick does on wax. Now, Plik began to isolate that wick from the rest of his body, sealing it within a cocoon woven from his desperate will to survive. He began within his core, preserving his vital organs and brain. Then, when these were safe, he moved to his extremities.

As he worked, Plik realized something of great value. The disease was very like a fire. Deprive it of fuel, and it would smother and die. Once he had isolated it, Plik experimented with such a smothering, closing the cocoon segment by segment, imagining himself as squeezing out the air. The fires burned hotter as he forced them into more contained areas. With their heat the pain grew in intensity until Plik thought he must give up and let himself be consumed.

But he remembered grief, and, holding on to the memory, he fought.

Eventually, he fell unconscious, dead even to pain. When he woke, he heard Isende's voice.

"The fever has definitely broken. He's through it!"

"Once dead or twice?" Tiniel said, his voice bitter.

"Stop it, idiot. He's alive. Alive!"

"Alive to be a captive."

"Alive."

"Alive."

Tiniel's voice softened, and Plik felt the young man's hand, gentle on his brow, and realized that testing touch had been there many times before over that long night's battle.

"Alive," Tiniel repeated, and this time he sounded truly happy.

Plik slept, clean, true sleep, not the unconsciousness of exhaustion. When he woke, he was aware that although he had come through querinalo he was not done with pain. Every muscle in his body, including those that moved his tail tip and his eyelids, ached from past convulsions. His throat was so raw he knew he had been screaming. A headache pounded beneath his brow, but after the pounding of the surf, it was almost welcome.

He opened his eyes and found Tiniel watching him. Isende lay on a heap of blankets on the floor. She was snoring slightly, and Plik thought with almost parental affection that the young woman looked cute in a rumpled sort of way.

"Once dead or twice dead?" Tiniel said as he had to his sister, but he redeemed himself with a self-mocking smile. "That's apparently the traditional question to ask someone who has survived querinalo."

Plik motioned for water, and when he had drunk deeply, he replied, "If I knew what you meant, I'd answer."

"Once dead means you went through querinalo but kept some of your magic intact. Twice dead means the fever burned it all away." He gave a hard, bitter laugh. "I'm twice dead. So's Isende."

Plik reached into himself. Ever since his waking experience, he had envisioned his ability to sense magic as sort of an extra set of ears. Now he pricked those ears—for to preserve himself from the pounding he had kept them flat—and listened.

Nothing. Maybe the faintest hint of surf sound, but that well could be his headache.

"Twice dead," Plik said, "but as I hardly knew the sense existed . . . It must be harder for you."

"There are times I feel like my heart has been cut out," Tiniel said. "I never realized how much I relied on that connection. . . . It was always there."

Isende stirred, and Tiniel lowered his voice. "She prefers we not speak of it. Let me help you to the pot. If I recall correctly from my own experience, you're going to need it."

He was right. Plik needed his help hobbling even that short distance. When they returned, Isende was awake, sitting up on the heap of blankets and finger-combing her hair into order.

"You're up," she said.

"And alive," Plik said, "barely."

"Hungry?"

"A little."

"Soup. Thick. I've asked the cook to keep some simmering."

She ran out, and when she returned insisted on feeding Plik. He wanted to protest. Now that he was more alert, he could see how exhausted both twins looked. They had probably sat up with him through the crisis, sleeping only once they were sure the fever had broken.

"Once dead and twice," Plik said, his voice rough, but his own to command. "You spoke of them before."

"The Once Dead are those who survived querinalo and have power left," Isende said promptly. "Most of them are horribly deformed in some way. They think themselves superior because they sacrificed their bodies to preserve their power. Some of them, though, they don't show any mark—at least on their bodies. Those are the ones you really should be scared of. The Twice Dead are, well, like us."

Plik nodded. "But these Twice Dead remain here?"

Tiniel glanced at the door as if fearing he might be overheard. "I'm not sure, but I don't think these sorcerers are universally loved. They certainly don't rule as their ancestors did."

"They'd like to, though," Isende whispered. "Oh, they really would like to. . . ."

XXIV

FIREKEEPER LOOKED UP from honing her Fang when Truth returned. Night had fallen since the Meddler's report had made them decide to trip the alarm and see what came through the gate. By the time they had their map drawn and had decided on details for every eventuality, even Firekeeper had agreed that waiting until the coming morning, after they had all had an opportunity to rest, would be wiser.

Eventually, Firekeeper and Blind Seer had wearied of how the humans insisted on rehashing what should be a simple plan, and had gone outside. The jaguar had left to tell Eshinarvash and Bitter of their intentions. She returned smelling of acrid concern.

"We have a small problem. Eshinarvash and Bitter insist on accompanying us."

"How can a horse help?" Firekeeper said. "And we have Lovable to fly and scout for us."

"And what about the pack and riding animals?" Blind Seer added.

"I asked those same questions," Truth said. She licked her shoulder with the odd, jerky motion that Firekeeper was coming to recognize as laughter.

"In answer to how a horse could help, Eshinarvash reared onto his hind legs and struck the air with his hooves. Then fast as a snake striking, he brought his head down and snapped at the air right above my ears. Stallions, as he reminded me, are warriors to be reckoned with."

"True," Firekeeper said, thinking of a battle witnessed years before. "Even the stupid ones can be brave and fierce. A Wise Horse . . . Yes. It would be foolish to dismiss him as a mere herbivore."

Truth sat and began grooming behind one ear. "I agree. As to the pack animals, Eshinarvash and Bitter have not sat quietly while we have been in here. Bitter needed to rebuild his flying muscles. He used those flights to scout for the yarimaimalom who are not here. Eventually, he found some: a small herd of elk who left this area soon after the blood briars made grazing unsafe. They have agreed to tend the pack and riding animals. The gear has already been stowed away."

Firekeeper did not ask how it had been gotten off the animals. She had seen Eshinarvash open gate latches with his teeth. Also, where one type of yarimaimalom had taken refuge, there might be others. Raccoons had very clever paws.

"And if Bitter can fly," Firekeeper said quickly, to distract herself from wondering how Plik was doing, "we would be lucky to have him with us. We are going into a place none of us has seen before. The Meddler admits the map he gave us may be useless. Even a one-eyed raven will add to our knowledge. Very well. Let us take them with us. Can you bring them both into the copse?"

"I think I could," Truth said, "but why should I risk tiring myself unnecessarily? We will need to touch the ring of false trees that hides this place. Why not do it by bringing those two through? I will go out at the appropriate time, and we will all come through together."

"I like it," Firekeeper said, "and tempted as I am to not tell the humans until the matter is concluded, they deserve to know."

Blind Seer rose and stretched.

"They most certainly do," he agreed, panting laughter. "Think how this new information will change all their plans."

DAWN THE NEXT MORNING found them all ready. Derian had gone to the door into the stronghold so he could hold back the alarm web.

Firekeeper and Blind Seer were guarding the gate itself, the blue-eyed wolf stationed to one side, Firekeeper with bow near the apple tree. Lovable, excited almost to incoherence at the thought of being reunited with her mate, was with Derian. Harjeedian admitted to little skill with weapons, and so waited in the section of the corridor where they had made their camp.

"It may be a long wait," the aridisdu reminded Firekeeper. "We don't know how much time will be needed for the alert to reach them or whether they will react immediately."

"I am better," she replied, "at long waiting than you think."

Privately, she did not expect a long wait. If she had kidnapped someone, then received warning that pursuit was possible, she would not delay. To do so would be to permit precisely the type of countertrap they had set.

Lovable winged down the corridor a few moments later.

"They are through! They are through! The bracken beasts are felled with the tree trunks. They wriggle like worms, but are broken beyond repair!"

She was gone, presumably to greet Bitter, before Firekeeper could frame an answer.

Harjeedian was looking expectantly at Firekeeper.

"They are through," Firekeeper said, bending her bow and fitting the string. "The deadfall broke the bracken beasts. There are blood briars still, but without the bracken frame to support them, they are little danger to us."

She tested the bow's pull, then relaxed it, but she kept an arrow in hand. No time would be wasted when the moment came to strike.

Harjeedian checked their map, then moved the tip of an old knife Firekeeper had sharpened the night before into the coals.

During the planning session, Derian had suggested that Harjeedian pose as the group's leader.

"Our usual extended debates," Derian had said with a laugh, "would be less impressive."

No one had disagreed, not even when Harjeedian suggested they show willingness to use torture.

Firekeeper had only nodded. "We not know how long until they is to howl back before their pack is to worry."

"Probably," Blind Seer had commented, "we will have some time. They will be expected to find out who the intruder is, then, if possible, take action."

"But every breath that we have before," Firekeeper said, "is worth giving some fear."

The clopping sound of horse hooves against stone announced the arrival of Eshinarvash. Bitter and Lovable were perched on his back, but even a glance showed that Bitter was not riding because he was too weak to fly. The blood briar poison was out of him, and like most wild things he healed quickly, because in the wild there is no leisure to do otherwise.

Derian led the procession.

"Anything?" he asked, strapping on his weapons.

"Not . . ." Firekeeper was beginning to say; then the stone of the wall began to transform from rough, lifeless grey to shimmering molten silver. She raised her bow, arrow to string, and pulled back. Blind Seer poised to spring. Truth bolted in to join them, crouching opposite the wolf.

The molten silver began to form shapes. Initially there was one: a blob against the smoother background. This elongated, jutting forward, rising to a second tier, then falling off slightly.

"*Strange,*" Blind Seer commented. "*When I look at whatever that is from the front, it seems to be moving forward, but when I look from the side, it remains behind the edge of the wall.*"

"*Let me know if it seems to pass the wall,*" Firekeeper said, "*and stay ready.*"

The blob was separating, becoming distinct shapes within the silver mass. Three groups, defined mostly by height. Then six distinct entities, walking in pairs. Two followed by two followed by two more, she thought. Details were becoming clear, as if whatever was there was coming closer, though neither Blind Seer nor Truth had indicated that the image had crossed the edge of the wall.

Derian moved closer, fascinated by the image that was taking shape. Although he wore his sword, the weapon he had to hand was a club.

"Back," Firekeeper warned. "Not between my arrow and that."

Derian stepped back. "Sorry. Trying to tell what that is. It reminds me of something, but I can't tell what. Maybe a . . ."

Harjeedian interrupted. "Four humans preceded by two large quadrupeds. It's like watching shadow plays. At first the figures overlapped, but now . . ."

Firekeeper nodded, her blood quickening with excitement and dread. There was something familiar in how that first pair of shapes moved, something she feared was going to ruin their entire plan.

"Those first," she said, "if they are yarimaimalom . . ."

"*Leave them to us!*" Truth hissed. "*Concentrate on the humans.*"

"*They are passing the wall!*" Blind Seer howled. "*I smell wolves!*"

The shadow pair charged forth then, yarimaimalom wolves, each as tall as Blind Seer. Their fur was reddish brown, shading into black, their coats less dense, but although this difference made them momentarily look smaller than the blue-eyed wolf, Firekeeper realized this was an illusion. They were as big and powerful, nor had their strange journey damaged their alertness.

Snarling, they lunged one-to-one at Blind Seer and Truth, attacking almost before their tails broke from the silver and into the closed courtyard.

Behind them emerged two men, burly and broad-shouldered. One was ruddy; the other had the darkest skin Firekeeper had ever seen on a human. However, they were matched in armor and equipment. In one hand each carried a metal-studded club. Packs were slung over their backs. Neither carried a shield, and Firekeeper thought that a good thing. She raised her bow, took careful aim.

But something was spoiling her aim. Two more were emerging from the silver-surfaced wall. These wore no armor and carried satchels in each hand. Weapons were slung at their waists, not held ready as with the preceding pair. Firekeeper thought one was male, the other female, but she couldn't be certain, for they wore elaborate caps and loose robes.

Firekeeper saw the features of these last two shift from blank alertness to alarm as they realized that they had not entered the quiet sanctuary they had clearly expected. Then satchels were dropped, weapons fumbled for, but Firekeeper was ready.

She fired her arrow. It sliced over the heads of the quadrupeds and landed, as she had intended, in the thick leather padding over the dark-skinned man's right shoulder. He bellowed something, and dropped his club.

Derian was yelling in Liglimosh, the language they had thought most likely to be understood.

"Drop your weapons! Call off the wolves!"

Firekeeper fired again, this time slicing the upper arm of one of those in the third tier. This one cried out in a high voice that seemed to confirm Firekeeper's guess at her gender. If these humans were like most humans she had met, the males would feel more alarm at damage to a female than to another male.

As she fit fresh arrow to string, Firekeeper glanced about.

Truth had leapt onto the back of one of the wolves, but the jaguar's effectiveness was hampered in that she was trying to overcome her opponent with her weight rather than anchoring her claws in the vulnerable flesh or setting her powerful jaws to break the wolf's neck. The wolf had no such qualms, but though he bent nearly in two, he could not quite reach the encumbrance on his back.

Blind Seer and his opponent were rearing onto their back legs, crashing into each other, snapping at ears and throats. Thus far one did not seem to have a great advantage over the other, and Firekeeper felt confident that Blind Seer would win.

Although the combatants had spilled forward into the courtyard, the crowded space was keeping any of Firekeeper's other allies from getting into the fracas. Eshinarvash stamped and trumpeted from the corridor, and the ravens circled above, looking for an opening but finding none that would not give their opponents too much of an advantage.

Derian continued shouting, "Surrender! We only need one of you, but we'll spare the lot. Just surrender!"

Firekeeper decided to add weight to Derian's words with another arrow. She targeted the weapon arm of the ruddy man and fired. He wore leather bracers, so she didn't hesitate to shoot for the limb, and her arrow anchored itself a hand's breadth over the elbow.

She howled in wordless glee, feeling the wildness of the hunt flow into her bones. Her howl blended with the startled cry of the wounded man, rising over the snarls and growls of the battling wolves, and over Truth's shriller screams.

The two who had emerged last had flattened themselves against the wall as if hoping to press themselves back from where they had come, but the surface was grey stone now, not yielding silver. Firekeeper loosed her next arrow to smash into the wall between their heads.

"Surrender!" Derian shouted again. "For your Ancestors' sake, stop before someone gets hurt and this stops being a game!"

There was worry in his voice, and perhaps that, rather than the threat of further injury, was what made the male of the pair against the wall shout something in a language Firekeeper did not know. It was a single word, but carried such authority that even the wolves ceased their battling, but cringed back, offering their throats in surrender. The armored men dropped their weapons and froze in place.

Firekeeper had been about to loose another arrow. Now she waited, her bowstring held taut so that any who attempted treachery would pay with his life.

The two stranger wolves bled but lightly. In the next rank, the dark-skinned man flexed his fingers and looked to the deep scar in his shoulder armor. Beside him, the ruddy man had clamped his fingers around where the arrow had gone through the leather protecting his upper arm. Blood seeped forth, but not in great quantities.

In the last rank, one held her hand around where blood leaked from her wounded arm. The other spoke in Liglimosh so strange in the shape of the words that Firekeeper could barely understand it.

"We have surrendered. Will you have these heads?"

"I said we would spare you, but I warn you. Break your surrender, and we will show no mercy." Derian turned slightly toward Firekeeper. "Do those wolves understand?"

"I find out."

Firekeeper glanced over where the two stiffly lay on their backs.

"You two," she said, *"you are beaten? Will you stay beaten?"*

The wolves seemed only mildly surprised to hear a human speak to them in their own language. Firekeeper wondered just how far tales of her and Blind Seer had traveled since their coming to Liglim over two years before.

"We were beaten before ever these two laid fang or paw in our flesh," said the one who had been fighting Truth. *"These humans hold our mates and packs."*

"That is a tight hold," Firekeeper said. She was not without sympathy. *"Can we break it?"*

"Defeat them," replied Blind Seer's opponent. *"We do not run with them from choice. Indeed, I think they meant us no kindness bringing us here."*

Truth's opponent only growled, a long, low rumbling, that sounded like a distant summer storm in that closed place.

"Firekeeper?" Derian asked. "The wolves?"

"They need to be put away from these," Firekeeper said. "Locked up. They are mean."

She looked at the reddish wolves. *"Go with Blind Seer and Truth. Pretend to cringe still. Best for your pack that these humans who go through walls think they still rule you."*

"We understand," said the one through his growling. They let themselves be herded off into another part of the building. Bitter winged stiffly above the cortege, untrusting, as well he might be. Firekeeper did trust these stranger wolves, though. She knew too well what it was like to have the life of someone you loved held over you, and wolves, even more than ravens, identified with their group.

Harjeedian had remained silent to this point, but now he spoke, and Firekeeper noted that his Liglimosh had taken on the same odd cast as that spoken by the strangers.

"Bring the prisoners before me," the aridisdu intoned.

Derian spoke with a hesitancy Firekeeper did not think was completely feigned. "Two of them are bleeding, Aridisdu. Can we do something about that first?"

"Bring the prisoners here," Harjeedian repeated. "If they please me, then perhaps we will tend these injuries they have so deserved."

"You heard him," Derian said, motioning with his club. "Aridisdu Harjee-dian wishes to speak with you."

The two men in armor, the ones who had carried weapons, glanced to the other two for orders.

"We will go to him," the male said.

"Leave all your gear here," Derian said, "those bags, the packs . . ."

The ruddy armored man looked as if he might protest, and Firekeeper made a great show of pulling back the bowstring she had gradually let slacken.

"I'll need help," the man said sulkily. "I can't move my arm."

"Help him," Derian said to the dark-skinned man. "And don't try anything clever. She's just a little crazy."

Firekeeper thought she heard the man mutter "A little?" but the comment did not displease her. She knew Derian wanted their captives to fear her. Right now these strangers couldn't be sure how many were in their company. When they learned there were only three humans, they might start reassessing the odds in their own favor.

That wouldn't do—at least not until they had learned what they needed to know in order to follow Plik. Then these Old World humans could make all the mistakes they wanted. Firekeeper would be quite happy to show them the danger involved in underestimating an angry wolf.

DERIAN WAS INCREDIBLY RELIEVED when the strangers surrendered. Firekeeper had been playing up until then—whether or not they realized it. The wolf-woman had her strengths, but an excess of imagination was not one of them.

She had attacked the newcomers as if they had no abilities she had not seen before—despite their arriving by walking through a solid stone wall. This time it seemed she had been right, but what if she had been wrong?

What if she had been wrong?

"This way," Derian said tersely, gesturing the four humans to where Harjee-dian prepared to hold court in front of their campfire. The four prisoners came obediently enough, and Derian took the opportunity to study them more closely.

Three men, one woman. Two of the men were dressed in light armor as if they had anticipated combat. Since they had responded so quickly, Derian guessed they were bodyguards, but he thought that the armor probably had been donned in anticipation of action once they left the stronghold rather than because they had thought to find trouble waiting right outside the gate.

One of these bodyguards looked like a Stoneholder, his build along straight, squared lines, the wisps of hair that slipped out from under his helmet pale white-blond. His skin was ruddy and lined from constant exposure to sunlight and weather, making it difficult to judge his age.

The other man had the darkest skin Derian had ever seen, a rich blackish brown that was slightly oily, and practically without lines. This made him seem younger than his companion, but from a contained, compact power in his movements that was completely missing from his partner, Derian wondered if the dark-skinned man might be older. Certainly, he was better-trained.

The male of the other pair might have been a citizen of Liglim in coloring and general appearance, the female could have been from Derian's own Hawk Haven. They wore robes similar to those Derian had seen worn by the thaumaturges of New Kelvin. Their heads were covered by close-fitting, embroidered caps, their hair braided tightly to fall behind. They moved in a studied, rhythmic fashion that made it difficult to judge their ages, although Derian felt fairly certain that neither was beyond forty, and that perhaps they were much younger.

Without comment, the four captives took the places Harjeedian indicated near the banked campfire. The two Derian thought of as "thaumaturges," because of their manner of dress, sat first. The bodyguards resisted sitting for a moment, but the dull twang of the tune Firekeeper played on her bowstring made them take seats fast enough. They positioned themselves behind the others, as if to guard their backs.

Derian took his own post in the corridor. Firekeeper and Lovable remained in the courtyard. Neither Truth nor Blind Seer had returned, but Bitter winged in as all were settling, and as Firekeeper did not say anything, Derian guessed the two stranger wolves remained under control.

Harjeedian gave the prisoners a tight-lipped smile and a stiff nod. Although he had rejected a suggestion that they assemble some sort of audience chamber for him, he had not neglected the little flourishes that would emphasize his position of power. He sat at ease on a low campstool, a mug of savory tea close to hand. A knife rested, edge to a red-hot coal, tacit promise of the mutilations heated metal could work on unprotected flesh. When Truth had gone to trip the alarm, Harjeedian had taken a moment to don a few of the amulets and other elaborate ornaments that he usually reserved for religious services.

Derian had seen Harjeedian through a stranger's eyes, through a prisoner's eyes, and knew perfectly well how intimidating the man could be, especially when he sat as he did now, studying those before him, his gaze saying without words that he knew far more about his prisoners than they realized.

"I am the aridisdu Harjeedian, of u-Nahal in Liglim," he began. "You are?"

Harjeedian's tone held only bored good manners, not the least hint of curiosity.

The male thaumaturge was obviously offended. "I am the Once Dead Lachen. My companion is the Once Dead Ynamynet. We are served by Verul and Skea of the Twice Dead."

Lachen spoke in Liglimosh, but the accent was odd, the sound of many of the vowels peculiar to Derian's ear.

Harjeedian did not react to the strange titles, although Lachen had definitely meant them to impress.

"Very good," the aridisdu said. "Now, unless you are interested in becoming permanently dead, you will answer my questions. Your answers must be accurate, for we will be testing them, and should those tests fall short of expectations, we will not hesitate to exact penalties."

"And if we refuse?" Once Dead Ynamynet said sharply. Her Liglimosh bore two accents, some vowels after Lachen's speech, others holding what sounded like the accent they had encountered in Gak. Her eyes were a pale blue-grey hazel in which the grey dominated, but the flat hue proved quite capable of flashing with anger. Derian noticed Ynamynet was dressed much more warmly than were any of her companions, with fur at her throat and wrists. He wondered that she wasn't stifled.

Harjeedian moved one shoulder in an almost shrug. "Someone will come after you. They may be all the more willing to tell us what we wish to know once they see what has happened to you."

This took some of the fire from the prisoners' eyes. Derian bet that Lachen was regretting introducing himself and his companion with that boastful title. If he had claimed to be nothing other than an apprentice or servant, vanguard to a greater power . . .

Too late, Derian thought. *What will you do?*

Harjeedian did not ask his promised questions, but sat sipping his tea, letting the silence stretch.

Neither of the Once Dead spoke, but dark-skinned Skea broke the silence. His accent was closer to Ynamynet's than Lachen's.

"You said to these ones that should we cooperate then healing would be given. Speak your questions. My comrades bleed."

Skea didn't mention his own shoulder, though that must have been badly bruised. Derian found himself reluctantly admiring the bodyguard's forthrightness. He noted with interest that neither Lachen nor Ynamynet was pleased by this solicitude.

Ynamynet held her hand to her injured arm, pressing the fabric of the robe over the cut as a makeshift bandage. She seemed to have stopped most of the bleeding. Verul could have no such relief until the arrow was drawn forth. He held himself very stiffly, and Derian thought he detected a hint of pallor beneath the ruddy skin.

Harjeedian showed no awareness of this, nor admiration for Skea's willingness to speak. If anything, he looked with disapproval upon this self-appointed spokesman.

"Very well. A member of our company, one called Plik, was taken from us. We have tracked him to this place, and know that from here he was taken far hence. We wish him back."

Skea gave a sharp jerk of his head that might have been a nod, might merely have been an acknowledgment that he understood.

"Short, fat, round," he said. "Very strange. I know where this Plik is kept."

"And do you know how to open the gate between this place and that?" Harjeedian asked.

"I know in theory," Skea replied, "but this one cannot open that way myself, for this one is among the Twice Dead."

Harjeedian did not ask for a definition of this strange term, but turned his gaze to Verul.

"And you?"

Verul grunted. "It is as Skea says. I am Twice Dead."

The interchange had meant little enough to Derian, but Lachen was clearly enraged.

"A small wound and you would betray these ones?" he said. "Such courage. No wonder you died twice."

Skea curled back his lips from teeth that were very large and white. He spoke deliberately in his odd Liglimosh, as if challenging Lachen with his new alliance—no matter how tenuous it might be.

"You heard this Harjeedian. If we do not tell, then we suffer and the next to come through the gate will view our tortured bodies."

His gaze dropped, and Derian realized that Skea, at least, had not missed the significance of the knife set edge to the hot coals.

Firekeeper spoke from behind them, her voice rough. "And others may tell . . . Speak quickly, for I do not like when my pack is broken."

She leaned against her unstrung bow, Lovable perched on one shoulder. Somehow Firekeeper seemed more dangerous for having put the weapon by. The posture said without words, "I am not afraid of you. Fear me."

Skea and Verul, perhaps because of their training, had the good sense to do so. Lachen and Ynamynet sat in thin-lipped silence.

Harjeedian looked at the bodyguards. "You show very good sense. I respect that. Verul, how deep has the arrow gone?"

"Into the muscle, not into the bone. The armor stopped much. The angle is bad, or I would pull it out myself."

"Is it barbed?" Skea asked.

Firekeeper spat. "No. I do not need such."

Harjeedian looked thoughtful. "Skea, pull out the arrow."

Skea began to raise his right arm, but let it drop.

"I . . . My shoulder . . ."

Firekeeper laughed softly. "Hold you both. I pull."

Derian wondered if she was being wise, walking in so close to where the prisoners might try and take her prisoner in turn. Perhaps Bitter, perched now on a heap of camping gear, shared this thought, for he croaked hoarsely. Firekeeper only smiled, and motioned for Lovable to take wing as she leaned her bow against the wall and padded forward.

Lachen and Ynamynet shifted nervously, but Skea and Verul held perfectly still as if afraid any motion on their part might be taken as a threat.

Firekeeper grasped the arrow firmly. As she gave a single sharp pull that brought the arrow out she said conversationally, "No barbs. I hit what I hit, how I hit."

Verul seemed transfixed by the words, only noticing the arrow was out when fresh blood coursed beneath his armor down his arm. Skea helped him undo the straps that held the bracer in place, stanching the wound with a loose edge of Verul's tunic.

Harjeedian spoke. "There is boiled water, and I have powders that will stay infection."

"I know enough field medicine to treat this," Skea said curtly. "Something to stanch the bleeding . . ."

Harjeedian pulled a bandage from his kit, poured boiled water into a cup, and passed it over to Skea. All through the process, he, like Firekeeper, seemingly ignored the Once Dead. Derian, however, kept a sharp eye on them, and saw their growing anger. They were not accustomed to being ignored. Moreover, enough time had passed that they were realizing how well and truly caught they were.

Blind Seer returned at this moment. Firekeeper had stepped back to the archway that led into the closed courtyard and now leaned against the stone. The great grey wolf sat beside her, and Derian did not doubt he was telling her whatever had been learned from the two captive wolves.

Lovable had returned to the boughs of the apple tree, so even if the strangers did not yet realize it, the gate was being watched. If the silver glow returned, warning would be issued with the first glimmer.

Harjeedian returned his attention to the Once Dead.

"Your companions have indicated they will tell us what we will find on the other side. From Skea's words we know, too, that Plik lives. Now, will you let us through before we are separated much longer, or will you force us to make you an example to those who will come looking to see the reason for your failure?"

Derian thought it was that single word, "failure," that melted through the remaining resistance.

"What good would our dying do?" Ynamynet said to Lachen. "Or our pain? Blood is to be shed for use, not to stain stone."

Lachen bent, head in hands.

"I suppose," he said, "we have no choice."

"Then you will teach us how to open the gate?" Harjeedian said, triumph ringing in his voice.

"Teach you," Lachen said, his words muffled for he did not raise his head. "Teach you, and even open the gate for you. It is not easily done."

"Good," Harjeedian said. "We will begin almost at once. First, I will make some arrangements to ensure that you and your associates do not trick us."

Lachen started, and Derian thought Harjeedian had been right to be careful.

Harjeedian looked to where the wolf-woman stood viewing the captives, her expression quizzical.

"Firekeeper, I wish these four separated, so I may question each privately and then compare their answers. Will you and the yarimaimalom guard them so none escapes or creates some sort of mischief?"

Firekeeper nodded. "There are many rooms here we can use to hold them. The stranger wolves are safe kept in other places."

"I will begin with Lachen," Harjeedian said.

Derian assisted with removing the other three to separate quarters in the crumbling stronghold. Bitter took Lovable's post in the apple tree, so Lovable might summon Truth and Eshinarvash.

After the three prisoners were secured, alone with their thoughts and very little else, for Firekeeper had insisted on searching each one to make sure there were no concealed weapons or other tools, Derian drew her and Blind Seer aside.

"It was too easy," he said to them. "Harjeedian is terribly pleased with his success. He's doing his best to make sure we don't get led down the garden path, but I can't help but feel it was too easy to get those four to surrender."

Firekeeper and Blind Seer both cocked their heads to one side, so natural that only seeing it in duplicate made the gesture look at all odd.

"Maybe yes," Firekeeper said. "Blind Seer and Truth have speaked with the other wolves. These have a tale to tell. From it, I think that maybe this taking is not too easy. Maybe what is waiting on the other side will be very hard to fight."

XXV

TRUTH LICKED BLOOD from between her claws and watched with a certain appreciation as the two stranger wolves tore into the rats they had cornered and killed within one of the cellars of the stronghold. They must be hungry indeed to eat such poor game with such enthusiasm.

Her bearing said as much. The slightly larger of the two wolves, one who had introduced himself as "Onion," looked up from his feeding, licking messy gobbets of flesh and fur from his muzzle.

"They fed us very little there," Onion said, "only enough to keep breath in body—and sometimes not enough to do that. Never was what we were given full of life's heat and strength."

Blind Seer, who had participated in the hunt but had not joined in the meal that followed, thumped behind one ear with a hind leg. He'd been shedding rather badly of late, probably because his body thought it should be putting on its winter coat, but the warmer southern temperatures were creating conflicting signals.

"So they captured you but did not kill you," Blind Seer said. "That is very odd."

"But fortunate for us," said the smaller of the wolves. He was called Half-Ear, and indeed part of his right ear—if not precisely half—was missing.

"But fortunate," Blind Seer agreed. "I do not mean to sound rude. These same people have stolen away one of our pack, a strange creature called Plik.

We have acted on the belief that they would not have stolen him merely to kill him; learning you were also kept alive gives us hope."

"I don't recall anyone who called himself Plik," Half-Ear said, licking a bit of viscera from the ground. "You called him a 'strange creature,' so he was not also a wolf?"

"He was more like a raccoon," Blind Seer said, "but with a bit of the human about him. As I said, an odd creature."

"Very," Onion said. "I certainly never saw him."

"Nor I," Half-Ear agreed. "Nor scented that strange mixture."

"Are you sure?" Blind Seer asked. "He smells more like a raccoon than otherwise."

"There were a few raccoons among those yarimaimalom who were taken, but not many," Onion said. "They do not have family feeling as wolves do. A few investigated the copse out of curiosity. When they did not return . . . I suspect their fellows were among those who had the sense to flee when things got bad."

Truth said, "We have heard something of this from an owl who still haunts the vicinity. However, she knows nothing of what happened to those who went into the copse."

"It's simple enough," Half-Ear said. "Do you know how some of us made pets of the human pair that came here?"

"We do," Blind Seer said.

"Well, when the twins vanished and that strange copse appeared, some of us went looking for our humans. What met us were tangles of a strange briar . . ."

"We have seen these," Truth said.

"And the bracken beasts," Onion asked. "Have you seen these, too?"

"We have."

"Then you know how we were captured. These did the battling. Humans did the binding. They took us through that silver wall—the gate—and we found ourselves in a place . . . How would you describe it, Half-Ear?"

Half-Ear considered. "It is not easy to describe. For one, mostly we are kept in one area, a series of pens no bigger than that over there."

He indicated a closet with a toss of his nose.

"One beast to a section. Exercise once daily in a sort of long loop. No contact between us but by howls and other cries—and what we could say by scents left for the next one to come to the exercise area."

"Those who kept us liked our sounds little enough," Onion added, "that they would withhold food and water if we were not quiet. Scents actually worked better. They did not think of scent, but there is little enough one can say in pee."

Blind Seer said carefully, "You two are lean, yes, but not starved."

"They feed us enough to keep spirit in body," Onion said. "Nor do I think they feed us always the same amount. Some days ago, my portion was increased."

"Mine, too," Half-Ear said. "They do that when they think they will have use for you."

"Use?" Truth asked.

Half-Ear shook as if he could physically separate the thought from his mind. "Do you know what they are?"

Truth said calmly, "We believe they are descendants of the Old World sorcerers."

"Cats are truly mad, great cats madder than most," Onion said, but the words were so evidently a proverb that Truth took no offense. "Your belief is correct. The ones that call themselves the Once Dead are able to do magic still, and the magic that they find easiest uses blood . . . preferably, someone else's blood."

"Those bracken beasts," Half-Ear said, beginning to pant in fear, "they are kin to the blood briars, but they are far worse. . . . I don't know how it is done, but the sorcerers have discovered how to . . ."

He was panting hard now. Onion licked his friend's unmangled ear and took over the recitation.

"It is worse for him. He has had it done. I have only heard."

"Heard what?" Truth didn't even growl. The wolves' fear was too obvious, too real, for impatience. She thought it was a wonder they could discuss this at all.

"They do something that takes your self and puts it within that frame of branches. You cannot hear or smell, but you can see after a fashion. Those who have had this done to them say the images are flat, like a reflection in a puddle broken by ripples, but good enough to navigate by."

"And not only are you there in the thing they have made," Half-Ear said, crouching as if he could protect himself from horrible memories by protecting his belly, "something else, one of them, is in the thing with you. It has the will. It feels like thorns in your eyes. It makes you be the thing, the bracken beast, but it chooses what the bracken beast will do."

Blind Seer froze as if he had spotted a herd of elk when the hunting was winter lean.

"And this is what they were going to do with you here, isn't it? They were going to use you to feed the next set of bracken beasts they left to guard the copse."

"After they had hunted you down and killed you," Onion agreed. "They learned soon enough—quite probably from the twins, but possibly from their own legends of the New World—that the yarimaimalom have more sense than do Cousins. They liked that very much, and they took to using those of us who could be made to act out of fear for our fellows. Wolves are easy to manipulate that way, but over time even bears and great cats—creatures who are not pack creatures—fell into their power. You see, there in the holding area, we became a tight community in our suffering. That closeness was used against us."

"Then that is why you fought us when you came through the gate?" Blind Seer asked. "Have they threatened your pack mates?"

"They have," Half-Ear said. "We have little pride left, but I can say with confidence that not one of us would let another be tortured to spare himself. To do otherwise is to be finally left alone, and still subject to torment."

"What happens," Truth said, trying to keep ears or tail from betraying how important this was, "to one who is eyes and skill for a bracken beast when that beast is broken?"

Onion swished his tail in a wolfish wag. "We know you and yours have broken many bracken beasts. Fear not that we will hold this against you. Indeed, we honor you for it."

"But what happens?" Truth asked. "Have we been killing yarimaimalom unknowing?"

"A few," Half-Ear said. "A puma, two wolves, a bear. Most, however, were merely freed from the webwork and their sense returned to their bodies. Believe me, as one who has been in that trap, those who perished died grateful for their freedom."

"Did you fight us?" Blind Seer asked.

"No," Half-Ear said. "My torment was some time ago, back when the Once Dead were hunting the yarimaimalom from these forests. They feared the yarimaimalom, you see, feared we would carry rumors away."

Onion added, "A foolish fear. Those on the outside knew too little to tell, but then fear motivates much of what these sorcerers do."

"Fear of what?" Truth asked.

"We are not certain," Half-Ear said, "but all agree that the Once Dead and Twice Dead are not universally loved even in the Old Country. I am sorry we cannot tell you more, but it is difficult to learn much when locked within a pen."

Blind Seer perked his ears and listened. "I think I should go and tell Fire-keeper what I have learned here. She may wish to pass it on to the other humans."

After the Royal Wolf had loped away, Onion said, "That Firekeeper, what is she? She speaks as a wolf, but smells human."

"She was raised by wolves," Truth said, "and is stranger even than Plik, for all she looks human. Take care to treat her as you would a wolf. She is very touchy on the subject."

"Once," Onion said, "this would have seemed odd. Now, though, compared to the Once Dead and their servants, this Firekeeper seems comfortably normal."

Truth flattened her ears. "That," she said, "may be the most frightening thing you have said so far."

ᘍᑦᕒ

"THEY WANT TO SEE YOU," Isende said, her voice tight.

Plik turned his gaze from the window to the young woman's face, moving his head as little as possible. The worst of the querinalo might have passed, but he by no means felt well. Even moving his eyes made his head ache. When he focused on where Isende stood at his bedside, the strain he had heard in her voice was evident on her features.

"Who?" he asked, hearing his voice come forth rough and deeper than usual. "Who wants to see me?"

"The leaders of the Once Dead," Tiniel replied, crossing the room to stand at his sister's side. "They sent word through Zebel."

Tiniel's tone shifted to something mincing and cold. "We did not bring the creature here in order for it to become a peculiar pet for the twins. It has answered one question already. Now we wish it to answer others."

"I don't suppose," Plik said, "we could send word I don't feel up to inter-rogation? I don't, honestly."

"The doctor already tried," Isende said, reaching and very gently squeez-ing his hand. "They said they have no time to wait."

Despite pain and fear, Plik felt a wash of hope, hope immediately followed by dread. The urgency might be because the others had done something that had alarmed the Once Dead. Plik had vague memories—memories he was not entirely sure were not hallucinations—of someone who had identified himself as the Meddler telling him the others were determined to find him.

That was the hope. The dread was that he could not forget that in coming after him the others would be exposed to querinalo. He had survived, as had the twins, but in the old days Divine Retribution had killed many.

Isende continued to stroke Plik's hand. "Don't be too afraid," she said. "We're coming with you. Some of the Once Dead speak a form of Liglimosh, but most do not. We have been asked to serve as interpreters."

Plik wasn't certain exactly what good having Isende and Tiniel with him would do, since they were little more than prisoners themselves. He supposed it was a good thing that someone who understood something of the New World would be translating. It would save the need for lengthy explanations.

"How long?" he asked.

"How long until they wish to see you?" Tiniel said. "As soon as you can be made presentable. The doctor sent an infusion that will help with the pain."

He produced a bottle from one pocket and mixed it with the mint tea re-maining in Plik's mug.

"It tastes vile," Tiniel said frankly. "I suggest you get it down in as few swal-lows as possible."

"But it does help," Isende said. "While we let the medicine take effect, we'll clean you up."

They did this. Isende brushed quantities of loose fur from Plik's coat. Tiniel took care of cleaning more intimate places. Plik found their respect for his gender amusing, but a promising sign that they thought him a person rather than otherwise.

A knocking at the door announced when the councillors felt they had been kept waiting long enough.

Plik's aches had receded fairly quickly following his drinking the doctor's brew, but he hadn't felt any particular desire to hurry to this interview. Nor did he think there was much advantage to giving away how much his thinking had cleared. Drugs that would work well on a human might not work well on a maimalodalu.

Therefore, Plik rose slowly to his feet and walked stiffly, leaning on the arm Isende offered him. But when Tiniel asked if they should summon a wagon or litter, Plik declined, wanting to show how cooperative he was.

"I'm fine. Really fine."

Walking, he thought, would also give him a chance to see something of his surroundings. He didn't know how useful that information would be, but if that conversation with the Meddler had not been just a hallucination maybe he could pass something on to the others.

The thought gave him courage, and he looked about with as much alertness and curiosity as he could without relinquishing his pretense of illness.

He'd been right about his own prison. "Cottage" might dignify the structure a bit too much, but it was a small, detached structure built for residence rather than for storage—a step up in some indefinable fashion from a "hut" but not really a house. A similar structure a short distance away answered the question of where the twins resided. Both buildings were enclosed within a hedge heavily intertwined with blood briar, the whole surrounded by a scrubby forest.

There was a guard posted at the enclosure's gate: a heavyset man, brown after the manner of the Liglim, but with a different style of features—wider lips and nose, very thick, coarse black hair. He wore a leather jacket that wasn't quite armor, but there was no mistaking the bow he strung as they emerged for anything but a weapon.

Isende spoke to the guard politely in the language of the Liglim, her manner that of the mistress of the household releasing a trusted servant from duty.

"We're going to be with the council, Wort. I don't know how long until we come back."

Wort answered in a fashion that didn't quite make a lie of Isende's pretense that he was something other than a jailer. His accent was that of the city-states, making clear from whom he'd learned Liglimosh.

"I'll walk with you to the council house, then stop by the kitchens for something. Can I order anything for you?"

"Well, they certainly won't be feasting us," Isende said, "so a meal of some sort would be welcome for when we return."

"I'll take care of that," Wort promised, "and I may drop in to see how things are going when I'm done."

Wort didn't look at Plik with anything like curiosity. This told Plik that the man had been in and out of the cottage, probably frequently. Plik wondered how many of the inhabitants of this place knew him, at least by sight, and what deductions they had drawn from his appearance.

The enclosure in which the twins and Plik had been residing proved to be on the lower edges of the inhabited area. As they climbed an upward-sloping path out of a protected hollow, the wind came strong enough that Plik's nose—congested from querinalo—finally caught the smell of the sea.

When they mounted the rise, the trees became shrubs, and Plik got his first good look around. His immediate reaction was a pang of homesickness. They were on an island, part of a grouping of other islands, and though the twisted evergreens and low-growing shrubs were nothing like the lush forests of Misheemnekuru, still, there was something here that cried out to his soul.

However, even on Center Island where the maimalodalum dwelt, there was nothing like the structures that dominated this island. The maimalodalum had preserved the five towers that had once been dedicated to the Elements worshipped by the Liglim and used by their sorcerers in their magical arts. But these had been New World buildings, constructed in an unsettled frontier, meant for service before beauty or ornament. When this place—wherever this place might be—had been built, something beyond mere serviceability had been intended.

"What are those round buildings?" Plik asked, indicating an area farther inland, on the highest ground the island offered.

"That's where the gates are," Tiniel said, attempting casualness, but his awe coming through nonetheless. "They're not round, not really. More like wedges of pie with the doors coming out into a central atrium. There are gardens between the wedges, places where people could wait for their guests or for a transit."

Plik realized that the rounded roofs were what created the illusion that each series of wedges made one round. They also offered some protection to the walkways and gardens between the wedges.

Those wedge shapes would assure that any going in or out of each gate area could be inspected, Plik thought. *They trusted, but not completely.*

The gate area showed evidence of having been abandoned for a long time, but also of recent attempts at cleaning and repair. Great effort had been made to clear an area surrounding these buildings, to expose their walls.

In the past, the outer walls of each of the wedges had been heavily ornamented, apparently with mosaics or bas-relief sculptures that would withstand the vicissitudes of ocean weather. Today's weather was fairly pleasant, but island-born Plik could tell from the twisted trunks of trees and the way any-thing alive and growing tended to lean in one direction that there were times when the winds must blow hard, steady, and strong.

Although the decorative medium on the wedge buildings was forced by ne-cessity into a few forms, the styles varied widely. Colors and themes clashed, creating in their very clashing an odd but definite agreement.

Among the scenes, Plik recognized one as a depiction of the step pyramids favored by the Liglim for their temples. The pyramid was extended slightly from the wall, tiny figures of both animals and humans ascending the steps. Beside this scene, however, was a mosaic showing a grassland so open and vast Plik had trouble believing any such place really existed. Surely there could not be a place completely without trees!

Each region, each sponsoring body, Plik thought, *felt a need to cry out its own importance, to stress its own unique qualities. Here, where cultures and peoples came together because of the gates, there seems to have been no blending. Instead, they felt more than ever the need to emphasize what made each culture worth preserving. Interesting . . . I wonder how these independent peoples reacted when querinalo swept through their numbers. Not well, I think, not well. Nor do I think their descendants would be too different. I wonder if the clearing-away was done to show off the art, or to make sure it would be hard for anyone to sneak into—or out of—the gates.*

Their own destination was not near these wedge-shaped buildings, but some distance away, down a slope. Here again, there was evidence that the area had been long abandoned, but also that time—years even—had been put into restoring the place. The buildings were again made of stone, but their structure spoke not of a need for security, but for easy access. There were many doors, some large, some small, numerous windows, some boarded, but many with glass intact or replaced. The buildings reconfirmed, through cov-ered walkways and bridges built connecting buildings, that the weather on these islands was often less than clement.

One building showed more than those around it both recent use and that it was meant to impress. Its doorways were wider than those around it. Carving had been lavished around windows and doors. The pillars that held up the porches were worked in the shape of strong, broad-shouldered humans. As they drew closer, Plik saw that many varieties of humans were depicted.

Again, the need to emphasize differences, even where they were coming to-gether. Why should I be surprised? None of our legends tell of the Old Country

rulers being particularly kind or beneficent to their colonies. Why should I think
they would have treated their Old World neighbors any differently?

This building was also guarded. Plik had the feeling that these guards were more a formality, an acknowledgment of the importance of those who dwelt within—a means of keeping the unwanted out, rather than the residents in.

However, when Wort handed them off to these others, Plik felt no desire to see just how alert these new guards were. He suspected they would prove completely able.

Once again, Isende acted as if the guards were an escort, rather than meant to keep her from doing as she liked. Plik sensed she was perfectly aware of the truth, and admired Isende for finding a facade that enabled her to maintain some degree of self-respect.

The twins told Plik to wait with the guards while they went in to announce him. They came back several minutes later, their expressions strained and tight. Wordlessly, they motioned for Plik to follow.

What he had seen depicted on the buildings outside gave Plik some idea what to expect in the council chamber. He had expected a hetcrogeneous grouping, one representing every variation of humanity he had ever encountered and a few he had not even imagined. What he had not expected, despite the twins' tales of querinalo and the price it took from those who battled to keep their magic, was the grotesque appearance of many of those who awaited him.

For a weird moment, he almost felt as if he were back among the maimalodalum, the peculiarity of appearance was so great. That impression left him once he had a second look.

For one, the maimalodalum, while often blending the characteristics of several types of beasts with those of humans, were in themselves healthy and functional creatures. These were not. Many of them bore a deformity or mutilation: a bandage over presumably blinded eyes; a missing limb, most often a hand or foot; hair bleached or entirely gone. Yet Plik had not forgotten what the twins had told him—that the Once Dead to fear the most were those who showed no obvious sign of what they had traded to maintain their magic. Remembering his own experience, he thought he understood, and that understanding made him shudder.

Another difference between these Once Dead and the maimalodalum was less obvious, yet once Plik noted it, it was so striking that the physical deformities vanished to unimportance in contrast. The maimalodalum were all too aware of their difference from any other creatures that walked the earth. They

were neither humans nor beasts, but combinations born of unwilling blend-
ings forced one upon the other. Aware of their heritage, the maimalodalum
shied from contact with other peoples, keeping to themselves with an inherited sense of shame.

These Once Dead possessed none of that shame. Indeed, their arrogant
self-confidence was so strong that it permeated the closed air of the chamber
with a rank scent. Whatever their original tales, the Once Dead were all bound
into a new one. They had defeated a plague that had slain many before them.
Though they had been wounded and bore the scars from that battle, they had
come through with what mattered most to them still intact.

Plik shivered. He understood for the first time something of what haunted
Tiniel. The youth not only mourned the loss of his magic, but suffered under
the onus of being forever assigned to the second rank—at least in the view of
these Once Dead whose attitude said before they had spoken a single syllable
that they considered that their successful battle against querinalo had made
them the rightful rulers of all they could reach.

And now, thanks to an old gate and a pair of twins with more dreams than
sense, the Once Dead could reach the New World and all those whom Plik
treasured. This thought chased the shivers from his bones. Here and now he
was the sole defender of his homeland. If he could make the New World seem
unattractive or not worth the effort to explore, he must do so.

Defiance cradled in his soul, Plik awaited the first question.

His interrogators were five. They sat in a semicircle at one end of a long,
narrow room. The other Once Dead, some couple dozen, sat on risers on either side. Plik and the twins were kept standing in the area between.

No routine questions were asked. No one bothered asking Plik's name or
after his health. Apparently, they already knew the answers to these questions.
Doubtless, the twins and the doctor had been reporting on a regular basis.

Or maybe the Once Dead simply didn't care.

The interrogators were two women, three men. None of them apparently
spoke Liglimosh—although Plik wondered about one man, who looked rather
like a Liglim. Plik noted that Isende translated for the women, Tiniel for the
men. They did this without prompting, so presumably they had received instructions before this. Plik wondered at the twins' ability to translate so freely,
but then they had been in these people's keeping for moonspans, and the
young did learn languages more easily, or so he had heard.

A skeletally lean woman with skin so brown it was almost black and hair like wool, twisted into long ropes, spoke first. She fired out a list of questions almost without waiting for the answers.

"When you came to the twins' stronghold, did you know about the gate?"

"No."

"Why did you come?"

"We were looking for the twins."

"Why?"

"We had heard of their powers."

"Why did this interest you?"

Plik had thought about how he might best answer this question. He didn't know how much the Once Dead had spied on them. He did not think he should tell them the full story. If these reacted to the idea of the Meddler with the same fear and fury that Harjeedian had, Plik didn't like to think about the consequences.

"Our group consists of misfits," Plik temporized. "We sought others like ourselves."

"This despite the fact that, as the twins tell it, all the New World hates and despises magic?"

"Just so."

The man who looked as if he might be from Liglim spoke next—or rather he didn't speak, but moved his hands in the air in elaborate patterns. Tiniel translated as if the man had spoken in words.

"What manner of creature are you?"

"I am called a maimalodalu."

"Are you a natural creature?"

Plik felt a pang of pain. "My mother bore me as mothers do."

"And your father?"

"I never knew him."

"And your mother's mother and your mother's father, back through the generations. Where were you formed?"

"I was formed by magic," Plik said bitterly, "or rather my mother was. 'Deformed' she would say, by one who sought to steal her shape for his own."

"But he did not succeed," the man said in an agitated waving of hands.

"He did not," Plik replied, and he knew there was pride in his voice.

The man stood and came around the edge of the table behind which the committee sat. To Plik's horror, he held a knife in his hand.

"Hold still," the man said, and Tiniel's translation gave the waving of the knife-holding hand sharpness and authority. "I am curious as to the structure of your features. The fur gets in the way of clear examination."

Plik stumbled back a step, uncertain as to whether the man meant to skin him then and there.

"Hold still!" the man ordered again. "I'm only going to shave off a bit of your fur."

Plik tried to turn and run, but the guard Wort had appeared from out of the watching group gathered along the wall. He grasped Plik firmly, pinning his arms. Wort smelled of a seafood stew, dark bread, and bitter beer.

"Hold still," Wort said to Plik. "They'll have their way in the end. Don't make it worse."

To the Once Dead who stood there knife in hand, blade held at an angle, Wort said something in another language.

"I told him he might want to use at least water, if not soap, if he wants to clean shave. They're sending for it."

Plik realized he was trembling. Acid rushed up the back of his throat, sour and bitter. He thought he might vomit. His world was restricted to the robes of the Once Dead before him and the scent and warmth of Wort behind him. Into this intruded the anomalous perfume of soap and roses.

"They're being gentle," Wort said. "Try and stop trembling or you're sure to get cut."

Plik tried, but his limbs shook despite his best efforts. He squeezed his eyes shut, but not knowing where the knife was made it worse. He opened his eyes and squeaked in terror at a glint of shiny metal directly beneath his eye. Had Wort not held him so tightly, Plik might have been badly cut. As it was, the knife glided smoothly over his skin, and he felt only the slightest tugging as the fur beneath his eyes fell away. The shaving continued over Plik's cheek and along his jaw.

The Once Dead spoke, and Tiniel's voice translated: "The fur masks how very human the features are. No wonder the creature can speak intelligibly. Whatever directed his mutation was careful to preserve certain advantages."

The Once Dead stepped back, and Wort relaxed his grip just a touch.

"Can you stand?" the guard murmured.

Plik nodded stiffly, but he was sorry when Wort's support was withdrawn. He felt his isolation all the more for this moment of solidarity.

The other woman, her hair silky black, her eyes long rather than round, her wide mouth dominating her features, one sleeve hanging limp and empty off her shoulder, spoke in a voice that managed to be both deep and musical, yet somehow reminiscent of the peeping of newly hatched chicks.

"We know you had magic before you died to querinalo. Are all maimalo-dalum magical?"

Plik shrugged, resisting the urge to raise a hand and touch the shaven portion of his face. "I did not know I was magical until I came here and the querinalo made me ill."

This caused a great deal of discussion, but none of it was translated for Plik.

A runner departed. When she returned, Zebel, the doctor who had treated Plik, was with her. He was bombarded with a great number of questions, and answered politely but not meekly. Twice Dead he might be, but apparently his skills gave him some status.

Plik had no idea what was being said, and neither of the twins offered explanation. They offered nothing, in fact, but prompt translation. Even Isende refrained from the small kindnesses that were usual for her. She stood still as the crystal statuette the Meddler had carved of her, moving only to breathe and translate. Even the automatic blinking of her eyes seemed stiff and rhythmic, as if she moved only when she must.

The twins must be terrified, Plik thought. *Both for themselves, and perhaps a little for me. I must be careful not to say anything that would bring harm to them.*

Before Zebel was dismissed, he made a final, uninvited statement. The content of this statement Plik could guess at, for soon after a slat-backed chair was brought for him. The legs were too long for his feet to reach the ground, but he hoisted himself up onto the hard wooden seat and relaxed against the back with real gratitude.

Another of the men on the committee took over the interrogation. This one was pink-skinned and hairless. He had been gifted by birth with a build that should have been powerful, but despite his size and musculature the man reminded Plik of a deflated bladder.

"We know your companions are seeking you. Do you believe they will persist?"

"Yes."

"Tell us about them. Start with the woman who is so frequently accompanied by the wolf."

The memory of the knife against his face was very fresh, and so Plik obeyed, but even in his obedience he tried to reserve some information.

He was careful not to lie outright because he didn't know just how much spying had been done, but he reserved what he could. He said nothing of Fire-keeper's ability to speak with Beasts, but didn't deny her fighting ability. One by one his interrogator asked about Derian, Harjeedian, the ravens, and Truth. With each, Plik tried to keep something secret. From the questions, he gathered that the Once Dead had spied upon them, but that the spying had been distant and somewhat lacking in detail.

Interestingly, Plik's newest interrogator asked nothing about Eshinarvash, so in turn Plik offered nothing. If the Once Dead's experience had been restricted to the local yarimaimalom, there might not have been Wise Horses among them.

At last the questions ended, and Plik thought he might be permitted to go back to his bed. The Once Dead who sat around the edges of the room were shifting as if they expected the meeting to be dismissed, but a voice broke the expectant silence, echoed by Tiniel's a moment later.

"I am not satisfied," the final member of the committee said. His voice was light and clear, and sounded like a woman's. Plik thought he knew what this one must have sacrificed to keep his magic. "The creature has not told us enough to explain everything we have seen."

"Perhaps," said the emaciated woman, twisting one of her woolly locks around a finger, "we have not asked the right questions."

"Make him tell us what we do not know," said the man who spoke with his hands.

"We might be here all night," the long-eyed woman said with a laugh, "and our translators will not last much longer."

"This will not matter," the final member said, "if we make his blood talk for him."

The room grew very still, and Plik scented anticipation mingled with dread.

"That will take time to prepare," said the man who spoke with a fluttering of hands, "and the doctor has warned us that the creature is not yet strong."

"Tomorrow then," the man said, resignation evident in his light voice even before Tiniel translated.

Plik sensed that he had narrowly escaped something very unpleasant. Relief broke through and swept away his waning strength, leaving him to sag limp in his chair. As from a distance, he heard the sounds of the meeting breaking up. Only after the Once Dead had left the room did Tiniel and Isende stir. Wort came over and lifted Plik from the chair without a comment, motioning for the twins to follow with a jerk of his head.

Wort carried Plik back to his cottage. Plik managed to say a few words of thanks, then collapsed into sleep. When he awoke, Isende was waiting beside his bed, working on some knitting. Late-afternoon sunlight was evident without. As the interrogation by the council had been in the morning, Plik realized that he had been truly exhausted by even that limited exertion.

Thick pease porridge and brown bread refreshed him, and he decided to ask Isende for her impressions of the session.

"I think they were trying to learn as much as they could about my friends," Plik said, "but do you think they mean to go after them or are they simply preparing in case my friends come here?"

"What do I think?" Isende replied. "I don't know. You see, I don't remember any of it."

"What?"

"I don't remember."

Isende looked up from her knitting, meeting his gaze for the first time since he had awakened, the warm brown of her eyes filled with anguish.

"It's like they took me over. I don't remember a single moment of that meeting after Tiniel and I went in to report your arrival, not a single thing."

XXVI

MIDDAY HAD COME AND GONE by the time Harjeedian finished interviewing the four who had come through the gate. Now the prisoners were locked in separate sections of the stronghold, guarded by unseen ravens, the dark birds' shadows hiding within the broken masonry or peering through breaks in the floorboards.

This left the remainder of the company free to hear Harjeedian's summation of what he had learned. Firekeeper had already reported on what they had been told by Onion and Half-Ear. Now she settled on the floor, one arm around Blind Seer, watching as Harjeedian shifted stacks of paper into order.

"First, and most importantly," the aridisdu began, "the prisoners do not expect anyone to miss them until sometime the middle of tomorrow—and even more time could pass before any on the other side would actually worry. This matches well with what the Meddler has already told us."

Harjeedian looked unhappy at having to take the Meddler's word for anything, but he was too intelligent to discard information for no other reason than that he did not like the source.

Firekeeper wondered if Harjeedian might have been heartened by the low growl that rose involuntarily in Blind Seer's throat at the mention of the Meddler. She wasn't about to ask. That would raise too many questions she had been deliberately avoiding even within the privacy of her own thought. She wasn't sure if she liked the Meddler, but there was something about him that drew her . . . well, that interested her, at least.

Harjeedian was proudly displaying a map he had drawn based upon the different information garnered from the four prisoners.

Firekeeper leaned forward to look, determined that this time the bird's-eye view would make sense to her. She was dismayed to find that Harjeedian's drawing represented nothing so much as a scattering of pebbles and twigs left by the retreating waters on the edge of a riverbank.

"This is a composite based on the four interviews," Harjeedian was saying. "I have also collated in information we were given by the Meddler. Interestingly"—Firekeeper heard the grudging note in his voice—"the Meddler seems to have been honest with us. Where there are differences, the passage of time is ample explanation for them."

"Passage of time?" Derian asked.

"New buildings, such as the entire New World gate complex," Harjeedian said, pointing to one carefully shaded section, "and several other buildings. These all could have been added since the Meddler was imprisoned, and so was less able to roam."

"I see," Derian said. "Go on."

Harjeedian tapped the map with a peeled length of apple wood. "Areas about which I am fairly certain have been shaded in. Those about which I have more doubts are left as outlines. I did my best, but sometimes the language barrier did get in our way."

"I wonder this," Firekeeper said. "Why they all speak Liglimosh?"

Harjeedian gave a crisp nod of approval. "I wondered that as well. Ynamynet deigned to explain. They knew they were coming after someone who had broken through the copse barrier. They had half expected a rescue attempt. Since Plik spoke Liglimosh, the group that was assembled was selected from those who spoke some form of the language. Lachen's native language is a form of Liglimosh. He had been teaching others."

Firekeeper could guess why. An invasion would go a whole lot more smoothly if some of the invaders could talk to the locals. She said nothing, though. If Harjeedian hadn't thought of this already, she had no desire to distract him from their immediate problem.

Derian tapped a series of roundish wedges that dominated the center of the map. "What are these?"

"Those are the gates," Harjeedian said. He indicated one set placed off at a distance from the others. "This is the assemblage that connects to the New World."

"So that's where we would arrive," Derian said. "Do you know which one?"

"Either this one, or this one," Harjeedian said, indicating two segments. "I don't think it matters much. The gates are housed in individual buildings, and each opens into the middle of the circle."

"Are they guarded?" Firekeeper asked.

"I'm not sure," Harjeedian admitted. "Both of the Once Dead did their best to assure me that they are. The Twice Dead were determinedly silent on the matter. What I think is that the general area is patrolled, but not each individual building. Let me finish the overview before we go into details."

Firekeeper nodded, and settled back.

"Over here to the southwest," Harjeedian said, indicating a shaded area, "is where Plik is being kept. I'm certain about this at least. I also have the impression the twins are nearby. One of the Twice Dead, Skea, mentioned something about having 'stood watch' there, so it seems fairly certain that Plik is under guard. It seems possible that the twins are as well."

"So they are prisoners, too," Blind Seer said. *"Interesting."*

"Or," Firekeeper said, *"they are numbered among his jailers. They would have the advantage of speaking a language he would understand. I wonder if Skea learned some of his Liglimosh while standing guard. Of them all, he is the one I liked the most, but if he has been ambitious enough to learn a language from elsewhere . . ."*

"He bears watching," Blind Seer agreed.

Harjeedian went on. "Something Lachen said—he is so angry at being captured that he let some interesting things slip—gave me the impression that human guards are not the only things we will need to attend to when we go after Plik. I think they used the blood briar to fence the area.

"These areas"—Harjeedian indicated various outlines west, southeast, and northeast of the central structures—"are where I have the impression that the Once and Twice Dead reside. My impression is that living quarters are communal and temporary.

"Over here"—Harjeedian pointed to a shaded section directly east of the gates—"is where the yarimaimalom are being held—caged and chained—in a menagerie."

He paused, clearly to control his temper. Firekeeper felt sympathy for him, knowing that her own indignation at this news was nothing to the aridisdu's. She was angry to learn that her worst suspicions were confirmed. Harjeedian was infuriated at the sacrilege that had been committed.

The people of Liglim would never even dream of holding the yarimaimalom against their will. They built facilities like u-Bishinti to house them, gave the yarimaimalom full run of their own cities and temples. Firekeeper found it mildly amusing that the imprisonment of Plik had not raised this same level of anger, but then Harjeedian did not believe that the maimalodalum spoke the deities' will. He did believe the yarimaimalom did so.

"They're alive, though," Derian said. "Right?"

"Some of them," Harjeedian said. "As Firekeeper has told us, some have died from the abuses heaped upon them."

"We free yarimaimalom, too," Firekeeper said. "I promise Onion and Half-Ear already. We free them all."

Derian was studying the map again, less personally offended by what had been done to the yarimaimalom than the rest—or perhaps merely determined that they not stray too far from the matter at hand.

"These rectangles," he said, pointing to structures to the northwest. "You have some of them shaded."

"Those are buildings used as headquarters," Harjeedian said, "and as residences for the higher ranking Once Dead."

"Strange place," Derian commented. "It doesn't seem quite real."

Harjeedian nodded. "I felt the same way. Finally, something Lachen said helped me understand. This is no longer the place that the Meddler described—an active transit center. Nor is it a living city or town. It is more like a university, devoted to teaching how to use the gates—and also to researching their intricacies. My impression is that the nexus has only been active a generation, perhaps less, that the facility was deserted for a long time after Divine Retribution spread through its environs."

"These Once Dead and Twice Dead," Firekeeper said. "What are they?"

"The Once Dead are in charge. They are served by the Twice Dead in a wide variety of capacities."

"So not every Twice Dead is a bruiser like Skea and Lachen?" Derian said. "I'm relieved."

"So am I," Harjeedian admitted with a small smile. "I am not completely certain what the relationship is between the two groups, nor would any tell me the source of those titles. All I could gather is that the Once Dead are superior to the Twice Dead—and that they consider themselves superior to just about anyone because they are the ones who actually work magic."

Truth grumbled, *"I was wondering if he was going to get around to that. Firekeeper, ask Aridisdu Harjeedian if he has learned how to make the gates work."*

Firekeeper didn't mind. She'd been wondering the same thing, and knew

Harjeedian was more likely to answer if a respected member of the yari-maimalom was asking.

"Truth say, 'Can you work gates?'"

Harjeedian pulled at his lower lip. "I can . . . or rather, Lachen and Ynamynet will work them for us. We need to provide them with the . . . fuel."

"Blood," Derian said bluntly. "It comes back to blood, doesn't it?"

Harjeedian's utter impassivity said more than any words would have done.

"Great." Derian looked disgusted.

Firekeeper felt equally sick at the idea, but there was apparently no way around it.

"Blood here," she said firmly. "How different than blood spilled there? We know we is to fight. We know we is maybe hurt. Still, we go."

Harjeedian looked at her with a certain amount of respect.

"I'd never fancied you as a philosopher, Firekeeper," he said.

Eshinarvash stamped one hoof.

"I can give a great deal more blood without it weakening me than can you little human things. Does the blood need to come from each who travels through the gates, or can one or two give more?"

Firekeeper relayed the question.

"I believe that the blood does not need to come from the travelers," Harjeedian replied, "or rather, each needs give only a token smear so the gate will know them. If Eshinarvash will be so generous . . ."

The Wise Horse stamped a hoof again and nodded, his black-and-white mane floating with the vigor of his reply.

"Then if the matter of making the transit work is settled," Harjeedian said, "we merely need to figure out what we will do on the other side."

They spent a long time discussing and refining plans, Firekeeper translating for the various beasts as they offered opinions. Onion and Half-Ear, who had politely kept a distance while the companions weighed their options, gladly accepted an invitation to join in the councils.

At last a plan was roughed out.

They would go that very night. Darkness would be a disadvantage only for the two humans. Like Firekeeper, the ravens and Eshinarvash had some practice functioning in the dark. Attacking that night would also mean that the group on the other side of the gate would not have begun to worry about their absent number. If all went well, only a few guards, drowsing on their presumably secure island, would be awake.

So that they did not need to reduce their numbers to leave a guard behind, the company decided that they would bring the four prisoners with them.

"It should make them more willing to cooperate," Harjeedian said cynically. "After all, they will be returning to familiar territory. The Meddler says the gates have only two end points, but what if he is wrong? What if the Old World sorcerers have learned some way to set someone adrift in a void that is neither here nor there?"

The prisoners would be bound, and the two Once Dead would be set up on Eshinarvash's back. The Twice Dead would be permitted to walk, but the ravens would ride on their shoulders. As a raven's horned beak could easily remove an ear or eye, this would be ample threat.

After they arrived, Bitter would go with one attack party, while Lovable went with the other, thereby enabling a message to be carried if something went wrong at either end. Truth and Eshinarvash would remain to hold the gate.

"And," Derian said with some satisfaction, "the closeness of four of their own to our people will be some protection for the ravens and Eshinarvash. It's almost a pleasure to be on the side taking hostages, rather than being one."

Firekeeper noticed that Harjeedian stiffened, as though unsure if Derian meant to insult him, but only a tang in Derian's sweat gave him away, and as Harjeedian could not smell this, he relaxed.

They decided that as soon as they left the gate building they would split their forces, mounting the rescues of Plik and the yarimaimalom simultaneously.

"When these are concluded," Harjeedian said, "we can make every effort to rendezvous and return back here through the gate. Unhappily, this may be more difficult."

"Why?" Firekeeper asked, although she had a fairly good idea.

"Because right now the Once Dead are cooperating for two reasons only. One, they know if they do not, we will capture those who come through the gate after them. Two, our eagerness to go through the gates is their best promise of returning to their fellows. Neither of those motives will prompt them to work their skills on our behalf again."

Truth growled, *"We will have seen how it is done by then. Perhaps threatening them with having their own blood used rather than ours will prompt them."*

"Perhaps," Harjeedian agreed, "but we cannot be certain of this."

Truth's tail lashed, her ears flattened to the rounded sides of her head. One did not need Firekeeper's skill for understanding the speech of Beasts to know she was saying, *"I can be very persuasive."*

"So," Derian said, "we could go there and find ourselves trapped, unable to return."

"We must consider that possibility," Harjeedian said. "However, there are ways we may be able to raise the odds of cooperation on the part of at least some of the Once Dead."

"What?" Firekeeper said.

"We will have with us a small army of very angry yarimaimalom. We will have you and your singular skills. Could we possibly take some of their leaders captive?"

Firekeeper enjoyed the praise, but she did not promise anything rash.

"Perhaps," she said. "How we know which are their Ones?"

"I have a few names," Harjeedian said. "Lachen started threatening at one point . . . I cannot imagine he would threaten me with promises of what a cook or guard captain would do."

"We can try," Firekeeper said, "but maybe we no need to do this. Maybe we will be in, out, and away."

"Maybe," said Blind Seer, slowly, as if he was tasting the idea, *"if we take the twins, they can work the gate for us. After all, didn't they manage at least once?"*

"That's brilliant!" Harjeedian said when Firekeeper had translated the idea. "I had forgotten the twins. When Plik is rescued, they can be rescued as well."

"Or taken prisoner," Firekeeper said. "Simple. We bring away three, not one. Now, who goes where?"

Derian said, "I imagine that Onion and Half-Ear would make the best guides to where their families are kept. I'll go with them. I'm used to taking orders from wolves, and they'll certainly need someone with hands to undo latches and locks."

Harjeedian gave a dry chuckle. "I cannot say I have Derian's experience taking orders from wolves, but I am willing to try. More than one set of hands would be useful."

Firekeeper nodded. "Blind Seer and I can get Plik and twins. Once free, Plik will be another to herd these twins if they not wish to come."

"I only wish," Harjeedian said, "that we had a third member of the wingéd folk to leave with the group at the gate. I hate to imagine our attack parties struggling back only to find that something has happened to the rear guard."

Blind Seer said, *"There was the owl, Night's Terror. She is not far from here.*

She said she has remained in hopes of being reunited with her mate. Perhaps, like Onion and Half-Ear, she will be willing to go after her mate."

Firekeeper translated, adding, "Owls are predator birds, and those night-sharp eyes would do well for us all. We have much time to the time of night when we will go. The copse no longer gives alarm. Let us go and find Night's Terror."

No one disagreed, but Onion and Half-Ear asked to go with the pair.

"It is long since we ran any distance. Let us stretch our legs and maybe hunt some decent game. Tonight's venture is the fulfillment of a dream."

The remainder agreed to take shifts watching the prisoners, and making preparations. Everyone was to eat well, then try to sleep.

Blind Seer reminded Firekeeper that she would need to sleep, too, but Firekeeper was glad to be away, out of the stronghold with its smells of spiders, mold, and dust.

"Time enough, dear heart," she said when they had safely passed through the barriers to emerge onto the grassy plain. "First, let us find this owl."

Night's Terror had not shifted her roost, so they located her without great difficulty. The owl listened to their proposal from her shadowed nest within the hollow tree, her white face glimmering like some phosphorescent growth on a rotting log.

"You have found a means to cross to where they took the yarimaimalom," Night's Terror said when they had concluded their proposal. "Impressive."

"Will you come with us, then?" Firekeeper asked. "Or if you cannot, is there another wingéd one to whom you can guide us?"

"I will go with you," Night's Terror said, "but only if you will have me after I tell you a certain tale."

Blind Seer sat and scratched vigorously behind one ear. "This tale . . . you don't think we're going to like it?"

"I think I don't like it," Night's Terror replied, "but I must tell it."

Firekeeper climbed a neighboring tree so that she could be nearer to the owl. It felt good to be away from the dank stone of the old stronghold, out in the sun again.

"Talk, owl," the wolf-woman said, leaning back against the trunk. "We will listen."

"You have already heard how the strange things came from the old stronghold," Night's Terror began, "and how my mate vanished. That is all true. What is not true is that I did not know what happened to him. I did. I knew he was a captive.

"A human male emerged from the copse one night when I was flying around, hoping to find some trace of my mate. I admit, I was afraid to cross into those trees, afraid that I would not find Golden Feather, that the only result would be my joining the flocks of the vanished. When this human came out from the trees, I would have fled, but Golden Feather's voice cried out to me.

"I banked air, nearly losing lift in my astonishment. Then I saw that the human held a cage dangling from one arm, and Golden Feather was packed into that cage.

"I rose in the air with no plan, nothing but the thought of breaking that man's hold on the cage, and setting my mate free. But Golden Feather's cry held me before I could begin my descent.

" 'Don't, Night's Terror. This cage is woven of blood briar. Even now the thorns are in my flesh. If the human ceases restraining them, they will drink me dry. The human has a proposal for you, beloved. Listen, if ever you wish me to fly again beside you.'

"What could I do? I brought myself into the human's line of vision, perching upon a tree well outside of his grasp. He made no move to grasp me, but instead began to speak. I could not understand his words, but Golden Feather translated for me."

Firekeeper guessed what the mysterious human would say, but she found she was holding her breath nonetheless.

"The human said he had a proposition for me," Night's Terror went on. "He said that he needed a watcher on the outside of the copse—a spy, to be completely honest. He was making his selection from among those creatures known to have strong pair bonds. He wanted a bird, because even a large bird can come and go relatively unseen. He had decided on a nightbird for the same reason.

"My task was to be simple. I would watch, and if any came to the area who seemed strange or different, I was to fly to the copse and land upon a certain tree. That would alert a human stationed within, and the human would choose what action to take. In return, once each moonspan Golden Feather would be brought forth so I could witness with my own eyes that he lived and breathed.

"If I refused, then Golden Feather would be killed, and his body flung out onto the plain so I would know how horribly he had died.

"I listened in increasing horror. There was my Golden Feather with his blood being drained from him, telling me what I must do to preserve his life—

or so I thought at first. But, although the human trusted that Golden Feather could understand him, and that Golden Feather could translate for him, the human in turn could not understand what my beloved mate said. Thus he did not hear what Golden Feather told me at the last.

" 'Night's Terror, you must not agree to this. I only agreed to come here so that I could urge you to fly free. I will die in peace knowing you are safe. Don't you understand? They wish you to warn them of possible enemies—and those enemies are the only chance for freedom the captive yarimaimalom have. Moreover, I do not think these humans will be long content with this small plain. As soon as they are prepared, they will come forth in strength. I would not have you betray our peoples—not to preserve my life. Go. Warn the other yarimaimalom. Tell them bad times have come again.' "

Night's Terror had puffed her feathers as she related her tale. Now she deflated so suddenly Firekeeper expected to feel a gust of wind. There was no wind, only a slender bird glimmering in the shadowed hollow.

"I couldn't do it," Night's Terror said softly. "I couldn't leave my mate to be tortured to death. To buy him life, even captive life, I spied for those who were my enemies. Each moonspan when they brought him out Golden Feather repeated his entreaty, telling me of some atrocity the humans had committed so I might realize that his one life meant little against anything that made these Old World humans stronger. He told me that if he could, he would kill himself so the humans would lose their hold over me, but that when he had tried to starve himself, they had forced food into him.

"For many moonspans, I had little enough to warn anyone about. The yarimaimalom had fled. The humans did not come here. Then one day I recognized purpose in the flight of a pair of ravens. For a moment I thought of confiding in them, but my heart nearly flew my breast at the thought of what the humans would do to my Golden Feather. How was I to know if I was the only watcher? Did they have other eyes watching from within the copse? Might my failure mean a horrible death for Golden Feather?

"Despise me if you will. I went into the copse, and sat in the appointed tree, and that night I said nothing when I saw the blood briars creep upward and begin to strangle the pair of ravens where they slept. I watched the female battle for her mate's life, but though I admired her courage, I could not go to her aide. My mate was wrapped in briars, too, and I think I even hated that raven a little. At least she could fight. I could only betray.

"Now you ask me to fly with you, to be your third set of eyes, to carry information between your groups. I would go. I would risk my life to set my Golden Feather free, and if I cannot free him, I will die with him. But knowing the hold they have over me, can you trust me?"

Firekeeper glanced down to Blind Seer and found his blue eyes raised to hers. She knew his heart and spoke for them both.

"Night's Terror, we know what it is to have your freedom taken from you because you dared make a true bond with another. Once not so long ago I swore that I had been pushed far enough, that never again would I let a hostage be used to force my actions. Wolves accept the risk that their mates may die in a hunt. Indeed, the Ones lead the pack and take the greatest risks. If I could be pressed hard enough to refuse any that power over me—even if it means that the only joy that would be left to me is revenge's cold meat—who am I to deny you that same choice?"

"Then you will trust me?" the owl said.

"Enough that I will let you go with the group that is to free the captive yarimaimalom. Two wolves whose mates are held there run with that pack. I think you will find yourself in good company."

Blind Seer rose onto all four paws and shook. Then he said to Night's Terror, "I have one question for you. In your tale, the human never laid a hand on you. Did they bind you in any other way than through your obligations?"

"You mean did they ensorcell me?" Night's Terror said. "No, they did not. Golden Feather warned me that they had skills in this way, and never did I let them touch me, nor have I been touched by any of their creations or plants. Whatever sorcery was done to make the copse let me enter and leave untouched was done to it, not to me. My mind and will are my own. It is my heart that is not."

"Are any of our hearts our own?" Blind Seer asked softly. "Sometimes I think the only way we know we have hearts is when we lose them."

Firekeeper leapt down from the tree and put her hand on the wolf's head for just a moment. Then she looked up to the hollow.

"Come down and ride on my shoulder," she said to Night's Terror. "I am sure you have learned to move in light as I have within darkness, but still, this will be easier."

Night's Terror glided down. Her motion reminded Firekeeper of the thaumaturge Grateful Peace of New Kelvin when his glasses had been broken. There was another who had learned the hard lesson that keeping faith sometimes meant doing what your loved ones would despise.

Blind Seer howled for Onion and Half-Ear.

"We'd better rest," the blue-eyed wolf said. "It's going to be a very busy night."

⚜

TRUTH WAS NAPPING, but only she knew how unrestful that sleep was. The Meddler had come to lounge within her dreams.

"So you're going through the gate," he said, "after my friends the twins."

"After our friend, Plik," Truth replied, burying her nose in her flank. "The twins . . . Well, they may be useful, but never make the mistake of thinking we are your lackeys."

"A dangerous mistake that would be," the Meddler said, and with her nose buried in her fur, Truth could not be certain whether or not he mocked her.

Truer than you imagine, the jaguar thought, and in this dream space her words came forth as speech.

"What must I do to gain your trust?" the Meddler said. "Didn't the map I gave you match on essential points with the details Harjeedian garnered for you from your prisoners? Haven't I led you fair to this point? Haven't I helped you?"

Truth gave up all pretense of sleeping, but rolled onto her back to groom her stomach.

"You have helped us, but always for your own reasons. I don't understand those reasons. I don't understand you."

"But don't the others have reasons?" the Meddler said. "All of them came to find the twins for reasons of their own. Noble reasons, certainly. I admire the desire to gain information that will enable homelands and hearths to be kept safe. Still, those remain reasons."

"That is so," Truth said. "Tell me your reasons and perhaps I will understand you."

"I have told you. I wanted my freedom. Now I seek to repay you for your kindness in setting me free by offering a little information here and there—an elder's perspective on events, you might say."

"Gratitude is a reason, I suppose," Truth said. "Yes. It can be a good reason, even. Gratitude is why Firekeeper first ventured to help me find the door back into myself."

"Then you understand me now," the Meddler said. "We are friends?"

"Friends trust each other," Truth said. "I do not trust you."

"But why? Haven't I been open and honest with you?"

Truth sat perfectly still for a moment, focusing her will on remembering. "There remains one reason I will not trust you."

"What? Tell me. Maybe I can give you a good answer and so make myself your friend."

"I doubt it," Truth said as at last she felt true sleep claiming her. "None who wished me for a friend would ever carve me in crystal and move me about as if I were nothing but a toy."

XXVII

TO HIS SURPRISE, Derian was actually sleeping soundly when Firekeeper gently touched his shoulder and whispered, "Time is come to go."

Derian sat up, scrubbing sleep from his eyes, and draining the mug of tepid water near his bedroll. He gathered his belongings and stacked them next to the wall. They were only taking what they thought they would need, and that wasn't much: weapons, a few useful tools, copies of Harjeedian's map.

They had decided to have a light meal before starting, but Derian noticed that neither he nor Harjeedian ate with much interest.

But then, Derian thought, *Firekeeper looks as if she's eating as a duty rather than otherwise. Only those new wolves—Onion and Half-Ear—seem to have any enthusiasm for the prospect. I wonder how a wolf came to be named "Onion"?*

Had he been with a human army, Derian might have asked, tried to lighten the mood with frivolous conversation. Once again, Derian felt the difference of this company. Here three wolves the size of ponies and an equally disproportionate jaguar shredded some fresh fish. There a horse stood looking with genuine thoughtfulness at some gouges cut into the stone of the freshly swept courtyard floor. In the boughs of the apple tree, two ravens and an owl were deep in what was obviously conversation.

Harjeedian was drinking strong tea and surreptitiously trying the weight of the club he was carrying as a weapon. He had a bow as well, one of those that had been carried by the Twice Dead, but Derian hoped Harjeedian wouldn't need to employ it as more than a threat. The aridisdu knew how to use it, but he wasn't very accurate.

When all was ready Firekeeper brought the prisoners forth. All of them had their hands bound behind their backs and their ankles hobbled. They made no protest, and not even a stumbling attempt to escape. Quite possibly, the three wolves flanking them and Truth's lazy presence near the gate were enough warning.

Firekeeper addressed Ynamynet and Lachen: "You already tell Harjeedian what we must do. Now tell again, slowly. Remember, no tricks. We not need you so much. There will be others."

Ynamynet shrugged. "We will need our hands unbound."

"All?" Firekeeper asked, a warning growl rumbling beneath the words.

"Not all of us," Ynamynet said, "only Lachen and myself. We work the magic."

Firekeeper cut their bonds without another word.

"Now," Lachen said, rubbing his wrists, certainly for no other reason than to make clear he had resented being tied, for the bonds had not even left a mark, "we need to anoint the gate area with sigils and signs drawn in blood, preferably human blood."

"Human?" Harjeedian asked. "Why human?"

"The spell seems to work better when the blood comes from an intelligent creature," Lachen replied, his tone holding the same lofty notes Derian had heard from snobbish nobles who believed that because they owned good horses they then knew something about them.

"Intelligence is not a problem for our volunteer donor," Harjeedian said, "and Eshinarvash can spare a little blood more easily than can any other of us."

Lachen looked mildly startled. Apparently, although the Once Dead had not hesitated to use the blood of the yarimaimalom in some of their creations, they had not adapted their thinking.

That comes from living in a place without Royal Beasts, Derian thought with a curious pride, given that he himself had not known about thinking beasts, Royal or Wise, until a few years ago.

"Yes, the horse's blood should do nicely," Ynamynet said, recovering more quickly than Lachen. "We'll need the small silver cup from my pack, and also one of the pads of clean cloth, and the green stoneware jar of ointment."

Harjeedian had already set these items by. When he brought them over, Eshinarvash walked over to Lachen, his hooves sounding a steady, determined tattoo as they struck the flagstone. When Derian walked to join the Wise Horse, the Once Dead looked puzzled.

"Are you also a donor?" Lachen asked. "You're certainly big enough to spare a bit."

"I'm going to make sure you don't do anything like nick a tendon," Derian said, "or make any other foolish move. If you do, well, then I think we know exactly who our 'donors' are going to be."

The fact that neither of the Once Dead made even a token protest against his threat told Derian far more than he wanted to know about their society.

They seem just as cruel as our legends tell, he thought. *I'm sure they're holding out on us. I wish I knew what we haven't thought to ask.*

Very, very carefully, Lachen made a wound in Eshinarvash's shining coat. He caught the blood that spilled forth with great care so the white hair surrounding the cut was hardly stained at all.

When the cup was full, Lachen handed Derian a clean cloth pad and the pot of ointment.

"Use this ointment to cover the wound, then hold the pad over it until it stops bleeding."

"What is this stuff?" Derian said, pressing the pad to the cut and sniffing the ointment suspiciously. It smelled vaguely familiar, and he didn't much like the memories it stirred. Judging from the raised hackles on the wolves, they shared his aversion.

"It contains the pulp of the blood briar vine suspended in a highly rendered fat," Lachen said. "It will make the wound heal quickly, without scarring."

"Are you willing to swear that's all it does?" Derian pressed.

Ynamynet gave a light laugh and dipped two fingers in the pot, smearing the ointment where Firekeeper's arrow had sliced her.

"Does that convince you?" she said. "Our ancestors first bred the blood briar because the numbing properties in the sap made it very useful for small area surgeries and stitching. Later, the plant was adapted to other uses."

Derian dipped his fingers in the stuff and smeared it on Eshinarvash's wound. The blood had already nearly stopped flowing, but he thought it couldn't hurt.

"Is that all the blood you'll need?" he asked.

"Not quite," Lachen said. His tone was abstracted, and Derian suspected he was already concentrating on the task at hand.

"If we might have the small book bound in pale leather," Ynamynet said, "this will go more quickly."

Harjeedian knew exactly which book she meant. Indeed, Derian had seen him leafing through it earlier, but when Derian had taken a peek at the pages the symbols that were neatly drawn, one or two to a page, meant nothing to him. Now the group all watched in relative silence as the two Once Dead painted emblems around the area where the gate should open. From time to time, Firekeeper would nod thoughtfully, and Derian took comfort in this. Apparently, Onion and Half-Ear had been present when the other side of the gate had been prepared. Firekeeper had asked them to review the process, and indicate if they noted any distortions.

Derian suspected that the wolves would not know if different signs were being drawn, but they certainly would notice if the Once Dead told the company to do something completely different—like take off their clothing or set aside their gear. So far, whether out of fear or merely from resignation, the Once Dead were holding true to their agreement.

Eventually, more blood was drawn from a fresh cut in Eshinarvash's hide. This was set in small, round-bottomed silver pots that balanced perfectly in the gouges cut in the courtyard paving. More was used to make a translucent wash over the bare grey stone where the gate would open.

All the preparations went smoothly, the Once Dead working with little discussion, the Twice Dead watching in sullen silence. The rest stood alert, attentive to any betrayal.

The only hitch in the detailed process came when Harjeedian explained that he wanted the two Once Dead to pass through the gate while on Eshinarvash's back. Lachen frowned, shaking his head, and Ynamynet actually took a step back.

"We shouldn't do that," Lachen said. "We've never transported more than two at a time. You see those ovals drawn to either side of the gate? That's where the blood of each passenger must be spread right before the transit. Then the appropriate words are said, and powders tossed in the brazier, and the gate opens. If three were to go through, we'd need to reconfigure everything and . . . honestly, I don't know if it would work."

There was no doubting their sincerity. Firekeeper spoke up in confirmation.

"These wolves say they never see more than two go."

Harjeedian frowned and pulled out the roster he had made on a wax tablet. He did some rubbing out and scratching in, then looked at the Once Dead.

"You said, I believe, that you need to do some small workings before each transit?"

"That is correct," Ynamynet said.

"Then one of you must be in the last pair . . ."

"With me," Firekeeper said. "Derian first with Blind Seer. Both are good at fighting. I wait. Come through with Ynamynet last. She not give me any trouble."

Harjeedian pursed his lips, considered, and rewrote his roster. "Very well. I have it so Onion and Half-Ear will be the second group. That way there will be four of our own on the other side before the first of the prisoners is brought over. We'll bring the Twice Dead, each with a raven, then Lachen with Eshinarvash, Harjeedian with Night's Terror, Truth alone, and finally Firekeeper and Ynamynet. That way Firekeeper will have backup until the last minute."

Derian thought Firekeeper might protest this insult to her prowess, but she was busy giving Blind Seer a hug. She crossed to Derian and said, "Have bow ready, and sword. You not know if trouble come close or far."

Derian nodded a little stiffly. The original plan—made before they realized that one of the Once Dead would need to be among the last to pass over—had assigned the final passage to himself and Harjeedian. It was a touch unnerving to find himself instead set in the vanguard.

A fleeting memory came of the first battle he had witnessed, and how hurt and angry he had been that he would not be among those on the "field of honor." He knew better now, and almost wished for the prideful confidence that had been his only a handful of years before.

There was no helping it, though. Other than Firekeeper, Derian was the best of their company at fighting a human-type fight. He also spoke at least a few words in three languages, and so could communicate as, say, two wolves could not.

He strung his bow and made sure his sword was at hand.

"Ready?" Lachen said, sounding mildly amused.

Blind Seer padded up to join Derian, standing to his left so as not to block Derian's sword arm. The blue-eyed wolf glowered at Lachen, and any amusement faded from the man's expression.

"I'll need to cut you," Lachen said to the wolf, his tone suddenly apprehensive.

"I do," Firekeeper said, stepping forward. "For all the Beasts I do. Give me little pot."

Someone passed forward the ointment.

"Let me treat the humans," Harjeedian said. "I think for now we still have guards enough."

Ynamynet shrugged as if it didn't matter much to her, but Derian didn't think he had imagined disappointment wrinkling her brow for just a moment. If Firekeeper hadn't been so suspicious, they might have found themselves suddenly under assault, and a gate neatly drawn through which the Once Dead could have made their escape.

Firekeeper balanced her Fang lightly in one hand, in a grip Derian knew could switch to one meant for throwing without any effort. She wasn't trusting, even now. He decided to make that a lesson.

But none of that distrust made its way into Firekeeper's bearing. She nicked a little cut in Blind Seer's ear and smeared the blood from it in the waiting circle. As she dabbed healing ointment on the cut, she grinned at Derian.

"See you in a little. Leave some fighting for me."

Derian, who knew well that Firekeeper was a hunter, not a warrior, recognized this salutation for what it was—another attempt to make sure their enemies saw her as a bloodthirsty killer. It worked, too. Ynamynet definitely looked unhappy as she began her part in the chanting and blood spilling that opened the gate.

Facing forward as he was, Derian saw little of the final stages of the ritual. Of one thing there was no doubt. When Eshinarvash's blood spilled down the gouges and touched the wall, the stone began to glow, turning luminous, then into molten silver. Just when he thought he could see a distorted image that could not have been reflected from behind him, Lachen's voice spoke.

"Walk in now. It will feel like fire for a moment, but the sensation will pass."

Blind Seer moved without hesitation, and Derian was only a moment slower. Nose and booted foot passed through as one. Then indeed there was a sensation of heat, more like immersion in bathwater that was just a little too hot than like fire. Then all grew dark.

For a moment, Derian thought they had been cast into some void. Then he realized that what he was seeing was the darkness of the interior of a building. At Firekeeper's insistence, the stronghold's courtyard had been lit only the bare amount necessary, and his eyes rapidly adjusted to seeing by the pale glow of the still active gate. He noted that there were a few functioning light blocks, similar to what he had seen on Misheemnekuru, near the doors. These gave little more light than would a couple of candles, but their light was steady, and did not flicker when the wolf walked between them.

As promised, they were standing at the wide end of a large, wedge-shaped building—or rather he was. Blind Seer was already padding off toward the narrower end, his nose high, doubtless scenting for trouble. The fact that the wolf did not indicate that he had sensed anyone close by gave Derian courage as he prepared himself. Remembering Firekeeper's advice, he held his bow ready, and followed the blue-eyed wolf.

The next group that was scheduled to come through would contain Onion and Half-Ear. Derian estimated that he had time to make sure the immediate area was indeed clear of other humans before he had to take charge of Twice Dead Verul.

Outside the air was cooler than it had been in the stronghold, the wind brisk. Derian found himself wishing for the heavier shirts that remained in his pack. Somehow no one had thought to ask about the weather on this side. The wolves with their thick coats and greater problems bearing up under heat rather than chill would not have thought to comment.

As if Derian's thinking had summoned them, the wall at the far end began to glow silver, and two low-slung shapes started taking form. Derian forced his gaze away from the molten images once he was sure they were indeed the wolves. There was a glow from the nearly full moon, and in its light Derian confirmed the locations of the other gate buildings. They were little more than dark solidity that broke the pattern of the starlit sky, but seeing them where he had been told they would be gave him a completely unwarranted sense of security.

How undeserved that sense was was confirmed when a moment later Blind Seer's damp nose touched the side of his arm. Derian swallowed a shriek and stepped back inside the building. The latent glow of the gate showed that Onion and Half-Ear had arrived.

"Anyone near?" Derian asked, keeping his voice low.

Blind Seer shook his head, a mannerism he had adopted some years ago, finding it useful for bridging the gap between humans and himself.

"But there are humans here," Derian persisted. "This place isn't deserted."

Blind Seer stared reproachfully at him. Derian colored as he realized that he had phrased his question in such a fashion that a simple nod couldn't answer it.

"There are humans here."

Nod.

"Any coming this way?"

Shake.

"Good. I'll step back to the gate and take charge of Verul when he comes through. Then Bitter can do some scouting."

Onion and Half-Ear had already slipped out, but with remarkable discipline. Given that their families were near and they hoped to rescue them, the two wolves stayed close by as they prowled and sniffed, glancing occasionally at Blind Seer. Obviously an agreement had been reached as to who was in charge.

When Verul and Bitter came through, Derian saw that someone had stuffed a gag into the Twice Dead's mouth and knotted it firmly behind his head.

Firekeeper again, Derian thought. *Wolves howl, and she remembered that humans can shout. This whole thing about the gates has made me forget my common sense. I expected guards, but not something as simple as one of our prisoners calling for help once he was on his own turf.*

Derian took no chances with Verul. Even hobbled and with his hands behind him, the man was big and obviously muscular.

"Sit down," Derian suggested gently. "The faster this is done, the faster you'll get that uncomfortable thing out of your mouth."

Done one way or another, Verul's glower seemed to say, but he sat where Derian had indicated, leaning back against the masonry wall, and remaining ostentatiously still.

Skea and Lovable came through next. Derian indicated that Skea should sit some distance from Verul, but where he could keep an eye on them both.

Lachen and Eshinarvash made the transit next, and Eshinarvash made amply clear that he would keep his burden.

"Harder for him to cause trouble up there, eh?" Derian said. He still felt odd about scratching another person behind his ears, but Eshinarvash angled his head in obvious invitation, so Derian gave in.

Harjeedian and Night's Terror came through next.

"We sped up the intervals," Harjeedian explained as the owl not so much flew as drifted noiselessly out to join the other avian scouts. "We feared that this much gate activity would alert someone sensitive to those 'ripples' of which the Meddler spoke."

"The wolves and ravens send no word that this is so," Derian said. "In any case, even if someone detected activity, would they necessarily think it was trouble? Only their people use these gates. I think they'll just figure that for some reason their New World party has come back."

"I hope so," Harjeedian said, his gaze fixed on where Truth was emerging from the molten glow.

The aridisdu's expression held mingled fascination and revulsion, emotions Derian shared, for the implications of this nearly instantaneous transit were enough to frighten any sane person. Yet, there were more immediate problems with which Derian could distract himself.

Derian was all too aware that the time for leaving this relatively safe place was coming, and he wondered at his own bravado in volunteering to help rescue the yarimaimalom. Certainly, if he hadn't said anything he would have been left on guard here.

"Firekeeper is taking quite a while," Derian said, for more time had passed since Harjeedian's arrival than had between that of the last several groups.

"Perhaps something must be done to close the gate properly from that side," Harjeedian said uneasily. "I never thought to ask."

As one they glanced at their captives, but three sets of eyes and three jaws locked over their gags made amply clear that now that they were on their own side of the gate, the prisoners would offer no more advice.

We expected that, Derian thought. *But where is Firekeeper? What could be keeping her?*

"NOW, US," Firekeeper said to Ynamynet, when Truth had passed through the gate. "You cut you or do you want me to?"

Ynamynet folded her arms across her chest.

"I'm not going to do it," she said. "Why should I? My people are back where they should be, and you are here without allies. You can kill me if you'd like, but you cannot make me open the gate so you may pass through and bring your violence to ruin the nexus project."

Firekeeper stared at the Once Dead for a moment unbelieving.

She held up her Fang, which she had been about to use to prick her own finger, in a wordless threat.

"Threaten me all you want," Ynamynet said. "You may find I have a greater ability to resist torture than you believe. There are many mysteries involved in my art, and not all of them are learned without pain."

Firekeeper had little stomach for the methodical torment involved in torture. Wolves killed their prey as cleanly as they could, not toying with it as cats did.

She was honest enough to admit that there was no great code of honor that had initiated that particular behavior. It was simply that a wolf pack's kill belonged to all the pack, and the one who brought the animal down usually got the first good bite. Therefore, there was no advantage to delay. Cats, however, killed for themselves alone, and if they found added amusement in prolonging the kill, there was no reason for them not to do so.

Firekeeper did not think that Ynamynet was bluffing. She scented excitement mingled with defiance in the woman's sweat, but very little fear.

"I must go through," Firekeeper said. "Blind Seer waits. The others need me to lead. Open the gate."

Ynamynet shook her head. Little wisps of hair that projected from beneath her close-fitting cap clung to the suddenly damp skin of her face.

"I won't open it, and there's nothing you can do to make me. Nothing at all. You're stuck here. And let me tell you why I'm so determined to hold out. I think you're absolutely right. I think they need you to lead them. Harjeedian might have done all the talking, but he's no war leader. In a fight, you would lead. The longer your friends flounder around waiting for you to show up, the longer my people have to notice something is wrong. Our community isn't huge, but it's large enough to deal with that handful you've stranded there. When the fighting is over, they'll ask Lachen or one of the Twice Dead, and then they'll send for me."

"Ynamynet's right you know," said a voice from over by the well. The Meddler, more translucent than ever he had appeared in one of these waking visions, stood leaning against the mortared stone.

Ynamynet started, her momentary arrogance vanishing. She didn't seem to see the Meddler at first. Then her eyes narrowed as she focused on the translucent image. Firekeeper wondered what the Once Dead saw. She doubted it was the same wolf-headed human with which she herself had become unwillingly familiar.

"Once Dead Ynamynet is correct," the Meddler said. "The others cannot succeed without you. You are the One who gives that pack direction. What are you going to do?"

Firekeeper was not to be toyed with. She didn't know if the Meddler had the gift of foretelling the future, but as his predictions matched her own, she saw no reason to argue.

"You have some thought—some plan. Tell. Time is going."

The Meddler grinned a wolf's grin that showed his fangs and was as much challenge as expression of amusement. "Very well, my dear, direct Firekeeper. You need the gate to be opened a final time. No one but a sorcerer can do this.

The one you had counted on has refused. By the way, you should have kept Lachen, he's much less intelligent and not nearly as strong-willed. Ynamynet says she will not give way before torture. She may be wrong about her ability to resist pain, but you don't have time for the extended process that would prove this."

"You talk too much," Firekeeper growled.

The Meddler's grin vanished and his ears flattened slightly. "Very well. You need a sorcerer. I know a sorcerer who will work the spell—for a price."

"Who?"

"Why, myself of course."

Firekeeper considered this. She should have known.

"What is the price?"

"A favor, to be redeemed later, at the time of my choice."

"Favor?"

"Something from you to me, nothing more. I will swear in advance that I won't involve another in any way, nor will I ask you to kill someone. I won't even ask you to stand by and let me kill someone. All I'll ask is a favor from you."

Firekeeper considered. She didn't trust the Meddler. She suspected he had something underhanded in mind, but she couldn't think of another way to get through the gate quickly enough.

Ynamynet was staring with rigid fascination at the Meddler. She was obviously frightened, but not so frightened that her resolve to resist casting the spell was about to break.

Moreover, Blind Seer was wherever he had gone without her. He had led trusting she would follow. That alone would have been enough to make Firekeeper accept the Meddler's offer.

"I give you this favor," Firekeeper agreed, "as you named it. Me to you. No one else between. Now, open this gate."

The Meddler's ears rose and his smile returned. He glanced at Ynamynet.

"Do you wish to take that woman with you? You know you can't trust her."

"Can't leave at back either," Firekeeper said, "and not know how long will be gone. Would be cruel to leave starve. I bring."

"I won't even charge an extra favor for transporting her," the Meddler said. "Perfectly free of charge. I will suggest that you tie her up."

"I not need your mind for that," Firekeeper said. She looked at Ynamynet. "Hands behind back. Fight me, and I will be very happy to hit you hard for the trouble you already cause."

Ynamynet apparently believed Firekeeper, because she was docility itself when Firekeeper bound and then gagged her.

"You need blood like she do?" Firekeeper asked the Meddler.

"Just the smear on the gate," the Meddler said. "Now that the gate is primed, that is enough. They didn't lead you astray in how the spell needed to be prepared."

"Good," Firekeeper said.

She saw fear in Ynamynet's eyes when Firekeeper drew her Fang, but Firekeeper had experienced too much already of torture and terror. She nicked the woman's forearm then moved her so the blood could flow directly onto the location marked earlier. Her own blood came from a similar spot, chosen so it would not impede her fighting when that time came.

"Ready?" the Meddler asked.

Firekeeper nodded and steered Ynamynet into place. The Once Dead resisted very little. No surprise in that. Ynamynet was going home to friends and allies. Firekeeper was the one who was hurrying into danger, hoping against hope that this delay had not left her with no option but that of seeking revenge for those the flaw in her plan had betrayed into defeat.

XXVIII

FIREKEEPER CAME THROUGH THE SILVER LIGHT, hardly feeling the burning that filled her inside and out through the chill certainty that her first sight on the other side would be the dead bodies of her friends. So convinced was she that her worst fears had come true that she hardly recognized Derian's voice when it spoke to her from a few paces away.

"What kept you so long, Firekeeper?"

The wolf-woman heard her own reply as from a distance, her voice rougher than usual.

"This one. She try a trick. Meddler is better at tricking, though. He bring me through. Is all well?"

Derian looked as if he wanted to ask for details, but her question reminded him of the urgency of their situation. He would continue wondering, though. Derian was smart, and he had heard the stories about the Meddler. Yes. He would wonder.

Well, for that matter, so would she.

Derian didn't ask, though. He took charge of Ynamynet, who went with him with flattering eagerness. While Derian moved Ynamynet to a place near but not too near her companions, he answered Firekeeper's question.

"I don't think we've been detected. At least none of our scouts returned bleeding or signaling we need to be ready to fight. Beyond that, well, we need you to translate."

"Then I go ask, tell you and Harjeedian what is where."

Firekeeper found Blind Seer waiting a few steps into the darkness beyond the doorway. He licked her bloodied arm, but unlike Derian did not ask why she had been delayed. Possibly, he had already heard her explanation. More probably, though, being a wolf he worried less about the past than the present—especially when the present was so very uncertain.

"Onion and Half-Ear have scouted," the blue-eyed wolf said, *"and say the kennels are much as they left them. They have snuffled some warning to their kin to expect a rescue and have cautioned them to silence."*

The night was quiet, so Firekeeper guessed that the warning had been taken seriously.

"And Plik?" she asked.

"Lovable is scouting where the others said they thought he might be. She should return very soon."

"Good."

Firekeeper hugged Blind Seer's head close to her. Later she would tell him how close she had come to not being able to reach him, but not now. She stroked his head, then turned to go back inside.

"I tell Harjeedian and Derian that they can go now. Eshinarvash and Truth still wish to hold here?"

"More than ever," Truth replied from the shadows. *"This island's air is filled with the reeks of blood and fear. I have no wish to have our one door out of here blocked from our use. The horse and I will guard it well."*

Firekeeper grinned. *"Good. Make sure the humans do not talk to each other, and remember, fingers are very clever at working loose ropes and things."*

Truth coughed a jaguar's laugh. *"Royal Beasts might forget about fingers and human wit, but those of us who have lived close to humans are too wise to underestimate how very clever they can be. Go now. Tell Derian and Harjeedian what they will need to know."*

Firekeeper did so, drawing the two humans out of earshot of the captives. As she spoke with the two men she noted something. Her sense of smell might not be a match for Blind Seer's, but it was good enough for her to catch the acrid stink of sweat on both men. The night was cool enough that dread and tension, not heat, must be the source.

"Are you good with this?" she asked, looking from the fair-skinned redhead to the darker-skinned aridisdu—so different to the eye, but alike in sensible fear. "The night is dark. Truth might trade with you."

Derian shook his head decisively. "I thought about asking, but Truth and

Eshinarvash can't work latches or use keys. The yarimaimalom will need human hands to help them."

Harjeedian nodded solemn agreement with Derian's position.

"I also thought about retreating, but what manner of aridisdu would I be if my service to the deities' messengers stopped when danger was involved? I will go forward as well. Just ask our guides to remember that we do not see as well in the dark as you do."

"I will," Firekeeper said. For a moment she thought about asking Onion or Half-Ear to trade places with Truth or Eshinarvash, so that one of the yarimaimalom who regularly associated with humans would be with the strike party. Then she thought how unhappy she would feel if she were asked to not be part of rescuing Blind Seer or even one of those who had made up her little pack on Misheemnekuru. She would just have to trust that the others would remember her cautions.

By the time these last-minute arrangements were made and the other group had started out, Lovable had returned. Firekeeper had the raven begin her briefing as they headed to where Plik was being held. The raven perched on Blind Seer's back, reminding Firekeeper of a peculiar knight mounted for war.

"I found the place," Lovable said, puffing out her feathers importantly. "It is much like we had been told. There is a high hedge into which that horrible blood briar is woven, but there is a gate in the hedge. A human guards the gate."

Lovable went on to describe the human's armor and weapons far more efficiently than Firekeeper herself could have done. Once again Firekeeper found herself recalling the differences between the Wise Beasts and the Royal. She was rather glad the Liglim seemed to have no desire for conquest. If the yarimaimalom sided with them, they would be formidable indeed.

"Inside the hedge there are two small buildings. I looked in through the windows. Plik sleeps in the smaller of the two buildings. Two who must be the twins sleep in the other."

Blind Seer had only one question.

"When we arrive, does the guard live or die?"

"Live, if possible," Firekeeper said. "But not at the price of either our health or our success. Harjeedian gave me rope and a gag for binding him."

Blind Seer huffed understanding.

"Loveable," Firekeeper said. "You go over the hedge and into Plik's house.

Wake him. Tell him to tell the twins that we come, and they are to cause no trouble. They will come with us. I will hurt them if they refuse."

"Shall Plik wake the twins if he thinks they will resist?" Lovable asked.

"No," Firekeeper said. "Easier to take them without hurting them if they are asleep."

The raven flapped off.

Soon they arrived in the vicinity of the hedged enclosure. Firekeeper could see the guard standing near the gate. As they watched, he shifted his weight from one leg to the other with the practiced economy of motion of someone who had stood numerous watches. Then he was still again.

Firekeeper actually liked most of the human guards she had met. They made more sense to her than warriors did, because, unlike warriors, their purpose was to preserve rather than to attack. Firekeeper had found many friends among the guards of Eagle's Nest Castle when they had realized she offered no threat to those they were sworn to protect.

In honor of the memory of those friends, the wolf-woman resolved not to harm the man who stood patiently a few paces outside the wrought-iron gate. This did make her task rather more difficult, however.

She studied the scene for a long moment.

"No one near?" she asked Blind Seer.

"I hear a rapping," he said, twitching one ear, "but that would be Lovable outside a window. Otherwise, no one is near."

"We will wait a moment longer," Firekeeper said. "Then I will go after the guard. If I move quickly enough, he will not have opportunity to warn any others who might be on patrol."

Using the darkness for cover, Firekeeper moved out and around so that she could approach the guard on a line parallel to the hedge. She was careful to keep out of the reach of the briars that stirred sluggishly as soon as they sensed the heat from her body. She didn't doubt that the briars were the reason the guard stood a few paces from the iron gate rather than leaning up against it.

Although the air was crisp and cold, the grass underfoot was not yet winter dry. Firekeeper knew she could glide over this smoothly and silently. The guard remained vigilant, but never once did he look behind him. His first indication that something was wrong was when a piece of rope slipped around his neck and tightened just shy of strangulation.

"Not move," Firekeeper whispered, "or I will pull all the way tight."

The man held very, very still, his breath coming in little whistling wheezes.

"*Blind Seer,*" Firekeeper said, "*come and let him see you.*"

The wolf emerged from the darkness and stood before the now terrified guard. Blind Seer's mouth gaped in what Firekeeper knew was laughter, but the expression showed off an impressive array of sharp teeth nonetheless.

"Now," she said to the guard, "make no noise or move when I loosen the rope or my friend will hurt you—and he bites very hard."

The guard gave a minor inclination of his head, the best nod he could manage with the rope around his neck. Firekeeper maintained the pressure on the rope with one hand while getting out lengths of cord and a gag she had prepared earlier.

When she loosed the stranglehold, the guard kept his frozen silence, but even so, Firekeeper felt it was best to gag him first. Then she secured his hands and feet, and finally roped him to the wrought-iron gate. She allowed the man enough play so that he did not come within reach of the blood briars, but tied him closely enough that he would still appear to be on watch.

The keys to the gate were in the guard's pocket. Firekeeper opened it only wide enough for her and Blind Seer to slip inside. Then she closed it and latched it, but did not lock it again.

Faint light glowed from the larger of the two cottages, and Firekeeper guessed that Lovable had awakened the twins. There were no screams or cries from anywhere. Events seemed to be progressing according to plan.

If she was honest with herself, Firekeeper had to admit that worried her.

"CAREFUL THERE, Harjeedian," Derian said softly. "Ground drops off a bit."

He could hear the aridisdu slide his foot along the path until he found the uneven place, then a brief grunt of thanks.

Night's Terror and the two local wolves had not forgotten Firekeeper's warning that neither of the humans could see in the dark, and they had come up with a rather ingenious method of guiding them.

After flying ahead to make sure all remained quiet, Night's Terror had landed on Derian's shoulder. For such a large bird, she was very light. More importantly, the grip of her claws was solid enough that Derian could feel it through his shirt. The owl pulsed her right foot to give him warning of something ahead, her left for something underfoot. It was a bit painful, but, then, so would crashing into something be.

There was light ahead now, bright spots at regular intervals. When they drew closer, Derian saw that there were oil lanterns set along the aisles in the menagerie, flames turned up just high enough to break the darkness into twilit shadow. After the darkness between the gate buildings and the menagerie, the area seemed comfortably bright.

Night's Terror seemed to sense Derian's greater assurance, for she launched off his shoulder and winged ahead. She landed on a gate and turned her white, heart-shaped face toward them. Derian needed no other invitation.

"I'll start here," he said, keeping his voice very low. "Show Harjeedian where to go."

The owl had, not surprisingly, led them first to an aviary. There was another barn owl here, a great horned owl, three young ravens, and a hawk that reminded Derian too much of his long-absent friend, the peregrine falcon Elation. Each was in a cage too small for flight, the floors and perches soiled with droppings, bits of feather, and other, less definable detritus.

The birds emerged gingerly, and Derian guessed that none of them would find flying easy. He didn't know if they had been held captive long enough for their wing muscles to actually atrophy, but certainly they were out of condition.

The great horned owl seemed in marginally better condition than the others. He—Derian had no idea of the actual gender, but he needed to think of the creature as *something*—hopped over to another series of cages. These held more birds of prey along with a few medium-sized animals: a raccoon, a bedraggled vixen crowded in with three half-grown kits, a spotted wildcat. There were a few empty cages as well. Derian wondered if they had once been inhabited, and if for those inhabitants rescue had come too late.

Subconsciously, Derian had expected the imprisoned animals to snarl or growl, even to slash out with beak or claw, but he had forgotten that these were yarimaimalom, Wise Beasts, and that they knew he was their rescuer. Even so, he was surprised when the wildcat paused in her limping progress out of her cage and bumped her round-eared head against his hand in mute thanks. He felt honored, as he had not felt since those early days when Elation had made clear that she considered him as fit a companion as she did Firekeeper.

Other figures were now milling around in the dimly lit darkness between the cages: wolves, far too lean, flickering in and out of sight as if partially made of shadows. A trio of lumbering bears, their fur patchy, their skin hanging loose. One bear rose onto his back legs to scout, his head rising higher than Derian's own, his black nose flared, his small eyes watchful.

A golden brown puma came into sight carrying what Derian thought was a kitten in her mouth. Then he realized it was a full-grown lynx, one paw swollen with some sort of infection. The weak-winged birds of prey flapped to ride on the bears' backs, and not a one grunted protest, though those taloned feet had to be sharp. Here it was as Onion had said, differences of species had been forgotten in their common captivity.

Harjeedian hurried over to the injured lynx, muttering about infection and amputation. Derian looked around for Onion and Half-Ear.

He found them in the midst of a milling throng of wolves. Derian did not need to have spent the better part of these last four years associating with Fire-keeper and Blind Seer to know that the snapping and snarling was not the usual ebullient greetings wolves shared among themselves. This was an argument, and he thought that Half-Ear and Onion were losing.

Taking a deep breath, and hoping the wolves would respect him for the fear they couldn't help but smell on him, Derian waded into the swirling reddish grey sea. The wolves stopped their bickering. One by one, eyes in shades of gold and amber focused on him, their stares cold but not without curiosity.

Derian located Half-Ear, grateful as never before for that truncated appendage which made identification certain.

"What is it?" He spoke softly, remembering a long-ago lesson that whispers carry as low voices do not. "We were to lead everyone to the gate."

Half-Ear tilted his head to one side, a gesture indicating puzzlement; then he nudged Derian's arm. When the wolf was certain he had Derian's attention, he pointed with his nose toward a darkened building at the end of the long aisle of cages. Instantly, Derian understood.

The building was a solidly built cottage, probably containing two rooms and a storage loft. Undoubtedly, those responsible for the yarimaimalom's daily care resided there, close to their charges. The reason the yarimaimalom were not fleeing was also immediately evident. Pinned to the outside of the cottage walls were the spread hides of various animals: several wolves, a bear, a pair of what Derian thought were lynxes, an eagle . . .

His stomach turned as he realized what he was seeing. These were not just the tanned hides of animals hung to finish curing. These were the hides of yarimaimalom, skinned, tanned, and hung to dry as a reminder to their kin of the penalty for disobedience.

Red anger flashed before Derian's eyes. He bent over, not certain that he could keep from vomiting. A damp nose against his cheek brought him to himself.

"I understand," he muttered, his voice shaking with rage. "I couldn't leave the bastards who did that either. Come on."

Derian glanced around and located Night's Terror, over atop a cage, nuzzling the owl he assumed was Golden Feather, her mate.

"Go," he said. "Tell Eshinarvash and Truth we'll be delayed a moment. Then tell Firekeeper."

Harjeedian had noticed the delay and come over. Like Derian, he needed no explanation. His skin seemed to tighten over his high cheekbones, as lips curled in a snarl of contained rage.

"There's evidence of mutilation among the living," Harjeedian said, keeping his voice low with difficulty. "That lynx is missing toes. One of the fox cubs lacks a tail. What they did to one of the eagles . . . Be careful—and try and keep it quiet."

The cottage door was latched but not locked. What was there to lock it against? Derian eased up the latch and opened the door. He felt a bump against his leg and looked down. Several of the wolves had already streamed past him.

The front room, illuminated by a lamp burning low on a table, proved to be empty. A small falcon flapped with painful labor to the loft and with his lack of interest in the contents indicated that it was also uninhabited.

A wolf with pale, almost icy fur was snuffling near a door. She raised her head and looked at Derian. He crossed over and lifted the latch as quietly as possible.

This room was darker than the outer room, but his eyes were well adjusted by now. He saw three beds set exactly equidistant from each other. Each appeared to be occupied. What he hadn't expected was for them to be occupied by women.

He couldn't make out the details, but he was sure. Maybe it was some scent in the air, maybe the lack of strong male odor, but Derian was absolutely certain. The one who lay curled on her side on the far left had skin as dark as that of Skea the Twice Dead. The one in the middle was huddled under her comforter—a bear-fur comforter, Derian noticed with increasing unease. The one on the far left was sitting up, her sheet falling back from milky pale, naked breasts.

The woman made an exclamation in a language Derian didn't know, and then the icy wolf was upon her. Two other wolves moved almost as quickly, and dark wetness stained the bedclothes. A new smell entered the closed room: the mingled odors of blood and bowel.

Derian stumbled back, knowing he had crossed some line without even knowing he had been making a choice. His hand touched a garment hanging on a rack near the door—a thick cloak sewn from some spotted fur. His fingers tightened on its softness. He imagined it worn by the milky-skinned woman as she went about her chores.

What had he done? He'd opened the door and let the wolves in on three sleeping women. He'd been angry and revolted, but this quick, efficient slaughter . . . it seemed worse than what had been done to the yarimaimalom—if those had been yarimaimalom hides he'd seen.

Was it worse? These women had died quickly in their sleep. Only one had even had a suspicion that anything was wrong.

But they'd been human. Did he really want to believe that the yarimaimalom had the right to dispense their form of justice and punishment? Where did that leave him?

It was the doubt as much as anything else that made Derian suddenly sick, his knees so weak he had to grasp the doorframe to turn himself around so he could get out of that room. The wolves were leaving now. Derian felt a peculiar relief. He'd known they'd been kept half-starved. He didn't know what he would have done if they'd stayed to eat their kill.

He staggered out, gulping the cool night air. Harjeedian appeared beside him, put a hand on his arm.

"Are you all right?"

"No," Derian said frankly, "but we'd better get out of here, even if there's no one left to raise an alarm."

"I took one of the lanterns," Harjeedian said. "It's a panel model. We can open only as much as we need to see our way back."

But even so, Derian needed to lean on the other man's arm as they headed back to the gate, surrounded by creatures that filled Derian with a deep, soul-twisting fear.

PLIK WAS DREAMING that he was eating shellfish and honey with Powerful Tenderness when some part of his sleeping mind registered that the tapping on the windowpane was not the sound of oyster shells being tossed on the growing heap between him and his friend.

He sat up and saw something large and dark darting outside the window, rapping erratically while performing some peculiar aerial dance. Plik moved to look more closely and the image resolved into a large raven dodging the slow but determined attempts of the blood briar that grew outside his windows to snag it.

Climbing onto the window seat, Plik opened the window and the raven flew in. Faithful to its training, the briar remained without, although Plik thought that it continued to rub against the glass longer than was necessary.

To Plik's amazement, the raven proved to be Lovable.

"We're here to rescue you," she said proudly. "All of us. Firekeeper and Blind Seer will be in soon. Firekeeper told me to have you awaken the twins and tell them they are coming with us—whether they want to or not."

Plik's still sleepy mind assimilated this torrent of information laboriously. He'd dreamed of rescue before, and most of those dreams made at least as much sense as this.

"Firekeeper and Blind Seer?"

"They are going to take out the guard."

"Not kill him!" Plik said with concern. The guards, as far as he could tell from his own experience and the twins' report, were fairly decent fellows. Mostly they were Twice Dead who had limited skills to offer their community beyond size and a certain amount of training with weapons. They served as guards when needed and general laborers when not.

"Probably they won't kill him," Lovable said. Plik thought the raven sounded disappointed, but then, given what had been done to Bitter, Lovable probably had little desire for mercy to be shown to any of these singularly bloodthirsty humans.

Plik considered his options.

"I'll tell the twins," he said.

To this point, Plik had been given no reason to go into the twins' cottage, but when he'd awakened that afternoon, he'd gone with Isende when she went to fetch more yarn. From the brief tour she had given him, he had a fair idea where everything lay.

The twins' cottage was somewhat larger than Plik's own. It possessed two rooms. One was used as general living quarters, and, at night, as Tiniel's bedroom. The other, much smaller room, was Isende's.

The cottage's front door was not locked. Not wanting to alert the guard in the event that Firekeeper had not yet put him out of action, Plik lifted the latch as quietly as he could and walked in without announcing himself. Lovable strutted in after him with that particularly raven gait that was both bold and alert.

As they entered, Tiniel stirred slightly on his cot near the hearth, but didn't awaken. Plik stirred up the fire so there would be light for the humans to see by, then shook the young man by one shoulder.

" 'Sende?" Tiniel murmured. He moved as if to draw Plik into bed with him. When his hand met fur, it stopped abruptly.

He woke more fully, and opened his eyes.

"Plik?"

"Wake up," Plik said, keeping his voice in the conversational range, and crossing to Isende's door. Unlike the outer door, this one was locked. He rapped on it sharply.

"What is it, Tin?" Isende's sleepy voice called a moment later. "Has Plik taken a turn for the worse?"

"This is Plik. I've something important to tell you—and, no, it can't wait until morning."

Clad in a long, shapeless robe, Isende emerged almost immediately. Tiniel was sitting up in his cot, staring at Lovable, who had taken a proprietary perch on his blanket-covered foot.

"Don't make my job more difficult," Plik scolded the raven. *"Go tell Fire-keeper how things stand."*

"What happened to your face?" the raven asked, getting her first look at the shaven section in the light from the fire.

"Later," Plik said. *"Go report to Firekeeper. Tell her not to kill the guard."*

Lovable chortled and obediently winged off through the door Plik held open. He closed it and immediately began talking.

"My friends have come for us," he said. "Get dressed and grab anything you need. Knowing Firekeeper, she's not going to wait for you to pack."

"Here?" Tiniel said, getting up and beginning to pull on trousers under his nightshirt. "They came through the gate?'

"I assume so," Plik said. "The season's all wrong here for this place to be close enough to home for them to have come overland. Further north for one, I'd guess, but maybe the Old World is colder overall. You did tell me this place was in the Old World."

"Right," Tiniel said. "Sorry. I think I was still asleep."

He'd buttoned his trousers and was thrusting his arms into shirt sleeves. Isende had vanished, but her voice came from her bedroom door.

"I don't understand. How could they figure out how to use the gate without notes? We took everything with us."

"They're pretty remarkable people," Plik said smugly. "My guess is that this is going to be a quick strike. In and out, then back through the gate. It's quite possible that the Once Dead and their people won't even know we're gone until daylight comes and you're not at the gate waiting for the breakfast tray."

"Oh!" Isende said, her voice rising with anxiety. "Do you think all of them came?"

"Probably the entire group," Plik replied, confused. What did this matter? Why didn't Isende sound happier?

"But don't you see . . ." Isende was beginning when the door swung open and Firekeeper came in, Blind Seer beside her.

Almost as if they were still linked, the twins gaped as one, staring at the intruder, expressions filled with mingled wonder and shock.

Plik had forgotten just how remarkable Firekeeper might appear to those who did not know her. He had now been around a sufficient number of humans to realize that Firekeeper didn't even move like a human. She didn't move like a wolf—that would have been impossible given that she was both bipedal and had excellent posture—but if a wolf could move like a human, that wolf would have been Firekeeper. Then there were her eyes. They were far, far darker than the amber and gold that glowed from the faces of most wolves, but Firekeeper's eyes held the same unfocused yet ever focused gaze of the pack predator, aware both of her prey and those with whom she hunted.

Firekeeper padded soundlessly into the center of the room, ran a hand through her already tousled hair, then dropped it onto Blind Seer's shoulder.

"Guard is out," Firekeeper said in Liglimosh, evidently pleased with herself. "He still stand, though, and so until relief come should look like is on duty. When relief due?"

Tiniel was gaping at the wolf-woman, but he closed his mouth and managed a question. "Is it past midnight?"

"Think so."

"Then not until dawn—probably. Might be sooner, though, now that the nights are getting longer."

"We have time, then," Firekeeper said. Those dark, dark eyes inspected Plik, and a smile touched them at finding him in one piece, then a frown as he turned his head and she saw the shaven place, but she didn't ask anything. "Ready to go?"

Isende found her voice. "But don't you see? You can't go back to the New World. If you go back, you'll carry Divine Retribution with you and who knows how many people will die!"

XXIX

TRUTH SAT, tail wrapped around her paws, watching the prisoners. Above their gags, the Once Dead glowered at her in undisguised hatred and resentment. The other two were more relaxed. Truth thought that Verul might even be asleep.

The difference, she thought, *between believing one has power, and knowing that one does not.*

Eshinarvash was standing near the opening to the outdoors.

"I hear sounds from the direction of the menagerie."

"An alarm?"

"No. Success, I think. Small whimpers and cries of joy. I doubt a human would even hear them."

"What do you smell?"

The stallion's nostrils flared. When he angled his head to catch the correct wind, his long mane danced on the currents. He was a beautiful enough beast that Truth could look at him with admiration uncolored by the least trace of hunger.

"Many beasts," Eshinarvash said. "Some tainted by illness and rot. There is a touch of blood as well. Human, I think. Yes. Human."

"Well, as long as it doesn't belong to either of our humans," Truth said, "that's all right. I am beginning to understand why the Royal Beasts strove to drive the Old Country rulers from the land. I wonder at the courage our ancestors showed in being willing to make truce with them."

"Courage," the horse said, stamping one hoof against the stone, "or necessity. Ah . . . Here come the first, led by Onion."

"It will be impossibly crowded if they all come in here," Truth said, "nor do I think these will have any love for walls. Suggest they remain outside, but remind them to be quiet."

The Wise Horse raised his tail and deposited a few round droppings on the floor.

"I will do so," he said with such mildness that Truth was left to ponder whether the defecation had been deliberate insult or not.

"Here come our humans," Eshinarvash added. He trotted out of the doorway and a few moments later returned with Derian and Harjeedian. Both men were quiet, and there was something odd about how Derian shied when Truth came over to greet him.

Harjeedian gave the Wise Jaguar a respectful bow, gathered up the pack of medical supplies he had not carried with him to the menagerie, and, after saying a few inconsequential words to Derian, quickly departed.

Truth lashed her tail. "Derian has never shown so much fear of me before, only healthy respect. Can you find out what happened?"

Eshinarvash snorted. "Maybe if you go outside. Ask the others what happened. Derian seems to take comfort from me. Together we can guard these four and I will see if Derian will talk."

Truth was glad enough to leave the enclosed building and her glowering prisoners. She leapt lightly over the still steaming horse apples, and padded over to where Onion was supervising Harjeedian's inspection of a paw-sized sore on a young wolf's shoulder.

"Derian is edgy," Truth said. "What happened?"

Onion gave his own shoulder a quick, nervous lick in sympathy for the injured wolf before offering reply.

"We told you some of what was done to us by those who imprisoned us here. We did not wish to be thought whining pups, so we did not tell you everything—all the torments they heaped upon us for no other reason than that it amused them."

Perhaps, Truth thought uncharitably, *you didn't tell us because you feared you would frighten us off and you needed our help.*

When the wolfling made as if to snap at Harjeedian, Onion leaned forward, grabbed the young wolf by the neck scruff, and shook him solidly.

"Be still and silent, pup! This human is helping you."

The young wolf subsided as wolves always did when chided by their seniors, but his yellow-eyed gaze remained distrustful and unkind.

Onion returned his attention to Truth. "The pup has reason for his fear. We told you that some of us had died here. What we did not tell you was what happened afterwards. Those who called themselves our keepers would skin the dead one, scrape the hide, and prepare it as they do those of Cousin-kin. When the weather grew cooler—and often at night when the winds from the ocean were brisk—they wore garments made of these hides when they tended us. It was mockery and reminder both.

"When young Derian saw some hides still drying, he instantly understood what had been done. Up to that moment, his scent had been filled with honest fear and apprehension—good things when on a hunt so uncertain. After he saw the drying hides, you could not smell the fear for the fury. Derian opened the keepers' den to us without our asking, and he opened the way into their sleeping lair as well. Only after we had made certain that these cruel ones would 'keep' no others did Derian's scent change. Now he smells sick and uneasy."

"And Harjeedian?"

"He, too, smelled of anger, but never this sickness. I do not understand."

"Derian's people know little of our kind," Truth said, "while Harjeedian's have lived side by side with us since Divine Retribution came. Tell this tale to Firekeeper when she returns. She may have words to comfort Derian where Harjeedian would not."

Half-Ear came to join them. "Bitter went searching for his mate on our return. The Firekeeper brings those she went to rescue."

"Intact?"

"Not a scent of blood on them, but Bitter says something is very wrong."

"Keep watch," Truth said. "Remind the others that silence must be kept no matter how great the pleasures of freedom."

"We will not easily forget," Half-Ear replied. "We know the insides of cages all too well to risk returning."

DERIAN LEANED HIS HEAD against Eshinarvash's flank. For the first time, he felt no wonder or awe in the presence of the Wise Horse, only a sense of comfort and security in the familiar odor of horse sweat and the smooth warmth of living horse beneath his brow.

Eshinarvash bent his neck and nuzzled Derian, nickering to him as a mare might to a nursling foal.

"Ancestors," Derian prayed softly. "Let me know that what I did was right."

A rough-edged voice broke him from his reverie.

"Fox Hair," Firekeeper said, "you must hear—we learn something."

Derian pulled himself upright. Firekeeper was standing just inside the doorway, her bearing tight and alert.

"What?"

"Trouble."

"Tell me."

"Not here," Firekeeper said. She tossed her head in the direction of the prisoners. "Others will guard them. You and Eshinarvash come."

Wolves were entering the building now accompanied by a puma longer than Truth, and quite a bit slimmer.

"Guard them." Derian heard his voice break. "You promise me. They will only guard. Nothing, absolutely nothing, else."

"Guard only," the wolf-woman replied.

Firekeeper didn't sound puzzled, so Derian guessed she had already been briefed as to what had happened over by the menagerie. She didn't sound happy, either, from which he took some reassurance. Even so, he was surprised when she waited for him to join her, then touched him lightly on the arm. The motion might have been taken as guiding him, for the building had grown darker as the light from the gate had faded, leaving only the dim illumination from the glowing blocks, but Derian knew comfort when it was offered.

Outside, Firekeeper led Derian to an area on the far side of the gate buildings where a few lanterns had been lit and a group of oddly disparate figures sat on the grass around the lanterns as around a campfire. There were blankets, too, presumably brought from wherever the twins and Plik had been staying. As he took a seat, Derian shrugged a blanket over his shoulders, grateful for the warmth.

Only then did he look to see who was part of this privileged council.

"Plik!" he cried, and felt joy warm parts of his soul that had been chilled by confusion and doubt. "You look pretty good."

Then he saw that half the raccoon-man's face had been shaved to the bare skin.

"Are you all right?"

"I've been through a lot," the raccoon-man said, his voice without its usual note of humor, "and indirectly that's what we need to talk about. First, let me introduce you to the twins we've come so far to find. This is Isende and this is her brother, Tiniel."

Derian looked the pair over as best he could in the lantern light. They looked less alike than he had imagined, siblings with a strong family resemblance rather than copies of one person. With their warm brown skin they looked rather like diluted Liglimom, but Derian had never seen anything quite like their thick, somewhat wavy hair. Seen in one light it appeared fair, but beneath it held a warmer brown.

Like it has been polished, Derian thought, *not sun-faded. The color is nice-enough-looking, once you get used to it.*

He remembered that Rahniseeta had said something similar about his freckles, and realized with weird relief that he was remembering his former fiancée without the same degree of heartache.

Derian inclined his head to each twin in neutral greeting. Then he glanced to see who else was included in the conference.

Blind Seer reclined near Firekeeper. Truth sat at the fringe of the lantern light, along with Half-Ear. Bitter and Lovable cuddled close, perched on a stone plinth that had probably once held a statue. Harjeedian was missing, and Firekeeper anticipated Derian's question.

"Harjeedian is treating some of the yarimaimalom as best he can. Some were very badly hurt by their keepers."

As Liglimosh was the one common language in this group now that the twins must be included, Firekeeper used the Liglimosh word "kidisdu." Her inflection made clear she found no likeness between those who had kept the yarimaimalom captive, and their Liglimom friends.

"Harjeedian say," Firekeeper went on, "that whatever we do, he will follow."

"So what's the problem?"

"We can't go back," Isende said. Her Liglimosh had the same accent they'd heard in Gak, but even so Derian could detect a note that told him she had said this before and was desperate that she be believed. "It's querinalo, Divine Retribution, the Plague. All of you have probably been infected. If we go back, you'll spread it."

Derian thought he had suffered enough shocks that he would be immune to another, but this announcement made the inside of his head vibrate as if he'd been physically hit.

"But how have we been infected?" he asked. "Was it contact with the Once

Dead and Twice Dead? If so, they've been into the New World. It's too late to stop the infection from spreading."

Tiniel shook his head. "We're not sure how the infection is spread, but neither one of us grew ill with it until we came through the gate and spent time here. The illness wasn't lingering in the stronghold or any of the old papers or anything like that."

"But," Isende said, "it's the experience of the yarimaimalom that makes me think that the infection is here in the Old World, but not yet in the New. After Tiniel and I made our transit, the Once Dead took us captive. When we were over querinalo, we were brought back to the stronghold for a time, so we could show them where everything was, explain what we had found where. That's how we know that they captured some of the yarimaimalom and held them there in the stronghold for a while before deciding to bring them into the Old World. It was only after the transit that some of the yarimaimalom felt the fires of Divine Retribution."

Firekeeper nodded. "I have asked Onion and Half-Ear, and they say the same. Only after they come here did this querinalo strike."

"So the New World is still safe," Derian said with relief.

"Unless you go back and infect it," Isende said. "We're safe, but it's going to take a day and a half or so before we know which ones of you are vulnerable."

"Then you have already had it?" Derian asked.

"Yes," Tiniel replied for them both.

The single word was so blunt and so bitter that Derian didn't ask more. "Plik?"

"Yes. It was . . . horrible. I nearly died. I saved myself by . . . I don't know how to say this, but by offering it my talent to burn instead of my body. I lived, but my ability to sense magic is gone. When I arrived, the magical energies being used here were like a surf pounding in my head. Now there is only silence."

"Are the stories true?" Derian asked. "The Plague—'keri-something,' I think you called it—only affects those who have magical abilities?"

"That seems to be the case," Tiniel said. "Plik could sense magic. We—Isende and I—could sense each other. That ability is gone."

Isende added, shyly, as if she thought the information unimportant, "The Once Dead are those who had the Plague but their magic still 'lives.' The Twice Dead—like us, like Plik—'died' twice. Once in having the disease, once in letting our talents die. Some of those here call those who don't catch querinalo the 'Never Lived.'"

"Does this querinalo," Derian said the word carefully, "still kill people?"

"Yes," Isende said, "but not as frequently as our legends tell us it did in the old days. Perhaps the disease has mellowed over time. Perhaps some long-ago sorcerer found a way to temper it, but couldn't eliminate it. Perhaps the really great talents that would fuel the fever to killing levels no longer exist. I don't know. These days, so we are told, if the victim is willing to fight—to sacrifice—the victim can live and even maintain magical ability. But it's not easy."

Derian scratched his neck where the wool blanket was making it itch. "And you're sure that if we go back before the disease runs its course we'll risk carrying it to others?"

"That's what the doctor who treated us believed," Isende said. "Maybe he's wrong, but do we want to take the risk?"

Firekeeper said, "We could go back. Stay in the stronghold. Let see what happens. Not meet any others."

Isende shook her head. "It's too big a risk."

"Is a big risk to stay," Firekeeper said, "especially if many of us may be ill."

Derian knew who the likely candidates for catching the Plague would be. Firekeeper almost certainly. Truth, unless she had really lost her ability to see the future rather than just having put it aside. And himself. He'd been told that his skill with horses consisted of training and education augmented by a touch of talent. He didn't know. There were no tests to tell the more subtle levels of talents. Talents simply manifested clearly—as in Doc's ability to speed the process of healing—or were suspected.

What about the others? Bitter, Lovable, Eshinarvash, Harjeedian, even Blind Seer? Were they also talented? Would they learn of these talents only when this querinalo hit?

Firekeeper was right. They would be in great danger if they stayed here, even with a horde of yarimaimalom to guard them. But Isende was right, too. Did they dare take the risk that they might carry this querinalo to the New World? A single talented creature coming in contact with them might carry away the disease all unknowing.

"So," he said, "what do we do?"

Firekeeper tilted her head to one side. "Either we go back, and wait in stronghold, or we take this place and stay here."

"Take this place," Derian said. "How many people are there here?"

Tiniel spoke up. "The numbers do shift, but I'd estimate somewhere around fifty to sixty. Not all of these are Once Dead—maybe a third. The remainder are Twice Dead, with a smattering of Never Lived. These are mostly family of one of the others."

Isende added, "You have to understand. The New World was not alone in having rather bad memories of the time before querinalo thinned the ranks of the magically talented. As in the New World, those with magical ability tended to rule or to support those who ruled. In the better cases, magic was used to improve lives immensely. Look at the lights inside the gate buildings: light without smoke or excessive heat. That's pretty wonderful. However, magic was also used to force the acceptance of unpopular measures and rulers. When querinalo struck, many people in many lands did as we did in the New World. They took advantage of the sorcerers' weakness to eliminate them."

"Night will not last forever," Firekeeper reminded. "We must decide."

Isende held up her hand. "But you have to understand. Those here—especially the Once Dead—have come from cultures where they were outcasts or grew up in isolation or hiding. It doesn't help that most of them follow the blood-magic path. You need to be a bit ruthless to do that. They have a reason for being the way they are, but not all of them are completely horrid."

Derian heard himself asking, "Do you know anything about those who were set to watch over the yarimaimalom?"

"A little," Isende said, "enough to know that they were far worse than the 'beasts' they were set to tend. They were the ones responsible for the initial creation of the bracken beasts. That took a lot of experimentation—we used to hear the cries. It made me sick."

Derian didn't know if Isende knew what had happened to those keepers, and judging from how Firekeeper kept glancing at the eastern horizon as if trying to judge how long they had until dawn, this wasn't the time to ask.

Plik looked as if he were about to say something when a red fox burst into the circle of lantern light, eyes wild, flanks heaving.

Firekeeper surged to her feet, her knife in her hand.

"Too late to talk more," she said. "This fox say that movement has been spotted. Someone—many someones—know we are here."

WITH AN EXPLOSION OF WINGS, Bitter and Lovable took to the night-dark sky. More soundlessly, Night's Terror glided in to take their place on the boulder.

"*One of the eagles spotted the movement first,*" she said. "*It was a human male. He came from one of the buildings up the hillside, stood and stared this way, then hurried down the hillside toward where many of the humans dwell. The eagle wished to give warning, but he had had his flying feathers pulled, and we had all been warned against screaming, so he had to find someone who could scout for him. By the time I was located . . .*"

"*Slow, slow,*" Firekeeper said, holding up her hand. "*First, how many come?*"

"*More than a fresh clutch of eggs,*" the owl replied promptly.

As Firekeeper knew nothing about the size of a barn owl's clutch, this did her no good. She indicated the group gathered around. "*More than this or the same or fewer?*"

Night's Terror swiveled her head around to assess the company. "*More, but not much more.*"

"*Do they carry weapons?*"

"*Some do,*" the owl replied. "*Some simply walk as if they are weapons—as a puma prowls or a wolf.*"

"*Or an owl flies in the night sky,*" Blind Seer said. He had been sniffing the air, but the wind clearly came from the wrong direction for him to get much good from it. "*Dear heart, I will go and scout. Many of these yarimaimalom know nothing of human ways. Their reports will tell us less than nothing.*"

Truth's tail was lashing. "*I will go with you, wolf. I see nearly as well in the darkness as does an owl.*"

Blind Seer gave a swish of his tail that acknowledged his willingness to have the jaguar as a companion, and then the two loped away.

Night's Terror squinted her eyes nearly shut. Firekeeper knew that Blind Seer's flattery had not soothed the owl's ire at being interrupted. No time now though to smooth ruffled feathers. Firekeeper knew she must give her attention to arraying her pack to best advantage.

"Derian," she said, "humans are coming. Some, perhaps all, are armed. I think we must get the wounded to cover lest they be taken and used as hostages."

Plik broke in. "We also need to make certain they do not get between us and our gate home."

"Can we combine the two needs?" Derian said, already moving toward where Harjeedian had set up a makeshift infirmary. "Bring the wounded into the building, and guard that?"

"Good," Firekeeper said. "You take charge. I need to speak to the yarimaimalom before they scatter."

"You think they'd run?" Derian said.

"I think they would hunt," Firekeeper replied, "and from what we have heard of these Once and Twice Dead, I think the hunters would find what looks like a buck in velvet might have very sharp antlers."

Derian nodded. "I'll take charge here. Try and let me know what's going on."

"I will," Firekeeper promised, wondering how she could manage it. Her gaze fell on Plik. "Are you up to a run?"

The raccoon-man shook his head. "Even at my best, I am not built for running, and I am far from my best."

Firekeeper cast around and saw a great reddish brown bear.

"Would you join us?" she asked. *"My friend here is too weak to run, but he is the only other who can speak both to Beasts and humans. I may need him to carry a message."*

The bear—a she-bear as it turned out—gave Firekeeper a long look from deceptively small eyes.

"I might, but I have been guarding my cubs."

"They will be watched," Firekeeper promised rashly. *"Or they can chase on your heels."*

"Hmm," the bear said. *"Very well. Comb Ripper, Grub Digger, follow me. I'll have your ears and tails if you stray."*

The bear cubs, half-grown already, but slim and stunted from their time in captivity, romped up.

Firekeeper left Plik to arrange the details of his transport. She let her ears and eyes probe the darkness, and almost immediately knew the direction from which the humans were coming.

Blind Seer came loping back, panting a little in excitement. *"There are a fair number,"* he said. *"A few carry bows, but shorter than the one you bear. They carry lanterns, too, so their night sight is ruined. We have the advantage, then."*

Firekeeper nodded. *"But advantage in what? What is it we wish to do?"*

The wolf tilted his head at her, momentarily puzzled. *"Defend ourselves, of course, so we can get home."*

Firekeeper frowned. *"If we are retreating, then, we should not spread ourselves out, racing around like a litter of excited pups. Everyone should get back to the gate. Find the twins. They can begin the opening. When they have done this, then we will send everyone through. Only those who have had the Plague or proven immune may leave the stronghold. The rest of us must remain within."*

The plan sounded good, but some element in it left Firekeeper vaguely uneasy. There was something, maybe several somethings she had overlooked. Yet the sense that the darkness that surrounded her was filled with figures seething toward violence filled Firekeeper with the urgent awareness that she needed to act now, and hope that refinements could come later.

"We should not fight unless we must," she said, hoping this was what she had forgotten. *"Remember that these take power from blood."*

"I will find the twins," Blind Seer promised.

"And I will send out the order to gather back at the gate building," Truth said.

Plik came up, riding directly behind the reddish brown bear's humped shoulders and looking no more awkward than he did on a pony. The half-grown cubs apparently thought the sight amusing, and kept rearing on their back legs to playfully swat at Plik's tail.

"Anything for us?" Plik asked in Pellish.

"Will the others listen and gather?" Firekeeper asked. *"I am not their One to order them here and there."*

"I think they will," the bear replied. *"All we want to do is go home, and you offer a means to do so. The worst offenders will not offend again. If there is a fight, we will fight, but winter is coming on fast, and my children and I need to go fatten ourselves for the long sleep."*

"Then help Truth tell the rest what we're doing," Firekeeper said. *"I will cry like a screech owl if I need Plik to carry some message to the humans."*

When the others had left, Firekeeper continued listening to the sounds of the advancing humans. They were closer now, coming over the rise. They were moving quietly for humans, with only a little jingling of metal and squeaking of leather. As Blind Seer and Truth had reported, they carried lanterns, but these were shielded so that the light fell low and mostly served to illuminate their trail.

Firekeeper bent her bow, stringing it as she tried to think what she had overlooked. She had a full quiver, and since Race Forester had first taught her this art, she had rarely missed her mark, even when shooting at night.

She was trying to gauge the distance between her and the nearest lantern, thinking that shooting it would certainly make the advancing group move even more slowly, when Blind Seer loped up. He was panting hard, and shedding little tufts of fur, a sure sign he was anxious.

"What is it, sweet hunter?" Firekeeper asked.

"The twins are gone," Blind Seer replied.

"Gone?"

"I sought them where we were all meeting. They were not there. The scent trails were muddled with so many coming and going. I found them at last by dropping below the area nearest to the gate building and circling the area. By bad luck, I went the wrong way—I thought they might head in the direction of their former lair, perhaps to bring some forgotten thing away. Never did I think they would head toward those who still believe they are sneaking up on us, undetected."

"They went to the Once Dead?" Firekeeper said, aghast. "They would warn them?"

"They did speak of some who had been kind to them," Blind Seer said. "Perhaps they felt some duty."

"Duty to those who kept them prisoner," Firekeeper growled. "I will show them duty. . . . Can you lead me? We must bring them back before they are with the others, else we will have no one who can open the gate."

There is the Meddler, she thought. *Would he barter for another favor?*

Then she remembered that the Meddler had said he could not reach this place, that it was shielded against such as him. He might have been lying, but that was a slim branch along which to slide her weight.

Blind Seer had indicated his willingness to lead her with a nudge of his nose against her hand. Slinging her bow over her shoulder, Firekeeper followed, and as she trotted after her guide she gave a barn owl's cry. As she had hoped, Night's Terror dropped out of the sky.

"We have been betrayed," Firekeeper said, and succinctly gave the owl the details. "Tell the yarimaimalom. Also tell Plik. He can tell Derian and Harjeedian. Blind Seer and I will go after them. Tell the others to stand ready."

"I will!" the owl said.

"You knew she was close," Blind Seer said. "I am impressed. Even I did not hear her on the wing."

"We damaged her sense of importance," Firekeeper explained with a dry chuckle. "I hoped she might be near, looking to redeem it."

"Now," Firekeeper said, "we can run at speed and possibly intercept the twins before they reach their masters."

"And if we cannot?" Blind Seer asked, breaking into a lope, his nose to the ground so as not to miss a nuance of the trail.

"They are our key to returning to the New World," Firekeeper said. "I suppose, although I would like nothing more than to leave them, we must do what we can to get them back."

XXX

THEY WERE CLOSE ENOUGH now to hear the murmur of human voices, but they had not overtaken the twins.

"Can you make out what they're saying?" Firekeeper asked Blind Seer, knowing the wolf's hearing was far better than her own.

"I can make out words," the wolf said, "but not the sense of them. Another language than the ones we know."

"Humans," Firekeeper commented, not for the first time, "are overly complex when it comes to language. Robins all know each other's songs. Wolves hear howling and understand the nature of the cry. Why do humans need to make communicating with each other so hard?"

Blind Seer glanced up at her, his teeth gleaming in a panting laugh. "For no other reason than to make life difficult for a certain Little Two-legs, no doubt."

Firekeeper kicked at him without pausing in her stride, but the wolf dodged easily. After a time, Blind Seer indicated that they should stop.

"We're too late," he said, letting out his breath in a shuddering sigh. "I cannot understand the words, but I know the voices. Tiniel and Isende are amid those who carry the lanterns."

"Are you sure?" Firekeeper asked. "You have only known them for a short time."

"Long enough," Blind Seer said. "Long enough. It is them."

"How do they sound? What is the note that underlies their words?"

Blind Seer pricked his ears forward to listen more intently. "There is no note. Neither joy nor sorrow. The words come with even rhythm and cadence. That is all."

The pair stood watching the flickering lights, then Blind Seer tossed back his head.

"You see differently than I do, dearest. Take a look. Those lights were holding still, but now . . ."

"They have begun to retreat," Firekeeper replied, "back to where they came from."

"If they take the twins to one of those buildings of which the Meddler spoke," Blind Seer said, "getting them out again alive and in one piece will be very difficult."

"If not impossible," Firekeeper agreed. "They are out in the open," Firekeeper went on after a moment of further consideration. "Here the advantage is ours. Shall we attempt to take back our keys?"

"Just the two of us?"

"I suspect we will not be alone for long," Firekeeper said, "especially if sounds of fighting are heard. Night's Terror should have spread her message by now."

"We need to get close enough that we can cut the twins from the greater herd," Blind Seer said.

"I have an idea how to slow them," Firekeeper said. "Without light, even the bravest humans become very cautious."

She fit arrow to bowstring and took aim. There were six lights there, brighter now, for the humans had clearly decided that they need not hide their retreat as they had their advance.

"What if you miss?" Blind Seer asked. "Your arrow might take out those we seek to rescue."

"Only one," Firekeeper said with calculated brutality. "We only need one of the pair to open the gate. Run light and low, off to one side. See if you can spot our strayed pups and perhaps drag one away."

She drew back the bowstring and aimed at what seemed to be the nearest lantern. Without waiting to see if she had hit, Firekeeper reached for another arrow. Her fingers were on the fletching when she saw heard glass breaking and saw a brilliant yellow-orange flare. Then the lantern was dropped.

She wasn't watching. Her attention was for the next lantern. She got that one and one beyond before the last three pools of light hit the ground and went out, dropped by holders who had finally realized what made them targets. She didn't think any of the arrows' momentum had carried them through and into the clustered group, but from the fuss the humans were now making she couldn't be sure.

"*To me! To me!*" Firekeeper howled, inflecting the call so that Blind Seer would know it was meant for reinforcements, not to bring him back. She heard answering calls, and knew that within moments she and Blind Seer would have a pack that could more than rival the humans milling in the night.

"I have come for the twins!" Firekeeper called out, first in Pellish, then in Liglimosh. "Give them to me and go your way unharmed."

She heard a male voice answer in a language she did not recognize. Then so closely behind that his words overlapped the first speaker, Tiniel spoke.

"You will not have them," Tiniel said, puzzling Firekeeper by this peculiar way of referring to himself. Then she recognized that he was translating for that first voice.

Despite the familiarity of Tiniel's city-state-accented Liglimosh, Firekeeper found the timbre of the young man's voice curiously flat. Something wasn't right here.

"What is to stop us from taking them?" Firekeeper asked defiantly.

"We'll kill them," Isende's voice came, speaking on the heels of a stiff female voice. "We'd prefer to keep them alive. They're interesting, and a true font of knowledge, but rather than give them to you, we will kill them."

Firekeeper's shoulder was suddenly heavier, and Night's Terror spoke.

"*She's not lying. One of the men has a knife to the one's back, another holds a blade to the other.*"

"And if you kill them," Firekeeper said, "what is to keep us from killing you? Be wise. Give us the twins, and walk away with your lives."

Isende spoke again, prefacing her comments with a dry, harsh laugh. "We have done some spying on you in a fashion you could only begin to comprehend, wolfling. We know how you came through the gate, and I do not think that key will work again. We only need to keep you here for a day or so more. Then you will be too ill to do anything to resist us. As I said before, we would prefer to keep the twins alive, but to seal you here, well . . ."

It was strange to hear Isende talk about her own death in such a dispassionate fashion, but the cry that came from Tiniel at that moment was in the youth's own voice.

"*They've cut him,*" Night's Terror said. "*The one who did so is holding a cloth to the wound, but I do not think this is a gesture of compassion. There is a hungry look in his eyes. He likes what he has done, and longs to do more.*"

Something in Firekeeper snapped. She was tired of being clever and patient, of making plans that didn't work out. They needed the twins—either that or she was going to have to torture Ynamynet and Lachen until one or the other would work the spell. Given that choice or an honest fight . . .

She drew back her bowstring, loosed the arrow she'd been holding. It smashed into the one of the shadowy shapes and someone screamed.

"Grab the twins!" she howled, high, fierce, and suddenly terrible.

She felt Night's Terror launch from her shoulder. Dropping her bow onto the ground, Firekeeper sprang forward. The darkness was filled with howls and snarls as the summoned yarimaimalom went with focused intensity after those who had held them prisoner.

Firekeeper's anger went cold as she focused on her purpose. She didn't pause as she saw a man fall, a puma on his chest. Her way was cleared by a hawk who swept down and latched on to the nose of a man who would have put a spear into her.

Blind Seer had arrived at her goal before her. His mouth was locked on Isende's arm, his fangs dimpling her plump flesh. The girl stared at him dreamily. She did not fight, but neither did she make any move to follow when he tugged at her.

Drugged? Firekeeper thought. *Drunk?* If so, there was no reasoning with Isende.

"Drag her," Firekeeper told Blind Seer. Then she saw Plik arriving, mounted on the reddish brown bear. *"Wait! Here's Plik. Let him take her."*

"I'll take care of Isende," Plik said. *"Get Tiniel. I don't like what I saw."*

Firekeeper had been content to let the yarimaimalom handle the fighting, but at Plik's words she spun, casting about for one human male among the shadowed mass.

Most of the Once Dead and their allies were down, not dead, perhaps, but certainly not doing anything that would attract the attention of the prowling beasts. A small group remained standing. These had centered on Tiniel and the man who held him. A lantern had been relit, and in its flickering light Firekeeper located the young man. Instantly, she understood Plik's apprehension.

Spears made a porcupine's screen around the edges of a cluster at whose center stood Tiniel and two people Firekeeper thought must be Once Dead. Arrows threatened any of the wingéd folk who might approach from above. In the middle of this protective circle, Tiniel stood unresisting while a short, fat, snaggletoothed man busily etched an elaborate pattern onto Tiniel's face with the tip of his knife.

The very strangeness of the scene held the yarimaimalom back, rather than the threat offered by the spears and arrows. Alongside the pair who worked on Tiniel, a skeletally thin woman with very dark skin had just begun to sing. Her voice was shrill and piercing, pitched high enough to make Firekeeper's throat ache just from listening.

Blood streamed from a long slice down Tiniel's arm. Every few notes, the singing woman would dip her hand into the red flood. When the blood touched her fingertips it stuck there, and when she raised her fingers to within a few inches of her mouth, the blood steamed.

Firekeeper shook her head, trying to clear the sound of the woman's singing from her ears. Her inner ears felt squashed, as if the pressure which builds before a thunderstorm was building around this group.

Firekeeper had seen enough, and too much. Her Fang was in her hand, but she did not rely upon it to breach the spears. Instead she trusted in her night vision. Knowing that darkness would hide her, she dropped, then rolled beneath the line of spear points. She came up onto her feet inside the circle, knowing that if the spear holders turned their weapons in on her, the waiting yarimaimalom would make sure those weapons were never brought into play.

The four within the circle seemed to be focused on something other than their immediate surroundings. They did not react with any speed to suddenly having an attacker in their midst. Firekeeper, remembering how these people drew power from blood, shifted her grip on her Fang, then hit the singing woman solidly in the mouth. Firekeeper felt teeth break beneath the blow, and the singing abruptly stopped.

The sense of pent-up force did not diminish in the least, but at least the surrounding area was quieter.

Wheeling to her right, Firekeeper now turned her attention to the man who was still tormenting Tiniel. The young man stood under his own power, and like his sister he seemed to lack any will to control his actions. Unlike Isende, Tiniel's expression was not in the least dreamlike. He was in the midst of a nightmare and knew it all too well.

Firekeeper grabbed at the snaggletoothed man's arm, meaning to get that knife away from Tiniel's face. Instead of encountering her target, she came up against something hard as ice. Flecks of light resembling sparks from a fire, if sparks could be a clean, hot metallic violet, scattered across her field of vision. One spark hit the exposed skin of her arm and burnt like salt in an open cut.

As if Firekeeper's blow had focused something that had remained inchoate until this moment, the blood in the elaborate pattern on Tiniel's face began to move, writhing and hissing, then rising in a column of violet steam that coalesced into light.

Firekeeper had learned the danger of lightning from her youngest days, and she sensed that same electrical violence now.

"Down!" she howled. *"Down and away, but down!"*

Then she flung herself forward, knocking Tiniel flat beneath her. In the same motion, Firekeeper kicked out and back with all the strength in her legs. Her feet impacted both of the flesh carver's knees.

Tiniel seemed content to lie still and bleeding, so Firekeeper twisted up and back, balanced on her shoulders, readying another kick. She poised with her legs curled in midstrike. The look of concentration had left the man's features, replaced by a wordless scream as he stared at where the hand wielding the knife had been.

A violet sphere of sparkling, prickly energy had formed around the carver's hand. It raced down the knife blade, devouring the blood, and leaving etched, broken metal to fall to dust and evaporate away.

Then the energy centered on the man's hand, forming a sphere that looked and smelled much like ball lightning. Desperately, the carver tried to shake it loose, but the violet light clung with animal tenacity.

The carver grabbed at the violet light. He tried to pull it off or shape it into some form, but he was rapidly losing any control of whatever it was he had summoned. Apparently the patterns on Tiniel's face, or perhaps the song of the woman who now stood with hands pressed to her mouth, oblivious to anything but the pain of her broken teeth—or perhaps both of these—had been what had kept this energy in focus.

The man could no longer control the close-packed ball of prickly light. It snaked down his arm, over his torso, losing mass, but covering the carver with a cushion of tiny violet pins that probed into his skin, seeking the blood that had been promised, then denied.

The man writhed, twisted, screamed; then he exploded in a starburst of light that colored all the surroundings a lurid purple for one eye-searing moment.

After that, the battle was over but for the taking of prisoners and regathering of Firekeeper's forces, for with that explosion the heart went out of all those who had not already been subdued by the yarimaimalom. Even those who remained in the buildings surrendered meekly when challenged, coming out when Firekeeper threatened to set the buildings afire and leave the gathering-up to the yarimaimalom.

"We've won," Firekeeper said, dropping Tiniel at Harjeedian's feet some time after. "Now, would someone tell me just what it is that we have won?"

I WONDER HOW OFTEN, Plik thought, *victory wears a face that a stranger would take for sure defeat. More often than the ballads tell, of that I feel certain.*

It was midmorning of the day following the night assault on the Nexus Islands. Plik was waiting for his New World allies while they slept. Some of the yarimaimalom were keeping watch over various groups of prisoners. Others watched in each of the gate buildings, whether there were signs the gates had been used or not. Before Firekeeper had sunk into exhausted sleep, she had reminded those of the yarimaimalom who were beginning to chafe under her authority how their rescuers had managed to arrive undetected. That had stopped the protests.

A final group of the yarimaimalom were prowling the island, making sure no one had escaped. In one building they had found a trio of frightened children, whom they returned to their parents. In another they found a defiant pair—lovers, it later turned out—who had slipped away for some private time, only to awaken to a changed order. Otherwise, it seemed that the surrender of the Once Dead and their allies had been complete.

The reason for the completeness of this surrender was becoming clearer, and Plik longed for his allies to awaken so that he could explain. However, he knew it was essential that they rest fully. There were too many decisions to make, and these too critical for them to be made by an increasingly exhausted and irritable cadre.

And there was querinalo to consider. Judging from what he had learned, they probably had at least a full day before the fevers would begin. Plik had located Zebel, the doctor who had treated him. He convinced the man to treat the new conquerors. Indeed, this proved simpler to do than Plik had anticipated, and it was from Zebel that Plik had also learned the reasons for the willing surrender of so many.

Eshinarvash, who had slept standing and half alert as wild horses did, was the first to awaken, followed soon thereafter by Derian.

Plik found himself wondering how Derian would feel once querinalo had destroyed his singular rapport with horses, yet surely that was the young man's only choice. Who would choose death or disfigurement to keep a mere talent?

Derian had been sleeping on a bedroll inside what they all now thought of as "their" gate building. Warmer clothes had been found for all of them, but Derian looked disheveled and mismatched in the heavy, midthigh-length sheepskin jacket he now wore over trousers of a heavy, dark blue fabric.

"Any of the others up?" Derian asked, gratefully accepting the steaming mug of broth Plik handed him.

Eshinarvash snorted at him, and Derian grinned. "I meant other than the obvious," he said. "I saw Harjeedian's nose peeking out of his bedroll, but no one else."

"The others found the building too enclosing," Plik said, "and chose to sleep out-of-doors. I suspect they will all arrive soon. Are you certain you had enough rest?"

"I'm not sure I'll ever feel like I've had enough rest," Derian said, something of the tight, tense look returning to his features, "but I know I'm not going to sleep any more right now. How are our prisoners behaving?"

Plik was partway through a report when Firekeeper and Blind Seer arrived, Truth a few steps behind. Roused by the sound of voices, Harjeedian came out of his bedroll. When Plik had assured him that the yarimaimalom were doing well, the aridisdu was more than happy to settle by the fire with a mug of hot broth.

In addition to the broth, there were fresh fish ready to go in the pan for breakfast, along with a nice porridge taken from the cookhouse stores. There'd been a barrel of apples as well, hardly touched with storage shriveling, and so they dined quite well.

"I've learned something about why so many surrendered last night," Plik said, "and why they are being such model prisoners now."

"Tell," Firekeeper said, spitting fish bones into the fire. "I think they are scared."

"That's certainly part of it," Plik agreed, "but it's not the whole. Remember what Isende and Tiniel told us about the Once and Twice Dead—how they're not exactly welcome even in their homelands? Well, it seems that most of our captives are, in fact, Twice Dead or Never Lived."

"I really don't like those terms," Derian said.

"I don't either," Plik agreed, "but I'd like to stay with them for now."

Derian nodded. "They're just so . . . so nasty."

"Exactly," Plik said. "Nasty. Consider the disdain they show for those who either gave up their magic or never had any. They explain a lot about the mind-set of this community. The Once Dead had power, and so they remained on top. The Twice Dead are the ones I pity—and not because that's where I would be ranked. They are exiles from their own birth lands, yet, in the place in which they have been forced to make their homes, they are classified as failures."

"I understand," Firekeeper said, and Plik knew her empathy came from feeling herself a wolf, but forever being separated from the people to whom she felt closest. "No belonging in either place. Not so bad for the Never Lived. Why they here anyhow?"

"Mostly because of some tie to one of the other two groups. Some are spouses. Some are children born to Once or Twice Dead parents who have never known any other life. A few are parents or siblings who went into exile rather than lose one they loved. But I wander from the point, though less than you might imagine.

"Among those who lived here on the Nexus Islands, the ones who rose to positions of authority were"—Plik reached up and touched the shaved side of his face—"not nice people at all. They had redeemed their images of themselves by viewing themselves as far better than anyone else. This ruthlessness came to extend even to their own small community. In addition to experimenting with the gates, they were working to expand their knowledge of blood magic. Since they did not have a bountiful donor like Eshinarvash, you can guess from where they were taking the blood."

"Their own people," Blind Seer said, shaking as he would to remove water from his coat.

"Their own people," Plik said, both in agreement and in translation. "Occasionally, they would take prisoners, but they didn't wish to make themselves too suspect in the lands where they had associates."

"I don't imagine that they made themselves too loved among their own people," Derian said. "Is that why so many surrendered?"

"That," Plik agreed, "and one other thing. When Firekeeper interfered with that spell, it seems she did more harm than she imagined. I can't claim to understand how blood magic works, but Zebel told me an interesting detail related to that one spell. It seems that the man and woman who were working it were only two of those who were intended to be able to use the final effect."

"And that was?" Truth interrupted.

Again Plik phrased his reply so it would translate the question.

"The spell they were preparing was meant to enable them to channel some form of electricity."

Harjeedian's eyebrows went up. "You mean the sorcerers of old really could throw lightning? I always thought that a storyteller's exaggeration."

"I can't be sure," Plik said. "In this case, it might have been more like a personal shield."

"I touched something that blocked me," Firekeeper said. "Maybe this spell then."

She looked distinctly unsettled by the thought.

"Well, as the doctor explained things," Plik said, "the initial stages of the spell had been prepared in advance, and one of the preparations had been a solution in which the blood of those who would be using the spell was already mingled. When the spell went wrong, its effect was most noticeable around the caster, but apparently wherever they were, the most powerful of the Once Dead died as their blood was replaced by this electricity."

"I'm not sure I understand," Eshinarvash said. *"It seems a poor protection that kills the one it is meant to protect."*

"The spell didn't work as intended," Plik explained. "Initially, they planned to use one of their own to provide the blood to power the spell, but when they took Tiniel back, they thought to use him as an object lesson about the penalties for defiance, and in the hope that any attacker would stop and negotiate to preserve Tiniel's life."

"Seems risky," Derian said dubiously. "I mean, they were under attack."

"You forget," Plik said, "they had no idea the extent of the danger they were in. They thought *they* were the attackers, that they were in control of the situation. Who knows? If they had completed their spell, they might have been."

Derian looked at the scars the out-of-control lightning had left on the landscape and nodded. Plik went on.

"When Firekeeper broke Tiniel from the sorcerer's grasp before the spell was completed, the spell had too much momentum to simply disintegrate. It found power where it could—and in this case, that was in those who would have used it at no cost to themselves."

"Nasty," Firekeeper said, "and I am glad that they died from their own working. Still, I am not sure that Tiniel should have been saved—not after he and Isende betrayed us."

"I have information about that, too," Plik said. "You and Blind Seer both mentioned how Tiniel and Isende seemed to lack the will to resist. We had to drag Isende away, not because she was fighting us, but because she couldn't be made to move on her own. You told how Tiniel just stood there while patterns were carved into his face. I don't think Tiniel and Isende meant to betray us. I think they were drawn away by sorcery."

Derian and Harjeedian looked inclined to be convinced, but Firekeeper remained stony-faced, unyielding in her conviction.

"Earlier that same day," Plik said, "I saw the twins used as translators for the Once Dead. They seemed to understand many different languages, languages I don't think they've had time to learn. Moreover, later, when I asked Isende for her opinion of the interrogation, she was deeply upset and admitted to remembering nothing at all."

Firekeeper's expression was softening. "I hear something like that, too. When first I spoke with the Once Dead and told them to give us the twins, they answered, but Isende and Tiniel translated and their voices were very—even too—calm."

Firekeeper looked happier now, and Plik thought with relief that she had no more liked believing the twins were traitors than he had.

"You put them in their cottage," she said, "with ravens and owls to watch over them. I am glad."

Plik knew that by "glad," Firekeeper meant glad that Plik had halted her initial impulse, which had been to give the pair a very wolfish battering to remind them of the consequences of their actions.

"Are the twins in control of their own minds again?" Derian asked.

"I think so," Plik said. "Onion and I escorted Zebel there this morning so he could look at Tiniel's injuries. The twins were badly upset by what had been done to them, but able to talk and reason."

"*So,*" Truth said with a long and luxurious yawn that showed every sharp and deadly fang, "*did any of the Once Dead survive this spell-storm?*"

"Several of the Once Dead did survive," Plik said. "Three who are, essentially, minimally talented. They did not practice sorcery as such, and were viewed as hardly better than the Twice Dead—or so I am told. Two others survived as well—our prisoners, Lachen and Ynamynet. Either the spell-storm or the yarimaimalom accounted for the rest."

"There are still a whole lot of people to deal with," Derian said. The tense expression, which had faded during Plik's report, had now returned. "I might as well say it up front and get it over with. I can't stomach the idea of slaughtering all these people. I'm sorry, but I can't. I'm no coward, but . . ."

He gave up trying to articulate his feelings and shrugged.

Firekeeper leaned over and patted Derian on the arm. "I don't want to do this either," she said. "Killing just to kill, to prevent possible wrong someday . . . it may be wise, but it is still not right."

Derian looked relieved. "But what are we going to do?" he asked. "We can't just leave them here, can we?"

Plik interrupted, knowing that the time had come for him to raise an issue that had been bothering him since they first began discussing their return to the New World.

"I don't think we can," he said. "That isn't the important issue though."

All eyes had turned on him. Plik went on, hearing his own voice rise with a passion that had been growing since he first realized the implication of these Nexus Islands.

"Not only can't we just leave these people here," he said, "we can't leave this place in other hands. We must take the Nexus Islands and we must hold them, or all we care about will be doomed."

XXXI

DERIAN INSTANTLY UNDERSTOOD the logic behind Plik's statement, but it didn't stop it from shocking him. He decided he was getting royally tired of being shocked.

Firekeeper was looking stubborn again, and Derian didn't think Plik should be stuck with explaining to her yet again why the course of events couldn't be as neat and tidy as she desired.

"It makes sense," Derian said aloud. "I mean, we can go back, and we can do everything we can think of to make sure the gate in the twins' ancestral stronghold is jammed so no one can ever open it again, but that doesn't solve the bigger problem."

"Bigger problem?" Firekeeper asked, glancing at Blind Seer. Derian wondered what the wolf had been saying.

"The bigger problem," Derian said, "that we know there are other gates from the Old World into the New. I counted eight buildings in this circle. From what the Meddler told us, the gates into the New World were all put in one place. That means there are at least seven other points from here that end up somewhere in the New World. Think about that for a moment."

Firekeeper did, and from her expression it was evident she didn't like the implications one bit.

"Not all in city-states, either," she said, "but probably one in each colony."

"That's how I see it," Plik said, "and the current nations in the New World don't match the old colonies, not precisely. At least that's what I've gathered.

Liglim pretty much has the same borders, but Hawk Haven and Bright Bay were originally parts of one colony."

Derian nodded, "And I've never quite figured out how things were divided up south of the Fox River. Stonehold has two dominant peoples, but I think there might have been more than two colonies there. New Kelvin says it used to own the area that's now Waterland. Do we count that as one or two colonies?"

Harjeedian frowned. "And if some of the materials in our libraries are to be taken as factual, rather than allegorical, the New World, as we term it, was probably more than one landmass. There may be areas out there with which we have completely lost touch. The Old Country rulers didn't like their colonists to know too much about anything that might diminish reliance on their founders."

"Think about what would happen," Derian said, looking at Firekeeper, "if a gate opened up in New Kelvin. Horse! The thaumaturges would probably declare a major festival. The sodalities would probably tell Toriovico to resign his rulership. I don't even want to think about what would happen next."

Truth licked a paw and Firekeeper said, obviously in partial translation, "So if we leave these gates here, it is like standing faithful watch at one side of a rabbit's burrow when the rabbit has gone out another hole."

"Gone out the other side," Derian said forcefully, "turned into a puma and come around to pounce on your unprotected backside. Plik's right. We've got to hold this place. Worse, we've got to understand it."

"Worse?" Harjeedian said with a dry laugh.

"Worse," Derian said, "because understanding it is going to mean understanding magic, and understanding magic is going to mean spending time with people who, quite frankly, make me want to vomit whenever I look at them and remember the things they've either participated in or at least let go on without interfering."

"Worse," Harjeedian agreed. "I see your point."

Completely unexpectedly, Firekeeper said, "I rather like Ynamynet, at least a little."

Derian gaped at the wolf-woman. "She tried to strand you! She would have killed you if she could have managed."

"Yes," Firekeeper agreed, "but she was very brave in how she do this. She risk having herself killed, and she take this risk without any help. She offer herself for her people's good. This is a wolf thing. I understand it. I like her a little because I can see a little how she thinks."

"You will never stop amazing me," Derian said with a sigh. "Next thing I know, you'll be telling me you want to adopt Lachen."

"Not adopt," Firekeeper said, "but maybe we can work with him. The Meddler tell me that Lachen is less brave than someone with his size might seem. These two are sorcerers. They are alive. Let us learn what we can about them before we talk to them, though. Plik, will this doctor talk more?"

"Zebel is trying rather desperately to show me that there are people here worth preserving," Plik said. "I think he will tell us anything we ask—although I would not count on him to bring up the worst about anyone. What is it we need to know?"

"About where they are from," Firekeeper replied. "Not the where of body, but the where of inside, of the heart. Like I am wolf . . ."

Plik nodded reassurance. "I understand. We need to know more about Ynamynet and Lachen's lives, what brought them here, if they are among the ones who have family or children in the community."

"Right," Firekeeper said, relieved. "Family would be good to know about. I not want to do hostage taking, but if that is a way to make behave, then we must, but maybe we can find some other hold."

Plik said, "Truth has raised an interesting point. She says, 'Let us look at their lairs as well—before we let them return to them. Remember Dantarahma? Remember what was found after he had gone? Sometimes humans give away a great deal with what they keep, what they hide.' "

"Good thinking," Firekeeper agreed.

Derian rubbed his temples. Ever since he had awakened, he'd had a touch of a headache. It was probably nothing more than the end result of too little sleep, but he wondered if it might be a sign of the onset of querinalo.

"I hate to bring this up," Derian said, "but if Plik's predictions are right, before long some of us are going to be very, very ill. Do we try and get back to the stronghold, or do we weather the illness here?"

Plik wrinkled the tip of his nose in a fashion that made him look distinctly raccoon-like.

"How exactly did you plan on opening the gate to get back? You did have a plan for this, didn't you?"

Derian frowned. "We did. We figured that since the twins had opened the gate at least once, they could open it again."

"There's a problem with that," Plik said. "Querinalo. I'm not sure the twins still possess the ability to make the gates work."

❧

FIREKEEPER WAS RELIEVED when the others agreed that theorizing among themselves was not the best way to resolve this new complication, not when the twins could be brought forward and given a chance to speak.

She also wanted an opportunity to take a look at the pair by daylight, and to learn what messages the beasts would read in their sweat.

"Let's go," Firekeeper said, "and talk with these two."

Eshinarvash said, *"I am a little large to fit into a cottage. Let me remain here and make certain our allies do not get ambitious in our absence."*

When the others arrived at the cottage, Bitter agreed with Eshinarvash's caution. *"Lovable and I will join Eshinarvash. Not only do our allies bear watching, but the humans do as well."*

The rest crowded through the wrought-iron gate, awakening the blood briars in the hedge into writhing motion. Firekeeper could see that Derian was torn between simply opening the cottage door and knocking as would be polite. The one would signal their distrust of the twins; the other might leave them in some doubt as to their status.

Before Derian could decide, the choice was taken from him. Isende opened the door and motioned for them all to enter. Tiniel, his face covered with a webwork of red tracery, stood near the hearth.

"It's warmer in here," she said. "Tiniel has just built up the fire."

That last might have been meant as a gesture of courtesy, but once all of them had crowded into the cottage's front room, they created heat enough.

"Tea?" Isende said, indicating a kettle on the hob.

Before she could go further with these social gestures, Firekeeper, seated back by a window she had opened so Blind Seer would not be too warm, spoke up: "Can you two open the gate anymore?"

Neither twin pretended they couldn't understand, and they answered almost as one.

"I don't think so," Isende said.

"It's like querinalo burned away a sense," Tiniel added.

"Forever?" Firekeeper pressed. "Maybe it will get better again?"

"Forever," Tiniel said bluntly, but Isende's reply was different.

"I'm not sure. I feel as if I kept some small . . . I don't know what to call it . . . Gem? Kernel? In any case, some small bit of ability might still be alive, buried deep inside. I remember sending the fires up around it, feeling a hard, glittering core preserved, maybe even refined, in all that heat."

The twins had been standing side by side in the area closest to the hearth, united against their interrogators, but now Tiniel spun and glowered at his sister.

"What? You never told me any of this!"

Isende stuck out her chin defiantly. "You were so upset. I didn't think it would make you happy. Has it?"

Firekeeper had the feeling that Tiniel at least had forgotten there was anyone else present. She remembered how the aridisdu in Gak had told them that the twins grew up being able to communicate their feelings without speaking aloud. She wondered if Tiniel had forgotten that the situation had changed.

"How could I be happy?" he said. "I remember what we had. I remember feeling the fires coming. I remember feeling your pain almost as if it was my own, but that didn't matter because we were united against whatever came. We might die together, but that didn't matter. Then . . ."

He stopped speaking, but the expression in his eyes grew wilder and wilder, as if he was remembering something that had been vague until this moment.

Isende prompted him, her tone cool and a touch mocking. "Yes? Yes, Tin. What then?"

"Then I felt a change," the young man said, the words coming in a rush, becoming staccato. "The heat . . . It began to . . . change? No, that isn't right. It didn't so much change as . . . move. For the first time in my life I didn't feel you. Where you had been was heat. Fever heat. Burning . . . surging through that intimacy. I felt like my heart was shriveling. I tried to drive it back. I tried to find you again, but there was always the heat where you should be. I tried to drive it back!"

The last phrase was shouted. Isende replied very, very quietly.

"I didn't. And you know why, Tin. You know why. I fed that fire, and I'm glad."

Tiniel looked at his sister, his eyes, so like hers, widening in horror and comprehension.

"But, 'Sende. I never meant anything wrong. I . . ."

Isende shook her head, a hard motion, direct as a slap. Tiniel shut his mouth, pressing his lips together so hard that they turned white against the brown of his skin. His agonized gaze remained locked on his sister, but she had turned her attention to the fascinated group who had listened to this interchange without sound or breath.

Isende spoke as if there had been no interruption.

"Despite this 'gem,' " she said, "I don't think I can work the gates. Not now, at least. Maybe later. Maybe someday."

Her tone had become dreamy with contemplation. Now she shook her head.

"But not now. Not soon, even. Tiniel and I wouldn't have managed what we did without the notes we found."

Derian was looking at Isende as if seeing her for the first time. "The Once Dead took those?"

"They did," Isende said with a bitter smile. "Took those and our freedom. Now, I've answered one of your questions. Would you answer one of ours?"

Firekeeper gave an answer that wasn't really an agreement, although she could tell Isende took it for one.

"What is the question?"

"What are you going to do with us?" Isende asked.

Plik replied with a question of his own. "How do you explain your deserting us to rejoin the Once Dead?"

Isende shrugged her round shoulders.

"I can't. Not really. I can tell you what I think happened, but I don't know, not for sure."

"Try," Plik suggested.

"I think that the Once Dead had put some sort of controlling spell on us. They did a lot of things to us when they first caught us—when we were so stupid as to walk right into their arms. I think they'd set some sort of sign or signal so that if they whistled, we'd come running like bird dogs to their master."

"And you think that's what happened," Plik pressed.

"I do," Isende said. She looked at her brother for the first time since ending their argument. "What do you think, Tin?"

The young man shook himself, as a dog might when waking from a deep sleep.

"I don't know what to think," he said softly, and Firekeeper wasn't at all certain he meant about the Once Dead. Then his tone became more direct. "All I can add to Isende's theory is that I have no memory of leaving that place where we were talking to you. I remember the fox. I remember Firekeeper saying something about people coming. I remember more animals than I had realized were near suddenly coming into the light. I remember someone asking if we could help move a few things into the gate building. That's it. After that, I remember nothing until there was noise and this brilliant violet light, and we were being hustled back to this cottage without a word of explanation."

Blind Seer gave a low laugh. *"That's quite a lot of 'not remembering,' but I will tell you this. Tiniel smells of many things, including something like rage, but there is none of the fear stink that so often comes when humans lie. If this one lies, he does it without compunction. I could believe that of the Meddler, but not of this one."*

Firekeeper agreed. She switched to Pellish in order to tell Derian and Har-jeedian what Blind Seer had said, then returned to Liglimosh to question the twins.

"How long until this querinalo comes?"

"My guess," Tiniel said with a bitter laugh, "is you'll be feeling the fever by tomorrow at this time."

Isende nodded agreement.

Firekeeper turned to her companions. "Then we have much to do before then. Let us set about making all secure."

"What about us?" Tiniel asked. "You haven't answered our question. What about us?"

Firekeeper looked at him in cool calculation. "Talk to us after querinalo has run its course. When we know who live or die, then we know what to do with you."

"Then we stay here?" Tiniel asked. "We stay locked up, just like always?"

"Why not?" Firekeeper said.

Before she could add anything further, Derian surprised Firekeeper by ask-ing Isende, "Would that be all right for you? Would you maybe like to move your things into the other cottage—the one Plik had?"

Isende shook her head, a small, tight smile making her seem suddenly quite old.

"I'll be fine," she said, "but I would like to suggest that if you're going to leave us locked up, you might want to move whoever comes down with queri-nalo here. Tiniel and I know a little about nursing those with the disease. Right, Plik?"

Plik nodded. "They do. I can testify to that. Really, this would be the best place I can think of."

Harjeedian interjected, "What about the buildings where the Once Dead lived? We have moved the survivors all into the building they were using as headquarters. It wouldn't have been my first choice, but not many of them were living there, so it was easy to search. Now they're crowded, but at least we can keep them guarded. The relocation leaves many other empty buildings we could use."

"We haven't had a chance to search those other buildings," Plik said. "I, for one, wouldn't feel comfortable using one of their residences as a refuge until we could make certain they didn't have any amulets or some such thing hidden that they could use against us. The few hours we have left aren't going to be enough."

Harjeedian nodded. "I have spoken to the doctor here in passing. Let me do so now in more detail."

"I'll go and review our prisoners," Derian said. "Plik, you'd better come with me. Once Firekeeper and I are down, playing jailer is going to be up to you and the yarimaimalom. You may have the advantage on me when it comes to your ability to talk to them, but I don't see how that's going to give you extra hands."

"Right," Plik said.

One by one, the members of the company moved to various jobs. Firekeeper found herself deputized to bring blankets and bedding that could be used to transform the cottages into a makeshift hospital. There were small donkeys in one of the stables, along with carts and harness. Firekeeper threatened one of the terrified creatures into service so she wouldn't need to carry load after load.

Blind Seer walked with her, just out of the range of the donkey's rolling eye, his mere presence coaxing the stubborn beast into unwonted cooperation.

Normally, Firekeeper would have been amused, but thoughts of the ordeal to come haunted her, keeping her from enjoying the present moment. Blind Seer left off his teasing of the donkey.

"Are you frightened, dear heart?" he asked gently.

She didn't try to pretend otherwise.

"Everyone seems so certain I will be among those to fall," she said, "but I do not feel magical."

"You are different from other humans," the wolf said, his gentleness unfailing.

"But I am a wolf, and my heart is a wolf's. Nothing that I do would be impossible for a wolf," Firekeeper protested, then added for fairness' sake, "at least if the wolf had hands and walked upright."

"Like the Meddler does in your visions," Blind Seer said. "I envy him."

It was the first time he had raised the matter directly. Firekeeper did not evade the scent of rivalry as a human might have done, but she gave the matter a twist no human would have anticipated.

"I envy him as well," she said. "He has almost everything I want."

"Almost?" Blind Seer asked.

"Well," Firekeeper said with a smile, "for one, he doesn't have you."

QUERINALO CAME THE NEXT DAY, as Zebel had predicted. First to be touched was the jaguar Truth. Midmorning, Bitter and Lovable brought a report to where Firekeeper and Blind Seer were talking with some of the others near the cottages where their field camp had been moved.

"Truth has found herself an isolated place near where a freshwater spring comes from the rock," Bitter said. "She says she will bite the first person to move her from it."

"I don't think she wants nursing," Lovable said, hopping and flapping her wings. "Do you think she can survive without it?"

Plik shrugged, "Truth has been mad and sane and near mad again. If anyone can cope with the hallucinations that come with querinalo, then it is she."

When told of Truth's decision, Isende admitted rather shamefacedly that she was relieved.

"Even Plik was difficult to handle at times," she said, "and his claws are not made for rending—not in the same way. Truth may be thinking of us as much as of anyone else."

Firekeeper nodded. "I think so, too. Truth knows how deadly she is, and how dangerous she can be in madness."

Derian was the next to fall ill, the symptoms coming on him some hours later. He grew quieter and quieter, but it was not until he began speaking to his younger sister, Damita, telling her how he missed her, that his friends realized he was already engulfed in the early hallucinations.

Firekeeper herded Derian into Plik's bed, knocking the tall redhead flat with little effort. Then, Blind Seer beside her, she went running for Zebel.

"Why didn't you smell the fever on Derian?" she asked Blind Seer reproachfully.

The blue-eyed wolf said nothing for several paces; then he looked at her with blank, unseeing eyes.

"I don't like this place," he said with flattened ears and drooping tail. Then he collapsed in midstride.

Firekeeper dropped beside him, lifted her head toward the sky, and howled.

Help came in four-legged droves, but none but Firekeeper could lift the enormous wolf. She might have been able to carry Blind Seer, but not without adding injuries to the fever that had brought him low.

Harjeedian came with the donkey cart, and helped Firekeeper lift and slide Blind Seer onto the boards.

"Can you get him to the cottage?" he asked. "I'll go for the doctor."

"Not need," Firekeeper said hoarsely. "There."

Zebel was coming, herded by a group of yarimaimalom that included a fox, a doe, and a bear. A golden eagle soared overhead, watchful, but the doctor showed no sign of deserting his trust.

"I'm not a veterinarian," Zebel began, hoisting himself onto the wagon bed and beginning to examine Blind Seer. "I know mostly about treating humans."

Firekeeper snarled at the donkey, who began trotting at a fair clip despite her burden. Firekeeper paced alongside, near enough to keep the donkey on course, while remaining near to Zebel. Thus far his examination matched those she had seen in the past, and she felt a certain amount of relief.

"But you know how to doctor for wolves?" she asked.

"A little," Zebel said. "There were a few in our number with better skills than mine in animal medicine. I haven't seen them since your group's, uh, assumption of administration, but one of them might be better able to treat your companion than I."

"Women?" Firekeeper asked. "Three, living in house near where yarimaimalom were kept?"

"That's right," Zebel agreed. He'd peeled Blind Seer's upper lip back and was examining the gum.

"Not here anymore," Firekeeper said tersely.

Zebel glanced at her as if he was about to ask for clarification, took one look at her face, and hurriedly returned his attention to Blind Seer.

"Well," he said, "I can do something. The important thing is trying to keep the fever down. Unhappily, when the fever rises, that's when the hallucinations are worse. Is someone willing to take the risk to sit with the wolf and do what needs to be done to tend the fever?"

"I will be with him," Firekeeper said.

Zebel glanced at her. "Forgive me, but I was told who were most likely to be my patients. Your name headed the list."

"I will be with Blind Seer," Firekeeper repeated stubbornly. "No matter."

The doctor sighed but said nothing more. Evidently, he thought it a waste of breath to argue with one who was clearly already suffering from the irrationalities of querinalo.

Firekeeper snorted. She felt fine. Maybe a little warm, but then she had done a great deal of running already that day. True the weather was cool, but she did not think she was feverish. She resisted the impulse to touch her fore-head as she had seen others do. Even contemplating the possibility that she could become ill might give the illness entry.

"I am fine," she said, and almost believed herself.

Plik met them at the gateway into the pair of cottages. The eagle perched on the gate, snapping at the blood briar vines that were trying to snare him, gave explanation for Plik's readiness.

"We're going to put Blind Seer in the same room as Derian," Plik said. "There's plenty of space, near . . ."

Firekeeper raised her eyebrows, daring Plik to finish his statement, which almost certainly would have been "near to where we've prepared a bed for you."

Plik looked at her and concluded, "Near one of the windows."

"Good," Firekeeper said.

"I've brought a heavy blanket we can use as a stretcher," Plik went on, "if you take one end, and Harjeedian the other."

Harjeedian, forgotten to this moment, came from behind where he had fol-lowed the donkey cart. Together they eased the unconscious but restive wolf onto the blanket. Firekeeper stayed close to Blind Seer's head. She wouldn't have blamed Harjeedian if he had dropped his share of the weight if Blind Seer had snapped at him. The wolf's fangs were very sharp, and his jaws could crack bone.

Isende and Tiniel watched in anxious silence as Blind Seer was carried in and made as comfortable as possible. Zebel took advantage of the delay to ex-amine Derian. The young man was tossing restlessly on his bed, talking in Pellish to people who weren't there.

"He was fairly lucid not long ago," Isende said. "I managed to get him to drink a good amount then—and he kept most of it down."

"You know what to do," Zebel said, "and this time I will be able to be here to assist."

Firekeeper found this statement, with the implication that Zebel had been prevented from attending more closely to Plik during the maimalodalu's ill-ness, interesting. Then again, Zebel might be licking the jaw of those he now saw as Ones. Humans were no less inclined to do such groveling than wolves. They were simply less honest about when they did it.

Blind Seer seemed to be coming conscious. He lifted his head, then rolled onto his breastbone and balanced there. The gaze of his blue eyes seemed truly blind now, casting about the room, fastening on things that Firekeeper could not see, looking through most of those present. He saw Firekeeper though, and nuzzled her hand when she sat beside him.

"*Can you drink, dear heart?*" Firekeeper asked anxiously. "*The doctor says you should drink as much as possible to combat the fires fever will set in your blood.*"

"*I will drink,*" the wolf replied, and tried to struggle to his feet. He could not, and Firekeeper held the bowl in her lap, ignoring how his sloppy lapping spilled water all over her.

When he had finished, Blind Seer slowly collapsed back onto his side, but he did not sleep.

"*Where are we, Firekeeper?*" he asked.

"*On the island with the gates,*" she replied. "*Do you remember?*"

"*I remember, but instead of salt air and stone I seem to smell the forests where we were born. It is summer there, early summer. The leaves are soft, giving shade and coloring the light in hues of green. There is moss underfoot, or soft duff. I am chasing a certain Little Two-legs, who runs surprisingly fast for being so hampered by her odd gait. Of course, she has the annoying habit of climbing trees.*"

"*I think,*" Firekeeper said, stroking along the bridge of his nose, "*you are remembering when you were a puppy. That's the last time I could run faster than you, when you were a fat little fur ball. Climbing, though, there I still have the better of you.*"

"*You have the better of me in so many things,*" the wolf replied. "*Those hands are marvelous—especially once you found human tools and skills to fit them. It seems there is nothing you cannot do. You can even hunt better than I can.*"

Firekeeper bent and kissed the wolf on one ear. "*Not hunt. Never hunt. Kill . . . perhaps. Certain kinds of kills. Coward kills from a distance. That I have learned. But you have the ears that can hear a butterfly landing on a rose petal. You have the nose that can tell you past as well as present. You can never be stripped of your abilities, but I can be stripped of my tools.*"

Blind Seer said nothing in reply. At first, Firekeeper thought he was thinking over what she had said. Then she looked to where his paws were moving just a little, but in a pattern clearly recognizable as that of running, and she knew that he had gone somewhere she couldn't follow.

Was he running in the forests of their childhood? Was he reliving one of their journeys? Was he somewhere that was real only in his own mind?

Plik had recounted how during his own illness he had met the Meddler, and spoken with him. Firekeeper wondered if Blind Seer would also meet that strange person, and if so what they would speak about. She had the distinct impression Blind Seer did not like the Meddler one bit. She was honest enough to admit that part of the reason for this was the Meddler's interest in her—and hers in him as well.

Oh, sweet hunter, my best and dearest friend, Firekeeper thought, *wherever you run, remember to turn your paws and find the trail that will bring you back to me.*

XXXII

TRUTH STRETCHED OUT IN A FRESHWATER streamlet that overflowed from a patch she'd found where the groundwater ran just below the surface—not quite a spring, but almost. Normally the water here seeped away through the porous, rocky soil. Now the jaguar's bulky body dammed the clear liquid, soaking it up, cooling her against the heat of querinalo.

Truth didn't feel well at all, but she wasn't about to go creeping down to those stone-walled cottages and have some feather-skinned human try to tend to her. Truth had enough guilt on her conscience without adding killing or maiming someone who was just trying to help.

Much had been made of the responsibility the Liglimom took toward the yarimaimalom. Less was said of the responsibility those same yarimaimalom took toward "their" humans. Truth had been reared with not merely the expectation, but—courtesy of her ability to read omens—the knowledge that in most time streams she would someday serve as jaguar of her year. She had grown to adulthood feeling a certain arrogant awareness of how fragile humans were, and a realization that if she were to serve the deities as their voice she must learn to accept human fragility.

So now Truth lay in a spreading puddle, hallucinations treading about the verges of her awareness, trying to decide whether living or dying was the better option.

So far her hallucinations had been mild. Truth had considerable experience telling reality from possibility, so she didn't even find the visions of the tangled forests of Misheemnekuru through which she now prowled particularly disorienting. Rather she welcomed them as she welcomed the coolness of the water in which she repeatedly dipped the hot leather of her nose.

Her mother came to talk with her, leaping down from the boughs of a moss-shrouded oak.

"Your friends are worried about you, fur ball," Mother said, licking damp earth from one of her front paws. "Do you see them watching you from the trees?"

Truth did. The raven pair, Bitter and Lovable, had kept a steady but non-intrusive watch since Truth had gone to ground. She had also glimpsed the white-faced barn owls, Night's Terror and Golden Feather, and thought she knew who would take over the watch come dark.

"What does their worry matter?" Truth asked. "It's not going to change what I do."

Mother studied her paw critically, noticed a speck of dirt still remaining, then began to lick it again. She'd always been a very clean cat.

"And what are you going to do?" she asked, starting on the other paw.

By reflex, Truth started to reach out and read the various omens to guide her to one choice or another. Then she pulled back. Madness was far, far too close here. If she ventured into unreality, especially when cloaked within hallucination, she might never return.

Truth pulled back, and when she did, her mother was no longer there. Truth remained in the forest, though, nestled in a damp space beneath a cluster of honeysuckle in early spring flower. A stream chattered over rocks within reach of her paw and little, bright, slim-sided fish darted between the rocks, sliding with the current.

Not in the least hungry, Truth watched the fish dance for a while. Not even the lumbering advent of a snapping turtle, usually one of her favorite foods, could draw her from the comfortable languor that was seeping into her bones. Deep down, if she chose to probe beneath the hallucination, Truth could tell that her body was suffering badly from fever. He joints ached. Her nose was dry. Even the folds of her ears hurt.

Truth plunged her nose into the stream. The fish scattered, and the snapping turtle did its best to become a rock. Truth rewarded them for speed and stealth by leaving them to their cold wet lives, but she couldn't resist using the snapping turtle's shell as a stepping-stone when she rose from her honeysuckle bower and went to follow a faint game trail.

She didn't remember the trail being there before, but now it called to her. She padded along it, going up from the declivity the stream had followed, along a slope so thick with duff that she didn't even need to watch her step. Everything was so lusciously damp that Truth couldn't have broken a twig if she'd tried.

(Deep inside, Truth knew the fever was bad now, so bad that someone had gone to the trouble of dumping water on her. She suspected the ravens. They'd find the act funny, as well as virtuous, a combination they couldn't resist. Truth tried to care enough even to be insulted, but she couldn't. That reality was too far away.)

She padded on, rising with the slope. Sunlight dappled down through the trees, warming her spots. She heard a sound from upslope and angled toward it. It was a warm sound, a deep sound, one that comforted her, easing a loneliness she hadn't wanted to admit was present until she had the remedy.

The ground underfoot was changing, the duff giving way to thick grass, soft as springtime, thick as midsummer when the rains were heaviest. The grass felt good underfoot, springing back when she passed so that even her weight left not the faintest of traces.

She was a spirit passing over, leaving even less impression than did the wind.

(Truth wondered if she was indeed a spirit. Her body seemed very far away now. She could hardly feel the heat, couldn't feel the pain.)

Truth followed the sound until it resolved into voices joined in easy conversation. She followed until she knew the voices. Three. All male. All familiar.

She arched her neck and sniffed the wind, peeling her lips back from her fangs so she might taste the scents as well as smell them. By scent and sound she knew the speakers long before she finished her wandering progress up the hill and they came into view through the thinning greenery.

Three. All male. All familiar. Derian. Blind Seer. And the Meddler.

The trio sat on enormous pale grey boulders arrayed in a rough grouping amid thick grass so interspersed with a riot of wild flowers that telling where the one began and the other ended was impossible.

Blind Seer reclined on his rock, paws outstretched in front of him, tail long behind. Derian and the Meddler sat upright, Derian as if his boulder were a rather uncomfortable backless chair, the Meddler sprawled on the grass, using his boulder as a rest. He had just plucked a stalk of clover with the rounded fuzz of the flower intact. As Truth approached, the Meddler set the stem between his teeth and began to slowly chew.

Truth leapt onto the remaining boulder, arranging herself so that her paws hung down the front, slightly to the sides. She rested her chin on a convenient protrusion, then let her eyes slide mostly shut, drowsing in the sun.

None of the men greeted her, but they clearly knew she was there. After a moment, Truth felt as if she had always been there, and the lazy cadence of their conversation had been a constant backdrop to her sleep.

Derian was saying, "I thought you couldn't come to the Nexus Islands, Meddler. Something about a barrier or shield or something."

The Meddler shifted the clover stem from his front teeth to his back so he could talk around it without losing the rhythm of his chewing.

"I haven't come to those islands. You've come here."

Blind Seer looked about appreciatively. There was a herd of red deer grazing in the far distance down one of the slopes. The prick of his ears said he was thinking how nice it would be to give the deer chase, if only he wasn't so very comfortable where he was. Wolves were like kittens that way.

"Here?" Derian asked.

Truth wondered at the human tendency to ask questions. Wasn't it enough that they were here and away from the worst pain of querinalo?

"Here," the Meddler said, taking the clover from his mouth and gesturing about their hilltop with the chewed end before popping the entire thing into his mouth and chomping down. Immediately, his fingers began a lazy quest for another flower-topped stem.

Truth had eaten the occasional mouthful of grass, but never with much pleasure. She wondered if the Meddler was working on a hairball.

Derian looked uneasy. "This is a nice place, but I don't remember it, and I can't think why I should be hallucinating about you of all people, Meddler. Earlier I was visiting my family back in Hawk Haven. That at least makes sense."

Blind Seer stopped watching the deer, and directed his uncomfortably penetrating blue-eyed gaze upon the Meddler. Truth thought that if the wolf were a cat the tip of his tail would be twitching.

"Here," Blind Seer said. "Bitter said something about meeting you in a place . . . I think Plik said something similar happened in his illness. A strange place . . ."

The Meddler nodded. "On the edges of life and death. That's right. That's where I am. That's where you are. I figured that once you folks went over to the Old World at least some of you would catch querinalo. Retreating from the pain and fever brought Plik here. I thought I might see who else would come to call. I must say, I didn't think to see you, Blind Seer, and I rather thought I might see someone else."

"Firekeeper." Blind Seer growled softly as he said the name. "Why won't you leave my Firekeeper alone?"

"Take care what you claim, wolf," the Meddler said easily, "especially now, when you're not even in full possession of your own life. That's not the time to be laying claim to someone else's."

"Why are you so interested in Firekeeper?" Blind Seer persisted, his hackles rising.

"Firekeeper is interesting," the Meddler said cheerfully. "Certainly you of all creatures should agree. Wherever Firekeeper goes, things change around her. She sees the world inside out and outside in. She's a beast with human form, and a human with a beast's soul. Just accepting Firekeeper for who she is can be enough to make most intelligent creatures reassess everything they've ever believed. I learned to meddle. She does it without even trying."

Derian had listened to this exchange with increased anxiety. Now the words he had been holding back came blurting out.

He looked at Blind Seer, his eyes so wide Truth could see the whites all around.

"I can understand you!" Derian said. "I just now realized it. We've been sitting here talking. Talking. Really talking, with words and everything."

Blind Seer cocked his ears and thumped his tail. "I can see why that would disturb you, Derian. It's not so odd for me. I've been listening to you talk all along. It's you who have not understood my speech."

Derian grinned, his expression just a bit crazed. "This is really great. Is this how it is for Firekeeper all the time?"

The Meddler replied when Blind Seer only wrinkled his brow in puzzled consideration.

"It is and it isn't. This place is—for lack of a better word—'translating' what Blind Seer, and Truth if she'd bother to say anything, are saying. Because you're accustomed to words, you're hearing things as words. Firekeeper doesn't always need words to understand what is being said—any more than you need your little brother to say the words 'I'm happy' when you see him smile."

"I think I understand," Derian said. "So this isn't another of my private hallucinations. We've all come to the same place."

"You're all dying," the Meddler said bluntly. "Or dangerously close to severe bodily injury from the fever that comes with querinalo. You all need to decide how you will manage your illness, or you may find your bodies in such unpleasant places that you will refuse to rejoin with them. In short, you will die."

Blind Seer narrowed his eyes. "You said you met Plik. Did he lose his talent because of your advice?"

The Meddler shrugged. "I prefer to think that I convinced him to live. He was close to dying, you know, closer even than you are now, for he had not yet recovered from blood briar poisoning before querinalo took hold. The twins cared for Plik as well as they could, but being neither animal nor human, Plik presented a very difficult case. I would imagine you will, too, unless those who watch over your body have specialists in animal medicine that they can consult."

Truth remembered the slaying of the three corrupted kidisdum.

"I suspect they do not," she said, and saw Derian's head snap around at the sound of her voice.

She tilted her head and curled her whiskers playfully at him. Derian relaxed just a little, focusing on their immediate problem to escape the strangeness.

"What is querinalo?" he asked. "I don't know much about medicine, but I do know that usually fever is a sign of infection."

"Or infestation," the Meddler said. "Many illnesses are caused by little creatures that enter your body through tainted water or food or even air. Your body raises its temperature to convince these creatures to leave."

"Interesting," Derian said. "Then is querinalo caused by some creature like this? Does it remain in the air of the Old World, but no longer in the New?"

The Meddler finished eating his clover and rubbed a finger under his nose. He pursed his lips, then bit his lower one.

"Stop avoiding Derian's question," Truth said, half raising a threatening paw. "You know something, don't you?"

The Meddler fell still, his gaze watchful, and Truth felt a little thrill of threat.

"Say instead that I suspect," the Meddler said, "and you will be closer to the point. I have wondered why querinalo lingered in the Old World and not the New. If it was a disease such as those caused by the little creatures of which I spoke, surely it should have found plenty of hosts among the talented—at least enough that there would be an occupancy or two as a child grew into strength. However, there seems to be none of that."

"So why the difference?" Derian pressed. "What is it you suspect?"

"I suspect," the Meddler said, "that querinalo is a curse, rather than a disease."

"A curse?" Derian said. "I know the word, but only in the general sense of an ill-wishing. The old stories contain references to powerful magical curses, though . . . Is that what you mean?"

"Exactly," the Meddler said. "An ill-wishing of great strength, one created to target those who possessed considerable magical power. What troubles me is that this explanation doesn't answer all my questions."

"What troubles me," Derian said forcefully, "is what querinalo may do to us three, right here, right now. Plik told us he had to let querinalo burn along his talent to save his life. I . . . I don't know if I can do that. I mean, I've lived all my life with horses. What if I find I don't have the same way with them anymore? I'm not sure I'd know myself. It would be like losing a sense . . . No, worse, like losing a part of my soul."

Blind Seer's gaze had become vague, and when he spoke, the words were clearly meant as much for himself as for any listener.

"I don't even know what my talent is. How can I destroy something I didn't know I had?"

The Meddler shrugged. "Unlike Derian, you'll never miss it."

Blind Seer didn't look pleased. "I would always wonder. Always. It would be like dying, in a way. Is there no alternative?"

"There is the way the Once Dead took," the Meddler said, "that of directing querinalo to cause some physical mutilation or transformation in order to spare the rest of the body."

Derian looked very uncomfortable, obviously remembering the monstrosities the Once Dead had become.

The Meddler went on. "The greater the talent, the greater hold querinalo has, and the greater the sacrifice must be."

Blind Seer rose and shook. "It seems to me there must be another way. A harder way, perhaps, but another way."

"What?" Derian asked, his tone equal parts trepidation and hope.

"Accepting the pain, running with it, not from it," the wolf said. "Taking the fever in one's teeth and twisting it."

The Meddler was looking distinctly alarmed.

"That course might kill you. It might drive you mad."

The wolf panted laughter. "You humans value life too much. We wolves know that a life spent merely protecting life isn't living at all. If I am to be a wolf, then I must live as a wolf."

Blind Seer rose onto all fours, stretched, and gave them each a bow that, in the Meddler's case, was accompanied by a mocking yawn. Then he leapt from his rock. He was running before his paws hit the soft ground.

"Tell Firekeeper," the Meddler said, rising to his feet so that he could catch a last glimpse of the running wolf. "Tell her that I really did try to save him."

❧

PLIK SAT WITH HARJEEDIAN one morning, huddled over cups of tea and slices of toasted bread near the hearth in the larger of the two cottages. The meal was breakfast for Harjeedian, dinner for Plik. They had divided their numbers into shifts, and Plik found night watch easier than did any of the humans. Last night he had taken it with Tiniel, and that young man had already gone to bed.

The weather outside had turned ugly. It was rapidly becoming apparent that the climate here—wherever it was they were—was much less mild than that of Liglim. Here a driving wind from the north brought bone-chilling cold and what one of the ospreys swore was a scent of snow.

However, the weather was their ally as well as a source of discomfort. In the sleet and rain, the remaining residents of the island were disinclined to wander. The yarimaimalom continued to guard them, and Harjeedian made regular trips to make certain nothing untoward was going on.

The situation was uncertain, but the memory of the Once Dead exploding and of Firekeeper's fury, and the rumors of what had happened to the three who dwelt near the menagerie, were all fresh enough that most of the survivors were content to be alive. This halting peace would not last, but soon querinalo would have run its course in the new arrivals, and decisions could be made.

"I want to go home," Plik said, hearing the longing in his own voice. "It is cold here. It was hardly autumn there when we left. My coat has not thickened."

"When the others are well," Harjeedian said in what Plik thought of as his formal "aridisdu" voice. "Then we shall check the omens. Hopefully, they will show us how we can go back to the New World, and still leave this place secure against use."

Harjeedian sighed then as if hardly believing the truth of his own words. He reached for the honey pot, stirring a dripping spoonful into his tea. When he spoke next, it was in much less formal tones.

"But I'd be lying if I didn't admit to wanting to go home. We keep our temple complex warm for the comfort of the reptiles. This wind goes straight to my marrow."

Plik nodded. He glanced over to where Isende was sponging Derian's forehead with cool water, then to where Firekeeper sat spooning an herbal infusion between Blind Seer's jaws. Much of this dribbled out along the sides of the long, slack jaw, but surely some of it got into the wolf.

"I don't know what astonishes me more," he admitted, keeping his voice low, "that Blind Seer who never showed the faintest whiff of magic should fall so to querinalo, or that Firekeeper who seemed a preordained victim should not."

Harjeedian nodded. "I have thought much the same, but the omens are indistinct on this point. Some seem to say that Firekeeper does indeed have the disease. Others that she does not. As for Blind Seer . . . I don't even know what questions to ask."

"I wonder," Plik said, "if Firekeeper does not succumb because she is so intensely focused on Blind Seer. Her fear for him is a fever that will admit no other."

"A reasonable thought," Harjeedian said. "Sometimes the best way to halt a wildfire is to set another blaze in anticipation. Tell me, Plik, are you certain you never sensed anything magical about Blind Seer?"

"Not that I recall. Of course, he and Firekeeper were so often in close company that if I did sense anything, I might have credited it to her rather than to him. You must understand, I did not consciously go about sniffing for magic. Indeed, until I was brought to the Old World, I was hardly aware of using the ability at all."

Harjeedian looked puzzled, so Plik tried to explain.

"When you use your hearing, unless you are trying to hear something—say someone whispering—you are not really aware of the sense at all. You hear sounds constantly, though, enough that if something were to strike you deaf, you would know instantly."

"Even if," Harjeedian said like a good student demonstrating he has grasped the lesson, "to that point I would have said that all about me was quiet."

"Exactly. So it was with me and my sensing of magic. Sometimes—as when taking my shift on the maimalodalum's traditional watch against the return of the Old World rulers—I would 'listen' consciously. Even then, I heard little, for there was little to hear. When I awoke in this place, I thought there must be a storm raging, so loud was the sound pounding in my head. Indeed, I did not sort it out all at once, and when I did I could hardly believe that there was so much to 'hear.' I had to learn how to fold my ears down to dampen the sound."

"My ears do not fold," Harjeedian said, chuckling slightly and touching his own stiff human ears, "but I believe I understand."

"Humans do have remarkably immobile sense organs," Plik said. "You cannot close your nostrils or ears, only your eyes. It must be dreadfully inconvenient."

"There are times," Harjeedian admitted. "So, essentially, what you are saying is that you never really 'sniffed' Blind Seer."

"Not really," Plik admitted. "By the time doing so began to seem important—as when I could have tried to learn which of our number was likely to come down with querinalo—it was too late. My ability had been burned away."

Harjeedian was about to say something when Isende rose from where she had been sitting by Derian and came hurrying over to them.

"Something's not right with Derian," she said without preamble, motioning for them to follow her. "He has been muttering for the longest time. I even thought the fever was diminishing. But now it's rising again, and . . . look."

They had reached the young man's bedside by now, and for a moment Plik could not see what Isende was talking about. Harjeedian had knelt by the bed and was touching Derian's forehead with the back of his hand.

"Has Derian swallowed any of the doctor's potion lately?"

"Yes," Isende said. "A good bit, and water as well. That's why I thought he was getting better. Then I noticed, well, noticed . . ."

She pointed, and this time Plik understood. Derian's flesh seemed to be—Plik struggled for a word—melting, rather like the wax on the edges of a thick candle melts, not turning liquid, but becoming soft. While it held its form, Plik did not doubt for a moment that if he reached out he would find the flesh malleable to the touch.

The idea both revolted and tempted him. He saw his own hand moving toward Derian's ear. Harjeedian's hand slapped him sharply away.

"Don't touch him!" he said. "I don't think we even dare continue the cold compresses while Derian is in this state. I don't like how the skin moved when I touched his forehead. I'm going for the doctor."

"I'll go," Isende said, already moving for the door. "You're closer to being a healer than I am. Stay with him!"

The doctor came promptly. He inspected Derian carefully, his expression growing more and more grave—then touched with fear when he saw that Firekeeper had left her vigil at Blind Seer's side and come to join them. The residents of the Nexus Islands had been given time to learn about those who had conquered them, and they knew that other than Blind Seer the one the dangerous and apparently unpredictable wolf-woman valued most was Derian.

Plik thought their assessment unfair only on one point. Firekeeper was not unpredictable when it came to those she viewed as her pack. If Blind Seer was One Male to her One Female, then Derian was a valued and trusted second—protected and honored as such.

However, for all the intensity in those dark, dark eyes, Firekeeper said nothing but stood head angled so she would hear the faintest sound from Blind Seer, waiting for Zebel's report.

"This . . ." the doctor gestured toward Derian, "is not an uncommon direction for querinalo to take. Indeed, we might call it a hopeful sign."

Isende frowned. "I remember nothing like this when Plik was ill—or when my brother and I were either."

"That is because," the doctor said gently, "you—as did I, as did Plik—chose the path that would lead to becoming Twice Dead. This manifestation occurs with those who are fighting to retain their magic—and in doing so are sacrificing some part of their bodies. This is why I say this can be seen as a hopeful sign. Derian has chosen to live, and that is the first step to recovery. We can even say that he has chosen what 'medicine' to take to effect his cure."

"Then is good?" Firekeeper said. She stepped closer and looked down at Derian, her lips pursed in concern. "He not look good. His ears is wrong. So is his hair, I think."

The doctor stepped back a step. "All I can tell you is what I know from the cases I have observed. Most who develop this melted skin recover."

"Most?" Firekeeper asked.

"Sometimes," the doctor looked increasingly nervous, "sometimes the melted skin heals in a manner that . . . that . . ."

"Speak," Firekeeper growled, "I do not bite."

Then don't look like you're going to do just that, Plik thought, but he didn't blame the wolf-woman for her reaction. Derian looked very strange. Zebel reeked of fear sweat. As far as Plik knew, Firekeeper had hardly dozed since Blind Seer's collapse. This did not make for an even temper.

Zebel swallowed, then went on, "Sometimes the melted skin heals in a manner that is fatal in itself. One woman's nose grew so long that it folded over onto itself and she smothered. A man grew fangs that pierced the roof of his mouth and curved into his brain. Those are extreme cases, though. You have seen how many of the Once Dead survive intact, if altered in appearance."

"I see," Firekeeper said. Again she inspected Derian, but although his exposed flesh showed that strange softness, there was no sign of disfiguring growths.

"We watch," she said, and turned to go back to Blind Seer.

Plik looked at Isende.

"Would you like a rest?" he asked, for although he had been up doing the night watch and had planned on sleeping, he didn't think he could now.

"No," Isende said, giving him a brave smile. "I don't want to leave now. Finish your meal. I'll call if anything seems to change. You can be sure of that."

Firekeeper looked over at Isende, and to Plik's surprise gave the younger woman a tired smile.

"I know you will call," she said. "I know."

XXXIII

FIREKEEPER HAD HEARD ALL of the soft-voiced conversation by the hearthside, but she had not felt any desire to participate. How could she? To answer would be to give away more about herself than she cared for any—other than Blind Seer—to know.

Querinalo had bitten into her soon after it had bitten Blind Seer. She had felt it probing through her system, chewing along her nerves, browsing for what would feed it, and then a rhythmic chant had started in her head: "Only a wolf may live. Only a wolf may live."

They were words that had haunted her dreams since her childhood, words she now knew had been spoken by the maimalodalu called Questioner when he sought a way around her stubborn refusal to accept the fresh meat that she needed to recover her strength after barely surviving the fire that had killed her human parents. Sickened with the deaths of friends and family, Firekeeper had revolted against living at the expense of another's life—yet Questioner had known she could not hope to heal without it.

He had charmed her into believing herself well and wholly a wolf, and now it seemed that charm was coming to her aid again. Firekeeper felt her own conviction that there was nothing magical about her, that she was wolf in mind and blood and soul, block querinalo of the sense that there was anything in the least magical about her. Querinalo quested, sought, probed, but finding nothing of the magic that was its anchor, it could not ravage her as it did its more usual prey.

Firekeeper, racked with fever, but knowing even at the worst that she would survive intact, supposed she was grateful.

On one matter, Plik was absolutely right. It was her intense fear for Blind Seer that kept her from sleeping. More than once since her vigil had begun had she cursed the impulsive revenge that had slain the three humans best schooled in the treatment of beasts.

True, they might have been more cruel than a weasel with rabies, but they knew things, and Firekeeper would have made certain they did not lie to her. As it was, she had to go by what Harjeedian and the doctor said, and both admitted that they knew little about illness in canines.

Harjeedian, who had studied some veterinary medicine in preparation for the venture that had brought Firekeeper and Blind Seer into the land of the Liglim, had been the most helpful. He had assured her that the willow bark infusion that they were using to bring the fever down in the humans should not harm Blind Seer. He had suggested placing cool, damp cloths on the wolf's ears, nose, and paw pads—places where the skin was close to the surface.

Plik had advised against shaving the wolf, saying that he recalled his own fever as being mingled with chills, and that there would be times when Blind Seer would welcome his fur. Firekeeper had agreed, for she was not certain that she could tell the difference between shivering from extreme heat or from the illusion of cold.

What no one but herself realized was how much pain Blind Seer was experiencing. He panted almost continuously, and not only to shed heat. He shuddered, and when Firekeeper stroked his flanks great washes of fur came loose, mostly from his undercoat, but tufts containing thick guard hairs as well. Wolves regularly shed—almost molting as birds did—but never when winter was coming on. This shedding was a response to pain, and probably to fear.

Unlike Derian, who had muttered in his sleep, Blind Seer was silent but for occasional whimpers. Usually Derian spoke in Pellish, although sometimes he spoke in Liglimosh. At these times, Firekeeper thought he might be talking to Rahniseeta, and she was saddened to think how her friend's heart still bled for the woman he had thought would be his mate.

Now, as Firekeeper resumed her watch beside Blind Seer, easing more water between his jaws, stroking gently along his ears, gazing down at those familiar blue eyes that tracked nothing she could see, Firekeeper thought how odd it was that apparently querinalo could give one the ability to alter one's physical form.

Could this much-feared disease actually be the means to the thing she had longed for as long as she could remember? If she had opened herself to queri-nalo's fires, could she have burned away her human form and given herself a wolf's in return? The idea was tempting, so tempting.

Firekeeper longed to lay her head on Blind Seer's flank and give herself to sleep and whatever came with it. Knowing what she did now, surely she could make use of it.

So easy, Little Two-legs? she chided herself. *I think not, pup. If querinalo was so easy to control, would those monsters you saw—those who boasted themselves Once Dead to hide their revulsion for themselves—would they have chosen those forms? I think not. There is a cost. Perhaps you could make yourself wolf indeed, but might you lose something else? What if you became as a Cousin, lacking in sense? What if you lost your memory? There are worse things than being human.*

But she couldn't help but wonder.

More time passed. With the wet weather blocking the sun, those within the cottage were trapped in an eternal, unchanging twilight. Time's passage was marked only in increasing exhaustion, in how the level of water in the pitcher dropped. In mild surprise when it rose after someone filled it.

Firekeeper ate what was put in front of her, but she didn't taste it. Her only exercise was rising to check on Derian, to use the pot, to throw away some rag soaked in wolf piss after Blind Seer urinated.

Isende kept her own vigil long after Harjeedian urged her to rest. Something was happening to Derian, but in Firekeeper's exhausted state all that registered was that whatever was happening did not seem to be threatening his life. Occasionally, one of the wingéd folk came to report that Truth continued to live and breathe, but that the jaguar had not stirred from the den she had made herself near a spring.

Firekeeper wondered what the jaguar saw in her hallucinations. She hoped it was more pleasant than whatever Blind Seer was encountering. The wolf's paws now moved as if he were running and climbing. Periodically, he snarled. Once, when Firekeeper was giving him water, he snapped, and the cut seamed across the back of her hand, missing the tendons, but drawing quantities of blood.

Firekeeper would take nothing for the pain, fearing it would dull her ability to stay awake, but she did let Harjeedian clean the wound and stitch it. She almost welcomed the pain of needle and thread moving through her flesh. It brought her the closest to alertness she had been for hours.

Zebel had warned them that the crisis in querinalo's progress should come that night. He also warned them that he was speaking mostly about Derian. Although some of the yarimaimalom had certainly passed through the disease, he had not treated them.

Tiniel replaced Isende when evening came, but Isende was back again by midnight, stating she could not sleep knowing what was happening. The wingéd folk reported that Truth was tossing and turning. They had carried small buckets of water and throughly dowsed her, but they had not dared draw too close. For all that Truth seemed to be in another world, she was too aware what was close, and had nearly taken Night's Terror on the wing.

"Derian's skin is changing again," Harjeedian said. Like Isende, he had napped following his shift, but returned. "It's losing that waxy look. I fear it is going to firm up in its current shape."

Firekeeper tried to remember what that shape was, but she could not. Something about ears. Nose. Hair. Fingernails?

Her focus was on Blind Seer. He had been running harder for a while now. The cloths with which she cooled his feet had been damp with blood the last few times she had changed them. There was not much blood; the appearance was as if those thick pads had been run raw.

There were other signs of a struggle. For a time Blind Seer had growled, but now the only sounds that came forth were whimpers. Firekeeper longed to hold him close, but the throbbing in her injured hand reminded her to take care near those formidable jaws. She settled for breathing on him, keeping her scent near his nostrils.

Come home to me, sweet hunter. Come home. Come home. Don't run away. Come home. Come home.

Firekeeper chanted the words softly under her breath, plucking occasionally at the stitches on her hand so the pain would keep her sharp and alert. Even so, she nearly missed the crisis when it began.

Blind Seer's paws flexed in one last convulsive effort. Firekeeper saw the stain of blood through the cloths on his feet. She saw pink in the foam on his jaws, pink darkening toward red. Blind Seer coughed, then growled. Then he wrenched upright, almost onto his feet.

"Firekeeper!" he howled.

Then, his last energy spent, he collapsed. Firekeeper clasped him up and to her, no longer dreading what those jaws could do to her fragile human skin, indeed, welcoming the rending if it would take her to him.

After a long moment, she realized that the wildly beating heart was not hers alone. Blind Seer was still breathing, more easily now, something almost like rest coming into his muscles.

She lowered Blind Seer back onto the floor, and saw him relax into real sleep. Looking up, she saw a circle of faces looking at her. Human, beast, and maimalodalu were weirdly alike in their expression of worry and fear.

"Derian?" she asked.

"He's going to make it," Plik said. "Altered, but alive. Blind Seer?"

"He will live," Firekeeper said, lowering her head and pillowing it at last on Blind Seer's flank. "I must sleep."

DERIAN WOKE SLOWLY, his muscles and joints aching as if he had spent the past week teaching a particularly stubborn horse how to jump. He opened his eyes carefully, and was relieved to find that his eyelids, at least, didn't hurt—much.

Isende was sitting in a chair near his bed, gaze unfocused, her fingers busy knitting a stocking from extremely fine yarn. She saw him shift, and a smile blossomed, rounding out her cheeks.

She's lost a little weight, Derian mused, aware of the inanity of the thought. *But then she would. We've been running her hard since we came to the "rescue."*

"Water?" Isende asked, filling a mug from a pitcher near at hand.

"Please," he croaked.

His voice sounded odd in his ears. In fact, everything sounded a little strange—sharper than usual. The water splashing into the pitcher plashed and gurgled like a stream running over rocks. He wondered if he still had a touch of a fever.

As she poured, Isende spoke, "Blind Seer seems to have made it through querinalo, but he's still asleep, so we don't know what it may have done to him. Truth is still in her self-chosen exile, but the ravens seem to think she's come through her crisis."

"Firekeeper?" Derian was again aware of the strangeness in the sound of his voice.

"Oh! That's right. You wouldn't know. She's either through it or she never got it. We can't tell."

Derian thought uncharitably that this was typical of Firekeeper. She seemed to thrive on being unpredictable. What had the Meddler said in that dream? Something about Firekeeper causing things to change around her?

Had it been a dream? He found himself hoping not. He'd rather liked talking with Blind Seer and Truth. It had been a confirmation that all those times he'd tried to speak with them as if they were—well, sort of odd humans, if he were honest with himself—hadn't just been craziness on his part.

"So we're all fine," he said, "or nearly so."

"At least no one has died," Isende said, and something in her expression made Derian instantly wary. "Are you hungry? The doctor said you could eat now that the fever has broken."

Derian realized he was starving.

"Do we have any porridge? Maybe oat porridge with raisins or grated carrots."

"I can manage that," Isende said with a smile. "There's a kettle going in the main kitchens."

That made Derian remember the tense, unbalanced situation before his collapse.

"Are we still in charge?"

"Fairly," Isende said. "Our prisoners are beginning to get restive, but so far the yarimaimalom are enough to keep them in line. It will be good to have more humans active, though. We're going to need to decide what to do with the Old Worlders. Now, let me go and get you that porridge."

Derian settled back on his pillows, vaguely pleased to be back in the present moment. He could hear Firekeeper's breathing across the room, Blind Seer's almost matching in cadence. Someone, Harjeedian, probably, from the clipped pace of the shod feet, had just come in and was crossing to his bedside.

"How do you feel?" the aridisdu asked.

"I hurt all over," Derian replied. "Even my finger joints ache, but otherwise, I actually feel pretty good. Am I the first to come around?"

"That right. You were also the first to go down, and your recovery is right on the doctor's schedule."

"So I'm recovered," Derian said. "I wasn't sure. I still feel sort of weird. Sounds are sharper, light seems a bit odd."

He was watching for it, so he saw the flicker of discomfort that crossed Harjeedian's features, similar to that he had seen on Isende's face. The aridisdu had better control, but Derian felt no doubt.

"Harjeedian," he said, "what has happened? What aren't you telling me?"

Harjeedian drew in his breath, and almost visibly shrugged into the mannerisms he used when acting in his role as aridisdu. Reaching for the chair Isende had been using, he sat down so his gaze was closer to level with Derian's own.

Derian felt his heart racing with dread. He felt as if he should know what Harjeedian was about to tell him, that he already knew on some gut level, but he couldn't retrieve the memories, so he looked at the other man, waiting for revelation.

"You must thank the deities, or your ancestors, who you believe act as intercessors between you and the divine," Harjeedian began, "that you still have your life."

Derian stared at him, refusing to say anything, willing the other to speak further.

"These people here—the Old World natives—would say you have something further for which to feel gratitude," Harjeedian went on. "We will not know until you are able to be up and about, but the indications are that you have also kept your talent."

"My talent," Derian said.

He remembered the conversation with the Meddler on that hilltop. He remembered saying how he wasn't sure he could sacrifice his talent even to save his life. He remembered other things, too, and found himself lying as still as he could.

"Your talent," Harjeedian repeated. "You see, every visible indication seems to show that you are Once Dead, not Twice."

"Visible indication," Derian repeated.

He flattened his ears in distaste, felt himself starting to show his teeth. Realized what he was doing, and froze.

"What has happened to me? Harjeedian, you've got to tell me!"

"Easier, perhaps, to show you," Harjeedian said reluctantly. "I have a mirror set by."

He bent and lifted a large hand mirror from below Derian's line of sight. He raised it and held it so Derian could see his own face. Derian drew in his breath and forced himself to look.

His own face looked out at him, but although it was unmistakably his own, it was also transformed. His ears were the most visibly changed. They were shaped like those of a horse, covered in short red—or chestnut—hair identical in color to the hair on his head.

That hair had also changed, not in color, but in how it grew from his scalp. Previously, it had tended toward a slight center part, making it easy for him to brush it back and tie it into a queue. Now a portion flopped across his fore-head in a distinct, unmistakable forelock. The rest had been braided back, but Derian didn't doubt that in subtle ways it would resemble a mane.

His eyes had also changed. They had been a green-brown hazel. Now they were purely brown, the irises filling his sockets more fully, showing less white.

He raised his hands to touch this altered face and saw that they, too, were different. The nails were heavier, harder, the tips a bit more blunt. He didn't doubt that his toenails were the same.

"I . . . I look like a human horse!" Derian exclaimed. "I remember telling the others that I didn't know if I would feel like myself if I didn't have my tal-ent, but I don't remember asking for this!"

Absorbed in his self-inspection, Derian had ignored the sounds of others entering the cottage. Now a new voice, that of Zebel, the doctor, spoke from near the foot of the bed.

"This is often the case with those who become Once Dead. Some remem-ber making a deal of some sort—sacrificing their sight or hearing or some physical feature in order to maintain their magical ability. Others, often those who have a talent specifically tied to some specific skill, find the transforma-tion is less predictable."

"So," Derian said, making himself speak very, very carefully, "I didn't want to lose my rapport with horses, so querinalo made me look like a horse?"

Isende, standing to one side, holding a bowl of porridge on a tray, said, "It's not that bad, Derian. Really. Once you get over being startled, you don't look bad at all."

Derian snorted, and felt his nostrils flare—not as a horse's would, but cer-tainly in a human form of the same mannerism.

"I woke up wanting oat porridge," he said, laughing and hearing the hyster-ical note in it. "With carrots! I'll be eating grass next."

A voice spoke from the window. *"Really, there are worse things. You'll never starve."*

Derian looked and saw Eshinarvash standing in the window. The Wise Horse snapped at the sluggishly moving blood briars with big, square teeth.

"Even these aren't too bad," the horse went on. *"Though a bit rank."*

"Eshinarvash," Derian said. "I . . . This isn't a joke, is it?"

"What isn't a joke?" Harjeedian said sharply.

Derian turned to look at the three humans gathered by his bedside. He re-alized from their expressions that although all of them were aware of the Wise Horse's presence, none of them had understood what Eshinarvash had said.

"I understood him," he said, "just like I did Blind Seer and Truth in my dream."

Harjeedian's eyes widened with awe and just a bit of envy. Derian found himself remembering how the Liglimom had coveted Firekeeper's ability to speak with the yarimaimalom, and now it seemed Derian was claiming the same ability. For a moment, Derian felt very important, then he caught his reflection in the mirror and his heart sunk.

"I can never go home," he said. "Not looking like this. I'd be a freak, an embarrassment to my family. What was I thinking? I could have done without my talent. Most of my life, I didn't even think of myself as being talented. I had skills. I'd still have those skills."

He raked the tips of his fingers across his face, felt a fine down of hair there, felt those hardened tips dig in and leave welts.

"Go away!" he shouted, pulling up the blankets to mask his face. "Don't look at me!"

WHEN PLIK AWOKE that evening, he found Tiniel awake before him and eager to report the changes in their situation.

"Firekeeper has slept all day, as has Blind Seer, but they're wakening now. I've just brought her some stew and him a huge bowl of meat stock. She says that when they're done, they're going for a run, but I don't think they'll be gone long."

"There's something else," Plik said. "I can hear it in your voice. Has Truth arisen from hiding?"

Tiniel paused before he replied, and when he did his tone held a note of indignation.

"I think so. The ravens came and spoke with Firekeeper, and she said something to Harjeedian and my sister that makes them think Truth came through the crisis. Firekeeper didn't give any details, though, and, of course, you're the only other one who can talk easily to the yarimaimalom. I guess Derian could, but he's . . ."

"He's what?" Plik said sharply, when Tiniel trailed off.

"He's hiding under the bedclothes. He won't speak with anyone."

"Then he's learned what happened to him?" Plik said, hurrying toward the door.

"He woke earlier, and Harjeedian broke the news to him very gently. It seems that Derian has come through even better than we imagined last night. Not only has he retained his talent, it has been enhanced. He could understand Eshinarvash when the Wise Horse came to the window to speak with him."

Plik thought he understood the change in Tiniel's manner. He had thought it was due to Firekeeper slighting the young man, but although that might play a part, clearly Tiniel could not understand why Derian should not be rejoicing in his survival. Tiniel had not stopped mourning his own loss. Apparently, he did not understand why Derian would mind being physically changed when he was magically enhanced.

"Derian comes from a land where magic is considered abhorrent," Plik explained.

They had come to the cottage that was being used as a sickroom, but he made no effort to lower his voice. Best if Derian heard what he had to say as well.

"I've wondered about that," Tiniel replied. "For a land that despises magic, they sure seem to have a good many talented people: Blind Seer, Derian, and probably Firekeeper as well, for all she didn't get as sick as the rest."

Harjeedian rose from where he had been reading at Derian's bedside, and crossed to join them.

"Tiniel said you were waking," he said, "and Isende has gone to get us all something to eat."

"Things continue well with the prisoners?" Plik asked.

"They do," Harjeedian said. "Zebel reported to his allies that all have passed through querinalo alive, and that Derian, at least, appears to be Once Dead. This changes the situation, at least to the doctor's way of thinking. I must admit, their way of thinking remains a mystery to me."

"Interesting," Plik said. He glanced over, but it was impossible to tell whether the lump of bedclothes that was Derian was awake or asleep. "And Firekeeper?"

"Am here," came a husky voice from behind him. "Us both. We went a little way, but Blind Seer is very weak."

"And amazingly hungry," the blue-eyed wolf added. *"Although I do not think I could stomach more than broth."*

"Isende is sure to bring more for both of you to eat," Plik said. "That young woman is proving very resourceful."

"We both are," Tiniel said defensively. "After our parents died, we were all we had left. No one was going to fetch and carry for us. Isende had to learn to manage an entire household."

Plik smiled to himself. Tiniel seemed unaware of the contradictions in his own statement. Then again, that seemed in keeping with the young man's character to this point. He had many good qualities, but an astonishing amount of self-absorption as well.

A great cat, Plik thought, *rather than some herd or pack animal. Survival of the self, rather than of the whole. Isende is not like her twin in that. I wonder if they are complementary opposites rather than a matched set as we have been led to believe.*

Firekeeper had settled Blind Seer on a folded blanket a comfortable distance from the hearth, and now she padded over to inspect Derian. She laid a gentle hand where the young man's shoulder should be, but he did not stir. Plik thought the wolf-woman might strip back the blankets and force Derian to communicate, but she did no such thing. Instead, shaking her head in sorrow, she returned to the group near the fire.

She was about to seat herself by Blind Seer when she jerked up her head. Plik caught the sound even as the wolf-woman did.

"Isende is back," Firekeeper reported, moving to the door.

Plik heard soft conversation between the two women, and a moment later they entered, carrying several packs between them. Firekeeper's interest in this menial task became evident when she set her burden down, and removed a large bottle from one of the packs.

"Zebel send broth cooked with plants so to make Blind Seer stronger," Firekeeper reported with satisfaction as she poured some into a large, shallow bowl and set it near the reclining wolf.

"And there is food for the rest of us as well," Isende laughed. "Eshinarvash helped me carry it over, or I would have had real problems."

They chattered rather stiltedly as they dished out portions for everyone, all too aware of Derian huddled under his blankets.

"Tiniel and I were talking," Plik said, deciding he must be the one to introduce the matter again, "about how odd it is that although the northerners claim to despise magic, they have so many talents among them."

Harjeedian nodded. "I discussed the matter with Derian long ago. Apparently, as he understands the tales told in his land, an effort was made to slaughter any who showed the gift for sorcery, but talents, especially those with a limited focus, were overlooked."

"Odd," Tiniel said.

"But reasonable," Harjeedian said. "After all, those very talents could help those who had been abandoned into war and chaos when their rulers fled to survive. However, while in our land we view talents as divine gifts, in Derian's land they simply don't think of them at all."

"I don't understand," Isende said.

"If talents manifest," Harjeedian said, "they are accepted, but neither praised nor censured. I have met a friend of theirs from the north—a Sir Jared Surcliffe—who is blessed with the healing talent. However, the man does not base his life around that talent as might one of the Liglimom so blessed. While that Liglimom would take his talent as an omen that he should follow the disdu's path, this friend delights in his nickname of 'Doc'—a name that affirms his gift. When he realized that his talent could not answer all medical needs, he devoted himself to learning medical arts."

Isende nodded now. "I see. So although Derian, say, has this rapport with horses, in his land there is no way he could become a kidisdu. He simply became a very talented horseman."

"That is correct," Harjeedian said. "I believe that gradually being forced to face that he had a magical talent and how much that talent meant to him has been very difficult for Derian. Querinalo only brought to a head an issue that had been troubling him for several years now."

Plik noted that not a single voice had been lowered during this discussion. He was not the only one who hoped Derian was listening, and perhaps learning that no one here blamed him for what had happened.

"Transformation," Plik said, "is very difficult to accept though, especially when it comes unwilling and unwanted. Do you remember how I told you all that 'Plik' was not my given name, but one I took for myself?"

The twins shook their heads, but Harjeedian nodded.

"I do. Derian asked you why your name was so unlike that borne by most of the maimalodalum. I don't think you ever told us why."

"Well," Plik said, reaching for another slice of bread and smearing it thickly with butter. "Since we have little to do this evening but wait, this would be the perfect time for me to tell that tale."

XXXIV

"you've all heard about how the maimalodalum were created as a merging of humans and yarimaimalom by sorcerers who wished to acquire the ability to change shapes," Plik began. "The maimalodalum are the victors of that struggle, those who did not die so another could steal their shape. What is not so often told is that not all those who found themselves made into maimalodalum were happy with that transformation. My mother was one such who felt nothing but misery and despair at her 'victory.'

"My mother was a raccoon in the prime of her life when she was captured by a sorcerer back in those days when querinalo had not destroyed all who practiced magic."

"But," Harjeedian said, "that was well over a hundred years ago!"

"Who knows?" Plik said with a sad smile. "Perhaps this sorcerer was one such as here would be termed Once Dead. In any case, my mother did not bear me until many years after her transformation, for reasons I will explain, nor am I as young as you seem to imagine."

Harjeedian nodded stiffly, his eyes filled with wonder mixed with calculation. Plik ignored this. He had a more important listener in mind for his tale.

"Strong and beautiful as she was, doubtless these qualities made my mother a target to the sorcerer who had captured and sought to corrupt her. This sorcerer, however, did not consider that my mother might equal him in strength of will. In the end, not only did my mother slay the sorcerer rather than being slain herself, she retained many of her raccoon qualities.

"However, there was no escaping the mark of the human upon her. Her eyes now saw color differently. Her ears were set lower upon her skull. Her legs moved oddly, so that quadrupedal motion was not her only choice. Her feet had changed so that she could bear her weight when walking on two legs as well as upon four. Her hands had changed, giving her a longer, more mobile thumb.

"Perhaps those of you who are humans will only see an improvement in all these changes, but my mother did not. Before she had been viewed as beautiful, and some said that every boar on Misheemnekuru (although the islands did not yet have that name) had come to court her, some traveling for moonspans to do so. Raccoons do not choose one mate as do wolves or ravens, but this does not mean that they take their breeding lightly. Indeed, it might be said that they take it much more seriously, for though a pair of ravens will raise many broods, a pairing of raccoons may only come together once.

"Now my mother was viewed as a curiosity by some, as a monstrosity by others. Whichever view was held, certainly no one thought her beautiful any longer, nor desirable. She had chosen which boar to mate with shortly before the sorcerer had captured her. Now he shunned her, moving several islands away to avoid her. Those who had come courting suddenly ceased their visits, and even those who had shared adjoining or overlapping territories before found reasons to move elsewhere.

"Representatives from the maimalodalum came to my mother and offered to give her home and companions, but my mother desired nothing but the life that had been taken from her. She chased them from her with growls and snarls, and though you might not think so, looking upon me who is a peaceful soul, an angry raccoon is a formidable opponent."

Both Blind Seer and Firekeeper grunted agreement, and Plik felt perversely pleased. He went on, however, as if he had not heard.

"My mother began to track down boar after boar, offering herself as mate to each one. Now indeed did she regret her dallying and coquettish behavior, for over and over she was rejected. After many years—decades—when her power to breed was ebbing, she found a boar who either did not find her repulsive or perhaps possessed more compassion than his fellows. In any case, she became pregnant, and after time had passed—longer time than if she had been carrying a litter of raccoons—she bore a litter of three.

"Two died within days, for they contained a combination of raccoon traits and human traits that would not mingle. One lived, and that one was me. However, although my mother suckled me and tried to accept me, each sight she had of me and of those human traits I had inherited reminded her of the taint in her own flesh—a taint that, indeed, she showed more visibly than did I.

"Eventually, she rejected me completely, but she did not leave me to die. Instead she went to what is now called Center Island and dropped me on the doorstep of the Tower of Magic. Then she vanished into the forests, and to the best of my knowledge has never again been seen by maimalodalum nor yarimaimalom."

Plik fell silent then. During his telling, he had seen a few restless motions beneath the bedclothes, and knew that Derian had heard all, but the young man had not come forth, nor would Plik force him.

After a moment, Isende said, "What about your father? Did he ever come to meet you?"

"He never did," Plik said. "Whether from shame or from ignorance of what he had engendered, he did not make himself known to me or to anyone. Boar raccoons, even of the yarimaimalom type, do not have much to do with raising their young."

Tiniel frowned. "Harjeedian indicated that you had another name than 'Plik.' Did your mother then name you? Perhaps she did care then, at least a little."

"I don't think so," Plik said, hearing his own sorrow, "for what she named me was 'Misbegotten.' "

"Oh!" Tiniel gasped, shocked. "I am sorry."

"You couldn't know," Plik reassured him. "In any case, the maimalodalum would have nothing of this. They called me baby names like 'Fuzzy Tail,' and 'Ring Bottom.' When I was an adult they encouraged me to call myself by a name of my choosing. I chose 'Plik,' for the sound of water falling on rock is a pleasant one. My companions have given me other names over time, affectionate names that recognize contributions I have made, but although I keep them as loving awards, I prefer Plik."

Silence followed Plik's concluding remark, a silence that stretched as everyone waited for a response that, so it seemed, would not come. Then, just as Harjeedian was opening his mouth, perhaps to put a pious moral on Plik's story, across the room the bedclothes were thrown back, revealing Derian in all his transformed glory.

He's grown a little hairier, Plik thought. *That red down is not unbecoming.*
But Derian clearly thought otherwise.

"I really thought," he said stiffly, "that I had outgrown the days when I would be lectured in such a fashion. If any of you think my behavior unbecoming, then by all means say so—but say so to this face!"

He pointed dramatically to his own features, a wide gesture that encompassed the elongated ears, the transformed line of nose and jaw, the wholly brown eyes. His obvious disdain for what he had become quelled even Plik, who found him far less odd than most of the maimalodalum. Only Firekeeper was unmoved.

"So you are changed," she said. "Who is not by life and what it does? Maybe you are changed more visibly than most, but you live and breathe and have gained new abilities. Tell me why I should weep for you?"

Derian glowered at the wolf-woman. "I dare say you would have welcomed something like this happening, but I'm not you. I'm happy being a human. I never asked to be a monster!"

Firekeeper looked at him. "Blind Seer say 'At least you know what manner of monster you are.' He has been through querinalo, and knows no more of himself than before. As for me, would I have welcomed? I cannot say. I have not run that trail. I chose another, and my head hurts nonetheless."

Derian blinked at the wolf-woman, but before he could frame a retort, Isende was heard to say softly into the unexpected silence, "Better to be a monster without than one within." Her voice was so low that she might have been speaking only to herself, but her gaze was fixed on Tiniel. Her twin's face had flamed scarlet. His expression mingled shock and betrayal.

"In any case," Isende went on more loudly, suddenly realizing that her comment had been overheard by everyone, "I don't think Derian looks like a monster at all. Different, sure, but not a monster."

Sharp retorts from both Tiniel and Derian canceled each other out, leaving the two young men staring at each other with a distaste that had never been between them before.

Someone might then have said something from which there would be no turning back, but at that moment Bitter and Lovable came battering at the door, beating it open with the sheer force of their wings.

"Something is horribly wrong with Truth!" Lovable squawked. "Hurry!"

Plik saw at that moment what querinalo had done to his wolf friends. No grey blur leapt for the door, Firekeeper hardly a step behind. Instead Blind Seer rose slowly, and was pushed back by his companion.

"*Wait,*" she said, "*the air without is too chill for you without your undercoat.*"

Plik had translated the raven's message for Harjeedian, and now offered to go and act as translator.

"No," Firekeeper said, "let me go. I began this madness in search of Truth. Let me continue as I began."

Before taking her leave, Firekeeper paused and looked at Derian, her dark eyes cold.

"None of us come through querinalo completely improved," she said. "Some of us do not even come through with talent intact."

With that Firekeeper turned to follow the raven, but she was a far cry from the lithe, strong figure who only days before had challenged an army on its own ground. Now she moved stiffly, and Plik knew how each joint cried out complaint to her.

When Eshinarvash intercepted Firekeeper outside and mutely knelt in offer to carry her, Firekeeper did not decline, but heaved herself wearily astride and sat shivering on the Wise Horse's broad back. So clumsy was the wolf-woman in her weakness that she nearly failed to catch the blanket Plik tossed up to her, but fumbled with her injured hand to catch and hold. Nor was she too proud to settle the blanket about her shoulders as Eshinarvash bore her away.

TRUTH DIDN'T KNOW exactly when the conclave on the hilltop broke up. She remembered watching Blind Seer run down the slope, and the Meddler speaking to her, but when she raised her head from where she didn't remember pillowing it on her paws, the Meddler and Derian both were gone and she was alone. Nor was she on the hilltop any longer, but in the high sanctuary of the five deities in the secret heart of u-Nahal.

All but one of the altars were cold, with no sense that the divine powers had ever looked upon them with any awareness of the mortals who so desperately turned to them for guidance. The exception was the altar of Fire, where a single candle burned. The flame of this candle bobbed and danced miraculously, for not the slightest touch of air moved within the sealed chamber.

As Truth focused on that brilliant yellow-orange flame, seeking to discover what made it move, the flame flared into a massive fireball. Truth shrank away into the farthest corner of the room and watched in wonder and awe as the fire-ball condensed into a jaguar who was the very image of Truth herself, but shaped entirely of fire, even to the spots which, though black, burned as brilliantly as all the rest.

The fire jaguar slunk from the altar and paced toward Truth, every hair on back and tail raised, each burning with its own eye-searing brilliance.

"I have come to devour you," the fire jaguar hissed, "though your cowardice will make your flesh bitter indeed."

Truth's own hackles rose at this and she retorted. "There is no cowardice in keeping one's whiskers from the fire, only wisdom and prudence."

"That is not the cowardice of which I speak," the fire jaguar replied, "and mine is not the only fire from which you flee. Is that not so, Truth, daughter of a long and prideful line of Truths? Are you not here before me because you have decided to give yourself to the fire rather than face what it brings?"

Truth snarled in faint defiance, but there was no denying that as she had lain there on that rock on the hilltop, basking in the warmth of the sun, she had contemplated the tremendous relief that would be hers if she gave in to querinalo. Death did not seem so terrible a thing in this place, for life with and yet without the talent that had defined her very being was becoming onerous indeed. Indecision haunted her every action. Madness stalked her dreams. Once Truth had thought she could not bear to live without her ability. On that hilltop, she had come to wonder if she could bear to live with it in its current, mutated form.

Now, facing this snarling image so like herself but undamped by doubt and fear, Truth faced something worse than the desire to die. She faced the bitter truth that in some fashion she had been dead from the moment she had fled into the peculiar comfort of insanity. Even when body and spirit had been reunited, still she had continued in that living death.

Truth was the name that had been divined for her, but a better name now would be Lie.

What had Derian Carter said? Something about not being sure whether he would know himself if he were to relinquish his talent? Truth confronted the honesty of those words. She knew that she who had once known so much about everything now knew nothing at all.

The fire jaguar paced toward Truth, and her fangs were white light and her eyes were more brilliant than the sun at noon.

"Then am I to die?" Truth said, bowing her head, for she knew her patron deity when Ahmyn, as the Liglimom called Fire, so manifested before her.

Ahmyn met Truth's humility with contempt. "You encountered a raging conflagration and fled, you who have been the very ornament of my year. Now you ask if you are to die, as if this is something I am inflicting upon you. Death is here and wears your shape, for you have invited her. Yes, you are to die, unless you choose to fight, but I have not given up *my* ability to read the omens, and thus I see myself dining upon your bitter flesh."

Truth felt some small flare of her former pride and a strange, weird emotion that after a moment she identified as hope. She knew better than most that no future was absolute. Even in a rainstorm there was the smallest chance that the drops might fall up.

Truth still thought she might like to die, but death this way, with Ahmyn whom she had served with such fierce fidelity glowering at her from those burning eyes . . .

Shutting her own eyes and bending her head as if in continued humility, Truth reached for the ability she had avoided since the day the Tower of Magic had fallen and in its tumbling rocks she had seen what the future held. In more futures than the sun had light Truth saw herself being rent and torn by the jaguar Ahmyn, but in one slim shadow she saw omens of hope. Into that shadow, Truth leapt.

She landed upon Ahmyn's back. Instantly, Truth felt her fur ripple and begin to smoke. She would burst into flame if she remained here long, but in all the futures offered to her, this insane course was the only one that led toward the possibility of life. Nor was that life certain. Truth delved again and saw herself consumed in flames, torn into bloody gobbets, asphyxiated as she rolled over and over trying to put out the fire in her fur and flesh. Each of these battles ended in a dark warmth Truth knew was death, but there was one in which the light still shone.

She dove into that light, battling Ahmyn, anticipating each dodge and bite the other jaguar ventured. She was Truth again, riding the strange streams of time and chance, alive in the insanity of knowing each outcome. She fought with claws and fangs, ripped into fur that parted only to spark and flame with greater force as it fed upon her body. Yet, even while Truth screamed in pain until her throat was raw, the moment came when there was not one streamlet that puddled into success in this eldritch battle, but two, then three, then more.

Ahmyn was powerful and her very substance devoured the mortal jaguar who fought against her with increasing skill and ferocity. Ahmyn was the manifestation of a deity, an elemental force only slightly younger than the Earth and Air who had birthed her, yet in this battle she had taken Truth's shape and form, and so she was limited by them.

For Ahmyn was Fire, but she was not Truth.

Ahmyn might claim to see into the ways the omen waters split, but in this ability Truth knew herself without peer. Sanity or insanity no longer mattered to Truth. She was herself again, one and whole, united as no one but herself could unite herself. Truth gloried as she battled for a life that she realized she did not care to relinquish, even to her own Ahmyn, that deity who she had served with such pride.

So Truth fought and so Truth won, and came to herself upon the damp earth with the sound of ravens shrieking in her ears, and the one called Fire-keeper's hand upon her flank, shaking her gently and saying, "Is this then Truth?"

❧

"TRUTH HAS BEEN FIGHTING something," Lovable explained, flying alongside Eshinarvash as the Wise Horse carried Firekeeper to where the jaguar had taken refuge when she had felt the first touches of querinalo. "She leapt and twisted so that we hardly dared move lest somehow she register our presence and attack us as well. I do not exaggerate when I say that Truth moved so swiftly I think she could have snagged a raven on the wing."

"Especially, this one," Bitter added. He was riding behind Firekeeper, claws gripped into the blanket she wore against the cold. "I can fly again, but I am less than dextrous, and Truth—she moved like a whirlwind or a raging flame."

"Then she fell very, very still," Lovable said, "and there was something . . . But you will see yourself. We are here."

Firekeeper slid from Eshinarvash's back, knees and ankles protesting bearing her weight. She laid a hand on the stallion's flank in mute thanks, then moved to where Lovable squawked from the tree limb.

"Here! Here!"

Firekeeper went where she was bid, and for a long moment could not believe that the ravens had taken her to the right place. A cat-like shape lay upon the damp earth, but it was not Truth as the wolf-woman had known her. The glossy golden fur was charcoal black, as if it had been burned. Where spots and rosettes had adorned that glossy pelt were now irregular markings the shape and color of a burning candle flame.

Disregarding her own safety and the complaints of her body, Firekeeper hurried over and knelt beside the figure on the ground.

She sniffed, hoping for some identifying scent, but all she smelled was ash and smoke. She laid her hand on the great cat's flank. The fur, for all that it looked burned, was soft and dense to the touch. Firekeeper said to the ravens, "Is this then Truth?"

At the sound of her voice, the great cat stirred, opening eyes no longer burnt orange, but the white of the hottest fire. The pupil was pale blue.

"I have been a lie," the creature said in Truth's voice, but the words and cadence were strange, "but I am again Truth. I have wrestled with a deity and the deity has won—but then so have I, if living is a victory. And you, bold one who calls herself Fire's keeper?"

Firekeeper answered levelly, forcing herself to meet those blue-white eyes. "I live, so do all the others, though none has come through without being changed."

Truth gazed at her unblinking. "All but you, eh, Firekeeper?"

"So they say," the wolf-woman replied, "but I know better. Can you walk or shall I send for a wagon? I would carry you but I do not think I could bear your weight." She gave a harsh laugh. "Indeed, I can hardly bear my own."

"I can walk," Truth said, "if we go slowly. Eshinarvash should not be asked to carry us both."

And so they walked slowly, side by side, and as they walked, Firekeeper told Truth what had happened over these past days of illness. Eshinarvash filled in details that Firekeeper, limited by her vigil beside Blind Seer, had not known. Truth, in turn, was more talkative than Firekeeper had ever known her to be, telling of her own long battle with such stark honesty that Firekeeper almost found herself longing for the jaguar's accustomed arrogance.

It was not that Truth had become humble, not in the least, but she embraced her own failing with such enthusiasm that Firekeeper wondered if such intense humility might be in its own way a new type of arrogance.

They entered the cottage and found the others—including Derian—seated near the hearth. All eyes widened and rounded when they saw what Truth had become. Blind Seer sneezed.

"You smell like a forest fire! No . . . Worse, for burning wood has one reek, but yours is that of singed fur and scorched flesh."

"*I have been in the fire,*" Truth said, "*but unlike brave Derian, I did not choose my fire until the choice was nearly taken from me.*"

To everyone's astonishment, Truth then crossed to where Derian sat, and gave a low bow.

"What . . . what is this?" Derian said, clearly flustered.

Plik translated what Truth had said, adding, "I wouldn't refuse her praise. She's been through a lot, even to believing she has wrestled with Ahmyn and barely come away with her life."

"I won't," Derian said, his eyes so wide that bits of white showed around them, making him look more than ever like a startled horse. "By my ancestors, I swear it!"

Truth now rose from her bow and padded to where she could sit closest to the hearth.

"*We live, we breathe,*" the jaguar said, "*some of us rather differently than before. Now I ask you, what will we do next?*"

"Can you divine the future as once you did, O holy Truth?" asked Harjeedian. Of all the company, the aridisdu had been the most deeply impressed by the jaguar's tale. "What would the deities have us do?"

"*Divination,*" Truth replied, "*has never been intended to substitute for thought, only to offer guidance. This much I can and will say: There is no one right answer before us. From this moment the future fragments and there are no clear omens as to how the deities wish us to reassemble it.*"

When Plik had translated this, Harjeedian inclined his head in acceptance. Then his face broke into a sheepish smile that astonished Firekeeper with its lack of pretense.

"So much for the easy answer," the aridisdu said. "Before querinalo struck, we were delving into the matter of what we should do about the Nexus Islands and the facilities they harbor."

"Can these facilities be destroyed?" Derian asked, his voice filled with loathing. "Can we take sledge and hammer to each of these cursed gates and ruin them beyond use? I, for one, think things of the Old World should remain in the Old World. Look what contact with it has done to us. Look at the twisted people we have found here. I say we break each and every gate to pieces—all but two. One we use to send these 'prisoners' of ours back where they came from. Then we break that gate. Then we go home through the gate we know will take us back to the stronghold, and we break that one from the other side."

No one immediately responded to Derian's harangue; then Tiniel spoke, and when he did, Firekeeper was reminded that Tiniel had not liked it in the least when his sister had praised Derian's new appearance.

"I suppose we could go and destroy these artifacts," Tiniel said. "Such acts would be in keeping with the traditions of our ancestors—and we know how much you northerners revere your ancestors. Tell me though, who will operate the gates? Isende and I cannot. Ynamynet and Lachen are the only Once Dead who survive. Can you trust them to be your agents?"

Firekeeper frowned and spoke quickly to cut off whatever retort Derian might make. It was not spring, but she could scent the rivalry of young males nonetheless.

"Tiniel has a good thought here," she said. "Who knows if any elsewhere has tried to use the gates?"

Bitter said, *"The yarimaimalom have kept watches on each of the gate buildings, even those that had not yet been brought back into use by those who nest here. So far there has been no indication of the gates coming alive, but will that last?"*

"Is there any way to know if those elsewhere share the secret of the gates?" Harjeedian asked.

Isende said, "If that matter was discussed in my hearing, I no longer remember, but since communication between areas depends on people passing between, my guess is that each active gate may have at least one on the other side who acts as custodian and who could, in an emergency, come across with information."

"That's not good," Derian said. "That means we need to decide quickly."

Firekeeper shook her head. "If destruction or fighting is what you wish, we cannot act too quickly. All of us who have been ill are weak, and the yarimaimalom cannot use these sledges and hammers of which you speak. These will take hands, and most of our strength lacks hands."

"And some of us," Plik added ruefully, "who have hands do not possess, even at our best, the muscle that would be needed to break solid stone. I certainly do not."

"I might manage some such labor," Harjeedian said, "but not all that would be needed."

"I'd be hopeless," Isende said with a self-deprecating laugh. "Tiniel and I haven't lifted anything heavier than a dinner tray or log for the fire since we first crossed over."

Tiniel didn't look as if he much cared for his sister's dismissal of his physical prowess, but neither did he deny the accuracy of her assessment.

"That," Firekeeper said, turning to Derian, "leaves you and me with some help from Harjeedian. Unless you mean to force these humans we have captured to labor for you."

Derian sank back, the intensity that had fueled his earlier speech draining from him. "Even for that—even if I could—I'm not strong enough now. Maybe when I've had more rest, but even at my strongest I was no Ox, awarded for my strength. Very well, if we cannot destroy this place we must either hold it or abandon it. Earlier we discussed how abandoning it invited future problems."

"I suppose," Isende said, "we could compromise and only destroy those gates we think lead to the New World."

"And if we missed one?" Tiniel retorted. "That would be wonderful, wouldn't it?"

"Tin . . ." His sister said the nickname like a warning. "This is serious, not a matter for bickering."

"I am serious," Tiniel said. "It would be horrible if we thought we were safe and then discovered we'd missed something and destroyed our only way of getting back and dealing with the problem, wouldn't it?"

Harjeedian broke in. "You two sound like Rahniseeta and me when we'd argue. You both have good points. I, for one, fear that Tiniel's argument is the stronger here."

Firekeeper, who had agreed with Derian's desire to destroy the entire nexus, was startled to hear Blind Seer taking Harjeedian's part.

"Rabbits have many ways out of their burrows. At the center of the burrow, the rabbit can watch all those tunnels, but to cover them from without would take a wolf pack. We have found the rabbit warren and are in its heart. We would be foolish to relinquish what we have so dearly won."

Firekeeper translated faithfully, then added, "And if later, when we are stronger, we wish to attempt to destroy the nexus, well then, we will be in a better position to do that as well. For now we must secure this place and its people as best we can. In a few days, when we have recovered more from querinalo, we will be able to do more."

"I never thought I would hear myself saying this," Harjeedian commented, "but I wish we could consult the Meddler in this matter. He knows far more than we do about these gates and how they are used."

Firekeeper grinned at the aridisdu.

"The Meddler keeps a good watch on us, I think, but since we are here, the only way we can meet with him is to nearly die. I, for one, have no wish to do this."

"Nor do I," Harjeedian replied with heartfelt sincerity. "I assure you, nor do I."

XXXV

SOME DAYS LATER, Truth padded up to Firekeeper where she stood on the hilltop upon which the majority of the gates were built. The jaguar's charcoal-black tail with its strange flame-colored spots lashed with such agitation that Firekeeper expected sparks to trail after.

"Are you stronger, wolfling?" the jaguar asked with a trace of her former arrogance.

"I can bend a bow again, and run from this cottage to the hilltop without losing my breath," Firekeeper said with some pride. It had taken hard and painful labor to achieve these goals. "But I am not what I was."

"And Blind Seer?"

"He is stronger as well, though less than pleased with having to wear a coat other than his own."

This last was an understatement. To the eye, Blind Seer was not much changed from what he had been before. If he were a bit leaner, well, that only made him look all the more fierce. Appearances, however, lied.

In battling querinalo's fever—an ordeal of which the wolf still would not speak except to say that he had learned things about himself no one should know—Blind Seer's body had sought to cool itself by shedding all of the thick undercoat that normally insulated the wolf from extreme cold. Blind Seer, once able to sleep within a drift of snow, now found himself unable to tolerate a passing breeze. He shivered uncontrollably, and grew quite short-tempered as a result.

Derian suggested the solution, an artificial coat crafted from a thick wool blanket.

"We make these for foals born too early in the spring," he said, "and I can make one for you that won't restrict your movements in the least."

Blind Seer growled, *"I will look the fool—and worse, weak, here where there are many wolves who may wish to challenge me."*

Firekeeper faithfully translated, wondering how Derian would respond, for the young man was still sensitive about his appearance. Derian surprised her.

Derian reached up and touched his horse's ears. "I think I know more than you ever will about looking a fool. Didn't I once dress up as a carrot? Stop whining and come over here and let me fit you."

Blind Seer slunk over, shamed by his insensitivity to his friend's distress. Now he wore a skillfully cut coat in a shade of grey not unlike his own fur. None of the yarimaimalom had challenged him, perhaps scenting the blue-eyed wolf's buried fury, perhaps from gratitude for what Blind Seer had done for them, certainly from respect for his prowess.

"I am glad that you both are stronger," Truth went on. "I fear we have overlooked something, and only hope that we are not too late to deal with it."

Blind Seer had padded over to join them in time to hear the jaguar's words. Now he looked about uneasily, head back as if he could catch some sense in Truth's words on the wind.

"As I have grown stronger," Truth continued, "I have resumed my prowling. It is interesting what these eyes can see."

She deliberately blinked those white eyes with their blue slit pupils. Oddly, they did not at all give the impression of blindness, but rather of seeing too much, so that Firekeeper shifted uneasily despite herself. Blind Seer was less impressed.

"I smell your tension, cat, though you try to hide it. Speak. Or is this matter not as urgent as your glands believe?"

"It is urgent," the jaguar said, "but I am not certain we can deal with it until darkness has fallen and the humans grow quiet."

"Then it has to do with our prisoners?" Firekeeper prompted. "What have those white eyes seen?"

"Great activity where there should be little," Truth replied. "Two missing who should be more visible. Anticipation and anger warring in the same breasts. I think that those we think are our captives have come up with some plan to turn against us, to transform the hunters into the hunted."

Firekeeper frowned. "Two missing?"

"Ynamynet and Lachen—not missing as such. They are seen at the evening meal and occasionally elsewhere. However, when I began my prowling, I realized I could not find them. I asked the yarimaimalom, and they assured me the two Once Dead were about, but admitted upon being pressed that there were long chunks of the day that one or the other of that pair were missing."

"And no one wondered about this?" Blind Seer growled. "No one felt concern that the Ones of this strange pack vanish?"

"Not all creatures are wolves," Truth said stiffly, "to think in such a fashion. Most of the watchers were wingéd folk, and although they flock, the flocks rarely have leaders as such."

Firekeeper evaded a budding argument by raising another question. "The humans have been watched continuously since we have taken them. Their actions have been restricted to the counsel building alone. Only those few who must go elsewhere to perform their duties have done so—and those under escort. How could they act against us?"

"Our error," Truth said obliquely, "was in forgetting that although these southwestern yarimaimalom are indeed yarimaimalom, they know little of humans. Moreover, these humans speak languages we do not, so that they could talk to each other. As long as they hid the emotional sense of what they said beneath bland faces our watchers could not understand what was being said. Even so, when I questioned them, a few of the more nose-oriented watchers admitted being troubled by a strange odor of triumph they scented from a few of the humans."

Firekeeper nodded. "Eshinarvash is too large to have been among the watchers, and the ravens spent their waking hours watching over you. You are right. The yarimaimalom from the southwestern forests could easily be fooled. But what could the humans do, confined as they are in one building? We inspected that building before it was turned into a prison. I thought that we had removed everything that could be turned into a weapon."

"I do not know what they are doing," Truth said, "but the omens are clear. If we do not investigate this soon—and without our investigation being known of—events will turn against us."

"I know little of divination," Blind Seer said, "but enough to draw some conclusions from what you have said. This need for secrecy and speed would seem to indicate that whatever the humans have been preparing, it is nearly done—close enough that were our purpose to be detected they might spring their trap early."

Truth's tail began lashing again. "I fear you are correct, wolf. My first impulse was to make my way inside and inspect immediately, but the smoothly flowing river of the immediate future broke into foaming white water."

"Then for now the future flows smooth?" Firekeeper asked.

"Fairly," Truth said. "Few things move from now to then unquestioned."

They waited until nightfall, but not without making preparations. Their allies were briefed, and the yarimaimalom cautioned that the least change in their usual manner might mean disaster for them all. Perhaps these Wise Beasts would have been more contentious, but they were of Truth's faith, and the words of a jaguar marked so clearly with Ahmyn's sign were not to be lightly disobeyed.

There was the usual wrangle as Firekeeper convinced the others that she, Blind Seer, and Truth were the best adapted to undertake the investigation of the administration building.

"We all see well by night," she said, "and there is no need to translate among us."

"But you've been ill," Derian protested. "I know how I feel. I can't imagine you feel much better."

"Wild things," Firekeeper responded, "are used to being 'not better.' I not think I was 'better' all the years of my life until I meet you. Besides, we need you with Plik and Eshinarvash. Someone must take charge of making certain that yarimaimalom do not act foolishly, and that the humans do not flee."

Finally, the others agreed, and Firekeeper and Blind Seer ate a large meal and settled in to sleep. The wolf-woman might have boasted how much stronger she felt, but in reality she feared that her own weakness might betray them all.

PLIK WOKE FIREKEEPER and Blind Seer after full dark.

"The others are awake already," he said. "I saved you for last since I knew you woke clearheaded."

In reality, the maimalodalu's motives had been different. He knew well how weak he had been following querinalo, and he had wanted to give the pair as much rest as possible.

The twins had been told they must wait in the cottage that had been their own. Firekeeper respected the nursing the pair had done, but she did not yet trust them at her back. Somewhat sadly, for he was growing fond of both Tiniel and Isende, Plik had agreed. A brace of eagles, not yet recovered from their captivity, but fully able to deal with two rather plump humans, would lurk on the rooftop in secret watch.

Neither twin had protested, but Plik could smell their mingled disappointment and relief as they returned to captivity. He thought the disappointment was stronger in Tiniel, the relief in Isende, and wondered just what had so dismayed the young man. Was Tiniel looking to prove himself to them, or did he have some other motivation? Much as he liked the young man, Plik could not forget that Tiniel had been willing to use blood magic, a thing any sane person should shun.

As those who would be venturing out into the chill dampness of the night spooned down hot, thick stew, and wiped their bowls with coarse brown bread, Bitter briefed them on what they might expect. The ravens felt deeply shamed that they had not realized that the humans were plotting against them, and nothing the others could say would keep them from attempting to make amends.

"*The building stands several stories high,*" Bitter began, "*but we are fairly certain that whatever it is you seek lies below ground, not above. Today we wingéd folk have looked in through every window, and various of the yarimaimalom have done their best to sniff around without raising suspicion.*"

"Won't this in itself arouse suspicion?" Derian asked when this was translated.

"*Not really,*" Bitter replied. "*The yarimaimalom have always had some of their number go within the headquarters building. They might not be wise in the ways of humans, but they knew full well that they could not see all the interior through the windows. Fearing that any representative of their number might be attacked or imprisoned, however, they tended to send the larger, more dangerous beasts—especially the bears, for there seemed no way a bear could be slain without first giving ample warning. But bears are very bulky, and not as inquisitive as wolves or cats.*"

Derian nodded. "I understand."

"*We have located the area that seems to be at the heart of the plotting,*" Bitter continued. "*In the oldest portion of the structure, near the center, there is a stairway leading down. We did not know of its existence until today, for the doors were always closed.*"

Firekeeper looked at the floor plan Plik had produced based on the reports of the various yarimaimalom.

"I remember that door," she said. "It was locked—not only locked, but swollen shut. We checked the workings of the lock and found them fused. There seemed no way it could be opened, and so we left it be."

"This door is unsealed now," Bitter said, *"but great care has been taken that it not appear to have been unsealed. That would be suspicious enough, but the bear who scouted today noted that both Lachen and Ynamynet's scents were strong around that area. However, she could not recall having seen either of them very frequently over the past several days."*

"Certainly Ynamynet and Lachen are at the center of this attempt," Plik said. "I wonder if they are attempting some sort of magic?"

"Perhaps," Harjeedian replied. "Perhaps something more mundane. We cannot forget that they are the last of the Once Dead here and so the leaders of this community. They may be fitting sharpened spoons onto broom handles to make spears."

Plik hid a smile as Firekeeper gave a characteristic, almost canine, shake of impatience.

"We know when we know," the wolf-woman said rising to her feet, "and we not know until we go. So let us go."

YOU SHOULDN'T EXPECT to come out of wrestling with a deity untouched, but Truth hadn't quite expected Ahmyn's touch to be so hard or so permanent.

What she hadn't told the others was how these new white eyes of hers Saw all the time. Before she'd been able to slip in and out of her omen visions at will. Now she saw them all the time. Truth guessed it was Ahmyn's way of reminding her what she'd been ready to give up.

Well, Truth certainly was reminded, and pretty much constantly confused. She thought that eventually she would learn to see what was real and what was shadow. When Firekeeper had roused Truth from querinalo's hold, Truth had seen a gaggle of Firekeepers: one shaking her with her right hand, one with her left, another toeing her with a bare foot (and toeing her with the other foot), one prodding her from a distance with the end of her unstrung bow, another calling from a perch on Eshinarvash's back.

That had been confusing enough. More confusing were the actions Truth saw herself taking: slashing out with a paw, rolling over and clawing with hind feet, bolting for cover and running. When she'd answered Firekeeper's words with words of her own, Truth had hardly believed that this was her own real action.

In the days that had passed, Truth had learned to discern reality from possibility. Reality had acquired a brighter hue (or the visions duller ones). Yet even so the visions remained, ghost dancers overlapping the world she moved in with worlds her actions might create.

No, Truth hadn't expected to come from wrestling with Fire untouched, but she hadn't realized just how severely she'd be burned.

Oddly, Truth saw reality more clearly after nightfall than at any other time. This was because the visions persisted in appearing tinted with color, a faint wash that darkness did not grant reality. So she headed for the administration building with a fair degree of confidence, Firekeeper and Blind Seer pacing her, all of them moving with a bit less speed and confidence than was their wont.

When they came to the administration building's main door, a dog-fox was waiting for them. (And Truth saw the realities in which they had been met by a bear, a puma, a doe, an osprey, by no one at all.)

"The humans are quiet," the dog-fox said. "If they are not sleeping within their night lairs, then they are feigning such sleep. A few are awake in the kitchen, brewing tea and talking."

"Are any of our own within the place?" Firekeeper asked.

"A bear dozes in the kitchen," the fox replied, "and my mate and several raccoons keep covert watch in the upper reaches."

"And the cellar?" Firekeeper asked.

"None are there. We have obeyed orders that we not give away our awareness of that section of the building, but from what we can hear all is quiet."

"Lachen and Ynamynet?"

"Among those who were watched going from the public areas to their own—separate—chambers."

Firekeeper grunted acknowledgment and glanced at the other two to see if they had anything to add. Blind Seer shook his head after the human fashion.

Truth looked at the options before her and saw many questions that could be asked and answered, but none that seemed imperative. Letting Firekeeper open the door with those useful hands, Truth followed the two wolves inside.

The large building was comparatively still. Somewhere in the upper reaches, a baby was shrieking in high, rhythmic cries. Booted footsteps moved purposefully down a corridor and in their cadence Truth recognized the patient doctor.

A woman's belly laugh came faintly from the back of the house. Truth wondered if the entertainment being pursued included something more intoxicating than tea. However, although visions sought to become reality by luring her to investigate, Truth kept her course, fixing her gaze on Blind Seer's tail to eliminate distracting images.

Exterior impressions invaded nonetheless, each tempting the jaguar's attention to wander: an odor of fish from an otherwise pristine bit of carpet, a creak as some building timber protested the damp weather, the sensation of her paws moving from carpet to stone flagging. Truth focused as hard as she could on the present moment, and was rewarded by seeing Firekeeper carefully unlatch the dusty double-sided door that led to the lower reaches of the administration building.

There was no lock, nor did the hinges creak under the weight of the old wood. A scent of fresh oil and ancient rust answered why, and Truth (fighting images of what might have happened had the door been locked, had the hinges squealed, had an alarm been rigged) found clarity in focusing on the quality of the hinges' construction and the care that had been taken that the door remain decrepit-looking, though the scent trails confirmed that this passage had seen steady use.

The area below was dark, and Firekeeper stepped back to let Blind Seer take the lead. She waited a moment to see if Truth cared to go before her, and when the jaguar hung back said softly, "Unless you can close the door, come quickly so I may do so."

Truth, her mind blossoming with all the possible ramifications of doors left open and shut, padded in and stood on the landing while Firekeeper carefully closed and latched the door. Not questioning why the jaguar did not go before her, Firekeeper hurried after her pack mate. Truth came last, struggling to dampen images of the ramifications of questions asked, not asked, answered and not.

The stair was carved from the rock on which the headquarter's building had been constructed. As they descended, their way was lit by a faint glow that came from blocks set intermittently in the masonry of the wall. These were at foot level and did little more than illuminate the treads, but Truth imagined that humans would have found them useful.

In this glow, Truth saw marks of chisel and hammer on the stone. This place then had been worked by human labor, not magic. She thought of the work involved, and wondered what had been so important that such work should be done. The stair angled right, then went farther down.

Now Truth saw what seemed to be native rock, untouched by tools. She understood that what seemed to be a cellar was actually a natural ravine. The building had been built over it, and again she wondered why. Surely the labor involved in cutting that staircase eliminated any benefit garnered from not having to excavate the cellar.

The stairway angled again, then, with a few almost anticlimactic steps, came to a halt. Wolves and jaguars are soft-footed creatures, but Truth thought that the sound of her breath indicated that they were in a large chamber. As she debated the merits of making a sound or not, perhaps a growl or a snarl or extending her claw and scraping the stone, Firekeeper's husky voice, pitched low but not whispering, broke the stillness.

"So?" she asked. "What do ears and noses tell?"

"Blood," Blind Seer said instantly. "Not in great quantities, but there."

"Fresh earth," Truth added, "broken stone. Familiar human scents: Ynamynet, Lachen, Skea, Verul, a few others."

"Beeswax and lamp oil and the ashes of old fires," Blind Seer said. "Perhaps Firekeeper would care to give us more light."

"You scent no one here?" Firekeeper asked.

"No one here in the now," Blind Seer reassured her. "As humans work by light, I think we will need light to see what they do here."

Firekeeper grunted soft agreement and let Blind Seer guide her to where he smelled lamp oil. Taking from the bag she wore about her neck the fire-making tools that—like her knife—never left her, she struck spark to tinder and soon had lit both candle and oil lamp.

To eyes accustomed to seeing with very little light, these two pale glows revealed a great deal—and for Truth revealed more than she wished to see. Visions assaulted her of vengeful humans, alerted somehow by the light as they had not been by soft conversation, clattering in booted feet down the stair. They rolled from hiding in secret chambers, came brandishing swords and long-hafted spears.

True, these last images were fainter than the others, for even in the confused state of her thoughts Truth had some sense of balance, but even so she reared on her hind legs and struck at one of the more persistent images.

"Truth?" said Blind Seer, his question pitched on a rumbling growl.

"I'm fine," she lied. "A bug or bit of ash."

She could tell from the cant of the wolf's ears that he did not quite believe her, but neither was he willing to challenge the veracity of her statement.

To distract herself from probing visions of what would happen if that challenge came, Truth forced herself to study the minute details of the chamber in which they stood.

She had been right when she had thought it a ravine, for that was precisely what it was—small by the standards of such in the open air, but making for a quite large, if irregularly shaped, room. Glancing up, she saw that the ceiling above was only partly human built.

"This must have been both cave and ravine," Truth said, "and the building was built above it. I wonder why."

She regretted the last statement, for Ahmyn's generosity offered her a wealth of possibilities. Firekeeper's blunt practicality broke these as a paw breaks a reflection.

"I wonder more," the wolf-woman said, "that this place is so uncluttered. I am no human, but I have lived in their dens, and places like this are usually filled with overflow from their lives: vegetables or discarded furniture or some such litter. I have seen this in castles and in common houses. Why is this place so empty?"

"Not all empty," Blind Seer said, indicating an area deeper in. "My nose tells me that some work is going on over there."

"Let us look then," Firekeeper said, but she continued to muse as she lifted lamp and candle, then followed the wolf. "True, this place was unused, the door swollen shut until a few days past, but I cannot believe that humans before querinalo were any less given to hoarding than those who have come after."

Blind Seer led them (for Truth was too distracted to track anything herself, but could only follow and hope not to stumble) to what his nose had found. At first all Truth's eyes saw was a jumble of rocks broken and moved back from a section of the wall rather smoother than those around. Then she heard Firekeeper hiss something that might have been a curse, and the random detritus fell into a recognizable pattern.

"There is a gate here," Firekeeper said. "It was buried beneath that rock fall, but it is here. That is what they have been doing. It is as you said, sweet hunter, rabbits and their burrows. No wonder some dared smell of triumph. They thought to leave by this and bring back allies."

Blind Seer was casting around, nose close to the ground. Here and there he sniffed deeply. Once he sneezed.

"The blood I have scented seems mostly to have come from this work," he reported. "Where rock cut or crushed, not shed for spellcasting."

"That is something," Firekeeper said. "Then this thing is not yet alive."

"I don't think so," Blind Seer said. "In a day or so, though . . . Truth has advised us well."

Truth lashed her tail back and forth, then seized on one image among the many.

"We should check," she said, "to make sure that this gate is the only such thing here. Above they built many gates close together."

"Good," Firekeeper said. "I will leave the lamp here, but take the candle."

She did so, moving quickly as if hot on some trail. Blind Seer cast his search in another direction, and Truth paused to inspect the gate they had found before joining in the search. This gate was different from the one at the stronghold, for no effort had been made to hide it. Here the markings were carved deeply into the surrounding rock, the channel that would carry blood to fuel the spell cut broad and wide.

Truth sniffed, but no blood scent remained, though much must have been spilled here. Even as she realized the ludicrousness of this gesture, she also re- alized that she was tense and alert, every part of her straining for something that had not yet happened, but that she was certain must come.

It was with something almost like relief that Truth heard a scrape of leather against stone, a footfall from somewhere, though not the stair down which they had come. It did not belong to either of her companions. Both of them were unshod.

Truth did not need to alert Firekeeper and Blind Seer. Both had heard, and upon hearing, Firekeeper had snuffed the flame of her candle. Truth consid- ered knocking over the lamp, but seeing the ramifications of this choice de- cided to leave it. The light had to have been seen, and humans were easily distracted by a bit of light. Instead, Truth took step after perfect step and melted soundlessly into the surrounding darkness.

XXXVI

FIREKEEPER RUBBED the still warm candle wick between thumb and forefinger to damp the last smouldering scent. Then she stood frozen and listened.

Footsteps, shod feet on stone stairs, more than one set. Three sets, perhaps, or five. Interestingly, they were not coming from the direction of the stair by which she and her companions had descended, but from another off in the darkness where her candlelight had not carried, in the direction in which Blind Seer had gone.

We might have guessed there would be another way into this place, she thought, *with all our talk of rabbits and their burrows.*

Firekeeper wasn't worried about Blind Seer. The wolf would have heard the footsteps even before she had. Doubtless he was somewhere in the shadowed chamber, listening as she was.

Firekeeper was more concerned about Truth. The jaguar had been acting very oddly—although Truth had always been hard to figure out. However, as the wolf-woman heard nothing, she trusted that the jaguar, too, was waiting to see what this intrusion might bring.

The first paces were regular and business-like; then there was hesitation.

"Who left a lamp burning?" Lachen's voice, the inflections accusatory, the language his odd version of Liglimosh.

Firekeeper felt fortunate he was speaking something she could understand, but then these mixed peoples must have a few languages that they chose to speak among themselves.

"The chamber was dark when we left." Skea, confident. "I blew out the lamps myself."

"Who's there?" Lachen called out. Then in a lower tone, "We told everyone to stay away from here lest those creatures become suspicious about comings and goings. Why won't they obey?"

The footsteps had resumed during this rant, and Firekeeper felt Blind Seer's nose cold against her arm.

"Five," he said. "The four who came to the stronghold and one male I do not know."

Firekeeper touched his head in acknowledgment. There was no need to say that the best thing they could do was to wait, listen, and learn what they could. She hoped Truth thought the same.

The footsteps had reached the room, their sound widening as they struck the stone floor. A silhouetted figure intercepted the lamplight. Ynamynet spoke.

"It's turned pretty low. It's possible that there was a spark in the wick that slowly kindled in the oil. I'll take a look around."

She had turned up the wick now, and Firekeeper took care not to look directly at the bright center of the new halo of light.

Ynamynet moved around the immediate area, lighting a series of lamps hung from hooks set into walls or support beams. Firekeeper studied what had been revealed.

In this greater range of light, the place looked less like the natural ravine it had begun as and more like a human structure fashioned after a ravine. Firekeeper was reminded of the caverns beneath Dragon's Breath in New Kelvin. There, too, the sorcerers had liked to work their incantations beneath the earth. Firekeeper wondered if they had reason for this other than the obvious security such places offered.

We know too little about magic, Firekeeper thought fleetingly, *and too much of what we know is wrong.*

Lachen had accepted Ynamynet's suggestions, perhaps because with the coming of light he no longer felt so afraid. Humans put far too much trust in light. Lachen had moved to the gate, holding one of the lamps close so he could inspect the markings on the wall.

"We should have the significant parts cleared in another few hours," he announced, "if we put our backs to it."

This appeared to be a command of sorts, for Skea, Verul, and the last person now moved forward and resumed clearing away the rocks. This last was a very large man who reminded Firekeeper a little of her friend Ox, for all this man was colored like the Winter Grass people of Stonehold, with their golden brown skin and shining black hair. Lachen helped, though he talked as much as he worked.

"Found anything, Ynamynet?"

Ynamynet had moved in the direction Blind Seer had gone, and Firekeeper felt a trace of apprehension. What if the wolf had left a paw print to mark his presence? She asked him, and the wolf replied confidently.

"If she can read sign on stone, then perhaps, but I smelled many trails there. The dust and grit have long been muddled by these humans' own passage. I ran clean-foot, so left nothing behind."

However, Blind Seer might have carried mud between each toe for all Ynamynet would have noticed. Firekeeper saw that Ynamynet's investigation was not for the floor, but for the various nooks and crannies about the edges of the room. Ynamynet stopped in one place, and Firekeeper's heart began to pound uncomfortably hard, certain that Ynamynet had found some sign of their passage, but the woman was only studying with idle speculation another heap of fallen rock.

"I wonder where this gate goes?"

"Elsewhere," Lachen grunted. He was helping Skea move a large slab. "When we are free of these intruders, perhaps we will look."

"Hmmm . . ." Ynamynet said.

She left her perusal of the wall and continued her search. There was no urgency about Ynamynet's progress, and Firekeeper suspected Ynamynet was searching mostly to humor Lachen and to avoid taking her own turn at moving rock.

Eventually, Ynamynet turned in the direction of the place from which Firekeeper and Blind Seer had been watching, but they had long since melted away, moving to where they could see both what Ynamynet had found and the men working over the stone heap behind them. Firekeeper had even remembered to take the candle with her so there would be no question of how it came to be there.

The wolf-woman had almost forgotten Truth, for the jaguar had been silent until now. Firekeeper had guessed that like them the great cat was watching and waiting, moving a few steps to avoid the traveling light.

Forgetting Truth proved to be a mistake.

Eventually, Ynamynet's path brought her into the vicinity of the stair by which the trio had descended. She raised her lamp to look up the stair, and there on the lowest landing crouched the jaguar.

Truth was frozen in midmotion, one paw raised as if she would climb further up the stairs, her head turned as if she would descend the few stairs that separated her from the room below. Even her tail was held stiffly in mid-lash. Her blue-white eyes were the only things that moved, darting back and forth, watching something that none of the others could see.

"She's gone mad again," Blind Seer breathed in resignation.

Ynamynet's response to finding the jaguar, so very strange with her charcoal coat and burning spots, was completely sensible as human reactions went. She screamed, her voice so shrill that in it Firekeeper heard the long-ago days when humans were still wild creatures, and such screams were meant to summon a distant pack.

The men responded as those long-ago men must have done, dropping their burdens and racing to the woman's side. All but Lachen bore makeshift clubs, crafted from the furniture left in the administration building. They ran with these raised, but swift as they were, Firekeeper and Blind Seer were the swifter.

They did not run to put themselves between Truth and those who now lunged toward her, but leapt from behind. Blind Seer bore the ox-built man over, and Firekeeper heard the man hit with a solid, sickening crack. She did not think he would trouble them soon—if ever.

She had chosen for her target Verul, the big, fair-skinned Twice Dead. Keeping in mind her promise to Derian that there would be as little killing as need be, Firekeeper did not leap upon Verul's back and put her Fang into his throat, but instead grabbed at his leg, tripping him so he stumbled and fell. In catching himself on his hands, Verul let his club drop and the solid bit of wood skittered off into the shadows.

But Verul was luckier than the other man, and caught himself successfully, rolling over onto his back and bounding to his feet with admirable ease. Firekeeper, joints and muscles still aching from fever, envied him and even hated him a little. That hate made what she must do next a little easier.

Verul was still casting about for who had hit him, for Ynamynet's one lamp, held in her shaking hand, cast as much dancing shadow as it did light. In the cover of those shadows, Firekeeper came low and fast. Her Fang was sharp, and Verul's light leather boots offered the blade little challenge. In one hard cut, Firekeeper sliced the tendon at the back of his ankle.

Verul bellowed in rage and pain, but for all his noise, his leg buckled beneath him nonetheless. He crashed to the floor, and this time he stayed down.

Blind Seer had now targeted Skea, but the dark-skinned man was proving more of a challenge than his fellows, and not only because he had some warning. Skea seemed able to root himself to the floor on which he stood, and also to understand that if Blind Seer leapt, the wolf would be for that moment vulnerable. Even so, there was no way that Skea would have attention for any other than Blind Seer for a good time to come.

Firekeeper glanced behind her. Lachen had fallen on his knees beside the big man Blind Seer had first attacked. His motions as he checked the man for signs of life were stiff and jerky. Clearly, he could hardly believe what had happened, that his plans had come to ruin so quickly. Ynamynet, however, remained on her feet, alert, standing between Firekeeper and Truth. It was to her the wolf-woman turned her attention.

The women locked eyes and Ynamynet tilted her chin up in defiance. Firekeeper shifted her grip on her blade, but she had been with humans too long. She could not bring herself to strike this unarmed opponent, especially with Derian's anguish fresh in her mind. She was struggling to remember the human forms for demanding surrender—for surely the wolf's way would only frighten this woman, if not kill her—when Ynamynet said something very strange.

"I have a daughter," she said, her tone so carefully conversational that Firekeeper could hear the fear vibrating beneath every note. "Do you have any children?"

"No," Firekeeper said, completely confused.

"Then perhaps you will not understand when I tell you I could not trust my daughter to the mercies of you and your allies—especially of you, given how I had betrayed our agreement there at the Setting Sun stronghold. Zebel attempted to assure me that you were a creature of honor, but I could not even trust him. I must do what I could to escape."

"I do not want your daughter," Firekeeper said. "I do not want you or this place or anything else, but having them I must deal with them."

"If I order Skea to surrender, will the wolf kill him?" Ynamynet asked in that same too conversational voice.

"If the surrender is real," Firekeeper said, "Blind Seer will not harm him."

Ynamynet raised her voice. "Skea. Surrender."

Firekeeper did not turn, did not trust this woman, but she heard the dull thud of wood as Skea dropped his club. She heard the crack as Blind Seer broke the piece of wood in his jaws, and hid a smile. Wolves had a sense of humor she understood perfectly.

"Are you surrender?" Firekeeper asked.

Ynamynet shrugged. "I am unarmed—unless I could turn this lamp into a weapon, which I cannot. There is a jaguar at my back, and you to the front. If you will accept my surrender I will give it."

"I accept," Firekeeper said. "Sit and . . ."

She stopped speaking, competing sounds claiming her attention. One was a rumbling growl from Truth, echoing from stone walls to reverberate like thunder. The other was an anguished shout from the almost forgotten Lachen.

"No! No! No! No!" Screaming on a rising note. "NO!"

Firekeeper wheeled and saw Lachen rolling on the floor. He was deliberately soaking himself in the blood that had flowed from Verul's cut leg before that man had stanched the flow. Verul, seated on the floor, both hands gripping the makeshift bandage he had bound around his wound, was staring at Lachen in horror, a horror that grew to terror as Lachen began to claw at Verul's hands, trying to force them from the wound.

Verul kicked out at Lachen with his sound leg, and Firekeeper heard bones break, probably in Lachen's hand, but Lachen seemed to be beyond pain. He looked at the limp hand and his own blood dripping from broken skin and seemed more pleased than otherwise. He was muttering to himself, and in the words Firekeeper recognized the cadences of the older form of Liglimosh.

Before she could act, steam began to rise around Lachen, steam the rusty red of blood. It rose so thickly that Lachen vanished entirely from view. Then the mist began taking a form that made Firekeeper's gut shrivel, something that touched her hindbrain with fear close to paralysis. The shape had something to do with long claws, something to do with fire. It was reaching for her, and she knew those long claws would pierce her brain, then penetrate directly into her heart.

Blind Seer snarled and interposed himself between Firekeeper and the mist, pushing her back. Claws meant to rip into her brain passed harmlessly over the wolf's head.

In Blind Seer's courage, Firekeeper found the will to move. Although every fiber of her wanted to bolt for some safe corner, she slashed out at the thing with her Fang. The keen blade met no more resistance than it would have in a mist, but one of those long claws connected with her knife hand and drew blood.

The mist darkened about her hand, and Firekeeper swore she could hear purring. She could hear Lachen laughing now, but there was nothing of merriment in the sound, only more fear.

Firekeeper jerked her hand free of the mist and stumbled back a pace. The mist could claw at her, but she apparently could not injure it. Blind Seer had also found his own attacks fruitless. Thus far, his fur and his cloth coat had protected him from injury, but that immunity would not last long.

"Back away!" Firekeeper cried. "We cannot hurt it this way."

At that moment, Truth's growl, which had been like thunder rumbling, cracked lightning into a snarl. The jaguar sprang directly into the place where the mist was darkest red, directly onto Lachen.

Truth landed squarely on Lachen's chest. Unlike a wolf, Truth did not go for the throat, but ripped directly into the man's face. Jaws that could break the thickness of a snapping turtle's shell found no challenge in the bones of a skull. There was one solid crack, and then another, this sounding a flatter note.

The lamplight showed Lachen's brains spilling onto the floor, but the rust red mist did not diminish. Firekeeper knew it was rooted in Lachen's blood now, draining the hot fluid into itself, drinking gleeful sustenance, rejoicing in freedom from its maker's death. With every moment the cloud grew larger and more dense.

Truth leapt free, contemplating what she had done—or at least contemplating something, for her gaze was active, though her body had frozen into immobility once again.

"Don't go near the mist!" Ynamynet called. "Don't let it touch you."

Firekeeper was willing to obey, but then her gaze fell on Verul. The fair-haired man was trying to get away, but he could not rise without letting more blood flow—a thing he was loath to do, for clearly it would attract the mist to him. Firekeeper dodged the groping tendrils of mist and darted to Verul's side. Grabbing him beneath the armpits, she dragged him away from the mist, avoiding the bright claws that continued to grope after her.

Skea had moved under his own power, bringing with him the inert form of the man Blind Seer had first attacked. Together, they watched as the mist struggled to reach them, but it seemed anchored on Lachen, and Lachen was not moving. Eventually, all that remained was Lachen's corpse with its ruined head—and numerous long slashes along his arms, where, unseen to them within the mist's red heart, he had apparently cut himself to feed the mist.

Firekeeper looked at Ynamynet.

"You did not help Lachen. You helped us. Why?"

"I had given you my surrender. I did not think you would accept it a second time. Better to stand and wait. Either way, I would have a victory of sorts."

Firekeeper tilted her head to one side, considering. There was something very wolf-like in such a practical solution—and she remembered that Ynamynet had mentioned a daughter. The Once Dead had good reason to want to live, on any terms.

"What manner of creature was that thing?" Blind Seer asked, and Firekeeper translated.

"Emotion given force through blood," Ynamynet said. "As you saw, Lachen used it as a weapon, a means to fight you without your being able to touch him yourself. His fear was the link that permitted the mist to make contact with you. Once the jaguar killed him, the mist was no longer able to do so."

Firekeeper mused that Ynamynet must have known the mist's vulnerability but had not chosen to reveal it when it might have aided them. No harm, yes, but no help until it was clear which way the fight must go. Something to remember.

Turning to Skea, Firekeeper jerked her head at the man on the floor.

"Live or not?"

"He breathes," Skea reported, "but he hit his head hard when the wolf jumped him. I'd like the doctor to see him."

"See him and Verul both," Firekeeper said, "but not until we settle a thing or two first."

She looked at Blind Seer. "Hold these while I get word to our pack above. Then we will talk about gates and prisoners and what will come hereafter."

FIREKEEPER DIDN'T WANT the wounded to receive treatment until all matters were settled, but despite how Derian felt about what querinalo had done to him—and the resentment he still harbored that no one had warned them what might happen if they came through the gate—Derian found himself among those working to convince the wolf-woman that this was not a good idea.

"What if someone dies?" Derian said. "We have the upper hand, but we can't forget two things: First, there are more of them than there are of us. Second, with Lachen dead, Ynamynet is now the only person we know of who can open our gate home."

"Three things," Plik added. "We can't forget three things. The third is that we have been very lucky so far, and in the many days we have been here no one has come through any of the active gates. Our luck won't last forever."

Firekeeper had at last been convinced. Watching her, Derian wondered how much of her willingness had been due to physical exhaustion. He knew that his turn as scout had worn him down. Firekeeper and Blind Seer had not just scouted, they'd had to fight.

So a meeting was scheduled for the following day at noon. It was to be held in the large hall the Once Dead had used for their own meetings. Harjeedian had suggested that the prisoners be permitted to nominate four representatives. Firekeeper had surprised everyone by saying that she felt every one of the prisoners had the right to speak.

"We decide if they live or die, stay or go. I say everyone come, everyone make a great howl, and when it is over, well . . ."

She had shrugged.

Derian stared at her. "But, Firekeeper, you hate debates."

"I hate more this being as One over those I have not beaten myself. This is serious, Derian, too serious for me."

In the end, a compromise had been reached between Firekeeper's suggestion and Harjeedian's. The prisoners would be asked to nominate four speakers, and to funnel their questions through these speakers. Moreover, the yarimaimalom would be present in force, reducing to nil any temptation on the part of the prisoners to revolt.

"I will stay outside," Eshinarvash said, and Derian felt a weird thrill that he could understand the Wise Horse's speech so easily, "and take command of those who continue to patrol the gates. Give me at least a few of the wingéd folk as messengers, and you will know almost as I do if anything untoward occurs."

Truth lashed her tail, and Plik translated for the jaguar, "I will go with Eshinarvash. These eyes see that my being at the council would not help—and perhaps my presence would hurt."

The jaguar did not clarify, and no one asked her to do so. Firekeeper's report of how Truth had been pushed over the borders of sanity once again was still fresh in all their memories—as was their relief that she had come back from wherever her odd visions had taken her.

There was one remaining problem. Although several of the prisoners spoke either Liglimosh or the odd version of the language that Lachen had used, and a few even spoke something close enough to Pellish that those who spoke that language could communicate with them, there was no one language common to them all.

Rather bravely, as Derian saw it, Isende offered herself as translator.

"If Ynamynet can do that spell again," Isende said, "I'm willing to help. I don't know a lot about whatever that spell did, but it doesn't seem to have hurt me, and, well, I think the Old World people will feel a lot more certain they're getting the truth if the translation is coming through something they're familiar with."

Faced with his sister's courage, Tiniel offered himself as well. "After all, last time they seemed to need a male speaker and a female."

Ynamynet was summoned and allowed that she knew the procedure.

"Does it have to work so that I don't remember anything afterwards?" Isende asked. "That's the part I really didn't like."

"That was a separate spell," Ynamynet said. "I can leave that one out."

"Then I'll do it," Isende said.

"And I," Tiniel added. "If that will make it easier."

"It will," Ynamynet agreed. "There is a gender-linked element. However, it will take me some time to prepare the necessary components and . . ."

She looked uncomfortable, and Tiniel gave a wry grin.

"Let me guess. You're going to need a little blood from each of us."

"That is right," Ynamynet said. "If it is any comfort, any of those who do not understand what the northerners call 'Liglimosh' will need to give a few drops as well. This is what will enable them to use your ears to hear their words."

Derian found himself unduly relieved that he wouldn't need to contribute. The idea of his blood being mingled with that of a bunch of other people made his skin crawl.

He hadn't missed how Ynamynet kept looking at him, nor had he missed that her gaze was admiring rather than otherwise. Strangely, Ynamynet's admiration made him feel better than had any of the kind or encouraging things his friends had said.

Maybe you should have been give jackass ears, Derian Carter, Derian thought ruefully. *You're at least as stubborn as one.*

When the meeting convened, at midday on the day following what Firekeeper was calling—with what Derian was certain was an attempt at humor—"the Battle of the Basement," not all the prisoners chose to attend. Some, overwhelmed by all that had happened in the past several days, were apathetic, already viewing their fates as something beyond their control. Some trusted the four appointed representatives. Some, Derian was astonished to learn, were as uncomfortable with blood magic as he was.

"They don't wish to give any of their blood," Zebel said dryly, "out of fear that some little may be held back for other purposes."

"Do you think Ynamynet would do this?" Derian asked.

"No, too much rests on this meeting for her to play games. In any case, the entire procedure is being closely watched—not only by our own people, but by several of the yarimaimalom."

"And keeping blood hidden from a fox's nose, or a wolf's," Derian said, understanding, "would be nearly impossible."

"Precisely," Zebel replied.

No one had been surprised when Zebel had been chosen as one of the four speakers. Ynamynet had been the other obvious choice. However, only Blind Seer wasn't surprised when Skea was chosen as a third. Nor was the wolf surprised when Ynamynet revealed that Skea was her husband.

"I scented the closeness between them," the wolf said. Firekeeper still had to translate, of course. "First in the stronghold, but there I thought it the closeness of a faithful guard to the one guarded. In the basement, I was more certain."

There had been some question as to whether Skea and Ynamynet both should be permitted to act as speakers, but in the end the New World contingent decided to let the Old Worlders decide this for themselves.

"They seem to see Skea as representative of those Twice Dead rather than as Ynamynet's spouse," Harjeedian said. "That, along with the fact that Skea speaks Liglimosh, makes him a good choice in their eyes."

The last speaker chosen was taken from the "Never Lived." Urgana was an older woman who had chosen long ago to march her fate in step with that of a beloved sister who had been Once Dead. The sibling had died a few years ago, but by then Urgana belonged more to the semi-exile world of the Once Dead than she did to the community she had left behind. Urgana spoke the same form of Liglimosh that Lachen had spoken, although she took pains to assure them that she and that particular Once Dead had not been close.

"He was arrogant," Urgana said, "and had long forgotten the faith of our ancestors—this despite the fact that his own father was an aridisdu and his mother's mother had been a kidisdu with an almost legendary rapport with birds of prey."

Derian thought that Urgana might already be on "their" side of things. Certainly, she had been horrified when she had learned that the beasts being kept in the menagerie were yarimaimalom. With her Once Dead sister now truly dead, Urgana had fewer ties to the resident community than did Ynamynet or the doctor.

But then, Derian thought as he settled into his assigned seat behind a long, slightly curved table, *the entire point here is to see if we can eliminate "their side" and "our side," and somehow construct an entirely new setup out of this mess.*

Harjeedian had been nominated as head of the meeting, a role he slipped into very easily, doubtless because in his calling, meetings were part of his routine. Plik was serving as main translator for the yarimaimalom, although he had made clear that he would offer his own opinions as well. Firekeeper sat, as usual, on the floor, arm around Blind Seer. The wolf had refused to wear his blanket coat in this public forum, and Derian, still dreadfully sensitive about his own altered appearance, could not blame him.

Firekeeper had been less kind in her reaction to Blind Seer's vanity, and Derian wondered if she was seeking to warm the wolf with her own body heat.

Harjeedian called the meeting to order with a statement that had been agreed upon in advance.

"This meeting is to serve two purposes: to decide the fate of the facilities on the Nexus Islands, and to allow the people who were in control of this place before our coming to have some say in what will be done with them."

A low murmur of consternation and surprise answered this, and Harjeedian held up his hand in sign that he needed to continue.

"Those of us from the New World came here with no desire to control this place, but now that we know that it exists, and now that we know that other gates may exist, we have reluctantly decided that either we must maintain control of the facility or we must destroy it. Our wish is to control it and to learn how to use it, for, as much as human—and indeed yarimaimalom—nature can embrace the desire to return to past innocence, a wise spirit knows that this cannot be done. However, we know that we cannot control the gates without your cooperation. Therefore, let us state plainly that if such cooperation is refused, we will do our best to destroy this facility, even if it means condemning ourselves to exile."

Those had been hard words to frame, and as Tiniel's voice concluded his translation, Derian scanned the surrounding faces for some sign of their impact. He thought that he saw consternation on those of both Skea and Ynamynet, and guessed that this frank admission of what the New Worlders

were willing to concede and what they were not willing to concede had under-
mined some carefully worked out strategies.

Firekeeper's doing, Derian thought, not bothering to hide his own amusement. *Trust our wolf-woman to decide that long debate and discussion merely to
reach the point at which we had already arrived was useless. It's not how King
Tedric would rule. He'd let his contentious counselors exhaust themselves concluding what he had already worked out, but we don't have time for that.*

Harjeedian made no effort to interrupt the low-voiced debate going on at
the separate table where the Old World speakers had been seated.

Indeed, the only member of their own group who stirred was Firekeeper,
and that was to say in a very soft voice, "Blind Seer say they speak some talk he
not know, but he not think they is angry, only herding their thoughts into a
good order, leaving the weak and sick behind."

Derian amused himself playing with her analogy, imagining written words
chasing themselves around a freshly written page. Even as he did so, some little part of his newly awakened horse self thought that the wolves were missing
the point. They seemed to feel contempt for a strategy that would let the herd
as a community survive.

At last Ynamynet, a herd mare if he'd ever seen one, spoke for the rest.

"Then we are to understand that on certain points you cannot be swayed?
We cannot, for example, suggest a treaty between ourselves and your group in
which we agree to send you home in return for a promise that we will do our
best to make certain that there is no further meddling with the New World
from this facility?""

The word "meddling" reminded Derian of that peculiar entity. He wondered if that strange spirit-man had found a way to contact any of them again.
If so, no one had mentioned it. The thought was fleeting. Harjeedian was
speaking, and his response demanded Derian's full attention.

"You are correct, Ynamynet. There are points on which we cannot be
swayed and one of these is regarding our feeling that either we must manage
this place or destroy it. There can be no middle ground."

Skea spoke next, his voice strong and deep, his mien reminding Derian of
the posturing dance through which a stallion tried to intimidate his rival before battle.

"Exile is a hard life. We who have been separated from homes and families
know this better than can you. How long have you been away from home? A
couple of moonspans only. Do you really wish to never see home and family
again?"

"I, personally, serve the deities wherever I am," Harjeedian said. Derian, knowing the aridisdu's attachment to his younger sister, admired his poise. "The rest of my company have considered their options, and when the choice is never seeing family again and protecting them from disease and distant conquerors, or returning home and letting chaos follow behind . . . Well, the answer is a simple one."

It wasn't, not really, but Derian agreed with it nonetheless.

Zebel, calm and practical, raised the next objection, still seeking to pierce their earlier resolve, rather than moving forward from the position Harjeedian had said they were determined to hold.

"And what if others come through the gates? Are you prepared to deal with them? We know them, are friends and allies with these various peoples. If we refuse to work with you, will you fight all the Old World?"

Firekeeper gave a dry laugh. "In twos, certainly, Blind Seer and I would fight all the Old World and New as well."

"Twos?" the doctor looked puzzled, then dismayed as he followed Firekeeper's logic.

Derian almost forgot his own new oddities in the familiar role of fleshing out Firekeeper's rather cryptic statements for other ears.

"Ynamynet, Skea, and the rest, when questioned by us back at the Setting Sun stronghold, told us that the gates are usually constructed to carry through no more than two at a time. Our own experience and our explorations of this facility seem to bear this out. Firekeeper is quite correct: two at a time, even two at a time through every gate that is active here, we are quite able to deal with intruders. In a pinch, we'd do something to block the gates, perhaps set cages at the ends so those who come through find themselves in less than ideal situations for invasion."

Plik spoke up. Something in his inflection said that he was translating for one of the many yarimaimalom who lingered with bright-eyed awareness about the council chamber.

"And in the New World we have not forgotten that iron is the death of more complex magics. We have sniffed and probed throughout this place, and taken heed that although there is bronze and brass and silver and even gold aplenty, there is scant iron. Thus we think that your antipathy to iron remains—and we have enough in our gear to eliminate your abilities completely."

Derian almost saw Ynamynet melt at this statement and knew that this remembered lore about iron was accurate. Knowing that they could have scotched her talent with a simple iron ring about her wrist or throat, yet they had not done so, must tell the proud sorcerer something about their own confidence in their strength.

"Now that we have dispensed with these preliminaries," Harjeedian said with a too pleasant smile, "shall we get to the matter at hand? Will you work with us in controlling this place, or must we destroy it and with it your own chances of ever returning to your homelands?"

XXXVII

WITH THE SAME CERTAINTY that he had once been able to scent magic, Plik could tell that the others were now ready to bargain. The feeling was so sharp he wondered if he had acquired a new talent to replace the old, but he knew he had not. Those first exchanges had been essential, enabling the four speakers for the residents of the Nexus Islands to assure those they represented that they had not surrendered their advantages too quickly. That done, the tricky part could begin.

Firekeeper spoke from where she sat beside Blind Seer. In a few words, she cut to what might have otherwise taken them hours to reach.

"So, you open gate home for us? Teach us how to do this or do we start breaking and making traps?"

Ynamynet didn't show surprise this time, but then she had clashed with Firekeeper twice before, and had some sense of the wolf-woman's temperament.

"Tell me what is in it for me if I do," the Once Dead said.

"You have a daughter," Firekeeper said, and paused.

"And if I do not do what you say, you will take her from me?" Ynamynet asked.

Her words were cool, but beside her Skea all but raised his hackles. Plik had seen the child in question, a cute girl darker than her mother, but lighter than her father. The child never walked where she could skip or dance. In her father's native language—which contained breath pauses most of the New

Worlders had trouble easing their throats around—her name meant "sunshine."

"No," Firekeeper replied. "We will not take her. I do not like this hostage-taking. But what is life for her on these cold islands with colder to come with winter? If the gates are broken, neither your daughter nor the other children here will see more than these few islands. Is this what you wish?"

Ynamynet looked thoughtful. "Perhaps it would be better than raising her in a war zone, for that is what these islands will become when the Once Dead who know of the gates learn that others have conquered them."

"Perhaps," Firekeeper shrugged, "but the New World would be there: green forests, fresh supplies, meat other than fish and seabirds."

"Medical supplies," Harjeedian added. "A land where querinalo does not seem to occur. If your daughter has inherited your abilities—as seems possible, given that you have and your husband had magical potential—then we may be offering a place where Sunshine can come into her own abilities without torturing fevers and threat of death."

Ynamynet pulled her heavy cloak more closely around her and shivered. Plik wondered what scars querinalo had left upon her. Whatever they were, they were not visible, but he had no doubt that they were there.

"Unless the seeds of querinalo are within Sunshine already," Skea said. "This is what is believed in my birth land."

"We cannot promise," Harjeedian said, "only offer hope. Trapped here there will be no hope."

Zebel looked interested in this, and Plik saw the stirring among the watching island residents. He wondered if this possible freedom from querinalo would be a deciding argument. Harjeedian, however, was too canny to rely on one point alone.

"If we make an alliance between us," he said, his tone officious, "we would initially need some restrictions to make certain we were not betrayed."

Ynamynet had the grace not to protest that such was not her way. Skea grinned slightly at her. He said in Liglimosh, so clearly the words were meant for more than his wife, "I told you your cleverness would play against you someday."

Ynamynet scowled at him, but her expression became neutral as she returned her attention to Harjeedian.

"And what manner of restriction do you have in mind?"

"There is having you wear something of iron," Harjeedian said. "My allies"—his gesture encompassed the watching yarimaimalom—"rather insist on this at least initially. Later, you could be paroled to some lighter restriction—a personal guard, perhaps. Several of the yarimaimalom have volunteered for this duty."

Ynamynet's scowl returned. "Am I then to be the only one so penalized?"

Harjeedian shook his head. "Consider it not a penalty, but a mark of respect. Ynamynet, you are the only of the Once Dead spellcasters who remains. Unless you can train another to share your duties, you are going to be both severely burdened and in a unique position within this new society."

"And if I do train someone?" Ynamynet said sharply. "Then will I find that iron locked to me permanently? Or might I simply not awaken some morning?"

Harjeedian glowered at her. "If you are going to refuse, then simply say so. I must note, however, that once the destruction of the active gates is decided upon, your usefulness will be ended. In a situation where you yourself have stated your unwillingness to cooperate, well, then why shouldn't we lock iron about you for the duration of your life? Why should we leave a person of great talent and considerable loyalty to her community free to harm us when she finds opportunity?"

That silenced Ynamynet, and in the silence Zebel began to ask questions about what the New Worlders intended to do with the place of gates, what they intended to do with the residents, with any who came through the gates uninvited.

To most of these questions Harjeedian gave a general reply, but over and over again he repeated that as time was of the essence he and his allies had not wasted any making plans that might not be needed. Not only did this tack raise a sense of urgency, but it made clear that the island's inhabitants would have some say in shaping their new lives.

Urgana had been the most silent of the speakers, mostly spending her time reading the notes passed from the surrounding listeners and passing them on to the appropriate speaker. Now she spoke and from the pitch of her voice, Plik guessed her words were meant as much for her own community as for the conquerors.

"Was what we had really so wonderful? Let us be honest. Most of us who chose to live here permanently did so because we had grown weary of the lives we were forced to live in what Skea has so poetically called our 'birth lands.' My sister was thrown out of our family when her talent became apparent, and those of you who knew her know how innocuous that talent was. I think our parents would have rejoiced if she had died from querinalo, but to have her survive, and with her talent intact—that was an unforgivable sin.

"The New World people may hate and fear magic, yet they let the talented live among them. In time they may even learn to welcome sorcery." This last was said with an open glower at Ynamynet. "We have a chance to take charge of our lives, rather than being driven. I say we should take it."

There was a great amount of confusion following this, with people shouting either in support or in protest. Isende and Tiniel struggled to translate the varying languages and were driven to yammering nonsense. Blind Seer broke through the confusion with a high howl, answered and amplified by the yari-maimalom wolves.

Into the sudden silence, Harjeedian spoke with calm control. "I think before we go any further there is a key question we must ask. What exactly is your relationship to the Once Dead of the Old World? Who rules whom?"

"Neither," Skea said. "We who choose to live here trade with those who would use the gates. The tariff we charge is high, high enough that we have ample supplies laid by."

Several of the yarimaimalom who had made themselves free of the various buildings said to Plik: *"He speaks the truth. We have found storehouses and root cellars both bulging full. They have poultry and goats they tend as well, even a few cows."*

"And if someone comes through who doesn't want to pay?" Derian asked.

"Then they would find themselves stranded," Skea said. "This has not happened for several years—examples were made."

Remembering some of the more ruthless of the Once Dead, Plik could imagine how gruesome those examples might have been. So apparently could the others, for no one asked for details.

"And given the high tariff you charge," Plik said, "transits are perhaps not as frequent as they might be."

"We need to support ourselves," Urgana said defensively. "After all, the endpoints of the gates are held outside of our sight. Some of those who hold them are reliable allies, but some are less than pleased to find the crossroads held by others."

"And the gate you were opening," Firekeeper said, "the one in the basement. Where would that one go?"

Ynamynet pressed her lips together tightly as if considering not to reply, then she blew out her breath in a long gust.

"We don't know for certain."

"Yet you would flee there?" Firekeeper clearly did not believe this.

"We had an idea . . ." Ynamynet began. Then she almost shouted, "It was better than being your captives. We had to try."

"You have said that or something like that before," Firekeeper said, unimpressed. "Tell us what you thought you'd find."

"When this nexus was first established," Ynamynet said, "the gates up on the hillside were not the first built. These islands were the refuge of a sorcerer who specialized in travel magics. Those ravine gates—those that are buried in the cellar of this building—were his boast, his proof that he could live in apparent isolation and still have all he desired. However, his boast pushed the tolerance of his fellows, and they showed him he was not as immune to retribution as he thought. Later, when the idea of a network of gates was proposed, these islands were considered perfect. They were in territory no one claimed, and there were already gates in place.

"After the gates you have seen were built, those in the ravine were covered over. A building was erected over them, and what was now the cellar was locked and sealed. I suspect those older gates were almost forgotten within a generation or so."

She paused. "You might understand our situation a bit better if you permit us to give a little history of the nexus today."

No one protested, not even Firekeeper, so Harjeedian inclined his head graciously and said, "Please, continue."

"As you know," Ynamynet began, "querinalo struck well over a hundred years ago. In the beginning, at least as we have heard the tales, it was violent. No one with anything other than the least talent survived. Here most of the great sorcerers perished, and from what I've heard about them, that may have been all for the good. They were so ruthless as to make those you caused to be destroyed here seem benevolent by comparison.

"So matters stood for a long while. When magical talent in any form cropped up, querinalo seized the holder and usually killed him or her. However, whether because various peoples grew wiser in learning how to deal with querinalo or the disease changed into a milder form over time, seventy-five years ago, some sufferers began to survive. Most were Twice Dead, but a few Once Dead lived. Ten years later more were living, and more were retaining some vestige of their talent.

"You've heard enough to know that this change was far from welcome in many places. In some, those who survived querinalo were executed. In others they were banded with iron. However, in some more enlightened areas, the talented were permitted to live."

Skea interrupted with a dry laugh. "Ynamynet gives you the simplified version, and I suppose she must. What she isn't saying is that in some areas memories of the horrors that sorcery could create were indeed remembered, but in some places there were rulers—especially those of smaller countries pressed by their neighbors—who thought that a horror or two might be useful. It was in a land ruled by one such ruler that the first attempt was made to reopen one of the remaining gates."

"My sister was part of the team that did the work," Urgana said, memory etching the notes of her voice. "She had a feeling for stone, a talent most had found useless, but it was useful for this. I remember how excited we all were when the old wreck was finally ready for use—and how disappointed we were when we found that only more ruin remained on the other side.

"Still, we set to work with a will. The would-be conqueror who was our patron wanted us to find which gate led into the land of his nearby rivals. We did, and when we opened it from the nexus side, we found heaped rubble in front of us. One man was killed by falling stones. The sorcerer with him barely escaped by using her companion's blood to work her spells. Even so, she was weeks healing.

"The next attempt was better prepared, and once the initial rubble had been cleared away, our patron was delighted to receive report that the gate opened into a cellar that, to all evidence, had not been opened since the coming of querinalo. By then some of our researchers—I was one—had found lists and guides indicating where the various gates led. To make the work of moonspan upon moonspan brief, our patron mounted a frontal assault on the borders of this neighboring land, and when the troops were drawn away, a force went through the gate and hit at the heart.

"This plan worked more than once, but gradually our patron's neighbors became suspicious that more than conventional espionage and betrayal was at work. They had heard rumor that our patron made those who had survived querinalo welcome in his land, and were not so convinced that magic was forever gone to dismiss the possibility that sorcery was behind these convenient conquests. Fear makes strange alliances, and our patron, overextended as he was, was defeated at last. By then, however, we had several gateways active, and the key members of the project had withdrawn to the nexus along with our research library. We negotiated a deal with those who had thought to make themselves our masters and . . ."

Urgana shrugged. "Here we are. Ten years have passed since we made ourselves independent. More gates have been opened. The New World was not high on our list of priorities, for our stories told how those lands had been difficult enough to conquer when the greater magics were commonly used. Then the twins came stumbling through, and we took them in. That was the worst thing we ever did, for you came after them—worst, I suppose, or best, depending on how we resolve this."

A long silence followed the conclusion of Urgana's account, as the various listeners shook themselves free from what had been and again faced the immediate reality.

"Maps, you said," Derian asked. "Of the Old World only, or are there any listings of the New World gates as well?"

"Old World mostly, but some of New," Urgana replied, ignoring Ynamynet's glower. "However, the names of the locations may mean little, especially if the twins told us rightly of the political upheavals and general chaos that followed the coming of querinalo. Perhaps all the old gate sites have been destroyed as bastions of sorcery."

"Not all," Harjeedian reminded. "The Setting Sun stronghold established by the twins' father's family still stands. Other places may as well."

"True, true," Urgana said.

Derian spoke very softly. "I wonder, could these New World gates be a faster way home?"

FIREKEEPER SAW THE HOPE that lit Derian's face, then that hope drowned almost immediately with despair as his hand went up to touch his horse-like ears.

She knew if she did not step in, the discussion was likely to become sidetracked.

"Where go not matter," she said, focusing her gaze on Ynamynet, "if we cannot open even one. I, for one, weary of this bicker and arguing of fine points that will not matter if one person, one only, set herself against us. What you say, Ynamynet?"

Ynamynet closed her eyes and pressed her fingers against them. Yet although she seemed to be trying to block out the world, Firekeeper saw her arm move and knew that Ynamynet had reached to hold Skea's hand. She sat this way for a long time, and not even Firekeeper stirred to hurry her along. When Ynamynet at last opened her eyes there was a strange fixedness in them, as if she saw her thoughts more clearly than anything in the room. She focused on Firekeeper with great effort and spoke in a voice so calm that it hardly seemed like her own.

"Firekeeper, sometimes in order to make a wise decision a person needs to consider what might be the result of that decision. Equally, there are times you need to know what came in the past in order to decide wisely what to do in the future. That's what we've been trying to do here."

Firekeeper nodded, but said nothing, hearing in the intake of Ynamynet's breath that the other woman had more to say.

"How long has it been?" Ynamynet went on. "Only ten days have passed since we went through the gate to the New World stronghold, thinking to find some confused or wounded yarimaimalom. Instead, we found ourselves captives. Even then I could tell there was something dangerous about you—not just your group, you in particular. I tried to stop you, even though that stopping meant I would never see my husband or daughter again. I don't know what power you called on to bring you through . . ."

Ynamynet paused and Firekeeper knew the other woman was hoping for information, but Firekeeper wasn't about to tell her—or this gathered throng—about the Meddler. Harjeedian might not be the only one who had grown up on tales of the Meddler's well-meant actions going awry.

Curling her lips into a slight smile was enough to let Ynamynet know this silence was all the answer she was going to get. After another ragged breath, Ynamynet continued.

"It's obvious that your people would rather take over this place than destroy it, equally obvious that you will destroy it if you must."

Harjeedian said conversationally, "We will begin with those gates that go to the Old World. It may be by the end that, faced with isolation on these islands, you will decide to change your mind."

Ynamynet nodded, "I supposed as much."

"And you should consider something else," Harjeedian said. "We have been speaking as if you are the one and only key to this facility. Thus far, this is true. However, one of these days someone on the other side of a gate is going to come through. Then there will be someone else with whom we can deal. The yarimaimalom watch even now. How long will your power to make deals last, Ynamynet? A moonspan or maybe only a few more minutes?"

Firekeeper had to admire how Harjeedian followed her lead and added pressure, but then the aridisdu had always been skilled with words.

Skea turned to his wife. "They're right, Nami, and they're well prepared. Right now it's our choice. Later, it's going to be someone else's."

Urgana added softly, "All the Old World was so certain that querinalo meant the end of the rule of the crueler type of sorcery, but it didn't take very long for someone to see the advantage of being willing to use a tool his neighbors shunned. Maybe the next ones to come through the gates will share your conviction. Maybe even the ones after that, but you know that not all who wield sorcery are ethical and loyal."

Zebel said, his tones so level they were almost flat, "Most are not. Querinalo forces people to make choices: to live or die, to decide what is valued, what is not. Many of those who kept their magical abilities feel they are owed something for what they gave up. This is not a state of mind that leads to valuing the good of the community over that of the self."

Again, but briefly this time, Ynamynet pressed her fingers to her eyes. When she lowered them, none of the vagueness remained. Her voice was loud and strong as she addressed not only those from the New World but her own community as well.

"Consensus has never been the way of the Once Dead—except occasionally among ourselves. Zebel is right. We have long taken the view that our sacrifices make us superior to any others. However, in this case, I cannot decide for everyone else. I must know that I am supported in whatever decision I make."

She turned to Harjeedian. "May we have a vote? A silent one, so none is swayed by what others choose?"

"We would rather have all of your cooperation," Harjeedian conceded.

He glanced at the others. Firekeeper nodded, as did the most of the others. Plik spoke for the yarimaimalom.

"They will agree—though many think this very strange."

The meeting was adjourned while arrangements were made for the secret vote and the discussion to this point was summarized for those who suddenly realized they had made an error in not attending. When Blind Seer howled the meeting to order again, the room was noticeably fuller and the air reeked of sour sweat and hastily dried tears.

There was a clicking and clattering as the humans shifted broken bits of ceramic from hand to hand. Skea rose from his place and held up an opaque jar.

"Voting will be very simple. If you favor an alliance, with Ynamynet agreeing to open gates for these New World peoples and to teach them—if possible—how they might do this themselves, put in the red piece. If you favor refusal to cooperate, waiting to see if assistance comes through one of the gates, then put in the green piece. It's that easy."

There were a few questions, most of them the type that made Firekeeper edgy, but that humans of all cultures seemed to need.

"It's like when all the pack howls as one," Blind Seer said, bumping his head against her in reassurance. *"They make all this chatter to assure themselves that they are a pack."*

"That may be," Firekeeper replied grumpily, *"but if I had fur it would be on end."*

"Then perhaps it is a good thing you don't have fur," Blind Seer replied dryly.

Firekeeper punched gently, noting tenderly how different his fur felt without the thick undercoat. She draped an arm around the wolf, and felt him press into her.

Side by side, they listened as the broken shards of pottery dropped into the jar, the bright sound dampening and becoming deeper as the jar filled. As far as they could tell, no one tried to peek inside the slit cut in the jar's top to see what others had decided, and most cupped their hand so that those close by could not see what their own vote would be.

Eventually, the jar was handed down from the surrounding seats. Skea dropped his own piece in, then handed the jar to Zebel. Last to vote was Ynamynet, and if her face was tight and strained as she did so, Firekeeper would be the last to call her a coward.

Skea met Harjeedian halfway across the room and handed the now full jar to the aridisdu. Harjeedian had not trained in reading omens without learning something about detecting the temper of a gathering. Rather than carrying the jar back to the table where the New World contingent sat, Harjeedian removed the covering from the jar. Bending slightly at the waist, he spread the gathered shards in a broad arc across the stone-flagged floor.

There was no need to count. A wash of red spilled out against the grey. Here and there a defiant bit of green showed, but overwhelmingly the color was red—the color signifying a choice to cooperate.

"It looks like blood," Firekeeper said softly to Blind Seer.

"You have been too much among the Liglim," Blind Seer replied. *"This is no omen, only a choice."*

But Firekeeper felt the wolf shudder, and knew that he too wondered just what had begun with that bright scattering of choice.

❦

AS FROM ONE THROAT, Truth heard the rumble of voices. She did not need to be from a long line of diviners to know what she heard.

"They have made a decision," she said to Eshinarvash.

The Wise Horse swiveled one ear back, but kept most of his attention for the gate complex they patrolled.

"I hear the howls of wolves and the yapping of foxes. Each says one word only: 'Home!' So it seems the humans here have decided to work with us rather than against us. That is good. I had wondered how well I might live on a diet of kelp. We wild horses have less finicky guts than our domesticated cousins, but I had wondered . . ."

Almost idly, Truth watched the folding and unfolding of futures triggered by Eshinarvash's statement. She was learning to accept Ahmyn's gift. Being constantly enwrapped in visions would never be easy, nor would she ever again be able to completely trust what she saw, but she was learning.

"Now you do not need to choose," Truth said. "I, for one, am glad. I am not overly fond of horsemeat."

Eshinarvash shivered his skin at this, but did not edge away. Really, he was very brave, especially for an herbivore.

" 'Home!' they howl," Eshinarvash said after a time. "Do they realize that not all of us can return? Not now, perhaps not for a long, long time to come?"

Truth rested on her haunches and began to lick her left front paw. (Visions of her beginning with her right paw or at the tip of her tail, milled at the edges of her vision, rather like gnats on a summer evening. She ignored them.)

"I will stay," Truth said. "The omens agree this would be my best course. These humans respect the Once Dead, even as they fear them. I am flamboyantly Once Dead."

"So is Derian," Eshinarvash said. "I think he can be convinced to remain—if the omens think this is wise."

Truth tilted her head and studied the various visions swirling around her.

"Derian must choose his own course," she said at last, "not be convinced either to stay or to go. All the omens agree that if he is persuaded against his will, evil events will follow."

Truth did not say what these events were, but watched in idle fascination as armies marched and a warrior in armor all of brass and silver led an invincible army two by two through a gate. It was only one of many visions, but it was certainly the most colorful.

"I will decide after Derian does, then," Eshinarvash said. "Wherever he goes, Derian will need someone with whom he can talk. I think that one should be me. He is of my people, at least a little bit."

Truth let the spiraling movements of army fade and concentrated on the question she heard in the Wise Horse's statement.

"Yes," she said. "Derian would benefit from your friendship, although he will not always be grateful for the reminder you give him of his changed state."

"I can live with that," Eshinarvash said, biting off a clump of stiff salty grass and chewing.

"Yes," Truth agreed, "you can."

XXXVIII

THE YARIMAIMALOM WERE THE FIRST to leave, a pair of wolves initially, followed by two bears in singularly bad humor as they contemplated trying to survive a winter for which they had not stored sufficient fat.

Firekeeper had listened to the bears discussing going farther south, as if they were some sort of enormous, furry birds. Harjeedian had politely suggested that the bears might find welcome in Liglim, where the appropriate temple would be happy to give them shelter.

Whatever decision the bears chose to make, the wolf-woman did not fancy the chances of any who crossed them as they inspected the other side to make certain all was well. However, when Night's Terror—who, along with Golden Feather, had been in the next pair to make the crossing—was brought back and reported that the surrounding area seemed as she remembered from before their departure, many of the yarimaimalom were eager to return.

For the carnivores, returning to the New World was more than a matter of at last escaping where they had been held captive. It was a question of getting in some hunting before winter moved in fully and made their prey lean and stringy. The herbivores felt a similar pressure, for although these lands farther south did not experience winters as severe as those Firekeeper had known in her childhood, still the plants became dormant and did not offer as much nourishment.

However, knowing full well that Firekeeper's small pack could not control their still untrustworthy allies without assistance, many of the yarimaimalom agreed to stay on. The wingéd folk and smaller hunters, like the foxes and wild cats, made up the larger part of the occupation force, so the Once and Twice Dead and their companions were aware that they were watched—and watched by creatures who had ample reason to interpret the least oddity in their behavior as threatening.

Given the situation, Derian resolved to remain. Teamed with Eshinarvash, he made a translator almost as adept as Firekeeper or Plik. Within days, the two were rarely seen one without the other, and Derian was too busy to brood over his altered condition.

Eshinarvash's choosing to remain brought to the fore the need for a regular source of supply, for the island did not provide good forage for a horse. Harjeedian and a contingent of yarimaimalom made their way to Gak and negotiated with Amiri and Layo for supplies. Lovable reported rather coyly that Harjeedian had spent a good deal of time visiting with an argumentative aridisdu, and Firekeeper speculated what this might mean for Harjeedian's own eagerness to return to Liglim.

The supply run into Gak meant formulating a story to cover their continued absence. Harjeedian did so with such facility that Firekeeper remembered all over again why she had once distrusted him. The explanation was that they had indeed located Tiniel and Isende, and had found them weak from an undefined illness. Given the lateness of the season and the fragility of the twins, the group had decided to stay with them and assure their care.

If anyone wondered at the gaps in this tale, the lingering fear all New World residents held regarding illnesses that might spread as the Plague had once done provided ample distraction. A pair of ospreys agreed to fly to Liglim and deliver written messages to Harjeedian's people and to the Bright Haven embassy so that there would be no worries on their account.

"Will Elise have whelped?" Firekeeper asked Derian as he scribbled out their own message. It was a long one, for although it had been agreed that nothing would be said about the gates or the Meddler, still there was a great deal to tell. He was also including a letter that would be forwarded to his family in Hawk Haven, because "Even if I can't tell them almost anything important, I am alive, and I'm beginning to realize that's a lot to be grateful for."

"Whelped?" Derian replied as he finished scratching out a sentence. His grin was almost as easy as it had been before querinalo, and Firekeeper felt warmed.

"You know, had the baby."

"Not yet. Humans take longer than wolves at this. You should remember. In the spring."

Firekeeper sighed, and Derian took pity on her.

"The ospreys have agreed to carry a return message, and I've specifically asked Elise to report on her condition. We should know how she is faster than it would take for us to travel to u-Bishinti."

"I know. I miss them, though. This would have been easier with them to help."

Derian nodded. "But remember, Doc would have had to go through querinalo. I can't wish that on anyone."

"I wonder," Firekeeper said thoughtfully, "if Ynamynet and the others didn't tell us because they thought we might be killed by it."

"Probably," Derian said. "Querinalo isn't like any disease I've ever heard of, but I do know that people develop resistances to diseases that touch their populations frequently—like that swamp fever that makes going to Waterland in summer so nasty for anyone but the people who live there. Ynamynet's not stupid. She may have hoped we would have no resistance and be killed as easily as those Old World sorcerers were back when the Plague first hit."

"We not know much," Firekeeper said. "So much we don't know."

She was thinking about how little they knew one of the times she made the transit back to the New World. Ynamynet had found an apprentice, or rather the apprentice had found her. It was Enigma, a puma who had been among the captive yarimaimalom. He had announced himself and his interest in learning the spell by padding up to Ynamynet as she was about to perform the ritual and going through the ritual with her. Afterward, when Ynamynet had time to consider, the Once Dead said that she had felt a familiar sense of someone else sharing the transmission of power with her, and although not a word was spoken between them, even in translation, she had known what Enigma wanted.

"So the name that was augered for me is fulfilled," the puma said, *"for I was a definite puzzle to those who viewed the omens of my birth."*

The spell had to be slightly adapted so Enigma could work it solo, but Ynamynet had admitted with a slight shiver that the puma had taken to blood magic "as if it were his first nature."

Knowing how carnivores loved blood-hot meat, Firekeeper only wondered that Ynamynet thought this worthy of comment. Indeed, although the yarimaimalom's tales of the days when magic had been more commonly in use did not include beast sorcerers, Firekeeper was growing cynical on what she had and had not been told.

"Paws," she said to Blind Seer, "and teeth are not the best for creating gates and other artifacts, but as Enigma's experience shows, when someone else makes the tools . . ."

Blind Seer didn't comment, not even with a proverb, but Firekeeper didn't see how he could do anything but agree. Still, the blue-eyed wolf did not like going through the gate, and so Firekeeper had made this return trip alone.

She was going to be gone only a few hours, checking with representatives from the various packs and herds, all of whom had promised to report if querinalo surfaced among any of their peoples. Thus far it had not, and since many days had passed since the return—more than it had taken for the illness to appear before—and no sign had occurred, there was reason to believe that querinalo could not be transmitted by one who had suffered it to one who had not.

Firekeeper was in the stronghold courtyard, eating a rather withered apple and waiting for Enigma to return from her hunting, when the Meddler stepped from behind the apple tree.

"So, Firekeeper, you've done it again."

"Me? What?" Firekeeper dropped the apple and reached for her Fang, although she was not at all certain the blade could touch whatever the Meddler was.

"Changed things around you."

"I did no more than all the others," Firekeeper protested, although she knew this was not true. What the others had done had been important, but not even Plik could have created the bridge between human and beast as she had done. "I am one with a very odd pack."

"You are One of a very odd pack," the Meddler said, and as they were speaking the language used by the wolves, there was no question as to his meaning.

Firekeeper shrugged, and the Meddler panted a wolfish smile.

"This is the first time," the Meddler continued, "since I helped you cross to the Nexus Islands, that I have been able to speak with you alone. I have come for my favor."

Firekeeper stiffened. Although she had done her best to keep the bargain she had made with the Meddler from her mind, it had always been there, lurking beneath the surface. In a sense she was glad he brought the matter up now. To live for moonspans or even years waiting for this "favor" to be called due would be unbearable.

She said aloud what she was thinking.

"Good. This is a relief. What do you want?"

"I want you to kiss me."

Firekeeper blinked at him. "What?"

"Kiss me." The wolfish visage was changing now, shifting into that of a man Firekeeper felt she vaguely recognized, yet at the same time she was certain she had never seen. "I want you to kiss me, mouth to mouth, as a woman kisses a man."

Firekeeper felt herself blushing, her skin prickling hot all over.

"But," she protested, "how can I do that? You aren't there, not really. You told us you lack a body."

The Meddler smiled, and the smile sent very strange sensations through Firekeeper—powerful sensations such as she had never felt before.

"I have been freed from my prison for several moonspans now. That is time enough even for someone insubstantial like myself to gather some power. Although I have spent some of that power—even on your behalf—still, I have enough to assure that we will close the gap between body and spirt long enough for you to touch your mouth to mine."

Firekeeper took an involuntary step back. "But why? Why do you wish this thing?"

The Meddler grinned at her. "I could say that I want you to learn what you're missing in refusing your love to any but wolves." The grin faded and that almost remembered visage grew sad. "But the truth is easier. I told you that I cannot cross into the Nexus Islands because it is guarded from any but those who cross by conventional routes."

"And now we are guarding from those, too," Firekeeper said, thinking with distinct satisfaction of the load of iron bars Harjeedian had brought with him from Gak.

"All too true," the Meddler said. "However, I would like to go there. Firekeeper, I was born in the Old World. When I was made captive, I was no isolated individual. Like you I had friends. I had family. I realize that hundreds of years have passed since I was imprisoned. Doubtless all those I loved are dead. Those who did not die from old age probably died from the very Plague that my imprisonment rather ironically protected me from. But I would like to know. I could make the journey in this spirit state I now occupy, but the distance would not be shortened. It would be a very long walk. Please, Firekeeper, give me the means to start my journey home."

Firekeeper stared at him. From the tales Harjeedian and Plik had told, she knew the Meddler was known for well-intentioned actions that somehow went awry. She wondered what she would be letting into the Old World if she helped the Meddler. Then she cheered up slightly. At least if he went through the gates into the Old World, she'd be removing him from the New. That would be a good thing without question. Even Harjeedian would praise her for it . . . if she told him, and she knew with a certain uneasiness in her gut that she wouldn't.

"So I can help you cross through the gate," she said, "by kissing you."

"That is correct." The Meddler smiled rakishly at her. "Kiss me and I believe I will have what I need to cross via the gate. You won't even know I am there."

Firekeeper frowned at him. "A favor you ask then, between you and me. I suppose this is such."

"That is right. I'm not going to steal your body or your soul, just in case you've heard stories of that sort. I'm simply going to create a link between us, a link that will let me follow you."

Firekeeper stared at the Meddler. Against her better judgment, she felt sorry for him. Ever since she had crossed the Iron Mountains and encountered humankind, she had felt isolated from what had been her home. However, nothing kept her from going to visit. Nothing barred her from learning what had happened to those she loved.

"I will kiss you then," she said, "and the favor is done."

"Don't look so miserable." The Meddler laughed. He walked toward her, measured step by step, becoming more substantial with every pace until she felt the heat of his body and smelled his sweat, a little human, a little wolf. "You might just enjoy it."

Firekeeper had meant to peck him on the lips, a fast kiss as was familiar to her between friends, but somehow the Meddler gathered her in his arms. Before Firekeeper quite knew what was happening, he was kissing her very intently, holding her close, his tongue slipping between her lips.

Before Firekeeper could jerk away, she felt the Meddler begin to lose substance. He released her, stepping back a pace.

"Thank you, my lady," he said, and he sounded a touch surprised. "I am very glad to have found you. I can promise you, we will meet again."

He stepped back a few more paces, and by the time he had reached the trunk of the apple tree, he had vanished. As if she herself was coming back from a long distance away, Firekeeper heard sounds and knew that Enigma, the puma, was returning.

I wonder, Firekeeper thought, staring where the Meddler had been, *what has happened here? When we left Misheemnekuru, I thought I was the one who was hunting. Perhaps the Meddler was doing the hunting, hunting those who could help him so he could find his way home again.*

With that unsettling thought, Firekeeper turned to where Enigma had begun the ritual that would open the gate. When the wall shimmered, Firekeeper stepped through stone, into fire, hurrying to where Blind Seer waited.

GLOSSARY OF CHARACTERS

Agneta[1] Norwood: (H.H.) daughter of Norvin Norwood and Luella Stanbrook; sister of Edlin, Tait, and Lillis Norwood; adopted sister of Blysse Norwood (Firekeeper).

Aksel Trueheart: (Lord, H.H.) scholar of Hawk Haven; spouse of Zorana Archer; father of Purcel, Nydia, Deste, and Kenre Trueheart.[2]

Alben Eagle: (H.H.) son of Princess Marras and Lorimer Stanbrook. In keeping with principles of Zorana I, given no title as died in infancy.

Alin Brave: (H.H.) husband of Grace Trueheart; father of Baxter Trueheart.

Allister I: (King, B.B.) called King Allister of the Pledge, sometimes the Pledge Child; formerly Allister Seagleam. Son of Tavis Seagleam (B.B.) and Caryl Eagle (H.H.); spouse of Pearl Oyster; father of Shad, Tavis, Anemone, and Minnow.

Alt Rosen: (Opulence, Waterland) ambassador to Bright Bay.

Amery Pelican: (King, B.B.) Spouse of Gustin II; father of Basil, Seastar, and Tavis Seagleam. Deceased.

Amiri: city-state of Gak; aridisdu.

Anemone: (Princess, B.B.) formerly Anemone Oyster. Daughter of Allister I and Pearl Oyster; sister of Shad and Tavis; twin of Minnow.

Apheros: (Dragon Speaker, N.K.) long-time elected official of New Kelvin, effectively head of government.

Aurella Wellward: (Lady, H.H.) confidante of Queen Elexa; spouse of Ivon Archer; mother of Elise Archer.

Barden Eagle: (Prince, H.H.) third son of Tedric I and Elexa Wellward. Disowned. Spouse of Eirene Norwood; father of Blysse Eagle. Presumed deceased.

Barnet Lobster: (Isles) sailor on the *Explorer*.

Basil Seagleam: see Gustin III.

Baxter Trueheart: (Earl, H.H.) infant son of Grace Trueheart and Alin Brave. Technically not a title holder until he has safely survived his first two years.

Beachcomber: a Wise Wolf.

Bee Biter: Royal Kestrel; guide and messenger.

Bevan Seal: see Calico.

Bibimalenu: (L.) member of u-Liall, representative for Air.

Bitter: a Wise Raven.

Blind Seer: Royal Wolf; companion to Firekeeper.

Blysse Eagle: (Lady, H.H.) daughter of Prince Barden and Eirene Kestrel.

Blysse Kestrel: see Firekeeper.

Bold: Royal Crow; eastern agent; sometime companion to Firekeeper.

Bright-Eyes-Fast-Paws: a Wise Jaguar.

Brina Dolphin: (Lady or Queen, B.B.) first spouse of Gustin III, divorced as barren.

Brock Carter: (H.H.) son of Colby and Vernita Carter; brother of Derian and Damita Carter.

---

[1] Characters are detailed under first name or best-known name. The initials B.B. (Bright Bay), H.H. (Hawk Haven), N.K. (New Kelvin), or L. (Liglim) in parenthesis following a character's name indicate nationality. Titles are indicated in parentheses.

[2] Hawk Haven and Bright Bay noble houses both follow a naming system where the children take the surname of the higher-ranking parent, with the exception that only the immediate royal family bear the name of that house. If the parents are of the same rank, then rank is designated from the birth house, greater over lesser, lesser by seniority. The Great Houses are ranked in the following order: Eagle, Shield, Wellward, Trueheart, Redbriar, Stanbrook, Norwood.

Brotius: (N.K., Captain) soldier in New Kelvin.

Calico: (B.B.) proper name, Bevan Seal. Confidential secretary to Allister I. Member of a cadet branch of House Seal.

Caryl Eagle: (Princess, H.H.) daughter of King Chalmer I; married to Prince Tavis Seagleam; mother of Allister Seagleam. Deceased.

Ceece Dolphin: (Lady, B.B.) sister to current Duke Dolphin.

Chalmer I: (King, H.H.) born Chalmer Elkwood; son of Queen Zorana the Great; spouse of Rose Rosewood; father of Marras, Tedric, Caryl Gadman, and Rosene Eagle. Deceased.

Chalmer Eagle: (Crown Prince, H.H.) son of Tedric Eagle and Elexa Wellward. Deceased.

Chutia: (N.K.) Illuminator. Wife of Grateful Peace. Deceased.

Cishanol: (L.) assistant to Meiyal, disdu in training.

Citrine Shield: (H.H.) daughter of Melina Shield and Rolfston Redbriar; sister of Sapphire, Jet, Opal, and Ruby Shield; adopted daughter of Grateful Peace.

Colby Carter: (H.H.) livery stable owner and carter; spouse of Vernita Carter; father of Derian, Damita, and Brock.

Columi: (N.K.) retired Prime of the Sodality of Lapidaries.

Comb Ripper: a Wise Bear cub.

Cricket: a Wise Wolf.

Culver Pelican: (Lord, B.B.) son of Seastar Seagleam; brother of Dillon Pelican. Merchant ship captain.

Daisy: (H.H.) steward of West Keep, in employ of Earl Kestrel.

Damita Carter: (H.H.) daughter of Colby and Vernita Carter; sister of Derian and Brock Carter.

Dantarahma: (L.) member of u-Liall, representative for Water. Deceased.

Dark Death: a Wise Wolf.

Dawn Brooks: (H.H.) wife of Ewen Brooks, mother of several small children. Deceased.

Dayle: (H.H.) steward for the Archer Manse in Eagle's Nest.

Derian Carter: (H.H.) also called Derian Counselor; son of Colby and Vernita Carter; brother of Damita and Brock Carter.

Deste Trueheart: (H.H.) daughter of Aksel Trueheart and Zorana Archer; sister of Purcel, Nydia, and Kenre Trueheart.

Dia Trueheart: see Nydia Trueheart.

Dillon Pelican: (Lord, B.B.) son of Seastar Seagleam; brother of Culver Pelican.

Dimiria: (N.K.) Prime, Sodality of Stargazers.

Dirkin Eastbranch: (knight, H.H.) King Tedric's personal bodyguard.

Donal Hunter: (H.H.) member of Barden Eagle's expedition; spouse of Sarena; father of Tamara. Deceased.

Edlin Norwood: (Lord, H.H.) son of Norvin Norwood and Luella Kite; brother of Tait, Lillis, and Agneta Norwood; adopted brother of Blysse Kestrel (Firekeeper).

Eirene Norwood: (Lady, H.H.) spouse of Barden Eagle; mother of Blysse Eagle; sister of Norvin Norwood. Presumed deceased.

Elation: Royal Falcon, companion to Firekeeper.

Elexa Wellward: (Queen, H.H.) spouse of Tedric I; mother of Chalmer, Lovella, and Barden.

Elise Archer: (Lady, H.H.) daughter of Ivon Archer and Aurella Wellward; heir to Archer Grant.

Elwyn: (Isles) also called "Lucky Elwyn"; a sailor on the *Explorer*.

Enigma: a Wise Puma.

Eshinarvash: a Wise Horse.

Evaglayn: (N.K.) senior apprentice in the Beast Lore sodality.

Evie Cook: (H.H.) servant in the Carter household.

Ewen Brooks: (N.K.) spouse of Dawn Brooks, father of several children.

Faelene Lobster: (Duchess, B.B.) head of House Lobster; sister of Marek, duke of Half-Moon Island; aunt of King Harwill.

Fairwind Sailor: (B.B.) ambassador to Liglim from Bright Haven.

Farand Briarcott: (Lady, H.H.) assistant to Tedric I, former military commander.

Feeshaguyu: (L.) member of u-Liall; representative for Earth.

Fess Bones: a pirate with some medical skills.

Firekeeper: (Lady, H.H.) feral child raised by wolves, adopted by Norvin Norwood and given the name Blysse Kestrel.

Fleet Herald: a pirate messenger.

Fox Driver: (H.H.) given name, Orin. Skilled driver in the employ of Waln Endbrook. Deceased.

Freckles: a Wise Wolf.

Gadman Eagle: (Grand Duke, H.H.) fourth child of King Chalmer and Queen Rose; brother to Marras, Caryl, Tedric, Rosene; spouse of Riki Redbriar; father of Rolfston and Nydia.

Garrik Carpenter: (H.H.) a skilled woodworker. Deceased.

Gayl Minter: see Gayl Seagleam.

Gayl Seagleam: (Queen, B.B.) spouse of Gustin I; first queen of Bright Bay; mother of Gustin, Merry (later Gustin II), and Lyra. Note: Gayl was the only queen to assume the name "Seagleam." Later tradition paralleled that of Hawk Haven where the name of the birth house was retained even after marriage to the monarch. Deceased.

Glynn: (H.H.) a soldier.

Golden Feather: a Wise Owl; mate to Night's Terror.

Grace Trueheart: (Duchess Merlin, H.H.) military commander; spouse of Alin Brave; mother of Baxter.

Grateful Peace: (Dragon's Eye, N.K.) also, Trausholo. Illuminator; Prime of New Kelvin; member of the Dragon's Three. A very influential person. Husband to Chutia; brother of Idalia; uncle of Varcasiol, Kistlio, Linatha, and others; adopted father of Citrine.

Grey Thunder: a Wise Wolf.

Grub Digger: a Wise Bear cub.

Gustin I: (King, B.B.) born Gustin Sailor, assumed the name Seagleam upon his coronation; first monarch of Bright Bay; spouse of Gayl Minter, later Gayl Seagleam; father of Gustin, Merry, and Lyra Seagleam. Deceased.

Gustin II: (Queen, B.B.) born Merry Seagleam, assumed the name Gustin upon her coronation; second monarch of Bright Bay; spouse of Amery Pelican; mother of Basil, Seastar, and Tavis Seagleam. Deceased.

Gustin III: (King, B.B.) born Basil Seagleam, assumed the name Gustin upon his coronation; third monarch of Bright Bay; spouse of Brina Dolphin, later of Viona Seal; father of Valora Seagleam. Deceased.

Gustin IV: (Queen, B.B.) see Valora I.

Gustin Sailor: see Gustin I.

Half-Ear: a Wise Wolf.

Half-Snarl: a Wise Wolf.

Hard Biter: a Wise Wolf.

Harjeedian: (L.) aridisdu serving the Temple of the Cold Bloods; brother of Rahniseeta.

Hart: (H.H.) a young hunter.

Harwill Lobster: (King, the Isles) spouse of Valora I; during her reign as Gustin IV, also king of Bright Bay. Son of Marek.

Hasamemorri: (N.K.) a landlady.

Hazel Healer: (H.H.) apothecary, herbalist, perfumer resident in the town of Hope.

Healer: a Wise Wolf.

Heather Baker: (H.H.) baker in Eagle's Nest; former sweetheart of Derian Carter.

High Howler: a Wise Wolf.

Holly Gardener: (H.H.) former Master Gardener for Eagle's Nest Castle, possessor of the Green Thumb, a talent for the growing of plants. Mother of Timin and Sarena.

Honey Endbrook: (Isles) mother of Waln Endbrook.

Hope: a maimalodalu.

Hya Grimsel: (General, Stonehold) commander of Stonehold troops.

Idalia: (N.K.) assistant to Melina. Sister of Grateful Peace, spouse of Pichero; mother of Kistlio, Varcasiol, Linatha, and others.

Indatius: (N.K.) young member of the Sodality of Artificers.

Integrity: a Wise Wolf.

Isende: a woman from Gak; twin sister of Tiniel.

Ivon Archer: (Baron, H.H.) master of the Archer Grant; son of Purcel Archer and Rosene Eagle; brother of Zorana Archer; spouse of Aurella Wellward; father of Elise Archer.

Ivory Pelican: (Lord, B.B.) Keeper of the Keys, an honored post in Bright Bay.

Jalarios: see Grateful Peace.

Jared Surcliffe: (knight, H.H.) knight of the Order of the White Eagle; possessor of the healing talent; distant cousin of Norvin Norwood who serves as his patron. Widower, no children.

Jem: (B.B.) deserter from Bright Bay's army.

Jet Shield: (H.H.) son of Melina Shield and Rolfston Redbriar; brother of Sapphire, Opal, Ruby, and Citrine. Heir apparent to his parents' properties upon the adoption of his sister Sapphire by Tedric I.

Joy Spinner: (H.H.) scout in the service of Earle Kite. Deceased.

Kalvinia: (Prime, N.K.) thaumaturge, Sodality of Sericulturalists.

Keen: (H.H.) servant to Newell Shield.

Kenre Trueheart: (H.H.) son of Zorana Archer and Aksel Trueheart; brother of Purcel, Nydia, and Deste Trueheart.

Kiero: (N.K.): spy in the service of the Healed One. Deceased.

Kistlio: (N.K.) clerk in Thendulla Lypella; nephew of Grateful Peace; son of Idalia and Pichero; brother of Varcasiol, Linatha, and others. Deceased.

Lachen: a Once Dead.

Layozirate: an important citizen of Gak; mother of Petulia.

Lillis Norwood: (H.H.) daughter of Norvin Norwood and Luella Stanbrook; sister of Edlin, Tait, and Agneta Norwood; adopted sister of Blysse Norwood (Firekeeper).

Linatha: (N.K.) niece of Grateful Peace; daughter of Idalia and Pichero; sister of Kistlio, Varcasiol, and others.

Longsight Scrounger: pirate, leader of those at Smuggler's Light.

Lorimer Stanbrook: (Lord, H.H.) spouse of Marras Eagle; father of Marigolde and Alben Eagle. Deceased.

Lovable: a Wise Raven; mate of Bitter.

Lovella Eagle: (Crown Princess, H.H.) military commander; daughter of Tedric Eagle and Elexa Wellward; spouse of Newell Shield. Deceased.

Lucho: (N.K.) a thug.

Lucky Shortleg: a pirate.

Luella Stanbrook: (Lady, H.H.) spouse of Norvin Norwood; mother of Edlin, Tait, Lillis, and Agneta Norwood.

Marek: (Duke, Half-Moon Island) formerly Duke Lobster of Bright Bay but chose to follow the fate of his son, Harwill. Brother of Faelene, the current Duchess Lobster.

Marigolde Eagle: (H.H.) daughter of Marras Eagle and Lorimer Stanbrook. In keeping with principles of Zorana I, given no title as died in infancy.

Marras Eagle: (Crown Princess, H.H.) daughter of Chalmer Eagle and Rose Rosewood; sister of Tedric, Caryl, Gadman, and Rosene; spouse of Lorimer Stanbrook; mother of Marigolde and Alben Eagle. Deceased.

Meddler: a spirit.

Meiyal: (L.) iaridisdu of the Horse.

Melina: (H.H.; N.K.) formerly entitled "lady," with affiliation to House Gyrfalcon; reputed sorceress; spouse of Rolfston Redbriar; mother of Sapphire, Jet, Opal, Ruby, and Citrine Shield. Later spouse of Torovico of New Kelvin, given title of Consolor of the Healed One. Deceased.

Merri Jay: (H.H.) daughter of Wendee Jay.

Merry Seagleam: see Gustin II.

Minnow: (Princess, B.B.) formerly Minnow Oyster. Daughter of Allister I and Pearl Oyster; sister of Shad and Tavis; twin of Anemone.

Moon Frost: a Wise Wolf.

Nanny: (H.H.) attendant to Melina Shield.

Neck Breaker: a Wise Wolf.

Nelm: (N.K.) member of the Sodality of Herbalists.

Newell Shield: (Prince, H.H.) commander of marines; spouse of Lovella Eagle; brother of Melina Shield. Deceased.

Night's Terror: a Wise Owl; mate of Golden Feather.

Ninette Farmer: (H.H.) relative of Ivon Archer; attendant of Elise Archer.

Nipper: a Wise Wolf.

Nolan: a sailor on the *Explorer*. Deceased.

Noonafaruma: (L.) member of u-Liall; representative for Magic.

Northwest: Royal Wolf, not of Firekeeper's pack. Called Sharp Fang by his own pack.

Norvin Norwood: (Earl Kestrel, H.H.) heir to Kestrel Grant; son of Saedee Norwood; brother of Eirene Norwood; spouse of Luella Stanbrook; father of Edlin, Tait, Lillis, and Agneta; adopted father of Blysse (Firekeeper).

Nstasius: (Prime, N.K.) member of the Sodality of Sericulturalists, sympathetic to the Progressive Party.

Nydia Trueheart: (H.H.) often called Dia; daughter of Aksel Trueheart and Zorana Archer; sister of Purcel, Deste, and Kenre Trueheart.

Oculios: (N.K.) apothecary; member of the Sodality of Alchemists.

One Female: also Shining Coat; ruling female wolf of Firekeeper and Blind Seer's pack.

One Male: also Rip; ruling male wolf of Firekeeper and Blind Seer's pack.

Onion: a Wise Wolf.

Opal Shield: (H.H.) daughter of Melina Shield and Rolfston Redbriar; sister of Sapphire, Jet, Ruby, and Citrine.

Oralia: (Isles) wife of Waln Endrook; mother of three children.

Ox: (H.H.) born Malvin Hogge; bodyguard to Norvin Norwood; renowned for his strength and good temper.

Paliama: (L.) a kidisdu.

Pearl Oyster: (Queen, B.B.) spouse of Allister I; mother of Shad, Tavis, Anemone, and Minnow.

Perce Potterford: (B.B.) guard to Allister I.

Perr: (H.H.) body servant to Ivon Archer.

Petulia: city-state of Gak; trainee kidisdu.

Pichero: (N.K.) spouse of Idalia; father of Kistlio, Varcasiol, Linatha, and others.

Plik: a maimalodalu.

Polr: (Lord, H.H.) military commander; brother of Tab, Rein, Newell, and Melina.

Posa: (Prime, N.K.) member of the Sodality of Il-luminators.

Postuvanu: (L.) a kidisdu of the Horse, son of Varjuna and Zira.

Powerful Tenderness: a maimalodalu.

Puma Killer: a Wise Wolf.

Purcel Archer: (Baron Archer, H.H.) first Baron Archer, born Purcel Farmer, elevated to the title for his prowess in battle; spouse of Rosene Ea-gle; father of Ivon and Zorana. Deceased.

Purcel Trueheart: (H.H.) lieutenant Hawk Haven army; son of Aksel Trueheart and Zorana Archer; brother of Nydia, Deste, and Kenre Trueheart. Deceased.

Questioner: a maimalodalu. Deceased.

Race Forester: (H.H.) scout under the patronage of Norvin Norwood; regarded by many as one of the best in his calling.

Rafalias: (N.K.) member of the Sodality of Lap-idaries.

Rahniseeta: (L.) resident in the Temple of the Cold Bloods; sister of Harjeedian.

Rarby: a sailor on the *Explorer*. Deceased.

Rascal: a Wise Wolf.

Red Stripe: also called Cime; a pirate.

Reed Oyster: (Duke, B.B.) father of Queen Pearl. Among the strongest supporters of Allister I.

Rein Shield: (Lord, H.H.) brother of Tab, Newell, Polr, and Melina.

Riki Redbriar: (Lady, H.H.) spouse of Gadman Eagle; mother of Rolfston and Nydia Redbriar. Deceased.

Rillon: (N.K.) a maid in the Cloud Touching Spire; a slave.

Rios: see Citrine Shield.

Rip: see the One Male.

Rolfston Redbriar: (Lord, H.H.) son of Gadman Eagle and Riki Redbriar; spouse of Melina Shield; father of Sapphire, Jet, Opal, Ruby, and Citrine Shield. Deceased.

Rook: (H.H.) servant to Newell Shield.

Rory Seal: (Lord, B.B.) holds the title Royal Physician.

Rose Rosewood: (Queen, H.H.) common-born wife of Chalmer I; also called Rose Dawn; his marriage to her was the reason Hawk Haven Great Houses received what Queen Zorana the Great would doubtless have seen as unnecessary and frivolous titles. Deceased.

Rosene: (Grand Duchess, H.H.) fifth child of King Chalmer and Queen Rose; spouse of Purcel Archer; mother of Ivon and Zorana Archer.

Ruby Shield: (H.H.) daughter of Melina Shield and Rolfston Redbriar; sister of Sapphire, Jet, Opal, and Citrine Shield.

Saedee Norwood: (Duchess Kestrel, H.H.) mother of Norvin and Eirene Norwood.

Sapphire: (Crown Princess, H.H.) adopted daughter of Tedric I; birth daughter of Melina Shield and Rolfston Redbriar; sister of Jet, Opal, Ruby, and Citrine Shield; spouse of Shad.

Sarena Gardener: (H.H.) member of Prince Barden's expedition; spouse of Donal Hunter; mother of Tamara. Deceased.

Seastar Seagleam: (Grand Duchess, B.B.) sister of Gustin III; mother of Culver and Dillon Peli-can.

Shad: (Crown Prince, B.B.) son of Allister I and Pearl Oyster; brother of Tavis, Anemone, and Minnow Oyster; spouse of Sapphire.

Sharp Fang: a common name among the Royal Wolves; see Northwest and Whiner.

Shelby: a sailor on the *Explorer*. Deceased.

Shivadtmon: (L.) an aridisdu.

Siyago: (Dragon's Fire, N.K.) a prominent member of the Sodality of Artificers.

Skea: Nexus Islands; a Twice Dead; spouse of Ynamynet; father of Sunshine.

Sky: also Sky-Dreaming-Earth-Bound, a maimalodalu. Deceased.

Steady Runner: a Royal Elk.

Steward Silver: (H.H.) long-time steward of Eagle's Nest Castle. Her birth-name and origin have been forgotten as no one, not even Silver herself, thinks of herself as anything but the steward.

Sun of Bright Haven: first born of Sapphire and Shad.

Sunshine: Nexus Islands; daughter of Skea and Ynamynet.

Tab Shield: (Duke Gyrfalcon, H.H.) brother of Rein, Newell, Polr, and Melina.

Tait Norwood: (H.H.) son of Norvin Norwood and Luella Stanbrook; brother of Edlin, Lillis, and Agneta Norwood.

Tallus: (Prime, N.K.) member of the Sodality of Alchemists.

Tangler: a Wise Wolf.

Tavis Oyster: (Prince, B.B.) son of Allister I and Pearl Oyster; brother of Shad, Anemone, and Minnow Oyster.

Tavis Seagleam: (Prince, B.B.) third child of Gustin II and Amery Pelican; spouse of Caryl Eagle; father of Allister Seagleam.

Tedgewinn: a sailor on the *Explorer*.

Tedric I: (King, H.H.) third king of Hawk Haven; son of King Chalmer and Queen Rose; spouse of Elexa Wellward; father of Chalmer, Lovella, and Barden; adopted father of Sapphire.

Tenacity: a Wise Wolf.

Tench: (Lord, B.B.) born Tench Clark; right hand to Queen Gustin IV; knighted for his services; later made Lord of the Pen. Deceased.

Thyme: (H.H.) a scout in the service of Hawk Haven.

Timin Gardener: (H.H.) Master Gardener for Eagle's Nest Castle, possessor of the Green Thumb, a talent involving the growing of plants; son of Holly Gardener; brother of Sarena; father of Dan and Robyn.

Tiniel: a man from Gak; twin brother of Isende.

Tipi: (N.K.) slave, born in Stonehold.

Tiridanti: (L.) member of u-Liall; representative for Fire.

Toad: (H.H.) pensioner of the Carter family.

Tollius: (N.K.) member of the Sodality of Smiths.

Toriovico: (Healed One, N.K.) hereditary ruler of New Kelvin; spouse of Melina; brother to Vanviko (deceased) and several sisters.

Tris Stone: a pirate.

Truth: a Wise Jaguar.

Tymia: (N.K.) a guard.

Ulia: (N.K.) a judge.

Urgana: Nexus Islands; Never Lived.

Valet: (H.H.) eponymous servant of Norvin Norwood; known for his fidelity and surprising wealth of useful skills.

Valora I: (Queen, the Isles) born Valora Seagleam, assumed the name Gustin upon her coronation as fourth monarch of Bright Bay. Resigned her position to Allister I and became queen of the Isles. Spouse of Harwill Lobster.

Valora Seagleam: see Valora I.

Vanviko: (heir to the Healed One, N.K.) elder brother of Toriovico; killed in avalanche.

Varcasiol: (N.K.) nephew of Grateful Peace; son of Idalia and Pichero; brother of Kistlio, Linatha, and others.

Varjuna: (L.) ikidisdu of the Horse; husband of Zira; father of Poshtuvanu and others.

Vernita Carter: (H.H.) born Vernita Painter, an acknowledged beauty of her day, Vernita became associated with the business she and her husband, Colby, transformed from a simple carting business to a group of associated livery stables and carting service; spouse of Colby Carter; mother of Derian, Damita, and Brock Carter.

Verul: Nexus Islands; a Twice Dead.

Violet Redbriar: (Ambassador, H.H.) ambassador from Hawk Haven to New Kelvin; translator and author, with great interest in New Kelvinese culture.

Viona Seal: (Queen, B.B.) second wife of King Gustin III; mother of Valora, later Gustin IV.

Wain Cutter: (H.H.) skilled lapidary and gem cutter working out of the town of Hope.

Waln Endbrook: (the Isles) formerly Baron Endbrook; also, Walnut Endbrook. A prosperous merchant, Waln found rapid promotion in the service of Valora I. Spouse of Oralia, father of two daughters and a son. Deceased.

Wendee Jay: (H.H.) retainer in service of Duchess Kestrel. Lady's maid to Firekeeper. Divorced. Mother of two daughters.

Wheeler: (H.H.) scout captain.

Whiner: a wolf of Blind Seer and Firekeeper's pack, later named Sharp Fang.

Whyte Steel: (knight, B.B.) captain of the guard for Allister I.

Wiatt: a sailor on the *Explorer*.

Wind Whisper: Royal Wolf, formerly of Firekeeper's pack, now member of another pack.

Wort: Nexus Islands; a Twice Dead.

Xarxius: (Dragon's Claw, N.K.) member of the Dragon's Three, former Stargazer.

Yaree Yuci: (General, Stonehold) commander of Stonehold troops.

Ynamynet: Nexus Islands; Once Dead; spouse of Skea; mother of Sunshine.

Zahlia: (N.K.) member of the Sodality of Smiths. Specialist in silver.

Zebel: Nexus Islands; a Twice Dead; a doctor.

Zira: (L.) kidisdu of the Horse; wife of Varjuna; mother of Poshtuvanu and others.

Zorana I: (Queen, H.H.) also called Zorana the Great, born Zorana Shield. First monarch of Hawk Haven; responsible for a reduction of titles—so associated with this program that overemphasis of titles is considered "unzoranic." Spouse of Clive Elkwood; mother of Chalmer I.

Zorana Archer: (Lady, H.H.) daughter of Rosene Eagle and Purcel Archer; sister of Ivon Archer; spouse of Aksel Trueheart; mother of Purcel, Nydia, Deste, and Kenre Trueheart.

DISCARD